THE CHARTERHOUSE
OF PARMA

STENDHAL

THE

CHARTERHOUSE

OF PARMA

Translated from the French by Richard Howard

Illustrations by Robert Andrew Parker

THE MODERN LIBRARY

NEW YORK

This translation was commissioned by
Ben Sonnenberg for the Grand Street Foundation

1999 Modern Library Edition

LIBRARY OF CONGRESS CATALOGING-IN-PUBLICATION DATA
Stendhal, 1783–1842.
[Chartreuse de Parme. English]
The charterhouse of Parma/Stendhal; translated from
the French by Richard Howard.
p.   cm.
ISBN 0-679-60245-3
I. Howard, Richard, 1929– . II. Title.
PQ2435.C4E5   1999
843′.7—dc21   98-36417

Modern Library website address: www.modernlibrary.com

Printed in the United States of America on acid-free paper

2 4 6 8 9 7 5 3

STENDHAL

Marie Henri Beyle—later known as Stendhal—was born in Grenoble on January 23, 1783. His mother, whom he idolized, died when he was seven, and he was raised by three people he detested—his bourgeois father, a prosperous lawyer; a jealous maiden aunt; and a tyrannical Jesuit tutor who inspired in him lifelong feelings of anticlericalism. The only person he felt any closeness to was his maternal grandfather, a respected physician who embraced the culture of the Enlightenment. In 1799, at the age of sixteen, the young man left for Paris to study mathematics at the École Polytechnique, but became a dragoon in Napoleon's army the following year. The invasion of Italy took him to Milan, the city he came to love above all others; over the next decade he served as an aide-de-camp in Bonaparte's campaigns in Germany, Austria, and Russia. In between wars he flourished in Parisian drawing rooms and devoted himself (unsuccessfully) to writing plays, all the while keeping elaborate journals that chronicled his travels and love affairs.

Following Napoleon's fall in 1814, Beyle retired permanently from the army and settled in Milan, where he began to write in earnest. He soon produced *Lives of Haydn, Mozart, and Metastasio* (1814), followed by the two-volume *History of Painting in Italy* (1817). His next book—

a travel guide entitled *Rome, Naples, and Florence in 1817* (1817)—was the first to bear the pen name Stendhal, the most famous of the more than two hundred pseudonyms he employed in his lifetime. During this period he fell in love with Matilde Dembowski (née Viscontini), who served as the basis for his heroines. Suspected of being a French secret agent and of involvement in left-wing plots, the writer was expelled from Italy in 1821 by the Austrian police.

Upon returning to Paris, Stendhal immediately resumed *la chasse au bonheur* (the pursuit of happiness) and writing. He quickly finished the semi-autobiographical treatise *On Love* (1822), the critical study *Racine and Shakespeare* (1823), and *Life of Rossini* (1824). *Armance*, the author's first novel, appeared in 1827. *A Roman Journal*, a guidebook that marked Stendhal's first real success, came out in 1829. Then in October of that year he began a novel based on a case reported in the *Gazette des Tribunaux:* the trial of a young man charged with the attempted murder of an ex-mistress. Published in 1830, *The Red and the Black* shocked the public with its incisive portrait of Restoration France, along with its probing psychological study of the complex protagonist, Julien Sorel. ("A novel is like a bow, and the violin that produces the sounds is the reader's soul," Stendhal liked to remind his audience.)

Following the July Revolution of 1830, which brought Louis Philippe to the throne, Stendhal returned to government service. In 1831 he was appointed consul to the port of Civitavecchia, some forty miles from Rome, where he spent many of his final years. During the 1830s Stendhal began two novels, *Lucien Leuwen* and *Lamiel*, both of which remained unfinished and were not published until long after his death. He also undertook two autobiographical works, *Memoirs of an Egotist* and *The Life of Henri Brulard*, which likewise appeared posthumously. In 1835 Stendhal was awarded the Legion of Honor for services to literature; the following year he returned to Paris on an extended leave of absence. There he started a biography of Napoleon and completed *Memoirs of a Tourist* (1838), a popular travel guide to France. Then, between November 4 and December 26 of 1838, the author dictated his last great novel, *The Charterhouse of Parma* (1839), a tale of political intrigue set in Italy. In failing health, he lived long enough to rejoice in Balzac's generous praise of it. Stendhal died in Paris, following a series of strokes, on March 23, 1842, and was buried the next day in the cemetery of Montmartre. "I will be famous around 1880," Stendhal once predicted. Indeed, at about this time he began to attract widespread attention, and many of his previously unpublished books appeared—including *A Life of Napoleon* (1876), *Journal of Stendhal* (1888), *Lamiel* (1889), *The Life of Henri Brulard* (1890), *Memoirs of an Egotist* (1892), and *Lucien Leuwen* (1894). In the twentieth century such writers as Paul Léautaud, André Gide, and Paul Valéry have acclaimed Stendhal's work. "We should never be finished with Stendhal," said Valéry. "I can think of no greater praise than that."

CONTENTS

FOREWORD

xiii

MAPS

xv–xvi

THE CHARTERHOUSE

OF PARMA

3

NOTES

497

AFTERWORD BY

RICHARD HOWARD

503

FOREWORD

This tale was written in the winter of 1830 and three hundred leagues from Paris; hence no reference to the events of 1839.

Many years before 1830, at the time when our armies were overrunning Europe, I happened to be billeted in the house of a Canon: this was at Padua, a charming town in Italy; my stay being prolonged, we became friends.

Passing through Padua again toward the end of 1830, I hastened to the good Canon's house: he was no longer alive, I knew, but I wanted another glimpse of the *salon* where we had spent so many pleasant evenings, so often regretted since. I found the Canon's nephew and this nephew's wife, who received me like old friends. Several people came in, and we made a long night of it; the nephew ordered an excellent *zabaione* from the Caffè Pedrocchi. What especially entertained us was the story of the Duchess Sanseverina, to which someone alluded, and which the nephew kindly told from beginning to end, in my honor.

"Where I am going," I told my friends, "there will be no parties like this one, and to while away the long evenings I shall make a novel out of your story."

"In that case," said the nephew, "I shall give you my uncle's journal, which under the heading *Parma* mentions several court intrigues from the days when the Duchess enjoyed absolute power there; but beware! the tale is anything but moral, and now that the French pride themselves on gospel purity, it may win you the reputation of an assassin."

I publish this tale without altering the 1830 manuscript, hence two possible drawbacks:

The first for the reader: the characters, being Italian, may interest him less, since hearts in that country differ altogether from those in France: Italians are sincere, honest people, and if not intimidated will say what they think; only intermittently are they subject to vanity, which then becomes a passion and goes by the name of *puntiglio.* Furthermore, they do not hold poverty up to ridicule.

The second drawback concerns the author: though I have ventured to leave untouched all my characters' irregularities of nature, I acknowledge having poured the deepest moral censure on many of their actions. Why ascribe to them the lofty morality and the graces of the French, who love money above all things and never sin out of love or hate? The Italians in this tale are virtually the opposite. Moreover, it seems to me that each time we venture two hundred leagues from South to North, we confront a new novel as well as a new landscape. The Canon's charming niece had known and even been devoted to the Duchess Sanseverina, and begs me to alter nothing in her affairs, blameworthy as they are.

January 23, 1839

LIECHTENSTEIN

HELVETIA

**EMPIRE OF
AUSTRIA**

TYROL

Republic
of Valais

*Lake
Maggiore* Como *Lake
Como*

Milan

Verona

Turin

**KINGDOM
OF
ITALY**

Venice

**EMPIRE OF
FRANCE**

Parma

Genoa

Modena

San
Marino

Adriatic Sea

Principality
of Lucca

Florence

Ligurian Sea

**KINGDOM
OF
ETRURIA**

❶

Ancona

Principality
of Piombino

**PAPAL
STATES**

ELBA

CORSICA

❷

**KINGDOM
OF
NAPLES**

❸

Rome

Principality
of Pontecorvo

**KINGDOM OF
SARDINIA**

Naples

ITALY IN 1806

**AT THE DISSOLUTION OF THE
HOLY ROMAN EMPIRE**

Tyrrhenian Sea

❶ Kingdom of Etruria to France, 1807
❷ Northern Papal States to Italy, 1808
❸ Southern Papal States to France, 1809

0   50   100

MILES

ITALY IN 1815
AFTER THE
CONGRESS OF VIENNA

1 Massa and Carrara
2 To Tuscany
3 Lucca

0   50   100
MILES

THE CHARTERHOUSE
OF PARMA

CHAPTER ONE

Milan in 1796

On May 15, 1796, General Bonaparte entered Milan at the head of that young army which had lately crossed the Lodi bridge and taught the world that after so many centuries Caesar and Alexander had a successor. The miracles of valor and genius Italy had witnessed in a few months wakened a slumbering nation: just eight days before the French arrived, the Milanese still regarded them as no more than a band of brigands who habitually fled before the troops of His Imperial and Royal Majesty: at least so they were told three times a week by a little news-sheet the size of a man's hand, printed on dirty paper.

In the Middle Ages, republican Lombards had displayed a valor equal to that of the French, and were entitled to see their city utterly razed by the German emperors. Since they had become *loyal subjects,* their chief concern was to print sonnets on tiny pink taffeta handkerchiefs for the weddings of a young lady belonging to some rich or noble family. Two or three years after that great event in her life, the same young lady would take a *cavaliere servente:* sometimes the name of the *cicisbeo* chosen by the husband's family occupied an honorable place in the marriage contract. It was a far cry from such effeminate manners to the deep emotions produced by the French army's unexpected arrival. Soon new and impassioned standards of behavior were observed. On May 15, 1796, a whole nation realized that whatever it had hitherto respected was sovereignly absurd and on occasion odious. The departure of the last Austrian regiment marked the fall of the old ideas: risking one's life became fashionable; happiness depended, after centuries of insipidity, upon loving one's country with a passion, upon seeking out heroic actions to perform. People had been plunged into darkness by the persistence of the jealous despotism of Charles V and Philip II; they pulled down their statues and were forthwith flooded with light. For the last fifty years, even as the *Encyclopédie* and Voltaire were exploding in France, the monks had adjured the good people of Milan that learning to read, or learning anything at all, was a worthless effort, and that by promptly paying one's tithe to the curé and by offering him a faithful account of all one's petty sins, a fine place in paradise was virtually assured. To complete the enfeeblement of this people once so argumentative and so bold, Austria had sold them cheap the privilege of not supplying recruits to her army.

In 1796 the Milanese army consisted of twenty-four wretches in red uniforms who guarded the city with the help of four magnificent regiments of Hungarian grenadiers. Moral freedom was extreme, but passion extremely rare; moreover, aside from the nuisance of having to tell one's curé everything (or be ruined even in this world), the good people of Milan were still subject to certain minor monarchical restrictions which continued to vex them. For instance the Archduke, who resided in Milan and governed in the name of his cousin the Emperor, had conceived the lucrative notion of speculating in wheat. Consequently, no peasant could sell his crop until His Highness's granaries were full.

In May 1796, three days after the entry of the French, a young miniaturist named Gros, slightly mad and subsequently famous, arrived with the army and overheard talk in the great Caffè dei Servi (fashionable at the time) of the exploits of the Archduke, who happened to be extremely fat. Snatching up the list of ices stamped on a sheet of coarse yellow paper, he drew on the back a French soldier thrusting his bayonet into the obese Archduke's belly: instead of blood out poured an incredible quantity of grain. The idea of caricature or cartoon was unknown in this nation of wary despotism. The sketch

Gros had left on the table of the Caffé dei Servi seemed a miracle from Heaven; it was printed overnight, and twenty thousand copies were sold the next day.

That same day, notices were posted of a war-tax of six million levied for the needs of the French army, which, having just won six battles and conquered twenty provinces, lacked only shoes, jackets, caps, and trousers.

So much pleasure and happiness poured into Lombardy with these Frenchmen, however ill-dressed, that only the priests and certain noblemen remarked this burden of six million, soon followed by many others. These French soldiers laughed and sang all day long; most were not yet twenty-five, and at twenty-eight their commanding general was accounted the oldest man in his army. Such youth, such gaiety, such free and easy ways offered a fine answer to the furious imprecations of the monks who for six months had preached that the French were monsters under orders, on pain of death, to burn down everything and cut off everyone's head; to which end, each regiment marched with a guillotine in its front ranks.

Throughout the countryside French soldiers could be seen dandling babies at farmhouse doors, and almost every evening some drummer scraping his fiddle would improvise a ball. Since French *contredanses* were far too intricate for the soldiers, who scarcely knew them themselves, to teach the local girls, it was the latter who showed the young Frenchmen the *monferrina*, the *saltarello*, and other Italian dances.

The officers had been billeted on the rich as often as possible; they were in great need of recuperation. For instance, a certain Lieutenant Robert was assigned to the Marchesa del Dongo's palace, which this unscrupulous young conscript entered with one *scudo* (worth six francs) as his sole wealth, having just received his pay at Piacenza. After crossing the Lodi bridge, he had stripped a handsome Austrian officer killed by a cannonball of a magnificent pair of brand-new nankeen trousers, and never had a garment been so timely. His officer's epaulettes were of wool, and the ragged fabric of his jacket was patched with the lining from its sleeves to hold the pieces together; sadder still, the soles of his shoes consisted of scraps of visors, similarly gleaned from the battlefield the other side of Lodi bridge. These extempore soles were quite visibly tied to the uppers of his shoes with bits of string, so that when the major-domo appeared in Lieutenant Robert's bedroom to invite him to dine with the Signora Marchesa, the officer was mortally embarrassed. He and his orderly spent the two hours until this fatal dinner attempting to patch the jacket and to conceal the lamentable pieces of string with black ink. At last the dreadful moment arrived. "I never felt so uncomfortable in all my life," Lieutenant Robert told me; "the ladies expected me to terrify them, and I was trembling much more than they. I glanced at my shoes and could not imagine how to walk gracefully. The Marchesa del Dongo," he added, "was then in the prime of her beauty: you have seen her yourself—those fine eyes of an angelic sweetness, that lovely dark-blond hair which so perfectly framed the oval of her charming face. In my bedroom hung a *Salomé* after da Vinci which seemed her portrait. Thank God I was so overcome by this divine beauty that I forgot how I was dressed. For two years I had seen nothing but ugliness and misery in the mountains around Genoa: I ventured to mention my rapture to her.

"But I had too much sense to waste my time on compliments. Even as I was turning my phrases, I noticed that the marble dining-hall was filled with lackeys and footmen dressed in what then seemed to me the height of magnificence. You realize, these wretches wore not only fine shoes, but silver buckles! Out of the corner of my eye I saw them all staring stupidly at my jacket, and perhaps at my shoes as well, which stabbed me to the heart. I might have terrorized every one of them with a word, but how to put them in their place without running the risk of alarming the ladies? For the Marchesa, to bolster her own courage (as she has told me a hundred times since), had summoned from the convent, where she was still at boarding-school, her husband's sister Gina del Dongo, who was later to become the charming Countess of Pietranera: in good times no one surpassed her in gaiety and sweetness of temper, just as no one surpassed her in courage and serenity of soul in adversity.

"Gina, who might have then been thirteen though she looked eighteen, vivacious and frank as you know her to be, was so afraid of bursting into laughter at the sight of my outfit that she dared not eat; the Marchesa, on the contrary, overwhelmed me with reserved attentions, having recognized hints of impatience in my expression. In a word, I cut a foolish figure as I swallowed my ration of scorn, a thing said to be impossible for a Frenchman. At last I was inspired by a Heaven-sent idea; I began describing my wretchedness to these ladies, and all we had suffered the last two years in the mountains around Genoa where we had been stationed by imbecilic old generals. There, I remarked, we were paid by promissory notes which had no currency in the region, and three ounces of bread a day. I had not spoken two minutes before the Marchesa had tears in her eyes, and Gina had become serious.

" 'What, Signor Lieutenant,' she exclaimed, 'three ounces of bread!'

" 'Yes, Signorina; but even so the supply failed three times a week, and since the peasants we were billeted on were even poorer than ourselves, we gave some of our bread to them.'

"Leaving the table, I offered the Marchesa my arm as far as the dining-hall door, then, swiftly retracing my steps, I gave the lackey who had served me that single scudo on whose expenditure I had built so many castles in Spain.

"Eight days later," Lieutenant Robert continued, "when it was widely acknowledged that the French were guillotining no one, the Marchese del Dongo returned from Grianta, his castle on Lake Como, where he had valiantly taken refuge at the French army's approach, abandoning his sister and his lovely young wife to the chances of war. The Marchese's hatred of us was equal to his fear, which is to say, incommensurable: it was amusing to see his pale and pious countenance as he uttered his polite formulas. The day following his return to Milan, I received three ells of cloth and two hundred francs out of the levy of six million: I feathered myself anew and became the cavalier of these ladies, for the ball-season had begun."

Lieutenant Robert's story was much the same as that of every Frenchman; instead of deriding the plight of these gallant soldiers, people took pity on them and came to love them.

This period of unforeseen happiness and intoxication lasted but two short years; the craze had been so excessive and so widespread that it would be impossible for me to give any notion of it, except for this profound historical reflection: these people had been bored for a hundred years.

The love of sensual pleasure natural to southern countries had once reigned at the court of the Viscontis and the Sforzas, those famous Dukes of Milan. But since 1624, when the Spaniards had seized the duchy, and seized it as arrogant, suspicious, taciturn masters ever fearful of rebellion, gaiety had fled. Assuming the manners of their masters, the Milanese pondered avenging the slightest insult by a dagger-thrust rather than delighting in the present moment.

Wild joy, gaiety, sensual pleasure, disregard of all sad or even sensible feelings reached such a pitch between May 15, 1796, when the French entered Milan, and April 1799, when they were driven out after the battle of Cassano, that instances have been cited of old millionaire merchants, old usurers, old notaries who, during this interval, had forgotten to be dyspeptic and obsessed with making money.

At most one could number several families of the higher nobility who had withdrawn to their country houses, as though to sulk amid the general cheer and expansiveness of all hearts. It is also quite true that these rich and noble families had been provokingly singled out in the distribution of war-taxes levied by the French army.

The Marchese del Dongo, vexed at the sight of so much gaiety, had been one of the first to retire to his splendid Castle of Grianta on the far side of Como, to which Lieutenant Robert now accompanied the ladies. This castle, in a situation possibly unique in all the world, on a plateau some hundred and fifty feet above that sublime lake, of which it dominates a large portion, had been a stronghold built by the del Dongo family in the fifteenth century, as was evidenced by the many marble escutcheons; here were still to be seen drawbridges and deep moats, though at present without water; but with walls some twenty-four feet high and six feet thick, this castle was safe from assault; for which reason it was dear to the suspicious Marchese. Surrounded by twenty-five or thirty servants whom he believed to be devoted, apparently because he never addressed them without some insult on his lips, he was less tormented by fear than in Milan.

Such fear was not entirely gratuitous: the Marchese was actively corresponding with an Austrian spy stationed on the Swiss frontier three leagues from Grianta, in order to effect the escape of prisoners taken on the battlefield, an enterprise which might have been regarded as a serious matter by the French generals.

The Marchese had left his young wife in Milan; there she managed family affairs, dealing with the taxes imposed on the *Casa del Dongo,* as the local expression had it; she sought to reduce these as much as she could, which obliged her to consult those members of the nobility who had accepted public functions, as well as certain highly influential persons not of noble birth. There now occurred a great event in this family. The Marchese had arranged the marriage of his young sister Gina to an extremely rich personage of the highest birth; but the man powdered his hair: on this account Gina received him with peals of laughter, and soon committed the folly of marrying Count Pietranera. Who was in fact a very fine gentleman, most attractive in appearance but ruined in fortune as his father had been before him and—a crowning disgrace—a fierce champion of the new ideas. Pietranera was a Second Lieutenant in the Italian Legion, a further cause of the Marchese's dispair.

After two such years of folly and happiness, the Directory in Paris, putting on the airs of a well-established sovereign, revealed a mortal hatred of anything not mediocre. The inept generals assigned to the army in Italy lost a series of battles on those same plains of Verona which two years earlier had witnessed the prodigies of Arcole and Lonato. The Austrians drew close to Milan; Lieutenant Robert, now commanding a battalion and wounded at the battle of Cassano, came to stay for the last time with his friend the Marchesa del Dongo. The farewells were sad; the Lieutenant left with Count Pietranera, who accompanied the French in their retreat to Novi. The young Countess, whose dowry her brother had refused to pay, followed the army, riding on a baggage-cart.

Then began that period of reaction and return to the old ideas, which the Milanese call *i tredici mesi* (the thirteen months), because it so happened that their happiness compelled this reversion to imbecility to last only thirteen months, until Marengo. Whatever was old, pious, dyspeptic reappeared in the leadership of affairs and resumed the guidance of society: soon those who had remained loyal to respectable doctrines reported in the villages that Napoléon had been hanged by the Mamelukes in Egypt, as he deserved on so many counts. Among these men who had withdrawn to sulk on their estates and who returned to Milan thirsting for vengeance, the Marchese del Dongo was distinguished by his fury; his exaggeration naturally carried him to the leadership of his party. These gentlemen, honest enough when they were not frightened, but perpetually in a funk, managed to impose on the Austrian general, a decent enough fellow who let himself be persuaded that severity was the best policy and ordered the arrest of some hundred and fifty patriots, the best men in all Italy at the time.

Soon they were deported to the *bocche di Cattaro*, where, flung into underground caves, humidity and especially lack of bread rendered a summary justice to all such wretches.

The Marchese del Dongo occupied a high position, and, since he united sordid greed with a host of other fine qualities, publicly boasted of not sending one scudo to his sister, Countess Pietranera: still deeply in love, she was unwilling to leave her husband and was starving to death with him in France. The good Marchesa was in despair; finally she managed to filch a few little diamonds from her jewel-case, which her husband took from her every evening to keep under his bed in an iron strongbox: the Marchesa had brought her husband a dowry of eight hundred thousand francs and received eighty francs a month for her personal expenses. During the thirteen months which the French spent outside Milan, this extremely timid woman found excuses for continually wearing mourning.

We must confess that, following the example of many serious authors, we have begun our hero's story a year before his birth. This essential personage is none other, indeed, than Fabrizio Valserra, *Marchesino* del Dongo, as they say in Milan.* He had just taken the trouble to be born when the French were driven out, and found himself, by the chance of birth, the second son of that great nobleman the

*By local custom, borrowed from Germany, this title is given to every son of a Marchese, *Contino* to every son and *Contesina* to every daughter of a Count, and so on.

Marchese del Dongo, with whose pale and heavy countenance, false smile, and limitless hatred of new ideas you are already familiar. The entire fortune of the house was entailed upon the elder son, Ascanio del Dongo, worthy portrait of his father. He was eight years old, and Fabrizio two, when suddenly that General Bonaparte whom all well-born people believed long since hanged, swept down from Mont Saint-Bernard and entered Milan. This moment is still unique in history; imagine a whole people insane with love. A few days later Napoléon won the battle of Marengo. No need to tell the rest. The intoxication of the Milanese was at its peak; but this time it was mixed with notions of revenge: these good people had been taught to hate. Soon the surviving patriots deported to the *bocche di Cattaro* were brought home; their return was celebrated by a national holiday, but their pale faces, huge staring eyes, and famished limbs contrasted strangely with the joy which exploded on all sides. Their arrival was the signal for the departure of the most compromised families. The Marchese del Dongo was among the first to flee to his Castle of Grianta. The heads of the noble families were filled with hatred and fear, but their wives and daughters remembered the delights of the first French occupation and regretted Milan and the gay balls organized at the *Casa Tanzi* immediately after Marengo.

A few days after the victory, the French general in charge of maintaining peace in Lombardy discovered that all the farmers and the old women on the estates of the nobles, far from marveling over that wonderful victory of Marengo which had changed the fortunes of Italy and reconquered thirteen fortresses in one day, were preoccupied exclusively by a prophecy of Saint Giovita, first patron of Brescia. According to these holy words, the prosperity of Napoléon and the French would cease precisely thirteen weeks after Marengo. What somewhat excuses the Marchese del Dongo and all the surly nobles of the countryside is that they really and quite seriously believed in this prophecy. None of these people had read four books in all their lives; they were openly preparing to return to Milan once the thirteen weeks had elapsed; but time as it passed marked new successes for the French cause. Returning to Paris, Napoléon, by astute decrees, rescued the Revolution from within just as he had saved it from foreign enemies at Marengo. Whereupon the Lombard nobles, having withdrawn to their castles, discovered first of all that they had misunderstood the prophecy of the patron saint of Brescia: it was not a matter of thirteen weeks, but of thirteen months. The thirteen months passed, and the prosperity of France seemed to increase with every day.

Let us skip ten years of progress and happiness, from 1800 to 1810; Fabrizio spent the first of them in the Castle of Grianta, giving and receiving many punches among the peasant boys of the village and learning nothing, not even how to read. Later, he was sent to the Jesuit College at Milan. The Marchese his father required that the Latin language be revealed to him, not according to those ancient authors who continually mentioned republics, but upon a magnificent volume embellished with over a hundred engravings, masterpieces of the artists of the seventeenth century; this was the Latin genealogy of the Valserras, Marchesi del Dongo, published in 1650 by Fabrizio del Dongo, Archbishop of Parma. The fortune of the Valserras was chiefly military, the engravings represented many a battle, and some hero of that name was invariably shown dealing mighty blows with his sword. This volume delighted young Fabrizio. His mother, who adored him, occasionally obtained permission to visit him in Milan; but since her husband never gave her money for these expeditions, it was her sister-in-law, the lovely Countess Pietranera, who loaned it to her. After the return of the French, the Countess had become one of the most brilliant ladies of the court of Prince Eugène, Viceroy of Italy.

Once Fabrizio had made his first Communion, she persuaded the Marchese, still in voluntary exile, to allow him to leave the College from time to time. She found her nephew to be singular, witty, very serious, but a fine-looking boy and by no means a liability to the *salon* of a fashionable lady; furthermore, he was quite ignorant, scarcely knowing how to write his name. The Countess, whose enthusiastic character was evident in all she undertook, promised her protection to the establishment if her nephew made remarkable progress and carried off many prizes by the year's end. In order to afford him the means of deserving them, she sent for Fabrizio every Saturday evening and frequently returned him to his masters only the following Wednesday or Thursday. The Jesuits, though dearly beloved by the Prince-Viceroy, were under sentence of expulsion from Italy by the laws of the realm, and the Superior of the College, a cunning fellow, perceived all the advantage he might derive from his relations with a woman omnipotent at court. He was careful not to complain of Fabrizio's absences, and at the year's end the boy, ignorant as ever, obtained five first prizes. On this stipulation, the brilliant Countess Pietranera, accompanied by her husband, commanding general of one of the divisions of the Guard, and by five or six of the greatest figures of the viceregal court, attended the prize-giving at the Jesuit College. The director was complimented by his superiors.

The Countess included her nephew in all those brilliant parties which marked the too brief reign of the lovable Prince Eugène. She had created him, by her authority, Officer of the Hussars, and Fabrizio, at twelve, wore their uniform. One day the Countess, delighted by his fine turnout, requested that the Prince give him a page's functions, which would mean that the del Dongo family was recovering its position. The following day she needed all her influence to keep the Viceroy from remembering this request, which lacked nothing but the consent of the future page's father, and this consent would have been vehemently refused. After this folly, which made the surly Marchese shudder, he found a pretext to recall young Fabrizio to Grianta. The Countess felt sovereign contempt for her brother; she regarded him as a grim fool who would commit any wickedness within his power. But she was wildly devoted to Fabrizio, and after ten years of silence, she wrote to the Marchese in order to reclaim her nephew: her letter was left unanswered.

On his return to that formidable castle built by the most bellicose of all his ancestors, Fabrizio knew of nothing better to do than to drill and to ride. Count Pietranera, as fond of the boy as his wife, had often put him on horseback and had taken him along on parade.

Arriving at the Castle of Grianta, Fabrizio, eyes still red with tears shed upon leaving behind his aunt's splendid *salon,* met with nothing but the passionate caresses of his mother and his sisters. The Marchese was shut up in his study with his elder son, the Marchesino Ascanio. Here they concocted letters in code which had the honor to be sent to Vienna; father and son appeared only at mealtimes. The Marchese repeated meaningfully that he was teaching his natural successor to keep double-entry accounts of what his estates produced. In fact, the Marchese was too jealous of his power to speak of such things to a son who was the inevitable heir to all these entailed properties. He kept him busy coding despatches of fifteen or twenty pages, which he forwarded to Switzerland two or three times a week, whence they made their way to Vienna. The Marchese claimed to inform his legitimate sovereigns of the internal condition of Italy, of which he himself knew nothing, though his letters enjoyed a great success. This is the reason: the Marchese's trustworthy agent counted the soldiers changing garrison in every French or Italian regiment, and in reporting this fact to the Austrian court, he scrupulously diminished by at least a quarter the number of soldiers in the field. Absurd as they were, these letters had the merit of giving the lie to more accurate ones, and they pleased their recipients. Hence, shortly before Fabrizio's arrival at the castle, the Marchese had received the Star of a renowed Order; it was the fifth one to embellish his Chamberlain's coat. True, he suffered the chagrin of not daring to sport this garment outside his study; but he never allowed himself to dictate a despatch without having first put on the coat embroidered with gold lace and embellished with all his decorations. He would have felt he was lacking in respect had he proceeded otherwise.

The Marchesa was astonished by her son's graceful manners. But she was still in the habit of writing two or three times a year to General-Count d'A—— (the current name of Lieutenant Robert). The Marchesa had a horror of lying to those she cared for; she questioned her son and was appalled by his ignorance.

"If he seems uneducated to me, ignorant as I am," she mused, "Robert, who is so learned, would find his education absolutely inadequate; yet nowadays it is true ability that counts." Another peculiarity which amazed her almost as much was that Fabrizio had taken seriously all the religious notions he had learned from the Jesuits. Though quite pious herself, her son's fanaticism made her tremble; "If the Marchese has the wit to divine this source of influence, he will rob me of my son's love." She shed a great many tears, and her passion for Fabrizio was thereby increased.

Life in this castle, inhabited by thirty or forty servants, was gloomy indeed; hence Fabrizio spent all his days hunting or rowing on the lake. Soon he was closely attached to the coachmen and the grooms; all were wild partisans of the French and openly derided the pious lackeys serving the Marchese or his elder son. The principal excuse for their mockery of these solemn personages was that they powdered their hair in imitation of their masters.

Chapter Two

... And when the evening darkens mortal eyes,
Seeking what's to come, I scan the skies,
Where God inscribes, in letters plain to see,
Of all who live, the changing destiny.
For He, discerning humankind astray,
Sometimes moved by pity, shows the way:
By Heaven's stars, which are His alphabet,
Foretells what good may rise, what evil set;
But men, by death and earthly error gripped,
Disdain the message and ignore the script.
—RONSARD

The Marchese professed a robust hatred of the Enlightenment: "It is ideas," he would say, "which have corrupted Italy." And he was uncertain how to reconcile his pious horror of learning with a desire to see his son Fabrizio perfect the education so brilliantly begun among the Jesuits. In order to incur the fewest possible risks, he entrusted the worthy Abbé Blanès, parish priest of Grianta, with the task of helping Fabrizio continue his studies in Latin. It would have been necessary that the Abbé himself possess some knowledge of this language, which happened to be the object of his scorn; his attainments in this realm were confined to reciting by heart the prayers of his missal, whose sense he could communicate, more or less, to his flock. Yet for all that this priest was deeply respected and even dreaded throughout the canton; he had always said it was not in thirteen weeks nor even in thirteen months that the famous prophecy of San Giovita, patron saint of Brescia, would be fulfilled. He would add, when speaking to friends he could trust, that this number thirteen must be interpreted in a manner which would astonish many, were he permitted to tell all (1813).

The fact is that Abbé Blanès, a figure of *primitive* virtue and honesty, and moreover a clever man, spent every night at the top of his belfry; he was obsessed with astrology. Having devoted his days to the calculation of the stars' conjunctions and positions, he employed the better part of his nights following them across the sky. Consequent upon his poverty, his only instrument was a lens in a long pasteboard tube. One may conceive his disdain for the study of languages, a man whose life was dedicated to the discovery of the precise date of the fall of empires, and of the revolutions changing the face of the earth! "Do I know more about a horse," he would remark to Fabrizio, "when I am told that its Latin name is *equus?*"

The peasants dreaded Abbé Blanès as a great magician: for his part, on account of the fear inspired by his belfry sessions, he kept them from stealing. His fellow priests in the neighboring parishes envied his influence and detested him accordingly; the Marchese del Dongo merely despised him because he reasoned too much for a man of such low station. Fabrizio worshiped him: in order to please him, he sometimes spent whole evenings adding or multiplying enormous sums. Then he would climb up into the belfry: this was a great privilege which the priest had never granted anyone; but he loved this child for his naïveté. "If you do not become a hypocrite," he would tell him, "you will perhaps be a man."

Two or three times a year, Fabrizio, bold and passionate in pursuit of his pleasures, risked drowning himself in the lake. He was the leader of all the exploits performed by the peasant boys of Grianta and Cadenabbia. These children had managed to obtain certain small keys, and after dark attempted to open the locks on the chains mooring the boats to some boulder or tree close to the water's edge. It must be explained that the fishermen on Lake Como set night-lines far out from shore, their upper ends attached to a cork-lined plank, and a supple hazel twig, tied to this plank, supported a little bell which jingled when a fish, taking the bait, shook the line.

The great object of these nocturnal sorties which Fabrizio commanded was to visit the night-line before the fishermen heard the warning given by the little bells. Stormy weather was the preferred time for these dangerous ventures, and the boys set out an hour before dawn. As they climbed into the boat, these children believed they were running the greatest dangers, this being the creditable aspect of their foray, and following their fathers' example they would devoutly recite an *Ave Maria*. Now it frequently happened that upon the moment of embarkation, and immediately after the *Ave Maria,* Fabrizio would be struck by an omen. This was all the fruit he had gathered from the astrological studies of his friend the Abbé, in whose predictions he otherwise had no confidence whatever. Spurred on by his boyish imagination, such omens informed him without question as to the success or failure of the expedition, and since he was more resolute than any of his comrades, the entire band gradually became so accustomed to omens that if, at the moment of pushing off, someone glimpsed a priest on the shore or a raven flying away to the left, the locks would be restored to the boat-chains at once, and everyone went back to bed. Thus Abbé Blanès had not imparted his rather abstruse learning to Fabrizio, but unwittingly had instilled in him a limitless trust in signs which can foretell the future.

The Marchese felt that an accident occurring to his coded correspondence might place him at his sister's mercy; hence every year, on the Feast of Saint Angela, Countess Pietranera's patron saint, Fabrizio was given permission to spend eight days in Milan. He lived the whole year in the hope or the recollection of these eight days. Upon this great occasion, to defray the expenses of this politic journey, the Marchese handed his son four scudi, and as was his habit, gave nothing to his wife, who was accompanying the boy. But one of the cooks, six lackeys, and a coachman and pair left for Como the eve of the journey, and every day in Milan the Marchesa would find a carriage at her disposal and a table set for twelve.

The sort of sullen life led by the Marchese del Dongo was anything but diverting, yet it had this advantage: it permanently enriched the families who were so good as to give themselves up to it. The Marchese, whose annual income exceeded two hundred thousand francs, did not expend a quarter of this sum; he lived on hopes. During the thirteen years that had passed since 1800, he continually and firmly believed that Napoléon would be overthrown before six months had passed. Judge of his delight when, early in 1813, he learned of the disasters of the Beresina! The capture of Paris and Napoléon's fall made him nearly lose his mind, and he permitted himself the most outrageous remarks to his wife and his sister. Finally, after a wait of fourteen years, he had the inexpressible joy of seeing the Austrian troops reenter Milan. Following orders from Vienna, the Marchese del Dongo was received by the Austrian general with a consideration bordering upon respect; an offer was immediately tendered of one of the highest positions in the government, which the Marchese accepted as the payment of a debt. His elder son received a lieutenancy in one of the Monarchy's finest regiments, but his younger obdurately rejected the proposed rank of cadet. The Marchese's triumph, in which he revelled with unusual insolence, lasted but a few months and was followed by a humiliating reversal. He had never possessed a talent for business, and fourteen years spent in the country among his lackeys, his notary, and his doctor, combined with the petulance of his advancing years, had rendered him utterly incompetent. Now it is impossible, under Austrian rule, to retain an important position without possessing the kind of talent required by the slow, complex, but entirely logical administration of that ancient Monarchy. The Marchese del Dongo's blunders scandalized the staff and even obstructed the progress of business. His ultra-monarchical observations irritated the very populations who were to be lulled into slumbrous apathy. One fine day, he learned that His Gracious Majesty had deigned to accept his resignation from the post he occupied in the government, and had simultaneously conferred upon him the rank of *Second Grand Major-domo Major* of the Lombardo-Venetian Kingdom. The Marchese was outraged by the cruel injustice of which he was the victim; he published a Letter to a Friend, he who so loathed the freedom of the press! And even wrote to the Emperor that his ministers were betraying him, being no better than Jacobins. These things done, he sadly returned to his Castle of Grianta. There was one consolation. After Napoléon's fall, certain powerful persons in Milan fomented a street attack upon Count Prina, former minister of the King of Italy and a man of the first order. Count Pietranera risked his life to save the Minister, who was beaten to death by umbrellas and whose agony lasted some five hours. A priest who happened to be the Marchese del Dongo's confessor might have saved Prina by opening the grille of San Giovanni, in front of which the unfortunate Minister had been dragged and even for a moment left in the gutter; but this priest jeeringly refused to open his grille, and six months later the Marchese had the happiness of securing for him a handsome preferment.

He loathed Count Pietranera, his brother-in-law, who, without fifty louis' income, dared to be content with his lot, determined to show himself loyal to what he had loved all his life, and had the insolence to display that spirit of justice without consideration of persons, which the Marchese called an infamous Jacobinism. The Count had refused to take service with Austria; this refusal was made known to the authorities, and some months after Prina's death the same persons who had hired his assassins managed to have General Pietranera thrown into prison. Whereupon his wife the Countess obtained a passport and requested post-horses for Vienna, in order to tell the Emperor the truth. Prina's assassins were intimidated, and one of them, a cousin of Countess Pietranera, brought her at midnight, an hour before she was to leave, her husband's order of release. The next day the Austrian general sent for Count Pietranera, received him with every possible distinction, and assured him that his pension as a retired officer would be paid on the most advantageous terms. The worthy General Bubna, a man of discernment as well as of feeling, appeared to be quite ashamed of Prina's murder and of the Count's imprisonment.

After this squall, staved off by the Countess's firm character, the pair lived as well as they could upon the retirement pension which, thanks to General Bubna's recommendation, was paid forthwith. Fortunately, it so happened that for the last five or six years, the Countess had enjoyed cordial relations with an extremely wealthy young man who was also an intimate friend of the Count, and who lost no time in placing at their disposal the finest pair of English horses to be seen in Milan, his box at La Scala, and his villa in the country. But the Count, whose generous spirit had the conscience of his very bravery, was a man readily carried away and at such times allowed himself to speak inopportunely. One day when he was hunting with some young men, one of them, who had served under other ensigns than the Count's, began making jokes about the courage of the soldiers of the Republic on the other side of the Alps; the Count slapped his face, a fracas immediately ensued, and the Count, who was the sole exponent of his point of view amid all these young men, was killed. There was a great deal of talk about this duel, if duel it was, and the persons involved then decided to make a journey to Switzerland.

That absurd courage known as resignation, the courage of a fool who lets himself be hanged without uttering a word, was not among the Countess's qualities. Outraged by her husband's death, she would have had Limercati, the wealthy young man who was her faithful friend, undertake the journey to Switzerland forthwith and there offer Count Pietranera's murderer either a slap in the face or a bullet in the breast.

Limercati treated such an enterprise as a consummate absurdity, and the Countess immediately realized that her disdain had killed her love. She multiplied her attentions to Limercati, seeking to awaken his love and subsequently to forsake him, reducing him to despair. In order to render such a scheme of revenge intelligible to French readers, I should explain that in Milan, a region quite remote from our own, a man may still be driven to despair by love. The Countess who, in her mourning robes, easily eclipsed all her rivals, flirted with the young men of good society, and one of them, Count Nani, who had long since observed that he had found Limercati's merit somewhat heavy, somewhat starched for a woman of such spirit, fell madly in love with the Countess. She wrote to Limercati:

Will you for once behave like a man with a brain? Imagine that you have never known me.
I remain, with a trace of contempt perhaps, your most humble servant.
Gina Pietranera

Upon reading this missive, Limercati departed for one of his castles; maddened by passion, he spoke of blowing his brains out, an unheard-of thing in countries where Hell is a reality. The day after he arrived in the country, he had written the Countess to offer her his hand and his income of two hundred thousand francs. She returned his letter unopened, employing Count Nani's groom for the commission. Whereupon Limercati was to spend three years on his estates, returning to Milan every two months but without ever having the courage to remain there, and boring all his friends with his passion for the Countess, and with a detailed narrative of the favors she had once shown him. In the early stages, he added that she was ruining herself with Count Nani, and that she would be dishonored by such a liaison.

The fact is that the Countess had no love whatever for Count Nani, as she declared to him once she was quite certain of Limercati's despair. The Count, a man of the world, implored her not to divulge the sad truth she had confided to him:

"If you will be so kind," he added, "as to continue receiving me, with all the marks of distinction granted to a reigning lover, I shall perhaps gain a suitable position for myself."

Having received this heroic declaration, the Countess had no further need of Count Nani's horses or his box at the opera. But for fifteen years she had been accustomed to a life of the greatest elegance: she was now obliged to solve this difficult or, frankly, impossible problem: how to live in Milan on a pension of fifteen hundred francs. She left her *palazzo*, rented a couple of rooms in an attic, and dismissed all her servants, even her chambermaid, whom she replaced by an old charwoman. This sacrifice was in fact less heroic and less painful than it appears to us; in Milan poverty is not a matter for ridicule, and therefore does not show itself to frightened souls as the worst of evils. After some months of such noble poverty, during which the Countess was besieged by continual letters from Limercati, as well as from Count Nani, who also sought her hand, it occurred to the Marchese del Dongo, in general so detestably stingy, that his enemies might well gloat over his sister's reduced circumstances. What! A del Dongo reduced to living on a pension from the Viennese court, which had given him such offense!

He wrote her that an apartment and an allowance worthy of his sister would await her at the Castle of Grianta. The Countess's volatile soul enthusiastically embraced the notion of this new kind of life; it had been twenty years since she had lived in this venerable castle rising majestically amid the old chestnut-trees planted in the days of the Sforzas. "There," she mused, "I shall find repose, and at my age, is that not happiness?" (Since she was all of thirty-one, she regarded herself as having reached the period of seclusion.) "On that sublime lake where I was born, a calm and happy life awaits me at last."

I do not know whether she was deceiving herself, but there can be no doubt that this passionate soul, who had just found it so easy to reject the offer of one enormous fortune after the next, brought happiness to the Castle of Grianta. Her two nieces were mad with joy. "You have brought back to me the happy days of my youth," the Marchesa exclaimed as she took her in her arms; "the day before you came I was a hundred years old!"

The Countess began revisiting, accompanied by Fabrizio, all those enchanting places surrounding Grianta, so celebrated by travelers: Villa Melzi, which affords such a fine view of the castle from the opposite side of the lake; beyond, the sacred grove of the Sfondrati and the bold promontory separating the lake's two arms, the one toward Como so voluptuously beautiful, and the one toward Lecco so austere: sublime and enchanting aspects which the most celebrated site in the world, the Bay of Naples, may equal but not surpass. It was with delight that the Countess regained the memories of her first youth and compared them to her present sensations: "Lake Como," she mused, "is not surrounded, like Lake Geneva, by great fenced-in fields cultivated according to the best modern methods, things suggestive of money and speculation. Here on all sides I see varying hills covered with groves of trees planted by Chance, and which the hand of man has not yet spoiled and forced *to bring in a return*. Amid these wondrously shapely hills sloping down to the lake, I may retain all the illusions of the descriptions in Tasso and Ariosto. Everything is noble and tender, everything speaks of love, nothing recalls the defects of civilization. The villages half-way up the hills are hidden by dense groves, and above the treetops rises the charming architecture of their lovely belfries. If some little field fifty paces wide occasionally interrupts the clumps of chestnuts and wild cherry-trees, the contented eye sees growing there crops more vigorous and happier than anywhere else in the world. Beyond these hills, whose crests afford a glimpse of hermitages one longs to take refuge in, one after the next, the astonished gaze perceives the Alpine peaks, ever covered with snow, and their austerity reminds one of life's miseries, and just how much of them are necessary to increase one's present joys. The imagination is stirred by the distant sound of the bell in some little hamlet hidden under the trees: such sounds, borne over the waves that sweeten them, assume a tinge of gentle melancholy and resignation, they seem to be telling man: life is fleeting, do not be so hard on the happiness which offers itself to you, make haste to enjoy it!" The language of these ravishing locales, which are unparalleled the world over, restored to the Countess her heart as it was at sixteen. How could she have lived so many years without seeing her lake again? "Is it when old age begins," she mused, "that happiness finds a refuge?" She bought a boat, which she and Fabrizio and the Marchesa decorated with their own hands, for there was not enough money to pay for such things, despite the castle's sumptuous state; ever since his disgrace, the Marchese del Dongo had multiplied its aristocratic splendors. For instance, in order to wrest ten feet from the lake, near the famous avenue of plane-trees leading to Cadenabbia, he was constructing an embankment which would cost eighty thousand francs. At its far end was rising, according to the plans of the famous Marchese Cagnola, a mortuary chapel made entirely of enormous granite blocks, and inside it Marchesi, the fashionable sculptor from Milan, was carving him a tomb on which numerous bas-reliefs were to represent the heroic deeds of his ancestors.

Fabrizio's elder brother, the Marchesino Ascanio, attempted to join the ladies in their excursions, but his aunt splashed water on his powdered hair, and each day had some new trick to play on his solemnity. Finally the merry group who dared no laugh in his presence was spared the sight of his fat, pale face. They realized he was spying for his father the Marchese, a severe and constantly raging despot who had to be placated ever since his obligatory resignation.

Ascanio swore to be revenged on Fabrizio.

There was a storm during which the boat was in some danger; although there was so little money, the two boatmen were paid to say nothing to the Marchese, who had already evidenced a great deal of bad temper at their taking his two daughters along. A second storm came up, unexpectedly severe on this lovely lake: squalls of wind suddenly emerged from opposite directions out of two mountain gorges, and waged battle over the waters. Despite the peals of thunder, the Countess wanted to disembark in the midst of the tempest; she claimed that, standing on a solitary crag about as high as a little room in the middle of the lake, she could witness a singular spectacle, assailed on all sides by the raging waves; but as she sprang out of the boat she fell into the water. Fabrizio instantly plunged in after her, and both were swept some distance away. Doubtless it is no pleasure to drown, yet for the time being boredom, taken by surprise, was banished from the feudal redoubt. The Countess was filled with enthusiasm for the Abbé Blanès, his primitive character and his astrological lore. What little money remained to her after the purchase of the boat had been used to buy a small second-hand telescope, and almost every evening, with her nieces and Fabrizio, she would climb up to the platform of one of the castle's Gothic towers. Fabrizio was the most knowledgeable of the party, and many pleasant hours were spent on those heights, far from prying eyes.

It must be confessed that there were days when the Countess spoke no word to a living soul; she was seen strolling under the tall chestnut-trees, absorbed in her gloomy reveries; she had too active a mind not to feel, occasionally, the tedium which comes from a failure to exchange ideas. But the following day she was as gay as she had been the day before: it was the grievances of her sister-in-law the Marchesa which produced such dark impressions on this naturally high-spirited creature. "Then must we waste what is left of our youth in this grim castle?" the Marchesa exclaimed.

Before the Countess's arrival, she had not had the courage to avow such regrets.

This was how they lived through the winter of 1814. Twice, despite her impecuniosity, the Marchesa went to spend a few days in Milan; once to see a sublime ballet by Viganò, given at La Scala, and the Marchese made no objection to his wife's being accompanied by his sister-in-law. The two women went together to cash the quarterly check of the Countess's little pension, whereupon it was the French general's poor widow who loaned a few sequins to the wealthy Marchesa del Dongo. These excursions were delightful; old friends were invited to dinner, and the company found consolation in laughing at everything, like children. This Italian gaiety, filled with *brio* and impulse, conjured away the melancholy which the glares of the Marchese and the Marchesino had spread around themselves at Grianta. Fabrizio, just sixteen, admirably represented the head of the house.

On March 7, 1815, the ladies had returned two days since from an agreeable little trip to Milan; they were strolling down the fine avenue of plane-trees recently extended to the water's edge when a boat appeared from the direction of Como, making strange signals. One of the Marchese's agents jumped out onto the embankment: Napoléon had just landed at the Gulf of Juan. Europe was sufficiently disingenuous to be surprised by this event, which failed to surprise the Marchese del Dongo; he wrote his sovereign a heartfelt letter, offering his talents and several millions, and informing him once again that his ministers were Jacobins in league with the ringleaders in Paris.

On March 8, at six in the morning, the Marchese, wearing all his orders, was having his elder son dictate the draft of a third political dispatch and solemnly transcribing the text in his fine painstaking hand on paper watermarked with the sovereign's effigy. At the same moment Fabrizio was shown into the Countess Pietranera's apartment.

"I'm leaving," he told her. "I shall join the Emperor, who is the King of Italy as well, and such a good friend to your husband! I shall travel by way of Switzerland. Tonight, at Menaggio, my friend Vasi, who sells barometers, has given me his passport; now you must give me a few napoleons, for I have only two; if you cannot, I shall go on foot."

The Countess wept for joy and anxiety. "Good God! Whatever made you think of such a thing!" she exclaimed, seizing his hands. She stood up and took out of her linen-closet, where it was carefully hidden, a little pearl-embroidered purse; this was all she possessed in the world. "Take it," she told Fabrizio, "but in the name of God, don't get yourself killed. What will your unhappy mother and I do if something should happen to you? As for Napoléon's success, my poor boy, it is impossible; our gentlemen will be sure to do away with him. Didn't you hear, last week, in Milan, the story of twenty-three assassination plots, each more cunning than the next, from which he escaped only by a miracle? And at the time he was omnipotent! And you've seen that our enemies haven't lacked the will to destroy him; France counted for nothing once he was gone." It was with the accents of the deepest feeling that the Countess described Napoléon's future destiny to Fabrizio. "By allowing you to join him, I am sacrificing what is dearest to me in the world," she said. Fabrizio's eyes filled with tears as he embraced the Countess, but his determination to leave was not shaken for a moment. He eagerly explained to this beloved friend the reasons which impelled him, and which we take the liberty of finding slightly absurd.

"Yesterday evening, at seven minutes to six, we were strolling, as you know, down the avenue of plane-trees to the lake shore above Casa Sommariva, and heading south. That was when I first saw the boat coming from Como, bringing such great news. As I was watching the boat without a thought of the Emperor, and simply envying the lot of those permitted to travel, I was suddenly seized by a powerful emotion. The boat landed, the agent whispered to my father, who turned white and took us aside to announce the *terrible news*. I turned toward the lake with no purpose but to conceal the tears of joy that filled my eyes. Suddenly, high in the sky to my right, I glimpsed an eagle—Napoléon's bird; it was soaring majestically toward Switzerland, and consequently toward Paris. And I too, I then resolved, would traverse Switzerland with the speed of an eagle, in order to offer that great man little enough but all I have: whatever strength resides in my weak right arm. He sought to give us a country, and he loved my uncle. While the eagle was still in sight, my tears suddenly dried; and as proof that this notion came from on high, without a moment's hesitation, I made my decision and discerned the means of making this journey. In the twinkling of an eye, all the sorrows which as you know poison my life, especially on Sundays, were somehow conjured away by a divine impulsion. I saw that great figure of Italy rise out of the mire in which the Germans keep her immersed, spreading her bruised and still enchainèd arms toward her king and her liberator. And I, I mused, the still unknown son of this unhappy mother, I shall depart, either to conquer or to die with this man chosen by fate, who would cleanse us of the obloquy we suffer from the vilest slaves of Europe!*

*The impassioned speaker translates into prose some lines by the famous poet Monti. [Stendhal's note.]

"As you know," he added in a low voice as he came closer to the Countess, staring at her with flaming eyes, "the winter I was born my mother planted with her own hands a young chestnut-tree beside a stream in our forest, two leagues from here: before taking action I was determined to have a look it. Spring is not yet far advanced, I reasoned: if my tree has already put forth leaves, that will be a sign. I too must emerge from the state of torpor in which I languish here in this cold and melancholy castle. Don't you see that these old and blackened walls, now the symbols and once the means of tyranny, are a true image of the melancholy winter? They are to me what winter is to my tree.

"Would you believe it, Gina? At seven-thirty last night I reached my chestnut-tree: it had leaves, lovely young leaves, already quite large! I kissed them without disturbing a single one, and respectfully spaded the soil around the beloved tree. And then and there, filled with new hopes, I crossed the mountain to Menaggio: I would need a passport in order to enter Switzerland. Time had flown, it was already one in the morning when I found myself at Vasi's door. At my first words he exclaimed, 'You are going to join Napoleon!' and flung himself into my arms. The others, too, embraced me passionately. 'Why am I a married man?' one of them asked."

Signora Pietranera had grown pensive; she regarded it as her duty to raise certain objections. If Fabrizio had had any experience of the world at all, he would have realized that the Countess herself did not believe in the good reasons she hastened to offer him. But though lacking such experience, he had his resolve; he did not even deign to listen to such objections. The Countess was soon reduced to making him promise that at least he would inform his mother of his plans.

"She will tell my sisters, and these women will betray me in spite of themselves!" cried Fabrizio, with a kind of heroic arrogance.

"Speak more respectfully," said the Countess, smiling through her tears, "of the sex which will make your fortune; for you will always displease the men—you have too much spirit for prosaic souls."

The Marchesa dissolved into tears upon learning of her son's strange plan; she was quite indifferent to such heroism and did everything she could to keep him from leaving. When she was convinced that nothing in the world but prison walls could keep him beside her, she gave him what little money she possessed, and then remembered that the day before the Marchese had entrusted her with eight or ten little diamonds, worth perhaps ten thousand francs, to take to Milan to be set. Fabrizio's sisters came into their mother's room while the Countess was sewing these diamonds into our hero's overcoat; he restored their scanty napoleons to these poor women. His sisters were so excited by his plan and embraced him so noisily that he snatched up the few diamonds still to be concealed and tried to leave then and there.

"You will betray me without even meaning to," he told them. "Since I am now so rich, there is no need for me to pack any clothes. I can buy them anywhere." He embraced these persons who were so dear to him, and left immediately, without even returning to his own room. He walked so fast, constantly fearing to be pursued by men on horseback, that he reached Lugano that very evening. Thank Heaven he was in a Swiss town, and no longer in danger of being attacked on a lonely road by officers in his father's pay. To the latter he wrote a noble letter from Lugano, a boyish weakness which added fuel to the Marchese's fury. Fabrizio took the post through the Saint-Gothard Pass, he traveled fast, and entered France through Pontarlier. The Emperor was in Paris. Here Fabrizio's misfortunes began; he had left with the firm intention of speaking to the Emperor; it had never occurred to him that this might be a difficult enterprise. In Milan, he had seen Prince Eugène ten times a day and could have addressed him on any occasion. In Paris, he went every morning to the courtyard of the Tuileries to watch Napoléon review his troops; but he could never approach the Emperor. Our hero supposed all Frenchmen were as deeply moved as himself by the extreme danger which threatened their country. At the hotel dining-table, he made no secret of his intentions and his devotion; the young men he met there were remarkably kind and even more enthusiastic than himself; in a few days they succeeded in relieving him of all the money he possessed. Fortunately, out of sheer modesty, he had not mentioned the diamonds his mother had given him. When he realized, one morning after a night's orgy, that he had certainly been robbed, he purchased two fine horses, hired one of the horse-dealer's grooms as his servant, and in his scorn of the well-spoken young Parisians, left to join the army, about which he knew nothing except that troops were mustering near Maubeuge. No sooner had he reached the frontier than he found it demeaning to stay indoors, with nothing better to do than warming himself in front of a good fire, while soldiers were in bivouac outside. Ignoring the words of his servant, a sensible man, he rashly set off for the camps that lined the road to Belgium. No sooner had he reached the first battalion bivouacked there than the soldiers began staring at this young civilian about whose clothes there was nothing to suggest a uniform. Night was falling, and a cold wind blowing. Fabrizio approached a campfire and offered to pay for hospitality. The soldiers exchanged astonished glances at the notion of payment, and kindly granted him a place at the fire; his servant made a shelter for him. But an hour later, when the regimental adjutant happened to pass by, the soldiers reported the arrival of this stranger speaking bad French. The adjutant questioned Fabrizio, who described his enthusiasm for the Emperor in his extremely noticeable accent; whereupon the adjutant requested our hero to accompany him to the colonel, billeted in a farmhouse nearby. Fabrizio's servant followed with the two horses, the sight of which struck the adjutant so forcibly that he immediately changed his mind and began interrogating Fabrizio's servant as well. The latter, an old soldier, instantly guessing his questioner's intentions, alluded to his master's influential protectors, adding that of course no one would *pinch* his fine horses. Immediately a soldier summoned by the adjutant collared the servant while another soldier seized the horses, and with a stern glance the adjutant ordered Fabrizio to follow him without a speaking a word.

After making him cover a good league on foot, in a night made even darker by the campfires which illuminated the horizon on all sides, the adjutant handed Fabrizio over to an officer of the *gendarmerie* who gave him a hard look and asked for his papers. Fabrizio produced the passport which described him as a dealer in barometers *bearing merchandise.*

"How stupid do they think we are?" the officer exclaimed. "This is too much!" He questioned our hero, who spoke of the Emperor and of liberty in terms of the liveliest enthusiasm; whereupon the officer burst into uncontrollable laughter.

"Now I've heard everything!" he exclaimed. "Who could believe they'd send us such fools!"

And though Fabrizio made every effort to explain that in reality he wasn't a barometer dealer at all, the officer sent him to prison in B——, a nearby town our hero reached at about three in the morning, beside himself with anger and tired to death.

Fabrizio, first astounded, then enraged, understanding absolutely nothing of what was happening to him, spent thirty-three long days in that wretched jail; he wrote letter after letter to the commandant of the place, and it was his jailer's wife, a handsome Flemish woman of thirty-six, who promised to deliver them. But since she had no desire to see such a handsome fellow shot, and since moreover he paid well, she never failed to toss every one into the fire. Late in the evening she deigned to come in and listen to the prisoner's complaints; she had told her husband that the young fool had money, whereupon the prudent jailer had given her carte blanche. She availed herself of this advantage and received several gold napoleons, for the adjutant had stolen only the horses, and the officer of the *gendarmerie* had confiscated nothing at all. One June afternoon, Fabrizio heard a burst of distant cannon-fire. So they were fighting at last! His heart leaped with impatience. He also heard a lot of commotion in the town; as a matter of fact a considerable maneuver was under way, three divisions passing through B——. When, around eleven at night, the jailer's wife came to share his woes, Fabrizio was even friendlier than usual; then, taking her hands in his: "Get me out of here—I swear on my honor to come back to this prison as soon as the fighting is over."

"Poppycock! Do you have what it takes?"

He looked troubled, not understanding her expression. The jailer's wife, seeing this, decided his funds were running low, and instead of stipulating gold napoleons as she had planned, now spoke only of francs. "Listen," she said, "if you can get hold of a hundred francs, I'll put double napoleons on the corporal's eyes when he comes on guard duty tonight. He won't be able to see you leave jail, and if his regiment has to march tomorrow, he'll agree to it."

The bargain was soon struck. The jailer's wife even consented to hide Fabrizio in her room, from which he could easily escape the following day.

The next morning, before dawn, this woman was overcome by a tender impulse and said to Fabrizio: "My boy, you're still much too young to go in for this nasty business: take my advice and don't come back here."

"Don't come back . . ." repeated Fabrizio. "Then is it a crime to want to defend one's country?"

"Enough of that. Just remember I saved your life; the case was clear—you would have been shot. But don't tell anyone, you'll lose both of us our jobs, my man *and* me. And above all, don't go telling that silly story of a Milanese gentleman disguised as a barometer salesman—it's too stupid! Listen to me now: I'm going to give you the uniform of a hussar who died in here a couple of days ago: don't open your mouth if you can help it, but if some billeting sergeant or an officer asks you questions you have to answer, say you were lying sick in some farmer's house after he found you trembling with fever in a roadside ditch and took you in out of charity. If they're not satisfied with an answer like that, say you're going back to your regiment. They may arrest you because of your accent, so then you say you were born in Piedmont and stayed in France last year after conscription, something like that . . ."

For the first time, after thirty-three days of rage, Fabrizio understood everything that had happened to him. He had been taken for a spy. He argued with the jailer's wife, who had been so tender that morning; and finally, while she was taking in the hussar's uniform with a needle, he managed to make sense of his story to the astonished creature. She believed it for a while, he seemed so naive and looked so handsome in his hussar's uniform!

"Since you're so eager to fight," she remarked, half-convinced at last, "you'd better enlist in a regiment once you get to Paris. If you buy some recruiting sergeant a drink, you'll get what you want!"

The jailer's wife added a good deal of advice for the future, and finally, at dawn, let Fabrizio out of her room, after making him swear a hundred times over that he would never utter her name, whatever happened. Once Fabrizio had left the little town, walking boldly along with the hussar's sword under his arm, he was overcome by a scruple: "Here I am," he mused, "with the uniform and the map of a hussar who died in jail, apparently because he stole a cow and some silverware! So I've inherited his identity, so to speak . . . without wanting to or expecting anything of the kind! Beware of prison! The signs are clear: I'll have a lot to suffer from prisons!"

Not an hour had passed since Fabrizio had parted from his benefactress, when it began raining so hard that the new hussar could barely walk, encumbered as he was by the heavy boots which were certainly not his size. He met up with a farmer riding on a sorry nag he purchased then and there with the help of sign-language; the jailer's wife had suggested he speak as little as possible, on account of his accent.

On that day the army, which had just won the battle of Ligny, was marching straight for Brussels; it was the eve of the battle of Waterloo. Around noon, the downpour still continuing, Fabrizio heard the sound of cannon-fire; such happiness immediately erased all memory of the dreadful moments of despair which his recent unjust imprisonment had forced upon him. He rode late into the night, and since he was beginning to gain a little good sense, he sought lodgings in a farmhouse quite far from the road. The farmer wept and claimed that everything had been taken from him; Fabrizio gave him an *écu,* and he found some oats. "My horse isn't much good," Fabrizio decided, "but even so, he might find favor with some adjutant," and he lay down in the stable beside the poor beast. An hour before daylight, Fabrizio was on the road again, and by lavishing caresses on his horse, he managed to persuade it to trot. By about five in the morning, he heard the cannonade: Waterloo had begun.

CHAPTER THREE

Fabrizio soon encountered some canteen-women, and his extreme gratitude to the jailer's wife in B—— moved him to speak to them; he inquired as to the whereabouts of the Fourth Regiment of Hussars, to which he belonged.

"Better not be in such a hurry, soldier-boy," one woman said, touched by Fabrizio's pale face and fine eyes. "Your wrist isn't strong enough yet for the saber-cuts being given today. Still, if you had a musket, you might fire a bullet as well as the next man."

Such advice did not please Fabrizio, but however much he urged on his horse, he could not pass the canteen-woman's cart. Now and then the sound of cannon-fire seemed to come closer and kept them from hearing each other, for Fabrizio was so beside himself with enthusiasm that he had begun talking once again. Each of the canteen-woman's remarks doubled his pleasure by making him understand it. Except for his real name and his escape from prison, he ended by confiding everything to this obviously kind woman. She was greatly astonished and understood nothing the handsome young soldier was telling her.

"Now I see what it is!" she finally exclaimed in triumph. "You're a civilian in love with the wife of some captain in the Fourth. Your mistress has given you that uniform, and you're running after her. Sure as

the Lord is God, you've never been a soldier in your life, but you're a brave boy, and now that your regiment's under fire, you want to be there and not let them think you're some pantywaist!"

Fabrizio agreed with all she said: it was his only way of obtaining good advice. "I haven't a clue how these French people behave," he said to himself, "and unless someone helps me, I'll get myself thrown into prison all over again, and my horse stolen into the bargain."

"First of all, my boy," said the canteen-woman, who was becoming an ever more intimate friend, "admit you're not yet twenty-one; at the very most you might be seventeen."

This was the truth, and Fabrizio confessed it freely.

"So you're not even a conscript; it's all because of Madame's pretty face that you're going to get your bones broken for you. Damn but she's none too particular! If you still have some of those gold pieces she gave you, first thing you do is buy a different horse. Look how your nag pricks up her ears when the cannons snore a little too close; that's a farm horse, and she'll be the death of you as soon as you reach the line. See that white smoke above the hedge over there? That's infantry fire, my boy! So get ready for a big scare when you hear the bullets whistling. You'd better get something into your stomach while there's still time."

Fabrizio followed this advice, and offering the canteen-woman a napoleon, asked her to accept what he owed her.

"It's pitiful!" she exclaimed. "The poor boy doesn't even know how to spend his money! Serve you right if I took your napoleon and then made Cocotte here trot right along. I'll be damned if your nag could follow us. What would you do, silly fool, when you saw me clearing out? Learn this much, at least: when the Big One grumbles, never show your cash. Here," she said, "take your eighteen francs fifty centimes, and your meal will cost you thirty sous. Now, we'll soon be having some horses for sale. If there's a small one, you offer ten francs, in any case never more than twenty, even if it's Lancelot's own!"

The meal over, the canteen-woman, who was still haranguing him, was interrupted by a woman crossing the fields and passing them on the road. "Hey there!" she shouted. "Margot! Your Sixth Light is over on the right."

"I must leave you, my boy," the canteen-woman remarked to our hero; "but I pity you, I really do; we're friends, after all, Lord knows! You really are an ignoramus, aren't you? And you're going to get yourself mowed down as sure as the Lord is God! You better come with me to the Sixth Light."

"I know I'm ignorant," Fabrizio replied, "but I want to fight, and I've made up my mind to go where that white smoke is."

"Look how your nag is pricking up her ears! Once she's over there, weak as she is, she'll take the bit between her teeth and start galloping and God knows where you'll end up. Listen to me! As soon as you're with the soldier-boys, pick up a musket and a cartridge-pouch, get yourself down beside the men, and do exactly what they do. But my God, I bet you don't even know how to tear open a cartridge!"

Fabrizio, stung to the quick, nonetheless admitted to his new friend that she had guessed correctly.

"The poor boy'll get himself killed right off. As God is my witness it won't take long. You better come with me," the canteen-woman continued imperatively.

"But I want to fight . . ."

"And fight you will. Come on, the Sixth Light is famous for fighting, and today there'll be enough for everyone."

"But will we find your regiment soon?"

"In a quarter of an hour at most."

"With this good woman's help," Fabrizio told himself, "I won't be taken for a spy, despite my ignorance, and I'll be able to do some fighting." At this moment the cannon-fire redoubled, each explosion coming immediately after the last. "It's like a rosary," Fabrizio thought.

"You can hear the infantry shots now," said the canteen-woman, whipping her little horse, which seemed quite excited by the gunfire.

The canteen-woman turned right and followed a road through the fields; the mud was a foot deep here, and the little cart was about to get stuck; Fabrizio gave the wheel a push; his own horse fell twice; soon the road, though less muddy, was no more than a path through high grass. Fabrizio had not ridden five hundred paces when his mare stopped short: a body was lying across the path, frightening both horse and rider.

Fabrizio's face, naturally pale, turned distinctly green; the canteen-woman, after glancing at the corpse, observed as if to herself: "Not from our division." Then, glancing up at our hero, she burst out laughing. "Here, my boy!" she exclaimed. "Here's something nice for you!"

Fabrizio was petrified. What struck him most was the dead man's filthy feet, already stripped of his shoes; the corpse was left with nothing but a blood-stained pair of ragged trousers.

"Come here," the canteen-woman ordered, "get off your horse. You've got to get used to this. Look!" she exclaimed. "He got it in the head." A bullet, entering one side of the nose, had come out through the opposite temple and hideously disfigured the corpse; one eyes was still open. "So get off your horse, boy," the canteen-woman said, "shake his hand for him, and see if he'll shake yours."

Without hesitation, though ready to expire with disgust, Fabrizio flung himself off his horse and took the corpse's hand, shaking it hard; then he remained standing where he was, as if paralyzed; he felt he had no strength to remount. What horrified him most was that open eye.

"She'll think I'm a coward," he realized bitterly, but he felt it was quite impossible to move: he would have fallen down. This was a terrible moment; Fabrizio was about to be sick. The canteen-woman realized this, jumped down from her cart and without a word offered him a shot of brandy, which he swallowed in one gulp; after that he could remount, and they continued along the path without speaking. The canteen-woman glanced at him from time to time out of the corner of her eye.

"You'll fight tomorrow, my boy," she said at last, "today you're staying with me. You see now, you've still got something to learn about soldiering."

"No, I want to fight right away," exclaimed our hero grimly, which the canteen-woman took for a good sign.

The cannon-fire redoubled and seemed to come closer. The explosions now formed a kind of *basso continuo;* there was no interval separating the explosions, and against this *basso continuo,* which suggested the sound of a distant stream, they could now make out the regimental gunfire.

Just then the road sloped down into a grove of trees: the canteen-woman caught sight of three or four French soldiers running toward her as fast as they could; she quickly jumped down from her cart and managed to hide fifteen or twenty feet off the road, crouching in a hole where a huge tree had been uprooted. "Now," Fabrizio decided, "now I'll find out if I'm a coward!" He stood beside the little cart the canteen-woman had abandoned and drew his saber. The soldiers paid no attention to him and ran past him through the grove to the left of the path.

"Those are our men," the canteen-woman said calmly, returning quite winded to her wagon. "If your horse could gallop, I'd send you to the edge of the woods to see what's out there on the field."

Fabrizio did not need to be told twice; he tore off a poplar branch, stripped its leaves, and began whipping his horse with all his might; the mare broke into a gallop for a moment, then returned to her customary trot. The canteen-woman had whipped her horse to a gallop as well.

"Now stop there, whoa!" she shouted to Fabrizio.

Soon both of them were out of the woods; at the edge of the field they heard a dreadful racket, cannon-fire and muskets rattling on all sides, to the right, to the left, and behind them. And since the grove they had just left covered a hill some eight or ten feet above the field, they saw a corner of the battle quite clearly; but there was no one to be seen in the field beyond the woods. This field was bordered, about a thousand paces from where they were, by a long row of bushy willows; above these appeared some white smoke circling upward into the sky.

"If only I knew where the regiment was!" said the canteen-woman, at a loss. "We can't cross this big open space. And by the way, you," she said to Fabrizio, "if you see an enemy soldier, run him through, don't bother trying to cut him down . . ."

At this moment the canteen-woman caught sight of the four soldiers just mentioned, coming out of the woods onto the field to the left of the path. One of them was mounted.

"There's what you want," she said to Fabrizio. "Hey, you there!" she shouted to the man on the horse. "Come over here and have some brandy."

The soldiers approached.

"Where's the Sixth Light?" she shouted.

"Over there, five minutes from here, on the other side of that ditch, behind the willows. And Colonel Macon's just been killed."

"How much do you want for your horse—will you take five francs?"

"Five francs! You're joking, Mother—this here's an officer's horse I can sell for five napoleons any time I want."

"Give me one of your napoleons," the canteen-woman murmured to Fabrizio. Then, approaching the mounted soldier: "Get off quick," she said, "here's your napoleon."

The soldier dismounted, Fabrizio leaped gaily into the saddle, and the canteen-woman unfastened the little portmanteau strapped to his mare. "All right, you men, help me!" she scolded the other soldiers. "Is this the way you let a lady do your work?"

But no sooner had the newly purchased horse felt the weight of the portmanteau than it began to rear, and Fabrizio, though an excellent rider, needed all his strength to control it.

"A good sign!" the canteen-woman said. "This fellow's not used to being tickled by a portmaneau!"

"A general's horse!" exclaimed the soldier who had just sold it. "A horse worth ten napoleons if it's worth a sou!"

"Here's twenty francs," Fabrizio said to him, beside himself with joy at feeling a spirited horse under him.

At this moment a cannonball sliced along the row of willows, affording Fabrizio the odd spectacle of all those twigs flying to either side as though sheared off by a scythe-stroke. "That's cannon-fire coming toward us," the soldier told him, taking his twenty francs.

It might have been two o'clock in the afternoon.

Fabrizio was still under the spell of this strange spectacle, when a group of generals, followed by some twenty hussars, galloped past a corner of the vast field, on the edge of which he was still standing; his horse whinnied, reared two or three times, then pulled violently at the bit. "So be it, go!" Fabrizio decided.

Left to himself, the horse galloped off to join the escort following the generals. Fabrizio counted four gold-braided hats. Fifteen minutes later, Fabrizio understood from a few words spoken by a hussar near him that one of these generals was the famous Marshal Ney. His happiness was complete; yet he could not tell which of the four was the Marshal. He would have given anything in the world to know, but remembered that he must not speak. The escort halted before crossing a broad ditch filled with rainwater from the night before; the ditch was lined with huge trees, forming the boundary of the field on the left, ' where Fabrizio had bought his horse. Almost all the hussars had dismounted; the side of the ditch was steep and slippery, and the water level was a good three or four feet below the brink. Fabrizio, wild with joy, was thinking more about Marshal Ney and glory than of his horse, which in its excitement leaped into the ditch; this raised the water level considerably. One of the generals was completely soaked by the sheet of water and swore aloud: "Damn the brute!"

Fabrizio was deeply wounded by this insult. "Can I demand an apology?" he wondered. Meanwhile, to prove he was not so clumsy, he tried to urge his horse up the opposite side of the ditch; but the slope was steep, and five or six feet high. He had to give it up, and rode upstream, the water up to his horse's head, and finally reached a sort of ford where the cattle came to drink; up this shallow slope he easily reached the field on the other side of the ditch. He was the first man of the troop to appear there; he began trotting proudly along the edge: the hussars were still floundering at the bottom of the ditch, struggling for a foothold, for in many places the water was five feet deep. Two or three horses took fright and tried to swim, which created a dreadful confusion. One sergeant noticed the maneuver just made by this youngster who seemed so unsoldierly.

"Back on your horses! There's a ford to the left!" he shouted, and gradually all the men clambered out of the ditch.

Upon reaching the other side, Fabrizio had found the generals there by themselves; the cannonade seemed twice as loud to him; he could scarcely hear the general he had just splashed shouting in his ear: "Where did you get that horse?"

Fabrizio was so distracted that he answered in Italian: *"L'ho comprato poco fa."* (I bought it just now.)

"What did you say?" the general shouted.

But the racket now grew so loud that Fabrizio could not answer. We must confess that at this moment our hero was anything but a hero. Still, fear was only his second reaction; he was chiefly outraged by this noise that was hurting his ears. The escort broke into a gallop, crossing a broad stretch of ploughed field on the far side of the ditch, strewn with corpses.

"Redcoats! Redcoats!" the hussars shouted with joy.

At first Fabrizio failed to understand; then he noticed that indeed almost all the corpses were wearing red. One circumstance made him shudder with horror: many of these wretched redcoats were still alive; they were obviously calling for help, and no one was stopping to give it to them. Our hero, a profoundly humane character, took all the pains in the world to keep his horse from planting its hooves on any redcoat.

The escort halted; Fabrizio, who was not paying sufficient attention to his duty as a soldier, galloped on, glancing down at a pathetic wounded soldier.

"Halt right there, you fool" the sergeant shouted at him.

Fabrizio realized he was twenty paces to the right, out in front of the generals, and precisely at the spot on which they were focusing their spyglasses. Returning to line up with the other hussars who had remained a few paces behind, he saw the fattest of these generals speaking to his neighbor with an authoritative, almost scolding expression; he was swearing. Fabrizio could not contain his curiosity, and in spite of the advice not to speak, which his friend the jailer's wife had given him, he worked out a very correct little French sentence and said to the man next to him: "Who is that general chewing out the one next to him?"

"Damn, that's the Marshal!"

"Which Marshal?"

"Marshal Ney, you idiot! Damn, where've you been fighting till now?"

Fabrizio, though extremely sensitive, had no thought of taking offense; he stared, lost in childish admiration of this famous Prince of the Moskova, "bravest of the brave."

Suddenly everyone galloped off. A few moments later Fabrizio saw, twenty paces ahead, a ploughed field that seemed to be strange in motion; the furrows were filled with water, and the wet ground that formed their crests was exploding into tiny black fragments flung three or four feet into the air. Fabrizio noticed this odd effect as he passed; then his mind returned to daydreams of the Marshal's glory. He heard a sharp cry beside him: two hussars had fallen, riddled by bullets; and when he turned to look at them, they were already twenty paces behind the escort. What seemed horrible to him was a blood-covered horse struggling in the furrows and trying to follow the others: blood was flowing into the mire.

"Aha! Now we're under fire at last. I've seen action!" he kept telling himself, with a certain satisfaction. "Now I'm a true soldier." At this moment the escort began galloping at breakneck speed, and our hero realized that these were bullets tearing up the earth. Though he tried to see where they were coming from, there was nothing but white smoke from the battery a great ways off, and amid the continuous roaring of cannon-fire he seemed to hear explosions much closer to him; he could make nothing of it.

At this moment the generals and their escort rode down into a little path filled with water five feet below the level of the field. The Marshal stopped and stared through his spyglass once again. Fabrizio, this time, could examine him at his leisure: he was very blond, with a huge red face. "We don't have faces like that in Italy," he said to himself. "Pale as I am, and with such dark hair, I'll never get to look like that," he concluded sadly. For him these words meant: "I'll never be a hero." He stared at the hussars; all but one had yellow moustaches. If Fabrizio stared at the hussars in the escort, they certainly stared back, and this stare made him blush. To put an end to his embarrassment, he turned his horse toward the enemy. These were long lines of red-coated men, but what astonished him most was how tiny these men appeared. Their long files, which were regiments or divisions, looked to him no higher than hedgerows. A line of red cavalry was trotting toward the sunken path where the Marshal and his escort were riding, stumbling through the mud. Smoke kept them from making out anything from the direction in which they were advancing; sometimes men on horseback were silhouetted against that white smoke as they galloped past.

Suddenly Fabrizio saw four men from the enemy lines galloping toward him. "Ah, now we're being attacked!" he told himself; then he saw two of these men speaking to the Marshal. One of the generals on the latter's staff galloped off toward the enemy, followed by two hussars of the escort and the four men who had just arrived. After everyone had crossed a ditch, Fabrizio found himself beside a sergeant who seemed friendly enough. "I must speak to this fellow," he decided, "maybe then they'll stop staring at me." He pondered a long while. "Monsieur, this is the first time I've seen battle," he finally said to the sergeant, "but is this a real battle?"

"Real enough. Who're you?"

"I'm a brother of the captain's wife."

"What's his name, your captain?"

Our hero was dreadfully embarrassed; he had not foreseen such a question. Fortunately the Marshal and his escort galloped off again once more. "What French name shall I say?" Fabrizio wondered. Finally he remembered the name of the innkeeper where he had lodged in Paris; he rode close to the sergeant's horse and shouted as loud as he could: "Captain Meunier!"

The man heard little enough because of the cannonade, and answered: "Captain Teulier, is it? Well, he's been killed."

"Fine, it's Captain Teulier: I must look sad," Fabrizio decided, and exclaimed: "Killed! Oh my God!" and assumed a woebegone expression.

They had left the sunken path and were crossing a little field, galloping through the hail of bullets, the Marshal heading for a cavalry division. The escort was riding over corpses and wounded men, but already such a spectacle made much less of an impression on our hero: he had other things to think about.

While the escort halted, Fabrizio noticed the little cart of a canteen-woman, and his affections for this worthy occupation prevailing over all else, he galloped over to join her.

"Stay where you are, damn you!" the sergeant shouted at him.

"What can he do to me here?" Fabrizio decided, and continued galloping toward the canteen-woman. As he spurred his horse on, he had some hope that this was his companion of the morning, the cart and horse being quite similar to those he remembered, but it was an entirely different owner that he approached, and our hero found her quite unwelcoming. As he came near, Fabrizio heard her saying: "... and such a good-looking one, too!"

A nasty sight awaited the new soldier; they were amputating a cuirassier's leg at the thigh, a handsome fellow almost six feet tall. Fabrizio closed his eyes and drank four brandies one after the next.

"Go for it, boy!" exclaimed the canteen-woman.

The brandy gave him an idea: "I must buy the good will of my comrades in the escort." And he told the canteen-woman to give him the rest of the bottle.

"Do you know I can get ten francs for this, on a day like today?"

As he galloped back to the escort, the sergeant exclaimed: "So you're bringing back something for us! That's why you deserted, is it? Hand it over."

The bottle circulated; the last one to drink tossed it into the air. "Thanks, comrade!" he shouted to Fabrizio. All eyes were on him, approvingly now, and these stares removed a hundred-pound weight from Fabrizio's heart, which was one of those hearts of excessive delicacy which required friendship from those around it. At last he was no longer disliked by his companions—there was a bond between them!

Fabrizio breathed deeply, then said to the sergeant in a loud voice: "And if Captain Teulier's been killed, where can I find my sister?" He regarded himself as a little Machiavelli for saying *Teulier* so cleverly instead of *Meunier*.

"You'll find that out tonight," the sergeant replied.

The escort set off again, heading for the infantry divisions. Fabrizio realized he was quite intoxicated; he had drunk too much brandy, and rolled a little in his saddle: opportunely enough, he remembered something his mother's coachman used to say: "When you've had one too many, look between your horse's ears and do what the man beside you does." The Marshal stopped for a long while beside several cavalry units he ordered to charge; but for an hour or two our hero had virtually no awareness of what was happening around him. He felt very tired, and when his horse was galloping, he fell back in the saddle like a lump of lead.

Suddenly the sergeant shouted to his men: "Don't you see it's the Emperor, you dolts ... ?"

Immediately the entire escort shouted *"Vive l'Empereur!"* at the top of their lungs. It will be conceived how intently our hero stared, but he saw nothing but galloping generals, followed by another escort. The long horsehair plumes dangling from their dragoon-helmets kept him from making out their faces. "So I failed to see the Emperor on the battlefield because of those cursed brandies!" he reflected, and found himself wide awake.

They rode back down into a path filled with water, where the horses wanted to drink. "Was that the Emperor who went past just now?" he asked the man beside him.

"Of course—the one without gold braid. How could you miss him?" his comrade answered good-humoredly.

Fabrizio longed to gallop after the Emperor's escort and join it. What bliss to be waging war in this hero's own company! That was why he had come to France! "I'm perfectly free to do as I choose," he mused, "after all, what other reason do I have for serving here but the will of my horse that has taken it into its head to gallop after these generals?"

What persuaded Fabrizio to remain was that his new comrades the hussars were smiling at him now; he was beginning to regard himself as the intimate friend of all these soldiers he had been riding with for several hours. Between them and himself he perceived the noble friendship of the heroes in Tasso and Ariosto. Were he to join the Emperor's escort, there would be new acquaintances to make; perhaps he would even be frowned at, for those other riders were dragoons, and he was wearing a hussar's uniform, along with all those serving under the Marshal. The way he was now being regarded delighted our hero, he would have done anything in the world for his comrades; his heart and soul were in the clouds. Everything seemed to have changed its appearance since he was with friends, and he was dying to ask questions. "But I'm still a little drunk," he decided. "I must remember what the jailer's wife said." He noticed as they left the sunken path that the escort was no longer with Marshal Ney; the general they were now following was tall, slender, and his expression was severe, his eyes terrible.

This general was none other than Count d'A——, our Lieutenant

Robert of May 15, 1796. How happy he would have been to see Fabrizio del Dongo!

It was already some time since Fabrizio had stopped noticing the earth exploding into black crumbs under the hail of bullets; now, as they came up behind a regiment of cuirassiers, he clearly heard the grapeshot landing on their breastplates, and saw several men fall to the ground.

The sun was already very low and about to set when the escort, leaving the sunken path, climbed a slope of some three or four feet into a ploughed field. Fabrizio heard a strange little noise right beside him, he turned to look: four men had fallen with their horses; the general himself had been knocked down but stood up again, covered with blood. Fabrizio stared at the hussars on the ground: three of them were still making convulsive movements, the fourth screamed: "Pull me out, get this beast off me!"

The sergeant and two or three men had dismounted to help the general who, leaning on his aide-de-camp, was trying to take a few steps; he wanted to get away from his horse that was struggling on the ground, its hooves lashing out furiously.

The sergeant came over to Fabrizio. At this moment our hero heard someone behind him say, quite close to his ear: "That's the only one still fit to gallop." He felt someone grab his feet; they were lifted out of the stirrups at the same time that his body was seized under the arms, and he was raised over the horse's tail and let slide to the ground, where he landed in a sitting position.

The aide-de-camp took Fabrizio's horse by the bridle; the general, with the sergeant's help, mounted and galloped off, rapidly followed by the remaining six men. Fabrizio stood up, furious, and began running after them, shouting: *"Ladri! Ladri!"* (Thieves! Thieves!) What a farce, to be running across a battlefield after horse-thieves!

The escort and the general (Count d'A———) soon disappeared behind a row of willows. Fabrizio, blind with rage, also reached this boundary and found himself at a deep ditch, which he waded across. Then, on the other side, he began swearing again as he once more caught sight—but far off now—of the general and his escort vanishing into the trees. "Thieves! Thieves!" he shouted, in French this time.

Despairing much less over the loss of his horse than on account of the betrayal, Fabrizio let himself collapse beside the ditch, exhausted and famished. If his splendid horse had been stolen by the enemy, he would have thought nothing of it; but to see himself robbed and betrayed by this sergeant he was so fond of and by these hussars he regarded as his brothers! That was what broke his heart. He could not console himself for such infamy and, leaning against a willow, began to weep bitter tears. One by one he was dispelling all his fine dreams of sublime and knightly comradeship like that of the heroes of *Gerusalemme Liberata*. To look death in the face was nothing, surrounded by tender and heroic souls, noble friends who clasp your hand at their last gasp! But to preserve your enthusiasm in the midst of knaves and scoundrels!! Fabrizio was exaggerating, like any offended man. After a quarter of an hour's emotion, he noticed that the bullets were beginning to reach the row of trees shading his meditations. He stood up and tried to figure out where he was. He stared at these fields bordered by a wide ditch and the row of bushy willows: he thought he recognized the place. He caught sight of a group of infantrymen crossing the ditch and walking into the field a quarter of a league ahead of him. "I was falling asleep," he realized; "I must be careful not to be taken prisoner," and he began walking very fast. As he proceeded he was reassured, recognizing the uniforms: the regiments by which he feared being cut off were French! He turned right to join them.

After the moral anguish of having been so basely robbed and betrayed, there was yet another which constantly made itself felt even more intensely: he was dying of hunger. So it was with extreme delight that after having walked, or rather run, for some ten minutes, he realized that the infantrymen, who were also moving very fast, were stopping as though to take up positions. A few minutes later he found himself among the first soldiers. "Comrades, can you sell me a piece of bread?"

"Here's someone who thinks we're bakers."

This harsh remark and the general mockery that followed it overwhelmed Fabrizio. So war was no longer that noble and mutual impulse of glory-loving souls which he had assumed it was from Napoléon's proclamations! He sat down, or rather let himself fall to the ground; he grew very pale. The soldier he had spoken to, who had stopped ten paces off to clean his musket-lock with his handkerchief, came over and tossed him a hunk of bread; then, seeing that he failed to pick it up, thrust it into his mouth. Fabrizio opened his eyes and chewed the bread without having the strength to speak. When at last he glanced around for the soldier in order to pay him, he found himself alone—the nearest soldiers were a hundred paces off, and marching away. He stood up mechanically and followed them. He entered a grove of trees; numb with fatigue, he was glancing around for a convenient place to sleep, but what was his joy upon recognizing first the horse, then the cart, and finally the canteen-woman of that morning! She ran over to him, alarmed by his appearance. "Walk a little farther, my boy," she exclaimed. "Are you wounded? Where's that fine horse of yours?" With such words she led him toward her cart, onto which she helped him, supporting him under the arms. No sooner on the cart than our hero, overcome with exhaustion, fell fast asleep.

CHAPTER FOUR

Nothing could wake him, neither the musket-fire so close to the little cart, nor the trotting horse which the canteen-woman was whipping with all her might. The regiment, unexpectedly attacked by a host of Prussian cavalry, after imagining victory all day long, was beating a retreat, or rather fleeing in the direction of France.

The colonel, a handsome, smartly dressed young fellow who had just succeeded Macon, was cut down; the battalion commander replacing him, an old man with white hair, ordered the regiment to halt. "Damn you!" he harangued the soldiers, "in the days of the Republic we didn't run away until the enemy forced us to.... Defend every inch of ground with your lives!" he shouted, swearing at them. "It's your native land these Prussians will be invading now!"

The little cart stopped, and Fabrizio woke with a start. The sun had long since set; he was astonished to discover that it was almost dark. Soldiers were running here and there in a confusion which amazed our hero; he thought they looked ashamed of themselves. "What's happening?" he asked the canteen-woman.

"Nothing much. Except that we're done for, my boy; that's the Prussian cavalry cutting us down. At first that fool of a general thought they were our men. Quick now, help me mend Cocotte's harness—it's broken."

Some shots were fired not ten paces away; our hero, cool and composed now, realized, "Actually, I didn't see battle once this whole day, all I did was escort a general." And he told the canteen-woman, "I must get into the fighting."

"Rest easy, you'll be fighting, and more than you bargained for! We're in for it. . . . Hey, Aubry boy!" she shouted at a passing corporal. "Keep an eye on the cart for me."

"Are you going to fight?" Fabrizio asked Aubry.

"No, I'm putting on my dancing-slippers!"

"I'll follow you."

"Take care of the little hussar," the canteen-woman called to him, "he's a gentleman with a heart."

Corporal Aubry walked on without a word. When eight or ten soldiers ran up and joined him, he led them behind a big oak in a briar patch. Here he posted them along the edge of the woods, still without a word, on a wide front, each man at least ten paces from the next.

"All right, you men!" the corporal shouted, and these were his first words. "Don't fire until you're ordered to—remember, all you've got is three rounds."

"What's happening here?" Fabrizio wondered. Finally, when he was alone with the corporal, he told him, "I have no musket."

"Shut up, then. Go over there: fifty paces into the woods you'll find one of those poor bastards of the regiment that's just been cut down— take his musket and his cartridge-pouch. But don't strip a wounded man; take the gun from someone who's good and dead, and hurry up about it so you don't get shot by our fellows."

Fabrizio ran off and quickly returned with a musket and pouch.

"Load your gun and get behind that tree, and be sure not to fire until I give orders. . . . God in Heaven!" the corporal broke off. "He doesn't even know how to load his gun . . . !" He helped Fabrizio do this while giving further directions. "If an enemy hussar gallops toward you with his saber up, duck behind your tree, and don't fire until he's on top of you—three steps off. Your bayonet should be almost

touching his uniform. And throw away that heavy saber," the corporal shouted, "you want it to trip you up, for God's sake . . . ! A fine lot of soldiers they're sending us these days!" And with these words he grabbed Fabrizio's saber and flung it angrily as far as he could. "All right, you, wipe your musket-flint with your handkerchief. Haven't you ever fired a gun?"

"I've done some hunting."

"God be praised!" the corporal answered with a sigh. "Be sure not to fire before I order you to." And he walked away.

Fabrizio was ecstatic. "At last I'll really be fighting," he said to himself, "killing an enemy! This morning we were under fire, and the only thing that happened was that I nearly got myself killed. . . . A fool's game!"

He looked all around him with great curiosity. In a moment he heard seven or eight shots fired quite close by. But receiving no orders to fire, he stood perfectly still behind his tree. It was nearly dark; he felt as if he were a lookout on a bear-hunt in the mountains of Tramezzina, above Grianta. A hunter's notion occurred to him, and he took a cartridge out of his pouch and removed the bullet. "If I see him," he realized, "I mustn't miss," and he slid a second bullet into his musket barrel. He heard two shots fired right next to his tree; at the same moment he saw a cavalryman in a blue uniform galloping in front of him, heading to his left. "He's more than three paces away," Fabrizio calculated, "but at this range I can't miss." He followed the horseman in his gun-sight and finally squeezed the trigger. The man fell with his horse. Our hero imagined he was out hunting and ran delightedly toward the game he had just bagged. He was already touching the apparently dying man when with incredible speed two Prussian cavalrymen galloped toward him, sabers raised to cut him down. Fabrizio ran toward the woods as fast as he could; to gain speed he threw away his musket. The Prussians were no more than three paces away when he reached another grove of oak saplings about as big around as his arm, at the edge of the woods. These stiff little trees halted the horsemen a moment, but they soon squeezed through and chased Fabrizio into a clearing. Once again they were almost upon him when he managed to slip behind seven or eight big trees. At this instant his face was almost scorched by the explosion of five or six shots fired from in front of him. He lowered his head; when he looked up again, he was facing Corporal Aubry.

"Did you kill your man?"

"Yes, but I lost my musket."

"We're not short of muskets. You're a good bugger, green as you look. You did well—these men here missed the two who were after you and coming straight for them. I didn't see them myself. Now we've got to get out of here; the regiment must be just over there, but first there's a field to cross where we can still be surrounded."

With these words the corporal marched ahead of his ten men. Two hundred yards on, entering the little field he had mentioned, they came upon a wounded general being carried by his aide-de-camp and an orderly.

"Give me four men," he said to the corporal in a faint voice, "I need to be taken to the ambulance—my leg's been shattered."

"Go fuck yourself," the corporal answered, "you and the other generals. You've all betrayed the Emperor today."

"What!" cried the general in a rage. "Are you disobeying orders? I am Count B——, the general in command of your division," and so on. He pulled some more rank, and his aide flung himself on the soldiers. The corporal stuck him in the arm with his bayonet, then ran off with his men on the double.

"Let them all get shot like that damn fool," the corporal kept swearing, "legs shattered and arms too! Pack of cowards! All of them sold to the Bourbons and traitors to the Emperor!"

Fabrizio listened in horror to this terrible accusation.

By ten o'clock the little troop reached the regiment outside a village consisting of several extremely narrow alleys, but Fabrizio noticed that Corporal Aubry avoided speaking to any of the officers.

"We can't get through!" the corporal exclaimed.

All these alleys were crowded with infantry, cavalry, and worst of all with artillery caissons and wagons. The corporal headed for the intersection of three of these narrow lanes; after about twenty paces he had to stop; everyone was in a rage and swearing.

"Another traitor in command!" the corporal exclaimed. "If the enemy had the wit to surround the village, we'd all be trapped like dogs. Follow me, you men!"

Fabrizio stared: there were no more than six soldiers with the corporal. Through a wide-open gate they entered a huge barnyard; from here they made their way into a stable whose rear door opened into a garden. Here they were lost for a moment, wandering this way and that, but finally, passing through a hedge, they found themselves in a huge field of buckwheat. In less than half an hour, guided by the shouts and confused noise of the regiment, they were back on the high road outside the village. The ditches beside this road were filled with abandoned muskets. Fabrizio chose one, but the road, though quite broad, was so crowded with fleeing men and carts that in another half hour the corporal and Fabrizio had advanced no more than five hundred yards; someone said that the road would take them to Charleroi.

As eleven o'clock was striking in the village steeple, the corporal shouted, "Let's cut across the fields again." The little troop now consisted of only three soldiers, the corporal, and Fabrizio. When they were less than a league from the high road, one of the soldiers said, "I can't go on."

"Me neither," said another.

"Nice news! We're all in this together," the corporal snapped; "follow my orders and you'll get through." He had noticed five or six trees along a little ditch in the center of a huge wheat field. "Get to those trees!" he told his men. "Lie down here," he ordered once they had reached the trees, "and not a sound. But before you sleep, who's got bread?"

"I do," said one of the soldiers.

"Give it here," the corporal commanded. He cut the bread into five hunks and took the smallest for himself. "Fifteen minutes before daybreak," he said between mouthfuls, "you'll have the enemy cavalry on your back. The point is not to get yourself cut down. If there were just one man here, he'd be done for, with the cavalry after him in these open fields, but five of us can get away: keep close to me, don't shoot except at close range, and tomorrow night I promise to get you to Charleroi."

The corporal wakened them an hour before dawn and ordered

them to reload their muskets. The racket on the high road continued, as it had lasted all night: it sounded like a rushing river in the distance.

"They're running away like a flock of sheep," Fabrizio observed to the corporal, innocently enough.

"Shut up, imbecile!" snapped the corporal, furious.

And the three soldiers who constituted his entire army along with Fabrizio stared angrily at the latter, as if he had uttered blasphemy. He had insulted the nation.

"That's a good one!" mused our hero. "I already saw it back in Milan, with the Viceroy: they never run away, oh no! With these Frenchmen you can't tell the truth if it offends their vanity. But I don't give a damn about their dirty looks, and I'd better let them know it." They kept on their way, five hundred yards from that river of fugitives on the high road. About a league farther, the corporal and his troop crossed a road that ran toward the high road, where a lot of soldiers were lying on the ground. Fabrizio bought a pretty good horse for forty francs, and among all the sabers lying about he carefully selected a huge straight one. "Since they say you have to stab with it," he decided, "this one's best." Thus armed, he galloped on and soon rejoined the corporal, who had marched ahead. He stood up in his stirrups, grasped the scabbard of his straight saber in his left hand, and cried to the four Frenchmen: "Those men running down the road look like a flock of sheep. . . . They're running like scared sheep . . . !"

Though Fabrizio emphasized the word *sheep*, his comrades no longer remembered having been offended by this word an hour before. Here appeared one of the contrasts between the Italian and French characters; the Frenchman is no doubt the better off of the two: he slides over the surface of events and bears no grudges.

We shall not conceal the fact that Fabrizio was quite pleased with himself after repeating the word *sheep*. The men marched on, talking of one thing and another. Two leagues farther, the corporal, still amazed at not seeing any sign of enemy cavalry, said to Fabrizio, "You be our cavalry: ride over to the farm up that little hill, ask the farmer if he'll *sell* us something to eat—explain that there are only five of us. If he hesitates, give him five francs of your own money in advance, but rest easy, we'll get it all back after we eat."

Fabrizio stared at the corporal, seeing an imperturbable gravity in his face, indeed an expression of moral superiority; he obeyed. Everything happened as his commander had foreseen, except that Fabrizio insisted that the five francs he had given the farmer not be recovered by force.

"It's my money," he told his comrades, "and I'm not paying for you, I'm paying for the oats he's given my horse."

Fabrizio pronounced French so poorly that his comrades imagined they detected a tone of superiority in his words; they were deeply offended, and from that moment a duel began to take shape in their minds for the end of the day. They considered him quite different from themselves, which distressed them all; Fabrizio, on the contrary, was beginning to feel warm friendship toward every man among them.

They had marched without speaking for two hours when the corporal, peering over at the high road, exclaimed in a transport of joy, "There's the regiment!"

They soon reached the road, but alas! there were less than two hundred men mustered under the eagle. Fabrizio immediately caught sight of the canteen-woman, on foot now, red-eyed and occasionally sobbing. He saw no sign of Cocotte or the little cart.

"Looted! Robbed! Ruined!" the canteen-woman cried, responding to our hero's anxious glance. Without a word, Fabrizio dismounted, took his horse by the bridle, and told the canteen-woman to mount. She did not wait for a second invitation. "Shorten the stirrups for me, my boy." Once in the saddle, she began telling Fabrizio all the night's disasters. After an endless narrative eagerly attended by our hero, who, to tell the truth, didn't understand a word but felt a tender comradeship for the canteen-woman, she ended her story with these words: "And just think, it was the French who beat me and robbed me and ruined me...!"

"You mean it wasn't the enemy?" Fabrizio asked with the naïve expression that made his pale, serious, handsome face so charming.

"You really are stupid, my poor boy!" The canteen-woman smiled through her tears. "But you're a sweet lad, all the same."

"And this same lad took care of his Prussian very nicely," said Corporal Aubry, who in the midst of the general confusion happened to be on the other side of the horse the canteen-woman was riding. "But he's stuck up . . ." Fabrizio gave a start. "By the way, what's your name?" the corporal continued. "If there's ever a report filed, I want to cite you in it."

"My name is Vasi," Fabrizio answered, making a peculiar face, "I mean, *Boulot*," he quickly corrected himself.

Boulot had been the name of the owner of the travel-permit the jailer's wife in B—— had given him; the night before, he had studied it carefully while on the march, for he was beginning to reflect a little now, and was no longer so surprised by things. Besides Hussar Boulot's travel-permit, he still possessed the precious Italian passport which entitled him to claim the noble name of Vasi, barometer-dealer. When the corporal had reproached him for his pride, it was on the tip of his tongue to answer: "Stuck up—me! Fabrizio Valserra, Marchesino del Dongo, and willing to be known as Vasi, barometer-dealer!"

While he was thinking these thoughts and telling himself: "I must remember my name's Boulot, or else it's back to prison for me," the corporal and the canteen-woman had been exchanging a few words about him.

"Don't think I'm being nosy, sir," the canteen-woman suddenly remarked, "it's for your own good I'm asking you, but who are you, really?"

Fabrizio did not immediately reply; he realized he would never find better friends of whom to ask the advice he so urgently needed: "We'll soon be in a town under wartime regulations, the governor will want to know who I am, and I'll be back in prison if my answers reveal I know no one in the Fourth Regiment of Hussars whose uniform I'm wearing!" As an Austrian subject, Fabrizio knew all about the great importance attached to a passport. The members of his family, though noble and devout, though belonging to the winning side, had been harassed twenty times over about their passports; hence he was not in the least offended by the canteen-woman's question. But since he made no reply, casting about for the simplest French words in which to express himself, the canteen-woman, her curiosity aroused, added: "Corporal Aubry and I are going to give you some good advice on how you should behave."

"I'm sure you are," Fabrizio replied. "My name is Vasi and I'm from Genoa; my sister's a famous beauty who married a captain. Since I'm only seventeen, she sent for me to show me something of France and to teach me a thing or two; since I couldn't find her in Paris and knowing she was following this army, I came here looking for her everywhere but not finding her. . . . The soldiers were suspicious of my accent and put me under arrest. I had some money then and gave it to the gendarme, who let me have a travel-permit and a uniform and told me to get lost and never mention his name."

"What was his name?" asked the canteen-woman.

"I've given my word," Fabrizio said.

"He's right," the corporal added, "the gendarme's a crook, but our friend here can't tell us his name. But what's the name of this captain, your sister's husband? If we knew who he was we could look for him."

"Teulier, Captain Teulier in the Fourth Regiment of Hussars," our hero answered.

"And it was because of you foreign accent," the corporal continued with considerable cunning, "that the soldiers took you for a spy?"

"That's the horrible word!" Fabrizio exclaimed, his eyes shining. "And that's what they called me, despite my love of the Emperor and the French! That's the insult which offended me most."

"It's no insult, you're wrong about that: the soldiers' mistake was quite natural," Corporal Aubry added gravely. He then explained, pedantically enough, that in the army one must belong to a corps and wear a uniform, otherwise it is quite natural to be taken for a spy. The enemy sends out any number: in this war, everyone betrays everyone else. The scales fell from Fabrizio's eyes; for the first time he understood how wrong he had been about everything that had happened to him for the last two months.

"But let the boy tell the rest of his story," the canteen-woman insisted, her curiosity sharper than ever. Fabrizio obeyed. When he had finished: "As it turns out," she said, addressing the corporal with a serious expression, "this boy is no soldier; we're going to have a nasty war on our hands, now that we're betrayed and defeated. Why should he get his bones broken, *gratis pro deo?*"

"Especially," the corporal added, "since he doesn't know how to load his musket, either on command or on his own. I'm the one who put in the bullet that brought down his Prussian."

"Besides, he shows his money to everyone," the canteen-woman continued; "he'll be robbed of everything he has as soon as he leaves us."

"The first cavalry officer he meets," said the corporal, "will commandeer it for his brandy, and maybe the boy will even be recruited by the enemy, since everyone's a traitor now. The first man he meets will order him to follow, and he'll follow—better for him if he joins our regiment."

"Not that, if you please, Corporal!" Fabrizio exclaimed. "It's a lot more comfortable on horseback, and besides I don't know how to load a musket! You've seen that I can manage a horse."

Fabrizio was quite proud of this little speech. We shall not recount the long argument concerning his future destiny which now ensued between the corporal and the canteen-woman. Fabrizio noticed that in their discussion these two repeated three or four times all the circumstances of his story: the soldiers' suspicions, the gendarme selling him a travel-permit and a uniform, how he had accidentally become a member, the day before, of the Field-Marshal's escort, the Emperor galloping past, the horse stolen from under him, and so on.

Her female curiosity aroused, the canteen-woman kept returning to how he had been dispossessed of the good horse she had told him to buy. "You felt someone pulling your feet, you slid over your horse's tail, and there you were on the ground!"

"Why keep repeating," Fabrizio mused, "what all three of us know perfectly well?" He hadn't yet realized that this was how the people of France arrive at their ideas.

"How much money do you have?" the canteen-woman suddenly asked him.

Fabrizio did not hesitate to answer; he was convinced of this woman's noble soul: such is the good side of France.

"All I have left is thirty gold napoleons and eight or ten five-franc pieces."

"In that case, you've got a clear field!" she exclaimed. "Get yourself away from this defeated army; find some way out—take the first good road to your right, get your horse moving and keep as far as you can from the army. The first chance you get, buy yourself some civilian clothes. Once you're eight or ten leagues away and you don't see any more soldiers, take the mail-coach and rest up for a couple of weeks in some nice town where you can eat beefsteaks. Never tell a soul you were in the army; the gendarmes will arrest you as a deserter; and nice as you are, my boy, you're not smart enough yet to answer their questions. As soon as you've got a gentleman's clothes on your back, tear up your travel-permit and use your real name—say you're ... Vasi. Where should he say he's from?" she asked the corporal.

"From Cambrai, on the Scheldt: that's a nice little town, you know? There's a cathedral there, and Fénelon, and everything."

"That's right," the canteen-woman continued, "never say you were in battle, and don't breathe a word about B——, nor about the gendarme who sold you the uniform. When you want to go back to Paris, get yourself to Versailles first, then enter Paris from that side, walk right in as if you were out for a stroll. Sew your napoleons into your trousers. And above all, when you have to pay for something, don't let anyone see more than what you need to pay. The saddest thing of all is that people are going to cheat you and gouge you out of all you have, and what will you do once you have no money, when you don't even know how to take care of yourself?" and so on.

The good woman went on for a long while; the corporal nodded agreement, unable to get a word in edgewise. Suddenly the crowd of men filling the high road broke into a run; then, in the twinkling of an eye, everyone jumped over the little ditch along the left side of the road and began running as fast as their legs would take them. "Cossacks! The Cossacks are coming!" was shouted on all sides.

"Back on your horse!" exclaimed the canteen-woman.

"God forbid!" said Fabrizio. "Be on your way, the horse is yours. If you need money for another cart, half of all I have is yours."

"Back on your horse, I tell you!" screamed the canteen-woman, furious now. And she began to dismount.

Fabrizio drew his saber. "Hold on tight!" he shouted, and smacked the horse's rump two or three times with the flat of his saber; the horse galloped off after the fleeing men.

Our hero stared down the high road; just now three or four thousand individuals had been crowded here, squeezed together like peasants at the end of a procession. After the word *Cossacks* he could see no one at all; the fugitives had abandoned shakos, muskets, sabers, and so on. Fabrizio, astounded, climbed up into a field to the right, about twenty or thirty feet above the road. He gazed up and down the high road and over the plain, but saw no trace of Cossacks. "Funny people, these French!" he mused. "Since I'm going to the right anyway, I might as well start walking now; it's possible all these men had some reason for running away that I don't know." He picked up a musket, checked to see that it was loaded, stirred the powder in the priming, cleaned the flint, then selected a well-filled cartridge pouch, and once again stared up and down the high road; he was absolutely alone in the middle of this vast plain so recently crowded with people. In the distance he caught sight of the fugitives, just vanishing behind some trees and still running. "Now, that's really strange!" he thought, and recalling the corporal's tactic of the night before, he proceeded to sit down in the middle of a wheatfield. He was not leaving, since he wanted to see his good friends the canteen-woman and Corporal Aubry again.

In this field, he discovered that he had only eighteen napoleons left, instead of thirty as he had thought, but there still remained the little diamonds he had sewn into the lining of the hussar's boots, that morning in the jailer's wife's bedroom, in B——. He concealed his napoleons as best he could, still pondering this sudden disappearance. "Is this a bad omen?" he wondered. His chief disappointment was not to have put one question to Corporal Aubry: "Did I really take part in a battle?" It seemed to him that he had, and he would have been overcome with delight to be sure of the matter. "All the same," he decided, "I took part in it under a prisoner's name, I had a prisoner's travel-permit in my pocket, and worse still, I was wearing his uniform! There's a sign for the future: what would Abbé Blanès have said? And that wretched Boulot dead in prison! It's all a grim omen—Fate will be leading me to jail!" Fabrizio would have given the world to know if Hussar Boulot had really been guilty; brooding over his memories, he seemed to recall that the jailer's wife in B—— had told him that the hussar was arrested for stealing not only silver plate but also a farmer's cow, and for beating the farmer half to death into the bargain: Fabrizio had no doubt that he would someday be imprisoned for a crime with some connection to Hussar Boulot's. He thought of his friend Father Blanès; if only he could consult him now! Then he remembered that he had not written to his aunt since leaving Paris. "Poor Gina!" he thought, and tears came to his eyes, when suddenly he heard a faint noise quite close by; it was a soldier allowing his three horses to graze on the wheat—he had taken the bits out of their mouths and was holding them by the snaffles. Fabrizio rose out of the standing grain like a partridge, startling the soldier. Our hero noticed this and yielded to the pleasure of playing the hussar for a moment. "One of those horses is mine, you bastard!" he shouted. "But I don't mind giving you five francs for the trouble you've taken to bring it here."

"What kind of fool do you take me for?" the soldier asked.

Fabrizio took aim at a range of six paces. "Let go of the horse or I'll blow your head off!"

The soldier's musket was slung over one shoulder, which he lowered in order to catch hold of his weapon.

"One more move and you're a dead man!" cried Fabrizio, rushing at him.

"All right, give me the five francs and take one of the horses," the soldier said, bewildered after a longing glance at the high road, where there was no one in sight. Fabrizio, keeping his musket raised in his left hand, tossed him three five-franc coins with his right. "Dismount or you're a dead man. . . . Saddle the black, and take the other two away. . . . I'll fire, the first move you make." The soldier sullenly obeyed. Fabrizio went over to the black horse and slid the reins onto his left arm without losing sight of the soldier, who was slowly walking away; when Fabrizio saw that he was some fifty paces off he quickly vaulted onto the horse. No sooner had he mounted, groping for the right stirrup with his right foot, than he heard a bullet whistling past his ear: the soldier was firing his musket. In a rage Fabrizio rushed toward him, but the soldier turned and ran, and soon Fabrizio saw him galloping off on one of his two remaining horses. "Good, now he's out of range," he decided. The horse he had just bought was a fine one but seemed nearly starved to death. Fabrizio returned to the high road, where there was still no one in sight, crossed it, and trotted his horse to a little fold in the terrain to the left, where he hoped to meet up with the canteen-woman; but when he reached the top of the little hill, all he could see, for more than a league, were a few scattered troops. "I'm fated never to see her again," he said to himself with a sigh, "what a good creature!" He soon reached a farm he had noticed in the distance, to the right of the high road. Without dismounting, and after paying in advance, he had the farmer give some oats to his poor horse, so famished that it was gnawing the manger. An hour afterward, Fabrizio was trotting down the high road, still hoping to meet the canteen-woman or at least Corporal Aubry. Riding on and peering in all directions, he reached a marshy stream crossed by a narrow wooden bridge. At the bridge, to the right of the high road, was a solitary house with a sign saying THE WHITE HORSE. "At least I'll get something to eat there," Fabrizio decided. A mounted cavalry officer with his arm in a sling stood at the bridgehead, looking extremely downcast; ten paces away, three more cavalrymen without horses were filling their pipes.

"Now those men," Fabrizio mused, "look to me as if they wanted to buy this horse for even less than it cost me." The wounded officer and the three men on foot watched him approach and seemed to be waiting for him. "I'd better not cross the stream by this bridge, I'll follow along to the right, that will be the road the canteen-woman told me to take in order to get away from here. . . . Yes," our hero decided, "but if I seem to be running away, I'll be ashamed of myself tomorrow; besides, my horse has good legs, and the officer's is probably worn out; if he tries to make me dismount, I'll gallop off." In the course of this reasoning Fabrizio reined in his horse, advancing as slowly as possible.

"Come on then, hussar!" the mounted officer shouted in a commanding tone of voice.

Fabrizio advanced a few steps and stopped. "You're after my horse?" he cried.

"No, of course not. Forward!"

Fabrizio stared at the officer: he had a white moustache and an honorable expression; the sling supporting his left arm was covered with blood, and his right hand, too, was wrapped in a bloody cloth. "It's the other two who will leap for my horse's bridle," Fabrizio speculated, but looking closely he saw that these men were wounded as well.

"In the name of honor," said the officer, who was wearing a colonel's epaulettes, "stay on guard here and tell every dragoon, cavalryman, and hussar who comes in sight that Colonel Le Baron is in that inn over there, and that I order them to join me there."

The old colonel seemed overcome with pain; by his first words he had made a conquest of our hero, who answered quite sensibly: "I'm too young, sir, for anyone to pay much attention to me; I should have an order written in your own hand."

"Right," the colonel said, observing Fabrizio closely; "write the order, La Rose, you've still got a right hand."

Without a word, La Rose took a tiny vellum notebook out of his pocket, scribbled a few lines, and, tearing off a sheet, handed it to Fabrizio; the colonel repeated his order, adding that after two hours on guard Fabrizio would be relieved, as was proper, by one of the three wounded cavalrymen who were with him. He and his men then went into the inn. Fabrizio watched them walk away and sat motionless at his end of the wooden bridge, struck by the grim and silent suffering of the three figures. "Like spirits under a spell," he mused. Finally he unfolded the sheet of paper and read the order, which ran as follows:

Colonel Le Baron of the Sixth Dragoons, commanding the Second Brigade of the First Division of Cavalry of the Fourteenth Corps, orders all dragoons and cavalrymen to join him at the White Horse Inn beside the La Sainte Bridge, at his headquarters.

June 19, 1815

For Colonel Le Baron, wounded in the right arm, and on his orders, Sergeant La Rose.

Fabrizio had been on guard duty no more than a quarter of an hour when he saw approaching six mounted men and three on foot; he showed them the colonel's order.

"We'll be back," said four of the riders, and they cantered across the bridge. Fabrizio then remonstrated with the other two. During the lively discussion which ensued, the three men on foot crossed the bridge. One of the remaining men on horseback ended by asking to see the order and took it with him, saying: "I'll bring this to my friends, they'll be sure to come back; you wait for them here." And he galloped off, his comrades following. All this happened in the wink of an eye.

Fabrizio, furious, called to one of the wounded soldiers, who appeared at a window of the White Horse Inn. This soldier, who was wearing a sergeant's stripes, came out of the inn and shouted to Fabrizio as he approached: "Draw your sword, soldier! You're on duty here."

Fabrizio obeyed, then told him: "They've taken the order."

"They're in a nasty mood after yesterday's business," the sergeant replied gloomily. "I'll give you one of my pistols; if anyone tries to get past you again, fire into the air. I'll come, or the colonel himself …"

Fabrizio had noticed the sergeant's gesture of surprise when he had informed him of the stolen order; he realized that this was a personal insult, and promised himself not to let such a trick be played on him again.

Armed with the sergeant's horse-pistol, Fabrizio had proudly returned to guard duty when he saw seven mounted hussars approaching: he took up a position barring access to the bridge and communicated the colonel's order, which seemed to annoy them a good deal, and the boldest sought to pass. Fabrizio, following the sage precept of his friend the canteen-woman, who only that morning had told him to stab and not to slash, lowered the point of his straight saber and prepared to thrust at the man who sought to force his way past him.

"So the young fool wants to kill us!" exclaimed one of the hussars. "As if we hadn't been killed enough yesterday!" At once all of them drew their sabers and fell on Fabrizio, who thought he was a dead man; but he remembered the sergeant's surprise, and did not want to be shamed again. As he retreated down the bridge, he tried to give a few thrusts with his saber. He presented such an absurd spectacle wielding this huge straight cavalry saber which was much too heavy for him, that the hussars soon realized whom they were dealing with, and now attempted no longer to wound him but to cut his uniform off his body. Thus Fabrizio received three or four tiny saber wounds on his arms.

For his part, still faithful to the canteen-woman's precept, he thrust and stabbed with all his might. Unfortunately, one of these thrusts wounded a hussar on the hand; furious at being touched by such a green soldier, he riposted by a deep thrust that wounded Fabrizio high on the thigh. What made the blow more telling was that our hero's horse, far from fleeing the engagement, seemed to delight in flinging itself upon the assailants. These, seeing Fabrizio's blood flow down his right leg, thought they had carried the game a little too far and, pushing him toward the left parapet of the bridge, went past at a gallop. As soon as he could, Fabrizio fired his pistol into the air to warn the colonel.

Four mounted hussars and two on foot, of the same regiment as the others, were approaching the bridge and were still two hundred paces off when the pistol was fired: they watched attentively what was happening on the bridge, and supposing that Fabrizio had fired on their comrades, the four mounted men galloped toward him, sabers high; it was a veritable charge.

Colonel Le Baron, warned by the pistol shot, opened the inn door and rushed out onto the bridge just as the galloping hussars reached it, and himself repeated the order to stop. "There is no longer any colonel here," exclaimed one of the hussars as he spurred his horse.

The colonel in exasperation interrupted the reprimand he was making, and with his wounded right hand grasped the bridle on the off-side of the horse. "Halt, you bad soldier!" he said to the hussar. "I know you, you're in Captain Henriet's company."

"And if I am, let the captain himself give me orders! Captain Henriet was killed yesterday," he added with a sneer, "so go fuck yourself!"

And with these words, he tried to force a passage and pushed the old colonel, who fell into a sitting position on the bridge pavement. Fabrizio, who was two steps farther along on the bridge, but facing the inn, spurred his horse, and while the breastplate on the hussar's horse knocked over the colonel, who had not released the off-side rein, Fabrizio, outraged, made a deep thrust at his assailant. Fortunately, the hussar's horse, feeling itself pulled downward by the bridle the colonel was still holding, made a sidelong movement, so that the long blade of Fabrizio's heavy-cavalry saber slid along the hussar's vest and its whole length passed in front of his face. Enraged, the hussar turned around and delivered a blow with all his strength, which cut through Fabrizio's sleeve and entered deep into his arm: our hero fell.

One of the dismounted hussars, seeing the two defenders of the bridge on the ground, seized the opportunity, leaped onto Fabrizio's horse, and tried to make away with it by spurring it to gallop across the bridge.

The sergeant, running out of the inn, had seen his colonel fall and supposed him to be seriously wounded. He ran after Fabrizio's horse and thrust the point of his saber into the thief's back: the man fell. The hussars, seeing only the sergeant standing on the bridge, galloped past and rode quickly away. The one who was on foot ran off into the fields.

The sergeant approached the wounded men. Fabrizio had already gotten to his feet; he was suffering little, but losing a great deal of blood. The colonel recovered more slowly; he was quite dazed by his fall, but had received no wound.

"I'm not hurt," he said to the sergeant, "except from the old wound in my hand."

The hussar stabbed by the sergeant was dying.

"To hell with him!" the colonel exclaimed. "But," he said to the sergeant and the two other cavalrymen who had run up, "look after this young fellow whom I have exposed to such unfair risks. I'll stay on the bridge myself and try to stop these madmen. Take the young fellow to the inn and dress his arm; use one of my shirts."

Chapter Five

This entire adventure had not lasted a minute; Fabrizio's wounds were nothing; his arm was bandaged with strips cut from the colonel's shirt. They wanted to arrange a bed for him upstairs in the inn.

"But while I'm being cared for upstairs," Fabrizio said to the sergeant, "my horse down in the stable will be lost without me and run off with some other master."

"Not bad for a conscript!" said the sergeant. And they installed Fabrizio on clean straw in the very manger to which his horse was tethered.

Then, as Fabrizio was feeling very weak, the sergeant brought him a bowl of mulled wine and stayed to chat awhile. A few compliments included in this conversation raised our hero to the seventh heaven.

Fabrizio did not awake till dawn the next day; the horses were neighing long and loud and making a fearful racket; the stable was filled with smoke. At first Fabrizio could make nothing of all this noise, and did not even realize where he was; finally, half-suffocated by the smoke, it occurred to him that the place was on fire; in the twinkling of an eye he was out of the stable and on his horse. He looked up; smoke was pouring out of the two windows above the stable, and the roof was covered with a layer of black smoke spiraling into the sky. A hundred fugitives had arrived during the night at the White Horse Inn; every man was shouting and swearing. The five or six whom Fabrizio could see at close range appeared to be completely drunk; one of them tried to stop him, shouting: "Where are you going with my horse?"

When Fabrizio was a quarter of a league away, he turned around to look; no one was following him, the inn was in flames. Fabrizio glimpsed the bridge and remembered his wound—his arm felt very hot in its tight bandages. "And the old colonel, what's happened to him? He gave up his shirt to bandage my arm." Our hero, that morning, was the coolest man in the world; the amount of blood he had lost had freed him from the whole romantic side of his character.

"To the right!" he said to himself. "And be quick about it." He began, quite calmly, to follow the course of a stream which, after passing under the bridge, flowed along the right side of the road. He recalled the canteen-woman's advice. "What a friend!" he mused. "What a generous character!"

After riding an hour, he felt quite weak. "And now am I going to faint?" he wondered. "If I faint, someone will steal my horse and maybe my clothes, and with my clothes all the money I have." He was no longer strong enough to manage his horse, and was trying to keep his balance, when a farmer digging in a field beside the road noticed his weakness and approached to offer him some bread and a glass of beer.

"When I saw you looking so pale, I thought you were one of the men wounded in the great battle!" the farmer told him. Never had help come more opportunely: just as Fabrizio took his first bite of black bread, his eyes were beginning to hurt when he looked straight ahead. When he felt a little stronger, he thanked the man.

"And where am I?" he asked. The farmer told him that three-quarters of a league farther he would find the town of Zonders, where he would be properly cared for. Fabrizio reached this town in the shakiest condition, his chief concern, at every step, being not to fall off his horse. He saw a doorway standing wide open; he went inside: this was the Currycomb Inn, and immediately the innkeeper's good wife appeared, an enormously fat woman who called for help in a voice resonant with pity. Two girls assisted Fabrizio off his horse; no sooner had his feet touched ground than he fainted dead away. A surgeon was fetched, and Fabrizio was bled. That day and those that followed, Fabrizio was uncertain what was being done to him; he slept almost continually. The saber-wound in his thigh threatened to become seriously infected. When his mind had cleared somewhat, he asked them to take care of his horse, and kept repeating that he would pay properly, which offended the innkeeper's wife and her daughters. They took good care of him for fifteen days, and he was beginning to recover his wits somewhat when he noticed one evening that his hostesses seemed quite upset. And a moment later a German officer entered his bedroom: they answered his questions in a language Fabrizio did not understand, though he realized they were talking about him; he pretended to be asleep. Soon afterward, when he believed the officer might have left, he summoned his hostesses:

"That officer came to put me on a list, and take me prisoner, didn't he?"

The innkeeper's wife assented, with tears in her eyes.

"Well, there's money in my jacket!" he exclaimed, sitting up in bed. "Buy me some civilian clothes and tonight I'll ride out of here. You've saved my life once by taking me in when I was on the point of falling down in the street; save it for me again by giving me the means of going back to my mother."

At this moment the innkeeper's daughters burst into tears; they were terrified for Fabrizio, and since they understood virtually no French, they came to his bedside to ask him questions. They argued in Flemish with their mother; but time after time they cast pitying glances his way; Fabrizio could tell they were willing to run whatever risk it was that he represented for them. He thanked them effusively, clasping his hands together. A Jew in the neighborhood would supply a suit of clothes, but when he brought it at around ten o'clock that evening these young ladies realized, comparing the suit with Fabrizio's jacket, that they would have to take it in along every seam. They set to work at once; there was no time to lose. Fabrizio showed them several napoleons hidden in his garments and requested that his hostesses sew them into the clothes he had just purchased. With these clothes had been brought a fine pair of new boots. Fabrizio did not hesitate to request these good girls to cut his hussar's boots where he showed them, and to conceal his little diamonds in the lining of the new boots. By a strange effect of his loss of blood and his consequent weakness, Fabrizio had almost entirely forgotten his French; he spoke Italian to his hostesses, who spoke a Flemish dialect, so that they communicated almost entirely by sign language. When the girls, though quite disinterested, saw the diamonds, their enthusiasm for Fabrizio knew no bounds; they believed him to be a prince in disguise. Aniken, the younger and more naïve of the two, embraced him straightaway. Fabrizio, for his part, found them both charming; and around midnight, when the surgeon had allowed him to take a little wine, on account of the distance he would have to cover, he almost yielded to an impulse to stay. "Where could I be better off than here?" he asked himself. Nonetheless, around two in the morning, he got dressed. At the moment of leaving his bedroom, his good hostess informed him that his horse had been taken by the officer who had visited the house a few hours earlier.

"Oh the swine!" Fabrizio exclaimed with an oath. "Robbing a wounded man!" Our young Italian was not sufficiently philosophical to recall the price he himself had paid for that horse.

With tears in her eyes, Aniken explained that a horse had been hired for him; she would have liked him to stay; the farewells were tender. Two tall young men, relatives of the innkeeper's wife, lifted Fabrizio into the saddle; out on the roadway, they supported him on his horse, while a third fellow, several hundred paces ahead of the little convoy, scoured the road to be sure there was no suspicious patrol in the area. After riding for two hours, they stopped at a house belonging to a cousin of the innkeeper's wife.

No matter what Fabrizio told them, the young men accompanying him were unwilling to leave him; they claimed that they knew the paths through the woods better than anyone. "But tomorrow morning when they find out I've escaped and you won't be found in the neighborhood, your absence will get you in trouble," Fabrizio protested.

They rode on. Fortunately, when day began to break, the plain was covered by a dense fog. Around eight in the morning, they approached a small city. One of the young men went ahead to see if the post-horses had been stolen. The post-master had had time to conceal them, and to procure wretched nags, with which he had filled his stables. Two horses were brought out of the marshes where they had been hidden, and three hours later, Fabrizio climbed into a rickety cabriolet, harnessed however to a pair of good post-horses. He had recovered his strength. The moment of separation from these young fellows, relatives of his hostess, was extremely affecting; on no condition, whatever friendly excuse Fabrizio might find, would they consent to accept his money. "In your condition, sir, you need it more than we do," these fine young fellows kept assuring him. Finally they left with letters in which Fabrizio, somewhat fortified by the agitation of the ride, had attempted to inform his hostesses of all that he felt for them. Fabrizio wrote with tears in his eyes, and there was certainly love in the note addressed to little Aniken.

The remainder of the journey was ordinary enough. Once in Amiens he suffered a good deal from the saber cut in his thigh; it had not occurred to the country surgeon to lance the wound, and despite the bleedings an abscess had formed. During the fifteen days Fabrizio spent in the Amiens inn, kept by an obsequious and greedy family, the Allies were invading France, and Fabrizio became an entirely different man, so many and so deep were his reflexions upon the things which had just happened to him. He remained a child only on this one point: had what he had seen been a battle and, furthermore, had this battle been Waterloo? For the first time in his life, he took pleasure in reading; he still hoped to find in the newspapers or in the accounts of battle some description that might allow him to recognize the places he had passed through with Marshal Ney's escort, and later with the other general. During his stay in Amiens, he wrote to his dear friends at the Currycomb almost every day. Once he had recovered, he came to Paris; at his former lodgings he found twenty letters from his mother and his aunt imploring him to return as soon as possible. A last letter from Countess Pietranera had a certain enigmatic turn of phrase which dismayed him, and dissolved all his tender reveries. Such was his character that a single word could inspire the greatest disasters; his imagination then compelled him to depict these disasters in the most horrible detail.

"Be sure never to sign the letters you write about what is happening to you," the Countess told him. "When you return, don't come to Lake Como right away: stop at Lugano, in Swiss territory." He was to arrive in this little town under the name of Cavi; he would find the Countess's footman at the main inn, who would explain what must be done. His aunt ended with these words: "Use every means possible to keep your foolish escapade from being known, and above all do not keep about your person any printed or written documents; in Switzerland you will be surrounded by the friends of Santa Margherita.* If I have enough money," the Countess continued, "I shall send someone to the Hotel des Balances in Geneva, and you shall have the details I cannot write and which you must nevertheless learn before you arrive. But in God's name, not one day more in Paris; you will be recognized there by our spies." Fabrizio's imagination began projecting the strangest things, and he was incapable of any pleasure but that of trying to guess what strange information his aunt might have to give him. Twice, crossing France, he was arrested, though both times he managed to escape; these inconveniences he owed to his Italian passport and the peculiar description of its owner as a barometer-dealer, which scarcely matched his youthful appearance and his arm in a sling.

Finally, in Geneva, he found the man in the Countess's service, who gave him her message: Fabrizio had been denounced to the Milanese police as having taken to Napoleon certain proposals from a huge conspiracy organized in the former Kingdom of Italy. If this had not been the purpose of his journey, ran the report, why had he bothered to use an assumed name? His mother was attempting to establish the truth, *i.e.*, first, that he had never left Switzerland; second, that he had left the castle unexpectedly, following a dispute with his older brother.

Hearing this, Fabrizio felt a thrill of pride. "I'm regarded as a sort of

---

*Silvio Pellico has made this name known throughout Europe: it is that of the street in Milan where the police headquarters and prisons are located. [Stendhal's note.]

ambassador to Napoléon!" he mused. "I am supposed to have had the honor of speaking to that great man—would to God I had!" He recalled that his ancestor seven generations ago, the grandson of the one who came to Milan in the service of the Sforzas, had had the honor of being decapitated by the Duke's enemies, who surprised him crossing into Switzerland bearing propositions to the Free Cantons and attempting to recruit soldiers. In his mind's eye he saw the engraving of this episode, placed in the family annals. Questioning this footman, Fabrizio discovered that he had been shocked by one detail, which he was finally persuaded to reveal, despite the Countess's repeated orders not to reveal it: it had been his older brother, Ascanio, who had denounced Fabrizio to the Milanese police. This cruel news nearly drove our hero out of his mind. In order to reach Italy from Geneva, one must pass through Lausanne; Fabrizio wanted to leave immediately, and on foot, thereby covering ten or twelve leagues, although the coach from Geneva to Lausanne would be leaving in two hours. Before leaving Geneva, he picked a fight in one of those dreary Swiss cafés with a young man who stared at him, he declared, peculiarly. Which was indeed the case, since the phlegmatic young Genevan, a rational creature with nothing but money on his mind, believed him to be mad; Fabrizio, entering the café, had glared furiously all around him, and then had upset the cup of coffee served him all over his trousers. In this dispute, Fabrizio's first impulse was quite that of the sixteenth century: instead of challenging the young Genevan to a duel, he drew his dagger and flung himself upon the fellow in order to stab him to the heart. In this moment of passion, Fabrizio had forgotten all he had learned concerning the rules of honor and returned to instinct or, to put it better, to the memories of earliest childhood.

The man in the Countess's service whom he found in Lugano increased his rage by supplying him with new details. Since Fabrizio was much loved at Grianta, no one would have spoken his name, and without his brother's kind intervention, everyone would have pretended to believe he was in Milan, and police attention would never have been drawn to his absence.

"Certainly the customs officers have your description," his aunt's employee told him, "and if we take the high road, you will be arrested at the Lombardo-Venetian border."

Fabrizio and his people were acquainted with the smallest paths across the mountain separating Lugano from Lake Como: they disguised themselves as hunters, that is as poachers, and since there were three of them of very determined aspect, the customs inspectors they encountered made no move beyond a greeting. Fabrizio arranged matters so as to arrive at the castle around midnight; at that hour, his father and all the powdered footmen had long been in bed. He easily climbed down into the moat, and entered the castle through a cellar window: here he was awaited by his mother and his aunt; soon his sisters ran in. The transports of affection and the fits of tears followed one another for a long while, and everyone was just beginning to speak rationally when the first hours of dawn came to warn these beings who imagined themselves so unfortunate that time was flying.

"I hope your brother has no suspicion of your arrival," observed Signora Pietranera; "I haven't spoken to him since that fine trick he played on you, and his conceit has done me the honor of being offended by my silence: tonight at supper I managed a few words—I needed some pretext for concealing my excitement, which might have roused his suspicions. Then, when I noticed how proud he was of our apparent reconciliation, I took advantage of his delight to make him drink too much, so there's no question of his lurking somewhere to continue his profession of spying."

"We must hide our hussar in your apartments," the Marchesa decided. "He can't leave right away; in these first moments we are not sufficiently in command of our reason, and we have to find the best way of misleading those terrible Milanese police."

This plan was followed; but the Marchese and his elder son noticed, the following day, that the Marchesa was constantly in her sister-in-law's bedroom. We shall not pause to depict the transports of tenderness and delight which all that day agitated these happy beings. Italian hearts are, much more than ours, tormented by the suspicions and wild notions afforded them by a volcanic imagination, but on the other hand their joys are much more intense, and last much longer. On that day the

Countess and the Marchesa were quite out of their minds; Fabrizio was obliged to tell all his stories over and over: finally it was decided to conceal their mutual joy in Milan, so difficult did it appear to avoid any longer the espionage of the Marchese and his son Ascanio.

They took the household boat to reach Como; any other behavior would have awakened a thousand suspicions; but upon reaching the harbor, the Marchesa recalled that she had left some papers of the greatest importance at Grianta—she instantly sent the boatmen back for them, so that no observation could be made as to how these two ladies spent their time in Como. Once there, they rented at random one of those carriages stationed for hire near the tall medieval tower rising over the Milan gate. They left at once, without giving the coachman time to speak to a living soul. A quarter of a league out of town, they met a young huntsman of the ladies' acquaintance, who quite readily, since they had no man with them, undertook to escort them to the gates of Milan, where his sport was taking him anyway. All was going well, and the ladies were having the most delightful conversation with the young sportsman, when at a turn the road makes to circumscribe the delightful hill and wood of San Giovanni, three policemen in plain clothes sprang at the bridles of their horses. "Ah! My husband has betrayed us!" the Marchesa exclaimed, and fainted.

A sergeant who had stayed a little behind his men approached the carriage, staggering a little, and said in a voice that seemed to emanate from the tavern: "I apologize for the duty I must now perform, but I arrest you, General Fabio Conti."

Fabrizio thought the sergeant was making a bad joke by calling him *General*. "You'll pay for this," he promised himself; he stared at the plain-clothes policemen and waited for the right moment to jump down out of the carriage and escape through the fields.

The Countess smiled quite at random, I believe, then remarked to the sergeant: "But my dear sergeant, can it be that you take this boy of sixteen for General Conti?"

"Aren't you the General's daughter?" asked the sergeant.

"Just take a look at my father," said the Countess, pointing to Fabrizio. The policemen were seized by fits of laughter.

"Show your passports without arguing," the sergeant intervened, annoyed by the general hilarity.

"These ladies never take passports to go to Milan," said the coachman in a cold and philosophical tone of voice; "they're coming from their Castle at Grianta. This is Madame the Countess Pietranera, and that is Madame the Marchesa del Dongo."

The sergeant, quite disconcerted, went forward to the horses' heads, where he took counsel with his men. The conference had lasted for some five minutes when the Countess Pietranera begged these gentlemen to permit the carriage to move a few feet forward so as to be placed in the shade; the heat was overwhelming, though it was but eleven in the morning. Fabrizio, who was staring intently all around him for a means of escape, saw the opening of a little path through the fields and, arriving along it at the highway, covered with dust, a girl of fourteen or fifteen who was weeping timidly into her handkerchief. She was walking along between two uniformed policemen, and three paces behind her, also between two policemen, came a tall, lean fellow assuming the dignified manner of a prefect following a procession.

"Where did you find them?" asked the sergeant, now completely drunk.

"Running across the fields, and no sign of a passport anywhere."

The sergeant seemed to lose his head completely; he had before him five prisoners instead of the two required. He withdrew a few paces, leaving but one man to guard the dignified prisoner and another to keep the horses from advancing.

"Stay where you are," said the Countess to Fabrizio, who had already jumped to the ground, "everything's going to be all right."

They heard a policeman exclaiming: "So what! If they have no passports, they're fair game anyhow."

The sergeant seemed not to be quite as certain; the name of the Countess Pietranera was worrying him; he had known the general, whose death he had not heard of. "The general is not a man to overlook his revenge if I arrest his wife by mistake," he said to himself.

During this extended deliberation, the Countess had entered into a conversation with the girl standing in the dust of the road beside the carriage; she had been struck by the child's beauty. "The sun will do you harm, Signorina; this good soldier," she added, speaking to the policeman stationed at the horses' heads, "will certainly allow you to get into the carriage."

Fabrizio, prowling around the carriage, approached to help the girl up into it. She had already stepped onto the footboard, her arm supported by Fabrizio, when the imposing old fellow, who was some six paces behind the carriage, cried out in a voice made louder by the desire to be dignified: "Stay down on the road, don't get into a carriage which doesn't belong to you."

Fabrizio had not heard this order; the girl, instead of climbing into the carriage, tried to get back down, and since Fabrizio continued to support her, she fell into his arms. He smiled, she blushed crimson; they remained a moment staring at each other, after which the girl released herself from his arms. "What a fellow-prisoner she would make," he thought, "what deep thoughts behind that forehead! She would know how to love."

The sergeant approached them with an air of authority: "Which of these ladies is named Clélia Conti?"

"I am," said the girl.

"And I," exclaimed the elderly man, "I am General Fabio Conti, Chamberlain to His Serene Highness Monseigneur the Prince of Parma; I find it quite improper that a man of my condition should be hunted down like a thief."

"Did you not, the day before yesterday, when embarking at the harbor of Como, unceremoniously dismiss the police-inspector who asked for your passport? Well then! Today he prevents you from taking your leave."

"My boat had already cast off, I was in a hurry, a storm was brewing; a man not in uniform shouted at me from the dock to return to port, I told him my name and continued my journey."

"And this morning, you fled from Como?"

"A man like myself does not take a passport to leave Milan and visit the lake. This morning, at Como, I was informed I would be arrested at the town gate; I left on foot with my daughter; I hoped to find some vehicle on the way which might take me to Milan, where you may be sure my first task will be to complain to the general in command of the province."

A great weight seemed to have been removed from the sergeant's mind. "Very well, General, you are under arrest, and I shall take you to Milan myself. And you—who are you?" he inquired of Fabrizio.

"He is my son," interrupted the Countess: "Ascanio, son of Division-General Pietranera."

"Without a passport, Countess?" asked the sergeant, much more mildly.

"At his age, he has never had one; he never travels alone; he is always with me."

During this discussion, General Conti had assumed an increasingly dignified demeanor with the police officers. "Not so much talk," one of them snapped. "You are under arrest, that's that."

"You will be glad to hear," said the sergeant, "that we are permitting you to hire a horse from some farmer—otherwise, despite the heat and the dust, and the rank of Chamberlain of Parma, you will be managing as best you can on foot among our horses." The General began swearing. "Will you be so good as to shut up?" the sergeant continued. "Where is your general's uniform? Anyone can come along and claim he is a general."

The General grew even angrier. Meanwhile, matters were improving inside the carriage. The Countess ordered the police officers about as if they were her servants. She had just given one of them a scudo to find some wine and, better still, some cold water in a farmhouse visible some two hundred paces away. She had found time to calm Fabrizio, who was intent on escaping at all costs into the woods covering the hillside. "I have good pistols," he said. She persuaded the outraged General to let his daughter ride in the carriage. On this occasion, the General, who enjoyed talking about himself and his family, informed the ladies that his daughter was but twelve years of age, having been born in 1803, on October 27 in fact; but that her perspicacity was such that everyone assumed she was fourteen or fifteen.

"Such a common man," signaled the Countess's eyes to the Marchesa. Thanks to the Countess, everything was settled after an hour's discussion. An officer, who happened to have some business in the neighboring village, rented General Conti his horse, after the Countess had said to him: "You shall have ten francs." The sergeant set off with the General; the other officers remained under a tree with four enormous wine-bottles, virtually demi-johns, which the officer dispatched to the farm had brought back, with the farmer's help. Clélia Conti was authorized by the dignified Chamberlain to accept, for the return to Milan, a seat in the ladies' carriage, and no one dreamed of arresting the son of the gallant Count Pietranera. After the first moments dedicated to good manners and to remarks upon the little incident just past, Clélia Conti noticed the degree of enthusiasm with which so lovely a lady as the Countess addressed Fabrizio; certainly she was not his mother. Her attention was particularly aroused by the repeated allusions to something heroic, bold, supremely dangerous he had just accomplished; but for all her intelligence, young Clélia could not guess what it might be.

With amazement she stared at this young hero whose eyes seemed still aglow with all the fire of action. For his part, Fabrizio was somewhat nonplussed by the singular beauty of this girl of twelve, and her glances made him blush.

A league before they reached Milan, Fabrizio said that he was going to see his uncle, and took leave of the ladies. "If I extricate myself from my difficulties," he remarked to Clélia, "I shall pay a visit to your fine paintings in Parma, and then you will perhaps do me the honor of remembering this name: Fabrizio del Dongo?"

"Fine!" exclaimed the Countess. "That's how you manage to keep your incognito! Signorina, do us the honor of remembering that this young scamp is called Pietranera and not del Dongo."

Very late that evening, Fabrizio re-entered Milan through the Porta Renza, which leads to a fashionable promenade. Sending their two servants to Switzerland had exhausted the modest savings of the Marchesa and her sister-in-law; fortunately, Fabrizio still had a few napoleons, and one of the diamonds, which it was decided he would sell.

The ladies were extremely popular, and knew everyone in town; the most notable personages in the Austrian and clerical party put in a word for Fabrizio with Baron Binder, the chief of police. These gentlemen could not imagine, they said, how anyone could take seriously the escapade of a boy of sixteen running away from home after a dispute with his older brother.

"It is my profession to take everything seriously," was the mild reply of Baron Binder, a man as melancholy as he was astute, who was then establishing the famous Milanese police, and determined to forestall a revolution like the one of 1746, which had driven the Austrians out of Genoa. This Milanese police, rendered subsequently so famous by the exploits of Silvio Pellico and Signor Andryane, was not precisely cruel in its rational and pitiless execution of harsh laws. Emperor Francis II sought to strike terror into these bold Italian imaginations. "Give me, day by day," repeated Baron Binder to Fabrizio's protectors, "a *proven* evidence of what the young *Marchesino* del Dongo has done; let us begin with the moment of his departure from Grianta, on March eighth, down to his arrival last night in this very city, where he has taken cover in one of the bedrooms of his mother's apartment, and I am ready to treat him as the most amiable and ingenious young man in town. If you cannot supply me with the young man's itinerary for every day following his departure from Grianta, whatever the grandeur of his birth and my respect for the friends of his family, is it not my duty to have him arrested? Must I not keep him in prison until I receive proof that he has not taken certain messages to Napoléon from certain malcontents who may exist in Lombardy among the subjects of His Royal and Imperial Majesty? Note further, gentlemen, that if young del Dongo manages to exculpate himself on this point, he still remains guilty of having gone abroad without a properly issued passport, and further of traveling under a false name and knowingly utilizing a passport issued to an ordinary workingman, that is, to an individual belonging to a class greatly beneath the one to which he belongs."

This cruelly reasonable declaration was accompanied by every mark of deference and respect which the chief of police owed to the high position of the Marchesa del Dongo and to that of the important personages who had intervened on her behalf.

The Marchesa was in despair when she learned of Baron Binder's response. "Fabrizio will be arrested," she exclaimed in tears, "and once in prison, God knows when he will get out! His own father will disown him!"

Countess Pietranera and her sister-in-law took counsel with two or three intimate friends, and whatever they advised, it was the Marchesa's determination that her son leave that very night. "But as you see," the Countess remonstrated, "Baron Binder knows your son is here; he is not a bad man."

"No, but he wants to please the Emperor."

"But if he felt that throwing Fabrizio into prison would advance his career, your son would be there already, and it will be seen as an insulting defiance of the Baron to help Fabrizio escape."

"But to tell us he knows Fabrizio's whereabouts is to authorize his escape! No, I shall not live another moment, so long as I can tell myself: 'In a quarter of an hour my son might well be behind bars!' Whatever Baron Binder's ambition," added the Marchesa, "he regards it as useful to his personal position in this country to publicize his concessions to a man of my husband's rank, and I see a proof of it in the singular frankness with which he admits he knows where to find my son. Moreover, the Baron has been so good as to describe the two offenses of which Fabrizio was accused by his wretched brother's denunciation, he has explained that either one of these involves prison—isn't that the same as telling us that if we prefer exile, we have the choice?"

"If you choose exile," the Countess kept repeating, "we shall never see him again in all our lives."

Fabrizio, present for this entire discussion, along with one of the Marchesa's old friends, now a councillor on the tribunal established by Austria, was strongly in favor of making his escape. And indeed he left the palazzo that very evening, concealed in the carriage in which his mother and his aunt were driven to the theater La Scala. The coachman, whom they mistrusted, spent his evening in a tavern as usual, and while the footman, who had their confidence, kept an eye on the horses, Fabrizio, disguised as a peasant, slipped out of the carriage and left the city. The next morning he crossed the border with the same good fortune, and a few hours later he was established on an estate of his mother's in Piedmont, near Novara, more exactly at Romagnano, where Bayard was slain.

It may be imagined with what attention these ladies, having entered their box at La Scala, listened to the performance. They had come to the theater only to be able to consult several of their friends belonging to the Liberal party whose appearance at the Palazzo del Dongo might have raised official suspicions. In the box, it was determined to make a further appeal to Baron Binder. There could be no question of offering money to this honest magistrate, and moreover these ladies were quite without means, having compelled Fabrizio to take with him whatever remained from the sale of the diamond.

It was nonetheless of the utmost importance to keep on the Baron's good side. The Countess's friends reminded her of a certain Canon Borda, an agreeable young man, who had once pressed his attentions upon her, though in a distinctly unpleasant fashion; unable to succeed, he had betrayed her friendship for Limercati to General Pietranera, whereupon he had been dismissed from their circle as unworthy of their society. Now it so happened that this very Canon went to Baroness Binder's every evening to play *tarocchi,* and naturally was an intimate friend of the husband's. The Countess determined to take the horribly painful step of going to see this Canon, and early the next morning, before he had left his apartments, she had herself announced.

When his one servant pronounced the name of the Countess Pietranera, the Canon was moved to the point of losing his voice; and he made no attempt to conceal the disorder of his extremely simple domestic attire. "Show her in, and leave us," he said in a whisper.

The Countess entered; Borda flung himself at her feet. "It is in this posture that a wretched madman must receive your commands," he said to the Countess, who, in a simple morning dress that seemed almost a disguise, was irresistibly attractive. Her despair over Fabrizio's exile, the violence she was doing her own feelings by appearing in the apartments of a man who had treated her so treacherously—everything combined to give her appearance an incredible charm. "It is in this posture that I wish to receive your commands," exclaimed the Canon, "for it is obvious you have some favor to ask of me, otherwise you would not have honored with your presence the humble house of a wretched madman: once transported by love and jealousy, he behaved toward you as a coward, when he discovered he could not win your favor."

These words were sincere and all the more pleasing, since the Canon now enjoyed a great power: the Countess was touched to the point of tears; humiliation and fear had gripped her soul; in an instant, pity and hope succeeded them. From a profoundly wretched state she passed in the twinkling of an eye to something very much like happiness.

"You may kiss my hand," she murmured to the Canon, offering it to him, "and please stand up." (She employed the intimate form of address, which in Italy, you must know, indicates a frank and sincere friendship quite as much as a tenderer sentiment.) "I have come to ask your help for my nephew Fabrizio. Here is the whole truth, without the least concealment, as one might offer it to an old friend. At sixteen and a half, he has just committed a signal indiscretion; we were at the Castle of Grianta, on Lake Como. One evening, at seven o'clock, we were informed by a boat from Como that the Emperor had landed on the shore of the Gulf of Juan. The next morning Fabrizio left for France, after having obtained the passport of one of his friends among the common people, a barometer-dealer by the name of Vasi. Since he does not look much like a barometer-dealer, he had scarcely ventured ten leagues into France when his fine features brought about his arrest; his enthusiastic forays into bad French appeared suspicious. In a short time however he made his escape and managed to reach Geneva; we sent to meet him at Lugano . . ."

"You mean Geneva," said the Canon, smiling.

The Countess finished her story.

"I shall do everything humanly possible for you," the Canon responded effusively; "I am entirely at your command. I shall even commit indiscretions," he added. "Tell me, what must I do, when this poor salon is deprived of the celestial apparition which has marked such an epoch in the history of my life?"

"You must go to Baron Binder and tell him that you have loved Fabrizio since his birth, that you saw him in his cradle when you came to our house, and that in the name of the Baron's friendship for you, you implore him to utilize every spy in his employ to verify that, before his departure for Switzerland, Fabrizio had not the slightest contact with any of those Liberals under his scrutiny. If indeed the Baron is properly served, he shall realize that what is involved here is entirely an escapade of extreme youth. You know that I had, in my private apartments in the Palazzo Dugnani, the engravings of the battles won by Napoleon: it was by studying the captions of these engravings that my nephew learned to read. When Fabrizio was five years old, my poor husband would describe those battles to him; we would put my husband's helmet on the child's head, and the boy would drag about my husband's huge saber. And then, of course, one fine day he learns that my husband's idol, the Emperor himself, has returned to France; he runs off to join him like a madman, but of course he fails utterly. Ask your Baron what penalty he would propose to chastise such a moment of folly."

"I was forgetting one thing," exclaimed the Canon. "You shall see that I am not altogether unworthy of the forgiveness you are extending to me. Here," he said, shuffling his papers on the desk, "here is the denunciation of that wretched *coltorto*"—hypocrite—"you see, signed *Ascanio Valserra del Dongo,* which is at the bottom of this whole business; I took it last night from police headquarters, and I went to La Scala in hopes of finding someone accustomed to visiting your box by whom I could pass it on to you. A copy of this document has been in Vienna a long while. Such is the enemy with whom we must do battle."

The Canon and the Countess read the denunciation together, and they determined that in the course of the day, he would obtain for her a copy of it made by a person in his confidence. It was with joy in her heart that the Countess returned to the Palazzo del Dongo. "Impossible to be more of a *galant'uomo* than this reformed rake," she observed to the Marchesa; "tonight at La Scala, and ten forty-five by the theater clock, we shall send everyone away from our box, we shall snuff the candles, we shall shut our door, and at eleven the Canon himself will come to tell us what he has managed. That will be the least compromising arrangement for him."

This Canon was a very shrewd man; he was careful not to break his appointment; once there he gave evidence of great kindness and an utterly open heart, such as is found only in those countries where vanity does not prevail over all other sentiments. His denunciation of the Countess to her husband General Pietranera was one of the greatest regrets of his life, and now he was finding the means of abolishing it.

That morning, when the Countess had left his apartment: "So she's making love with her nephew," he told himself bitterly, for he had by no means recovered. "Proud as she is, to have come to me! . . . When that poor wretch Pietranera died, she repulsed with horror my offers of service, polite and nicely presented as they were by Colonel Scotti, her former lover. The lovely Countess Pietranera, living on fifteen hundred francs a year!" added the Canon, striding up and down his room. "And then going to live in the Castle of Grianta with an abominable *seccatore* like the Marchese del Dongo! . . . Now I see it all! Indeed, young Fabrizio has all the graces—tall, well built, a smiling face . . . and better still, a certain voluptuous charm in his glance. . . . A Correggio countenance," the Canon added bitterly.

"The difference in age . . . not too great . . . Fabrizio born after the French came in, around '98, I would guess; the Countess might be twenty-seven or twenty-eight, impossible to be more charming, more adorable; in this country rich in beauties, she outdoes them all, Marini, Gherardi, Ruga, Aresa, Pietragrua: she transcends all these women. . . . And so they lived happy together, hidden on that lovely Lake Como when the young fellow wanted to join his Napoléon. . . . There are still souls in Italy! And no matter what we do! Beloved country! . . . No," continued this heart inflamed by jealousy, "how else to account for that submission to a life of boredom in the country, with the horror of seeing every day, at every meal, the hideous face of the Marchese del Dongo, and that wretched pale physiognomy of the *Marchesino* Ascanio, who will be worse than his father! . . . Well, I shall serve her turn, at least that way I shall have the pleasure of seeing her closer than through my opera-glasses."

Canon Borda explained the matter quite clearly to the two ladies. Actually, Binder was quite well disposed to their suit; he was delighted that Fabrizio had made his escape before the orders which might arrive from Vienna; for Binder had no power to determine matters, he was waiting for orders in this case as in all others; he sent to Vienna every day the exact copy of all the information he received: then he waited.

It was essential that during his exile at Romagnano, Fabrizio:

1. Must go to Mass every day, and take as his father confessor an intelligent priest devoted to the cause of the Monarchy, and in the confessional avow to him only the most irreproachable sentiments.
2. Be certain to frequent no person reputed to be intelligent, and on every occasion to speak of rebellion with horror, as a thing never to be countenanced.
3. Never allow himself to be seen at the café, never read any papers but the official gazettes of Turin and Milan; and in general betray a certain dislike of reading, and above all never read any work printed after 1720 except, if need be, the novels of Walter Scott.
4. Finally, the Canon added with a certain malice, he must pay the most observable court to some one of the attractive women of the community, of the noble class naturally; this would show that he does not possess the grim and malcontent spirit of a nascent conspirator.

Before going to bed that night, the Countess and the Marchesa wrote two endless letters to Fabrizio, in which they explained with a charming anxiety all the advice Borda had given.

Fabrizio had no desire to be a conspirator: he loved Napoléon, and, as a young nobleman, believed himself created to be happier than other men and regarded all bourgeois as absurd. He had never opened a book since leaving school, where he had read only the books prescribed by the Jesuits. He took up residence a certain distance from Romagnano, in a splendid palazzo; one of the masterpieces of the celebrated architect Sanmicheli; but no one had lived in it for thirty years, so that rain leaked into every room, and not one window closed properly. Fabrizio took possession of the steward's horses, which he rode quite casually at any hour of the day; he spoke to no one, and brooded. The advice to take a mistress in an *ultra* family struck him as quite agreeable, and he followed it to the letter. He selected for his confessor an ambitious young priest who wanted to become a bishop (like the confessor of the Spielberg*); but he walked three leagues a day and wrapped himself in a mystery he believed impenetrable, in order to read the *Constitutionnel,* a newspaper he considered sublime. "As fine as Alfieri or as Dante!" he would frequently exclaim. Fabrizio had this in common with the young men of France, that he was much more concerned with his horse and his newspaper than with his *bien-pensant* mistress. But there was not yet room for the *imitation of others* in this naïve and resolute nature, and he made no friends in the society of the big country town of Romagnano; his simplicity passed for pride; no one knew what to make of such a character. "He's a younger son resentful of not being the eldest," said the parish priest.

---

*See Andryane's curious memoirs, as amusing as a novel and as relevant as Tacitus. [Stendhal's note.]

CHAPTER SIX

We shall frankly admit that Canon Borda's jealousy was not entirely unfounded; upon his return from France, Fabrizio seemed to Countess Pietranera's eyes a handsome stranger she might have known well in days gone by. Had he spoken of love, she would have loved him; had she not, already, an admiration for his conduct and for his person that was passionate and, so to speak, limitless?

But Fabrizio embraced her with such an effusion of innocent gratitude and honest friendship, that she would have horrified herself had she sought any other sentiment in this virtually filial affection. "After all," the Countess told herself, "a few friends who knew me six years ago, at Prince Eugène's court, may still find me pretty and even young, but for him I am a respectable woman . . . and, to confess the whole affair without any concessions to my self-regard, an elderly one." The Countess was deceiving herself as to the stage of life she had reached, but not in the manner of vulgar women. "At his age, moreover," she added, "the ravages of time tend to be somewhat exaggerated; a man of riper years . . ."

The Countess, who was pacing up and down in her salon, stopped before a mirror, then smiled. It must be told that for some months Signora Pietranera's heart had been attacked quite seriously and by a singular personage. Soon after Fabrizio's departure for France, the Countess, who, without quite admitting it to herself, was already beginning to be quite preoccupied with him, had fallen into a deep depression. All her occupations seemed to her to lack pleasure, and, if we may say so, savor; she told herself that Napoléon, seeking to draw the Italian people to himself, would make Fabrizio his aide-de-camp. "He is lost to me!" she exclaimed in tears. "I'll never see him again; he'll write to me, but what would I be for him in ten years?"

It was in such a frame of mind that she journeyed to Milan; she was hoping to learn fresher news of Napoléon and, who knows? perhaps of Fabrizio in consequence. Without admitting it to herself, this volatile spirit was beginning to weary of the monotonous life she was leading in the country. "It's staying alive," she said, "not living." Seeing these *powdered* creatures every day, her brother, her nephew Ascanio, their footmen! What would their strolls along the lake shore be without Fabrizio! Her one consolation was the friendship which united her with the Marchesa. But for some time, this intimacy with Fabrizio's mother, who was older than she and a woman without hope, had begun to be less enjoyable to her.

Such was Countess Pietranera's singular position: with Fabrizio gone, she had little hope for the future; her heart needed consolation and novelty. In Milan, she became obsessed with the latest fashionable opera; she would shut herself up all alone, for hours at a time, in the box of her old friend Colonel Scotti, at La Scala. The men she attempted to meet in order to have news of Napoléon and his army struck her as crude and vulgar. Back at home, she improvised at her piano till three in the morning. One evening, at La Scala in the box of one of her friends, where she had gone hoping for news from France, someone introduced Count Mosca, Minister of Parma: an agreeable man who spoke of France and of Napoléon in such a way as to give her heart new reasons to hope or to fear. She returned to that box the next evening: this clever person reappeared, and throughout the performance she took pleasure in speaking with him. Since Fabrizio's departure, she had not experienced so lively an evening. This man who entertained her, Count Mosca della Rovere Sorezana, was then Minister of War, of Police, and of Finance of that famous Prince of Parma,

Ernesto IV, so famous for his severities, which the Milanese Liberals called cruelties. Mosca might have been forty or forty-five; he had large features, no trace of self-importance, and a simple, cheerful manner which people found attractive; he would have appeared even more so had a whim of his Prince not compelled him to powder his hair as a pledge of sound political sentiments. Since Italians have little fear of wounding one another's vanity, people there quite soon reach a tone of intimacy, and manage to speak quite personally. The antidote of this practice is to stop seeing one another if feelings are wounded.

"But why, then, do you powder your hair, Count?" asked Countess Pietranera the third time she encountered him. "For a man like you to wear powder, so agreeable, still young, and who fought on our side in Spain!"

"Precisely because I stole nothing in that very Spain, and because one must live. I was mad for glory; a flattering remark from the French general, Gouvion-Saint-Cyr, our commander, was everything to me, at the time. When Napoléon fell, it so happened that while I was devouring my patrimony in his service, my father, an imaginative man who already saw me a general, was building a *palazzo* for me in Parma. By 1813, my sole worldly possessions were a huge *palazzo* to finish and a pension."

"A pension: thirty-five hundred francs, like my husband?"

"Count Pietranera was a division-general. My pension, as a mere head of a squadron, was never more than eight hundred francs, and even that was not paid to me until I became Minister of Finance."

Since the only other person in the box was the lady of strongly Liberal opinions to which it belonged, the conversation continued with the same degree of frankness. Count Mosca, when questioned, spoke of his life in Parma. "In Spain, under General Saint-Cyr, I faced enemy fire to win a cross and a little glory thereafter, now I dress like an actor in a comedy in order to support a great household and earn a few thousand francs. Once I began playing this sort of chess, offended by the insolence of my superiors, I sought to fill one of the highest offices; I succeeded: but my happiest days are still those I can occasionally spend in Milan; here still beats, so it seems to me, the heart of your army of Italy."

The frankness, the *disinvoltura* with which this minister of so formidable a prince expressed himself, piqued the Countess's curiosity; from his title, she had expected to find a self-important pedant, and she encountered a man who was ashamed of the gravity of his position. Mosca had promised to provide her with all the news from France he could obtain: this was a great indiscretion in Milan, during the months before Waterloo; for Italy at that moment, the question was to be or not to be; everyone was in a fever, in Milan, of either hope or fear. Amid this universal upheaval, the Countess made inquiries about a man who spoke so casually of so envied a position which was his sole means of support.

Some curious things, and of a fascinating oddness, were reported to Signora Pietranera:

—Count Mosca della Rovere Sorezana, it is said, is about to become Prime Minister and declared favorite of Ranuccio-Ernesto IV, absolute sovereign of Parma and, furthermore, one of the richest princes in Europe. The Count would have already achieved this supreme position had he consented to assume a more dignified manner; it is said that the Prince often reprimands him in this regard: "What difference does my manner make to Your Highness," he answers boldly, "if I manage his affairs properly?"

—The felicity of this favorite, it was further reported, is not unalloyed: he must please a sovereign who is, no doubt, a man of sense and discernment, but who, since his accession to an absolute throne, seems to have lost his head and shown, for example, suspicions worthy of a silly old woman.

—Ernesto IV is courageous only in war. On the battlefield, we have seen this brave general leading a column to the attack; but after the death of his father, Ernesto III, upon returning to his territories where, to his misfortune, he wields unlimited power, he has begun ranting and raving against Liberals and liberty alike. Soon he reached the conclusion that he was hated; and finally, in a moment of bad temper, he actually ordered the hanging of two Liberals who may well have been blameless, advised in this by a wretch named Rassi, a sort of Minister of Justice.

—Since that fatal moment, the Prince's life has been changed; he is evidently tormented by the strangest suspicions. He is not yet fifty, and fear has so diminished him, if one may say so, that as soon as he mentions the Jacobins and the plans of the Central Committee in Paris, his physiognomy becomes that of an old man of eighty; he gives way to the chimerical fears of earliest childhood. His favorite, Rassi, Presiding Magistrate (or Chief Justice), has influence only by his master's fear; whenever he is apprehensive about his own position, he makes haste to discover some new conspiracy of the blackest and most fantastic nature. Say thirty rash fellows meet to read a number of the *Constitutionnel,* Rassi declares them to be conspirators and sends them as prisoners to that famous citadel of Parma, the terror of all Lombardy. Since it is built on an eminence, apparently of some hundred and eighty feet, it is visible from a great distance in the center of that vast plain; and the physical shape of this prison, of which such horrors are whispered, crowns it—by fear alone— the queen of that entire region extending from Milan to Bologna.

—Would you believe, another traveler asked the Countess, that at night, on an upper floor of his palace, guarded by eighty sentries who shout out an entire sentence every quarter of an hour, Ernesto IV trembles in his private apartments? All the doors are sealed with ten bolts, and the adjoining rooms, on the floors above and below as well, are filled with soldiers: he is terrified of the Jacobins. If a floorboard creaks, he reaches for his pistols, convinced that a Liberal is hidden under his bed. Immediately all the alarm-bells of the castle are set off, and an aide-de-camp goes to waken Count Mosca. Once in the castle, this Minister of Police is very careful not to deny the conspiracy; on the contrary, once he is alone with the Prince, and armed to the teeth, he visits every corner of the apartments, peers under the beds, and in a word performs a host of absurd actions worthy of an old woman. All these precautions would have seemed quite degrading to the Prince himself in the happy days when he was waging war and had killed no one save by musket-fire. Since he is a man of considerable intelligence, he is ashamed of these very precautions; they seem absurd to him, even at the very moment he is taking them, and the source of Count Mosca's enormous influence is that he employs all his skill in managing to spare the Prince any embarrassment in his presence. It is himself, Mosca, who in his rank as Minister of Police, insists on looking under the furniture and, it is said in Parma, even in the cases of the orchestra's double-basses. It is the Prince who raises objections, and teases his Minister on his excessive *puntiglio.* "It is a choice," Count Mosca answers him. "Think of the satirical verses with which the Jacobins would overwhelm us if we were to permit you to be killed. It is not only your life we are protecting here, it is your honor." But it appears that the Prince is only half duped, for if someone in the city should take it into his head to say that no one has slept a wink last night at the castle, Chief Magistrate Rassi sends the wretched joker to the citadel; and once in this lofty structure and *up in the air,* as people say in Parma, it takes a miracle for anyone to remember the prisoner's very existence. It's because he is a soldier, and because in Spain he managed a score of escapes, pistol in hand, from one tight corner after another, that the Prince prefers Count Mosca to Rassi, who is much more flexible and less principled. Those wretched prisoners in the citadel are in the strictest confinement imaginable, and all kinds of stories are spread about them. According to the Liberals, it is one of Rassi's ideas that the jailers and confessors are under order to convince them that virtually every month, one of them is put to death. On that day the prisoners are allowed to climb up onto the platform of the huge tower and from there to watch the procession with a spy playing the part of a poor devil being marched to his death . . .

These tales and a score of others of the same sort, and of no less authenticity, deeply interested Countess Pietranera; the following day she sought certain details from Count Mosca himself, whom she teased mercilessly. She found him entertaining, and kept insisting to him that in his heart of hearts he was a monster without suspecting it.

One day, returning to his lodgings in an inn, the Count said to himself, "Not only is the Countess Pietranera a delightful woman, but when I spend the evening in her box, I manage to forget certain matters in Parma, the very thought of which pierces me to the heart."

This Minister, despite his frivolous manner and his brilliant remarks, did not possess a soul *à la française;* he was not able to *forget* his griefs and grievances. When his pillow revealed a thorn, he was compelled to snap it off and blunt its point against his own throbbing limbs. (I apologize for this paragraph, translated from the Italian.)

Soon after making this discovery, the Count realized that despite the business which had summoned him to Milan, the day was inordinately long; he could not stay in one place; he exhausted his carriage-horses. Toward six in the evening, he took a horse to ride in the *Corso,* where he had some hopes of encountering Signora Pietranera; not having found her there, he recalled that the theater of La Scala would open at eight; he went in and found no more than ten persons in that enormous hall. He suffered a certain embarrassment at being there. "Is it possible," he said, "that at the age of forty-five, I should be indulging in follies that would make a sub-lieutenant blush! Fortunately no one suspects them." He made his escape and attempted to pass the time strolling through those attractive streets around the theater, lined with cafés which at that hour are overflowing with people; in front of each one, crowds of onlookers are perched on chairs in the middle of the street, taking ices and commenting on the passers-by, among whom the Count was remarkable; hence he enjoyed the pleasure of being recognized and greeted. Three or four importunate souls, of those who cannot be avoided, seized this occasion to have an audience with so powerful a Minister. Two of these tendered petitions; the third confined himself to addressing him with extensive advice on his political behavior. Intelligence, he reminded himself, is not taken unawares; nor does high office appear in the streets. He returned to the theater, where it occurred to him to rent a third-tier box; from here he could observe, without fear of detection, the second-tier box where he hoped to find the Countess. A wait of two whole hours did not seem too long to this lover; certain of not being seen, he happily abandoned himself to the full extent of his folly. "After all," he told himself, "isn't old age precisely the time when one is no longer capable of such delicious childishness?"

At last the Countess appeared. Armed with his opera-glasses, he examined her in a transport of delight. "Young, brilliant, light as a bird," he said to himself, "she can't be twenty-five. Her beauty is the least of her charms: where else to find a soul ever sincere, which never acts *with discretion,* which abandons itself wholly to the impression of the moment, which asks only to be swept away by some new object? How well I understand Count Nani's follies!"

The Count gave himself excellent reasons for his extravagance, completely absorbed in conquering the felicity he saw under his gaze. He found none so good when he came to consider his own age and the occasionally melancholy cares which filled his existence.

"A capable man whose wit is overpowered by his fears affords me a superior style of life and a great deal of money to be his Minister; but if he were to dismiss me tomorrow, I should be left old and poor, in other words, everything the world most despises; a fine figure of a man to offer the Countess!" Such thoughts were too somber, and his gaze returned to Signora Pietranera; he could not tear his eyes away, and to keep his mind focused upon her, he decided not to go down to her box. "She accepted Nani, I am told, only to put that imbecile Limercati in his place for his reluctance to take up a sword, or a dagger, against her husband's murderer. I would do battle for her twenty times over," the Count exclaimed in a transport. From one moment to the next he consulted the theater clock, which in luminous figures against a black background informed the audience, every five minutes, of the time when it was permissible to visit a friend's box. "I cannot," the Count mused, "spend more than half an hour in her box, recent acquaintance as I am; were I to remain longer, I should be making a spectacle of myself, and thanks to my age and worse still to this damned powdered hair, I should have all the attractions of the old fool in the *commedia dell'arte.*" But a further reflection made up his mind for him: "If she were to leave that box to visit another, I should be paid as I deserve for the greed with which I am hoarding such pleasure." He stood up to go down to the Countess's box, when all of a sudden he felt no further desire to present himself there. "Ah, now here's a pretty mess!" he exclaimed, laughing at himself and stopping on the stairs. "An impulse of authentic timidity—it's been twenty-five years since I've experienced such a thing."

He entered the box with a certain effort of will, and taking advantage, as a man of intelligence, of what had just occurred to him, he made no effort to seem at ease or to be clever by telling some entertaining story; he had the courage to be shy, he employed his wit in revealing his disturbance without being ridiculous. "If she takes it amiss," he told himself, "I'm lost for good. So! Timid with powdered hair which would be gray without it! But it's all true, so it can only be ridiculous if I exaggerate the fact or boast about it." The Countess had so often been bored to death at the Castle of Grianta by the powdered heads of her brother, her nephew, and several respectable bores of the neighborhood that it never occurred to her to concern herself with her new admirer's coiffure.

The Countess's mind being shielded from the notion of deriding his entrance, she was entirely concerned with the news from France which Mosca always brought when he appeared in her box; no doubt he made it up. In discussing such matters with him this evening, she noticed his warm and benevolent expression.

"I suppose," she said, "that in Parma, among your slaves, you would not permit yourself such a friendly aspect—it would spoil everything and give them some hope of not being hanged."

The complete absence of self-importance in a man who was regarded as the leading diplomat in all Italy struck the Countess as singular; she actually found him to possess a certain charm. Finally, since he spoke so well and so passionately, she was not distressed that he had felt it appropriate to assume, for an evening, and without further consequence, an admirer's part.

This was a great step forward, and a very dangerous one; fortunately for the Minister, to whom in Parma no lady was cruel, the Countess had arrived from Grianta only a few days before; her mind was still stiff with the tedium of country life. She had virtually forgotten the spirit of mockery, and all those things which belong to an elegant and frivolous style of life had assumed in her eyes a tincture of novelty which made them virtually sacred; she was not disposed to make fun of anything, not even a timid lover of forty-five. Eight days later, the Count's temerity might have been welcomed quite differently.

At La Scala, it is customary for these little visits to the boxes to last only some twenty minutes; the Count spent the whole evening in the box where he had the happiness of finding Signora Pietranera. "This is a woman," he told himself, "who gives me back all the follies of my youth!" But he sensed the danger: "Will my rank as lord and master some forty leagues from here gain forgiveness for this nonsense? I'm so bored with life in Parma!" Nonetheless, every quarter of an hour he promised himself he would take his leave.

"I must confess, Madame," he said to the Countess, smiling, "that at Parma I am perishing of tedium, and I must be allowed to intoxicate myself with pleasure when I find it in my path. So, without ulterior consequences and for this one evening, permit me to play a suitor's part with you. Alas! in a few days I shall be far away from this box which dispels all problems and even, you may say, all proprieties!"

Eight days after this scandalously extended visit to the box at La Scala, and in the wake of several minor incidents of which a narrative might seem tedious, Count Mosca was absolutely mad with love, and the Countess already thinking that his age should be no objection, if in other respects she found him attractive. Matters had reached this stage when Mosca was recalled to Parma by a courier. It appeared that his Prince, left to himself, was in a state of fear. The Countess returned to Grianta; now that her imagination no longer embellished that lovely spot, it seemed to her a desert. "Can I have become attached to this man?" she wondered. Mosca wrote and had no need for pretence, absence having deprived him of the source of all his thoughts; his letters were entertaining, and, prompted by a little eccentricity to which no exception was taken, in order to avoid the remarks of the Marchese de Dongo, who did not like having to pay for the delivery of letters, Mosca sent couriers who posted his at Como, at Lecco, at Varese, or some other charming little town in the environs of the lake. This was done in hopes that the courier might bring back her replies; he did so.

Soon the courier-days became an event for the Countess; these couriers brought flowers, fruit, trifling little gifts which diverted her, and her sister-in-law as well. Recollections of the Count mingled with the notion of his great power; the Countess had become interested in everything that was said of him; even the Liberals paid tribute to his talents.

The chief source of the Count's ill repute was that he was regarded as the leader of the *ultra* party at the court of Parma, and that the Liberal party was headed by a schemer capable of anything, even of succeeding, the Marchesa Raversi, an immensely rich woman. The Prince took great care not to discourage this opposition party; he was well aware that he would always be the master, even with a Ministry formed in Signora Raversi's salon. A thousand details were discussed at Grianta concerning her schemes; the absence of Count Mosca, whom everyone described as a Minister of extraordinary talent and a man of action, permitted the abandonment of powdered hair, symbol of everything sad and dull; it was a trivial detail, one of the obligations of the court at which he played, moreover, so important a part.

"A court is absurd," the Countess said to the Marchesa, "but entertaining; it's a game that interests me, though one must play by the rules. Who ever thought to protest the absurdity of the rules of whist? Yet once one has grown used to the rules, it is great fun to take your adversary's tricks."

The Countess often thought about the writer of so many amusing letters; the day they were delivered was a pleasure for her; she took her boat and went to read them in the beauty-spots along the lake shore, at Pliniana, at Belan, in the Sfondrata woods. These letters seemed to console her somewhat for Fabrizio's absence. At least she could not forbid the Count to be head over heels in love; a month had not passed before she was thinking of him with the tenderest feelings. On his side, Count Mosca was almost sincere when he offered to present his resignation, to leave the Ministry, and to come spend his life with her in Milan or somewhere else.

"I have four hundred thousand francs," he added, "which will always afford us an income of fifteen thousand."

"A box at the theater once again, horses! and so on," the Countess told herself; these were sweet dreams. The sublime beauties of the shores of Lake Como began to delight her once again. She went to daydream there about this return of a brilliant and exceptional life, which, despite all appearances, would once more become possible for her. She saw herself on the Corso, in Milan, happy and gay, as in the days of the Viceroy. "Youth, or at least a life of activity, would begin again for me!"

Sometimes her eager imagination concealed things from her, but she never entertained those deliberate illusions produced by cowardice. Above everything else, she was a woman honest with herself. "If I am a little too old to indulge such follies," she reminded herself, "envy, which creates as many illusions as love, can poison life in Milan. After my husband's death, my noble poverty enjoyed a certain success, as did the rejection of two great fortunes. My poor little Count Mosca hasn't the twentieth part of the wealth which those two wretches Limercati and Nani laid at my feet. The pathetic widow's pension so arduously obtained, the dismissal of the servants which produced a certain effect, the little room on the fourth floor which brought twenty carriages to the door—all this once produced a remarkable show. But I shall have some unpleasant moments, whatever my skill, if all I have is my widow's pension with which to return to life in Milan with the nice little bourgeois comforts supplied by the fifteen thousand francs which are all Mosca will have left after he resigns. A powerful objection, which will constitute a terrible weapon in envy's armory, is that the Count, though long separated from his wife, is a married man. Everyone knows about that separation in Parma, but it will be news in Milan, and attributed to me. So, my lovely theater of La Scala, my divine Lake Como ... adieu! adieu!"

Despite all these anticipations, if the Countess had had any fortune at all, she would have accepted Mosca's offer of resignation. She regarded herself as an older woman, and the court alarmed her; but what will seem highly unlikely on this side of the Alps is that the Count would have gladly handed in his resignation. At least so he managed to convince his dear friend; in all his letters he sought with mounting urgency a second meeting in Milan; it was granted.

"To promise you I feel a mad passion for you," the Countess observed to the Count, one day in Milan, "would not be the truth; I should be only too happy to love today, at thirty-some years, as I once loved at twenty-two! But I have seen the collapse of so many things I once believed eternal! For you I feel the tenderest friendship, I trust you completely, and of all men, you are the one I prefer."

The Countess believed herself to be perfectly sincere; yet at the end, this declaration contained a little prevarication. Perhaps, if Fabrizio had been willing, he would have triumphed utterly over her heart. But Fabrizio was merely a child in Count Mosca's eyes; he arrived in Milan three days after the young scatterbrain's departure for Novara, and he made haste to use his influence in the boy's favor with Baron Binder. His exile, the Count believed, was irremediable.

He had not come to Milan unaccompanied; in his carriage was the Duke Sanseverina-Taxis, a comely little old man of sixty-eight, enormously rich though not sufficiently noble. It was no one more remote than his grandfather who had amassed millions as tax-collector of the State of Parma. His father had persuaded the Prince of Parma to appoint him Ambassador to the Court of ——, as a consequence of the following argument:

"Your Highness grants thirty thousand francs to his Envoy to the Court of ——, who cuts a very mediocre figure there. If you were to deign to grant me this post, I shall accept a salary of six thousand francs. My expenditures at the Court of —— will never be less than one hundred thousand francs a year, and my steward will annually deposit twenty thousand francs in the Foreign Affairs Treasury at Parma. With this sum, you can attach to me any embassy secretary you like, and I shall show no jealousy concerning diplomatic secrets, should there be any. My goal is to give a certain luster to my house, still a new one, and to render it illustrious by one of the great positions of the realm."

The present Duke, son of this ambassador, had been so inept as to show himself something of a Liberal, and for the last two years he had been in despair. In Napoléon's time, he had lost two or three million by his insistence upon remaining abroad, and yet, since the re-establishment of order in Europe, he had not been able to obtain a certain Grand Cordon which embellished the portrait of his father, and the absence of which was gradually killing him.

At the degree of intimacy which in Italy follows upon love, vanity presented no further obstacle between the two lovers. Thus it was with utmost simplicity that Mosca said to the woman he adored:

"I have two or three possible schemes to offer you, each quite ingeniously worked out; I have thought of nothing else for the last three months.

"Firstly, I hand in my resignation, and we live as good bourgeois in Milan, in Florence, in Naples, or wherever you like. We have an income of fifteen thousand francs, independent of the Prince's favors, which will last a certain interval, more or less.

"Secondly, you will consent to come to the country where I have some power; you buy an estate, *Sacca,* for instance, a charming house surrounded by a forest, overlooking the valley of the Po—you can have the bill of sale signed eight days from now. The Prince invites you to his Court. But here an enormous obstacle arises: you will be well received at Court; no one will dream of raising the slightest objection. Moreover, the Princess regards herself as ill-treated, and I have just done her some favors with an eye to your interests. But I must remind you of one capital difficulty: the Prince is utterly bigoted, and as you are well aware, fate would have it that I am a married man. Whence a million embarrassments of detail. You are a widow, a fine title which must be surrendered for another, and this brings us to the object of my third proposition.

"We might find a new and not unaccommodating husband. But first of all, he would have to be extremely advanced in years, for why should you deny me the hope of eventually replacing him? Well then! I have devised this singular arrangement with the Duke Sanseverina-Taxis, who of course knows nothing of his future Duchess's name. All he knows is that she will make him an Ambassador and will present him a Grand Cordon possessed by his father, the absence whereof makes him the unhappiest of mortals. Apart from this, the Duke is not entirely a fool; he orders his suits and his wigs from Paris. He is not at all a man of *deliberate* ill nature; he seriously believes that honor consists in having a Cordon, and he is ashamed of his wealth. He came to me a year ago offering to fund a hospital in order to achieve that Cordon; I laughed at him, but he by no means laughed at me when I suggested a marriage to him; my first stipulation, of course, was that he would never set foot in Parma."

"But you realize that what you are suggesting is utterly immoral?" exclaimed the Countess.

"Not more immoral than many another thing that is done at our Court and at twenty others. Absolute power has the advantage that it sanctifies everything in the eyes of the people; now, what is an absurdity which no one perceives? Our policy, for twenty years, will consist in fearing the Jacobins, and what a fear that will be! Each year we shall believe ourselves on the eve of '93. You will hear, I trust, the observations I shall make thereupon at my dinner-parties! A fine affair! Everything that might somewhat diminish this fear will be *sovereignly moral* in the eyes of the nobles, and of the religious. Now, in Parma, whatever is not noble or religious is in prison, or is preparing to go there; be persuaded that such a marriage will appear strange in my country only on the day I am disgraced. Such an arrangement is an offense to no one; that, I believe, is the essential point. The Prince, on whose favor we are trading, has set but one condition to his consent, which is that the future Duchess be of noble birth. Last year, my position, all calculations made, earned me a hundred and seven thousand francs; my income must have amounted *in toto* to one hundred and twenty-two thousand. I have invested twenty thousand at Lyons. Very well! Choose: either a splendid existence based on a hundred and twenty-two thousand francs to spend, which, in Parma, would amount to at least something like four hundred thousand in Milan; but with this marriage which gives you the name of a decent man whom you will never set eyes on except at the altar. Or else the meager bourgeois life on fiftenn thousand francs in Florence or in Naples, for I agree with you, you have been excessively admired in Milan; envy would persecute you there, and perhaps manage to spoil our dispositions. The splendid existence at Parma will have, I trust, certain aspects of novelty, even in your eyes which have seen the Court of Prince Eugène; it would be politic to experience it before rejecting it forever. Do not suppose I am attempting to influence your choice. My own decision is clear—I prefer to live with you in an attic than to continue this splendid existence alone."

The possibility of this strange marriage was discussed daily by the two lovers. The Countess saw the Duke Sanseverina-Taxis at the Ball of La Scala, and he struck her as quite presentable. In one of their last conversations, Mosca summarized his proposition as follows:

"You must make a decision, if we wish to spend the rest of our lives in an agreeable fashion, and not turn old before our time. The Prince has given his approval; Sanseverina has a number of advantages to his credit; he possesses the finest palazzo in Parma, and a limitless fortune; he is sixty-eight years old, and obsessed by the Grand Cordon; only one defect shadows his life—he once commissioned a bust of Napoléon from Canova for ten thousand francs. His second sin, which will cause his death if you fail to come to his rescue, is to have loaned twenty-five napoleons to Ferrante Palla, a madman of our country, though something of a genius, whom we have subsequently condemned to death, fortunately *in absentia*. This Ferrante has produced two hundred verses in his entire life, quite beyond compare; I shall recite them for you, they are as fine as Dante. The Prince is sending Sanseverina to the Court of ———, he will marry you the day of his departure, and the second year of his journey, which he will call an Embassy, he will receive that Cordon of ———, without which he cannot survive. In him you will have a brother by no means unpalatable, one who will sign in advance all the papers I request, and moreover you will see him seldom or never, as you choose. He asks nothing better than never to show his face in Parma, where his tax-collector grandfather and his professed Liberalism embarrass him. Rassi, our hangman, claims that the Duke has been a secret subscriber to to the *Constitutionnel* through Ferrante Palla, the poet, and this calumny has long constituted a serious obstacle to the Prince's consent."

Why should the historian who faithfully follows the least details of the narrative supplied him be held responsible? It is his fault if the characters, seduced by passions he does not share, unfortunately for himself, descend to profoundly immoral actions? It is true that such things are no longer done in a country where the sole passion surviving all the rest is for money, the means of vanity.

Three months after the events hitherto recounted, the Duchess Sanseverina-Taxis astonished the Court of Parma by her easy affability and by the noble serenity of her mind; her house was incomparably the most agreeable in the city. This was what Count Mosca had promised his master, Ranuccio-Ernesto IV, the ruling Prince, and the Princess, his wife, to whom the Duchess was presented by two of the greatest ladies of the realm, received her with every mark of distinction. The Duchess was curious to see this Prince who was master of the fate of the man she loved; she sought to please him and succeeded all too well. She encountered a man of more than average height, though inclined to stoutness; his hair, his moustaches, and his enormous sideburns were of a splendid golden color, according to his courtiers; elsewhere they would have provoked, by their pallor, the ignoble word *flaxen*. Out of the center of his broad countenance jutted a tiny, almost feminine nose. But the Duchess noticed that in order to realize all these ugly points it was necessary to catalogue the Prince's features one by one. The general impression was that of a man of lively intelligence and firm character. His bearing, his movements were not without majesty, though he frequently sought to impress his interlocutor; then he grew embarrassed himself and would begin shifting from one foot to the other almost continually. Furthermore, Ernesto IV had a penetrating and commanding gaze; his arm gestures implied a certain nobility, and his words were at once measured and concise.

Mosca had warned the Countess that the Prince kept, in the grand bureau where he held audiences, a full-length portrait of Louis XIV, and a very fine inlaid-marble table from Florence. The imitation, she found, was striking, evidently he had tried for the gaze and the noble distinction of the Sun King, and he leaned upon the *scagliola* table in such a fashion as to assume the pose of Joseph II. He seated himself immediately after the first words he addressed to the Duchess, in order to give her an occasion to employ the *tabouret* befitting her rank. At this court, only Duchesses, Princesses, and the wives of the Grandees of Spain are entitled to seat themselves; all the other ladies wait until the Prince or the Princess invite them to sit, and to mark the differences in rank, these august personages are always careful to allow a certain interval of time to pass before inviting those ladies not Duchesses to be seated. The Duchess Sanseverina-Taxis found that now and again the Prince's imitation of Louis XIV was a little too marked; for instance, in his manner of smiling benevolently, tipping back his head.

Ernesto IV wore an evening-coat of the latest fashion from Paris; he was sent, every month, from this city he abhorred, an evening-coat, a frock coat, and a hat. But by a strange mixture of outfits, the day the Duchess was received at court the Prince had put on red knee-breeches, silk stockings, and very close-fitting shoes, models for which might be found in the portraits of Joseph II.

He received the Duchess Sanseverina graciously; he made several witty and delicate remarks; but she immediately discerned that there was nothing excessive in the warmth of his reception.

"Do you know why?" Count Mosca explained to her after the audience, "It is because Milan is a larger and more beautiful city than Parma. He might have feared, granting you the welcome I expected and which he had led me to hope for, that he would seem a provincial overwhelmed by the manners of a lovely lady from the capital. Doubtless too he is still vexed by a detail which I dare not tell you: the Prince sees no woman at his court who might rival you for *beauty*. That was the sole subject of his conversation, last night when he retired to bed, with Pernice, his chief valet, who is well-disposed toward me. I foresee a little revolution in court etiquette: my greatest enemy here is a fool known as General Fabio Conti. Just imagine an eccentric who has seen perhaps a day's service on the field of war in his whole life, and who thereby considers himself entitled to imitate the bearing of Frederick the Great. Furthermore, he insists on posing with all the noble affability of General Lafayette, and this because he is the leader, here, of the Liberal party. (God knows what kind of Liberals!)"

"I know this Fabio Conti of yours," said the Duchess. "I had a glimpse of him not far from Como; he was having an argument with the police." She described the episode, which the reader may well remember.

"You shall someday know, Madame, if your mind ever succeeds in penetrating the depths of our protocol, that young ladies appear at Court only after their marriage. Well then! The Prince has for the superiority of his Parma over all other cities a patriotism so intense that

I wager he will find some way of having little Clélia Conti, our Lafayette's daughter, presented at Court. She is, I must say, quite charming, and a week ago passed for the loveliest person in the Prince's domain.

"I don't know," the Count continued, "if the horrors which my sovereign's enemies have spread about him have reached as far as the Castle of Grianta; he passes for a monster, an ogre. The fact is that Ernesto IV was filled to bursting with many little virtues, and it might be added that if he had been as invulnerable as Achilles, he would have continued to be a model potentate. But in a moment of tedium and vexation, and also somewhat to imitate Louis XIV cutting off the head of some Frondist hero discovered living peacefully and impudently on his estate close by Versailles, fifty years after the Fronde, Ernesto IV managed one day to hang two Liberals. It appeared that these indiscreet fellows foregathered on a certain day to speak ill of the Prince and to address eager hopes to heaven that the plague might come to Parma and deliver them from the tyrant. The word *tyrant* was textual evidence. Rassi called this conspiring; he had them condemned to death, and the execution of one of them, Count L——, was a horror. This occurred before my time. Since that fatal moment," added the Count, lowering his voice, "the Prince is subject to fits of terror *unworthy of a man,* but which are the sole source of the favor I enjoy. Without such sovereign fear, I should have a variety of distinction all too sudden, too harsh for this Court, where imbecility is rampant. Would you believe that the Prince looks under the beds of his apartment before retiring, and expends a million, which in Parma is the equivalent of four million in Milan, to have a powerful police force, and you see before you, my lady Duchess, the chief of this dread force. By police, that is, by fear, I have become Minister of War and of Finance; and since the Minister of the Interior is my nominal chief, insofar as he has the police on his staff, I have had this portfolio given to Count Zurla-Contarini, an idiot who is greedy for such labors as the pleasure of writing eighty letters a day. I received one just this morning, in which Count Zurla-Contarini has had the satisfaction of writing in his own hand the number 20,715."

The Duchess Sanseverina was presented to the melancholy Princess of Parma, Clara-Paolina, who because her husband had a mistress (the

Marchesa Balbi, rather a pretty woman), regarded herself as the most unfortunate person in the universe, which may well have made her the most tedious. The Duchess found herself confronting a very tall, angular woman who was not yet thirty-six and looked a good fifty. A regular and noble countenance might have passed for beautiful, though somewhat marred by huge round eyes that were half blind, if the Princess had not given up on herself. She received the Duchess with so marked a timidity that some of the courtiers hostile to Count Mosca ventured to say that the Princess had the look of the woman being presented, and the Duchess of the Sovereign. The Duchess, surprised and virtually disconcerted, desperately sought words to assume a position inferior to that which the Princess assigned to herself. In order to restore some self-possession to this wretched Princess who did not altogether lack a certain native intelligence, the Duchess could find nothing better than to start in on and to continue a long lecture on botany. The Princess was in fact quite learned in the matter; she had several fine hothouses with many tropical plants. The Duchess, quite simply trying to escape an awkward situation, made the permanent conquest of Princess Clara-Paolina, who from her initial timidity and silence at the beginning of the audience found herself at its end so at ease that, against all the rules of etiquette, this first audience lasted no less than an hour and a quarter. The following day, the Duchess sent for some exotic plants, and described herself as a great lover of all things botanical.

The Princess passed her life with the venerable Father Landriani, Archbishop of Parma, a man of learning and even of intelligence, and a thoroughly decent person who nonetheless presented a singular spectacle when he sat in his crimson velvet chair (to which his office entitled him), opposite the Princess's armchair, surrounded by her ladies-in-waiting and her two *lady-companions*. The old prelate with his long white hair was even more timid, if possible, than the Princess; they saw each other every day, and every audience began with a silence that lasted a good quarter of an hour. It was only natural that the Countess Alvizi, one of the lady-companions, had become a sort of favorite, since she had the art of encouraging them to speak to each other and of making them break the silence.

In order to end the series of presentations, the Duchess was admitted to the presence of His Serene Highness the Crown Prince, a personage taller than his father and more timid than his mother whose strong point was mineralogy and who was sixteen years old. He blushed violently when he saw the Duchess come in, and was so disoriented that he could never find a word to say to this lovely lady. He was a fine-looking boy, and spent his life in the woods, hammer in hand.

At the moment the Duchess stood up to bring this silent audience to a close: "My Lord, Madame, how pretty you are!" exclaimed the Crown Prince, an observation not regarded as being in excessively bad taste by the lady presented.

The Marchesa Balbi, a young woman of twenty-five, could still have passed, two or three years before the Duchess Sanseverina's arrival in Parma, for the ideal type of Italian beauty. Now she still possessed the finest eyes in the world, and the most charming little airs and graces; but at close range, her skin was reticulated with countless tiny wrinkles which made the Marchesa into a young grandmother. Glimpsed at a certain distance, for example in her box at the theater, she was still a beauty; and people in the pit commended the Prince's excellent taste. He spent every evening at the Marchesa Balbi's, though frequently without opening his lips, and the boredom she observed in the Prince had caused this poor woman to decline into an extraordinary thinness. She laid claim to limitless subtlety, her constant smile tinged with malice; she had the finest teeth in the world, and on every occasion, though without any meaning, she sought by a cunning smile to suggest much more than what her mere words expressed. Count Mosca used to say that it was her continual smiles, even as she was inwardly yawning, that gave her so many wrinkles. Countess Balbi was a party to everything that was going on, and the State did not make a contract for a thousand francs without there being a *souvenir* (that was the polite expression in Parma) for the Marchesa. According to common gossip, she had invested six million francs in England, but in reality her fortune, quite recent in fact, did not amount to more than 1,500,000 francs. It was to be protected from her subtleties, and to be sure of her dependence upon himself, that Count Mosca had had himself appointed Minister of Finance. The Marchesa's sole passion was fear masked as sordid greed: "I shall die in the poorhouse," she occasionally remarked to the Prince, who was shocked by this prophecy. The Duchess noticed that the antechamber of the Palazzo Balbi, resplendent with gilding, was lit by a single candle that guttered on a precious marble table, and that the doors of her salon were blackened by the footmen's fingers.

"She received me," the Duchess remarked to her friend, "as if she were expecting me to give her a tip of fifty francs."

The Duchess's triumphal progress was to some degree interrupted by her treatment at the hands of the cleverest woman at court, the famous Marchesa Raversi, a consummate schemer who headed the faction opposed to Count Mosca's. She intrigued for his destruction, especially in the last few months, since as the niece of Count Sanseverina she feared to see her inheritance jeopardized by the charms of the new Duchess.

"Marchesa Raversi is not a foe to be despised," the Count observed to his mistress. "I believe her to be so dangerous that I separated from my wife solely because she insisted on taking as her lover Cavaliere Bentivoglio, one of Marchesa Raversi's friends."

This lady, a tall virago with coal-black hair, remarkable for the diamonds she wore all day, and for the rouge with which she covered her cheeks, had declared herself the Duchess's enemy from the start and opened hostilities immediately upon receiving her in her own home. The Duke Sanseverina, in the letters he sent from ———, seemed so delighted by his embassy, and especially by his expectation of the Grand Cordon, that his family feared he would leave a share of his fortune to the wife upon whom he was now lavishing so many trifling gifts. Marchesa Raversi, homely as she was, had for a lover Count Balbi, the best-looking man at court: in general she succeeded at whatever she undertook.

The Duchess maintained a splendid establishment. The Palazzo Sanseverina had always been one of the finest in the city of Parma, and the Duke, on the occasion of his embassy and of his future Grand Cordon, expended enormous sums upon its embellishment: the Duchess was in charge of the alterations.

The Count had guessed correctly: a few days after the Duchess was presented, young Clélia Conti came to court, having been made a Canoness. In order to parry the blow this mark of favor might seem to strike at the Count's credit, the Duchess gave a party on the pretext of opening her palace gardens, and, by her charming manners, she made young Clélia, whom she called her little friend from Lake Como, the queen of the evening. Her monogram appeared as though by accident upon all the principal lanterns of the garden. Though somewhat pensive, young Clélia had a charming way of referring to their little adventure beside the lake, and to her deep gratitude. She was said to be very religious and a lover of solitude.

"I'll wager," said the Count, "that she's bright enough to be ashamed of her father."

The Duchess made this young girl her friend, feeling attracted to her; she did not want to seem jealous, and included her in all her social occasions; ultimately her scheme was to try to diminish all the hostilities of which the Count was the object.

Everything smiled upon the Duchess, who was delighted by this court life where a storm is always to be feared; she felt as if she was beginning to live again. She was tenderly devoted to the Count, who was literally mad with happiness. This agreeable situation had afforded him a perfect *sang-froid* with regard to everything concerning his professional interests. Hence scarcely two months after the Duchess's arrival, he obtained the patent and honors of Prime Minister, which closely approach those paid to the Sovereign himself. The Count had complete control over his master's spirit, as all Parma was to learn in the most striking manner.

To the southwest, and ten minutes from the city, rises that citadel so famous throughout Italy; its huge tower a hundred and eighty feet high can be seen from a great distance. This tower, built in imitation of Hadrian's mausoleum in Rome by the Farnese family, grandsons of Paul III, early in the sixteenth century, is so large in diameter that on its upper platform has been built a palace for the governor of the Citadel and a new prison known as the Farnese Tower. This prison, built in honor of Ranuccio-Ernesto II, who had become the cherished lover of his step-mother, was regarded throughout the region as singularly beautiful. The Duchess was curious to see it; on the day of her visit, it was overpoweringly hot in Parma and up there, in that elevated position, she found refreshment, and was so delighted by doing so that she spent several hours in the place. A point was made of showing her all the rooms of the Farnese Tower.

On the platform of the big tower, the Duchess encountered a wretched Liberal prisoner, who had emerged to take the half-hour's exercise granted him every three days. Having come back down to Parma, and not yet in possession of that discretion requisite in an absolute monarchy, she mentioned this man who had told her his entire history. The faction of the Marchesa Raversi seized upon these remarks of the Duchess and repeated them widely, hoping they would distress the Prince. Indeed, Ernesto IV frequently repeated that it was crucial to impress the imagination of the people. "*Perpetual* is a big word," he would say, "and more terrible in Italy than elsewhere."

Consequently, he had never once in his life granted a pardon. Eight days after her visit to the fortress, the Duchess received a letter of commutation, signed by the Prince and the Minister, with the name left blank. The prisoner whose name she would write in this space was to obtain restitution of his possessions and permission to spend the rest of his days in America. The Duchess wrote the name of the man who had spoken to her. Unfortunately, this person turned out to be something of a rogue, and a weak spirit as well; it was upon his confession that the famous Ferrante Palla had been condemned to death.

The exceptional nature of this pardon had intensified the delights of the Duchess's position. Count Mosca was mad with happiness, this was a splendid period of his life, and was to exert a decisive influence upon Fabrizio's destiny. The latter was still in Romagnano, near Novara, going to confession, hunting, never reading, and paying court to a noble lady according to his instructions. The Duchess was still slightly shocked by this last necessity. Another sign which meant little or nothing to the Count was that though she was entirely frank with him on every subject imaginable, and virtually thought aloud in his presence, she never mentioned Fabrizio to him without first carefully choosing her words.

"If you like," the Count said to her one day, "I shall write to that charming brother of yours on the shores of Lake Como, and shall compel that Marchese del Dongo, with a certain pressure from me and my friends in ———, to seek pardon for your charming Fabrizio. If it is true, as I am far from doubting, that he is somewhat superior to the young fellows who ride their English thoroughbreds through the streets of Milan, what a life for a man of eighteen, doing nothing and with the prospect of nothing ever to do! Had Heaven granted him a real passion for anything at all, even for fishing, I should respect it; but what will he do in Milan, even after he has been pardoned? At a certain hour of the day he will ride a horse he has obtained from England, at a certain hour his idleness will take him to his mistress, whom he will care for less than his horse . . . But if you so desire it, I shall try to procure just such a life for your nephew."

"I should like him to be an officer," said the Duchess.

"Would you advise a Sovereign to confide a position which, on a given date, may be of some importance to a young man who first of all is capable of enthusiasm and who secondly has shown that enthusiasm for Napoléon, to the point of joining him at Waterloo? Think of where we should all be if Napoléon had won! We should have no Liberals to fear, true enough, but the sovereigns of our old families could continue to reign only by marrying the daughters of Bonaparte's marshals. Thus a military career for Fabrizio is the life of a squirrel in a revolving cage: plenty of movement but getting nowhere. He will have the disappointment of seeing himself outstripped by every plebeian devotion. The first virtue of a young man today—that is, for the next fifty years perhaps, as long as we live in fear, and religion has regained its powers—is to be incapable of enthusiasm and not to have much in the way of brains.

"One thing occurs to me, that will at first make you cry out in protest, and will give me infinite trouble long afterward—an act of madness that I will perform for your sake. But tell me, if you can, what madness would I not perform to obtain a smile . . ."

"Well?" said the Duchess.

"Well! we have had, as Archbishops of Parma, three members of your family: Ascanio del Dongo, who wrote something or other in sixteen hundred something or other, Fabrizio in 1699, and another Ascanio in 1740. If your Fabrizio is willing to enter the priesthood and display virtues of the first order, I shall make him a Bishop somewhere, then Arshbishop here, provided my influence lasts. The real objection is this: will I remain Minister long enough to achieve this fine plan which requires several years? The Prince may die, he may have the poor taste to dismiss me. But in any case, this is the one means I have to do something for Fabrizio which will be worthy of you."

There followed a lengthy argument: the Duchess found this notion repugnant in the extreme. "Show me again," she said to the Count, "that any other career is impossible for Fabrizio."

The Count showed her. "You will regret," he added, "the brilliant uniform. But in that regard, I don't know what I can do."

After a month, which the Duchess had required in order to reflect, she consented with a sign to the Minister's sage views.

"To ride haughtily on an English horse through some big city," the Count repeated, "or to assume a condition which in no way contradicts his birth—I see no middle ground. Unfortunately, a gentleman can become neither a physician nor a lawyer, and the age belongs to lawyers.

"Remember, Madame," the Count repeated, "that you are offering your nephew, in the streets of Milan, the fate enjoyed by the young men his age who pass for the most fortunate. Once his pardon is obtained, you will give him fifteen, twenty, thirty thousand francs; the amount matters little to you; neither you nor I make any claim to saving money."

The Duchess was sensitive to questions of glory; she did not want Fabrizio to be simply a wastrel; she returned to her lover's plan.

"Observe," the Count told her, "that I make no claim of turning Fabrizio into an exemplary priest, such as you see all around you. No; he is a nobleman first and foremost; he may remain quite ignorant if he chooses, and will become no less of a Bishop, and an Archbishop, if the Prince continues to regard me as a man useful to him.

"If your orders deign to change my proposal into an immutable decree," the Count added, "Parma must not see your protégé as a man living on modest means. His style of life will be regarded as shocking if he is seen to be a simple priest; he must appear in Parma only with a suitable establishment and *purple stockings.** Then everyone will realize that your nephew is destined to be a Bishop, and no one will be shocked.

"If you believe me in this, you will send Fabrizio to seminary, and he will spend three years in Naples. During his vacations from the Ecclesiastical Academy, he may visit Paris and London if he likes, but he must never show his face in Parma."

On hearing this sentence, something like a shudder passed through the Duchess. She sent a courier to her nephew, and arranged to meet him at Piacenza. Need it be said that this courier was the bearer of all the necessary moneys and passports?

Being the first to arrive at Piacenza, Fabrizio hastened to meet the Duchess when she appeared, and embraced her with transports which made her dissolve into tears. She was glad that the Count was not there; since their affair had begun, this was the first time she had experienced this sensation.

Fabrizio was deeply touched, and then distressed by the plans the Duchess had made for him; his hope had always been that, once his Waterloo business was settled, he would end by being a soldier. One thing struck the Duchess and further increased her romantic opinion of her nephew: he absolutely refused any thought of leading a café life in one of the great cities of Italy.

"Can't you see yourself on the *Corso* in Florence or Naples," said the Duchess, "with thoroughbred English horses! A carriage for the evening, a handsome apartment, and so on."

She delicately insisted on the description of this vulgar felicity, which she found Fabrizio rejecting with disdain. "The boy is a hero," she mused.

"And after ten years of this pleasant life, what will I have accomplished?" asked Fabrizio. "What will have I have become? A young man *of a certain age* who must give way to the first good-looking youth who turns up in society, also mounted on an English horse."

Fabrizio at first utterly rejected the notion of entering the priest-

---

*In Italy, young men who have patrons or who are learned become *Monsignori* or *prelati*, which does not mean *Bishop*; they then wear purple stockings. To be a *Monsignore* does not require vows of celibacy: a man may discard his purple stockings and marry. [Stendhal's note.]

hood; he spoke of going to New York, of becoming a citizen, a soldier in the Republic of America.

"What a mistake you're making! There will be no war for you to wage, and you'll fall back into café life, only without elegance, without music, without love affairs," the Duchess responded. "Believe me, for you as for me, an American life would be a sad business." She explained to him the cult of the god dollar, and the respect that must be paid to merchants and artisans in the street, who by their votes determine everything. They returned to the question of the Church.

"Before you fly into a passion," said the Duchess, "understand what it is that the Count wants you to do: there is no question of being a more or less exemplary and virtuous little priest like your Abbé Blanès. Remember what your uncles the Archbishops of Parma once were— read over the accounts of their lives in the Supplement to your *Genealogy*. Above all, it is important for a man bearing your name to be a great lord, noble, generous, protector of justice, destined from the first to find himself at the head of his order . . . and throughout his life committing only one dishonorable action, and that a very useful one."

"So all my illusions are shattered," exclaimed Fabrizio, sighing deeply. "It is a cruel sacrifice! I admit I had not contemplated this horror to enthusiasm and intelligence, even when wielded to their advantage, which will henceforth prevail among absolute sovereigns."

"Just think that a proclamation, a heartfelt whim casts a man of enthusiasm into the faction contrary to the one he has served his whole life long!"

"I an enthusiast!" repeated Fabrizio. "A strange accusation! I cannot even be in love!"

"What do you mean?" exclaimed the Duchess.

"When I have the honor to pay court to a beautiful woman, even well born, and religious to boot, I never think of her except when she is in front of me."

This avowal made a strange impression on the Duchess.

"I ask you for a month," Fabrizio continued, "to take my leave of Madame C—— in Novara and, what is still more difficult, of the castles in Spain of my whole life. I shall write to my mother, who will be kind enough to visit me in Belgirate, on the Piedmont side of Lake

Maggiore, and thirty-one days from now, I shall be in Parma, incognito."

"Anything but that!" exclaimed the Duchess. She did not want Count Mosca to see her speaking to Fabrizio.

This same pair saw each other once again at Piacenza; this time the Duchess was greatly agitated; a storm had broken at court; the Marchesa Raversi's faction was about to prevail; it was possible that Count Mosca would be replaced by General Fabio Conti, leader of what in Parma was called the Liberal party. Except for the name of the rival growing in the Prince's favor, the Duchess reported everything to Fabrizio. Once more she discussed the possibilities of his future, even with the prospect of lacking the Count's omnipotent protection.

"I shall be spending three years at the Ecclesiastical Academy in Naples!" exclaimed Fabrizio. "But since I must be a young gentleman first and foremost, and since you are not obliging me to lead the severe existence of a virtuous seminarian, this stay in Naples holds no terrors for me, such a life will certainly be as agreeable as that at Romagnano; the respectable folk there are beginning to find me something of a Jacobin. In my exile I have discovered that I know nothing, not even Latin, not even how to spell! I intended to start my education anew in Novara; in Naples I shall gladly study theology, a complex subject, I understand."

The Duchess was enchanted. "If we are driven out of Parma," she told him, "we shall come to see you in Naples. But since you accept the purple stockings for the time being, the Count, who knows the situation of Italy at the present time, has given me a suggestion for you. Believe what you are taught or not, *but never offer any objection.* Imagine that you are being taught the rules of a game of whist; what objections could you possibly have to the rules of whist? I told the Count that you were a believer, and he is pleased with the fact; it is useful in this world and in the next. But if you are a believer, do not fall into the vulgarity of speaking with horror of Voltaire, Diderot, and all those harebrained Frenchmen who have paved the way to a government of Two Chambers. Let these names rarely come to your lips, but when you must, speak of these gentlemen with a calm irony—they have long been refuted, and their attacks are no longer of any importance. Believe blindly everything you are told at the Academy. Realize that there are people keeping careful account of your slightest objections; you will be forgiven some minor amorous intrigue, if it is properly conducted, but not a doubt; now age suppresses intrigue and increases doubt. Act on this principle in the tribunal of Penitence. You will have a letter of recommendation to a Bishop who is the factotum of the Cardinal-Archbishop of Naples; to him only may you confess your escapade in France, and your presence, on June 18, in the environs of Waterloo. For the rest, greatly abridge—diminish this adventure, acknowledge it only so you cannot be reproached for having concealed it; you were so young at the time!

"The Count's second suggestion is this: If there should occur to you some brilliant reasoning, a victorious retort which would change the course of the conversation, do not yield to the temptation to shine, hold your tongue; intelligent people will see your wit in your eyes, there will be plenty of time to be witty when you are a Bishop."

Fabrizio entered Naples with a modest carriage and four servants, good Milanese, which his aunt had sent him. After a year's study, no one described him as a man of wit; he was regarded as a diligent and generous nobleman, perhaps something of a libertine.

This year, rather an entertaining one for Fabrizio, had been terrible for the Duchess. The Count had been three or four times within an inch of losing everything; the Prince, more fearful than ever because he was ill that year, believed that by dismissing the Count he would be rid of the odium of the executions performed before the Count had entered his Ministry. Rassi was the cherished favorite who would be retained at all costs. The dangers incurred by the Count gained him the Duchess's passionate attachment; she no longer brooded over Fabrizio. In order to put a good face on their possible retirement, it was given out that the air in Parma, somewhat humid as a matter of fact, like the air in all of Lombardy, was rather injurious to his health. Finally, after certain intervals of disgrace, which for the Count, as Prime Minister, meant not seeing his master for as long as twenty days at a time, Mosca prevailed; he had General Fabio Conti, the so-called Liberal, appointed Governor of the Citadel, in which Rassi's Liberal judges were imprisoned. "If Conti shows indulgence toward his prisoners," Mosca observed to his mistress, "he will be disgraced as a Jacobin whose political ideas have caused the neglect of his duties as a general; if he shows himself to be severe and pitiless, and it strikes me that he will incline to this position, he thereby ceases to be the leader of his own faction and alienates all the families who have some member in the citadel. This poor fellow knows how to put on a respectful face at the Prince's approach; if need be he will change his uniform four times a day; he can argue a question of etiquette, but his is not a mind capable of following the arduous path by which alone he can save himself; and in any case, I am there."

The day after General Fabio Conti was appointed, ending the ministerial crisis, it was learned that Parma would have an ultra-monarchist newspaper.

"How many disputes this paper will engender!" exclaimed the Duchess.

"This paper, whose idea is perhaps my masterpiece," replied the Count with a laugh, "I shall gradually allow, in spite of myself, to pass into the hands of the raging *ultras.* I have had splendid salaries attached to the editorial positions. Everyone will seek such offices; this business will occupy us a month or two, and the dangers I have just run will soon be forgotten. The weighty figures of P—— and D—— are already on the list."

"But such a paper will be disgustingly silly!"

"I rely on it," retorted the Count. "The Prince will read it every morning and admire the doctrines of its founder, myself. As for the details, he will approve or be shocked; of the hours he devotes to work, two will be taken up in this fashion. The paper will get into difficulties, but by the time serious complaints are registered, in eight or ten months, it will be entirely in the hands of the fanatical *ultras.* This will be the faction that will annoy me when I must answer for them, and it will be I who raises objections to the paper; as it turns out, I prefer a hundred wretched absurdities to one hanged man. Who recalls a piece of nonsense two years after the publication of the official paper? Better than having the sons and the family of a hanged man vowing a hatred that will last as long as I do and that may well shorten my life."

The Duchess, always passionate about something, always active, never idle, had sharper wits than the whole court of Parma; but she lacked the patience and impassivity requisite to success in scheming. Still, she had managed to follow devotedly the interests of the various coteries; she was even beginning to enjoy a certain amount of personal credit with the Prince. The Crown Princess, Clara-Paolina, surrounded by honors but imprisoned within the most outmoded etiquette, regarded herself as the unhappiest of women. The Duchess Sanseverina paid court to her, and undertook to prove to her that she was nowhere near so unhappy. It must be remarked here that the Prince saw his wife only at dinner; this repast lasted some thirty minutes, and the Prince spent whole weeks without addressing a word to Clara-Paolina. The Duchess attempted to change all that; she entertained the Prince, all the more frequently since she had managed to retain all her independence. Even had she wished to, she could never have avoided wounding the crowd of fools that swarmed around the court. It was this utter lack of skill on her part which made her loathed by the ordinary courtiers, all those Counts and Marchesi who enjoy an income of about five thousand a year. She realized this unfortunate fact after the first few days, and concerned herself exclusively with pleasing her sovereign and his wife, the latter exerting an absolute dominion over the Crown Prince. The Duchess managed to entertain the Sovereign, and benefited from the extreme attention he granted her slightest words in order to set the hostile courtiers in a ridiculous light. Since the foolish actions Rassi had made him perform, and the foolish actions of noble blood which are irreparable, the Prince was occasionally terrified and frequently bored, which had brought him to the point of melancholy desire; he realized that he was never entertained, and became grim when he supposed that others were having a good time; the appearance of happiness enraged him. "We must conceal our affections," the Duchess told her friend; and she let the Prince guess that she was now only passably taken with the Count, estimable a man though he was.

This discovery had given His Highness a happy day. Occasionally the Duchess dropped a few words of her intention to take a leave of a few months each year, which she would devote to seeing the Italy she knew nothing of: she would visit Naples, Florence, Rome. Now nothing in the world could cause greater pain to the Prince than such an appearance of abandonment: this was one of his most salient weaknesses; any behavior resembling disdain for his old capital pierced him to the heart. He felt that he had no means of keeping the Duchess Sanseverina with him, and the Duchess Sanseverina was by far the most brilliant woman in Parma. An unparalleled phenomenon, given Italian laziness, was that people came in from the surrounding countryside to attend her *Thursdays;* these were veritable parties; almost always the Duchess provided something new and entertaining. The Prince was dying to attend one of these *Thursdays,* but how was he to manage it? To visit the residence of a mere subject was a thing which neither he nor his father had ever done!

On a certain Thursday, it was cold and rainy; all evening the Prince heard the carriages rolling up the cobblestones from the palace square to the Palazzo Sanseverina. He was overcome by a feeling of impatience: other people were being amused, and he, the Sovereign Prince, the absolute master, who ought to be amused more than anyone else in the world—he was bored! He rang for his aide-de-camp, it was necessary to take the time to put a dozen trusty men in the street between His Highness's palace and the Palazzo Sanseverina. Finally, after an hour which seemed a century to the Prince, and during which he was twenty times tempted to brave the assassins' daggers and emerge quite spontaneously and taking no precaution, he appeared in Countess Sanseverina's first salon. A thunderbolt falling in that salon would not have produced as much astonishment. In the twinkling of an eye, and as the Prince advanced, a silence of amazement fell in these gay and noisy rooms; all eyes, fixed upon the Prince, opened excessively wide. The courtiers seemed disconcerted; only the Duchess showed no surprise. When at last people had regained the power of speech, the great concern of all present was to decide this important question: had the Duchess been informed of this visit, or had she been as surprised by it as everyone else?

The Prince was entertained, and the reader will judge of the utterly spontaneous character of the Duchess, and of the infinite power which certain vague hints of departure, cleverly dropped, had allowed her to assume.

As she was accompanying the Prince to the door while he was making a number of extremely agreeable remarks, a singular notion occurred to her which she ventured to express to him quite simply, and as if it were the most ordinary matter. "If Your Serene Highness wished to address three or four of these charming sentences lavished upon me to the Princess, you would make me happier far than by telling me here and now how pretty I am. For I would not for anything in the world distress the Princess by the particular marks of favor with which Your Highness has honored me."

The Prince stared at her fixedly, and replied in a dry tone of voice: "I was under the impression that I am empowered to go where I please."

The Duchess blushed. "I merely wished," she replied at once, "not to expose Your Highness to the risk of performing a futile errand, for this Thursday will be the last; I shall be going to spend a few days in Bologna or in Florence."

As she returned through her salons, everyone supposed her at the height of royal favor, and she had just ventured what in the memory of man no one had dared in all of Parma. She made a sign to the Count, who left his whist table and followed her into a little salon that was lighted but empty.

"You have done a very bold thing," he told her; "I should not have advised it; but in fond hearts," he added with a smile, "happiness augments love, and if you leave tomorrow morning, I shall follow you tomorrow night. I shall be delayed only by that task at the Ministry of Finance which I have been so foolish as to assume, but in four well-occupied hours, one can dispose of a good many treasury accounts. Let us return to the party, dear friend, and accomplish our ministerial fatuities in all freedom, and without any appearance of constraint; it is perhaps the last performance we shall be giving in this city. If he believes himself to be challenged, a man is capable of anything; he will call this *setting an example*. When these people will have gone, we shall determine the means of barricading the palace for the rest of the night; best perhaps to leave without delay for your estate of Sacca, near the Po, which has the advantage of being but a half-hour's distance from Austrian territory."

This was a delicious moment for the Duchess's love and for her self-esteem; she gazed at the Count, and her eyes brimmed with tears. So powerful a Minister, surrounded by this host of courtiers overwhelming him with compliments equal to those they addressed to the Prince himself—to leave everything for her and so readily!

Returning to her salons, she was wild with joy. Everyone bowed before her. "How happiness has changed our Duchess," said the courtiers on all sides, "she is quite unrecognizeable. Finally that noble Roman soul, so high above us all, deigns to appreciate the extreme favor of which she has just been the object on the part of our Sovereign!"

Toward the evening's end, the Count came to her: "I have news for you . . ." Immediately the persons surrounding the Duchess moved away. "The Prince, returning to his palace," continued the Count, "had himself announced at his wife's apartments. Imagine the surprise! 'I have come to tell you,' he said to her, 'of a fine evening which I have spent at the Duchess Sanseverina's. It is she who has requested me to tell you about all she has done with that musty old palace.' Then the Prince, who had taken a chair, began to describe each of your salons. He spent more than twenty minutes in those apartments of his wife, who was weeping for joy; despite her intelligence, she could not manage a word to keep the conversation in the light key His Highness sought to give it."

This Prince was by no means a bad man, whatever the Italian Liberals might say of him. In truth, he had thrown into his prisons a considerable number of them, but this was out of fear, and he sometimes murmured as if to console himself for certain memories: "Better to kill the Devil than let the Devil kill us." The day after the party we have just described, he was quite merry, having performed two fine actions: to attend a *Thursday* and to speak to his wife. At dinner, he spoke to her again; in a word, the Duchess Sanseverina's *Thursday* effected an internal revolution that echoed throughout all Parma; Marchesa Raversi was dismayed, and the Duchess had the double joy of having been able to be useful to her lover, and having found him more in love with her than ever.

"All this on account of a very imprudent notion that happened to pass through my head!" she said to the Count. "I might surely be freer in Rome or in Naples, but would I find there so entrancing a game to play? No, indeed, my dear Count, and it is you who constitute my happiness."

CHAPTER SEVEN

It is with minor details of court life as insignificant as the one we have just related that the history of the next four years should be filled. Each spring, the Marchesa and her daughters came to the Palazzo San-severina or to the estate of Sacca, on the bank of the Po, for a stay of two months; many agreeable hours were spent there, and Fabrizio was often mentioned, but the Count would never permit him to pay a single visit to Parma. The Duchess and the Minister had indeed to make amends for certain follies, but in general Fabrizio followed quite obediently the line of conduct that had been drawn for him: a nobleman studying theology and not entirely relying on his virtue to achieve his advancement. At Naples, he had developed a deep interest in the study of antiquity, he made excavations; this passion had almost replaced the one for horses. He had sold his English thoroughbreds in order to continue certain diggings at Miseno, where he had found a bust of Tiberius as a young man, which now ranked among the finest remains of antiquity. The discovery of this bust was nearly the keenest pleasure he had experienced at Naples. His soul was too noble to imitate the other young men, for example, to play a lover's part with any seriousness. No doubt he had no dearth of mistresses, but they were quite without consequence for him, and in spite of his youth one might say of him that he knew nothing of love; for which reason he was loved all the more. Nothing prevented him from behaving with utter self-possession, for to him one pretty young woman was always the same as any other pretty young woman; it was always the one he had met last who seemed most attractive. One of the most admired ladies of Naples had thrown herself at him for the last year of his stay, which had initially amused him and ultimately got on his nerves to such a degree that one of the felicities of his departure was to be released from the attentions of the charming Duchess of A——. It was in 1821 that, having passed all his examinations more or less satisfactorily, having bestowed a gift and a cross upon his director of studies, or tutor, Fabrizio finally left to see something of the city of Parma, of which he thought so often. He was a Monsignore, and four horses drew his carriage; at the post-stage before Parma, he took only two, and in town drew up in front of the church of San Giovanni. Here could be seen the elaborate tomb of his great-great-uncle, the Archbishop Ascanio del Dongo, author of the Latin genealogy. He prayed at the tomb, then walked to the palazzo of the Duchess, who expected him several days later. There were a number of people in her salon, but soon they were left alone.

"And are you satisfied with me now?" he asked her as he rushed into her arms. "Thanks to you, I have spent four quite happy years at Naples, instead of boring myself to death in Novara with a mistress authorized by the police."

The Duchess could not get over her amazement—she would not have recognized Fabrizio if she had passed him in the street; she found him to be what indeed he was: one of the best-looking men in Italy; it was his physiognomy, above all, that was charming. She had sent him to Naples with the manners of a daredevil; the riding-whip he always used to carry in those days seemed to be an inherent part of his being: now he had the noblest, and the most reserved expression in the presence of strangers, yet in private she recognized all the fire of his first youth. He was a diamond that had lost nothing in being polished. Fabrizio had not been there an hour before Count Mosca appeared, perhaps a little too soon. The young man spoke to him in such good terms of the Cross of Parma bestowed upon his tutor and expressed his deep gratitude for other benefits to which he dared not refer so openly with such perfect tact that the minister immediately formed a favorable impression.

"This nephew of yours," he murmured to the Duchess, "is made to embellish any high position to which you wish to advance him in due course."

So far, everything was going wonderfully, but when the Minister, very pleased with Fabrizio and hitherto concerned only with his words and gestures, happened to glance at the Duchess, he observed a singular expression in her eyes. "This young man is doing something peculiar here," he said to himself. This reflection was a bitter one; the Count had reached the age of *fifty*, a cruel number whose entire resonance can affect only a man desperately in love. Count Mosca was very kind, very worthy of being loved, whatever his severities as a Minister. But in his eyes, this cruel number of *fifty* darkened his whole life and would have been capable of eliciting cruelty on his own account. In the five years during which he had persuaded the Duchess to come to Parma, she had frequently roused his jealousy, especially in the early times, but never had she given him occasion for any real complaint. He even believed, and with reason, that it was in the intention of securing his affections all the more closely that the Duchess had resorted to these appearances of favor in regard to several handsome young men at court. He was certain, for instance, that she had rejected certain offers on the part of the Prince, who had even, on that occasion, had uttered an instructive remark.

"But if I were to accept Your Highness's offer," the Duchess had said to him with a laugh, "how should I dare to face the Count?"

"I should be almost as much out of countenance as you. The dear Count! My friend! But there is a simple solution to the difficulty, which I have already considered: the Count shall be sent to the Citadel for the rest of his days."

At the moment of Fabrizio's arrival, the Duchess was so transported with happiness that it had not occurred to her that the expression in her eyes might give the Count ideas. The effect was profound and the suspicions without remedy.

Fabrizio was received by the Prince two hours after his arrival; the Duchess, foreseeing the good effect this impromptu audience might produce in public, had sought it for two months: this favor put Fabrizio in an exceptional position from his first moment at court; the pretext had been that he was merely passing through Parma on his way to see him mother in Piedmont. At the moment when a charming little note from the Duchess was delivered to the Prince explaining that Fabrizio was awaiting his orders, His Highness was feeling bored. "Now I shall see," he told himself, "some saintly little dunce, a dull face or a cunning one." The City Commander had already reported on Fabrizio's first visit to the tomb of his uncle the Archbishop. The Prince saw coming toward him a tall young man whom, had it not been for his violet stockings, he would have taken for some young officer.

This little surprise dispelled his boredom. "Here is a fine fellow," he said to himself, "for whom I shall be asked Lord knows what favors— doubtless all I can give. He's just arrived, probably embarrassed: I'll try a little Jacobin politics on him, and we'll see how he manages to deal with that."

After the first gracious words on the Prince's part: "Well, Monsignore! Are the Neapolitans happy? Is the King popular?"

"Serene Highness," Fabrizio replied without a moment's hesitation, "I used to admire, passing them in the street, the fine bearing of His Majesty's various regiments; the better classes are properly respectful of their masters; but I must confess that never in my life have I permitted the members of the lower orders to speak to me of anything but the work I pay them to do."

"Plague!" said the Prince. "The falcon's well trained! I know the Sanseverina's touch when I see it." Becoming interested, the Prince employed a good deal of skill in making Fabrizio enter into this scabrous subject. The young man, excited by the danger, was fortunate enough to make some admirable remarks: "Would it not be something like insolence to parade one's love for one's King?" he asked. "Blind obedience is what is owed."

Observing such prudence, the Prince was almost vexed: "Apparently Naples has sent us a young man of wit, not a breed I would choose; even though a man of wit flashes the highest principles, and quite sincerely too, there is always, somewhere, a certain blood brotherhood to Voltaire and Rousseau."

The Prince found himself virtually defied by the proper manners and the impregnable replies of the young man just out of his seminary; what he had anticipated was not happening; in the twinkling of an eye he assumed the tone of good fellowship, and returning, in a few words, to the broad principles of government and society, he uttered, adapting them to the occasion, a few phrases out of Fénelon he had been made to learn by heart since childhood for public audiences. "These principles surprise you, young man," he said to Fabrizio, whom he had called Monsignore at the start of the audience, and he intended to use Monsignore at its close, but in the course of conversation, he found it more adroit, more suited to affecting phrases, to address the fellow in a more familiar fashion; "these principles surprise you, young man, I admit that they hardly match the ready-made slogans of absolutism [his very expression] you might read any day of the week in my court paper. . . . But Good Lord! What good is it quoting such things to you? Our journalists are quite unknown to you . . ."

"If His Serene Highness will excuse me, not only do I read the Parma newspaper, which strikes me as quite well written, but I agree with its editor that everything done since the death of Louis XIV, in 1715, is at once a crime and a folly. Humanity's greatest concern is its salvation, there cannot be two ways of regarding such a subject, and that is a felicity which lasts for all eternity. Such phrases as *liberty, justice, the happiness of the greatest number* are infamous and criminal: they give men's minds the habit of argument and resistance. A Chamber of Deputies *challenges* what such people call *the Ministry.* And once this fatal habit of resistance sets in, human weakness applies it to everything, humanity reaches the point of suspecting the Bible, Holy Orders, tradition, etc.; at which point it is lost. Even if, as it is horribly false and criminal to say, such resistance to the authority of princes *established by Divine Right* might afford a degree of happiness for the twenty or thirty years of life that might fall to each of us, what is a half-century, or a whole one, compared to an eternity of torment? and so on."

It was evident, from the fervor with which Fabrizio spoke, that he was seeking to present his ideas so as to make them as accessible as possible to his listener; clearly he was not just reciting a lesson.

Soon the Prince lost interest in matching wits with this young man whose simple and serious manners were beginning to annoy him. "Farewell, Monsignore," he said abruptly, "I see that the Ecclesiastical Academy at Naples affords an excellent education, and it is evident that when these good precepts fall upon a mind so well prepared, brilliant results may be obtained. Farewell." And he turned his back.

"I have not pleased this creature," Fabrizio said to himself.

"Now it remains to be seen," mused the Prince once he was alone, "if this handsome young fellow is capable of passion for something; in that case, he would be complete. . . . Who could repeat more cleverly his aunt's lessons? It's as if I were hearing her talk; if we had a revolution here, she's the one who'd be writing for the *Monitore,* the way the Marchesa San Felice used to do in Naples! But the Marchesa, for all her twenty-five years and her beauty, managed to get herself hanged for her trouble! A good example for ladies of a little too much wit." In supposing Fabrizio his aunt's pupil, the Prince was mistaken: men of wit born to the throne or beside it soon lose all finesse of touch: they proscribe, around them, that freedom of conversation which to them seems crudity; they wish to see only masks and claim to judge beauty by its complexion; amusingly enough, they believe themselves to possess a great deal of tact. In this instance, for example, Fabrizio happened to believe virtually everything we have heard him say; it is true that he never thought more than twice a month about such broad principles. He had lively tastes, he had a certain amount of wit, but he also had faith.

The love of liberty, the fashion and the cult of *the happiness of the greatest number,* by which the nineteenth century was so taken, was in the Prince's eyes merely another *heresy* which would pass like the rest, but after having slain many souls, just as the plague while it reigns in any one region slays many bodies. And despite all this Fabrizio used to delight in reading the French newspapers, and even committed certain indiscretions in order to obtain them.

When Fabrizio returned quite flustered from his audience and the palace, he reported to his aunt the Prince's various modes of attack. "The first thing you you must do," she explained, "is to pay a visit to Father Landriani, our excellent Archbishop; go there on foot, climb the stairs quite deliberately, make no noise in the antechambers; if you are kept waiting, all the better, in fact, all the best! In a word, be *apostolical!*"

"I understand," Fabrizio said, "our man is a Tartuffe."

"Not a bit of it, he is virtue itself."

"Even after the way he behaved when Count Palanza was executed?" Fabrizio asked in amazement.

"Yes, my friend, after the way he behaved: our Archbishop's father was a clerk in the Ministry of Finance, a petit-bourgeois, which explains everything. Monsignor Landriani is a man of lively intelligence, wide learning, deep thoughts; he is sincere, he loves virtue: I am certain that if the Emperor Decius were to return to the world, the Archbishop would undergo martyrdom like Polyeuctes in the opera they performed last week. That is the good side of the medal. This is what's on the reverse: once he's in the Sovereign's presence, or even the Prime Minister's, he is dazzled by so much greatness, he becomes disturbed, he blushes; it is physically impossible for him to say *no*. Hence the things he has done, and which have afforded him that cruel reputation throughout Italy; but what people do not know is that, when public opinion managed to enlighten him concerning Count Palanza's trial, he gave himself the penance of living on bread and water for thirteen weeks, as many weeks as there are letters in the name *Davide Palanza*. We have in this very court a very shrewd rascal named Rassi, a Chief Justice or Fiscal Magistrate, who, when Count Palanza died, cast a spell over Father Landriani. During his thirteen-week penitence, Count Mosca, out of pity and a certain malice, invited him to dinner once, even twice a week; the good Archbishop, to show his good manners, dined like everyone else. He might have believed that it was a matter of revolution and Jacobinism to parade penitence for an action approved by the Sovereign. But it was known that for each dinner, when his duty as a loyal subject had obliged him to eat like the other guests, he imposed upon himself a penance of two more days of bread and water.

"Monsignor Landriani, a superior soul, a scholar of the first rank, has only one weakness: *he wants to be loved.* Hence, show your feelings when you look at him, and on your third visit, love him indeed. That, combined with your birth, will win you immediate adoration. Show no surprise if he accompanies you out onto the stairs as you leave, appear to be quite accustomed to such manners; he is a man born kneeling to the nobility. For the rest, be simple—be apostolic, no wit, no brilliance, no quick replies; if you don't frighten him, he will be pleased with you; remember that it must be of his own accord that he makes you his Vicar-General. The Count and I will be surprised and even vexed by this excessively rapid promotion, which is essential in dealing with the Sovereign."

Fabrizio hurried to the Archbishop's Palace: by a singular stroke of luck, the good prelate's footman, being a trifle deaf, did not hear the name *del Dongo;* he announced a young priest by the name of Fabrizio; the Archbishop happened to be seeing a parish priest of questionable behavior whom he had summoned for disciplinary action. He was in the course of delivering a reprimand, a painful affair for himself, and hoped to be soon rid of such a distressing business; hence he kept waiting for some three-quarters of an hour the young descendant of Archbishop Ascanio del Dongo.

How to describe his excuses and his despair when, after having shown out the parish priest to the second antechamber, and having asked as he again passed by the young man who was waiting *how he might serve him,* he noticed the violet stockings and heard the name Fabrizio del Dongo. This business struck our hero as so amusing that upon this very first visit he ventured to kiss the venerable prelate's hand, in a transport of affection. One had to have heard the Archbishop's voice as he repeated in despair, "A del Dongo waiting in my antechamber!" And he felt obliged, in apology, to tell him the parish priest's whole story, his transgressions, his own replies, and so on.

"Can it be possible," Fabrizio wondered as he returned to the Palazzo Sanseverina, "that this is the man who accelerated the execution of poor Count Palanza?"

"What does Your Excellency think?" he gaily inquired of Count Mosca, seeing him enter the Duchess's salon (the Count did not want Fabrizio to call him Excellency). "Myself, I am amazed; I know nothing of human character: I would have wagered, had I not known his name, that this man cannot see a chicken bleed."

"And you would have won your wager," replied the Count; "but when he is in the Prince's presence, or even mine, he cannot say *no*. In truth, for me to produce my entire effect, I must be wearing my yellow ribbon of the Grand Cordon over my coat; in ordinary evening dress, he would contradict me; hence I always wear my full uniform when I receive him. It is not up to us to destroy the prestige of power, the French newspapers are demolishing it quite rapidly enough; there is some question whether the *mania of respect* will last our time, and you, nephew, you will outlive such manners. You will be no more than a fellow-man!"

Fabrizio greatly enjoyed the Count's company: this was the first superior man who had deigned to speak to him frankly; moreover, they shared an enthusiasm for antiquities and excavations. The Count, for his part, was flattered by the extreme attention with which the young man listened to him; but there was one capital objection: Fabrizio occupied an apartment in the Palazzo Sanseverina, spent his life with the Duchess, and revealed in all innocence that he was enchanted by such intimacy; and Fabrizio's eyes and his complexion were of a mortifying brilliance.

For a long time, Ranuccio-Ernesto IV, who rarely met with resistance from the Fair Sex, had been stung by the fact that the Duchess's virtue, so widely known at court, had not made an exception in his favor. As we have seen, Fabrizio's wit and presence of mind had startled him at their first encounter. He took amiss the extreme intimacy the young man and his aunt so rashly displayed; he listened carefully to his courtiers' gossip, which was endless. The young man's arrival and the unprecedented audience he had obtained constituted the principal topic of conversation and amazement for a month at court, whereupon the Prince had an idea.

Among his palace guard, he had a simple soldier who held his wine admirably; this man spent his life in taverns, and reported on the morale of the troops directly to his Sovereign. Carlone lacked education, or he would have obtained advancement long since. Now, his orders were to be at the Palace every day on the stroke of noon by the tower clock. The Prince himself proceeded a little before noon to arrange the blinds of a vestibule adjoining His Highness's dressing-room. He returned to this vestibule shortly after noon had struck, and found the soldier there; in his pocket the Prince had a sheet of paper and an inkstand, and dictated the following letter to the soldier:

> Your Excellency is doubtless very intelligent, and it is as a consequence of that great wisdom of yours that our State is so well governed. But, my dear Count, such great successes are never obtained without a certain amount of envy, and I very much fear the laughter at your expense, if your sagacity fails to discern that a certain handsome young man has been so fortunate as to inspire, perhaps in spite of himself, a singular sentiment of love. This lucky mortal is apparently but twenty-three years old, and, Dear Count, to complicate matters, the fact is that both you and I are much more than twice this age. In the evening, at a certain distance, the Count is charming, scintillating, a man of great intelligence and as attractive as can be; but mornings, at close range, to put matters frankly, the newcomer may possess superior attractions. Now, we women set great store by such youthful freshness, especially when we are past thirty ourselves. Has there not already been talk of establishing this appealing youth at our court, in some splendid position? And who indeed is the person who most frequently speaks of it to Your Excellency?

The Prince took the letter and gave the soldier two scudi. "This is a supplement to your pay," he told him solemnly. "Not one word to anyone, or else the dankest dungeon in the Citadel."

In his desk, the Prince kept a collection of envelopes addressed to most of his courtiers, in the handwriting of this same soldier who was believed to be illiterate, and who never even wrote out his own police reports: the Prince selected the envelope he required.

A few hours later, Count Mosca received a letter by post; the time it would arrive had been carefully calculated, and as soon as the courier, who had been seen coming in with a small envelope in his hand, left the Ministerial Palace, Mosca was summoned to His Highness's quarters. Never had the favorite seemed overwhelmed by a deeper depression: to enjoy the situation at greater leisure, the Prince exclaimed upon catching sight of him, "I need to relax a little by chatting at ease with my friend, and not by working with my Minister. I have had a dreadful headache this evening, and gloomy thought have given me no respite."

Need we speak of the abominable mood which distressed the Prime Minister, Count Mosca della Rovere, as soon as he was allowed to leave his august master? Ranuccio-Ernesto IV was quite adept at tormenting a heart, and it would not be excessively unfair to offer here the comparison with a tiger which enjoys toying with its prey. The Count had himself driven home at a gallop; he shouted as he entered the door that no one was to be allowed upstairs, informed the clerk on duty that he was free to go (the knowledge that a human being was within range of his voice was hateful to him), and hastily shut himself up in the great picture gallery. Here at last he could give free rein to all his rage; here the evening was spent in darkness, wandering about like a man beside himself. He sought to silence his heart, in order to concentrate all his powers of attention upon what course of action to take. Plunged into anguish which would have wrung pity from his cruelest enemy, he reasoned with himself as follows:

"The man I abhor is living in the Duchess's palace, spending all his time with her. Ought I to try making one of her chambermaids speak? Nothing is more dangerous; she is so kind; she pays them well! They adore her! (By whom, indeed, is she not adored?) Here is the question," he continued furiously: "Am I to reveal the jealousy which is devouring me, or never speak of it at all? If I keep silence, she will not attempt to keep anything from me. I know Gina, she is a woman of impulse from head to toe; her behavior is unforeseen, even by herself; if she wishes to play a part in advance, she loses her way; invariably, at the moment of action, some new idea occurs to her which she follows in ecstasy, as if it were the most wonderful inspiration in the world, and which ruins everything.

"Not ever mentioning my torment, nothing will be concealed from me and I shall know everything that may be happening . . .

"Yes, but by speaking, I create other circumstances; I cause her to think about what she is doing; I suggest any number of the horrible things that may well happen . . . Perhaps he will be sent away"—the Count breathed again—"whereby I have virtually triumphed; even so, there will be some sort of vexation at the moment, I shall calm her . . . and what could be more natural than such vexation? . . . for fifteen years she has loved him like her own son. There lies all my hope: *like a son* . . . but she had stopped seeing him after his Waterloo escapade; but on his return from Naples, for her at least, he has become another man. *Another man*," he repeated furiously, "and this man is charming; above all he has that naïve and tender quality, and that smiling glance, which promise so much happiness! And it is just such eyes which the Duchess is hardly accustomed to find at our court! . . . Here they have been replaced by gloomy or sardonic looks. I myself, pursued by affairs, prevailing only by my influence over a man who would enjoy making me look like a fool—what must my own glances suggest more often than not? Ah, whatever precautions I take, it is my eyes above all which have made me old! Even my good humor borders on a kind of irony most of the time. . . . Moreover, and here I must be honest, does not my good humor itself suggest something very close to absolute power . . . and a certain nastiness? Do I not say as much to myself on occasion, especially when I am thwarted: I can do whatever I like? And I even add this foolishness: I must be happier than the next man, since I possess what others do not have—sovereign power in three matters out of four. Well then! Be fair; the habit of thinking in such fashions must have spoiled my smile . . . must give me a selfish, self-satisfied expression. . . . And how charming *his* smile appears! It breathes the easy happiness of first youth, and indeed engenders it."

Unfortunately for the Count, the weather was warm that evening, stifling, and a storm was imminent; the kind of weather, in a word, which in these regions leads one to make extreme resolutions. How to account for all the arguments, all the ways of regarding what was happening to him, which for three mortal hours kept this impassioned man in torment? Ultimately, the party of discretion prevailed, solely as a consequence of this reflexion: "I am mad, most likely; imagining I can reason, I am doing anything but; I am merely circling about to find a less painful position, passing blindly over some decisive argument. Since I am blinded by excessive pain, let us follow that rule, approved by all elderly men, which is called *prudence*. Moreover, once I have uttered the fatal word *jealousy*, my role is determined forever. On the contrary, by saying nothing today, I may speak tomorrow, and remain master of the whole situation."

The crisis was too acute; the Count would have gone mad indeed had it lasted. He was comforted for few moments, his attention lingering over the anonymous letter. Where could it have come from? There ensued a search for names and a judgment of each, which produced a certain diversion. Finally the Count recalled a flash of malice that had appeared in his Sovereign's eye when he had reached the point of saying, toward the end of the audience:

"Yes, dear friend, let us agree on this, the pleasures and cares of the happiest ambition, even of limitless power, are nothing compared to the inner happiness caused by relations of tenderness and love. I am a man before I am a prince, and when I have the good fortune to love, my mistress speaks to the man and not to the prince."

The Count compared that moment of malign felicity with this phrase of the letter: *It is as a consequence of that great wisdom of yours that our State is so well governed.* "The Prince wrote that!" he exclaimed. "From a courtier, that remark would be of a gratuitous indiscretion; the letter comes from His Highness!"

This problem solved, the minor satisfaction produced by the pleasure of guessing correctly was soon erased by the cruel apparition of Fabrizio's charming graces, which obsessed him anew. It was as if an enormous weight had once again fallen upon the wretched man's heart.

"What does it matter whom the anonymous letter comes from!" he exclaimed in a fury. "Does it make the fact that it gives me away exist any the less? This whim may change my life," he mused, as though to excuse himself for such insanity. "At the first opportunity, if she loves him in a certain fashion, she leaves with him for Belgirate, for Switzerland, for some corner or other of the world. She is rich now, and even if she had to live on no more than a few louis a year, what would that matter to her? Didn't she confess to me herself, not eight days ago, that her palace, for all its comfort, all its splendor, bores her? A soul so young at heart craves novelty! And how readily that new happiness presents itself! She will be carried away before having realized the danger, before having thought of pitying me! And yet I am so wretched!" cried the Count, bursting into tears.

He had sworn not to visit the Duchess that evening, but to no avail; never had he thirsted so to see her. Around midnight he appeared at her door; he found her alone with her nephew; at ten she had dismissed all her guests and closed her doors.

At the sight of the tender intimacy which reigned between these two beings, and of the Duchess's naïve joy, a hideous difficulty rose before the Count's eyes, all unexpectedly! During the long deliberation in the picture gallery he had not thought of it: how was he to conceal his jealousy?

Uncertain what excuse to use, he claimed that this evening he had found the Prince excessively ill-disposed toward him, contradicting each of his assertions, and so on. He had the pain of seeing the Duchess scarcely heed what he was saying, and pay no attention to those circumstances which, as recently as the evening before, would have inspired endless speculations. The Count looked at Fabrizio: never had that handsome Lombard countenance seemed to him so simple and so noble! Fabrizio paid more attention than the Duchess to the difficulties he was describing.

"Really," he told himself, "that countenance combines an extreme sweetness of expression with a certain tender and naïve joy which makes it irresistible. It seems to say: there is nothing but love and the happiness it bestows which are serious matters in this world. And yet were we to stumble over some detail in which mind might be necessary, its vigilance wakens and astonishes you, and you are left dumbfounded.

"Everything is simple in his eyes because everything is seen from such a height. Good God! How to oppose such a foe? And after all, what is life without Gina's love? With what delight she seems to listen to the charming sallies of that young mind, which for a woman must appear unparalleled in the whole world!"

A cruel notion gripped the Count like a cramp: "Stab him here before her eyes, and then kill myself?" He walked once around the room, barely keeping on his feet, but one hand convulsively clutching the

handle of his dagger. Neither Fabrizio nor the Duchess paid any attention to what he might have done. He said he was going to give some
order to the footman—they did not even hear what he said; the
Duchess smiled tenderly at some remark Fabrizio had just made to
her. The Count went over to a lamp in the first salon and examined the
point of his dagger. "One must be gracious and show this young man
perfect manners," he told himself, returning to the room where they
were.

He was going mad; it seemed to him that they were leaning toward
each other, exchanging kisses, here, in front of his very eyes. "This is
impossible in my presence," he told himself; "I am losing my reason. I
must try to calm myself; if I behave coarsely, the Duchess is quite capable, out of wounded vanity, of following him to Belgirate; and there,
or during the journey, chance might produce a word which will give a
name to what they feel for one another; and afterward, in an instant, all
the consequences . . .

"Solitude will make that word decisive, and moreover, once the
Duchess is far away, what is to become of me? And if, after so many difficulties surmounted with regard to the Prince, I should show my old
and care-worn face in Belgirate, what part would I play beside this pair
so mad with happiness?

"Here too, what am I but the *Terzo incomodo?* (This beautiful Italian
tongue is ready-made for love!) *Terzo incomodo*—a third presence
which discommodes the other two! What pain for a man of intelligence to realize that he is playing that hateful part, and to be unable to
bring himself to stand up and leave the room!"

The Count was about to explode or at least to betray his suffering
by losing control of his features. As he wandered about the salon, he
found himself near the door and suddenly made his escape, shouting
in a friendly tone: "Good night, you two!"

To himself he said, "One must avoid bloodshed."

The day after this horrible evening, following a night spent sometimes in poring over Fabrizio's advantages, sometimes in the hideous
transports of the cruelest jealousy, it occurred to the Count to summon a young footman; this man was paying court to a young girl
named Cecchina, one of the Duchesses's favorite chambermaids. As

luck would have it, this young servant was quite reserved in his behavior, actually miserly, for he hoped for employment as a concierge in one of the public buildings of Parma. The Count ordered this man to call Cecchina, his mistress, immediately. The man obeyed, and an hour later the Count appeared quite unexpectedly in the room where this young woman and her betrothed were waiting. The Count alarmed both of them by the quantity of gold he gave them, then addressed these few words to the trembling Cecchina, staring into her eyes: "Does the Duchess make love with Monsignore?"

"No," replied the girl, forcing herself to speak after a moment's silence. . . . "No, *not yet,* but he often kisses Madame's hands, laughing as he does so, it is true, but with rapture."

This testimony was completed by a hundred answers to as many furious questions from the Count; his painful passion made these poor wretches labor hard for all the money he had bestowed upon them: he ended by believing what he was told, and was less unhappy.

"If the Duchess should ever suspect this conversation has taken place," he said to Cecchina, "I shall send your betrothed to the Citadel for twenty years, and the next time you see him again his hair will be white."

Several days passed, during which it was Fabrizio's turn to lose all his gaiety. "I assure you," he said to the Duchess, "Count Mosca feels a genuine antipathy toward me."

"So much the worse for His Excellency," she replied, with a certain edge to her voice.

This was not the real reason that Fabrizio's gaiety had vanished. "The position in which chance has placed me is untenable," he told himself. "I am quite certain she will never speak, she would be as horrified by any word that was too specific as she would be by incest itself. But suppose some evening, after a wild and indiscreet day, she should search her conscience and decide that I might have guessed her feelings for me—how would I look to her then? Exactly like the *casto Giuseppe!* (An Italian proverb, alluding to Joseph's absurd role with the wife of the eunuch Potiphar.)

"What if I made her understand, by a fine burst of confidence, that I am incapable of loving seriously? I haven't enough strength of mind to express such a thing without seeming to be simply impertinent. The only resource I have left is a grand passion abandoned in Naples, in which case I should return there for twenty-four hours; a clever plan, but is the game worth the candle? What about a minor affair here in Parma, which might cause a certain amount of irritation, but anything is preferable to the hideous role of the man who will not guess the truth. This latter course might be prejudicial to my future, of course; by exercising discretion and purchasing prudence, I should have to diminish the dangers . . ."

What was especially cruel in the midst of all these thoughts was that in truth Fabrizio loved the Duchess much more than anyone else in the world. "I would have to be very clumsy," he told himself in a rage, "to be so afraid of not being able to convince her of what is so obvious!" Lacking skill to escape this situation, he became somber and sullen. "What would become of me, for God's sake, if I were to quarrel with the one being in the world for whom I passionately care?" On the other hand, Fabrizio could not bring himself to spoil such perfect felicity by an indiscreet word. His situation was so full of charm! The intimate friendship of so delightful and so lovely a woman was so sweet! From the crudest point of view, her protection afforded him so pleasant a position at this court, whose great intrigues, thanks to her explanations, entertained him like a play! "But at the first moment, I can be awakened by a thunderbolt!" he realized. These gay and affectionate evenings, spent almost tête-à-tête with so amusing a woman, if they were to lead to something still better, she would imagine she would find in me a lover; she would expect me to have raptures, madness, and I would still have nothing to offer her but the liveliest friendship, though without love; nature has deprived me of such sublime follies. How many reproaches have I not had to accept in this regard! I can still hear Duchess of A———, and I didn't care a fig for her! She will suppose I feel no love for her, whereas I feel no love for anyone; she will never be willing to understand that. How often, after a story she has told about the court with that grace and abandon that only she possesses, and so necessary to my education as well, I kiss her hands and sometimes even her cheeks. What would happen if that hand should press mine in a certain way?"

Fabrizio appeared every day in the most highly regarded and least amusing houses of Parma. Instructed by the Duchess's astute advice, he paid careful respects to the two princes, father and son, to Princess Clara-Paolina and to Monsignore the Archbishop. Success was his, but it failed to console him for his mortal fear of falling out with the Duchess.

CHAPTER EIGHT

So, less than a month after his arrival at court, Fabrizio suffered all the vexations of a courtier, and the intimate friendship which constituted the happiness of his life was poisoned. One evening, tormented by such notions, he emerged from that salon of the Duchess where he had all too much the look of a reigning lover; wandering at random through the town, he passed in front of the theater, which he saw was lit up; he went in. This was a gratuitous imprudence for a man of the cloth, one he had sworn to himself he would avoid in Parma, which is after all only a small town of forty thousand inhabitants. It is true that from his first days there he had discarded his official costume; on the evenings when he was not going into society, he dressed very simply in black, like a man in mourning.

In the theater, he took a box in the third ring in order not to be seen; Goldoni's *La Locandiera* was being performed. He examined the architecture of the hall, scarcely glancing at the stage. But the large audience kept bursting into laughter; Fabrizio glanced at the young actress playing the mistress of the inn, who struck him as entertaining. He looked more closely: she seemed extremely appealing and altogether natural, a naïve young girl who was the first to laugh at the clever remarks Goldoni had put in her mouth and which she appeared quite surprised to be saying. He asked what her name was, and was told *Marietta Valserra*. "Ah," he thought, "she has taken my name, that's odd." Despite his plans, he did not leave the theater until the play was over. The next evening he returned; three days later, he knew Marietta Valserra's address.

The same evening of the day on which, with some difficulty, he had obtained this address, he noticed that the Count was smiling at him. The poor jealous lover, having a world of trouble keeping within the bounds of prudence, had set spies on the young Monsignore, whose escapade in the theater delighted him. How to describe the Count's joy when, the day after the one on which he had been able to bring himself to show Fabrizio some friendliness, he learned that the young man, in truth half-disguised by a long blue frock-coat, had climbed the stairs to the wretched apartment which Marietta Valserra occupied on the fourth floor of an old house behind the theater? His joy was doubled when he discovered that Fabrizio had introduced himself under a false name and had had the honor to provoke the jealousy of a scamp named Giletti, who played Third Servant in town and in the country danced on the tightrope. This noble lover of the Valserra launched into abuse of Fabrizio and kept repeating that he wanted to kill him.

Opera companies are formed by an impresario who hires wherever he can find them the performers he can afford or are at liberty, and the company, gathered at random, remains together for a season or two at most. This is not the case for the comedy troupes; proceeding from town to town and changing lodgings every two or three months, these nonetheless form a kind of family, all of whose members love or hate one another. In such troupes there are established households, which the *galants* in the town where the troupe is playing sometimes find it very hard to disrupt. This is precisely what happened to our hero: little Marietta was quite attracted to him, but she was dreadfully afraid of Giletti, who claimed to be her sole master and kept a close watch upon her every move. He protested everywhere that he would kill the Monsignore, for he had followed Fabrizio and had managed to discover his name. This Giletti was indeed the ugliest of creatures, hardly suited to be a lover: excessively tall, he was alarmingly thin, deeply pitted with smallpox scars, and inclined to squint. Furthermore, filled with the graces of his trade, he usually appeared in the wings where his colleagues were gathered by turning cartwheels or some other such stunt. He triumphed in the parts where the performer must appear with his face whitened with flour, giving and receiving countless beatings with a stick. This worthy rival of Fabrizio earned a salary of thirty-two francs a month and considered himself the most fortunate of men.

It seemed to Count Mosca that he was returning from the grave when his spies gave him proof of all these details. His cheerful spirits revived; he seemed gayer and better company than ever in the Duchess's salon, and was careful not to disclose to her the little episode that was bringing him back to life. He even took certain precautions to keep her from finding out what was happening for as long as possible. At last he had the courage to listen to reason, which for a month now had been vainly informing him that each time a lover's virtues begin to fade, that lover must take a journey.

Urgent business summoned him to Bologna, and twice a day cabinet couriers brought him far fewer official papers than news of little Marietta's amours, of the terrible Giletti's rage, and of Fabrizio's enterprises.

One of the Count's agents requested several times *Arlecchino Fantasma e Pasticcio,* among Giletti's triumphs (he emerges from the pie just when his rival Brighella is cutting into it and gives him a beating); this was an excuse to slip him a hundred francs. Giletti, riddled with debts, was careful not to mention this windfall, but became amazingly conceited.

Fabrizio's whim turned into wounded pride (at his age, worries had already reduced him to having whims!). Vanity took him to the performance; the girl acted quite winningly, and he was delighted; leaving the theater, he was in love for an hour. The Count returned to Parma upon receiving word that Fabrizio was running real dangers; Giletti, who had served in Napoleon's crack regiment of Italian dragoons, was talking seriously about killing Fabrizio, and taking measures to flee the country into Romagna afterward. If the reader is quite young, he will be scandalized by our admiration for this splendid sign of Virtue. Yet it was no small effort of heroism on the Count's part to return from Bologna; for it was frequently the case that his features appeared quite worn in the morning, and Fabrizio was so fresh, so serene! Who would have dreamed of blaming him for Fabrizio's death, occurring in his absence and for so silly a cause? But the Count had one of those rare natures which make a possible generous action left unperformed into an eternal regret; moreover, he could not endure the thought of seeing the Duchess melancholy, and himself the cause.

He found her, upon his arrival, taciturn and glum; here is what had occurred: Cecchina, the little chambermaid, tormented by remorse and judging the scope of her transgression by the enormity of the sum she had received for committing it, had fallen sick. One evening, the Duchess, who was very fond of her, climbed up to her bedroom. The girl could not resist this evidence of kindness and burst into tears, trying to return to her mistress what she still possessed of the money she had received, and finally daring to confess her answers to the questions the Count had put to her.

The Duchess rushed to the lamp, blew it out, and then told little Cecchina that she forgave her, on condition that she would never speak a word of this strange episode to a living soul. "The poor Count," she added quite gaily, "is so afraid of ridicule! Men are all like that."

The Duchess hastened downstairs to her own apartments. No sooner had she locked herself in her bedroom than she burst into tears, finding something horrible in the notion of making love with this Fabrizio whom she had known from his infancy; yet what else did her conduct mean?

Such had been the first reason for the deep depression in which the Count found her plunged; once he had arrived, she suffered fits of impatience against him, and perhaps against Fabrizio as well; she felt as though she wanted not to see either of them again; she was annoyed by the absurd role which, in her eyes, Fabrizio was playing with little Marietta; for the Count had told her the whole story, like a true lover incapable of keeping a secret. She could not inure herself to this disaster: her idol had a flaw; finally, in a moment of friendly feeling, she asked the Count's advice; for him this was a delicious moment and a fine reward for the honest impulse that had brought him back to Parma.

"Nothing simpler!" said the Count, laughing. "Young men want to win all hearts, and then forget all about it the next day. Should he not go to Belgirate and visit the Marchesa del Dongo? Well, let him go then. During his absence I shall request the comedy troupe to take their talents elsewhere, and I shall defray their travel expenses. Soon, though, we shall find him in love with the first pretty woman chance throws in his path; this is in the order of things, and I wouldn't have him otherwise.... If necessary, ask the Marchesa to write..."

This notion, given with an expression of utter indifference, was an inspiration for the Duchess, who was terrified of Giletti. That evening the Count announced quite by chance that there was a courier who, on his way to Vienna, was passing through Milan; three days later Fabrizio happened to receive a letter from his mother. He left, quite annoyed at not yet having, thanks to Giletti's jealousy, taken advantage of the excellent intentions little Marietta had communicated to him through the services of a *mammaccia,* an old woman who acted as her mother.

Fabrizio found his mother and one of his sisters at Belgirate, a big Piedmontese village on the right bank of Lake Maggiore; the left bank is Milanese, and consequently Austrian. This lake, parallel to Lake Como, which also extends from north to south, is located some twenty leagues farther west. The mountain air, the calm and majestic aspect of this splendid lake, which reminded him of the one on which he had spent his childhood—everything contributed to changing into gentle melancholy Fabrizio's disappointment, which was so close to anger. It was with an infinite tenderness that thoughts of the Duchess now occurred to him; it seemed to him that from a distance he was presently feeling the kind of love he had never experienced for any woman; nothing would have been more painful for him than to be permanently separated from her, and in this frame of mind, had the Duchess deigned to resort to the slightest coquetry, she could have won this heart, for example, by offering it a rival. But far from taking so decisive a step, it was not without blaming herself severely that she found her thoughts still attached to the young traveler's footsteps. She reproached herself for what she still called a caprice, as if it had been a monstrosity; she redoubled her attentions and kindness to the Count, who, seduced by such graces, turned a deaf ear to the voice of reason, which was prescribing a second journey to Bologna.

The Marchesa del Dongo, busy with the nuptials of her elder daughter, whom she was marrying to a Milanese duke, could spare only three days to her beloved son; never had she found in him so tender an affection. Amidst the melancholy which had increasingly occupied Fabrizio's soul, one bizarre and even absurd notion had occurred to him and suddenly produced results. Shall we dare say that he wished to consult the Abbé Blanès? This excellent old man was quite incapable of understanding the sufferings of a heart wrenched apart by childish passions of almost equal strength; moreover, it would have taken him a week to have even glimpsed all the interests which Fabrizio was having to contend with in Parma; but in thinking of consulting him, Fabrizio was rediscovering the innocence of his feelings at the age of sixteen. Will this be believed? It was not simply as a man of wisdom, as an utterly devoted friend that Fabrizio sought him out; the object of this errand and the feelings which agitated our hero during the fifty hours it lasted are so absurd that doubtless, in the interests of the narrative, it would have been better to suppress them. I fear that Fabrizio's credulity will deprive him of the reader's sympathy; but after all, this is what he was like, why flatter him more than any other man? I have certainly not flattered either Count Mosca or the Prince.

Fabrizio then, since the whole truth must be told, Fabrizio accompanied his mother to the port of Laveno, on the left, or Austrian, bank of Lake Maggiore, where she landed at about eight in the evening. (The lake is regarded as neutral territory, and no passport is required of those who do not set foot on shore.) But no sooner had night fallen than he had himself set ashore on this same Austrian side, in a little grove of trees that juts out into the waves. He had hired a *sediola,* a sort of fast rustic tilbury in which he could follow, at some five hundred yards' distance, his mother's carriage; he was disguised in the livery of the *Casa del Dongo*, and none of the customs officers or the numerous employees of the police dreamed of asking to see his passport. A quarter of a league from Como, where the Marchesa and her daughter were to stop for the night, he took a path to the left, which, skirting the town of Vico, then joined a little road recently laid along the far side of the lake. It was midnight, and Fabrizio could well hope to encounter no member of the police. The trees of the groves which the little road kept passing through silhouetted the black outlines of their foliage against a starry sky, veiled by a light mist. The waters of the lake and the sky itself were profoundly calm; Fabrizio's soul could not resist this sublime beauty; he stopped, then sat down on a boulder jutting up out of the lake, forming a sort of tiny promontory. The universal silence was troubled only, at regular intervals, by the lapping of the little waves that expired on the beach. Fabrizio had an Italian heart; I seek no pardon for him: this defect, which will make him less lovable, consisted chiefly in this: his vanity came only in sudden bursts, and the mere aspect of such sublime beauty plunged him into tenderness and dulled the sharp ache of his sufferings. Seated on his solitary boulder, no longer having to remain on guard against the agents of the police, protected by the darkness and its immense silence, he found there, with little or no effort, the happiest moments he had known in a very long time, and his eyes filled with gentle tears.

He resolved never to tell the Duchess any falsehoods, and it is because he loved her to the point of adoration at this moment that he swore to himself never to tell her that *he loved her*; never would he utter the word *love* to her, since the passion so called was alien to his heart. In the enthusiasms of generosity and virtue which at this moment constituted his entire happiness, he determined to tell her everything at the first opportunity: his heart had never known love. Once this courageous decision had been taken, he felt somehow relieved of an enormous weight. "She may have something to say to me about Marietta: well then! I shall never see little Marietta again," he gaily assured himself.

The oppressive heat that had prevailed during the day was beginning to be tempered by the morning breeze. Already dawn was outlining against a pale whitish glow the Alpine peaks rising to the north and east of Lake Como. Their masses, whitened by the snow-fields, even in June, were silhouetted against the clear blue of a sky forever pure at these great heights. A spur of the Alps thrusting south toward happy Italy separates the slopes of Lake Como from those of Lake Garda. Fabrizio gazed at all the spurs of these sublime mountains, the brightening dawn coming to mark the valleys which separate them by dissipating the faint mist which rose from the depths of the gorges.

Some minutes before, Fabrizio had begun walking again; he passed the hill which forms the Durini peninsula, and then caught sight of that steeple of the village of Grianta, where so often he and Abbé Blanès had observed the stars. "How ignorant I was in those days! I couldn't understand," he reminded himself, "even the absurd Latin of those astrological treatises my master would pore over, and I believe I respected them especially because, understanding no more than a word here, a word there, my imagination undertook to grant them a meaning—the most fantastical one possible."

Gradually his reverie took another turn. "Might there be something real about this science? A certain number of fools and scholars agree among themselves that they know *Mexican,* for instance; they impose themselves upon society, which respects them, and upon governments, which pay them. They are overwhelmed with favors precisely because they have no minds to speak of, and because the powers that be need not fear that they will rouse populations and move men's hearts by the help of generous sentiments! Take the example of Father Bari, to whom Prince Ernesto IV has just granted a pension of four thousand francs and the Cross of his Order for having restored nineteen verses of a Greek dithyramb!

"But good God! Am I entitled to regard such things as absurdities? Have I the right to complain?" he suddenly asked himself, stopping where he stood. "Hasn't that same Cross just been bestowed upon my tutor in Naples?" Fabrizio experienced a feeling of profound uneasiness; the fine enthusiasm of virtue that had just made his heart beat faster turned into the vile pleasure of sharing in the spoils of a theft. "Well then!" he said to himself at last, with the lusterless gaze of a man dissatisfied with himself. "Since my birth gives me the right to benefit by such abuses, it would be a signal imbecility not to avail myself of my share; but I must not permit myself to denounce them in public." Such reasoning had its good points, but how far Fabrizio had fallen from that height of sublime felicity to which he had been transported an hour before. The thought of privilege had withered that ever-delicate plant known as happiness.

"If I am not to believe in astrology," he continued, seeking to divert his mind, "if this science is, like three-quarters of all the non-mathematical sciences, a collection of enthusiastic fools and clever hypocrites paid by those they serve, how is it that I think so often and so intensely of this one fatal circumstance: I did escape from the prison at B——, but in the uniform and with the marching orders of a soldier thrown into jail for good reason."

Fabrizio's reasoning could never penetrate further; he approached the difficulty in a hundred ways without managing to overcome it. He was still too young; in his leisure moments, his soul was delighted to enjoy the sensations produced by the romantic circumstances his imagination was ever ready to provide. He was far from devoting his time to patient consideration of the real particularities of things in order to divine their true causes. Reality still seemed to him flat and muddy; I can agree that one is not fond of considering it, but then one ought not to reason about it. Above all, one ought not to raise objections against it with the various fragments of one's ignorance.

It was in this fashion that, without lacking intelligence, Fabrizio could not succeed in seeing that his half-belief in omens was a religion for him, a profound impression received upon his entrance into life. To think of this belief was to feel, was a happiness. And he persisted in questioning how astrology could be a true *proven* science, like geometry, for example. He ardently ransacked his memory for all the circumstances when omens he had observed had not been followed by the fortunate or unfortunate consequences they had seemed to foretell. But even while believing he was reasoning properly and heading in the direction of truth, his attention halted delightedly over the memory of those cases where the omen had been amply followed by the fortunate or unfortunate accident which it had seemed to predict, and his spirit was filled with reverence and affection; he would have felt an invincible repugnance for anyone who might have denied the omens, and especially if he had employed irony in so doing.

Fabrizio walked on without realizing the distance he was covering, and he was at this point in these impotent reasonings when, looking up, he saw the wall of his father's garden. This wall, which supported a splendid terrace, rose to a height of more than forty feet above the road, to the right. A row of rough-hewn stones at the very top, near the balustrade, gave it a monumental appearance. "Not bad," Fabrizio mused coldly, "the design is good, almost Roman in taste." He was applying his new knowledge of antiquities. Then he turned away in disgust; the severities of his father and especially his brother Ascanio's denunciation of him upon his return from France came to mind.

"This unnatural denunciation was the origin of my present way of life; I might hate it, I might despise it, but after all it has changed my destiny. What would I have become, back there at Novara, being no more than tolerated by my father's man of business, if my aunt had not made love with a powerful minister at court? If that same aunt had happened to have a dry and ordinary soul, say, instead of that tender and passionate spirit devoted to me with a sort of enthusiasm which amazes me still? Where would I be now if the Duchess had had the soul of her brother the Marchese del Dongo?"

Overcome by these cruel memories, Fabrizio began to walk hesitantly; he reached the edge of the moat just opposite the castle's splendid façade. Yet he scarcely cast a glance at this great time-blackened structure. The noble language of architecture found him quite unresponsive; the memory of his father and his brother closed his soul to any sensation of beauty, and he was conscious only of maintaining his vigilance in the presence of hypocritical and dangerous foes. He stared a moment, but with an evident disgust, at the little window of the third-floor bedroom he had occupied before 1815. His father's character had stripped the memories of early childhood of all their charm. "I have not come back here," he thought, "since March seventh at eight o'clock in the evening. I left to take possession of Vasi's passport, and the next day the fear of spies made me hasten my departure. When I passed by again after the journey to France, I had no time to go up there, even to have another look at my print collection, and all thanks to my brother's denunciation of me."

He turned his head away in horror. "Abbé Blanès is over eighty-three years old," he realized sadly; "he almost never comes to the castle anymore, according to what my sister tells me; the infirmities of old age have produced their effect. That resolute and noble heart has been chilled by the years. God knows how long it's been since he's been up in his steeple! I'll hide in the cellar, under the casks or the wine-press until he wakes up; I don't want to trouble the good old man's sleep; he will probably have forgotten what I look like, six years can do such a lot at that age! I shall find in him no more than the tomb of a friend! Indeed it is a piece of childishness," he added, "to have come here to face the disgust inspired by my father's castle."

Fabrizio then entered the little square in front of the church; it was with an amazement bordering on delirium that he saw, on the second floor of the ancient steeple, the long narrow window illuminated by the Abbé Blanès's little lantern. The Abbé was in the habit of setting it there when he climbed up to the cage of planks which formed his observatory, so that the light would not keep him from reading his planisphere. This star-map was hung on a huge terra-cotta pot which had once belonged to an orange-tree of the castle grounds. In the opening, at the bottom, burned the tiniest of lamps, its smoke led by the slenderest of tin pipes out of the pot, and the shadow of the pipe marking north on the star-map. All these memories of such simple things flooded Fabrizio's soul with emotions and filled it with happiness.

Almost unconsciously he made between his hands the tiny low whistle which used to be his signal to be let in. Immediately he heard the rope being drawn up by several tugs, opening the latch of the steeple door from up in the observatory. He rushed up the stairs, moved to the point of rapture; he found the Abbé sitting in his wooden armchair in the usual place, his eye pressed against the tiny glass of a mural quadrant. With his left hand, the Abbé gestured not to interrupt him in his observation; a second later he wrote a figure on a playing card, then, turning in his chair, he opened his arms to our hero, who flung himself into them, dissolved in tears. Abbé Blanès was his true father.

"I was expecting you," he said, after the first words of tender affection. Was the Abbé speaking in his professional character of a *savant*; or else, since he frequently thought of Fabrizio, had some astrological sign announced his return by pure chance? "And now my death is close at hand," said Abbé Blanès.

"What!" exclaimed Fabrizio, with deep emotion.

"Yes," the Abbé went on in a serious tone of voice, though not at all sadly: "five and a half months or six and a half after I have seen you again, my life, having found its fulfillment of happiness, will ... go out.

"*Come face al mancar dell'alimento*
[Like the little lamp when the oil runs dry]

Before that supreme moment, I shall probably live a month or two without speaking, after which I shall be received into our Father's bosom, if it so happens that I have fulfilled my duties in the post where he has placed me as a sentry.

"But you, you must be exhausted, your feelings have prepared you for sleep. Since I was expecting you, I have hidden away some bread and a bottle of brandy in the chest where I keep my instruments. Give yourself some sustenance, and try to gain strength enough to listen to me for a few moments more. It is in my power to tell you certain things before the night is quite overcome by day; I see them now, such things, more clearly than I may see them tomorrow. For my child, we are always weak, and we must always take our weakness into account. Tomorrow perhaps the old man, the man of this earth, will be concerned with preparations for my death, and tomorrow night at nine o'clock, you must leave me."

Fabrizio had obeyed in silence, as was his habit. "So, is it true," the old man continued, "that when you tried to see Waterloo, the first thing you found was a prison?"

"Yes, Father," Fabrizio replied, astonished.

"Well, that was a rare piece of luck, for warned by my voice, your soul may now prepare itself for another prison, one much harsher and more terrible! Most likely you will escape it only by a crime, but thanks be to Heaven, this crime will not be committed by you. Never succumb to crime, however violently you are tempted; I believe I can see that there will be some question of killing an innocent person who, without realizing it, has usurped your rights; if you resist the violent temptation that will seem justified by the laws of honor, your life will be very happy in men's eyes ... and reasonably happy in those of the wise man," he added, after a moment's reflection; "you will die like me, my son, seated on a wooden chair, far from all luxury, and disabused of such things, and like me with no serious reproach to lay upon your soul.

"Now that the affairs of a future state have ended between us, I can add nothing more of any importance. It is in vain that I have tried to see how long that imprisonment will last; can it be for six months, for a year, for ten years? I have no way of knowing; apparently I have committed some sin, and Heaven wishes to punish me by the suffering of this uncertainty. I have seen only that after prison—but I do not know if it is at the very moment of escape—there will be what I am calling a crime, but fortunately I believe I can be certain that it will not be committed by you. If you have the weakness to involve yourself in this crime, all the rest of my calculations are no more than one long error. Then you will not die with peace upon your soul, sitting upon a wooden chair and dressed in white."

As he spoke these words, Abbé Blanès attempted to stand up; it was then that Fabrizio noticed the ravages of time; it took the old man almost a minute to stand up and to turn around to face Fabrizio, who remained motionless and without a word. The Abbé took him in his arms several times; he embraced him very tenderly. After which he continued with all his old cheerfulness:

"Try to find a place among my instruments to sleep in some comfort, take my fur blankets; you will find several very costly ones which the Duchess Sanseverina sent me four years ago. She asked me for some prediction about you, which I was careful not to send her, though I kept her furs and her fine quadrant. Any prediction of the future is a breach of the rule, and incurs the danger of possibly changing the outcome, in which case all our knowledge falls to the ground like a veritable child's toy; and besides there were things hard to say to that Duchess, still so lovely a woman. . . . By the way, don't be alarmed in your sleep by the bells, which will be making a dreadful racket right next to your ears when they ring for seven o'clock mass; later, down below, they will set the great tenor bell ringing, the one that shakes up all my instruments. Today is the feast of San Giovita, martyr and soldier. You know the little village of Grianta has the same patron saint as the great city of Brescia, which, by the way, so amusingly misled my illustrious master Giacomo Marini of Ravenna. On more than one occasion he told me that I would enjoy some splendid ecclesiastical fortune, he supposed I would be the priest of the magnificent church of San Giovita in Brescia; I was parish priest of a little village of seven hundred and fifty hearth-fires! But all has been for the best. I have seen, and not ten years from that prediction, that if I had been a priest at Brescia, my fate was to be shut up in the Spielberg, a prison on a hill of Moravia. Tomorrow I'll bring you all kinds of delicacies stolen from the great banquet I am giving for all the priests of the countryside who are coming to sing at my high mass. I will put them downstairs, but don't try to come to see me, nor come down to take possession of these good things until you have heard me leave. You must not see me again *by daylight,* and the sun setting tomorrow evening at seven twenty-seven, I shall come to embrace you only around eight, and you must leave while the hours are still numbered singly, that is, before the clock has sounded ten. Take care not to be seen at the steeple windows: the police have your description and they are, in a manner of speaking, under the orders of your brother, who is a famous tyrant. The Marchese del Dongo is weakening," Blanès added sadly, "and if he were to see you again, he might give you something from his hand to yours. But such benefits, tainted by fraudulence, do not suit a man like yourself, whose strength will one day be in his conscience. The Marchese abhors his son Ascanio, and it is to this son that the five or six million he possesses will pass. That is justice. You, upon his death, will have a pension of four thousand francs, and fifty ells of black cloth for your servants' mourning."

CHAPTER NINE

Fabrizio's soul was exalted by the old man's talk, by his own close attention, and by extreme fatigue. He found it quite difficult to fall asleep, and his slumber was troubled by dreams, omens perhaps of the future; at ten in the morning, he was awakened by the general vibration of the belfry, a dreadful racket that seemed to come from outside. He got up in bewilderment, convinced that it was the end of the world, then he supposed he was in prison; it took him some time to recognize the sound of the great bell which forty peasants were tolling in honor of the great San Giovita; ten would have sufficed.

Fabrizio looked for a convenient place from which to see without being seen; he realized that from this great height, his gaze overlooked the gardens and even the inner courtyard of his father's castle. He had forgotten it. The notion of his father reaching the end of his life changed all his feelings. He made out the very sparrows pecking for bread crumbs on the great terrace of the dining hall. "These are the descendants of the ones I used to tame," he mused. This terrace, like all the other castle balconies, was filled with many orange-trees in earthenware pots of various sizes: this prospect touched him; the aspect of that inner courtyard, embellished by brilliant sunshine and sharply defined shadows, was truly impressive.

He recalled his father's failing health. "But how odd that is," he said to himself, "my father is just thirty-five years older than I; thirty-five and twenty-three make only fifty-eight!" His eyes, fixed on the bedroom windows of that severe man who had never loved him, filled with tears. He shuddered, and a sudden chill ran through his veins when he believed he recognized his father crossing a terrace decorated with orange-trees, which adjoined his bedroom; but it was only a footman. Immediately under the belfry, a number of young girls dressed in white and divided into various groups were busy making patterns with red, blue, and yellow flowers on the paving-stones of the streets where the procession would pass. But there was one spectacle which touched Fabrizio's soul more deeply: from the steeple, his gaze swept over the two branches of the lake for a distance of several leagues, and this sublime view soon made him forget all the rest; it awakened in him the loftiest sentiments. All the memories of his childhood laid siege to his mind, and this day spent shut up in a belfry was perhaps one of the happiest of his life.

Happiness carried him to a zenith of thoughts quite alien to his character; he considered the events of his young life as if he had already reached its ultimate limits. "It must be confessed, since I came to Parma," he realized at last, after several hours of delicious reverie, "I haven't had a moment of that perfect and peaceful joy I knew in Naples trotting through the lanes of Vomero or along the shores of Miseno. All the complicated intrigues of this wicked little court have made me wicked as well. . . . I take no pleasure in hatred, I even think it would be a melancholy satisfaction for me to humble my enemies, if I had any; but I have none whatever. . . . Wait a moment!" he suddenly realized. "I have Giletti. . . . The odd thing is, the pleasure I would take in sending this ugly fellow to the devil survives my rather vague feelings for little Marietta. . . . She is no match for the Duchess of A——, whom I was obliged to make love to in Naples, once I had told her I was in love with her. Great God! How bored I was during the many long assignations I was granted by that lovely Duchess! Which was never the case in that shabby little bedroom, which served as a kitchen as well, where little Marietta received me twice, and for two minutes each time.

"And Lord only knows what those people eat! It's pitiful! I should have settled on her and the *mammaccia* a pension of three beefsteaks, payable daily. . . . Little Marietta," he added, "would distract me from the evil thoughts inspired by the proximity of that court.

"I might have done well to live the café life, as the Duchess Sanseverina calls it; she seemed to incline in that direction, and she has much more sense than I ever will. Thanks to her favors, or else even with that pension of four thousand francs and the fund of forty thousand which my mother has invested for me at Lyons, I will always have a horse and some cash to spend on excavations and collections. Since I am destined, apparently, never to know love, these will always be a major source of happiness for me; I'd like, before I die, to revisit the battlefield at Waterloo and try to find the field where I was so gaily robbed of my horse and dumped on the ground. Once that pilgrimage is accomplished, I would frequently return to this sublime lake; nothing as lovely as this can be seen in all the world, at least to my mind and heart. What is the use of seeking happiness so far afield—it is here, right under my nose!

"Ah!" Fabrizio mused, "there is one objection: the police drive me away from Lake Como, but I am younger than those who give orders to the police. Here," he added with a laugh, "I shall find no Duchess of A——, but rather one of those girls down there arranging flowers on the cobblestones, and whom I would love quite as much: hypocrisy freezes my heart in love as in everything else, and our great ladies aim at effects all too sublime. Napoléon has given them notions of conduct and constancy.

"The Devil!" he said to himself all of a sudden, pulling his head in from the window as if he had feared being recognized despite the shadow of the enormous wooden shutters that protected the bells from the rain. "Here comes a troop of police in full uniform." Indeed, ten gendarmes, including four non-commissioned officers, appeared at the top of the village street. The Quartermaster posted them every hundred yards along the course the procession would take. "Everyone knows me here; if I am seen, I'll go straight from the shores of Lake Como to the Spielberg prison, where they'll fasten to each leg a chain weighing a hundred and ten pounds: and what pain that will be for the Duchess!"

Fabrizio needed no more than two or three minutes to recall that first of all he was stationed some eighty feet above ground, that the place he was standing was relatively dark, that the eyes of anyone who might be looking at him would be blinded by dazzling sunshine, and finally that they were strolling about and staring wide-eyed through the streets, where all the houses had just been whitewashed in honor of the Feast of San Giovita. Despite the lucidity of such arguments, Fabrizio's Italian soul would have been henceforth powerless to enjoy any pleasure whatever, had he not interposed between the police and himself a strip of old canvas, which he tacked against the window and in which he made two holes for his eyes.

The bells had been stirring the air for ten minutes, the procession was emerging from the church, the *mortaretti* (or little mortars) were audible. Fabrizio turned his head and recognized that little terrace embellished with a parapet and overlooking the lake, where so often, in his youth, he had risked his safety to watch the *mortaretti* explode between his legs, which made his mother prefer that he spend the holiday mornings by her side.

It must be said that these *mortaretti* are nothing more than rifle barrels sawed off to be no more than four inches long; it is for this purpose that the peasants greedily gather the gun-barrels which European politics since 1796 have been strewing across the plains of Lombardy. Once reduced to this length, these tiny cannons are loaded to the muzzle, thrust vertically into the ground, and a train of powder laid from one to the next; they are arranged in three rows like a battalion, two or three hundred of them, in some emplacement near the place where the procession will pass. When the Blessed Sacrament approaches, the train of powder is ignited, and then begins a running fire of successive explosions, irregular and absurd to the highest degree; the women are entranced. Nothing is so gay as the noise of these *mortaretti* heard from across the lake, and softened by the lapping of the waves; this singular noise, which had so often constituted the delight of his childhood, dispelled the somewhat over-solemn notions to which our hero had fallen prey; he set about finding the Abbé's big telescope and by it recognized most of the men and women following the procession. Many of the charming little girls whom Fabrizio had left at the age of eleven or twelve were now splendid women, in all the flower of the most vigorous youth; they restored our hero's courage, and he would have defied any number of gendarmes to speak to them.

Once the procession had passed and re-entered the church by a side door which Fabrizio could not see, the heat soon became extreme even high up in the belfry; the villagers returned to their houses and a great silence reigned. Several boats were filled with peasants returning to Bellagio, to Menaggio, and to other villages along the shores of the lake; Fabrizio could make out the sound of each oar-stroke, a simple detail which enchanted him; his present delight consisted of all the discomfort and all the wretchedness he found in the complicated life of courts. How happy he would have been, at this moment, to row a league on this lovely calm lake which reflected so clearly the depths of the heavens! He heard the door at the foot of the belfry open: it was the Abbé Blanès's old servant carrying a huge basket; it cost him a great deal to keep from speaking to her. "She is nearly as fond of me as is her master," he told himself, "and besides I'm leaving tonight at nine; would she not keep a sworn secret for these few hours? But my friend," Fabrizio decided, "would be distressed! I might compromise him with the police!" And he let old Ghita leave without a word. He made an excellent dinner, then lay down to sleep for a little while: he awoke only at eight-thirty that evening; the Abbé was shaking his arm and night had fallen.

Blanès was extremely tired; he had aged fifty years since the night before. He spoke no more of serious matters; seating himself in his wooden armchair, he said to Fabrizio: "Embrace me," and he clasped him over and over in his arms.

"Death," he said at last, "which is about to end this long life of mine, will have nothing so painful in it as this separation. I have a purse which I shall be leaving for Ghita, with orders to draw upon it for her own needs, but to give you what is left if ever you come to ask for it. I know her; upon such instructions, she is capable of buying meat no more than four times a year in order to accumulate savings for you, unless you give her very specific orders. You yourself may be reduced to penury, and an old friend's obol will come in handy. Expect nothing from your brother but harsh measures, and try to earn money by labors which will make you useful to society. I foresee strange tempests; perhaps in fifty years the world will have no use for idlers. Your mother and your aunt may fail you, your sisters will have to obey their husbands.... Go now, leave—make your escape!" the Abbé exclaimed urgently.

He had just heard a tiny sound in the belfry which indicated that ten o'clock was about to strike, and he was even reluctant to permit Fabrizio to embrace him one last time. "Hurry! hurry!" he cried to him: "You will take at least one minute to get down the stairs; be careful not to fall, that would be a terrible omen."

Fabrizio rushed down the stairs, and once out in the square began to run. No sooner had he reached his father's castle than the bells rang ten o'clock; each stroke echoed in his breast and left a strange disturbance there. He stopped to think, or rather to abandon himself to the impassioned sentiments inspired by the contemplation of this majestic edifice which he had regarded so coldly the day before. Human footsteps roused him from his reveries; he looked up and found himself surrounded by four gendarmes. He was armed with a brace of fine pistols whose priming he had just renewed while he was having his dinner; the tiny sound they made as he cocked them now alerted one of the gendarmes, and he was on the point of being arrested. He realized the risk he was running and decided to fire first; he was within his rights to do so, for this was his only way of resisting four well-armed men. Fortunately, the gendarmes, in making their rounds to clear the taverns, had not shown themselves entirely unresponsive to the welcome they had received in several of these agreeable resorts; they were not sufficiently swift in determining to do their duty. Fabrizio took to his heels, and the gendarmes ran a few paces after him, shouting, "Stop! Stop!"

Then everything returned to silence. After three hundred yards Fabrizio stopped to catch his breath. "The noise of my pistols almost got me caught—how right the Duchess would be to tell me, if ever I catch sight of her lovely face again, that my soul delights in pondering what will happen in ten years, and forgets to see what is going on right under my nose!"

Fabrizio shuddered at the thought of the danger he had just avoided; he walked faster, but could not keep from breaking into a run, which was anything but prudent, for he attracted the attention of several peasants who were returning to their homes. He could not bring himself to stop until he had reached the mountains, over a league from Grianta, and even once he had stopped, he broke into a cold sweat at the thought of the Spielberg.

"A fine fright you're in!" he told himself. (At the sound of this word, he was almost tempted to be ashamed.) "But didn't my aunt tell me that what I needed most of all was to learn to forgive myself? I keep comparing myself to a perfect model which cannot exist. Well! I forgive myself my fear, for on the other hand I was quite ready to protect my freedom, and certainly all four would not have remained on their feet to haul me off to prison. What I am doing at this moment," he added, "is not soldierly; instead of gaining a swift retreat, after having gained my goal and perhaps having aroused my foes, I am indulging in a caprice more absurd, perhaps, than all the good Abbé's predictions."

Indeed, instead of taking the shortest distance between two points and reaching the shores of Lake Maggiore, where his boat was moored, he was making a huge detour to visit *his tree*. The reader may recall the affection Fabrizio bore this chestnut-tree planted by his mother twenty-three years previously. "It would be just like my brother," he mused, "to have had it chopped down, but such creatures are not sensitive to such things; it would never have occurred to him. And besides, that would not be a bad omen," he added with conviction. Two hours later he was distressed to find that malefactors or a storm had broken one of the main branches of the young tree, which hung down, withered. Fabrizio cut it off respectfully, with the help of his dagger, and smoothed the place of the incision neatly, so that rainwater could not get inside the trunk. Then, though his time was precious, for day was about to break, he spent a good hour digging up the earth around the beloved tree. All these follies performed, he swiftly returned to Lake Maggiore. On the whole, he was not at all sad; the tree had grown quite well, and was more vigorous than ever; in five years it had almost doubled its size. The broken branch was only an unimportant accident; once cut off, it would do no further harm to the tree, which would grow all the straighter, if its branches began higher from the ground. Fabrizio had not covered a league when the peaks of the Resegone di Lecco, a famous mountain of the region, were silhouetted against a brilliant stripe in the eastern sky. The road he was taking was frequented by peasants; but instead of giving himself over to military ideas, Fabrizio indulged himself in the sublime or affecting aspects of these forests which surround Lake Como. They are perhaps the loveliest in the world; by which I do not mean that they bring in more *new-minted coins,* as they say in Switzerland, but that they speak most deeply to the soul. To heed this language in Fabrizio's circumstances, while prey to the attentions of the gentlemen of the Lombardo-Venetian police, was truly childish.

"I am half a league from the frontier," he told himself at last, "I am going to meet up with customs-officers and police on their morning rounds: this fine suit of mine will waken suspicions; they will ask to see my passport, which is inscribed quite explicitly with a name doomed to prison; hence I am faced with the pleasant necessity of committing a murder. If, as is usually the case, the police patrol in pairs, I cannot honestly wait to fire until one of them grabs me by the collar; supposing he manages to hold on to me for even a second as he falls, off I go to the Spielberg."

Fabrizio, horror-stricken above all at this necessity of firing first, perhaps at some old soldier of his uncle Count Pietranera's, ran to hide in the hollow trunk of a huge chestnut-tree; he was renewing the priming of his pistols when he heard a man walking through the woods singing a lovely tune of Mercadante's, so popular in Lombardy at the time. "Now that's a good omen!" he told himself. The tune, which he listened to religiously, defused the tiny element of rage which was beginning to blur his arguments. He gazed attentively at the high-road on both sides, and saw no one. "The singer must be coming along some path through the forest," he decided. Almost at the same moment he saw a footman, in English-style livery and mounted on a horse, heading toward him at a walk, leading a fine thoroughbred, though perhaps a little too thin. "Ah, now if I were to reason like Mosca," Fabrizio said to himself, "when he keeps telling me that the dangers a man runs are always the measure of his rights over his neighbor, I would blow this footman's brains out, and no sooner mounted on the thin horse, I would defy all the police in the world. No sooner back in Parma, I would send money to this man, or to his widow.... But it would be the act of a monster!"

Chapter Ten

As he moralized, Fabrizio sprang down onto the main road that runs from Lombardy into Switzerland: at this point, it is a good four or five feet below the level of the forest. "If my man is alarmed," Fabrizio said to himself, "he'll gallop away, and I'll be stranded here looking like the fool I am." At this moment, he found himself only ten steps from the footman, who was no longer singing: Fabrizio could see in his eyes that the man was frightened; perhaps he would turn his horses. Without having reached any decision, Fabrizio leaped forward and grabbed the lean horse by the bridle.

"My friend," he said to the footman, "I'm not your usual thief; I'll give you twenty francs right off, but I'm obliged to borrow your horse; I'll be killed if I don't clear out of here—the four Riva brothers are after me, those poachers you've probably heard of; they just caught me in their sister's bedroom, I jumped out the window and here I am! They're out here in the woods with their dogs and their guns. I managed to hide in this hollow tree when I saw one of them cross the road, but their dogs will track me down! I'm going to get on that horse of yours and gallop a good league beyond Como; I'll throw myself on the Viceroy's mercy in Milan and leave your horse at the post-house with two napoleons for yourself, if you'll be good enough to consent. If you put up any resistance, I'll kill you with one of these pistols. If you alert the police once I'm out of here, my cousin, that's Count Alari, Equerry to the Emperor, will be sure to break your bones for you." Fabrizio was inventing this harangue as he went along, speaking in a calm and measured tone of voice. "Besides," he said with a laugh, "my name's no secret; I'm the Marchesino Ascanio del Dongo; my castle is close by, at Grianta. Damn you!" he exclaimed, raising his voice. "Let go of that horse!"

The footman, stupefied, did not utter a word. Fabrizio shifted his pistol to his left hand, grabbed the bridle as the man released it, jumped onto the horse, and cantered off. When he was some three hundred yards away, he realized he had forgotten to give the fellow the twenty francs he had promised; he halted: there was still no one on the road but the footman, who was following him at a gallop; he signaled to him with his handkerchief to come closer and, when he judged him to be about fifty yards away, tossed a handful of coins onto the road and set off again. Looking back, he saw the footman picking up the money. "Now, there's a truly sensible fellow," Fabrizio said to himself with a laugh. "Not one unnecessary word." He rode on at a good pace, stopped toward noon at a lonely inn, and a few hours later was on his way. By two in the morning he was on the shore of Lake Maggiore, where he soon glimpsed his boat, drifting to and fro at its mooring. There was no one in sight to leave the horse with, so he turned the noble creature loose, and three hours later he was in Belgirate. There, finding himself on friendly ground, he took some rest; he was extremely happy, everything having turned out for the best. Dare we indicate the true causes of his joy? His tree had grown splendidly, and his soul had been refreshed by the profound sympathy he had found in the Abbé Blanès's embrace. "Can he honestly believe," he wondered, "in all those predictions he made to me? Or since my brother's described me as a faithless Jacobin capable of anything, does he just want to spare me the temptation of murdering some brute who's done me a bad turn?"

Two days later, Fabrizio was in Parma, where he greatly entertained the Duchess and the Count with the story of his journey, down to the last detail, as was his custom.

Upon his arrival, Fabrizio had found the porter and the other servants of the Palazzo Sanseverina wearing emblems of mourning on their livery. "Whom have we lost?" he now asked the Duchess. "That excellent man people call my husband has just died at Baden. He has left me this palace, according to our agreement, but as a sign of true friendship he has added a legacy of three hundred thousand francs, which I don't know what to do with. I have no desire to renounce it in favor of his niece, the Marchesa Raversi, who plays the most damnable tricks on me every day. You're an art-lover, you must find me some good sculptor who will carve the Duke's tomb for three hundred thousand francs."

The Count began telling funny stories about the Marchesa Raversi.

"I've had no luck trying to win her over," the Duchess observed. "As for the Duke's nephews, I've had them all made colonels or generals. In return for which, not a month passes when they don't send me some horrible anonymous letter—I've had to hire a secretary just to read such things."

"And these letters are the least of their sins," Count Mosca continued; "they continue fabricating loathsome denunciations. I could have had the whole clique dragged into court twenty times over, and Your Excellency may be assured," he added, addressing Fabrizio, "that my good judges would have convicted them one and all."

"Well, that's what spoils everything else for me," Fabrizio replied with a naïveté which court circles found quite entertaining. "I'd prefer seeing them convicted by magistrates who judge according to their conscience."

"You will do me a great favor, traveling as you do to widen your knowledge, if you furnish me the address of such magistrates. I'll write to them before I go to bed this evening."

"If I were Minister, this lack of honest judges would offend my self-esteem."

"But it strikes me," the Count retorted, "that Your Excellency, who is so fond of the French, and who on one occasion even managed to lend them the support of his invincible arm, is momentarily forgetting one of their great maxims: 'Better kill the Devil than let the Devil kill you.' I'd like to see how you'd govern these ardent souls who read *The*

History of the French Revolution every day by appointing judges who would acquit the people I accuse. They'd release the most obviously guilty rascals, and regard themselves as so many Brutuses. But I have a bone to pick with you; doesn't your sensitive soul suffer a certain remorse on account of that fine if somewhat emaciated horse you just abandoned on the shores of Lake Maggiore?"

"I fully intend," said Fabrizio, with the utmost seriousness, "to recompense the owner for whatever it costs him to advertise for his lost property, and any other expenses he may have incurred to recover his horse from the peasants who may have found it—I'll be careful to read the Milan papers, in order to find any notices of a lost horse; I know the description of this one very well."

"He is a true *primitive*," said the Count to the Duchess. "And what would have become of Your Excellency," he continued with a smile, "if while he was galloping hell for leather, his borrowed horse had happened to stumble? You'd be in the Spielberg right now, my dear nephew, and all my influence would scarcely manage to reduce by thirty pounds the weight of the chains attached to each of your legs. You'd be spending a good ten years in that agreeable resort; perhaps your legs would become swollen, infected, gangrenous—and in due course they would be amputated on the spot..."

"Ah, for pity's sake, stop your grim story there!" exclaimed the Duchess, with tears in her eyes. "Here he is back with us..."

"And I'm even happier about that than you are, if you can believe it," replied the Minister, quite seriously. "But why didn't this cruel child ask me for a passport inscribed with a suitable name, since he wants to cross Lombardy? At the first news of his arrest, I'd have set off for Milan, and my friends there would be happy to close their eyes and pretend to believe their police had arrested a subject of the Prince of Parma. The story of your excursion is certainly entertaining, I won't deny it for a minute," resumed the Count with a little less gravity in his voice, "your sortie out of the forest onto the road is quite thrilling, but *entre nous*, since that footman held your life in his hands, you had every right to take his. We're about to arrange a brilliant future for Your Excellency, at least so I am commanded by Madame, and I don't believe my worst enemies can accuse me of ever having disobeyed her orders. What a deadly disappointment for both of us if, during that steeplechase of yours, your famished horse had happened to stumble! It might almost have been better," the Count added, "if your horse had broken your neck."

"You're quite tragic this evening, my friend," said the Duchess, deeply moved.

"That is because we are surrounded by tragic events," replied the Count, also moved; "we are not in France, where everything ends with a song or a couple of years in prison; and it is quite wrong of me to speak lightly to you of such matters.... Well now, my young nephew, suppose I should find the means to make you a bishop one of these days—for in all conscience we can hardly begin with the Archbishopric of Parma, as Madame the Duchess here so reasonably desires. In such a bishopric, where you will be quite remote from our sage counsels, can you tell us something of what your politics will be?"

"To kill the Devil rather than letting him kill me, as my friends the French put it so nicely," Fabrizio replied, his eyes shining. "To preserve by all possible means, including pistols, the position you will have secured for me. I've read in the del Dongo genealogy about our ancestor who built the Castle of Grianta. At the end of his life, his dear friend Galeazzo, Duke of Milan, sent him on a mission to a fortress on our lake shore; there was some danger of another invasion on the part of the Swiss. 'Let me just dash off a word or two to our commander,' the Duke said to him as he was leaving. He wrote a couple of lines and handed him the note; then he asked for it back in order to seal it. 'A matter of *politesse*,' said the Prince. Vespasiano del Dongo left, but as he was sailing across the lake, he remembered an old Greek story, for he was a learned man; he opened his good master's letter and found orders addressed to the commander of the fortress that he be put to death upon his arrival. Galeazzo, all too intent on the trick he was playing on our ancestor, had left a gap between the last line of the note and his signature; in that space Vespasiano del Dongo wrote an order acknowledging himself governor-general of all the fortresses along the lake, and snipped off the original message. Having reached the fortress and been duly acknowledged, he flung the commander into a dungeon, declared war on Galeazzo and all the Sforzas, and after a few years exchanged his fortress for the vast estates which have made the fortunes of every branch of our family, and which will some day provide me personally an income of four thousand lire."

"You talk like an academician!" exclaimed the Count with a laugh. "Your story's a good one, but the opportunity of performing such entertaining feats occurs only once a decade. Any fellow with half a brain who's aware of what he's doing and keeps his eyes open often enjoys the pleasure of getting the better of men of imagination. It was such follies of the imagination that induced Napoléon to surrender to a prudent John Bull rather than trying to escape to America. John Bull in his counting-house had a good laugh at Bonaparte's letter quoting Themistocles. In every age, a base Sancho Panza triumphs over a sublime Don Quixote. If you confine yourself to doing nothing out of the ordinary, I have no doubt that you will be a highly respected if not a highly respectable bishop. Nonetheless my observation stands: Your Excellency behaved frivolously with regard to the horse, and came within an inch of a life sentence."

This last remark made Fabrizio shudder; he remained plunged in the deepest amazement. "Could this," he wondered, "have been the prison threatening me? Is this the crime I must not commit?" The Abbé's predictions, which he had taken so lightly at the time, now assumed in his eyes all the importance of veritable omens.

"Now what's come over you?" asked the astonished Duchess. "Has the Count overwhelmed you with gloomy thoughts?"

"I am illuminated by a new truth, and instead of rebelling against it, my mind has adopted it. It is true that I had a close call with life imprisonment, but that footman looked so handsome in his English livery: what a shame it would have been to kill him!"

The Minister was delighted by Fabrizio's air of discretion. "He is remarkable in every respect," he said, with his eyes on the Duchess. "Let me tell you, my friend: you've made a conquest, and perhaps the most desirable one of all."

"Ah!" thought Fabrizio. "Now comes a joke at my expense about little Marietta." He was mistaken.

"Your *evangelical* simplicity," the Count continued, "has won the heart of our venerable Archbishop, Father Landriani. One of these days we'll be making you a Grand Vicar, and the cream of the jest is that the present three Grand Vicars, men of great merit, hard workers, and two of whom, I believe, were Grand Vicars since before you were born, will be sending an eloquent letter addressed to their Archbishop, requesting that you rank first among them. These gentlemen base their arguments first of all upon your virtues and then upon the fact that you happen to be the grand-nephew of the famous Archbishop Ascanio del Dongo. When I discovered the respect in which your virtues were held, I immediately promoted the oldest Grand Vicar's nephew to the rank of captain; he's been a lieutenant since Marshal Suchet's siege of Tarragona."

"Go right away, dressed just as you are, and pay an affectionate visit to your Archbishop!" exclaimed the Duchess. "Tell him about your sister's wedding; when he learns that she's to be a Duchess, he'll regard you as altogether apostolical. And remember, you know nothing of what the Count has just confided to you concerning your future nomination."

Fabrizio hastened to the Archbishop's palace; there he was simple and modest, a manner he assumed all too readily; on the other hand, it required a tremendous effort to play the *grand seigneur*. While listening to Monsignore Landriani's extended narratives, he kept asking himself: "Should I have shot the footman leading the lean horse?" His reason told him as much, but his heart could not inure itself to the bloody image of the handsome young fellow falling disfigured from his horse. "That fortress which would have swallowed me up, had the horse stumbled—was that the prison all these omens threaten me with?" This question was of the utmost importance to him, and the Archbishop was pleased by his air of profound attention.

CHAPTER ELEVEN

On leaving the Archbishop's Palace, Fabrizio hurried off to little Marietta; from a distance he could hear the loud voice of Giletti, who had sent for wine and was enjoying himself with his friends the prompter and the candle-snuffers. Only the *mammaccia*, who played the mother's part, answered his call.

"New things have happened since you left!" she exclaimed. "Two or three of our actors have been accused of celebrating the great Napoléon's feast-day with an orgy, and our poor troupe, they call us Jacobins, has been ordered to leave the State of Parma, and bravo Napoléon! But they say the Minister spit in the cuspidor, and one thing's for sure: Giletti's got some money, I don't know how much, but I've seen him with a handful of scudi. Our manager's given Marietta five scudi for the trip to Mantua and Venice, and one for me. She's still in love with you, but Giletti scares her; three days back, at our last performance, he really wanted to kill her; he gave her two good smacks, and the worst thing is he tore her blue shawl. If you wanted to be nice, you'd give her a blue shawl and we'll say we won it in a lottery. The drum-major of the *carabinieri*'s giving an assault-at-arms tomorrow, you'll see the schedule posted at every street corner. Come and see us; if he's gone to watch the assault, so we can count on his being gone a while, I'll be at the window and signal you to come on up. Try to bring us something nice, and Marietta will love you madly."

Coming down the winding staircase of this wretched slum, Fabrizio was filled with compunction: "I haven't changed one bit," he said to himself; "all those fine resolutions I made at our lake shore when I was looking at life so philosophically have evaporated. My soul was wandering at the time; it was all a dream and dissolves at the touch of real life. This would be the moment for action," he mused as he returned to the Palazzo Sanseverina at about eleven that evening. But it was in vain that he sought in his heart the courage to speak with that sublime sincerity which had seemed so easy to him during the night he had spent on the shores of Lake Como. "I'm going to disappoint the person I love best in the world; if I speak, I'll seem no more than a bad actor; I'm worthless really, except in certain moments of exaltation."

"The Count has treated me admirably," he said to the Duchess after describing his visit to the Archbishop's Palace; "I am all the more appreciative of his conduct since I realize that he is not particularly fond of me; my behavior toward him must therefore be correct in the extreme. He has his excavations at Sanguigna, which he is still quite enthusiastic about, at least judging from his trip the day before yesterday when he galloped twelve leagues to spend two hours with his workmen. If they find fragments of statues in that antique temple, the foundations of which he has just unearthed, there's always the fear of their being stolen, and I thought I might offer to spend thirty-six hours at Sanguigna—tomorrow, around five, I must see the Archbishop again, and then I could leave in the evening and take advantage of the cool night air on the journey."

The Duchess did not at first reply. Then, with extreme affection, she remarked, "One might think you were looking for excuses to get away from me; no sooner are you back from Belgirate than you find reasons for leaving again."

"Here," thought Fabrizio, "is a good opportunity to speak. But at the lake I was a little mad, I didn't realize in my enthusiasm for sincerity that my compliments turn to impertinence; I should be saying something like: I love you with the most devoted friendship, and so on, but my soul is incapable of love. And isn't that as much as to say: I see that you're in love with me, but beware, I cannot repay you in the same coin? If she is in love with me, the Duchess may be annoyed to be found out, and she will be disgusted with my impudence if all she feels for me is mere friendship. . . . That kind of offense is never forgiven." While he was pondering these important notions, Fabrizio, without realizing it, was striding up and down the salon, his expression filled with the lofty gravity of a man who sees disaster straight ahead of him.

The Duchess watched him admiringly; he was no longer the boy she had seen grow up, he was no longer the ever-obedient nephew; he was a serious man by whom it would be delicious to be loved. She stood up from the ottoman on which she had been sitting and, passionately flinging herself into his arms, exclaimed: "So you want to run away from me?"

"No," he replied, with the expression of a Roman emperor, "but I want to conduct myself properly."

This remark was capable of various interpretations; Fabrizio lacked the courage to proceed any further and to run the risk of wounding this adorable woman. He was too young, too susceptible to emotion; his mind supplied him with no graceful turn of phrase to express all he meant. In a natural transport of feeling and despite all his reasoning, he took this charming woman in his arms and covered her with kisses. At the same moment, they heard the sound of the Count's carriage entering the courtyard, and at almost the same moment the Count himself appeared in the salon; he seemed greatly moved.

"You inspire very singular passions," he said to Fabrizio, who remained nearly thunderstruck by the remark. "Tonight the Archbishop had the audience which His Serene Highness grants him every Thursday; the Prince has just informed me that the Archbishop, seeming quite troubled, began with a set speech he had got by heart, filled with learned allusions which at first left the Prince completely in the dark. Landriani ended by declaring that it was important for the Church of Parma that Monsignore Fabrizio del Dongo be named his first Vicar-General, and then, immediately after his twenty-fourth birthday, his Coadjutor *with eventual succession.* I must confess this expression alarmed me," the Count continued, "and I feared some sort of outburst from the Prince. But he merely looked at me with a smile and

said in French: 'I recognize your hand in this, Monsieur.' 'I swear before God and Your Highness,' I exclaimed with all possible unction,
'that I am perfectly unaware of the expression *future succession.*' Then I
told the truth, the very thing we've been saying right here for the last
few hours; I added, with some feeling, that in the future I should consider myself extremely favored by His Highness if he deigned to grant
me a minor bishopric to begin with. The Prince must have believed
me, for he found it suitable to be gracious; with tremendous simplicity, he told me: 'This is official business between the Archbishop and
myself, you have no say in the matter. The good man,' the Prince went
on to say, 'then delivered an extremely long and quite tedious report,
after which came an official proposal; I replied rather coolly that the
person in question was still quite young and, moreover, a very recent
arrival at my court; that I would risk giving the impression that I was
honoring a bill of exchange drawn upon me by the Emperor, by offering so high a dignity to the son of one of the principal officers of his
Lombardo-Venetian realm. The Archbishop protested that no such
recommendation had ever been made. This was a stupid thing to say
to me; it surprised me coming from a man of his understanding; but he
always loses his head when he has to speak to me, and that evening he
was more troubled than ever, which suggested to me that he passionately desired the thing. I remarked that I knew better than he that
there was no higher recommendation in del Dongo's favor, that no one
at my court denied his abilities, that no one spoke too badly of his
morals, but that I feared he was liable to *enthusiasm,* and that I had determined never to raise to high office such lunatics with whom a
prince could never be sure of anything. And then,' his Highness continued, 'I was forced to endure a pathetic narrative almost as long as
the first: the Archbishop launched into praises of the House of God.
Bungler! I said to myself, he is losing his way and compromising an
appointment which was virtually granted; he should have stopped
there and thanked me effusively. Nothing of the sort: he continued his
homily with absurd insistence; I tried to find a response which would
not be too unfavorable to young del Dongo; I managed this, indeed a
rather felicitious one, as you will judge: "Monsignore," I said to him,
"Pius VII was a great pope and a great saint; he alone of all sovereigns

dared to say *no* to the tyrant who held all Europe at his feet! Yet he too was liable to enthusiasm, which led him, when he was Bishop of Imola, to write his celebrated *Pastoral Letter of the Citizen-Cardinal Chiaramonti* in favor of the Cisalpine Republic." My poor Archbishop appeared quite stupefied, and to complete the effect I told him, as seriously as I could manage: "Farewell, Monsignore, I shall take twenty-four hours to reflect upon your proposition." The poor fellow added several rather clumsy and inopportune supplications after I had pronounced the word *farewell*. And now, Count Mosca della Rovere, I request that you inform the Duchess that I do not wish to delay by twenty-four hours a thing which may be agreeable to her; sit down here and write to the Archbishop that letter of approval which will conclude this whole business.' I wrote the letter, the Prince signed it, and said: 'Take it immediately to the Duchess.' Here, Madame, is the letter, and it is this matter which has afforded me a pretext for the happiness of seeing you once again this evening."

The Duchess read the letter with rapture. During the Count's long narrative, Fabrizio had had time to recover himself: he did not appear the least surprised by this incident, but took the matter like a true *grand seigneur* who quite naturally believed he was invariably entitled to such extraordinary advancements, to these strokes of fortune which would unhinge any bourgeois person; he referred to his gratitude, but in moderate terms, and ended by remarking to the Count: "A good courtier must indulge the ruling passion; yesterday you expressed the fear that your workmen in Sanguigna would steal the fragments of whatever ancient statues they might unearth; I too am very fond of such excavations; if you will be so good as to permit me, I shall go and supervise the workmen. Tomorrow evening, after the suitable expression of gratitude to the Prince and the Archbishop, I shall leave for Sanguigna."

"But can you guess," the Duchess asked the Count, "the source of our good Archbishop's sudden passion for Fabrizio?"

"I have no need to guess; the Grand-Vicar, whose brother is one of my captains, told me only yesterday: 'Father Landriani proceeds on this unwavering principle, that the Titular Bishop is superior to the Coadjutor,' and he is beside himself with joy at having a del Dongo under his orders and at having put him under obligation. Anything which emphasizes Fabrizio's high birth adds to his secret happiness: that he should have such a man as his aide-de-camp! In the second place Monsignore Fabrizio delighted him, did not intimidate him at all; and lastly for ten years he has been nourishing a well-watered hatred for the Bishop of Piacenza, who has publicly paraded the claim to succeed him to the See of Parma, and worse still, is merely the son of a miller. It is with this prospect of a future succession that the Bishop of Piacenza has formed very close relations with the Marchesa Raversi, and now these liaisons greatly alarm the Archbishop as to the success of his cherished scheme, to have a del Dongo on his staff, and to give him orders."

Two days later, early in the morning, Fabrizio was overseeing the excavations at Sanguigna, opposite Colorno (the Versailles of the Princes of Parma); these diggings extended across the plain quite close to the high-road leading from Parma to the bridge of Casalmaggiore, the first town over the Austrian border. The men were working on a long trench eight feet deep but as narrow as possible; they were engaged in searching, along the old Roman road, for the ruins of a second temple which, according to local report, still existed in the Middle Ages. Despite the Prince's orders, several peasants regarded these long ditches across their property with a certain hostility. No matter what they were told, they imagined that a treasure hunt was being conducted there, and Fabrizio's presence was particularly suitable to prevent the outbreak of any little disturbance. He was far from bored, and followed the excavations with passionate interest; occasionally, some medal would be unearthed, and Fabrizio endeavored to keep the workmen from conspiring to make off with it.

The day was fine; it was about six in the morning: he had borrowed an old single-loading rifle and had shot a few larks, one of which, wounded, would land on the high-road; pursuing it, Fabrizio noticed in the distance a carriage from Parma heading for the Casalmaggiore frontier. He had just reloaded his gun when the carriage, an extremely dilapidated one, approached so slowly that he recognized little Marietta, flanked by the lout Giletti and the old woman she passed off as her mother.

Giletti imagined that Fabrizio had posted himself there in the middle of the road, holding his rifle, to insult him and perhaps even to rob him of little Marietta. As a man of valor, he jumped out of the carriage; in his left hand he was holding a huge rusty pistol, and in his right a sword still in its scabbard, which he used when the company's needs obliged him to assume the part of some nobleman.

"So, you brigand!" he exclaimed. "I'm glad to find you here a league from the border; I'll take care of you now, where you're no longer protected by your purple stockings."

Fabrizio was busy smiling at little Marietta and quite unconcerned with Giletti's jealous cries when suddenly he noticed three feet from his chest the barrel of the rusty pistol; he had just time to knock the weapon away with his own rifle: the pistol went off, but without wounding anyone.

"Stop here, you asshole!" Giletti shouted to the coachman. At the same time he was shrewd enough to leap at the barrel of his adversary's gun, holding it away from his body; Fabrizio and he each pulled at the gun with all their might. Giletti, a much stronger man, placing one hand in front of the other, kept moving up toward the trigger, and was about to seize the weapon when Fabrizio, to prevent this, managed to fire. He had previously noticed that the gun barrel was more than three inches above Giletti's shoulder: the detonation occurred quite close to the man's ear. He remained stunned a moment, then recovered almost at once. "So you want to blow my brains out, you scum! I'll settle your hash for you now." Giletti threw away the scabbard of his nobleman's sword and with admirable dispatch made for Fabrizio, who was unarmed and gave himself up for lost.

He ran toward the carriage, which had stopped a dozen paces behind Giletti; he passed to the left and, grabbing the carriage-spring, quickly turned around and passed beside the door on the right-hand side, which stood open. Giletti, who had started forward on his long legs and who had not thought of catching hold of the carriage-spring, made several steps in the wrong direction before he could stop. At the moment Fabrizio passed the open door, he heard Marietta whisper: "Watch out, he'll kill you! Here!"

At the same moment, Fabrizio saw what looked like a big hunting-knife falling out of the carriage-door; he leaned down to pick it up, but at that very second was touched on the shoulder by a swipe of Giletti's sword. Straightening up, Fabrizio found himself six inches from Giletti, who gave him a furious blow on the face with his sword-hilt; the blow was launched with such force that it left Fabrizio completely dazed; at this moment he was on the point of being killed. Fortunately for him, Giletti was still too close to be able to run him through. Coming to his senses, Fabrizio took to his heels as fast as he could run, and as he did so threw away the sheath of the hunting knife and then, quickly turning around, found himself three paces away from his pursuer. Giletti was upon him; Fabrizio struck at him with the tip of the knife; Giletti had time enough to push the knife upward with his sword, but received the wound full in his left cheek. He passed right by Fabrizio, who felt a stab in his thigh—this was Giletti's knife, which the latter had had time to open. Fabrizio leaped to the right; he turned around, and now the two adversaries found themselves at a proper fighting range.

Giletti was swearing like a lost soul. "Now I'll slit your throat for you, you damned priest!" he kept repeating.

Fabrizio was quite out of breath and unable to speak; his face was hurting terribly where the sword-hilt had struck it, and his nose was bleeding copiously; he warded off several blows with his hunting-knife and made a number of lunges without really knowing what he was doing; he had a vague sense of being on display. This notion had been suggested to him by the presence of his workmen, who had formed a circle of some twenty-five or thirty men around the combatants, but at a very respectful distance, for at every moment the two men would leap up and fling themselves upon each other.

The duel seemed to be slackening a little; the blows no longer succeeded each other with the same speed, when Fabrizio said to himself: "From the pain I feel in my face, he must have disfigured me." Furious at this idea, he leaped upon his foe, knife-point at the ready, so that it entered the right side of Giletti's chest and emerged near the left shoulder; at the same instant, Giletti's sword ran at full length into Fabrizio's upper arm, but the blade slid under the skin, and the wound was not serious.

Giletti had fallen; at the moment when Fabrizio advanced toward him, staring at his left hand, which was holding a knife, this hand opened quite mechanically and released his weapon. "The bugger is dead," Fabrizio said to himself.

He looked at Giletti's face: blood was pouring out of his mouth. Fabrizio ran to the carriage. "Do you have a mirror?" he shouted to Marietta, who had gone dead white and stared at him without answering. The old woman opened a green workbag with great aplomb and handed Fabrizio a little mirror with a handle, no bigger than his hand. Studying his face, Fabrizio worked his features. "My eyes are all right," he said to himself, "which is something, anyway." He looked at his teeth, none of which was broken. "Why am I in such pain?" he asked himself half-aloud.

The old woman answered: "Because the top of your cheek was crushed between Giletti's sword-hilt and the bone there. Your cheek is horribly swollen and discolored: put some leeches on it right away and it will be nothing."

"Oh yes, leeches, right away," Fabrizio said with a laugh as he recovered his composure. He saw that the workmen had surrounded Giletti and were staring at him without daring to touch him.

"Help that man!" he shouted to them. "Open his coat . . ." He was going to continue, but looking up he saw five or six men about three hundred yards away on the high-road, walking deliberately toward the scene of the action. "Those must be the police," he realized, "and since there's been a man killed, they'll arrest me and I'll have the honor of making a solemn entry into the city of Parma. What a story for the courtiers on Marchesa Raversi's side who detest my aunt!"

With lightning speed, he tossed all the money in his pockets to the workmen and leaped into the carriage. "Keep the police from coming after me," he shouted to his men, "and I'll make your fortunes for you; tell them I'm innocent, tell them this man *attacked me and tried to kill me.* And you," he said to the coachman, "see how fast your horses can gallop. Four gold napoleons for you if you cross the Po before those men can get hold of me."

"Right you are!" the coachman said. "But there's no need to fear: those men back there are on foot, and even trotting these little fellows of mine would leave them far behind." With these words, he put his horses to a gallop.

Our hero was startled by the word *fear* the coachman had employed: the fact is that he had indeed been in extreme fear after receiving the sword-hilt blow to his face.

"We might run into people riding toward us," the cautious coachman remarked, thinking of his four napoleons, "and the men behind us might call out to them to stop us." Which meant, reload your weapons . . .

"Oh, how brave you are, my dearest Abbé!" exclaimed Marietta, embracing Fabrizio.

The old woman looked out the door of the carriage; after a little while she pulled her head back inside. "No one is after you, sir," she said to Fabrizio quite coolly; "and there's no one on the road ahead. You know how finicky the Austrian police can be: if they see you coming at a gallop like this, along the banks of the Po, they'll be sure to stop you, have no doubt about that."

Fabrizio looked out the carriage door. "Trot the horses," he told the coachman. "What passport do you have?" he asked the old woman.

"Three, instead of one," she answered, "and each one cost us four francs: isn't it a shame for poor dramatic artists like ourselves, traveling all year round! Here's Monsieur Giletti's passport, *dramatic artist,* that will be you; here are our two passports, for Marietta and me. But Giletti had all our money in his pocket; what will become of us?"

"How much did he have?" asked Fabrizio.

"Forty good scudi worth five francs," the old woman answered.

"In other words, six francs and change," said Marietta laughing; "I don't want anyone cheating my dearest Abbé."

"Isn't it only natural, sir," the old woman went on with the greatest *sang-froid,* "that I should try to gouge you out of thirty-four scudi? What are thirty-four scudi to you? And we—we've lost our protector; who will take care of us and find us lodgings and argue about charges with the coachman when we're traveling, and scare everyone off? Giletti may not have been handsome, but he was very useful, and if the child here weren't such a fool as to have fallen in love with you first,

Giletti would never have noticed a thing, and you would have given us good money. I can promise you we're poor as church mice."

Fabrizio was touched; he took out his purse and gave the old woman several napoleons. "As you see," he told her, "fifteen are all I have left, so there's no use trying any more tricks on me." Little Marietta threw her arms around his neck, and the old woman kissed his hands. The carriage trotted on. When they saw the black-and-yellow-striped barriers up ahead announcing Austrian territory, the old woman said to Fabrizio:

"It would be better if you were to cross on foot, with Giletti's passport in your pocket; we're going to stop here for a while with the excuse of refreshing our *toilette*. Besides, the customs officers will be going through our things. If you trust me, you'll stroll quite casually through Casalmaggiore; you might even go into a café and drink a glass of brandy; once past the village, don't waste any time. The police are watchful as the devil in Austrian territory: they'll soon know there's been a man killed: you're traveling with a passport that's not your own; that's enough to get you two years in prison. Head for the Po on your right as you leave town, rent a boat, and make your escape to Ravenna or Ferrara; leave the Austrian States as fast as you can. With two louis you should be able to buy another passport from some customs-officer—the one you have would be fatal to you; remember that you've killed the man."

Approaching the pontoon-bridge of Casalmaggiore on foot, Fabrizio carefully reread Giletti's passport. Our hero was in a state of fear: he vividly recalled what Count Mosca had told him about the danger he would incur by entering the Austrian States; now, two hundred paces ahead, he saw the terrible bridge which would afford him access to that country whose capital, in his eyes, was the Spielberg. But what else could he do? The Duchy of Modena, which borders the State of Parma to the south, returned fugitives to Parma according to a special convention; the frontier of the State extending over the mountains toward Genoa was too far; his misadventure would be known in Parma long before he could reach those mountains; so nothing remained but the States of Austria on the left bank of the Po. Before anyone had time to write the Austrian authorities requesting his arrest, perhaps some thirty-six hours or two days would have passed. Having duly considered all these matters, Fabrizio set fire to his own passport with his cigar: in Austrian territory he would do better as a vagabond than as Fabrizio del Dongo, and it was quite possible he would be searched.

Aside from his natural repugnance to entrusting his life to the unfortunate Giletti's passport, this document presented certain material difficulties: Fabrizio's height reached at most some five feet five inches, and not five feet ten as the passport specified; he was nearly twenty-four years old and looked younger, Giletti thirty-nine. We will confess that our hero paced a good half an hour along the Po embankment near the pontoon-bridge before making up his mind to cross it. "What would I advise someone else to do in my place?" he asked himself at last. "Obviously: cross the bridge: it is dangerous to remain in the State of Parma; police might be sent in pursuit of a man who has killed another, even in self-defense." Fabrizio examined the contents of his pockets, tore up all the papers he found there, and retained only his handkerchief and his cigar-case: it was essential to shorten the examination he would have to undergo. He thought of one terrible objection that might be raised, to which he found only poor answers: he was claiming that his name was Giletti, and all his linen was initialled F.D.

As we see, Fabrizio was one of those unfortunates tormented by their imagination; this is frequently the defect of intelligent men in Italy. A French soldier of equal or even inferior courage would have ventured to cross the bridge immediately, without brooding in advance upon the difficulties; but he would also have proceeded with all his composure when, at the end of the bridge, a short fellow dressed in gray said to him: "Go into the police office and show your passport."

This office had dirty walls studded with nails on which hung the officials' dirty hats and pipes. The big pinewood desk behind which they were entrenched was stained with ink and wine; two or three big ledgers bound in green leather bore stains of all colors, and the edges of their pages were blackened by fingerprints. On the ledgers piled one on top of the other were three splendid laurel crowns which had done duty, a few days back, in one of the Emperor's festivals.

Fabrizio was struck by all these details, which made his heart sink;

such was the price he paid for the immaculate luxury of his pretty apartment in the Palazzo Sanseverina. He was obliged to enter this dirty office and represent himself as his social inferior; he was about to be interrogated.

The official, who held out a yellow hand to take Fabrizio's passport, was short and dark, and wore a brass pin in his necktie.

"A nasty bourgeois if ever I saw one," thought Fabrizio. The fellow seemed excessively surprised as he read the passport, which reading lasted a good five minutes.

"You have had an accident," he said to the stranger, glancing up at his cheek.

"The coachman ran us into the embankment of the Po."

Then silence resumed, and the official stared fiercely at the traveler.

"That does it," Fabrizio said to himself, "he's going to tell me he regrets to inform me that I'm under arrest." All sort of wild ideas ran through our hero's mind, which at this moment was not very logical. For instance, he thought of making his escape through the office door, which had remained open.

"I take off my coat, I jump into the Po, and probably I can swim across. Anything is better than the Spielberg." The police official stared hard at him during this moment while he was calculating the chances of a successful escape; they afforded a fine contrast in physiognomy. The presence of danger bestows genius upon the man of reason; it raises him, so to speak, above himself; in the man of imagination it inspires romantic notions, bold it is true, but frequently absurd.

You had to have seen our hero's outraged expression beneath the searching eye of the police official embellished with his brass jewelry. "If I were to kill him," thought Fabrizio, "I'd be convicted of murder and condemned to twenty years in the galleys or put to death, which is not so bad as the Spielberg with a hundred-and-twenty-pound chain on each foot and eight ounces of bread a day, for twenty years! I'd be forty-four when I got out...." Fabrizio's logic was forgetting that, since he had burned his own passport, there was nothing to indicate to the police that he was the rebel Fabrizio del Dongo.

Our hero was sufficiently frightened, as we have seen; he would have been much more so had he known the thoughts that were agitating the police official. This man was a friend of Giletti's; imagine his surprise when he saw his friend's passport in another man's possession; his first impulse was to have this other man arrested; then he realized that Giletti might well have sold his passport to this handsome young fellow, who had apparently just done some nasty business in Parma. "If I arrest him," he said to himself, "Giletti will be compromised; it will easily be discovered that he has sold his passport; on the other hand, what will my superiors say if they manage to find out that as a friend of Giletti's I stamped his passport when someone else submitted it to me?" The official stood up with a yawn and said to Fabrizio: "Wait a moment, sir." Then, out of official habit, he added: "A difficulty has arisen."

To himself, Fabrizio murmured: "What will arise is my escape."

As a matter of fact, the official went out of the office, leaving the door open and the passport on the pinewood table. "The danger is clear," Fabrizio thought; "I'll take my passport and slowly walk back across the bridge; I'll tell the officer there, if he questions me, that I forgot to have my passport stamped by the police commissary in the last village on the Parma side." Fabrizio already had his passport in his hand when, to his inexpressible astonishment, he heard the official with the brass jewelry saying: "Lord help me, I can't take any more of this; the heat is stifling; I'm going to the café for a demi-tasse. Go into the office when you're done with your pipe, there's a passport to stamp; the traveler's in there."

Fabrizio, who was making a stealthy exit, found himself face to face with a handsome young fellow who was humming to himself. "All right, all right, where the devil is this passport? I'll put my scrawl on it somewhere. . . . Where does the gentleman wish to go?"

"To Mantua, Venice, and Ferrara."

"Ferrara then," the clerk replied, still humming. He picked up a stamp and pressed the blue-ink *visa* onto the passport, scribbling the words *Mantua Venice Ferrara* in the space left blank on the stamp; then he waved his hand several times in the air, signed the passport, and dipped his pen in the ink to make his flourish, which he executed slowly and taking infinite pains. Fabrizio followed every movement of that pen; the clerk glanced at his flourish with satisfaction, added five or six dots, and finally handed the passport back to Fabrizio, saying quite casually: "Have a good journey, sir."

Fabrizio was walking away with a rapidity he was attempting to conceal when he felt something pulling his left arm: instinctively his hand closed around the pommel of his dagger, and had he not seen houses all around him, he might have done something rash. The man who was touching his left arm, noticing his expression of alarm, remarked by way of apology: "But I called the gentleman three times, without his answering; does the gentleman have anything to declare to customs?"

"All I have on me is my handkerchief; I'm going somewhere quite close to here, for some shooting with one of my relatives."

He would have been altogether at a loss, had he been asked to name such a relative. Given the terribly warm weather and the intensity of these emotions, Fabrizio was as soaked as if he had fallen into the Po.

"I have courage enough to confront actors, but clerks with brass jewelry are too much for me; I'll try to write a funny sonnet about it to entertain the Duchess."

Entering Casalmaggiore, Fabrizio took a mean street to the right, sloping down toward the Po. "What I need now," he told himself, "is the succor of Bacchus and Ceres," and he went into a shop outside of which was hanging a gray rag attached to a stick; on the rag was written the word *Trattoria*. A filthy bedsheet supported by two thin wooden hoops and hanging down to within three feet of the ground sheltered the trattoria door from the direct rays of the sun. Here a half-naked and quite pretty woman received our hero with respect, which caused him the liveliest pleasure; he hastened to inform her he was dying of hunger. While she prepared his breakfast, a man of about thirty came in; he had not greeted anyone upon entering, but all of a sudden he sprang up from the bench onto which he had flung himself quite familiarly, and said to Fabrizio:

"*Eccellenza*, your servant!"

Fabrizio was in high spirits at that moment, and instead of forming sinister plans, he replied with a laugh: "And how the devil do you know My Excellency?"

"What, doesn't Your Excellency recognize Ludovic, one of Her Grace the Duchess Sanseverina's coachmen? At Sacca, the country house where we went every summer, I always caught the fever, and I asked Her Grace for my pension and I've retired. I'm rich now; instead of the pension of twelve scudi a year which was all I was entitled to, Her Grace told me that in order to ensure me the leisure to write sonnets—for I am a poet in the vernacular—she would grant me twenty-four scudi, and His Lordship the Count told me that if I was ever in need, I had only to come and speak to him. I have had the honor of driving Monsignore for a stage when he made his retreat like a good Christian at the Charterhouse of Velleja."

Fabrizio stared at the man, whom he faintly recognized. He was one of the smartest coachmen of the *Casa Sanseverina:* now that he was rich, as he said, his entire outfit consisted of a torn overshirt and a pair of canvas breeches dyed black some time past, which barely reached his knees; a pair of slippers and a wretched hat completed the picture. Moreover, he had not shaved his beard for at least two weeks. As he ate his omelette, Fabrizio made conversation with him quite between equals; he decided that Ludovic was his hostess's lover. Rapidly finishing his breakfast, he whispered to Ludovic, "I want a word with you."

"Your Excellency can speak freely in front of her, she's a really good woman," said Ludovic tenderly.

"Well then, my friends!" Fabrizio resumed without hesitating. "I'm in terrible trouble and I need your help. First of all, there's nothing political about my trouble, I've simply killed a man who was trying to murder me because I was talking to his mistress."

"Poor young fellow!" sighed the hostess.

"Your Excellency can count on me!" exclaimed the coachman, his eyes shining with the liveliest devotion. "Where would His Excellency like to go?"

"To Ferrara. I have a passport, but I'd prefer not to run into the police, who may have found out about the business."

"When did you do away with this fellow?"

"At six o'clock this morning."

"Has Your Excellency any blood on his clothes?" asked the hostess.

"I was wondering about that," said the coachman, "and besides, the material of those clothes is too fine—you don't see much like that in our part of the country, it would catch people's eye; I'm going to buy some clothes from the Jew: Your Excellency is about my height, only thinner . . ."

"For pity's sake, stop calling me Excellency, that will attract attention."

"Yes, Excellency," the coachman replied as he left the shop.

"All right, all right!" Fabrizio exclaimed. "And what about the money? Come back here!"

"Don't mention money!" said the hostess. "He has sixty-seven scudi which are at your service. I myself," she added, lowering her voice, "I have a good forty which I'd be glad to let you have; one doesn't always have money on one when these accidents happen."

Fabrizio had removed his coat because of the heat when he came into the trattoria. "You have a vest there that might make some trouble for us if someone were to come in: that fine *English cloth* would attract attention." She gave our fugitive a black-dyed cotton vest belonging to her husband. A tall young man entered the shop through an inner door, dressed with a certain elegance.

"This is my husband," the hostess said. "Pietro-Antonio, this gentleman is a friend of Ludovic's; he had an accident this morning on the other side of the river; he wants to get away to Ferrara."

"Then we'll get him there," the husband observed very politely; "we've got Carlo-Giuseppe's boat."

By another of our hero's weaknesses, which we shall confess as naturally as we have described his terror in the police office at the end of the bridge, he had tears in his eyes; he was profoundly moved by the perfect loyalty he was encountering among these peasants: and he was thinking as well of the kindness so characteristic of his aunt; he would have liked to be able to make these people's fortunes. Ludovic came in carrying a bundle.

"Over and done with," the husband said to him, in the friendliest possible tone.

"Anything but," Ludovic retorted, sounding quite alarmed. "People are beginning to talk about you; they've noticed that you hesitated when you left the high-road and turned down our alley, like a man who was trying to hide."

"Go up to the bedroom right away," the husband said.

This bedroom, large and handsome, had gray canvas instead of glass at the two windows; in it were four huge beds each one six feet wide and five high.

"Quick now, quick!" Ludovic said. "There's a conceited ass of a policeman who's just been put on duty here and who began trying to make love to the pretty lady downstairs; I've told him that when he does his rounds in the country, he might meet up with a bullet here or there; if that dog hears tell of Your Excellency, he'll try to play some trick on us—he'll try to arrest you here to give Theodolina's trattoria a bad name.

"And all this!" Ludovic continued, seeing the blood-stained shirt and the wounds bound with handkerchiefs. "The *porco* put up a fight, did he? A hundred times more than it takes to get yourself pinched; I didn't buy a shirt."

He opened the husband's wardrobe without a moment's hesitation and gave one of his shirts to Fabrizio, who was soon dressed as a prosperous country merchant. Ludovic unhooked a net from the wall, rolled up Fabrizio's clothes in the creel, ran downstairs, and rapidly left the house through a rear door; Fabrizio followed him.

"Theodolina!" he shouted, passing beside the shop. "Hide what's upstairs, we're going to wait in the willows; and you, Pietro-Antonio— you send us a boat on the double, we'll pay for it."

Ludovic made Fabrizio cross more than twenty ditches. There were long, springy planks which served as bridges over the widest of them; Ludovic removed these planks after crossing on them.

Having reached the last canal, he carefully pulled the plank away.

"Now we can breathe," he said; "that dog of a policeman would have more than two leagues to cover if he wanted to reach Your Excellency now. How pale you look," he said to Fabrizio; "I haven't forgotten the little bottle of brandy."

"Just in time: the wound in my thigh is beginning to throb, and besides I was scared to death in the police office at the bridge."

"I can believe it," said Ludovic, "with a shirt full of blood like yours, I can't see how you even dared go into a place like that. As for the wounds, I can manage that: I'll get you to a nice cool place where you can sleep a good hour; the boat will come for us there, if there's some way of getting hold of a boat; if not, when you've rested a little, we'll do another couple of leagues, and I'll take you to a mill where I can get you a boat myself; Your Excellency knows a lot more people than I do: Her Grace will be in despair when she hears of the accident; they'll tell her you've been mortally wounded, and perhaps even that you killed the other fellow in some underhand way. The Marchesa Raversi will be sure to tell some nasty stories that will hurt the Duchess. Your Excellency might write . . ."

"And how will I get the letter to her?"

"The boys at the mill where we're heading earn twelve soldi a day; in a day and a half they can reach Parma, so four francs for the trip, two francs wear and tear on the shoes: if the job was done for a poor man like me, that would be six francs; since it's for the service of a gentleman, I'd give them twelve."

When they reached a resting-place in a cool, shady grove of alders and willows, Ludovic disappeared for over an hour in search of ink and paper.

"Great God, how good it is here!" Fabrizio exclaimed. "Fortune, farewell! I shall never be an Archbishop!"

Returning, Ludovic found him fast asleep and was reluctant to waken him. The boat would arrive only at sunset; as soon as Ludovic saw it coming downstream, he roused Fabrizio, who wrote two letters.

"Your Excellency knows so much more than me," said Ludovic with a pained expression, "and I would do anything not to offend you, but I hope you'll permit me to add a certain thing."

"I'm not such a fool as you think," Fabrizio answered, "and whatever you may say, in my eyes you will always be a loyal servant of my aunt, and a man who has done everything in the world to get me out of a very nasty scrape."

Many further protestations were required to convince Ludovic to speak, and when he finally determined to do so, he began with a preface lasting a good five minutes. Fabrizio grew impatient, then reasoned with himself: "Who's at fault here? It's all due to our vanity, which this man has seen quite clearly from his seat on the box." At last Ludovic's devotion persuaded him to risk speaking plainly:

"How much the Marchesa Raversi would give to the fellow you're going to send to Parma if she could have these two letters! They're in your hand, and they can offer legal proof against you. Youe Excellency will take me for a nosy fellow as well as an indiscreet one, and also you may be ashamed of showing Her Grace my bad coachman's hand; but after all your safety has opened my mouth, though you may think me impertinent. Couldn't Your Excellency dictate those two letters to me? That way I'm the only person compromised, and little enough; if need be I'll say that you showed up in the middle of a field with an inkhorn in one hand and a pistol in the other, and that you forced me to write."

"Give me your hand, my dear Ludovic!" exclaimed Fabrizio. "And to prove to you that I will have no secrets from a friend like you, copy these two letters just as they are."

Ludovic understood the extent of this sign of confidence, and was extremely touched by it, but after a few lines, as he noticed the boat rapidly approaching down the river: "The letters will be finished sooner," he said to Fabrizio, "if Your Excellence will take the trouble of dictating them to me."

When the letters were done, Fabrizio wrote an *A* and a *B* on the last lines, and on a tiny scrap of paper which he then crumpled up, he wrote in French: "Believe A and B." The messenger was to hide this scrap in his clothes.

The boat having come within hailing distance, Ludovic called to the boatmen by names which were not theirs; they did not answer and landed five hundred yards downstream, scouring both banks to make sure they had not been seen by some customs-officer.

"I'm at your orders," Ludovic said to Fabrizio; "do you want me to take these letters to Parma myself? Or would you rather I accompany you to Ferrara?"

"Accompanying me to Ferrara is a service I hardly dared ask. I'll have to land somewhere and try to enter the city without showing a passport. I can tell you I have the greatest repugnance to traveling under the name of Giletti, and I can't think of anyone but you who can buy me another passport."

"Why didn't you mention it at Casalmaggiore! I know a spy who would have sold me a first-rate passport, and cheap, for forty or fifty francs."

One of the two boatmen who was born on the right bank of the Po, and consequently had no need of a passport in order to enter Parma, offered to take the letters. Ludovic, who knew how to handle an oar, was ready to manage the boat with the other man.

"When we reach the lower branch of the Po," he said, "we'll find several armed boats belonging to the police, but I'll be able to keep out of their way."

More than ten times they were obliged to hide among the islets at water level, covered with willows. Three times they set foot on land to let the empty boat drift past the police craft. Ludovic took advantage of these long intervals of leisure to recite several of his sonnets. Their feelings were true, but somehow blunted by their expression, and the verses were scarcely worth transcribing; oddly enough, this ex-coachman had passions and visions that were lively and picturesque; they turned cold and commonplace as soon as he wrote them down. "It's just the opposite of what we see in society," mused Fabrizio; "nowadays we can express anything and everything gracefully enough, but our hearts have nothing to say." He realized that the greatest pleasure he could offer this faithful servant would be to correct the spelling of his sonnets.

"They make fun of me when I lend them my notebook," Ludovic said; "but if Your Excellency would be good enough to show me how to spell the words letter by letter, the envious fellows would have nothing to say: spelling doesn't make a genius."

It was not until the third night of his journey that Fabrizio could land safely in an alder grove, one league above Pontelagoscuro. He remained hidden in a hemp-field for a whole day, and Ludovic went on ahead to Ferrara; there he rented inconspicuous lodgings from a poor Jew, who immediately understood that there was money to be made by keeping his mouth shut. By sunset Fabrizio entered Ferrara riding on a pony; he was greatly in need of this support, for the heat had affected him on the river; the knife-wound in his thigh and Giletti's sword-thrust in his shoulder at the start of their combat were inflamed and had brought on a fever.

Chapter Twelve

The Jew, owner of their lodgings, had obtained a discreet surgeon who, realizing in his turn that there was money in someone's purse, told Ludovic that his *conscience* compelled him to make his report to the police concerning the wounds of the young man whom Ludovic called his brother.

"The law is clear," he added; "it is only too obvious that your brother has not wounded himself, as he claims, falling from a ladder, when he happened to be holding an open knife in his hand."

Ludovic coldly replied that if this honest surgeon took it into his head to yield to the inspirations of his conscience, he, Ludovic, would have the honor, before leaving Ferrara, of falling on him precisely with an open knife in his hand. When he reported this incident to Fabrizio, the latter reproached him sharply, but there was no longer a moment to lose if they were to escape. Ludovic told the Jew that he wanted his brother to try the effect of some fresh air; he went to find a carriage, and our friends left the house, never to return. The reader doubtless finds overlong the narrative of all these undertakings made necessary by the absence of a passport: such preoccupations no longer exist in France; but in Italy, and especially in the region of the Po, everyone talks passports. Once Ferrara was left behind them without hindrance, as though they were taking a ride, Ludovic dismissed the fiacre, then returned to town by another gate, and went back for Fabrizio with a *sediola* he had hired to take them a dozen leagues. On the outskirts of Bologna, our friends had themselves driven cross-country to the Florence road, spending the night in the worst inn they could find, and the next morning, Fabrizio feeling strong enough to walk a little, they strolled into Bologna. Giletti's passport had been burned: the actor's death was surely known, and there was less danger in being arrested as men without passports than as bearers of the passport of a murdered man.

In Bologna Ludovic knew two or three servants in great houses; it was determined that he would find out the latest news from them. He told them that he had been traveling from Florence with his young brother; the latter, overcome by the need for sleep, had let him go on ahead an hour before sunrise. He was to join him in the village, where Ludovic would stop to avoid the heat of midday. But Ludovic, not seeing his brother arrive, had decided to retrace his route; he had discovered his brother bruised by a blow from a stone and by several knife wounds, and robbed in the bargain by men who had picked a quarrel with him. This brother was a handsome fellow, knew how to groom and drive horses, as well as to read and write, and was eager to find a place in some good house. Ludovic reserved for future use, should the occasion arise, the detail that once Fabrizio had fallen, the thieves had run off with the little bag holding their linens and their passports.

Arriving in Bologna, Fabrizio, feeling extremely tired and not daring, without a passport, to present himself at an inn, had entered the vast church of San Petronio. He found it deliciously cool inside; soon he felt quite reinvigorated. "Ingrate that I am," he immediately reproached himself, "I walk into a church and sit myself down as if it were a café!" He fell to his knees and effusively thanked God for the evident protection which had been vouchsafed him since he had had the misfortune to kill Giletti. The danger, which still made him tremble, was being recognized in the police offices of Casalmaggiore. "How," he asked himself, "could that clerk whose eyes showed so many suspicions and who reread my passport at least three times have failed to notice that I am not five feet ten inches tall, that I am not thirty-eight years old, that I am not badly scarred by smallpox? How many mercies I owe you, O my Lord! And I have delayed until this very moment to fling my nothingness at your feet! My pride has chosen to believe that it was to a vain human precaution that I owed the good fortune of escaping the Spielberg already yawning to swallow me up!"

Fabrizio spent over an hour in this state of extreme emotion, in the presence of God's enormous goodness. Ludovic approached noiselessly, and took a position facing him. Fabrizio, whose forehead was buried in his hands, raised his head, and his loyal servant saw the tears that furrowed his cheeks.

"Come back in an hour," Fabrizio told him quite harshly.

Ludovic forgave this tone, which he attributed to piety. Fabrizio recited several times the seven psalms of penitence, which he knew by heart; he lingered a long time over the verses which related to his present situation.

Fabrizio asked God's forgiveness for many things, but—remarkably enough—it did not occur to him to include among his sins the plan to become Archbishop solely because Count Mosca was Prime Minister and regarded this situation and the splendid existence it afforded as suitable for the Duchess's nephew. He had desired it without passion, it is true, but finally had aspired to it, exactly as if it were a position as Prime Minister or general.

It had not occurred to him that his conscience might be concerned in the Duchess's plan. This is a remarkable feature of the religion which he owed to the teachings of the Milanese Jesuits. Such religion does away with the courage to think of inhabitual things, and above all forbids *personal examination* as the most heinous of sins; it is a step toward Protestantism. To know what it is of which one is guilty, one must question one's priest, or read the list of sins as it may be found printed in the books entitled *Preparations for the Sacrament of Penitence.* Fabrizio knew by heart the list of sins drawn up in Latin, which he had learned at the Ecclesiastical Academy of Naples. Thus, while reciting this list, having reached the article *murder,* he had thoroughly accused himself before God of having killed a man, but in defense of his own life. He had rapidly, and without paying the slightest attention, passed over the various articles relative to the sin of *simony* (to obtain ecclesiastical offices by money). Had someone offered to give him a hundred louis to become the First Grand Vicar of the Archbishop of Parma, he would have rejected such a notion with horror; but though he lacked neither wit nor above all logic, it never occurred to him that Count Mosca's influence, employed in his behalf, was a form of *simony*. Such is the triumph of a Jesuitical education: to form the habit of not paying attention to matters more obvious than the nose on one's face. A Frenchman, brought up among features of personal interest and of Parisian irony, might in good faith have accused Fabrizio of hypocrisy at the very moment when our hero was opening his heart to God with the deepest sincerity and the profoundest emotional transport.

Fabrizio left the church only after having prepared the confession he proposed to make the following day; he found Ludovic sitting on the steps of the enormous stone peristyle built on the great square in front of the façade of San Petronio. As after a great storm the air is purer, so Fabrizio's soul was tranquil, happy and, so to speak, refreshed.

"I seem to be quite well, I scarcely feel my wounds," he said to Ludovic as he came up to him; "but above all I want to ask your forgiveness for my harsh words when you spoke to me in church while I was examining my conscience. Well now, how have we left matters?"

"As well as can be expected: I've rented lodgings, in truth scarcely worthy of Your Excellency, with the wife of one of my friends, a very pretty woman quite intimately attached to one of the most powerful agents of the police. Tomorrow I shall visit him and declare that our passports have been stolen; this declaration will be taken in good faith; but I shall pay the costs of the letter the police will write to Casalmaggiore to learn whether there exists in that commune a certain Ludovic San Micheli, who has a brother, by name Fabrizio, in the service of Her Grace the Duchess Sanseverina, in Parma. Everything is arranged; *siamo a cavallo*." (An Italian proverb meaning: we are saved.)

Fabrizio's countenance had suddenly turned very grave: he begged Ludovic to wait for him a moment, almost ran back into the church, and no sooner was he there than he fell to his knees and humbly kissed the stone pavement. "It's a miracle, Lord!" he exclaimed, his eyes filling with tears. "When you saw my soul prepared to assume its duties, you rescued me! Good Heavens, it is perfectly possible that someday I may be killed in some business or other: remember when I die how my soul was disposed at this very moment!" It was with the most intense transports of joy that Fabrizio once again recited the seven psalms of penitence. Before leaving he approached an old woman sitting in front of a huge Madonna and alongside an iron triangle placed vertically on a pedestal of the same metal. The edges of this triangle bristled with a great number of nails intended for the little candles which the piety of the faithful light before the celebrated Madonna of Cimabue. Only seven candles were lighted as Fabrizio approached; he placed this circumstance in his memory with the intention of pondering it later at greater leisure. "How much do the candles cost?" he asked the old woman.

"Two *baiocchi* apiece."

As a matter of fact they were scarcely thicker than a quill pen, and less than a foot long.

"How many more candles will fit on your triangle?"

"Sixty-three, since there are seven lighted."

"Ah!" Fabrizio said to himself. "Sixty-three and seven make seventy: I should take note of that as well." He paid for the candles, placed and lighted the first seven himself, then knelt to make his offering and, as he rose, said to the old woman: "It's *for Grace received.*"

"I'm dying of hunger," Fabrizio said to Ludovic as he joined him.

"Let's not go to some tavern, we'll go back to our lodgings; the woman there will buy you what we need for a meal; she'll steal twenty sous and will be all the fonder of the new arrival."

"That merely means I'll have to go on dying of hunger for a good hour longer," Fabrizio said with the laughing serenity of a child, and he went into a tavern near San Petronio.

To his immense surprise, he saw, at a table close to the one where he had been placed, Pepe, his aunt's first footman, the very man who had once come to meet him in Geneva. Fabrizio made a sign that he should say nothing; then, after a rapid meal, a happy smile stealing over his lips, he stood up; Pepe followed him, and for the third time our hero entered San Petronio. Out of discretion, Ludovic remained walking back and forth in the square.

"Well, my Lord, Monsignore! How are your wounds? Her Grace the Duchess is dreadfully worried; for a whole day she thought you were lying dead on some island in the Po; I'll go and send her a message right away. I've been looking for you the last six days; I've spent three in Ferrara running from one inn to the next."

"Have you a passport for me?"

"I have three different ones: one with the names and titles of Your Excellency; the second with just your name, and the third made out in an assumed name, Joseph Bossi; each passport is issued in duplicate, depending on whether Your Excellency wants to be coming from Florence or from Modena. All you have to do is take a stroll around the town. Count Mosca would be pleased if you would stay at the Albergo del Pellegrino, where the innkeeper is a friend of his."

Fabrizio, seeming to be strolling at random, walked into the right-hand nave of the church to the place where his candles were lighted; his eyes were fixed on the Cimabue Madonna, and he said to Pepe as he knelt: "Just a moment, I must give thanks."

Pepe did the same. As they left the church, Pepe noticed that Fabrizio gave a twenty-franc piece to the first poor man who asked him for alms; this beggar uttered cries of gratitude which attached to the heels of this charitable being swarms of the many paupers who ordinarily embellish the Piazza San Petronio. All wanted to have their share of the napoleon. The women, despairing of penetrating the crowd which surrounded him, hurled themselves upon Fabrizio, shrieking to him to tell whether he intended his napoleon to be divided among all God's poor. Pepe, brandishing his gold-pommeled cane, ordered them to leave His Excellency in peace.

"Oh, Excellency," all these women repeated still more shrilly, "give another gold napoleon for the poor women!"

Fabrizio increased his pace; the women following and shrieking, and many men as well running toward them through all the streets, made a sort of minor riot. This whole dreadfully filthy crowd energetically echoed the word: "Excellency!"

Fabrizio had great difficulty in releasing himself from this mob; the scene brought his imagination back to earth. "It's only what I deserve," he told himself, "rubbing elbows with the rabble."

Two women followed him to the Saragossa gate, by which he left the city. Pepe halted them, seriously threatening them with his cane and tossing them some coins. Fabrizio climbed the charming hillock of San Michele in Bosco, circled a section of the city outside the walls, followed a path which brought him five hundred paces out onto the Florence road, then re-entered Bologna and gravely presented to the police clerk a passport on which his description was minutely indicated. This passport identified him as Joseph Bossi, a student of theology. On it Fabrizio happened to notice a tiny fleck of red ink that appeared as though by accident on the lower right-corner of the sheet. Two hours later he had a spy on his heels, on account of the title *Excellency* which his companion had given him in the presence of the poor of San Petronio, though his passport bore none of the titles which afford a man the right to be called *Excellency* by his servants.

Fabrizio saw the spy and passed it off as a joke; he was no longer concerned about either the passports or the police, and like a child was entertained by everything. Pepe, who had been ordered to stay with him, observing how pleased he was with Ludovic, preferred to take such good news to the Duchess on his own. Fabrizio wrote two very long letters to the persons who were dear to him; then it occurred to him to write a third to the venerable Archbishop Landriani. This letter produced a wonderful effect, containing as it did a very precise account of the fight with Giletti. The good Archbishop, greatly moved, did not fail read the letter to the Prince, who was quite interested in hearing it, being rather curious to see how this young *Monsignore* managed matters so as to excuse so dreadful a murder. Thanks to the many friends of the Marchesa Raversi, the Prince, as well as the whole city of Parma, had believed that Fabrizio had obtained the assistance of twenty or thirty peasants to do away with a wretched actor who had the insolence to question his rights to little Marietta. In despotic courts, the first adroit intriguer controls the *truth,* as fashion controls it in Paris.

"What the Devil!" exclaimed the Prince to the Archbishop. "One gets someone to perform such actions; but to do them oneself is hardly the thing; moreover, one does not kill an actor like this Giletti, one buys him off."

Fabrizio was far from suspecting what was going on in Parma. As a matter of fact, there was some question as to whether the death of this actor, who in his life earned perhaps thirty-two francs a month, would bring down the *ultra* ministry and with it its leader, Count Mosca.

Upon learning of Giletti's death, the Prince, stung by the airs of independence the Duchess was assuming, had ordered his Chief Justice Rassi to deal with the entire case as if it had concerned a Liberal. Fabrizio, for his part, supposed that a man of his rank was above the law; he did not consider that in countries where the great names are never subject to punishment, intrigue can accomplish everything, even against them. He frequently mentioned to Ludovic his "perfect innocence," which would soon be proclaimed, his chief reason being that he was not guilty. Upon which Ludovic remarked to him one day: "I can't understand how Your Excellency, who has so much native wit and education, can take the trouble to speak of such things to a man like myself, your devoted servant. Your Excellency is taking too many precautions. Such things had best be spoken in public or before a court."

"This man regards me as a murderer and loves me none the less for it," Fabrizio realized, suddenly struck down.

Three days after Pepe's departure, he was quite amazed to receive an enormous letter sealed with a silk ribbon as in the days of Louis XIV and addressed to *His Most Reverend Excellency Monsignore Fabrizio del Dongo, First Grand Vicar of the Diocese of Parma, Canon,* and so on.

"But am I still all that?" he said to himself, laughing. Archbishop Landriani's epistle was a masterpiece of clarity and logic; it consisted of no less than nineteen enormous pages, and described quite accurately what had taken place in Parma on the occasion of Giletti's death.

A French army commanded by Marshal Ney and marching upon the town would not have produced a greater effect, *wrote the good Archbishop;* with the exception of the Duchess and myself, my dear son, everyone here believes that you gave yourself the pleasure of killing the actor Giletti. Had this misfortune fallen upon you, these are the sorts of things which are passed off with two hundred louis and an absence of six months; but the Raversi seeks to topple Count Mosca by means of this incident. It is not the horrible sin of murder which the public reproaches you for, but solely the clumsiness or rather the insolence of not having deigned to resort to a bulo (*a sort of hired assassin*). I am translating for you here into explicit terms the talk which surrounds me, for since this forever-deplorable disaster, I visit every day some three of the most considerable houses of the town in order to have occasion to justify you. And never have I believed I made a holier use of what little eloquence Heaven has consented to grant me.

The scales fell from Fabrizio's eyes; the Duchess's many letters, filled with transports of friendship, never deigned to tell him such news. The Duchess swore she would leave Parma forever if he did not soon return to it in triumph.

"The Count will do for you everything humanly possible," she wrote him in the letter that accompanied the Archbishop's. "As for me, you have altered my character with this fine escapade of yours; I am now as avaricious as the banker Tombone; I have dismissed all my workmen, I've done more, I've dictated to the Count the inventory of my fortune, which turns out to be much less considerable than I had thought. After the death of the excellent Count Pietranera, which, parenthetically, you would have done much better to have avenged instead of exposing your life to such a creature as Giletti, I was left with an income of twelve hundred francs and five thousand francs of debts; I recall, among other things, that I had thirty pairs of white satin slippers from Paris and one pair of shoes to wear in the street. I have virtually made up my mind to take the three hundred thousand francs the Duke left me, a sum which I wished to devote exclusively to erecting a splendid tomb for him. Moreover, it is the Marchesa Raversi who is your chief enemy, which is to say mine; if you find it tedious being alone there in Bologna, you have only to say a word, and I shall come and join you. Here are four more bills of exchange, and so on."

The Duchess did not breathe a word to Fabrizio of the opinion held in Parma of his affair; she wished above all to console him and, in any case, the death of so absurd a creature as Giletti hardly seemed to her of a nature to be seriously held against a del Dongo.

"How many Gilettis have our ancestors not sent to the next world," she asked the Count, "without its occurring to anyone to blame them for it?"

Fabrizio, flabbergasted, and for the first time glimpsing the true state of affairs, began to study the Archbishop's missive. Unfortunately, the Archbishop himself imagined him better informed than was actually the case. Fabrizio realized that what constituted the Marchesa Raversi's special triumph was that it was impossible to find *de visu* witnesses of the fatal combat. The footman who first brought the news to Parma had been at the village inn at Sanguigna when it had occurred; little Marietta and the old woman who acted as her mother had vanished, and the Marchesa had bought the *vetturino* who drove the carriage and who had now made an abominable deposition.

Although the proceedings are surrounded by the deepest mystery, *wrote the good Archbishop in his best Ciceronian style,* and conducted by Chief Justice Russi, of whom Christian charity alone can restrain me from speaking evil, but who has made his fortune by oppressing the wretched victims of justice even as a greyhound pursuing a hare; though this Rassi, I say, whose turpitude and venality cannot, by your wildest imagination, be exaggerated, has been granted control of the case by a vexed Prince, I have managed to read the vetturino's three depositions. By a signal stroke of fortune, this wretched person has contradicted himself. And I shall add, because I am speaking here to my Vicar General, to the person who, after myself, is to have the charge of this diocese, I shall add that I have sent for the curate of the parish in which this strayed sinner resides. I may tell you, my dearest son, but under the secrecy of the confessional, that this curate already knows, through the vetturino's wife, the number of scudi he has received from the Marchesa Raversi, and I dare not say that the Marchesa has insisted that he calumniate your name, but the fact is highly likely. The scudi were sent by a wretched priest who fulfills certain venal functions for this Marchesa, and whom I have been obliged to forbid to say Mass for the second time. I shall not weary you with the account of several further proceedings which you are entitled to expect of me and which, moreover, constitute a part of my duties. A canon, your colleague at the Cathedral, and one who, moreover, occasionally recalls a bit too vividly the influence he enjoys on account of his family's wealth, of which, by divine permission, he has remained the sole heir, having allowed himself to say, at the house of Count Zurla, Minister of the Interior, that he regarded this trifle as proved against you (*he was speaking of the murder of the unfortunate Giletti*),

I have summoned to appear before me, and there, in the presence of my three other Vicars-General, of my Chaplain, and of two curates who happened to be in the antechamber, I requested him to communicate to us, his brethren, the elements of the complete conviction which he claimed he had acquired against one of his colleagues at the Cathedral; the wretched fellow has been able to articulate only inconclusive reasons; everyone has risen against him, and though I have not believed it necessary to add more than a very few words, he dissolved into tears and made us witnesses of the full confession of his complete error, whereupon I promised him secrecy in my name and in that of all the persons present at this meeting, though stipulating that he employ all the zeal at his command to rectify the false impressions most likely caused by the speeches made by him during the last fifteen days.

I shall not repeat to you, my dear son, what you must have known long since, which is to say that of the thirty-four peasants who are employed in the excavations undertaken by Count Mosca and whom the Raversi woman claims you paid to assist you in committing your crime, thirty-two were at the bottom of a ditch, entirely busy with their task, when you seized your hunting-knife and employed it to defend your life against the man who unexpectedly attacked you. The other two workmen, who were not in the excavations, shouted to the others: *Monsignore* is being murdered! Which cry alone reveals your innocence in all its purity. Imagine, then, that Chief Justice Rassi claims that these two men have vanished, and that moreover eight of the men who were in the ditch have been apprehended; at their first interrogation, six declared having heard the shout "*Monsignore* is being murdered!" By indirect means I have learned that in their fifth interrogation, which took place yesterday evening, five declared that they did not clearly recall whether they had distinctly heard this shout or if they had merely heard it described by one of their comrades. Orders have been given that I be informed as to the residence of these workmen, and their priests will make it quite clear to them that they will be damning their own souls if, in order to gain a few scudi, they permit themselves to alter the truth.

The good Archbishop entered into an infinity of details, as may be judged by those we have just reproduced. Then he added, using the Latin tongue:

This affair is nothing less than an attempt to effect a change of government. If you are condemned, it can only be to the galleys or to death, in which case I shall intervene declaring, from my Archiepiscopal Throne, that I know that you are innocent, that you quite simply defended your own life against a ruffian, and that finally I have forbidden you to return to Parma so long as your enemies are in triumph there; I even propose to stigmatize, as he deserves, the Chief Justice; hatred of this man is as common as esteem for his character is rare. But as a last resort, on the eve of the day that this Chief Justice pronounces so unjust a decree, the Duchess Sanseverina will leave the city and perhaps the State of Parma as well: in that case there can be no doubt that the Count will hand in his resignation. Then, most likely, General Fabio Conti will be made Prime Minister, and the Marchesa Raversi will triumph. The real difficulty with your affair is that no skilled person has been put in charge of the necessary steps to bring your innocence to light and to lay bare the attempts made to suborn the witnesses. This is a role the Count believes he can assume, but he is too much of a *grand seigneur* to stoop to certain details; furthermore, in his position as Minister of Police, he has been obliged, initially, to issue the severest orders against you. Lastly, dare I say it, our Sovereign Prince believes you to be guilty, or at least simulates such a belief, and that contributes a certain bitterness to this affair. (*The words corresponding to* our Sovereign Prince *and* simulates such a belief *were in Greek, and Fabrizio was infinitely grateful to the Archbishop for having dared to write them at all. He took his pen-knife and cut this line out of his letter and destroyed it on the spot.*)

Fabrizio interrupted his reading of this letter a score of times, seized as he was by transports of the deepest gratitude: he immediately replied by a letter of some eight pages. Frequently he was obliged to turn aside his head so that his tears might not fall upon his paper. The following day, just as he was sealing this letter, he read it over and found it too worldly. "I shall write it in Latin," he said to himself, "that will make it appear seemlier to the worthy Archbishop." But in attempting to construct his fine suitably extended Latin sentences in the manner of Cicero, he recalled that one day the Archbishop, referring to Napoléon, chose to call him Buonaparte; instantly all the emotion which had touched him to the point of tears disappeared. "O King of Italy!" he exclaimed. "That loyalty which so many have sworn to you in your lifetime I shall perpetuate even after your death. He cares for me, no doubt, but because I am a del Dongo and he the son of the bourgeoisie." In order that his fine letter in Italian not be wasted, Fabrizio made a few necessary alterations in it and addressed it to Count Mosca.

That very day, Fabrizio met up with little Marietta in the street; she blushed with happiness and gestured to him to follow her without speaking. She rapidly made for a deserted archway, where she tightened the black lace shawl which, according to the custom of the country, covered her head, in order that she not be recognized; then, quickly turning around: "How can it be," she said to Fabrizio, "that you are walking freely in the street like this?"

Fabrizio told her his story. "Good heavens, you were in Ferrara! I was there, looking for you everywhere! You must know that I quarrelled with the old woman because she wanted to take me to Venice, where I was sure you would never go, since you are on the Austrians' blacklist. I sold my gold chain to come to Bologna, since I had a feeling I would be lucky enough to meet you here, as I have; the old woman got here two days after I did. So I will not ask you to come to where we live; she would make more of her base requests for money which cause me so much shame. We have lived quite comfortably since the fatal day you recall, and we have not spent a quarter of what you gave her. I don't want to visit you at the Albergo del Pellegrino, that would be a *pubblicità*. Try to rent a little room in an empty street somewhere, and at the Ave Maria"—nightfall—"I will be here, under this same archway."

With these words, she ran off.

CHAPTER THIRTEEN

Every serious idea was forgotten upon the unexpected appearance of this charming person. Fabrizio took up life in Bologna in the profoundest joy and security. This naïve tendency to be happy with whatever filled his life was quite apparent in the letters he wrote to the Duchess, to such an extent that she took offense. Fabrizio scarcely noticed; he wrote, however, in a sort of code on the face of his watch: "When I wrote to the D. never say *when I was prelate, when I was in the Church;* that annoys her." He had bought two little horses with which he was highly pleased; he harnessed them to a hired carriage whenever little Marietta wanted to visit one of those delightful spots in the environs of Bologna; almost every evening he drove her to the *Cascata del Reno,* and upon their return he would call on that agreeable fellow Crescentini, who regarded himself as Marietta's father, more or less.

"My word, if this is the *vie de café* I used to consider so unworthy of a gentleman, I was quite wrong to reject it," Fabrizio said to himself. He was forgetting that he never went to a café except to read the *Constitutionnel,* and that since he was a complete stranger to anyone in Bologna's high society, the delights of vanity counted for nothing in his present happiness. When he was not with little Marietta, he might be seen at the Observatory, where he attended lectures on astronomy;

the professor had taken a great liking to him, and Fabrizio would lend him his horses on Sundays so that he might cut a figure with his wife on the *Corso della Montagnola*. He hated the very idea of doing harm to anyone at all, however disagreeable he might be. Marietta insisted that he not see the old woman; but one day when she was in church he went up to visit the *mammaccia*, who flushed with rage when she saw him come in. "Now is the time to act the del Dongo," Fabrizio said to himself.

"How much does Marietta earn a month, when she has a theatrical engagement?" he inquired, with the air of a self-respecting young man entering the balcony of the Bouffes Parisiens.

"Fifty scudi."

"You're lying as usual; tell me the truth, or by God you'll not get one centesimo."

"All right, she made twenty-two scudi in our company while we were in Parma, when we had the misfortune of meeting you; myself I earned twelve scudi, and we each gave Giletti, our protector, a third of whatever we made. Out of which, almost every month, Giletti used to give Marietta a present as well, and that was easily worth two scudi."

"You're still lying; you never made more than four scudi in your life. But if you're good to Marietta, I'll hire you as if I were an *impresario;* every month you'll receive twelve scudi for yourself and twenty-two for her; but if I see that she's been crying, I'll cut you off without a centesimo."

"Hoity-toity, but your generosity will be the ruin of us," the old woman answered angrily; "we're losing our *avviamento*" (our custom). "When we suffer the enormous misfortune of being deprived of Your Excellency's protection, there won't be a troupe in Italy that knows us, they'll all be full up; we won't find any work, and all on account of you we'll starve to death!"

"Go to the devil!" Fabrizio exclaimed as he left the room.

"I shall not go to the devil, you impious villain, but only to the police office, where they shall hear from me that you are a Monsignore who has thrown his cassock in a ditch and that you're no more Joseph Bossi than I am."

Fabrizio was already half-way down the stairs; he returned.

"First of all the police know better than you what my real name happens to be; but if you take it into your head to give me away, if you do anything so infamous," he told her with the greatest seriousness, "Ludovic will have something to say to you, and it will not be six little cuts with a knife that your old carcass will get, but two dozen, and you'll find yourself in the hospital for six months at least, and not a pinch of snuff."

The old woman turned pale and grabbed at Fabrizio's hand, which she tried to kiss. "I thankfully accept the provisions you have made for Marietta and for me. You have such a kindly face that I took you for a simpleton; and you ought to realize that others besides myself might make the same mistake; my advice to you is to look more like a nobleman." And then she added with splendid impudence: "It's good advice—you'd better think it over. And since winter is coming soon, suppose you make us each a present, Marietta and me, of a good coat of that fine English cloth they sell in the big shop in the Piazza San Petronio."

The love of pretty Marietta afforded Fabrizio all the delights of the sweetest friendship, which soon reminded him of the same sort of felicity he might have met with at the Duchess's hands.

"But how odd it is," he would occasionally tell himself, "that I'm not susceptible to that exclusive and impassioned preoccupation known as love? Among all the relationships chance has bestowed upon me at Novara or in Naples, have I ever met a woman whose presence, even in the first days, I preferred to a ride on a fine new horse? Is what they call love," he added, "only one more lie? Doubtless I love the way I have a good appetite at six o'clock! And could it be this rather vulgar propensity which our liars have made into Othello's jealousy and Tancred's passion? Or must I assume I am constituted differently from other men? Why should it be that my soul lacks this one passion? What a singular fate is mine!"

In Naples, especially toward the end of his visit, Fabrizio had encountered women proud of their rank, their beauty, and their position in the society of the suitors they had given up for him, women who had tried to dominate him. No sooner had he realized their intentions than Fabrizio had broken with them in the swiftest and most scandalous fashion. "Now," he said to himself, "if I ever let myself be carried away by the doubtless intense pleasure of being intimate with that pretty woman known as the Duchess Sanseverina, I shall be precisely like that idiot Frenchman who one day killed the goose that laid the golden eggs. It is to the Duchess that I owe the only happiness I have ever derived from tender sentiments; my friendship for her is my very life, and besides, without her what am I? A poor exile reduced to a pathetic existence in a crumbling castle outside Novara. I remember how during the terrible autumn rains I would have to fasten an umbrella over my bed to avoid an accident. I rode the horses of our notary, which he permitted me to do out of respect for my *blue blood* (for my high birth), but he was beginning to find my stay a bit extended; my father had granted me an allowance of twelve hundred francs and considered himself damned for supporting a Jacobin. My poor mother and my sisters did without dresses to enable me to make a few little presents to my mistresses. This way of being generous pierced me to the heart. And furthermore, people were beginning to suspect I was a poor man, and the young nobles of the region were taking pity on me. Sooner or later some fool would have revealed his scorn for the poor Jacobin whose plans had come to nothing, for in the eyes of such people that is precisely what I was. I would have given or received a good saber-thrust, which would have landed me in the Fortress of Fenestrelles, or else I would once again have fled to Switzerland, with no more than an income of those same twelve hundred francs. I have the good fortune to owe the Duchess the absence of all these miseries; moreover it is she who feels for me the transports of friendship which I should be feeling for her . . .

"Instead of this absurd and mean existence which would have made of me a melancholy mindless beast, I have lived the last four years in a great city and kept an excellent carriage, which has prevented me from suffering envy and all the low emotions characteristic of the provinces. This over-indulgent aunt always complains that I never take enough money from her banker. Would I ruin forever this admirable position? Would I lose the one friend I have in the world? All I need do is utter a single lie, merely say to a charming and perhaps incomparable woman for whom I feel the warmest friendship, "I love you," though I haven't the faintest notion of what it is to feel love. She would spend her days reproaching me for the lack of precisely those transports which are unknown to me. Marietta, on the other hand, who knows nothing of my heart and who takes a caress for a rapture of the soul, believes I am madly in love and regards herself as the happiest of women.

"As a matter of fact, all I have ever known, I believe, of that tender preoccupation known as love was what I felt for young Aniken in that inn at Zonders, near the Belgian border."

It is with regret that we shall record here one of Fabrizio's worst actions: in the midst of this tranquil life, a wretched *pique* of vanity seized this heart so refractory to love and led it far astray. At the same time as Fabrizio, there happened to be in Bologna the celebrated Fausta F——, one of the finest singers of our day, and perhaps the most capricious woman the world has ever seen. That splendid Venetian poet Burati had made her the subject of a famous satirical sonnet which was to be heard in those days on the lips both of princes and of the poorest street urchins:

> In a single day to desire and to refuse,
> to worship and detest, and in betrayal
> alone of all a lover's enterprise
> to be content, to scorn what the world adores,
> while the world adores her alone:
> these are Fausta's faults, and many more.
> Therefore never look upon this serpent.
> For if, foolhardy fellow, you but once
> allow your gaze to fall upon her form,
> you will forget her follies and her whims.
> Fortunate to hear her sing, you will forget
> yourself as well, and in an instant Love
> will make of you what Circe long ago
> made of the companions of Odysseus.

For the moment this miracle of beauty was under the spell of the enormous sideburns and haughty insolence of young Count M——, to the point of not being disgusted by his abominable jealousy. Fabrizio observed this nobleman in the streets of Bologna and was shocked by the air of superiority with which he monopolized the promenade and deigned to reveal his graces to the public. This Count was extremely rich, regarded himself as entitled to everything, and, since his *prepotenze* had incurred certain threats, he now appeared in public only surrounded by eight or ten *buli* (cut-throats), whom he had dressed up in his livery and imported from his estates near Brescia. Fabrizio's eyes had once or twice met those of this terrible Count, when as chance would have it he heard Fausta sing. He was amazed by the angelic sweetness of her voice; he had never imagined anything like it; it afforded him sensations of supreme happiness which presented a striking contrast to the placidity of his present existence. "Would this be love?" he asked himself. Intensely curious to experience this sentiment, and moreover quite entertained by the notion of defying Count M——, whose expression was more terrible than that of any drum-major, our hero gave himself up to the childishness of passing much too often in front of the Palazzo Tanari, which Count M—— had rented for Fausta.

One day, as it was beginning to grow dark, Fabrizio, attempting to attract Fausta's notice, was greeted by emphatic peals of laughter from the Count's *buli,* who happened to be standing in the doorway of the Palazzo Tanari. He hurried to his lodgings, quickly armed himself properly, and returned to the palazzo. Hidden behind her blinds, Fausta was awaiting his return, and gave him due credit for it. The Count, jealous of the world, became particularly so of Signor Joseph Bossi, and permitted himself some absurd remarks; whereupon every morning our hero saw to it that a letter was delivered to him which contained no more than these words:

Signor Joseph Bossi destroys noxious insects, and lodges at the Pellegrino, Via Larga, No. 79.

Count M——, accustomed to the respect assured by his enormous fortune, his blue blood, and the bravura of his thirty servants, declined to understand the language of this little communication.

Fabrizio wrote still others to Fausta; the Count set spies upon this rival, who might have had his charms; first of all he discovered his real name and, subsequently, that for the moment he could not show himself in Parma. A few days later, Count M——, his *buli*, his splendid horses, and Fausta left for Parma.

Fabrizio, lured on by the game, followed them the next day. It was to no avail that the faithful Ludovic made his touching remonstrances; Fabrizio refused to listen, and Ludovic, himself a brave fellow, admired him for it; moreover this journey brought him closer to his own pretty mistress at Casalmaggiore. With Ludovic's connivance, eight or ten former soldiers of Napoléon's regiments entered Signor Joseph Bossi's service as "domestics." "If," Fabrizio said to himself, as he undertook the madness of following Fausta, "if I am careful to have no communication with Count Mosca, the Minister of Police, or with the Duchess, I am exposing no one but myself to danger. Later on, I shall tell my aunt that I was going to Parma in search of love, that splendid thing I have never encountered. The fact of the matter is that I think of Fausta even when I don't see her. But is it the memory of her voice I love, or her person?" No longer mindful of his ecclesiastical career, Fabrizio was now sporting moustaches and sideburns which were almost as terrible as the Count's and which somewhat disguised him. He established his headquarters not in Parma, which would have been too rash, but in a nearby village in the woods on the Sacca road, where his aunt's castle happened to be. Following Ludovic's advice, he gave himself out in this village as the private servant of a great and eccentric English lord, who expended a hundred thousand francs a year to indulge in the pleasures of the chase, and who would soon be arriving from Lake Como, where he was detained by the trout-fishing. Fortunately, the pretty little palazzo Count M—— had rented for his lovely Fausta was located at the southern end of the city of Parma, specifically on the Sacca road, and Fausta's windows overlooked the fine *allées* of great trees extending beneath the high towers of the Citadel. Fabrizio was quite unknown in this lonely neighborhood; he lost no time in having the Count followed, and one day when the latter had just left the admirable singer's residence, he had the audacity to appear in the street in broad daylight; to tell the truth he was riding an excellent horse, and was well armed to boot. Some musicians, of the kind that are to be found on every street corner in Italy and who are sometimes excellent, came to plant their double-basses under Fausta's windows: after a brief prelude, they sang quite nicely a certain cantata in her honor. Fausta appeared at the window and easily noticed a very well mannered young man who, halting his horse in the middle of the street, made a gesture of greeting and then proceeded to stare in a manner anything but equivocal. Despite the exaggeratedly British costume Fabrizio had adopted, she soon recognized the author of the impassioned letters which had brought about her departure from Bologna. "What an odd man!" she said to herself. "I believe I'm falling in love. I have a hundred louis to spare, I can easily dispense with this terrible Count M——. As it happens, he has little enough wit and never surprises me, and the only thing the least bit entertaining about him is the dreadful appearance of his bodyguard."

The following day, Fabrizio having learned that at eleven every morning Fausta went to hear Mass in the center of town, in that same church of San Giovanni which housed the tomb of his great-uncle Archbishop Ascanio del Dongo, Fabrizio made so bold as to follow her. As it happened, Ludovic had procured for him a splendid English wig of the finest auburn hair. Apropos of the color of this embellishment, which was that of the flames which consumed his heart, Fabrizio produced a sonnet which Fausta purported to find delightful; an unknown hand had taken care to place it upon her piano. This little skirmish lasted some eight days, but Fabrizio found that for all his enterprise in these matters, he was making no real progress; Fausta refused to receive him. His eccentricity was being carried too far; she has subsequently remarked that she was alarmed by him. Fabrizio was now sustained only by a faint hope of managing to feel what is called *love*, but he frequently felt bored.

"*Monsignore*, let us be on our way," Ludovic kept urging him, "you are not in love; I observe you possessed of a mortifying good sense and *sang-froid*. Besides, you are making no progress; out of pure shame, let us decamp!"

Fabrizio was about to leave at the first moment of ill-humor when he learned that Fausta would be performing for the Duchess Sanseverina. "Perhaps that sublime voice will finally inflame my heart," he mused to himself, and actually dared to introduce himself, in disguise, into this palazzo where he was known to all eyes. Judge of the Duchess's emotion when suddenly, as the concert was ending, she noticed a man in *chasseur*'s livery standing near the door of the grand salon; his attitude reminded her of someone. She consulted Count Mosca, who only then informed her of Fabrizio's extreme and really quite incredible folly. He was taking it very well. This infatuation for someone besides the Duchess delighted him; a perfect gentleman in all things but politics, Count Mosca acted upon the theory that he himself could find happiness only so long as the Duchess was happy.

"I shall save him from himself," he told her. "Imagine our enemies' delight if he were to be arrested here in this palazzo! That is why I have more than a hundred men in my service here, and that is why I have asked you for the keys of the great reservoir. He lets it be known that he's madly in love with Fausta and that till now he cannot separate her from Count M——, who affords the absurd creature a queenly existence."

The Duchess's countenance betrayed the keenest pain. "Then Fabrizio is nothing but a libertine quite incapable of serious and tender feelings. Not even to come to see us! That is what I shall never forgive him," she said at last; "and here I've been writing him in Bologna every day!"

"I greatly admire his restraint," the Count replied; "he does not wish to compromise us by this episode, and it will be amusing to hear him tell us about it later on."

Fausta was too silly a creature to be able to keep her concerns to herself: the day after the concert, whose every aria her eyes had addressed to this tall young man in *chasseur*'s livery, she mentioned the existence of an unknown admirer to Count M——.

"Where do you see him?" demanded the Count in a rage.

"In the streets, in church," Fausta answered unthinkingly, and then immediately attempted to counteract her imprudence or at least to get rid of whatever might suggest Fabrizio: she immediately produced an elaborate description of a tall young man with red hair and blue eyes; no doubt it was some rich and clumsy Englishman, or some prince or other. At this word Count M——, who was hardly distinguished for the accuracy of his perceptions, conceived the notion, quite flattering to his vanity, that his rival was none other than the Crown Prince of Parma. This wretched and melancholy young man, guarded by five or six tutors, assistant tutors, instructors, and so on, who permitted him to venture into the world only after holding council, cast strange glances upon any passable woman he was allowed to come near. At the Duchess's concert, his rank had placed him in front of all the guests, on a separate armchair three feet away from lovely Fausta, and her glances had deeply offended Count M——. This folly of extreme vanity—having a prince for a rival—greatly entertained Fausta, who delighted in confirming it by a hundred naïvely furnished details.

"Isn't your lineage," she asked the Count, "just as venerable as that of the House of Farnese to which this young man belongs?"

"What do you mean, *just as venerable*! In my family there is no bastardy, if you please!"*

As chance would have it, Count M—— never had an opportunity to observe this imaginary rival, which only confirmed him in the flattering notion of having a Prince as his antagonist. For when the interests of his project did not summon Fabrizio to Parma, he kept to the woods around Sacca and the banks of the Po. Count M—— was much more arrogant, but also more prudent now that he believed himself in a position to dispute Fausta's heart with a Crown Prince; he requested her quite seriously to exercise the greatest restraint in all her behavior. After falling to his knees as a madly jealous lover, he informed her quite curtly that his honor was involved in her not becoming the young Prince's dupe.

"I should hardly be his dupe, you know, if I loved him; I've never happened to see a Prince at my feet."

"If you yield," the Count continued with a haughty stare, "perhaps I cannot take revenge on the Prince, but I will most assuredly take revenge." And he left, slamming the doors behind him.

---

*Pier-Luigi, first sovereign of the Farnese family, renowned as he was for his virtues, was widely believed to be a natural son of His Holiness Pope Paul III. [Stendhal's note.]

If Fabrizio had presented himself at this moment, he would have gained his cause.

"If you value your life," Count M—— said to Fausta that evening as he left her after the performance, "make certain I never learn the young Prince has entered your house. I can do nothing against him, damn his eyes, but don't remind me of what I can do against you!"

"Ah, my dear little Fabrizio," Fausta exclaimed, "if only I knew where to find you!"

Wounded vanity can take a long ways a young man who is rich and surrounded from the cradle by flatterers. Count M——'s authentic passion for Fausta awakened with a fury: he was not stopped by the dangerous prospect of doing battle with the sole scion of the sovereign in whose territory he was now living; nor had he any mind to see this Prince or at least to have him followed. Unable to attack him in any other way, Count M—— dared contemplate making him appear ridiculous. "I shall be banished forever from the State of Parma," he said to himself, "but what does that matter to me?" Had he sought to reconnoiter his enemy's position, Count M—— would have learned that the poor young Prince never left the palace without being followed by three or four old men, tiresome guardians of protocol, and that the only pleasure of his own choosing he was permitted in all the world was mineralogy. By day as by night, the little palazzo Fausta occupied, to which the best society in Parma thronged, was surrounded by observers; Count M—— knew hour by hour what she was doing and above all what others were doing around her. This much can be said in praise of the Count's jealous precautions: this whimsical woman at first had no notion whatever of this redoubling of surveillance. The reports of all his agents informed Count M—— that a very young man in a red wig appeared quite frequently under Fausta's windows, though always in a different disguise. "Obviously it's the young Prince," Count M—— said to himself, "or else why assume a disguise? And damn it all, a man like me is not made to yield to him. Were it not for the usurpations of the Republic of Venice, I too should be a Sovereign Prince!"

On the Feast of San Stefano the spies' reports assumed a darker coloring; they seemed to indicate that Fausta was beginning to respond to the stranger's suit. "I can take this woman away with me upon the instant!" Count M—— said to himself. "But no, in Bologna I retreated from del Dongo; here I would be retreating from a Prince! But what would this young man say—he might think he has succeeded in scaring me off! And by God, I am of as good a house as he ...!"

Count M—— was in a rage, but the climax of his misery was that he was determined not to appear in Fausta's eyes, knowing her as he did to be of a facetious temperament, in the absurd character of a jealous lover. On the Feast of San Stefano, then, after spending an hour with her, and having been received with an ardor he regarded as the height of insincerity, Count M—— left her around eleven, getting dressed for Mass at the church of San Giovanni. He returned home, put on the shabby black coat of a young seminarian, and hurried to San Giovanni; he selected a hiding-place behind one of the tombs which embellish the third chapel on the right; he saw everything that was happening in the church under the arm of a cardinal represented kneeling on his tomb; this statue cut off the light at the back of the chapel and concealed the Count adequately. Soon he saw Fausta arrive, lovelier than ever; she was in her finest clothes, and twenty admirers from the highest society in Parma escorted her into the church, a smile on her lips and pleasure in her eyes. "Obviously," the jealous wretch decided, "she means to meet here the man she loves and whom, thanks to me, she may have loved long since and could not see." Suddenly the sparkle of delight seemed to redouble in Fausta's eyes. "My rival is here," Count M—— realized, and his rage of vanity knew no bounds. "What a figure I cut here, no more than a pendant to a young Prince in disguise?" But whatever efforts he made, he never managed to discover this rival, whom his eager glances sought on all sides.

After repeatedly looking around the church in every direction, Fausta would let her loving gaze rest on the dark corner where Count M—— had concealed himself. In an impassioned heart, love is likely to exaggerate the slightest nuances, to draw from them the most absurd consequences, and so poor Count M—— ended by convincing himself that Fausta had seen him, that despite all his efforts she had perceived his mortal jealousy, and that she sought to blame and at the same time console him for it by these tender glances.

The cardinal's tomb, behind which Count M—— had taken up his observation post, was four or five feet above the church's marble pavement. The fashionable Mass was over at one, and most of the faithful were leaving, when Fausta dismissed the town *beaux* on the excuse of her devotions; remaining on her knees against a chair, she fixed her eyes, ever more brilliant and tender, on Count M——; since there were now only a few people left in the church, her glances no longer bothered to move about the building before coming to rest so happily upon the cardinal's effigy. "What delicacy!" thought Count M——, believing himself observed. Finally Fausta stood up and suddenly left the church, after making several peculiar movements with her hands.

Count M——, intoxicated with love and almost entirely disabused of his mad jealousy, had left his post in order to rush to his mistress's palazzo and thank her a thousand times when, as he passed in front of the cardinal's tomb, he noticed a young man all in black; this funereal being had remained there all this time, kneeling against the epitaph of the tomb so that the jealous lover's gaze seeking him out might have passed over his head and never discovered him.

This young man stood up, walked quickly, and was instantaneously surrounded by seven or eight rather clumsy persons of odd appearance who seemed to be in his service. Count M—— hurried after him but, without there being anything too noticeable, he was halted in the passageway formed by the wooden drum of the entrance-door by these clumsy men who were protecting his rival; finally, when he reached the street after them, all he could see was the closing door of a rather shabby carriage, which, by a strange contrast, was harnessed to two excellent horses, and which in a moment was out of sight.

He returned home breathless with rage; soon his spies arrived, reporting coldly that today the mysterious lover, disguised as a priest, had knelt quite piously against a tomb placed at the entrance to a dim chapel in the church of San Giovanni. Fausta had remained in the church until it was nearly empty, and then had rapidly exchanged certain signs with this stranger; she seemed to be making some sort of crosses with her hands. Count M—— hastened to his inconstant mistress, who for the first time could not conceal from him her perturbation; she told him with all the lying innocence of a passionate woman that as usual she had gone to San Giovanni, but that she had not seen there this man who was persecuting her. Upon these words Count M——, beside himself, called her the vilest names and told her all that he himself had seen, and since the boldness of her lies increased with the intensity of his accusations, he seized his dagger and flung himself upon her. With great composure Fausta said to him:

"All right, then, everything you accuse me of is quite true, though I have tried to conceal it from you in order not to force your audacity into mad plots of vengeance which might ruin both of us; for you should know once and for all, according to my observation, the man who is persecuting me with his attentions is not likely to find any obstacles to his intentions, at least in this country."

Having skillfully reminded Count M—— that after all he had no rights over her, Fausta ended by saying that she would probably never return to the Church of San Giovanni. Count M—— was head over heels in love, a little coquetry had managed to add itself to the prudence in this young woman's heart, and he felt completely disarmed. It occurred to him that he might leave Parma; the young Prince, powerful though he might be, could scarcely follow him, or if he did so would no longer be anything but his equal. But pride once again reminded him that such a departure would always seem a retreat, and Count M—— forbade himself to think of such a thing.

"He doesn't suspect my little Fabrizio's presence," the singer realized with delight, "and now we can make a perfect fool of him!"

Fabrizio never guessed his good luck, finding the singer's windows sealed tight the next day; catching no glimpse of Fausta he was beginning to find the joke a little long. He was having second thoughts. "In what position am I putting poor Count Mosca, who after all is the Minister of Police! He will be thought to be my accomplice, and I will be supposed to have come here to destroy his fortunes! But if I abandon a plan made so long ago, what will the Duchess say when I tell her of my attempts at love?"

One evening, ready to throw up the game, he was reasoning matters thus to himself as he prowled under the big trees dividing Fausta's palazzo from the Citadel. He noticed that he was being followed by a spy of extremely small stature; it was in vain that in order to shake him he turned into one street after another; nonetheless this microscopic being seemed glued to his footsteps.

Impatient, he ran down a solitary street along the River Parma, where his men were waiting in ambush; on a sign from him they leaped upon the poor little spy, who flung himself at their feet; this was *Bettina,* Fausta's chambermaid; after three days of boredom and seclusion, disguised as a man in order to escape Count M——'s dagger, of which both she and her mistress were terrified, she had undertaken to come and tell Fabrizio that he was passionately loved and that her mistress was burning to see him; but they could no longer appear in the church of San Giovanni. "Just in time," Fabrizio said to himself. "Hurrah for persistence!"

The little chambermaid was quite pretty, which did away with Fabrizio's moral reveries. She informed him that the promenade and all the streets through which he had passed that evening were cunningly watched, without his having to appear there, by Count M——'s spies. They had rented rooms on the ground floor or the first floor; hidden behind the blinds and maintaining absolute silence, they watched everything that was happening in the street, apparently so lonely, and heard everything that was said there.

"If these spies had recognized my voice," said little Bettina, "I would be repeatedly stabbed upon returning home, and perhaps my poor mistress with me."

Her terror rendered her charming, in Fabrizio's eyes.

"Count M——," she continued, "is furious, and Madame knows that he is capable of anything. . . . She has asked me to tell you that she wishes she were a hundred leagues away from here—with you!"

Then Bettina described the scene of the Feast of San Stefano and Count M——'s fury, having missed none of the glances and signs of love which Fausta, madly in love with Fabrizio that day, had made to him. The Count had drawn his dagger, had seized Fausta by the hair, and without her presence of mind she would have been lost.

Fabrizio took pretty Bettina upstairs into a little apartment he kept nearby. He told her that he was from Turin, the son of a great figure who for the moment was staying in Parma, which obliged him to exercise the utmost discretion. Bettina answered with a laugh that he was a much greater gentleman than he chose to appear. Our hero required a little time to realize that the charming girl was taking him for no less a personage than the Crown Prince himself. Fausta was beginning to be afraid and to love Fabrizio; she had determined not to reveal his name to her chambermaid, and to speak of him as the Prince. Fabrizio ended by confessing to this pretty girl that she had guessed correctly:

"But if my name is mentioned," he added, "despite the grand passion I have revealed so many times to your mistress, I shall be forced to stop seeing her, and immediately my father's ministers, those wicked scarecrows I shall one day get rid of myself, will not fail to send her orders to leave the country, which hitherto she has so embellished by her presence."

Toward morning, Fabrizio and the pretty chambermaid worked out several plans enabling him to meet Fausta: he sent for Ludovic and another of his cunning servants, who came to an understanding with Bettina while he was writing the most extravagant letter to Fausta; the situation involved all the exaggerations of tragedy, and Fabrizio made good use of them. It was only at dawn that he parted from the little chambermaid, herself quite satisfied with the manners of the young Prince.

It had been repeated a hundred times over that, Fausta having now reached an understanding with her lover, the latter was no longer to pass beneath the windows of the little palazzo except when he could be received there, and at those times a signal would be given. But Fabrizio, infatuated with Bettina and believing himself on the verge of a *dénouement* with Fausta, could scarcely remain in his village two leagues away from Parma. Toward midnight the following evening, he arrived on horseback, and with a considerable escort, to sing under her windows a serenade fashionable at the time, though he altered the words. "Isn't this how those gentlemen the lovers behave?" he asked himself.

Ever since Fausta had shown a desire to meet him, this entire pursuit seemed quite tedious to Fabrizio. "No, I am certainly not in love," he said to himself, singing rather badly beneath the windows of the little palazzo; "Bettina strikes me as infinitely preferable to Fausta, and it's with her I'd rather be at this moment." Quite bored, Fabrizio was returning to his village when at five hundred paces from Fausta's palazzo fifteen or twenty men threw themselves upon him, four of them seizing his horse's bridle, two others holding his arms. Ludovic and Fabrizio's own *bravi* were attacked but managed to escape; a few pistol-shots were fired. It was all the affair of a moment: fifty lighted torches appeared in the street in the twinkling of an eye and as if by magic. All these men were well armed. Fabrizio had leaped down from his horse, despite the men holding him; he attempted to break away, and even wounded one of the men holding his arms in a vise-like grip; but he was astounded to hear this man say in the most respectful tone of voice:

"Your Highness will grant me a good pension for this wound, which will be worth more to me than committing the crime of *lèse-majesté* by drawing my sword against my Prince."

"This is the just punishment for my foolishness," Fabrizio said to himself, "I shall have damned myself for a sin which didn't even seem attractive to me."

No sooner was the little skirmish over when several lackeys in full livery appeared with a gilded and brightly painted sedan-chair, one of those grotesque chairs the maskers use during Carnival. Six men, daggers drawn, requested His Highness to go inside, observing that the cool night air might do harm to his voice; the most respectful forms of address were employed, the title of Prince was repeated several times over, almost at a shout. The procession began to move past. Fabrizio counted more than fifty men in the street carrying lighted torches. It might have been one in the morning; people were at every window; the whole episode occurred with a certain gravity. "I was afraid of dagger-thrusts from Count M——," Fabrizio said to himself; "he is satisfied with making a fool of me; I didn't think he had so much taste. But does he really think he's dealing with the Prince? If he knows that I am only Fabrizio, watch out for daggers!"

These fifty men bearing torches and the twenty armed men, after having stood for a long time under Fausta's windows, proceeded to parade in front of the finest palaces of the town. Major-domos walking on either side of the sedan-chair occasionally asked His Highness if he had orders to give them. Fabrizio kept his head; by the light of the torches, he saw that Ludovic and his men were following the procession as closely as they could. Fabrizio said to himself: "Ludovic has only eight or ten men and dares not attack." From inside the sedan-chair, Fabrizio saw clearly that the men carrying out this bad joke were armed to the teeth. He pretended to laugh with the major-domos assigned to look after him. After over two hours of triumphal procession, he saw that they were about to pass the end of the street where the Sanseverina palazzo was situated.

As they were turning the corner of the street that led to it, he quickly opened the door in the front of the sedan-chair, leaped over one of the poles, and with a blow of his dagger felled one of the bullies who thrust his torch in his face; he received a dagger-cut in the shoulder; a second bully burned his beard with his lighted torch, and finally Fabrizio reached Ludovic, to whom he shouted:

"Kill! Kill anyone carrying a torch!"

Ludovic wielded his sword and released Fabrizio from the two men determined to pursue him. He raced to the door of the Sanseverina palazzo; out of curiosity, the porter had opened the little door three feet high that was cut into the main door and was watching in astonishment as this huge number of torches went by. Fabrizio leaped inside and slammed this tiny door behind him; he ran to the garden and escaped through a gate which opened onto a deserted street. An hour later, he was outside the city; by daybreak he had crossed the frontier of the State of Modena and was safe. That evening he reached Bologna. "Here's a fine expedition," he said to himself; "I haven't even been able to speak to my lovely." He hastily wrote letters of apology to the Duchess and Count Mosca, prudent letters which, describing what was transpiring in his heart, could give no information to an enemy. "I was in love with love," he wrote to the Duchess; "I did everything possible to gain knowledge of it, but it seems that nature has not granted me a heart with which to love and be melancholy; I cannot raise myself higher than vulgar pleasures, and so on."

The effect of this incident in Parma was indescribable. The mystery excited curiosity: any number of people had seen the torches and the sedan-chair. But who was this man who had been carried off and toward whom every form of respect had been shown? The next day, no person of note was missing from town.

The townsfolk who lived in the street from which the prisoner had escaped were sure they had seen a corpse, but in daylight, when the inhabitants dared emerge from their houses, they found no further traces of combat but a good deal of blood spilled on the pavement. More than twenty thousand idlers came to have a look at the street by daylight. The cities of Italy are used to singular spectacles, but generally they know the *why* and the *how*. What shocked all Parma on this occasion was that even a month afterward, when people no longer spoke solely of the torchlight procession, no one, thanks to Count Mosca's discretion, had been able to guess the name of the rival who had attempted to take Fausta away from Count M———. This jealous and vindictive lover had taken flight at the very start of the procession. On Count Mosca's orders, Fausta was taken to the Citadel. The Duchess laughed a good deal at the little act of injustice which the Count was obliged to commit in order to arrest the curiosity of the Prince, who might otherwise have managed to discover Fabrizio's name.

There was to be seen in Parma a learned man who had come from the North in order to write a history of the Middle Ages; he was seeking manuscripts in the various libraries, and Count Mosca had given him every possible authorization. But this scholar, though still a young man, behaved in an irascible manner; he believed, for instance, that everyone in Parma was attempting to make fun of him. It is true that children occasionally followed him through the streets on account of an enormous shock of bright-red hair, proudly displayed. This scholar imagined that his inn was charging him exorbitantly for every item, and he would not pay for the merest trifle without looking up the price in the travel-journals of one Mrs. Starke, which had achieved its twentieth edition by indicating to the prudent Englishman the cost of a turkey, an apple, a glass of milk, and so on.

The red-maned scholar, the very afternoon of the day when Fabrizio entered upon his forced procession, made a terrible scene at his inn and took out of his pocket two tiny pistols in order to revenge himself upon the waiter who was asking two soldi for a mediocre peach. He was arrested for the serious crime of carrying pocket pistols!

Since this irascible scholar was tall and thin, it occurred to the Count, the next morning, to pass him off in the Prince's eyes as the foolhardy adventurer who, having attempted to steal Fausta from Count M——, had been hoaxed. Carrying pocket pistols is punishable in Parma by three years in the galleys; but this penalty is never applied. After fifteen days in prison, during which the scholar had seen no one but a lawyer who had inspired him with a dreadful fear of the harsh laws enacted by the cowardice of the officials in power upon those bearing concealed weapons, another lawyer visited the prison and described to the scholar the procession inflicted by Count M—— upon a rival who had remained unknown.

"The police are reluctant to confess to the Prince that they have not been able to determine the identity of this rival: confess that you sought to win Fausta for yourself, that fifty brigands kidnapped you while you were singing under her window, that for an hour you were paraded in a sedan-chair without hearing a single disrespectful word. Such a confession has nothing humiliating about it, you are merely being asked to utter the word. As soon as you do so, you will have relieved the police of their embarrassment, you will be sent off in a postchaise and taken to the border and wished good evening . . ."

For a month the scholar resisted: two or three times the Prince was on the point of having him brought before the Ministry of the Interior and being himself present at the interrogation. But finally he gave up any such notion when the historian, exhausted, decided to confess everything and was taken to the border. The Prince remained convinced that Count M——'s rival had a thicket of red hair.

Three days after the procession, while Fabrizio, in hiding in Bologna, was determining with Ludovic's help how to find Count M——, he learned that he as well was in hiding in a mountain village on the road to Florence. The Count had only three of his *buli* with him; the following day, at the moment when he was returning from a prom- enade, he was kidnapped by eight masked men who led him to believe they were police agents from Parma. He was taken, once he had been blindfolded, to an inn two leagues farther on in the mountains, where he was treated with every possible consideration and a copious supper. He was served the finest wines of Italy and Spain.

"Then am I a prisoner of State?" asked the Count.

"Not at all!" answered Ludovic very politely under his mask. "You have insulted a private individual by deciding to parade him through the streets in a sedan-chair; tomorrow morning, he wants to fight a duel with you. If you kill him, you will find two good horses, some money, and post-relays readied on the road to Genoa."

"What is the name of this bully?" asked the Count in some irrita- tion.

"His name is Bombace. You will have the choice of weapons and good, loyal witnesses, but it is necessary that one of you two die!"

"But that's murder!" the Count exclaimed in alarm.

"Heaven forbid! It's merely a duel to the death with the young man whom you paraded through the streets of Parma in the middle of the night, and who would remain dishonored if you were to remain alive. One of the two of you is superfluous on this earth, so try to kill him; you will have foils, pistols, sabers—all the weapons we have managed to obtain in a few hours, for haste is of the essence; the police in Bologna are extremely diligent, as you may know, and must not be permitted to prevent this duel necessary to the honor of the young man of whom you made such a fool."

"But if this young man is a Prince . . ."

"He is a private individual like yourself, and indeed much less rich than you, but he seeks a duel to the death, and he will oblige you to fight, I warn you."

"I am afraid of nothing in the world!" exclaimed Count M——.

"That is what your adversary most passionately desires," replied Ludovic. "Tomorrow, very early in the morning, prepare yourself to defend your life; it will be attacked by a man who has reason to be highly incensed and who will spare you nothing; I repeat that you will have the choice of weapons; and draw up your will."

Toward six the following morning, Count M—— was served breakfast; then a door of the bedroom where he was kept under guard was opened and he was requested to pass into the courtyard of a country inn; this yard was surrounded by rather high hedges and walls, and the doors had been carefully closed.

In a corner, on a table which Count M—— was requested to approach, he found several bottles of wine and brandy, two pistols, two foils, two sabers, as well as paper and ink; some twenty peasants were at the windows of the inn overlooking the yard. The Count begged for mercy. "They're going to murder me!" he screamed. "Save my life!"

"You deceive yourself, or you seek to deceive others," exclaimed Fabrizio, who was in the opposite corner of the yard, beside a table covered with weapons.

He was in shirtsleeves, and his face was concealed by one of those wire masks such as are found in fencing establishments.

"I invite you," Fabrizio added, "to put on the fencing-mask which is beside you, and then to advance upon me with a foil or with pistols; as you were told last night, you have the choice of weapons."

Count M—— made countless objections, and seemed quite reluctant to fight; Fabrizio, for his part, feared the arrival of the police, though they were in the mountains some five leagues outside Bologna; he ended by addressing the vilest insults to his rival; finally he had the good fortune to enrage Count M——, who snatched up a foil and advanced toward Fabrizio; the duel began rather languidly.

After a few minutes, it was interrupted by a tremendous noise. Our hero had been well aware that he was involving himself in an action which might be a subject of reproach or at least of calumnious imputations for the rest of his life. He had sent Ludovic into the countryside to recruit witnesses. Ludovic gave some money to some strangers passing through a nearby woods; they came running in, shouting, imagining that they were expected to kill an enemy of the man who was paying them. Having reached the inn, Ludovic requested them to keep their eyes open and to determine whether one of these two young men engaged in combat was acting unfairly or taking illicit advantage of the other.

The duel momentarily interrupted by the shouts of these peasants was slow in starting over; Fabrizio once again offered insults to the Count's conceit. "Signor Conte," he shouted to him, "when one is insolent, one must be brave. I recognize that such a condition is hard for you; you prefer to pay others to be brave for you."

The Count, stung once more, began shouting that he had long frequented the fencing-hall of the celebrated Battistin in Naples, and that he would punish such insolence; Count M——'s anger having finally reappeared, he fought with considerable determination, which did not keep Fabrizio from giving him a good deep thrust in the chest, which kept him in bed for several months. Ludovic, bestowing first aid upon the wounded man, whispered in his ear: "If you report this duel to the police, I shall have you stabbed in your bed."

Fabrizio escaped to Florence; since he had remained in hiding in Bologna, it was only in Florence that he received all the Duchess's reproachful letters; she could not forgive him for having come to her concert without attempting to speak to her. Fabrizio was delighted by the letters from Count Mosca, which breathed a sincere friendship and the noblest sentiments. He guessed that the Count had written to Bologna, in such a manner as to allay the suspicions which might weigh upon him with regard to the duel; the police behaved with perfect fairness: they reported that two strangers, of whom only one, the wounded man, was known (Count M——), had fought a duel with foils, before more than thirty peasants, among whom were found, toward the end of the skirmish, the village priest who had made vain efforts to separate the combatants. Since the name of Joseph Bossi had not been uttered, less than two months later Fabrizio made so bold as to return to Bologna, more convinced than ever that his fate had doomed him never to know the noble and intellectual side of love. This he indulged himself in explaining at great length to the Duchess; he was quite weary of his solitary life and passionately desired, now, to return to the charming evenings he had spent with the Count and his aunt. He had not tasted the pleasures of good society since that time.

I find so tedious the thought of the love I attempted to enjoy with Fausta, *he wrote to the Duchess,* that were her whims to favor me now, I would not travel twenty leagues to hold her to her word; therefore have no fears, as you say you have, that I will go to Paris, where I hear she is performing with tremendous success. I shall travel any number of leagues to spend an evening with you and with the Count, who is so good to his friends.

CHAPTER FOURTEEN

While Fabrizio was pursuing love in a village near Parma, Chief Justice Rassi, who had no idea he was in the vicinity, continued to deal with his case as if he had been a Liberal: he feigned being unable to find, or rather intimidated, any witnesses for the defense; and finally, after an extremely learned labor of nearly a year, and around two months after Fabrizio's return to Bologna, on a certain Friday, the Marchesa Raversi, intoxicated with joy, informed her salon that the following day the sentence pronounced only an hour ago against young del Dongo would be presented for the Prince's signature and approval. A few minutes later the Duchess learned of her enemy's words. "The Count must be very ill served by his agents!" she mused. "Only this morning he believed that the sentence could not be rendered for another week. Perhaps he would not be sorry to send my young Grand Vicar away from Parma; but," she added with a lilt in her voice, "we shall see him back here, and one of these days he will be our Archbishop." The Duchess rang: "Gather all the servants in the antechamber," she said to her footman, "even the cooks; go ask the officer on duty for the necessary permission to obtain four post-horses, and then have these horses harnessed to my landau within half an hour."

All the women of the household were busily packing trunks, while the Duchess hurriedly selected a traveling costume, all without a word to the Count; the notion of playing a little trick on him filled her with delight.

"My friends," she said to her assembled staff, "I have learned that my poor nephew is about to be condemned *in absentia* for having had the audacity to defend his life against a madman, that Giletti who attempted to kill him. Each of you has had occasion to observe how sweet and harmless Fabrizio's character is. Rightfully outraged by this cruel insult, I am leaving for Florence: I am leaving each of you ten years' wages. If you are unhappy, write me, and as long as I have a single sequin, there will be something for you."

The Duchess believed just what she was saying, and at her last words the servants dissolved in tears; she too had moist eyes, and added in a moved tone of voice: "Pray to God for me and for Monsignore Fabrizio del Dongo, First Grand Vicar of the Diocese, who tomorrow morning will be sentenced to the galleys or, which would be less absurd, to the death penalty."

The servants' tears redoubled and gradually changed to virtually seditious cries; the Duchess got into her carriage and had herself driven to the Prince's palace. Despite the undue hour, she had General Fontana, the aide-de-camp on duty, request an audience; she was not in court dress, which cast the general into a state of profound astonishment. As for the Prince, he was not at all surprised, and still less annoyed by this request for an audience. "We shall see tears shed by these fine eyes," he said to himself, rubbing his hands. "She is coming to ask for a pardon; at last this proud beauty will be humbled! She was all too unendurable with her little airs of independence! Those expressive eyes always seemed to be telling me, whenever the slightest thing annoyed her, *Naples and Milan would provide a sojourn much more agreeable than your little town of Parma.* True, I do not rule over Naples or Milan, but finally this great lady is coming to ask me for something that depends on myself alone, something she is burning to have; I've always thought that this nephew's arrival would bring me some advantage or other."

While the Prince was smiling at these thoughts and indulging himself in all these pleasant anticipations, he was striding up and down his study, at the door of which General Fontana had remained standing stiff as a soldier presenting arms. Seeing the Prince's shining eyes and recalling the Duchess's traveling costume, he imagined the dissolution of the monarchy. His amazement knew no bounds when he heard the Prince inform him: "Request Her Grace the Duchess to wait a quarter of an hour or so."

General Fontana turned on his heel like a soldier on parade; the Prince smiled once more: "Fontana is not accustomed," he said to himself, "to seeing this proud Duchess kept waiting: the astonished expression with which he will tell her about the *quarter of an hour or so* will prepare the way for the touching tears this very room will soon see shed." This quarter of an hour or so was delightful for the Prince; he strode up and down with a firm and steady gait, he *reigned.* "Nothing must be said here that is not perfectly appropriate; whatever my feelings toward the Duchess, it must not be forgotten that she is one of the greatest ladies of my court. How did Louis XIV speak to the princesses his daughters when he had occasion to be displeased with them?" And his eyes stopped at the portrait of the *Roi Soleil.*

Amusingly enough, it never occurred to the Prince to wonder if he would pardon Fabrizio, and what such a pardon would mean. Finally, after some twenty minutes, the faithful Fontana reappeared at the door, but without saying a word.

"Let Duchess Sanseverina come in," the Prince exclaimed quite theatrically. "The tears are going to begin," he said to himself, and as if to be prepared for such a spectacle, he drew out his handkerchief.

Never had the Duchess been so gay, and so pretty; she looked no more than twenty-five. As he watched her tiny steps skim across the carpets, the poor aide-de-camp was about to lose his wits.

"I have many pardons to ask of Your Serene Highness," the Duchess said in her light, gay little voice, "I have taken the liberty of presenting myself here in a costume which is not precisely suitable, but Your Highness has so accustomed me to your kindness that I have ventured to hope you would deign to grant me one more."

The Duchess spoke quite slowly, in order to give herself time to enjoy the Prince's countenance: it was delicious on account of its profound astonishment as well as the remainder of the grand airs which the position of the head and arms still retained. The Prince had remained as though thunderstruck; in his shrill, troubled little voice he kept exclaiming, though almost inaudibly: *"What's this? What's this?"*

The Duchess, as though out of respect, having finished her compliment, left him plenty of time to reply; then she added:

"I venture to hope that Your Serene Highness will deign to forgive the incongruity of my dress."

But in speaking so, her mocking eyes shone with so lively a luster that the Prince could not endure it; he stared up at the ceiling, which in him was the last sign of the most extreme embarrassment. *"What's this? What's this?"* he said again. Then he was lucky enough to hit upon a phrase: "Your Grace, be seated."

He even pushed a chair toward her with a certain ease. The Duchess was not insensible of this sign of politeness and subdued the intensity of her gaze.

"What's this? What's this?" the Prince repeated a third time, wriggling in his armchair, where he seemed unable to find a firm support.

"I shall be taking advantage of the cool night air to travel by post," the Duchess continued, "and since my absence may last some time, I did not want to leave Your Serene Highness's territories without thanking you for all the kindnesses you have deigned to show me over the last five years."

At these words the Prince understood at last; he turned pale: this was a man who suffered more than anyone in the world at finding himself mistaken in his anticipations; then he assumed an air of grandeur quite worthy of the portrait of Louis XIV which was before his eyes. "At last," the Duchess said to herself, "he is behaving like a man."

"And what is the reason for this sudden departure," the Prince inquired in a steady tone of voice.

"I had been planning on it for some time," the Duchess replied, "and a little insult offered to *Monsignore* del Dongo, who tomorrow will be sentenced to death or the galleys, has made me hasten my departure."

"And to what city will you be going?"

"To Naples, I suppose." And as she stood up, she added: "There remains for me only to take leave of Your Serene Highness and to thank you very humbly for all your *former kindnesses.*"

In her turn she spoke so steadily that the Prince realized that in two seconds everything would be over; the scandal of the departure having occurred, he knew that any compromise was impossible; she was not a woman to go back on her word. He ran after her. "But you know quite well, Your Grace," he said, taking her hand, "that I have always cared for you, and that it was entirely up to you to give my friendship another name altogether. A murder has been committed, that is what cannot be denied; I have entrusted the investigation of the case to my best judges . . ."

At these words, the Duchess drew herself up to her full height; every appearance of respect and even of urbanity vanished in a twinkling of an eye: the outraged woman stood revealed, and the outraged woman addressing herself to someone whom she knew to be acting in bad faith. It was with the expression of the liveliest anger and even of contempt that she observed to the Prince, weighing each of her words: "I am leaving forever Your Serene Highness's territories, in order never to hear the name of Justice Rassi and the other infamous assassins who have sentenced to death my nephew and so many others; if Your Serene Highness prefers not to intermix a sentiment of bitterness with the last moments I have to spend with a Prince so refined and witty when he is not deceived, I humbly implore you not to bring to mind the very idea of these infamous judges who sell themselves for a thousand scudi or a decoration."

The admirable and especially sincere accent with which these words were spoken made the Prince shudder; for a moment he feared seeing his dignity compromised by an even more direct accusation, but on the whole his sensation soon turned to one of pleasure: he was admiring the Duchess; the whole of her person at this moment attained to a sublime beauty. "Great God! How lovely she is," the Prince said to himself; "something must be conceded to a woman so unique— there may not be another like her in all of Italy. . . . Well now, with a little diplomacy it shouldn't be impossible to make her my mistress one of these days; what a difference between such a creature and that doll of a Marchesa Balbi, who every year still manages to steal at least three hundred thousand francs from my poor subjects. . . . But did I hear her correctly?" he suddenly realized. "She said *sentenced to death my nephew and so many others.*"

Whereupon rage overcame him, and it was with an hauteur worthy of his supreme rank that the Prince said, after a silence: "And what must be done to keep Your Grace from leaving us?"

"Something of which you are incapable," the Duchess retorted with the accent of the bitterest irony and the most ill-concealed scorn.

The Prince was beside himself, but he owed it to the habit of his position as absolute sovereign that he had the power to resist a first impulse. "I must have this woman," he said to himself, "I owe it to myself, and then I must kill her with contempt. . . . If she leaves this room, I shall never see her again." But, intoxicated with rage and hatred as he was at this moment, how was he to find the words which might satisfy what he owed himself and at the same time convince the Duchess not to abandon his court that very moment? "A gesture," he said to himself, "a gesture can neither be reported nor made into a joke," and he went over to stand between the Duchess and the door of his study. At that moment he heard someone scratching at that very door.

"Who is the damned idiot," he roared at the top of his lungs, "who is the damned idiot who is foisting his imbecile presence upon me here?"

Poor General Fontana showed his pale and agonized countenance, and it was with the expression of a man in his final agony that he uttered these barely audible words: "His Excellency Count Mosca requests the honor to be introduced."

"Have him come in!" shouted the Prince. And as Mosca was bowing: "All right, all right, here is Her Grace the Duchess Sanseverina, who says she is leaving Parma this moment for Naples, and who is offering me any amount of insolence!"

"What's that?" asked Mosca, turning pale.

"You mean you knew nothing of this plan of hers?"

"Not the first syllable; I left Her Grace at six o'clock, happy and, I believe, satisfied."

This remark produced an incredible effect upon the Prince. First he stared at Mosca, whose growing pallor revealed that he was speaking the truth and was no accomplice in the Duchess's enterprise. "In which case," the Prince said to himself, "I am losing her forever; pleasure and revenge, everything is vanishing at the same time. In Naples, she will be composing epigrams with her nephew Fabrizio on the great wrath of the little Prince of Parma." He stared at the Duchess; the most violent contempt was disputing with the most violent anger for possession of her heart; her eyes at this moment were fixed upon Count Mosca, and the delicate contours of that lovely mouth expressed the bitterest disdain. Her entire countenance said: *Vile courtier!* "So," thought the Prince, after scrutinizing her, "I am losing this means of getting her back in my court. At this very moment, if she leaves the room, she is lost to me. God knows what she will say about my judges in Naples. . . . And with that wit and that divine power of persuasion Heaven has given her, she will make the whole world believe her. To her I shall owe my reputation as an absurd tyrant who gets up in the middle of the night to look under his bed . . ." Then, by an adroit gesture, as though attempting to stride back and forth in the room to diminish his agitation, the Prince once again put himself in front of the door; the Count was three paces to his right, pale, undone, and trembling so greatly that he was obliged to lean on the back of the armchair the Duchess had occupied at the beginning of the audience and which the Prince, in an impulse of rage, had pushed away. The Count was in love. "If the Duchess leaves, I shall follow her," he was saying to himself; "but will she want me in her entourage? That is the question."

To the Prince's left, the Duchess was standing, arms crossed and pressed against her breast, staring at him with a splendid insolence; a complete and profound pallor had succeeded the vivid colors which just now had animated this sublime countenance.

The Prince, unlike the other two persons in the room, was redfaced and evidently anxious; his left hand toyed convulsively with the Cross attached to the Grand Cordon of his Order which he wore under his coat; with his right hand he stroked his chin. "What is to be done?" he said to the Count, without quite knowing what he himself was doing and carried away by his habit of consulting him on every occasion.

"I have no idea, Your Serene Highness," the Count replied with the look of a man in the last agonies. He could barely speak the words of his answer. The tone of his voice gave the Prince the first consolation his wounded pride had been able to find in this entire audience, and this grain of happiness afforded him a phrase that did his vanity good.

"Well then," he said, "I am the most sensible of the three of us; I am quite willing to set aside my position in the world; I shall speak here *as a friend.*" And he added, with a fine smile of condescension carefully imitated from the happy days of Louis XIV: "*As a friend speaking to friends.* Your Grace," he went on, "what must be done in order to make you forget such an untimely resoluion?"

"I have no idea," the Duchess replied with a deep sigh. "To tell the truth, I have no idea, so greatly do I hold Parma in horror."

There was no epigrammatic impulse in this remark; it was evident that sincerity itself was speaking through her mouth.

The Count suddenly turned to one side; his courtier's soul was scandalized; then he cast an imploring glance at his Prince. With great dignity and *sang-froid,* the Prince let a moment pass; then he addressed the Count: "I see," he said, "that your charming friend is quite beside herself; it is simple enough: she adores her nephew." And, turning toward the Duchess, he added, with a glance filled with gallantry and at the same time with the kind of expression assumed for quoting a line from a play: *"What is to be done to please these fine eyes?"*

The Duchess had had time to reflect; in a slow and steady tone of voice, as if she were dictating her ultimatum, she replied: "Your Highness would write me a gracious letter of the kind you know so well how to compose; it would tell me that, not convinced of the guilt of Fabrizio del Dongo, the Archbishop's First Grand Vicar, you will not sign the sentence when it is presented to you, and that this unjust procedure will have no future consequences."

"What do you mean *unjust!*" exclaimed the Prince, reddening to the whites of his eyes and growing angry all over again.

"Nor is that all," the Duchess replied with a Roman pride; "*as of this evening,* and," she added glancing at the clock, "it is already a quarter past eleven, as of this evening Your Serene Highness will send word to the Marchesa Raversi that she is advised to proceed to the country to recover from the fatigue which must have been caused by a certain trial of which she was speaking in her salon earlier this evening."

The Prince was walking back and forth like a man in a fury. "Whoever saw such a woman . . . ?" he exclaimed. "She has no respect for me."

The Duchess replied with complete equanimity, "In all my life it has never occurred to me to lack respect for Your Serene Highness; your Highness has had the extreme condescension to say that you were speaking *as a friend to friends.* Moreover, I have no desire to remain in Parma," she added, glancing at the Count with utter contempt.

This glance galvanized the Prince, hitherto quite uncertain, though these words might have seemed to herald a commitment; little he cared for words.

A few more remarks were exchanged, but finally Count Mosca received orders to write the gracious letter sought by the Duchess. He omitted the phrase *this unjust procedure will have no future consequences.* "It suffices," the Count said to himself, "that the Prince promise not to sign the sentence which will be presented to him." The Prince thanked him, as he signed, with a glance.

The Count was greatly mistaken, for the Prince was tired and would have signed anything; he believed he was well out of the episode, and in his eyes the entire situation was dominated by these words: "If the Duchess leaves, I shall find my court a bore before the week is out." The Count noticed that his master corrected the date, and substituted that of the following day. He glanced at the clock, which showed that the time was nearly midnight. The Minister saw in this corrected date no more than the pedantic desire to give proof of exactitude and good government. As to the Marchesa Raversi's banishment, it was of no special account; the Prince took a special pleasure in banishing people.

"General Fontana!" he exclaimed, opening the door.

The general appeared, his face so amazed and so inquisitive that there was a lively glance exchanged between the Count and the Duchess, and this glance made peace between them.

"General Fontana," said the Prince, "you will take my carriage waiting in the colonnade, you will go to the Marchesa Raversi's, you will have yourself announced; if she is in bed, you will add that you come on my behalf, and once you are in her bedroom, you will say these very words and no others: 'Marchesa Raversi, His Serene Highness advises you to leave tomorrow, before eight in the morning, for your Castle at Velleja; His Highness will inform you when you may return to Parma.' "

The Prince's eyes sought those of the Duchess, who, without thanking him as he expected, made a deep and extremely respectful curtsy and quickly left the room.

"What a woman!" said the Prince, turning toward Count Mosca.

The Count, delighted by the banishment of Marchesa Raversi, which would facilitate all his functions as Minister, spoke for a good half-hour as the consummate courtier he was; he sought to console his Sovereign's vanity and took his leave only when he saw the Prince was indeed convinced that the anecdotal history of Louis XIV had no finer page than the one he himself had just furnished his future historians.

Returning to her palace, the Duchess closed her door and gave orders that no one was to be admitted, not even the Count. She wanted to be alone with her thoughts, and to determine how she should regard the scene which had just occurred. She had acted impulsively and to grant herself the pleasure of the moment; but whatever she had been led to do, she had done it with a certain steadiness of manner. She had nothing to reproach herself for, and she recovered her usual *sang-froid* with the notion that there was even less to regret: such was the character she owed it to herself to display as the prettiest woman at court at the age of thirty-six.

She speculated at this moment as to what Parma might have to offer by way of entertainment, as she might have done upon returning from a long journey, so deeply had she been convinced, between nine and eleven, that she would be leaving this country forever.

"The poor Count cut a funny figure when he learned, in the Prince's presence, that I was leaving. . . . Well, he's a lovable man and a true heart! He would have abandoned his ministries to follow me. . . . But it's also true that for five long years he hasn't had a single distraction to reproach me for. What women married at the altar could say as much to their lord and master? It must be admitted that the Count is neither self-important nor pedantic; he never tempts me to deceive him; in my presence he always seems to be ashamed of his own powers. . . . What a figure he cut in the presence of his lord and master; if he were here I would throw my arms around him. . . . But for nothing in the world would I take it upon myself to console a Minister who has lost his portfolio—that is a sickness cured only by death . . . and the cause of death as well. What a misfortune it would be to be a young Minister! I must write him, that's one of those things he should know officially before quarreling with his Prince. . . . But I am forgetting my good servants."

The Duchess rang. Her women were still busy packing her trunks; the carriage had come to the door and was being loaded; all the servants who had no work to do were standing around this carriage, tears in their eyes. Cecchina, who on great occasions was the only one entitled to enter the Duchess's bedroom, informed her of all these details. "Have them come upstairs," said the Duchess.

A moment later, she walked into the antechamber. "I have been promised," she told them, "that the sentence against my nephew will not be signed by the Sovereign"—this is the word used in Italy—"I am postponing my departure; we shall see if my enemies will have the power to change this resolution."

After a brief silence, the servants began exclaiming, "Long live Her Grace the Duchess!" and applauding furiously. The Duchess, already in the next room, reappeared like an actress taking a bow, curtsied gracefully to her people, and said, "*My friends, I thank you.*"

Had she said the word, all of them, at that moment, would have marched upon the Palace to attack it. The Duchess beckoned to a postilion, a former smuggler and a devoted servant, who followed her.

"You will dress as a prosperous farmer, you will leave Parma any way you can, you will hire a *sediola* and go as fast as you can to Bologna. You will enter the town as a stroller, and through the Florence gate, and you will hand Fabrizio, who is at the *Pellegrino*, a package which Cecchina will give you. Fabrizio is in hiding and is known there as Joseph Bossi; do not betray him by some stupidity, and don't appear to know who he is; my enemies may set spies on your heels. Fabrizio will send you back here in a few hours or a few days: it is especially on the return journey that you must redouble your precautions not to betray him."

"Ah! the Marchesa Raversi's people!" the postilion exclaimed. "We'll be waiting for them, and if Your Grace gives the word, we shall exterminate them all."

"Some day, perhaps! But promise on your life to do nothing without my orders."

It was a copy of the Prince's letter which the Duchess intended to send to Fabrizio; she could not resist the pleasure of entertaining him, and added a word concerning the scene which had produced the letter; this "word" became a letter of ten pages. She called back the postilion. "You cannot leave," she told him, "until four in the morning, when the gates are opened."

"I was going to make my way out through the main sewer, there would be water up to my chin, but I'd get through . . ."

"No," the Duchess said, "I don't want to expose to a fever one of my most faithful servants. Do you know anyone in Monsignore the Archbishop's household?"

"The second coachman is a friend of mine."

"Here is a letter for that saintly prelate: make your way into his Palace without any fuss, get yourself taken to his footman; I don't want Monsignore to be awakened. If he's already in his bedroom, spend the night in the Palace, and since he usually gets up at dawn, at four tomorrow morning have yourself announced on my behalf, ask for the holy Archbishop's blessing, and give him this package, and take whatever letters he may give you for Bologna."

The Duchess was sending the Archbishop the original of the Prince's letter; since this letter concerned his First Grand Vicar, she requested him to deposit it in the archiepiscopal archives, where she hoped that the Grand Vicars and the canons, her nephew's colleagues, would be so good as to become familiar with it; all under conditions of the profoundest secrecy.

The Duchess wrote to Monsignore Landriani with a familiarity which would enchant this good bourgeois; her signature alone took up three lines; the letter, an extremely agreeable one, was followed by these words: *Angelina-Cornelia-Isola Valserra del Dongo, Duchess Sanseverina.*

"I haven't written so much, I suspect," the Duchess said to herself with a smile, "since my marriage contract with the poor Duke; but these people can only be managed by such things, and in the eyes of the bourgeois, it is a caricature which constitutes beauty." She could not end the evening without yielding to the temptation of writing a letter of persiflage to the poor Count; she informed him officially, *for his guidance,* she said, *in his relations with crowned heads,* that she did not feel herself capable of consoling a Minister in disgrace. "The Prince frightens you; when you can no longer see him, will I be the one to frighten you?" She had this letter delivered immediately.

For his part, at seven the next morning, the Prince summoned Count Zurla, Minister of the Interior. "Once again," he said, "give the strictest orders to all the magistrates that they must arrest Signor Fabrizio del Dongo. We are informed that he may venture to reappear in our territories. While this fugitive from justice is in Bologna, where he appears to defy the pursuits of our tribunals, post *shirri* who are personally acquainted with him: (1) on the road from Bologna to Parma; (2) around the Duchess Sanseverina's castle, at Sacca, and around her house at Castelnovo; (3) around Count Mosca's castle. I venture to hope that your sagacity, my dear Count, will manage to conceal these orders of your Sovereign from the penetration of Count Mosca. Understand that I want Signor Fabrizio del Dongo arrested."

As soon as this Minister had left, a secret door admitted into the Prince's study Chief Justice Rassi, who advanced bent double, bowing still lower at every step. The countenance of this rascal was a picture: it did justice to the entire infamy of his role, and, while the rapid and chaotic movements of his eyes betrayed what knowledge he had of his merits, the arrogant and grimacing assurance of his mouth showed that he was well able to measure himself against contempt.

Since this personage will be acquiring considerable influence over Fabrizio's destiny, we may say a word concerning him here. He was tall, with fine, extremely intelligent eyes, but a face ruined by smallpox; as for reason, he had plenty of that, and of the subtlest variety; he was considered to know all there was to know about the law, but it was especially by his talents of resourcefulness that he shone. Whatever aspect a case might present, he readily found, and in very short order, the appropriate legal means of arriving at a conviction or an acquittal; above all he was a past-master in the subtleties of prosecution.

This man, whose services great kingdoms might well have envied the Prince of Parma, was known to have but one passion: to converse intimately with great personages and to entertain them by his buffooneries. It mattered little to him that the eminent man laughed at what he said, or at how he looked, or made disgusting jokes about Signora Rassi; provided he was seen to laugh and provided he treated Rassi himself with familiarity, he was satisfied. Occasionally the Prince, not knowing how to insult the dignity of this great jurist any further, would give him a kick; if the kicks hurt, Rassi would begin to cry. But his sense of buffoonery was so powerful that he might be seen any day of the week preferring the salon of a Minister who flouted him to his own, where he reigned despotically over every black gown of the country. Rassi had made a special position for himself, in that it was impossible for the most insolent nobleman to humiliate him; his way of taking revenge for the insults he suffered all day long was to relate them to the Prince, who had granted him the privilege of saying anything at all; it is true that the response was frequently a well-aimed slap, and one that stung, but Rassi took no umbrage at that. The presence of this great jurist distracted the Prince in his moments of ill humor, when he found it amusing to tease the fellow. It is evident that Rassi was a virtually perfect courtier: without honor and without humor.

"Secrecy above all!" the Prince exclaimed without any form of greeting, and treating Rassi—he who was so polite with everyone—as if he were some sort of scullion. "From when is your sentence dated?"

"As of yesterday morning, Serene Highness."

"How many judges have signed it?"

"All five."

"And the penalty?"

"Twenty years in the fortress, as Your Serene Highness told me."

"The death penalty would have caused some sort of rebellion," said the Prince, as though speaking to himself, "but it's a pity! What an effect on that woman! But he *is* a del Dongo, and this name is revered in Parma, on account of the three Archbishops virtually in succession.... You said twenty years in the fortress?"

"Yes, Serene Highness," replied Justice Rassi, still standing bent double, "with, beforehand, a public apology before Your Serene Highness's portrait; furthermore, bread and water every Friday and on the eve of all chief holidays, *the subject being of notorious impiety.* This for the future and to ruin his career."

"Write," said the Prince:

"His Serene Highness, having graciously deigned to grant a hearing to the humble supplications of the Marchesa del Dongo, mother of the guilty party, and of the Duchess Sanseverina his aunt, who have testified that at the time of the crime their son and nephew was extremely young and moreover deranged by an insane passion for the wife of the unfortunate Giletti, has consented, despite the horror inspired by such a murder, to commute the penalty to which Fabrizio del Dongo has been sentenced to that of twelve years in the fortress.

"Give it to me to sign." The Prince signed and dated the document as of the previous day; then, handing it back to Rassi, he said to him: "Write immediately under my signature:

"The Duchess Sanseverina having once again flung herself at his Highness's feet, the Prince has granted the guilty party one hour of exercise every Thursday on the platform of the square tower commonly known as the Farnese Tower.

"Sign that," said the Prince, "and keep your mouth shut, whatever you hear people say in town. You will inform Councillor De Capitani, who voted for two years' imprisonment and who even ventured to hold forth in favor of this absurd opinion, that I require him to reread the laws and regulations. Once again, silence and good night."

Justice Rassi, very slowly, made three deep bows, to which the Prince paid no attention.

This occurred at seven in the morning. A few hours later, the news of the Marchesa Raversi's banishment spread through the city and in the cafés, everyone talking at once about this great event. For some time the Marchesa's banishment rid Parma of that implacable foe of small towns and minor courts, boredom. General Fabio Conti, who had regarded himself as the new Minister, claimed to have suffered an attack of gout, and for several days did not emerge from his fortress. The bourgeoisie and subsequently the populace concluded, from what was happening, that evidently the Prince had resolved to confer the Archbishopric of Parma upon Monsignore del Dongo. The political pundits of the cafés went so far as to claim that Father Landriana, the present Archbishop, had been obliged to feign ill health and present his resignation; he would be receiving a generous pension based on tobacco duties: this rumor reached the ears of the Archbishop himself, who was greatly alarmed by it, and for several days his zeal for our hero was paralyzed to a great extent. Two months later, this fine piece of news appeared in the Paris newspapers, with one minor alteration, that it was Count de Mosca, nephew of the Duchess de Sanseverina, who was to be made Archbishop.

Marchesa Raversi raged in her castle at Valleja; she was not the sort of woman who regards herself as revenged by saying scandalous things about her enemies. The day following her disgrace, Cavaliere Riscara and three more of her friends presented themselves upon the Prince's orders, and requested his permission to visit the lady in her castle. The Prince received these gentlemen with consummate graciousness, and their arrival at Valleja was a great consolation for the Marchesa. Before the end of the second week, she had thirty persons in her castle, all those whom the Liberal Ministry was to put in office. Each evening the Marchesa held a regular council of war with the best informed of her friends. One day when she had received many letters from Parma and from Bologna, she retired quite early: the favorite chambermaid introduced first the reigning lover, Count Baldi, a young man of fine appearance and utter insignificance, and later, Cavaliere Riscara, his predecessor: the latter was a short man, dark in character as in physique, who, having begun as a geometry tutor at the College of Nobles in Parma, now found himself Councillor of State and a Knight of several Orders.

"I have the good habit," the Marchesa said to these two gentlemen, "of never destroying any document, and lucky it is for me: here are nine letters which Her Grace the Duchess Sanseverina has written me on various occasions. The two of you will leave for Genoa, and you will search among the convicts there for an ex-notary named Burati, like the great Venetian poet, or Durati. You, Count Baldi, sit at my desk and write what I am about to dictate to you:

"An idea has occurred to me, and I am writing you this note. I am going to my farm near Castelnovo; if you would like to come and spend a day with me there, I should be delighted: there appears to me to be no great danger after what has just happened here; the clouds are parting. Nonetheless, stop before you enter Castelnovo; you will find one of my people on the road, they are all extremely fond of you. You will of course continue to keep the name Bossi for this little journey. They say your beard resembles that of the most admirable Capuchin, and no one has seen you in Parma save with the decent countenance of a Grand Vicar.

"Do you understand, Riscara?"

"Perfectly; but the journey to Genoa is an unnecessary luxury; I know a man in Parma who, it is true, is not yet condemned to the galleys, but who will not fail to find himself there. He will admirably counterfeit the Duchess's hand."

At these words Count Baldi opened his fine eyes extremely wide; only now did he understand.

"If you know this worthy personage in Parma, whose interests you seek to advance," the Marchesa said to Riscara, "apparently he knows you as well; his mistress, his confessor, his friend may be in the Duchess's pay; I prefer to postpone this little joke for a few days, and not expose myself to any accident. Leave in two hours, like good little lambs, see no living soul in Genoa, and return as soon as you can."

Cavaliere Riscara departed with a laugh, and, speaking through his nose like Punchinello, "We must pack our traps," he whined, running along in a comical manner. He wanted to leave Baldi alone with the lady. Five days later, Riscara brought back to the Marchesa her Count

Baldi flayed alive: to shorten the journey by six leagues, they had made him cross a mountain on muleback; he swore that no one would ever again make him take *long journeys*. Baldi presented the Marchesa with three copies of the letter she had dictated to him, and five or six other letters in the same hand, composed by Riscara, which might perhaps be put to some subsequent use. One of these letters contained some very entertaining remarks concerning the Prince's nocturnal anxieties, and the deplorable skinniness of the Marchesa Baldi, his mistress, who it was said left the mark of a pair of tongs on any armchair cushion she sat on for even a moment. Anyone would have sworn that all these letters were written in the Duchess Sanseverina's hand.

"Now I know without the shadow of a doubt," said the Marchesa, "that the beloved Fabrizio is in Bologna or somewhere thereabouts . . ."

"I am too unwell," exclaimed Count Baldi, interrupting her; "I ask the favor of being excused from this second journey, or at least I should like to be granted a few days' rest in order to recover my health."

"I shall go plead your cause," Riscara said, standing and whispering something to the Marchesa.

"Very well, I consent," she answered with a smile. "Take comfort, you will not be leaving," the Marchesa said to Baldi with a somewhat contemptuous expression.

"Thank you!" exclaimed the Count with a heartfelt look.

And as a matter of fact, Riscara rode alone in the post-chaise. He had been in Bologna no more than two days when he glimpsed Fabrizio and little Marietta in an open *calèche*. "What the Devil!" he said to himself. "Apparently our future Archbishop doesn't waste any time; the Duchess must hear of this, she will be charmed by the news." Riscara had only to follow Fabrizio in order to discover his lodgings; the next morning, our hero received by courier the letter of Genoese manufacture; he found it a bit brief, but otherwise suspected nothing. The notion of seeing the Duchess and the Count again made him wild with happiness, and no matter what Ludovic could say, he took a post-horse and set off at a gallop. Without being aware of it, he was closely followed by Riscara, who, arriving some six leagues from Parma at the post-stop before Castelnovo, had the pleasure of seeing a considerable throng in the square in front of the local prison; our hero had just been installed there, recognized at the post-stop, where he was changing horses, by two *sbirri* selected and sent there by Count Zurla. Cavaliere Riscara's tiny eyes sparkled with delight; with exemplary patience he verified everything that had just occurred in this little village, then sent on a courier to Marchesa Raversi. After which, strolling through the streets as though to examine the remarkable church, and then to seek out a painting by Parmigianino he had been told was to be found somewhere in the place, he finally encountered the magistrate, who eagerly offered his respects to a Councillor of State. Riscara appeared amazed that this personage had not immediately sent to the Citadel of Parma the conspirator he had been so fortunate as to have arrested. "One might fear," Riscara added coldly, "that his numerous friends who the day before yesterday attempted to gain passage for him through the States of His Serene Highness might encounter the police; there were indeed some twelve or fifteen of these rebels, all mounted."

"*Intelligenti pauca!*" the magistrate exclaimed with a sly expression.

CHAPTER FIFTEEN

Two hours later, poor Fabrizio, fitted with handcuffs and attached by a long chain to the very *sediola* into which he had been made to climb, left for the Citadel of Parma, with an escort of eight members of the police. These had orders to bring with them all the police stationed in the villages the procession would pass through; the magistrate in person followed this important prisoner. At seven in the evening, the *sediola*, escorted by all the urchins of Parma as well as by thirty members of the police, crossed the fine promenade, passed in front of the little palazzo Fausta had inhabited some months previously, and finally presented itself at the outer gates of the Citadel just when General Fabio Conti and his daughter were about to leave. The Governor's carriage stopped before reaching the drawbridge in order to allow the *sediola* to which Fabrizio was attached to enter; the General immediately shouted that the Citadel gates were to be closed, and hurried down to the turnkey's office in order to see what was happening; he was not a little surprised when he recognized the prisoner, who had become quite stiff, chained as he was to his *sediola* for such a long journey; four members of the police had lifted him down and were carrying him into the turnkey's office. "So now he's in my power," the conceited Governor said to himself, "this famous Fabrizio del Dongo who, it would seem, all of Parma's high society has vowed to concern itself with exclusively for almost a year now."

Twenty times the General had encountered him at court functions, at the Duchess's, and elsewhere; but he took care not to indicate he recognized Fabrizio for fear of compromising himself.

"Draw up," he shouted to the prison clerk, "a full report of the transfer of this prisoner by the good magistrate of Castelnovo into my hands."

Barbone, the clerk, an alarming personage for the volume of his beard and his martial bearing, assumed a more important air than usual, as if he were a German jailer. Believing he knew that it was chiefly the Duchess Sanseverina who had kept his master the Governor from becoming Minister of War, he was more than usually insolent toward the prisoner; he addressed him in the second-person plural, the form of speech used in Italy to speak to servants.

"I am a prelate of the Holy Roman Church," Fabrizio said to him firmly, "and Grand Vicar of this Diocese; my birth alone entitles me to your respect."

"I know nothing about that!" the clerk retorted rudely; "prove your assertions by showing the documents which give you a right to these highly respectable titles."

Fabrizio had no documents, and did not answer. General Fabio Conti, standing beside his clerk, watched him write without raising his eyes to the prisoner, in order not to be obliged to say that he was indeed Fabrizio del Dongo.

All of a sudden Clélia Conti, waiting in the carriage, heard a dreadful racket in the guard-room. The clerk Barbone, who was writing up a long and insolent description of the prisoner's person, ordered him to open his garments so that the number and the condition of the flesh-wounds received during the Giletti business could be attested and verified.

"I cannot do so," said Fabrizio smiling bitterly; "I am not in a condition to obey the gentleman's orders, prevented as I am by these handcuffs."

"What!" exclaimed the General quite naïvely. "The prisoner is handcuffed, inside the Fortress! That is counter to regulations, it requires an *ad hoc* order; take off the handcuffs."

Fabrizio looked at him. "There's a joking Jesuit," he said to himself; "he's seen these handcuffs, which are hurting me horribly, for at least an hour, and he pretends to be surprised!"

The handcuffs were removed by the police; they had just learned that Fabrizio was the nephew of the Duchess Sanseverina, and hastened to show him a honeyed politeness which contrasted with the clerk's rudeness; the latter seemed annoyed by their behavior and said to Fabrizio, who stood stock still: "All right then, hurry up! Show us those scratches you got from poor Giletti, at the time of his murder."

In one leap, Fabrizio threw himself on the clerk and gave him such a blow that Barbone fell off his chair against the General's legs. The police seized Fabrizio's arms, which remained motionless; the General himself and the two policemen beside him hurried to pull the clerk to his feet, for his face was bleeding profusely. Two other policemen ran to close the office door, in case the prisoner tried to escape. The brigadier in command thought that young del Dongo could not make a serious attempt at an escape, since he was inside the Citadel; nonetheless, by a professional instinct he went over to the window to prevent any disorder. Just outside this open window, and two steps away, stood the General's carriage: Clélia had shrunk back inside it, in order not to witness the sad scene taking place in the office; when she heard the noise, she looked up.

"What is happening?" she asked the brigadier.

"Signorina, it is young Fabrizio del Dongo, who has just delivered a good blow to that insolent Barbone."

"What, is it Signor del Dongo they're taking to prison?"

"That's for sure," the brigadier said; "it's on account of that poor young fellow's high birth that they're taking so much trouble. I thought the Signorina knew all about it."

Clélia remained at the carriage window; when the police surrounding the table drew away, she caught sight of the prisoner.

"Who would have guessed that the next time I saw him, after our first encounter on the road from Lake Como, would be in this unfortunate situation? . . . He gave me his hand to help me into his mother's carriage. . . . He was already with the Duchess! Had their affair already begun back then?"

The reader must be informed that members of the Liberal party directed by Marchesa Raversi and General Conti chose to believe in the tender intimacy which doubtless existed between Fabrizio and the Duchess. The abhorred Count Mosca was the object of endless jokes for the deception being practiced upon him.

"So," thought Clélia, "here he is a prisoner, and a prisoner of his enemies! For after all, Count Mosca, angel though one would like to believe him, will be enchanted by this capture."

A burst of loud laughter rang out in the guard-room.

"Jacopo," she said in a moved voice to the brigadier, "what's happening now?"

The General questioned the prisoner severely about why he had struck Barbone: Monsignore Fabrizio answered coldly: "He called me a *murderer,* and for that he must show me the documents which authorize him to call me by such a name"; and everyone laughed.

A jailer who could write replaced Barbone, whom Clélia saw leave, mopping the blood streaming from his hideous face with his handkerchief; he was swearing like a trooper. "That bastard Fabrizio!" he shouted. "This is the hand that will put him out of his misery! I'll get there before the hangman," and so on.

He had stopped between the office window and the General's carriage to stare at Fabrizio, and his oaths redoubled.

"On your way," the brigadier said to him; "no such swearing in front of the Signorina."

Barbone raised his head to look into the carriage; his eyes met Clélia's, from whom a cry of horror escaped; she had never seen at such close range so hideous an expression on a human face. "He will kill Fabrizio!" she said to herself. "I must warn Don Cesare." This was her uncle, one of the most respected priests in the city; his brother General Conti had obtained for him the position of steward and principal chaplain of the prison.

The General climbed back into his carriage. "Would you prefer to go to your room," he said to his daughter, "or wait what may be a long while in the palace courtyard? I must account for all this to the Sovereign."

Fabrizio came out of the office escorted by three policemen; he was taken to the room selected for him. Clélia looked through the window; the prisoner was very close to her. At that moment she answered her father's question by these words: *I will go with you.*

Fabrizio, hearing these words spoken so close to him, raised his eyes and met those of the girl. He was chiefly struck by the expression of melancholy in her face. "How much lovelier she is," he thought, "since our meeting near Como! What an expression of deep feeling! . . . She's really comparable to the Duchess—an angelic countenance if there ever was one!"

Barbone, the wounded clerk, who had intentionally taken up his place beside the carriage, made a gesture to stop the three policemen leading Fabrizio and, walking behind the carriage in order to stand at the window where the General was sitting, said to him: "Since the prisoner committed an act of violence within the Citadel, by virtue of Article One fifty-seven of the regulations, would it not be a good idea to keep him in handcuffs for the next three days?"

"Go to the Devil!" exclaimed the General, still greatly embarrassed by this arrest. He was determined to avoid provoking either the Duchess or Count Mosca; moreover, how would the Count react to this business? Actually the murder of a Giletti was a trifle, and only political intrigue had managed to turn it into a matter of any importance.

During this brief exchange, Fabrizio stood proudly amid these police, showing his noblest expression; his delicate, clear-cut features and the scornful smile that flickered over his lips contrasted charmingly with the coarse appearance of the policemen around him. But all this formed, in some sense, merely the external part of his physiognomy; he was delighted by Clélia's celestial beauty, and his eyes betrayed all his astonishment. She, deep in thought, had not remembered to withdraw her head from the carriage window; he greeted her with the most respectful half-smile; then, after a moment: "I believe, Signorina, that on another occasion, beside a lake, I have already had the honor of encountering you with a police accompaniment."

Clélia blushed and was so taken aback that she found no words with which to reply. "How noble his expression among these coarse beings!" she said to herself at the very moment Fabrizio spoke to her. The profound pity and, we might almost say, the tender feelings which overcame her deprived her of the presence of mind necessary to utter even the most ordinary phrase; she was conscious of her own silence and blushed still more deeply. At this moment the bolts of the great gate of the Citadel were violently drawn; had not His Excellency's carriage been waiting at least a minute? The noise was so loud under this vaulted roof that even if Clélia had managed to answer something, Fabrizio could not have heard her words.

Swept away by the horses, which had broken into a gallop as soon as they had crossed the drawbridge, Clélia said to herself: "How silly he must have thought me!" Then all at once she added: "Not just silly; he must have decided my soul was vile—he thought I didn't answer his greeting because he's a prisoner and I'm the Governor's daughter." This idea cast the girl into despair, for she had a lofty soul. "What makes my behavior altogether degrading," she added, "is that before, when we met the first time, also *with a police accompaniment,* as he said, I was the one who was a captive, and he did me a service, and released me from a very awkward situation. . . . Yes, I must admit it, my behavior is inexcusable, both coarse and ungrateful. Alas! The poor young man! Now that he is in misfortune, everyone will turn against him. Didn't he say to me *back then:* 'Will you remember my name in Parma?' How he must despise me now! It was so easy to say a kind word! Yes, I must confess, my behavior with him has been dreadful. Once, without his mother's generous offer of a carriage, I would have had to follow those police on foot in the dust of the street or, what is even worse, to ride pillion behind one of those men; then it was my father who was arrested and I who was helpless! Yes, my case is complete. And how intensely such a man as he must have felt it! What a contrast between his noble countenance and my behavior! What nobility! What serenity! He looked just like a hero surrounded by his vile foes! Now I understand the Duchess's passion: if he conducts himself this way in the midst of such distressing circumstances which may have dreadful consequences, what might he be like when his soul is happy!"

The Governor's carriage had remained over an hour and a half in the palace courtyard, and nonetheless, when the General returned from his visit to the Prince, Clélia did not feel he had been gone a moment too long. "What is His Highness's will?" she asked.

"On his lips the word was *prison*! And in his eyes it was *death*!"

"Death! Good Heavens!" Clélia exclaimed.

"All right, that's enough of that!" the General retorted crossly; "I'm a fool to answer a child's questions."

Meanwhile, Fabrizio was climbing the three hundred and eighty steps leading to the Farnese Tower, a "new" prison built on the platform of the great tower, at a prodigious height. Not once did he think, distinctly at least, of the great change which had just taken place in his destiny. "What a look she gave me!" he was saying to himself; "how much it expressed, what depths of pity! She seemed to be saying: life is such a web of misfortunes! Don't suffer too much over what is happening to you—aren't we put on earth to be wretched? How her lovely eyes lingered on mine, even when the horses were clattering under the arch!"

Fabrizio completely forgot to be miserable.

Clélia followed her father through several salons; at the beginning of the evening, no one yet knew of the *great criminal*'s arrest, though such was the name the courtiers, two hours later, bestowed on this poor rash young man.

That evening people noticed more animation than usual in Clélia's face; yet animation, the look of participating in her surroundings, was precisely what this lovely creature lacked.

When people compared her beauty to the Duchess's, it was chiefly this appearance of being quite unmoved, this way of being somehow above everything, which tipped the balance in her rival's favor. In England, in France, nations of vanity, people would probably have been of an entirely different opinion. Clélia Conti was a young lady still a trifle too slender who might be compared to the lovely creations of Guido Reni; we shall not conceal the fact that, according to the canons of Greek beauty, her features were a little too marked; for instance the lips, though filled with the most touching grace, were a little too full.

The admirable singularity of this countenance in which shone the naïve grace and the celestial stamp of the noblest soul was that, though of the rarest beauty, she bore no resemblance whatever to the heads of Greek statues. The Duchess, on the contrary, possessed a little too much of the *known* beauty of the ideal, and her truly Lombard head recalled the voluptuous smile and the tender melancholy of Leonardo's beautiful Salomes. As much as the Duchess appeared brilliant, sparkling with wit and malice, passionately attaching herself, so to speak, to every subject the course of conversation brought before the eyes of her soul, just so much Clélia showed herself to be calm and slow to catch fire, whether out of disdain for what surrounded her, or out of regret for some absent chimera. People had long supposed that she would end by embracing the religious life. At twenty she was believed reluctant to appear at balls, and if she followed her father to them, it was only out of obedience and in order not to jeopardize the interests of his ambition.

"So it will be impossible for me," the General's vulgar soul had mused, "Heaven having bestowed upon me for a daughter the loveliest and the most virtuous girl in our Sovereign's territories, to derive any advantage whatever from that fact for the advancement of my fortunes! My life is too isolated, I have nothing but Clélia in the world, and what I need is a family which will support me in the world, which will give me *entrée* into a certain number of salons, where my merit and above all my talents at the Ministry might be presented as unchallengeable in any political circumstance whatever. And here is my lovely, dutiful, pious daughter, who turns to stone as soon as soon as any young man properly established at Court attempts to present his respects. Once such a suitor is shown the door, her character immediately becomes less somber, and I find her almost gay, until another suitor enters the lists. The handsomest man at Court, Count Baldi, presented himself and was refused; the richest man in His Highness's territories, Marchese Crescenzi, followed him, and she claims he would make her wretched.

"Unquestionably," the General had decided on other occasions, "my daughter's eyes are finer than the Duchess's, especially since on certain rare occasions they are capable of a deeper expression; but when is it that this magnificent expression is to be seen? Never in a salon, where she might do it honor, but more likely on the promenade, alone with me, where she will let herself be touched, for example, by the wretchedness of some hideous lout. 'Preserve some remnant of that sublime gaze,' I sometimes tell her, 'for the salons we shall be visiting tonight.' No such thing: if she deigns to follow me into society, her pure and noble countenance presents the rather haughty and anything but encouraging expression of passive obedience." The General spared no efforts, as we see, to find himself a suitable son-in-law, but what he said was true.

Courtiers, who have nothing to examine in their souls, notice everything: they had observed that it was chiefly on days when Clélia could not bring herself to emerge from her beloved reveries and feign an interest in things that the Duchess chose to linger beside her and attempt to make her talk. Clélia had ash-blond hair, affording a gentle contrast with her delicately tinted cheeks, which were usually a little too pale. Only the form of her forehead might have indicated to an attentive observer that this noble expression, this attitude so superior to the vulgar graces, derived from a profound lack of interest in everything vulgar. It was the absence and not the impossibility of interest in anything.

Since her father had been Governor of the Citadel, Clélia considered herself to be happy, or at least exempt from distress, in her lofty apartment. The dreadful number of steps to be climbed in order to reach the Governor's Palace, located on the esplanade of the great tower, discouraged tedious visits, and Clélia, for this quite material reason, enjoyed the freedom of a convent; here was almost the entire ideal of happiness which, in the future, she dreamed of seeking in the religious life. She was affected by a sort of horror at the mere thought of putting her beloved solitude and her innermost thoughts at the disposition of some young man, whom the title of husband would authorize to disturb this entire inner life. If by such solitude she did not attain to felicity, at least she had managed to avoid sensations that were only too painful.

The day when Fabrizio was taken to the Fortress, the Duchess encountered Clélia at a party given by the Minister of the Interior, Count Zurla; everyone formed a circle around the two women: that evening, Clélia's beauty outstripped the Duchess's. The girl's eyes had an expression so singular and so profound that they were almost indiscreet: there was pity, and also indignation and anger in her glances. The Duchess's gaiety and her brilliant notions seemed to cast Clélia into moments of pain reaching the point of horror. "What will be the cries and groans of the poor woman," she asked herself, "when she learns that her lover, this young man of such a great heart and so noble a physiognomy, has just been thrown into prison! And that look in the Sovereign's eye which condemns him to death! O absolute power, when will you cease oppressing Italy! O base and venal souls! And I am a jailer's daughter! Nor have I belied that noble position by deigning to answer Fabrizio! Though once he was my benefactor! What must he think of me at this moment, alone in his room with his little lamp as his only companion?" Repelled by this notion, Clélia cast glances of horror upon the splendid illumination of the salons of the Minister of the Interior.

"Never," people were saying in the circle of courtiers forming around the two fashionable beauties, attempting to join their conversation, "never have they spoken to each other so animatedly and yet so intimately. Has the Duchess, always eager to dispel the hatreds excited by the Prime Minister, devised some great match for Clélia?" This conjecture was based on a circumstance which had hitherto never presented itself to the Court's observation: the girl's eyes had more fire, and even, one might say, more passion than the lovely Duchess's. The latter, for her part, was astonished and, one might say to her credit, delighted by the new graces she was discovering in her young solitary; for an hour she observed her with a pleasure rather rarely experienced at the sight of a rival. "But what can have happened?" the Duchess was wondering. "Never has Clélia been so lovely, and even so touching: can her heart have spoken? . . . But in that case, surely, it is a doomed love, there is a dark distress within this new animation. . . . But unhappy love keeps silent. Can it be that she is summoning an inconstant lover by thus shining in society?" And the Duchess carefully observed the young men who surrounded them. Nowhere did she find a singular expression, but everywhere a pronounced complacency. "Yet there is some miracle here," the Duchess said to herself, stung at not being able to solve the mystery. "Where is Count Mosca, that subtle soul?

No, I am not mistaken, Clélia is looking at me as attentively as if I were the object of an entirely new attention for her. Can this be the effect of some order given by her father, that vile courtier? I always believed her young soul to be noble and incapable of sinking to interests of money. Has General Fabio Conti some decisive request to make of the Count?"

Around ten o'clock, a friend of the Duchess's approached and whispered two words into her ear; she turned excessively pale; Clélia took her hand and ventured to squeeze it.

"I thank you, and I understand you now. You have a noble soul!" said the Duchess, making an effort to control herself. She had scarcely the strength to utter these few words. She smiled a great deal at the mistress of the house, who stood up to accompany her to the door of the last salon: such honors were due only to Princesses of the blood and made, for the Duchess, a cruel contrast with her present position. So she smiled gaily at Countess Zurla, but in spite of desperate efforts did not succeed in speaking a single word to her.

Clélia's eyes filled with tears as she watched the Duchess pass through these salons crowded with all that was most brilliant in the society of Parma. "What will become of this poor woman," she asked herself, "when she finds herself alone in her carriage? It would be an indiscretion on my part to offer to accompany her! I dare not. . . . Yet how much consolation it would be for the poor prisoner, sitting in some wretched room with his little lamp, if he knew how greatly he is loved! What dreadful solitude it is in which he has been cast! And we— we are here in these brilliant salons: how horrible it is! Could there be some way of getting a message to him? Good God! That would mean betraying my father; his situation between the two factions is so delicate! What would become of him if he were to expose himself to the Duchess's impassioned hatred, controlling as she does the Prime Minister's will, and he the master of three-quarters of the Kingdom's affairs!

"On the other hand the Prince is forever concerned with all that happens in the Fortress, and he will hear no jokes on this subject; fear makes him cruel. . . . In any case, Fabrizio"—Clélia no longer said Signor del Dongo—"is much more to be pitied! . . . For him it is quite another matter than the danger of losing a lucrative position!... And the Duchess!... What a terrible passion love is!... And yet all these worldly deceivers speak of it as a source of happiness! Old women are pitied because they can no longer feel or inspire love!... I shall never forget what I have just seen; what a sudden transformation! How the Duchess's eyes—so lovely, so radiant—turned dim and lifeless after the fatal message Marchese N—— came to give her!... Fabrizio must indeed be worthy of being loved!..."

Amid these highly serious reflections which absorbed Clélia's whole soul, the complimentary remarks which constantly surrounded her seemed even more distasteful to her than usual. To be rid of them, she went over to an open window half-veiled by a taffeta curtain; she was hoping no one would be so bold as to follow her into this sort of retreat. The window overlooked a little grove of orange-trees planted just below it: of course each winter it was necessary to put up a roof over the trees. Rapturously Clélia breathed in the perfume of these blossoms, and this pleasure seemed to restore a little peace to her soul.... "I thought he looked so noble," she reflected; "but to inspire such feelings in a woman of such distinction!... She has had the glory of refusing the suit of the Prince, and had she deigned to accept it, she might have been queen of his territories.... My father says that the Sovereign's passion went so far as to promise to marry her if he ever became free!... And this love of hers for Fabrizio has lasted so long! For it must have been five years ago that we met up with them on the shores of Lake Como!... Yes, it was five years ago," she said to herself after a moment's reflection. "I was struck by it at the time, when so many things passed unnoticed before my child's eyes! How much those two ladies seemed to admire Fabrizio!..."

Clélia noticed with delight that none of the young men who had spoken to her so ardently had dared approach her balcony. One of them, Marchese Crescenzi, had taken several steps toward her, then had stopped beside a gaming-table. "If only," she was thinking, "if only under my little window in the Fortress palace, the only one that ever gets any shade, I had the view of some pretty orange-trees like these, my thoughts would not be so sad! But the only view I have is of the enormous stone blocks of the Farnese Tower.... Ah!" she exclaimed, making a sudden gesture, "maybe that's where they've put him! I must lose no time in speaking to Don Cesare! He will be less severe than the General. My father will certainly tell me nothing when we return to the Fortress, but I'll find out everything from Don Cesare. . . . I have some money; I could buy some orange-trees and plant them under the window of my eyrie, that would keep me from seeing that huge wall of the Farnese Tower. How much more hateful it will seem to me now that I know one of the prisoners it hides from the light of day! . . . Yes, that was only the third time I have seen him; once at Court, at the Prince's birthday ball; today, surrounded by three policeman while that horrible Barbone was requesting handcuffs for him; and then the time at Lake Como. . . . That was five years ago; what a naughty boy he looked like then! What stares he gave the police, and what looks his aunt and his mother gave him! Surely there was some secret that day, something special between them; at the time it seemed to me that he too was afraid of the police . . ." Clélia shuddered. "But how ignorant I was! Doubtless, even back then, the Duchess had taken an interest in him. . . . How he made us laugh after a few moments, when those ladies, despite their evident concern, had become somewhat accustomed to a stranger's presence! . . . And tonight I could not reply to his greeting! . . . O ignorance and timidity, how often you resemble all that is worst in us! And that's how I behave when I'm over twenty! . . . I was quite right to long for the cloister; truly I am good for nothing but retirement from the world! *Worthy daughter of a jailer!* he will be saying. He scorns me, and as soon as he can write to the Duchess, he will mention my lack of concern, and the Duchess will think of me as a deceitful little girl; for finally tonight she was able to see me as full of sympathy for her troubles."

Clélia realized that someone was approaching, apparently with the intention of taking a place beside her on the iron balcony of this window; she was annoyed, though she reproached herself for it; the daydreams from which she was about to be torn were not without their sweetness. "Here comes some importunate fellow, and I'll give him a fine reception!" she thought. She turned her head with a haughty expression, when she glimpsed the timid countenance of the Archbishop approaching her balcony by tentative little movements. "This holy man has no manners," Clélia mused; "why come and disturb a poor girl like me? My peace and quiet is all I have." She was greeting the Archbishop respectfully, but with a certain remoteness, when the prelate said to her:

"Signorina, have you heard the dreadful news?"

The girl's eyes had already assumed a very different expression; but in accordance with the instructions her father had repeated a hundred times, she answered with a look of ignorance, which the language of her eyes clearly contradicted: "I have heard nothing, Monsignore."

"My First Grand Vicar, poor Fabrizio del Dongo, who was no more guilty of that ruffian Giletti's death than I am, has been captured in Bologna, where he was living under the assumed name of Joseph Bossi; he has been imprisoned in your Citadel; he arrived there *chained* to the very carriage he was riding in. Some jailer or other named Barbone, who was pardoned not long ago after having murdered one of his own brothers, sought to inflict an act of personal violence upon Fabrizio; but my young friend is not the man to suffer an insult. He flung his wretched adversary to his knees, after which he himself was handcuffed and cast into a dungeon twenty feet underground."

"Not handcuffs, no."

"Ah, you've heard something!" the Archbishop exclaimed, and the old man's features lost their intense expression of discouragement. "But right now someone might come over to this balcony and interrupt us: would you be so charitable as to see to it yourself that this pastoral ring of mine is put in Don Cesare's hands?"

The girl had taken the ring, but had no idea where to put it to avoid losing it.

"Put it on your thumb," said the Archbishop, and he placed it there himself. "May I count on you to convey this ring?"

"Yes, Monsignore."

"And will you promise me to keep secret what I shall now tell you, even should you not find it easy to fulfill my request?"

"Certainly, Monsignore," the girl replied, trembling as she saw the somber and serious expression the old man had suddenly assumed. . . . "Our worthy Archbishop," she continued, "can give me no orders unworthy of himself and of me."

"Tell Don Cesare that I commend my adopted son to his care: I know that the *sbirri* who captured him have not given him time to take his missal, and I beg Don Cesare to let him have his own, and if your good uncle will be so good as to send to the Archiepiscopal Palace tomorrow, I shall take it upon myself to replace the book he has given to Fabrizio. And I request Don Cesare to pass on as well the ring worn by this pretty hand to Signor del Dongo."

The Archbishop was interrupted by General Fabio Conti, who was coming to collect his daughter for the carriage-ride home; there was a moment of conversation which was not unskillfully managed by the prelate. Without in any way alluding to the new prisoner, he succeeded in turning the conversation so that he was able to utter quite appropriately certain moral and political observations; for instance: There are moments of crisis in Court life which determine for long periods the existence of the greatest figures; it would be notably imprudent to transform into *personal hatred* the state of political distance which is frequently the very simple consequence of contrary positions. The Archbishop, letting himself be somewhat carried away by his deep distress caused by an unexpected arrest, went so far as to say that certainly it was correct to maintain the positions of one's choice, but that it would be a quite gratuitous imprudence to bring down upon oneself furious hatreds that would be the consequence of certain deeds not to be forgotten.

Once the General was in his carriage, he said to his daughter:

"Now that is what I call threats—threats to a man of my position!"

No other words were exchanged between father and daughter for some twenty minutes.

On receiving the Archbishop's pastoral ring, Clélia had certainly intended to speak to her father, once in the carriage, of the little favor the prelate had asked of her. But after the word *threats*, so angrily spoken, she was convinced that her father would intercept the commission; she covered the ring with her left hand and squeezed it hard. During the whole time it took to drive from the Ministry of the Interior to the Citadel, she wondered if it would be a crime on her part not to speak to her father. She was a very pious, very timid girl, and her heart, usually so tranquil, was beating with unaccustomed violence;

but finally the *Who goes there?* of the sentry on the ramparts above the gate rang out at the approach of the carriage, before Clélia had found words likely to incline her father not to refuse, so fearful was she of being refused! As she climbed the three hundred and sixty steps to the Governor's Palace, Clélia could think of nothing to say.

She hastened to speak to her uncle, who scolded her and refused to lend himself to anything.

CHAPTER SIXTEEN

"Well!" exclaimed the General, catching sight of his brother Don Cesare, "here is the Duchess about to spend a hundred thousand scudi to make a fool of me and help our prisoner escape!"

But for the moment we are obliged to leave Fabrizio in his prison, at the very top of the Citadel of Parma; he is well guarded, and perhaps we shall find him, when we return to him, somewhat changed. Meanwhile we shall concern ourselves chiefly with the Court, where some extremely complicated plots, and above all the passions of an unhappy woman, will determine his fate. As he climbed the three hundred and eighty steps to his prison in the Farnese Tower, under the Governor's eyes, Fabrizio, who had so dreaded this moment, discovered that he had no time to brood over his misfortunes.

Returning home after Count Zurla's party, the Duchess dismissed her serving-women with a gesture; then, collapsing fully dressed onto her bed: *"Fabrizio is in the power of his enemies,"* she exclaimed aloud, *"and perhaps on my account they will poison him!"*

How to describe the despairing moment which followed this account of the situation, in a woman so little swayed by reason, so much the slave of the present sensation, and, without confessing it to herself, so wildly in love with the young prisoner? There were inarticulate cries, transports of rage, convulsive movements, but not a single tear. She had dismissed her serving-women for the sake of concealment, expecting to burst into sobs as soon as she was alone, but the tears, that first relief of great sufferings, failed her completely. Rage, indignation, the sense of her inferiority when matched with the Prince, over-whelmingly ruled this proud spirit.

"Am I not humiliated enough!" she kept exclaiming. "I am being flouted and, worse still, Fabrizio's life is in danger! And I have no way of seeking revenge! Stop there, my Prince! Kill me, if you like, you have the power; but afterward I shall have your life. But alas, poor Fabrizio, what good will that do you? How different from that day when I sought to leave Parma! And yet then I believed I was unhappy . . . what blindness! I was about to break all the habits of a pleasant life: alas, without knowing it, I was on the brink of an event which would decide my fate forever. If, by his miserable habits of a fawning courtier, the Count had not removed the phrase *unjust proceedings* from that fatal leter the Prince's vanity granted me, we would be saved. I had had the luck (rather than the skill, it must be confessed) to involve his vanity with regard to his beloved Parma. When I threatened to leave is when I was free! Good God! What a slave I am now, stuck here in this wretched sewer, and Fabrizio chained in the Citadel, that prison which for so many great spirits has been the antechamber of death! And I can no longer restrain that tiger by the fear of seeing me leave his den!

"He is too clever not to realize I shall never leave behind that infa-mous tower where my heart is imprisoned. Now the man's injured vanity can inspire him with the oddest notions; their strange cruelty will merely encourage his amazing conceit. If he brings up his old notions of stale gallantry, if he goes back to saying 'Accept the homage of your slave, or else Fabrizio dies,' then we have the old story of Judith. . . . Yes, but if that is no more than a suicide for me, it is a murder for Fabrizio; that idiot heir to the throne our Crown Prince and the vile executioner Rassi will see to it that Fabrizio is hanged as my accomplice."

The Duchess screamed aloud: this apparently inescapable alterna-tive tormented her wretched heart. Her troubled brain could find no other likelihood in the future. For ten whole minutes she struggled like a madwoman; finally a sleep of exhaustion replaced this horrible condition for a few moments; life was overwhelmed. Minutes later, she wakened with a start, and found herself sitting on her bed; she seemed to be seeing the Prince ordering Fabrizio's execution in her very presence. What wild glances the Duchess cast around her! When at last she managed to persuade herself that she was seeing neither the Prince nor Fabrizio, she fell back on her bed and was on the point of losing consciousness. Her physical debility was such that she no longer felt strong enough to change her position. "Good God! If I could only die!" she murmured. . . . "But what cowardice! To abandon Fabrizio in his wretchedness! I am raving. . . . Come now, let us get back to reality, with a cool head let us consider the dreadful position in which I have thrust myself as though of my own free will. What a fatal mistake—to take up residence in the Court of an absolute monarch! A tyrant who knows every one of his victims! To whom their every glance seems a test of his power. Alas! Neither the Count nor I saw as much when I left Milan: I was thinking of the pleasures of an agreeable court life; something of lesser quality, it is true, but something in the style of the happy days of Prince Eugène!

"From a distance, we can have no notion of the powers of a despot who knows all his subjects by sight. The outer form of such despotism is the same as that of other governments: there are judges, for instance, but they are Rassis; the monster would find nothing remarkable about having his father hanged if the Prince were to order him to do it . . . he would call that his duty. . . . To seduce Rassi! What a wretch I am! There is no way for me to do it. What can I offer him? Maybe a hundred thousand francs! And they claim that, during the last dagger-thrust which Heaven's wrath against this miserable country allowed him to escape, the Prince sent him a chest filled with ten thousand gold sequins! Moreover, what mere sum of money could seduce the man? This base soul, which has never seen anything but scorn in men's eyes, now has the pleasure of seeing fear and even respect—he may become Minister of Police, and why not? Then three-quarters of the country's inhabitants will be his vile toadies and will tremble before him as basely as he himself trembles before the Sovereign.

"Since I cannot flee this hateful place, I must at least be useful to

Fabrizio while I am in it: what can I do for him living alone, in solitude and in despair? Come now, *Forward, march, wretched woman!* Do your duty, go into society, pretend you no longer have Fabrizio on your mind.... Pretend to forget you, beloved angel!..."

At this word, the Duchess dissolved in tears; at last she was able to weep. After an hour granted to this human weakness, she saw with a degree of consolation that her mind was beginning to clear. "If I had a magic carpet," she said to herself, "if I could carry Fabrizio off from the Citadel and take refuge with him in some happy country out of reach of our pursuers. Paris, for instance. We would live, at first, on the twelve hundred francs his father's notary allows me with such pleasing exactitude. I might gather together a hundred thousand francs from the ruins of my fortune!" The Duchess's imagination reviewed with moments of inexpressible pleasure all the details of the life she would lead three hundred leagues from Parma. "There," she said to herself, "he could enlist under some assumed name.... As an officer in some regiment of these brave French, young Valserra would soon win a reputation; at last he would be a happy man."

These rosy images brought back her tears all over again, but this time they were gentle ones. Then happiness did exist somewhere! This last state persisted a long time; the poor woman was in terror of returning to the contemplation of the dreadful reality. Finally, as the dawn was beginning to mark the summit of the trees in her garden with a white line, she struggled violently to rouse herself. "In a few hours, I shall be on the battlefield; it will be a question of taking action; and if something vexing should happen to me, if the Prince should take it into his head to say something to me about Fabrizio, I am not sure of being able to keep my wits about me. Therefore I must, without wasting another moment, *make plans.*

"If I am declared a State criminal, Rassi will seize everything in this *palazzo.* On the first of this month the Count and I burned, as is the custom, all the papers the police might have turned to advantage, and he is the Minister of Police—that's the joke. I have three diamonds worth something: tomorrow Fulgenzio, my old boatman from Grianta, will set off for Geneva, where he will put them in a safe place. If ever Fabrizio manages to escape (Lord, be good to me now!)"—here she crossed herself—"the Marchese del Dongo's unspeakable cowardice will discover that it is a sin to send bread to a man pursued by a legitimate Prince, though then, at least, he will find my diamonds and he will have bread.

"Dismiss the Count. . . . Being alone with him, after what has just happened, is the one thing impossible for me. The poor man! He is not a bad sort, quite the contrary; he is merely weak. That common soul is not up to our level. Poor Fabrizio! If only you could be here with me for a moment, to talk over our dangers!

"The Count's meticulous prudence will ruin all my plans, and besides I must not destroy him in my wake. . . . For what's to prevent this tyrant's vanity from throwing me into prison as well? For 'conspiring.' . . . What could be easier to prove? If he sent me to his Citadel and I could buy my way to a conversation with Fabrizio, if only for a moment, how bravely we would stride together toward death! But enough of such madness; his Rassi would advise him to get rid of me by poison; my presence in the streets, standing on a tumbril, might trouble the sensibility of his beloved Parmesans. . . . But what is this? More romantic dreams! Alas, such follies must be forgiven a poor woman whose actual fate is so sad! The truth of all this is that the Prince will never send me to death; but what could be easier for him than to throw me into prison and keep me there; he will secrete in some corner of my *palazzo* all sorts of damning papers, as was done in the case of that poor L——. Then three judges, not even too corrupt, for there will be what are called *documentary proofs*, and a dozen false witnesses will suffice. So I can be sentenced to death as a conspirator, and the Prince, in his infinite mercy, considering that in the past I have had the honor to be admitted to his Court, will commute my sentence to ten years in the Fortress. But as for me, not to betray that violent character which has led the Marchesa Raversi and my other enemies to say so many stupid things, I shall bravely take poison. At least the public will be kind enough to believe it; but I wager that Rassi will appear in my cell, gallantly bringing me, on the Prince's behalf, a little flask of strychnine, or Perugia opium.

"Yes, I must very publicly break off relations with the Count, for I do not wish to involve him in my ruin, that would be infamous; the poor man has loved me so sincerely! My mistake has been to believe that a true courtier would retain enough soul to be capable of love. Very likely the Prince will find some pretext to throw me in prison; he will fear that I might pervert public opinion concerning Fabrizio. The Count is a man of honor; immediately he will commit what the syco- phants of this Court, in their astonishment, will call a folly, he will leave the Court. I have flouted the Prince's authority the evening of that letter, I can expect anything and everything from his wounded vanity: does a man born a Prince ever forget the sensation I afforded him that evening? Moreover the Count separated from me is in a bet- ter position to be useful to Fabrizio. But if the Count, whom my re- solve will bring to the point of despair, sought revenge? . . . Now there is a notion that will never occur to him; he lacks the fundamentally base nature of a man like the Prince: the Count might, with a sigh, countersign a vile decree, but he is a man of honor. And then, what would he be taking revenge for? For the fact that, after having loved him five years without committing the slightest act of damage to his love, I say to him: 'Dear Count, I had the happiness to love you: well, this flame has died, I no longer love you! But I know the depths of your heart, and I preserve the deepest esteem for you, and we shall always be the best of friends.' What can a man of honor reply to so sincere a declaration? I shall take a new lover, or at least that is what people in society will believe. I shall tell him: 'Actually the Prince is right to punish Fabrizio's folly; but on his saint's-day our gracious Sovereign will doubtless grant him his liberty.' That way I gain six months. The new lover selected by prudence would be that forsworn judge, that in- famous hangman, that Rassi . . . he would find himself ennobled, and in point of fact, I should be giving him *entrée* into good society. Forgive me, dear Fabrizio! Such an effort is beyond my powers. What! That monster, still covered with the blood of Count P—— and of D——! I would faint with horror the minute he approached me, or rather I would snatch up a knife and plunge it into his infamous heart. Do not ask me to do impossible things!

"Yes, above all forget Fabrizio! And not the shadow of vexation shown to the Prince, resume my usual gaiety of manner, which will appear agreeable enough to these wretched souls, first of all because I will seem to be submitting with a good grace to their Sovereign, and second because, far from mocking them, I shall take care to play up all their pretty little virtues; for instance, I shall compliment Count Zurla on the beauty of the white feather in his hat which he has imported by courier from Lyons and which constitutes his chief happiness . . .

"To choose a lover from the Raversi faction. . . . If the Count goes, that will be the Ministerial party, and the power will be there. It will be a friend of the Marchesa Raversi's who will rule over the Citadel, for Fabio Conti will move up to the Ministry. How can the Prince, a man of good society, a man of intelligence, accustomed to the Count's delightful collaboration—how can the Prince conduct affairs with the assistance of this ox, this prize fool who has spent his whole life worrying one crucial problem: should His Highness's soldiers wear seven buttons on their jackets or nine? These are the creatures, and all insanely jealous of me, who constitute your danger, dear Fabrizio! These are the animals who will decide my fate and yours! So we must not permit the Count to resign his post! Let him remain, even though he must suffer certain humiliations! If he still supposes that handing in his resignation is the greatest sacrifice a Prime Minister can make; and each time that his mirror tells him he is growing older, he offers me that sacrifice: hence, complete break; yes, and reconciliation only in the case where there will be no other means of keeping him from leaving his post. Naturally I shall give him his dismissal in the friendliest way possible; but after the diplomatic omission of the words *unjust proceedings* in the letter to the Prince, I feel that in order not to hate him, I need to spend some months without seeing him. On that decisive evening, I had no need of his cleverness; all he had to do was to write what I dictated to him, just that message, *which I had obtained* by my own character: his courtier manners carried him away. He told me the next day that he had not been able to make his Prince sign anything so absurd, that was what was needed was a *letter of pardon*: well, good Lord! With such people, such monsters of vanity and rancor known as the *Farnese*, you take what you can get."

At the thought of this, all the Duchess's rage revived. "The Prince has deceived me," she said to herself, "and in such a cowardly fashion! . . . There is no excuse for this man: he has wit, discernment, the capacity to reason; it is his passions which are the vile part of him. Twenty times the Count and I have noticed it—his mind becomes vulgar only when he imagines someone has tried to offend him. Well! Fabrizio's crime has nothing to do with politics; it was one of those little murders that are counted by the hundreds in these happy territories, and the Count has sworn to me that he has obtained the most exact information, and that Fabrizio is innocent. That Giletti was not without courage: finding himself two steps away from the border, he was suddenly tempted to rid himself of an all too attractive rival."

The Duchess paused a long while to consider if it was possible to believe in Fabrizio's guilt: not that she considered it much of a sin, on the part of a gentleman of her nephew's rank, to rid himself of an actor's impertinence; but in her despair, she was beginning to feel somehow that she would be obliged to do battle in order to prove Fabrizio's innocence. "No," she said to herself at last, "here is a decisive proof; he is like poor Pietranera; he always has weapons in all his pockets, and on that day he was carrying only a miserable single-barreled rifle, and even that was borrowed from one of the workmen.

"I hate the Prince because he has deceived me, and deceived me in the most dastardly fashion; after his letter of pardon, he had the poor boy captured in Bologna, and so on. But these accounts will be settled." Toward five in the morning, the Duchess, overwhelmed by this long fit of despair, rang for her serving-women, who shrieked when they saw her lying on her bed fully dressed, with all her diamonds, pale as her sheets and with her eyes closed: it was as if they were seeing her laid out on her bier after her death. They would have supposed her quite unconscious had they not remembered that she had just rung for them. A few scattered tears occasionally ran down her lifeless cheeks; her serving-women understood by a gesture that she wished to be put to bed.

Twice that evening after Count Zurla's party, the Count had called at the Duchess's *palazzo:* refused admittance each time, he wrote her that he needed her advice for some business of his own: "Should he keep his position after the affront they had dared to offer him?" The Count added: "The young man is innocent; but, even guilty, should they have arrested him without informing me, his acknowledged protector?" The Duchess did not see this letter until the next day.

The Count had no principles; one might even add that what the Liberals mean by *principles* (seeking the happiness of the greatest number) seemed to him a deceit; he considered himself obliged to seek above all the happiness of Count Mosca della Rovere; but he was altogether honorable and perfectly sincere in speaking of his resignation. In all his life he had never told the Duchess a lie; she herself, for that matter, paid no attention whatever to this letter; her decision, painful as it was, was taken: *to pretend to forget Fabrizio;* after this effort, everything was a matter of indifference to her.

The next day, around noon, the Count, who had passed in front of the Palazzo Sanseverina some ten times, was finally admitted; he was astounded by the sight of the Duchess. . . . "She is forty!" he said to himself. "And yesterday she was so brilliant! So young! . . . Everyone told me that during her long conversation with Clélia Conti, she looked every bit as young and much more seductive."

The Duchess's voice and manner were as strange as the aspect of her person. This manner, divested of all passion, of all human interest, of all anger, made the Count turn pale; he remembered the behavior of one of his friends who, a few months ago, on the point of death, and having already received the Sacraments, had asked to speak to him.

After a few moments, the Duchess was able to speak. She looked at him, and her eyes remained lifeless: "Let us part, my dear Count," she said to him, in a faint but clearly articulated voice which she attempted to make agreeable, "let us part, as we must! Heaven is my witness that for the last five years, my conduct toward you has been irreproachable. You have given me a brilliant existence, instead of the tedium which would have been my mournful lot at the Castle of Grianta; without you I should have encountered old age several years sooner. . . . For my part, my sole occupation has been to try to make it possible for you to find happiness. It is because I love you that I am suggesting this separation *à l'aimable,* as they would say in France."

The Count did not understand; she was obliged to repeat her words several times. He turned pale as death, and flinging himself on his knees beside her bed, he said everything which the deepest astonishment, and then the most intense despair can inspire in an intelligent man who is passionately in love. He kept offering to hand in his resignation and to follow his beloved to some place of retreat a thousand leagues from Parma.

"You dare speak to me of leaving, and Fabrizio is here!" she exclaimed, half rising.

But when she realized that Fabrizio's name produced a painful impression, she added after a moment's silence, and faintly pressing the Count's hand:

"No, dear friend, I shall not say that I have loved you with that passion and those transports which one no longer feels, I believe, after thirty, and I am already much older than that. People will have told you that I loved Fabrizio, for I know that such rumors have run through this *wicked* court." Her eyes shone for the first time in this conversation, when she uttered the word *wicked.* "I swear to you before God, and on Fabrizio's life, that there has passed between him and myself not the smallest thing which the eye of a third person might not have tolerated. Nor shall I tell you that I love him altogether like a sister; I love him by instinct, if I may put it that way. I love in him his courage, so simple and so perfect that one might say that he is not even aware of it himself; I recall that this sort of admiration began upon his return from Waterloo. He was still a child, despite his seventeen years; his great anxiety was to know if he had truly participated in the battle, and in case he had, if he could say he had fought, since he had marched to the attack of no enemy battery or column. It was during the serious discussions we had together on this important subject that I began to discern a perfect grace in my nephew. His great soul revealed itself to me; how many knowing lies would a well brought up young man have proffered in his place! In short, if he is not happy I cannot be happy. There, that is the phrase which perfectly describes the state of my heart; if it is not the truth, at least it is all the truth I can perceive."

Encouraged by this tone of frankness and intimacy, the Count attempted to kiss the Duchess's hand: she pulled it away from him with a sort of horror. "Those times are past," she said; "I am a woman of thirty-seven, I stand on the threshold of old age, and already I feel all of its discouragements, and perhaps I am even close to the grave. This is a terrible moment, people say, and yet it seems to me that I desire it. I am feeling the worst symptom of old age: my heart is stifled by this dreadful misfortune, I can no longer love. In you, dear Count, I see nothing, now, but the shadow of someone who once was dear to me. What's more, it is gratitude alone which makes me speak to you in this fashion."

"What will become of me?" the Count kept repeating. "I, who feel that I am attached to you even more passionately than those first days when I saw you at La Scala!"

"Shall I tell you something, dear friend? This talk of love bores me and seems indecent to me. Come now," she said, attempting to smile, though in vain. "Courage! Be a man of sense, a man of judgment, a man of resource on this occasion. Be with me what you really are in the eyes of strangers, the most skillful man and the greatest politician Italy has produced in centuries."

The Count stood up and walked back and forth in silence for a few moments. "Impossible, dear friend," he said at last; "I am struggling with the lacerations of the most violent passion, and you ask me to consult my reason! There is no longer any such thing as reason for me!"

"Let us not speak of passion, I implore you," the Duchess said dryly. And this was the first time, after two hours of conversation, that her voice assumed any expression whatever.

The Count, in despair himself, sought to console her.

"He has deceived me!" she exclaimed without making any reply to the reasons for hope the Count set before her. "He has deceived me in the most dastardly fashion!" And her deadly pallor left her for a moment, but even in a moment of violent excitement the Count noticed that she lacked the strength to raise her arms.

"Good God! Could it be possible," he wondered, "that she is merely indisposed? But in that case it would be the onset of some very serious illness." Then, filled with anxiety, he suggested calling in the famous Rasori, the best physician in the State and in all Italy.

"Do you wish to give a stranger the pleasure of knowing the whole extent of my despair? . . . Is this the behavior of a friend or of a traitor?" And she stared at him with unseeing eyes.

"It is all over," he said to himself in despair, "she has no love left for me! And even worse, she no longer even considers me among the men of ordinary honor.

"I may tell you," the Count added, speaking carefully, "that above all I have wanted to obtain the details concerning the arrest which has brought us to despair, and strangely enough, I still know nothing distinct; I have had the police in the neighboring station questioned; they saw the prisoner coming on the Castelnovo road, and they received orders to follow his *sediola*. I immediately sent off Bruno once again— you know his zeal no less than his devotion—with orders to proceed backward from station to station until he finds out where and how Fabrizio was arrested."

Hearing the name Fabrizio, the Duchess suffered a slight convulsion. "Forgive me, my friend," she said to the Count once she was able to speak; "such details are of the greatest interest, tell me everything, let me understand even the most minor circumstances."

"Well, Madame," the Count went on, attempting a certain lightness of tone in the attempt to distract the Duchess a little, "I have a notion to send a confidential messenger to Bruno and to order him to proceed to Bologna; it is there, perhaps, that our young friend was seized. What is the date on his last letter?"

"Tuesday, five days ago."

"Had it been opened in the post?"

"No trace of tampering. I must tell you that it was written on dreadful paper; the address is in a woman's hand, and this address bears the name of an old laundress related to my chambermaid. The laundress thinks it has to do with a love affair, and my Cecchina pays her for the cost of the letters without giving her anything more."

The Count, who had now assumed the tone of a man of business, tried to learn, in his discussion with the Duchess, what could have been the day Fabrizio was seized in Bologna. Only then did he realize, he who ordinarily was so subtle, so tactful, that this was the one tone to take. Such details interested the wretched woman and seemed to distract her somewhat. If the Count had not been in love, this simple notion would have occurred to him upon entering the room. The Duchess gave him leave to go so that he could immediately send new orders to the faithful Bruno. When in passing the question arose as to whether there had been a sentence before the moment when the Prince had signed the letter addressed to the Duchess, the latter eagerly seized the occasion to say to the Count: "I shall not reproach you for having omitted the words *unjust proceedings* from the letter you wrote and he signed—that was the courter's instinct which controlled your hand; without realizing it, you preferred your master's interest to your mistress's. You have submitted your actions to my orders, dear Count, and have done so for a long time, but it is not in your power to change your nature; you have great talents for being a Minister, but you also have the instincts of the profession. Suppressing the word *unjust* has ruined me; but far be it from me to reproach you in any way: this was the fault of instinct, and not of will.

"Bear in mind," she added, changing her tone and with the most imperious expression, "that I am not overly suffering because of Fabrizio's abduction, that I have not had the slightest impulse to leave this country, that I am full of respect for the Prince. That is what you must say, and this is what, for my part, I want to say to you: since I plan in the future to manage my own affairs, I wish to separate from you *à l'aimable*, that is, as a good old friend. Think of me as sixty; the young woman in me is dead, and I can no longer consider anything in the world with exaggerated feelings, I can no longer love. But I would be even more wretched than I am if I were to compromise your destiny. It may enter into my plans to appear to have a young lover, and I do not want to see you distressed by such a thing. I can swear to you on the happiness of Fabrizio"—and she paused an instant after this word—"that I have never been unfaithful to you, and this for five whole years. A long time," she said, and tried to smile; her pale cheeks trembled, but her lips could not manage to part. "I even swear to you that I had never had any such intention or desire. And now that this is understood, leave me."

The Count, in despair, left the Palazzo Sanseverina: he realized the Duchess's firm intention of parting from him, and never before had he been so desperately in love with her. This is one of the matters to which I am compelled to return quite frequently, for they are unlikely outside of Italy. Upon returning home, he dispatched as many as six different persons along the road to Castelnovo and to Bologna, and entrusted them all with letters. "But this is not all," the unhappy Count said to himself; "it may have occurred to the Prince to put this wretched boy to death, and this to take revenge for the Duchess's tone the day she sent him that fatal letter. I felt that the Duchess was exceeding a limit that should never be crossed, and it is to mend matters that I had the incredible foolishness to suppress the words *unjust proceedings,* the only ones that bound the Sovereign. . . . But are such men bound by anything? That is doubtless the greatest mistake of my life— I've risked everything which might have made it rewarding; now I must compensate for my folly by all the activity and skill I can manage; but after all if I get nowhere, even by sacrificing a little of my dignity, I leave this man high and dry; with all his dreams of high diplomacy, his notions of making himself the constitutional monarch of all Lombardy, we'll see how he'll manage to replace me. . . . Fabio Conti is no more than a fool, and Rassi's talent comes down to finding legal reasons for hanging a man disliked by the authorities."

Once he had determined to renounce the Ministry if the rigors shown to Fabrizio exceeded those of mere detention, the Count said to himself: "If a whim of this man's vanity, rashly defied, costs me my happiness, at least my honor remains. . . . Apropos, since I am abandoning my portfolio, I can allow myself a hundred actions which even this morning would have seemed unfeasible. For instance, I shall attempt everything humanly possible to help Fabrizio escape. Good God!" the Count exclaimed, breaking off and opening his eyes wide, as though glimpsing an unexpected felicity. "The Duchess never mentioned escape; could she have been insincere once in her life, and might her quarrel with me be nothing but a desire that I betray the Prince? My word, as good as done!"

The Count's eye had recovered all its satirical subtlety. "That lovable Judge Rassi is paid by his master for all the sentences which dishonor us throughout Europe, but he is not the man to refuse to be paid by me to betray that master's secrets. The creature has a mistress and a confessor, but the mistress is too vile a sort for me to be able to talk to—the next day she would report our conversation to every fishwife in the neighborhood." Resuscitated by this gleam of hope, the Count was already on his way to the Cathedral; amazed by the lightness of his step, he smiled despite his distress: "What a thing it is," he said, "to be no longer a Minister!" Like so many churches in Europe, this Cathedral served as a corridor from one street to another; as he entered, the Count saw one of the Archbishop's Grand Vicars crossing the nave.

"Since we've met here," he said to the religious, "will you be so good as to spare my gout the mortal fatigue of climbing the stairs to His Grace the Archbishop. I should be infinitely grateful to him if he would deign to come down to the sacristy."

This message delighted the Archbishop, who had a thousand things to tell the Minister concerning Fabrizio. But the Minister guessed that these things were merely fine phrases, and would not hear a word.

"What sort of man is Dugnani, the Vicar of San Paolo?"

"A small mind and a great ambition," the Archbishop replied, "few scruples and extreme poverty, for we too have our vices!"

"Indeed, Monsignore!" exclaimed the Minister. "You depict the man like Tacitus himself." And he took his leave, laughing.

No sooner had he returned to the Ministry than he had the Abbé Dugnani summoned. "You are the spiritual director of my excellent friend Chief Justice Rassi. Would he have nothing to say to me?"

And without another word or further ceremony, he dismissed Dugnani.

CHAPTER SEVENTEEN

The Count regarded himself as out of office. "Let us calculate," he said to himself, "how many horses we'll be able to have after my disgrace, for that is what my resignation will be called." The Count reckoned up his fortune: he had entered the Ministry with eighty thousand francs to his name; to his considerable astonishment, he found that, all told, his present holdings did not come to five hundred thousand francs: "At most it's an income of twenty thousand lire," he mused. "What a fool I am, it must be confessed! Every bourgeois in Parma believes I have an income of a hundred and fifty thousand; and the Prince, on this subject, is more bourgeois than any of them. When they see me in the gutter, they'll say that I know how to hide my fortune. Damn it all, if I'm still Minister three months from now, we'll see that fortune of mine doubled." In this notion he found the occasion to write to the Duchess, and seized it greedily; but to be forgiven for a letter, considering the terms they were now on, he filled this one with figures and calculations. "We shall have no more than twenty thousand a year," he wrote her, "for the three of us to live on in Naples—Fabrizio, you, and myself. Fabrizio and I will share a saddle-horse between us." No sooner had the Minister sent off his letter than Fiscal General

Rassi was announced; the Count received him with a hauteur that verged on rudeness.

"What is this, sir?" he inquired. "You manage to seize in Bologna a so-called conspirator who is under my protection, and furthermore you intend to cut off his head, and you tell me nothing about it! At least you must know the name of my successor? Is it General Conti, or perhaps you yourself?"

Rassi was dumbfounded; he was insufficiently accustomed to good society to guess whether the Count was speaking seriously: he blushed deeply, stammered a few unintelligible words; the Count stared at him, delighting in his embarrassment. Suddenly Rassi pulled himself together and exclaimed with considerable ease and the expression of Figaro caught red-handed by Almaviva: "My word, Signor Count, I won't beat about the bush with Your Excellency: what will you give me if I answer all your questions as I would those of my confessor?"

"The Cross of San Paolo"—the Parmesan Order—"or money, if you can give me an excuse for granting it to you."

"I'd prefer the Order, since it gives me some rank as a noble."

"My dear Fiscal, you don't mean you still set some store by our wretched nobility?"

"If I had been born noble," Rassi replied with all the insolence of his métier, "the relatives of the men I've had hanged would hate me, but they wouldn't scorn me."

"Very well, I shall save you from scorn," said the Count; "cure me of my ignorance. What do you plan to do with Fabrizio?"

"My word, the Prince is in a terrible pickle: he fears that, seduced by the fine eyes of Armida—forgive these rather racy terms, they are the Sovereign's very words—he fears that, seduced by the very fine eyes which have rather stirred him himself, you might abandon him, and there is no one but you to manage the affairs of Lombardy. I'll go so far as to say," Rassi added, lowering his voice, "that you might make a good thing out of this occasion, something well worth the Cross of San Paolo you're going to give me. The Prince would grant you, as a national recompense, a nice estate worth six hundred thousand francs which he will set apart from his own domains, or a gratuity of three hundred thousand scudi, if you agree not to concern yourself with the fate of Fabrizio del Dongo, or at least to mention it to him only in public."

"I was expecting something better than that," said the Count; "not to concern myself with Fabrizio means a quarrel with the Duchess."

"Well, that's just what the Prince says: as a matter of fact he's horribly annoyed with the Duchess, just between ourselves; and he's afraid that to compensate yourself for the break with this lovely lady, now that you are a widower, you might request the hand of his cousin, old Princess Isotta, who is no more than fifty."

"He's guessed right!" the Count exclaimed. "Our master is the subtlest man in his own territories."

The Count had never had the fantastic notion of marrying this ancient Princess; nothing would have less suited a man whom the Court ceremonies bored to death. He began playing with his snuffbox on the marble top of a little table next to his armchair. Rassi regarded this nervous gesture as the chance of a windfall; his eyes gleamed.

"Forgive me, Signor Count," he cried; "if Your Excellency will accept either the estate or the gratuity in cash, I beg you not to choose any other intermediary but myself. I shall do everything possible," he added, speaking still lower, "to increase the gratuity, or even to add a good-sized forest to the estate. If Your Excellency deigned to instill a little amiability and tact into his way of speaking to the Prince of this puppy they've put away, it is quite possible that the estate offered as a national recompense might be elevated to a Duchy. I repeat to Your Excellency, the Prince, for the time being, loathes the Duchess, but he is dreadfully embarrassed, even to the point where I have sometimes supposed that there was some secret circumstance he dared not acknowledge to me. As a matter of fact, there may be a gold mine here, I selling you my most intimate secrets and with all the good will in the world, for I am believed to be your sworn enemy. Actually, even if he is furious with the Duchess, he also believes, as do we all, that only you in all the world can carry out the secret negotiations having to do with the Milanese. Will Your Excellency permit me to repeat to him the very words of our Sovereign?" Rassi inquired, warming to his theme. "There is often a physiognomy in the position of the words which no translation can depict, and Your Excellency may see more in them than I."

"I permit everything," said the Count, continuing, quite coolly, to tap the marble tabletop with his gold snuffbox, "I permit everything and I shall be grateful."

"Grant me a patent of hereditary nobility independent of the Order, and I shall be more than satisfied. When I mention ennoblement to the Prince, he replies: 'A rascal like you, noble! We'd have to shut up shop tomorrow; no one in Parma would ever wish to be ennobled again!' To return to the matter of the Milanese, the Prince was telling me, not three days back: 'There's no one but that scoundrel to follow the thread of our intrigues; if I drive him away or if he follows the Duchess, I might as well abandon all hope of someday seeing myself the liberal and adored leader of all Italy.'"

At this expression the Count breathed again: "Fabrizio will not die," he said to himself.

In all his life Rassi had not been able to hold so intimate a conversation with the Prime Minister: he was beside himself with happiness; he saw himself on the eve of being able to abandon the name Rassi, which had become synonymous the country over with everything low and vile; the peasants called mad dogs *Rassi;* only recently some soldiers had fought a duel because one of their comrades had called them *Rassi.* Indeed, not a week passed without this wretched name managing to embellish some cruel sonnet or other. His son, a young and innocent schoolboy of sixteen, was driven out of the cafés on account of his name.

It was the burning memory of all these amenities of his position that made him commit an imprudence. "I have an estate," he said to the Count, drawing his chair closer to the Minister's armchair, "called Riva—I'd like to become Baron Riva."

"Why not?" said the Minister.

Rassi was beside himself. "Well then, Signor Count, I shall permit myself an indiscretion, I'll make so bold as to divine the goal of your desires: you aspire to the hand of Princess Isotta, and that is a noble ambition. Once you are related, you are sheltered from disgrace, you *tie our man's hands.* I shall not conceal from you that he regards such a marriage with Princess Isotta with horror; but if your affairs were entrusted to someone skillful and *well paid,* we might not despair of success."

"Myself, dear Baron, I should despair; I disavow in advance any words that you might repeat in my name; but the day when this illustrious alliance finally manages to fulfill my hopes and to afford me so high a position in the State, I myself shall offer you three hundred thousand francs of my own money, or else I shall advise the Prince to grant you a sign of favor which you yourself will prefer to this sum."

The reader finds this conversation lengthy: yet we are sparing him over half of it; it went on for another two hours. Rassi emerged from the Count's chambers wild with happiness; the Count remained with high hopes of saving Fabrizio, and more determined than ever to hand in his resignation. He found that his credit had need of being renewed by the presence in the government of such men as Rassi and General Conti; he delighted in the possibility he had just glimpsed of being revenged on the Prince: "He can force the Duchess out," he exclaimed, "but by God he will give up all hope of being a constitutional monarch of Lombardy." (This chimera was absurd: the Prince was a clever man, but by dint of dreaming of it, had fallen madly in love with the notion.)

The Count could not contain his joy as he hurried to the Duchess to tell her of his conversation with the Fiscal. He found her door closed to him; the porter scarcely dared tell him of this order received from his mistress's own lips. The Count sadly returned to the Ministerial *palazzo;* the misfortune he had just experienced entirely eclipsed the joy he had been given by his conversation with the Prince's confidant. No longer having the heart to concern himself with anything, the Count was wandering sadly through his picture gallery when, a quarter of an hour having passed, he received a message which ran as follows:

> Since it is true, my dear good friend, that we are now no more than friends, you must only come to see me three times a week. In fifteen days, we shall reduce these visits, still so dear to my heart, to two each month. If you wish to please me, let this sort of rupture be widely known; if you wished to repay in kind almost all the love I felt for you, you would choose a new

mistress. As for myself, I have great plans for dissipation: I intend to go into society a great deal, perhaps I shall even find a man of intelligence to distract me from my woes. Doubtless as a friend, the first place in my heart will always be reserved for you; but I no longer want people to be saying that my conduct has been dictated by your policy; above all I want it to be known that I have lost all influence over your decisions. In a word, dear Count, rest assured that you will always be my dearest friend, but never anything else. Do not, I implore you, entertain any notion of a resumption, everything is really over. Rely on my eternal friendship.

This last stroke was too much for the Count's courage: he indited a fine letter to the Prince resigning from all his posts, and addressed it to the Duchess with a request to send it on to the Palace. A moment later, he received his resignation torn into four pieces and, on one of the blank scraps of the paper, the Duchess had deigned to write: *No, a thousand times no!*

It would difficult to describe the poor Minister's despair. "She is quite right, I see that," he kept saying to himself; "my omission of the words *unjust proceedings* is a dreadful misfortune; it may cause Fabrizio's death, and that will lead to my own." It was with death in his heart that the Count, who was reluctant to appear at the Sovereign's Palace before being summoned there, wrote in his own hand the *motu proprio* which created Rassi a Knight of the Order of San Paolo and conferred upon him hereditary nobility; to this the Count joined a report of half a page in length which explained to the Prince the reasons of State which favored such a measure. He took a sort of melancholy pleasure in making two fair copies of these documents, which he sent to the Duchess.

He lost himself in suppositions; he tried to guess the future plans of the woman he loved. "She knows no more than I," he told himself; "only one thing remains certain; nothing in the world would make her go back on the resolutions she has told me she made." What intensified his suffering was that he could not find it in his heart to blame the Duchess. "She was good enough to love me; she has ceased doing so after a mistake that was unintentional, it is true, but one that may involve horrible consequences; I have no right to complain." The next morning, the Count learned that the Duchess had begun going into society once again; she had appeared the evening before in all the houses which used to receive her. What would he have done had he encountered her in the same salon? How would he speak to her? What tone would he use? And how could he avoid speaking to her?

The next day was a gloomy one; everyone was saying that Fabrizio would be put to death, and the whole city was moved. It was observed that the Prince, out of regard for his high birth, had deigned to order this decapitation.

"I'm responsible for his death," the Count said to himself; "I can no longer hope to see the Duchess ever again." Despite this rather elementary reasoning, he couldn't keep from passing her door some three times; in truth, in order not to be noticed, he went there on foot. In his despair, he even had the courage to write her. He had sent for Rassi twice; the Fiscal had not shown up. "The scoundrel has betrayed me," the Count said to himself.

The following day, three great pieces of news stirred the high society of Parma, and even the bourgeoisie. Fabrizio's execution was more certain than ever; and, a curious complement to this news, the Duchess did not appear too upset about it. To all appearances, she suffered only moderate regrets on account of her young lover; nonetheless she benefited with infinite art from the pallor due to a rather serious indisposition, occurring at the same time as Fabrizio's arrest. The bourgeois easily recognized, from these details, the cold heart of a great lady of the Court. Yet out of decency, and as a sort of sacrifice to the shade of young Fabrizio, she had broken with Count Mosca.

"How immoral!" exclaimed the Jansenists of Parma.

But already the Duchess, incredibly enough, seemed disposed to listen to the flatteries of the handsomest young men at Court. It was noticed, among other singularities, that she had been extremely gay in a conversation with Count Baldi, the present lover of the Raversi woman, and had teased him mercilessly on his frequent visits to the Castle of Velleja. The petite bourgeoisie and the peasants were outraged by the death of Fabrizio, which these good people attributed to Count Mosca's jealousy. Court circles were also much concerned with the Count, but to deride him. The third of the great pieces of news we announced was none other, indeed, than the Count's resignation; everyone was making fun of an absurd lover who, at the age of fifty-six, had sacrificed a magnificent position to the disappointment of being left by a heartless woman who had long since preferred a younger man. Only the Archbishop had the wit, or rather the heart, to divine that honor forbade the Count to remain Prime Minister in a country where a young man who was his protégé was to be decapitated without his even being consulted. The news of the Count's resignation had the effect of curing General Fabio Conti of his gout, as we shall relate in the proper place, when we shall be speaking of how poor Fabrizio was spending his time in the Citadel, while the whole city was wondering about the hour of his execution.

The following day, the Count saw Bruno, that loyal agent he had sent to Bologna; the Count was waiting for the moment when this man would enter his cabinet; the sight of him recalled the happy state which he had enjoyed when he sent the man to Bologna, more or less in agreement with the Duchess. Bruno arrived from Bologna, where he had learned nothing; he had not been able to find Ludovic, whom the magistrate of Castelnovo had kept in the prison of that village.

"I'm sending you back to Bologna," the Count said to Bruno; "the Duchess insists on the melancholy pleasure of learning all the details of Fabrizio's misfortune. Inquire of the brigadier of police in command of the Castelnovo station. . . . No, wait!" the Count exclaimed, breaking off. "Leave right now for Lombardy, and distribute a good quantity of money to all our agents there. My purpose is to obtain reports of the most encouraging nature from all of these people."

Bruno, having perfectly understood the purpose of his mission, set about writing his letters of credit; as the Count was giving him his final instructions, he received a patently false but very well written letter; it appeared to be from a friend writing to a friend to ask a favor. The friend who was writing was none other than the Prince. Having heard something about certain plans of a resignation, he beseeched his friend Count Mosca to remain at his post; he asked this of him in the name of friendship and with regard to the *dangers to the fatherland;* and commanded as much as his Sovereign. He added that since the King of —— had just put two Cordons of his Order at the writer's disposal, he would keep one for himself and send the other to his dear Count Mosca.

"This creature will be the ruin of me!" exclaimed the furious Count in the presence of a stupefied Bruno, "and he expects to seduce me by those same hypocritical phrases we so often devised together to beguile some fool or other . . ."

He rejected the Order that had been offered, and in his answer spoke of the state of his health as leaving him only very faint hopes of being able to perform the heavy duties of the Ministry in the future. The Count was furious. A moment later, the Fiscal Rassi was announced, whom he treated like a blackamoor.

"So now that I've made you a noble, you start playing the insolent with me! Why didn't you come yesterday to thank me, as was your bounden duty, Baron Lackey?"

Rassi was beyond any such insults; this was the tone by which the Prince received him every day; but he craved being a Baron and excused his behavior with a certain wit. Nothing was easier.

"The Prince kept me nailed to a desk all day yesterday; I could not leave the palace. His Highness made me copy in my wretched attorney's hand any number of diplomatic documents that were so stupid and so prolix that I truly believe that his sole purpose was to keep me prisoner. When I was finally able to take my leave, around five o'clock, dying of hunger, he ordered me to proceed directly home and not to go out at all that evening. As a matter of fact, I saw two of his private spies, well known to me, strolling up and down my street until midnight. This morning, as soon as I could, I sent for a carriage, which took me as far as the Cathedral doors. I got out very slowly and then, walking through the church as fast as I could, I came here. Your Excellency is at this very moment the one man in the world I most desire to please."

"And I, Baron Joker, I am not in the least deceived by all these more or less plausible stories of yours! You refused to speak to me about Fabrizio the day before yesterday; I respected your scruples and your oaths of secrecy, though oaths for a creature like yourself are at most no more than means of evasion. Today I want the truth: what are these absurd rumors about condemning this young man to death as the murderer of the actor Giletti?"

"No one can account for these rumors to your Excellency better than I, since it is I who started them on the Sovereign's orders; and come to think of it, it may be to prevent me from informing you of such an incident that he kept me prisoner all day yesterday! The Prince, who does not take me for a madman, could have no doubts that I would come to you with my Cross and request that you fasten it in my buttonhole."

"To the point!" exclaimed the Minister. "No more fine speeches."

"Certainly the Prince would prefer to pass a death sentence upon Signor del Dongo, but he has been sentenced, as you doubtless know, to no more than twenty years in irons, commuted by His Highness the very day following the sentence to twelve years in the Fortress with fasting on bread and water every Friday, and other religious observances."

"It is because I knew of this sentence to imprisonment only that I was alarmed by the rumors of imminent execution spreading through town; I remember the death of Count Palanza, so cleverly devised by you."

"That was when I should have had my Cross!" exclaimed Rassi, in no way disconcerted. "I should have turned the screws while I held him in my hand, and while our man was eager to secure this death. What a fool I was then, and it is armed with this experience that I dare advise you not to follow my example today." This comparison appeared in the very worst taste to his interlocutor, who was obliged to restrain himself to avoid kicking Rassi. "First of all," he continued, with the logic of a jurist and the perfect assurance of a man whom no insult could offend, "first of all there can be no question of the execution of the said del Dongo; the Prince would not dare! Times have changed! And then too, I, a nobleman hoping by your intervention to become a Baron, I would not lend a hand. Now, as Your Excellency knows, it is exclusively from me that the executioner can receive orders, and I swear to you, Cavaliere Rassi will never give any against Signor del Dongo."

"And you will be acting wisely," said the Count, staring at him intensely.

"Let us make a distinction here," Rassi continued with a smile. "I am involved only in the official deaths, and if Signor del Dongo were to die of a colic, I am not to be held responsible! The Prince is in a frenzy, and I do not know why, against the Sanseverina." (Three days earlier, Rassi would have said "the Duchess," but like the rest of the town, he knew of her break with the Prime Minister.)

The Count was struck by the suppression of the title in this man's mouth, and what pleasure it gave him can be imagined; he shot Rassi a glance filled with the most intense hatred. "My beloved angel!" he said to himself later. "I can only show you my love by blindly obeying your orders."

"I confess to you," he observed to the Fiscal, "that I take no very passionate interest in Signora the Duchess's whims; however, since she had introduced me to this unfortunate Fabrizio, who should indeed have remained in Naples and not come here to meddle in our business, I insist that he not be put to death during my tenure, and I am quite willing to give you my word that you shall be named Baron within the eight days which follow his release from prison."

"In that case, Signor Count, I shall be a Baron only after twelve years have passed, for the Prince is furious, and his hatred against the Duchess is so intense that he seeks to conceal it."

"His Highness is only too kind! What need has he of concealing his hatred, since his Prime Minister no longer protects the Duchess? I merely choose not to be accused of baseness, and above all not of jealousy: it is I who invited the Duchess to Parma, and if Fabrizio dies in prison, you shall not be a Baron, but you may well be stabbed. But enough of such details: the fact is that I have examined my fortune; I have found an income of scarcely twenty thousand a year, on which I intend to offer my humble resignation to the Sovereign. I have some hopes of being employed by the King of Naples: that great city will offer me certain distractions which I need at this moment, and which I cannot find in a hole like Parma; only if you might enable me to obtain the hand of Princess Isotta would I remain," and so on.

The conversation on this subject was endless. As Rassi stood up to take his leave, the Count said to him with an indifferent expression: "As you know, it has been said that Fabrizio was deceiving me, since he is accounted one of the Duchess's lovers; I put no credence in such a rumor, and to give it the lie, I want you to see to it that this purse is given to Fabrizio."

"But Signor Count," said Rassi with alarm, eyeing the purse, "what you have there is an enormous sum, and the regulations . . ."

"For you, my dear, it may be enormous," the Count continued with an expression of the most sovereign disdain. "A bourgeois like you, sending money to a friend who happens to be in prison, imagines he is ruining himself by bestowing ten sequins; it is my *wish* that Fabrizio receive these six thousand francs, and in particular that the Palace know nothing of such a gift."

Even as the terrified Rassi sought to reply, the Count impatiently closed the door on him. "Such people," he said to himself, "see power only when it is behind insolence." Whereupon this great Minister gave himself up to an action so absurd that it affords us some pain to report it; he ran to take a miniature portrait of the Duchess out of his desk, and covered it with passionate kisses. "Forgive me, my darling angel," he exclaimed, "if I failed to throw this lackey out of the window with my own hands, who dares speak of you in such familiar tones, but if I behave with such excessive forbearance, it is out of obedience to your wishes! And he will lose nothing by waiting!"

After a long conversation with this portrait, the Count, who felt his heart dying in his breast, had the notion of an absurd action to which he gave himself up with childish eagerness. He sent for a coat bearing all his decorations, and paid a visit to the old Princess Isotta; in all his life he had been presented in her apartments only once, on the occasion of New Year's Day. Now he found her surrounded by a number of little dogs, and decked out in all her finery, including her diamonds, as if she were going to Court. When the Count instanced a certain fear of disturbing Her Highness's arrangements, since she was doubtless about to leave for some occasion, Her Highness replied to the Minister that a Princess of Parma owed it to herself always to be in such array. For the first time since his misfortunes began, the Count experienced an impulse of gaiety. "I did well to come here," he said to himself, "and here and now I must make my declaration." The Princess had been delighted to receive a visit from a man so renowned for his wit and a Prime Minister as well; the poor old maid was anything but accustomed to such attentions. The Count began by an adroit prologue, relative to the enormous distance which will ever separate the members of a ruling family from a mere nobleman.

"There are distinctions to be drawn," the Princess said; "the daughter of a King of France, for instance, has no hope of ever succeeding to the Throne; but such is not the course of events in the family of Parma. That is why we Farnese must always preserve a certain external dignity; and I, a poor Princess as you find me today, I cannot say that it is absolutely impossible that one day you might indeed be my Prime Minister."

The unexpected fantasy of this notion gave the poor Count a second moment of complete gaiety. As he left the apartments of the Princess Isotta, who had blushed deeply upon receiving the avowal of the Prime Minister's passion, the Count encountered one of the palace footmen: the Prince had sent for him, and required his presence with all possible celerity.

"I am ill," the Minister replied, delighted to be able to offer an affront to his Prince. "Aha, you drive me to the brink," he exclaimed in a rage, "and then you want my services! But you will learn, my Prince, that to have received power from Providence no longer suffices in this day and age—it requires a great deal of intelligence and a strong character to succeed in being a tyrant."

After dismissing the footman, who was deeply scandalized by this invalid's perfect health, the Count found it agreeable to visit the two men of the Court who had the most influence over General Fabio Conti. What made the Minister tremble most particularly and robbed him of all courage was that the Governor of the Citadel was accused of having in the past done away with a captain, his personal enemy, by means of the *aquetta di Perugia*.

The Count knew that in the last eight days the Duchess had expended enormous sums to obtain informants in the Citadel; but in his opinion there were few hopes of success, all eyes being, at this time, still too wide open. We shall not describe for the reader all the attempts at corruption made by this unfortunate woman: she was in despair, and agents of all kinds, utterly devoted to her service, were assisting her. But there is perhaps only one kind of business which is performed to perfection in the courts of minor despots, which is the custody of political prisoners. The Duchess's gold produced no effect other than securing the dismissal from the Citadel of eight or ten men of all ranks.

CHAPTER EIGHTEEN

Thus, for all their devotion to the prisoner, the Duchess and the Prime Minister had been able to do very little for him. The Prince was in a rage; the Court as well as the people were *vexed* by Fabrizio and delighted to see him come to grief; he had been too happy. Despite the gold disbursed by the handfuls, the Duchess had not advanced a step in her siege of the Citadel; no day passed without the Marchesa Raversi or Cavaliere Rassi having some new report to communicate to General Fabio Conti. They buttressed his weakness.

As we have said, on the day of his imprisonment, Fabrizio was first taken to the Governor's *palazzo:* this was a pretty little building erected in the last century on Vanvitelli's plans, who placed it one hundred and eighty feet above ground on the platform of the huge round tower. From the windows of this little *palazzo*, isolated on the back of the enormous tower like a camel's hump, Fabrizio could glimpse the countryside and far in the distance the Alps; at the Citadel's foot, he followed by sight the course of the River Parma, a sort of torrent which, turning right four leagues from the town, flung itself into the Po. Beyond the left bank of this river, which formed something like a series of huge white patches amid the green fields, his delighted eyes clearly identified each of the peaks of the vast wall by which the Alps enclose northern Italy. These peaks, perennially covered with snow, even in August as it now was, provide a certain reminder of coolness in the midst of this scorching countryside; the eye can follow their tiniest details, and yet they are more than thirty leagues from the Citadel of Parma. This extensive view from the handsome Governor's *palazzo* is interrupted toward the south corner by the Farnese Tower, in which a room was being hastily prepared for Fabrizio. This second tower, as the reader may recall, was built upon the platform of the great tower in honor of a certain Crown Prince who, unlike Hippolytus the son of Theseus, had not rejected the advances of a young stepmother. The Princess died in a few hours; the Prince's son regained his freedom only seventeen years later, ascending the throne upon his father's death. This extremely ugly Farnese Tower, to which, after waiting three-quarters of an hour, Fabrizio was led, was built another fifty feet above the platform of the main tower and adorned with any number of lightning-rods. The Prince, who, in his displeasure with his wife, had ordered the construction of this prison visible from all parts of the country, had had the singular notion of convincing his subjects that it had existed for ages: hence he gave it the name *Farnese Tower.* It was forbidden to speak of this edifice, though from every point of the city of Parma and the neighboring plains it was easy enough to see the masons laying each of the stones which composed this pentagonal structure. In order to prove its great age, there had been placed above the entrance door two feet wide and four feet high a magnificent bas-relief representing the celebrated General Alessandro Farnese forcing Henri IV to withdraw from Paris. This Farnese Tower, granted such an eminence, consisted of a ground-floor hall at least forty feet long, of comparable width, and filled with squat columns, for this disproportionately large room was no more than fifteen feet high. It was used as a guard-room and in its center an openwork iron staircase no more than two feet wide led upward, spiraling around one of the columns. Up this staircase, which trembled under the tread of the jailers escorting him, Fabrizio reached some huge rooms over twenty feet high, forming a splendid *piano nobile;* they had once been furnished with the greatest luxury for the young Prince who was to spend the best seventeen years of his life there. At one end of this apartment the new prisoner was shown a magnificent chapel, the walls of its vault entirely covered with black marble; black marble columns as well, and of the noblest proportions, were placed in rows along black walls though without touching them, and these walls were embellished with any number of white marble skulls, of colossal size, elegantly carved and supported, each one, by crossbones. "Now here is an invention of the hatred which cannot kill," Fabrizio said to himself, "and what a devilish notion to show me this!"

A light openwork iron staircase, also spiraling around a column, led up to the second floor of this prison, and it was in the rooms of this second floor, which were some fifteen feet high, that for a year now General Fabio Conti had given proof of his genius. First of all, under his direction, the windows of those rooms once occupied by the Prince's servants, and which were more than thirty feet above the flagstones forming the platform of the great round tower, were solidly barred. It was by a dark corridor located in the center of the structure that one reached these rooms which each possessed two windows; and in this very narrow corridor Fabrizio noticed three successive iron gates formed of enormous iron bars and extending up to the ceiling. For two years, the plans, cross-sections, and elevations of all these fine inventions had entitled the General to a weekly audience with his master. A conspirator placed in one of these rooms could not complain to public opinion that he was being treated inhumanely, indeed could have no communication with the outside world, nor make the slightest movement without being heard. The General had had placed in each room huge oak planks forming a sort of trestle some three feet high, and this was his capital invention, the one which entitled him to a claim to the Ministry of Police. Upon these trestles he had set up an echoing cell of planks about ten feet high, which touched the wall only on the window side. On the three other sides there was a narrow corridor some four feet wide between the actual wall of the prison, composed of enormous stone blocks, and the plank walls of the cell. These walls, formed of four double planks of walnut, oak, and maple, were solidly attached together by iron bolts and countless nails.

It was in one of these rooms, constructed a year earlier as General

Fabio Conti's masterpiece and given the splendid name of *Passive Obedience*, that Fabrizio was placed. He ran to the windows; the view from these barred windows was sublime: one tiny corner of the horizon was hidden, to the northwest, by the terraced roof of the Governor's *palazzo*, which was only two stories high; the ground floor was occupied by the staff offices; and immediately Fabrizio's eyes were drawn to one of the windows of the second story, where many birds of all kind were kept in a great number of cages. Fabrizio was delighted to hear them sing and to see them greet the last rays of the setting sun, while his jailers busied themselves around him. This aviary window was not more than twenty-five feet away from his own, and was five or six feet lower, so that he gazed down upon the birds.

There was a moon that evening, and just when Fabrizio entered his prison it was rising majestically above the horizon on the right, above the chain of the Alps, toward Treviso. It was only eight-thirty, and at the other end of the horizon, to the west, a brilliant red and orange sunset distinctly outlined the contours of Monte Viso and the other Alpine peaks which lead from Nice toward Mont-Cénis and Turin; without another thought for his misfortunes, Fabrizio was moved and delighted by this sublime spectacle. "So it is in this ravishing world that Clélia Conti lives! With that pensive, serious soul of hers, she must delight in this view more than anyone in the world; here we seem to be alone in the mountains a hundred leagues from Parma." It was only after having spent more than two hours at the window, admiring this horizon which spoke so intimately to his soul, and often too glancing down at the attractive Governor's *palazzo*, that Fabrizio suddenly exclaimed: "But is this really a prison? Is this what I have dreaded so much?" Instead of noticing at each step certain discomforts and reasons for bitterness, our hero let himself be charmed by the attractions of the prison.

All of a sudden his attention was abruptly returned to reality by a dreadful racket: his wooden room, which closely resembled an echoing cage, was violently shaken; the barks of a dog and tiny shrill cries completed the strangest uproar. "What is this? Am I going to escape so soon?" wondered Fabrizio. A second later he laughed as perhaps no one has ever before laughed in a prison. On the General's orders, there had been sent up, along with the jailers, a savage English dog intended to guard important prisoners; this brute was to spend the night in the passageways so ingeniously devised all around Fabrizio's room. Dog and jailer were to sleep in the three-foot space between the stone blocks of the prison wall and the wooden planks where the prisoner could not take a single step without being heard.

Now, upon Fabrizio's arrival, the room of *Passive Obedience* happened to be occupied by some hundred enormous rats which fled in all directions. The dog, half spaniel and half fox terrier, was anything but handsome though on the other hand appeared extremely alert. It had been attached to the flagstones under the planks of Fabrizio's cell; but upon hearing the rats running so close by, it made such extraordinary efforts that it managed to slip its head out of its collar; then occurred that splendid battle whereof the uproar awakened Fabrizio from the least melancholy reveries. The rats that had managed to escape the first attack took refuge in the wooden cell; the dog pursued them up the six steps leading from the stone floor to Fabrizio's chamber. Then began an even more dreadful racket: the cell was shaken to its foundations. Fabrizio laughed like a madman till tears ran down his cheeks: his jailer Grillo, laughing no less, had closed the door; the dog, pursuing the rats, was not impeded by any piece of furniture, for the room was quite bare; the dog's leaps were hampered only by an iron stove in one corner. When the beast had triumphed over all its enemies, Fabrizio called to it, petted it, and managed to win its favors: "If ever this fellow sees me jumping over some wall," he said to himself, "he won't be barking." But this subtle policy was a boast on his part: in his present state of mind, he found his happiness in playing with this dog. As a result of a strange mood to which he paid no attention, a secret joy prevailed deep in his soul.

After he had grown quite breathless from running with the dog, Fabrizio asked his jailer his name.

"Grillo, at Your Excellency's service in everything the regulations allow."

"Well then, my dear Grillo, as it happens a certain Giletti has tried to murder me on the highway, I defended myself and managed to kill him; I would kill him again if I had to; but that won't keep me from leading the best life I can while I am your guest. Request your superiors' permission and see if you can't bring me some linens from the Palazzo Sanseverina; and buy me a good supply of *nebiolo d'Asti* while you're at it."

This is quite a good sparkling wine made in Piedmont, which is Alfieri's homeland, and highly esteemed, especially by the class of connoisseurs to which the jailers belong. Eight or ten of these gentlemen were busily transporting into Fabrizio's wooden cell some old and heavily gilded pieces of furniture which they were bringing up from the Prince's apartment; all of them religiously took note of this request favoring the wine of Asti. In spite of all their efforts, Fabrizio's establishment for this first night was lamentable; but he appeared upset only by the absence of a bottle of good *nebiolo*.

"He seems like a good boy . . . ," the jailers were saying as they left, "and there is only one thing to be hoped for, that our bosses will let money be sent to him."

Once he was alone and a little recovered from all this uproar: "Can this be a prison?" Fabrizio said to himself, staring at that vast horizon from Treviso to Monte Viso, the long chain of the Alps, the snow-covered peaks, the stars, and so on. "And my first night in prison as well. I imagine that Clélia Conti delights in this lofty solitude; here we are a thousand leagues above the pettiness and the nastiness which occupy us down below. If those birds which are here under my window belong to her, I shall be seeing her. . . . Will she blush when she catches sight of me?" It was in the articulation of this great question that the prisoner found sleep at a very advanced hour of the night.

On the day following this night, the first spent in prison and during which he did not feel a moment's impatience, Fabrizio was reduced to making conversation with *Fox*, the English dog; his jailer Grillo gave him any number of friendly looks, but new orders made him keep silent, and he brought neither linens nor *nebiolo*.

"Shall I see Clélia?" Fabrizio asked himself, as he awoke. "But are those birds hers?" The birds were beginning to utter little cries and to sing, and at this altitude that was the only sound that could be heard upon the air. It was a sensation full of novelty and pleasure for Fabrizio, this vast silence that reigned at this height: he listened with delight to the intense little irregular cheeping by which his neighbors the birds greeted the day. "If they belong to her, she will appear for a moment in that room, right under my window," and even as he considered the enormous chains of the Alps, opposite the first hills of which the Citadel of Parma seemed to rise like a redoubt, his glances kept returning to the fine cages of orange-wood and mahogany, embellished with gilded wires, that filled the bright room which served as an aviary. What Fabrizio learned only later was that this room was the only one on the second floor of the *palazzo* which had shade from eleven till four in the afternoon; it was sheltered then by the Farnese Tower.

"How disappointed I shall be," Fabrizio said to himself, "if instead of that heavenly and thoughtful face I am expecting, and which may blush a little if she catches sight of me, I should see coming the vulgar countenance of some ordinary chambermaid, assigned the task of tending the birds! But if I do see Clélia, will she deign to see me? Upon my soul, I'll have to do something out of the ordinary to be noticed; my situation ought to have some privileges; besides, we're both alone here and so far away from the world! I'm a prisoner, apparently what General Conti and the other such wretches call one of their inferiors. . . . But she has so much sense, or I should say so much soul, as the Count imagines, that perhaps, according to what he says, she despises her father's profession; hence her melancholy! A noble source of sadness! But after all, I am not quite a stranger to her. With what modest grace she greeted me last night! I remember well how during our meeting near Como I told her: Some day I'll come and look at your fine paintings in Parma, will you remember this name: Fabrizio del Dongo? Will she have forgotten? She was so young back then!

"But that reminds me," Fabrizio said to himself, suddenly astonished and interrupting the course of his thoughts, "I was forgetting to be angry! Could I be one of those courageous men of the kind antiquity has revealed to the world? Am I a hero without suspecting it? What! I who was so afraid of prison—here I am, and I don't even recall being melancholy! How true it is that fear has been a hundred times worse than its object. So! I need to reason with myself to be distressed by this prison which, as Blanès used to say, can last ten years as easily as ten months? Might it be the amazement of all these new circumstances which distracts me from the pain I should be feeling? Perhaps this good humor independent of my will and quite without reason will suddenly vanish, perhaps in an instant I shall fall into the black despair that I ought to be feeling.

"In any case, it is quite surprising to be in prison and to have to reason with myself in order to be sad. My word, it brings me back to my supposition—perhaps I have a great character."

Fabrizio's reveries were interrupted by the carpenter of the Citadel, who had come to take the measurements for a window-blind; this was the first time that this prison had been used, and the authorities had forgotten to complete it down to this essential detail.

"So," Fabrizio said to himself, "I shall be deprived of this sublime view," and he tried to feel sad about this privation. "But what are you doing?" he suddenly exclaimed to the carpenter. "Am I no longer to see those pretty birds?"

"Oh, the Signorina's birds that she's so fond of!" the man said good-naturedly. "Hidden, eclipsed, overshadowed like all the rest."

The carpenter, like the jailers, was strictly forbidden to speak, but this man had taken pity on the prisoner's youth: he told him that these enormous shutters, placed over the sills of the two windows and slanting away from the wall, would block out everything but the prisoners' view of the sky.

"This is done to effect their morale," he told him, "in order to increase a salutary sadness and the desire for self-correction in the prisoners' souls; the General," the carpenter added, "has also devised a way of removing the panes of glass and having the windows replaced by oiled paper."

Fabrizio greatly appreciated the epigrammatic turn this conversation was taking, a rare phenomenon in Italy.

"I'd like to have a bird to distract me here, I love their songs; buy me one from Signorina Clélia Conti's chambermaid."

"You mean you know her?" exclaimed the carpenter. "You say her name so readily."

"Who has not heard of this famous beauty? But I've had the honor of meeting her several times at Court."

"The poor young lady leads a very dull life here," the carpenter added; "she spends all her time down there with her birds. This morning she's just bought some splendid orange-trees which she's ordered planted at the gates of the tower under your window; if it weren't for the cornice you could see them."

These were precious words for Fabrizio in this observation, and he found a tactful way of giving the carpenter some money.

"I'm committing two sins at once," this man said to him. "I'm speaking to Your Excellency and I'm taking money. The day after tomorrow, when I come back for the blinds, I'll bring a bird in my pocket, and if I'm not alone, I'll pretend to let it fly away; if I possibly can, I'll bring you a missal; you must be suffering from not being able to say your prayers."

"So," Fabrizio said to himself once he was alone, "these birds are hers, but in two days' time, I shall no longer be seeing them!" With this observation, his thoughts took on a sorrowful tinge. But at last, to his inexpressible delight, after such a long wait and so much gazing, toward noon Clélia came to tend her birds. Fabrizio stood motionless, hardly daring to breathe as he leaned against the huge bars of his window. He noticed that she did not look up toward him, but her gestures had the awkwardness of someone who feels watched. Had she wished to, the poor girl could not have forgotten the faint smile that she had seen flickering over the prisoner's lips, the evening before, when the police were taking him out of the guard-room.

Although, from all appearances, she was paying close attention to her actions, at the moment she approached the aviary window she blushed very noticeably. Fabrizio's first thought, leaning against the iron bars of his window, was to indulge in the child's play of tapping against these bars, which would produce a faint noise; then the mere notion of this indelicacy horrified him. "I should deserve eight days of having her send her chambermaid to tend her birds." This delicate notion would scarcely have occurred to him at Naples or at Novara.

He eagerly followed her with his eyes: "Certainly," he said to himself, "she'll leave without deigning to glance up at this poor window, and yet she's just opposite . . ." But in returning from the rear of the room which Fabrizio, thanks to his higher position, could see quite clearly, Clélia could not keep herself from glancing up, as she was walking, and this was enough for Fabrizio to consider himself authorized to greet her. "Are we not alone in the world here?" he said to himself to work up his courage. Upon this gesture, the girl stood stock-still and lowered her eyes; then Fabrizio saw them look up very slowly; and obviously making a great effort to control herself, Clélia greeted the prisoner with the most serious and *distant* movement, but she could not impose silence upon her eyes; probably without her being aware of it, they expressed for a moment the deepest compassion. Fabrizio noticed that she was blushing so deeply that the pink hue rapidly spread to the upper part of her shoulders, from which the warm air had just caused her to remove, upon entering the aviary, a black lace shawl. The involuntary glance by which Fabrizio responded to her greeting redoubled the girl's confusion.

"How happy that poor woman would be," she was saying to herself, thinking of the Duchess, "if only for a moment she could see him as I am seeing him now."

Fabrizio had had some faint hope of greeting her again upon her departure; but in order to avoid this new salutation, Clélia made a cunning retreat by stages, from cage to cage, as if, ultimately, she had had to tend the birds placed closest to the door. Finally she left the room; Fabrizio stood motionless staring at the door through which she had just vanished; he was another man.

From this moment the sole object of his thoughts was to know how he might manage to continue seeing her, even when this horrible blind had been put in place over the windows which overlooked the Governor's *palazzo*.

The previous evening, before going to sleep, he had given himself the tedious obligation of concealing the best part of what gold he had in the various rat-holes which embellished his wooden cell. "And tonight I must hide my watch. Haven't I heard it said that with patience and a jagged watch-spring, you can cut through wood and even iron? So I might be able to saw through that blind . . ." This labor of hiding his watch, which lasted two long hours, did not seem long at all to him; he brooded over the various ways of achieving his goal, especially over what he knew about carpentry. "If I could manage it," he said to himself, "I might cut out a square of the oak board that will form the shutter, near the part that will rest on the window-sill; I could remove and replace this piece depending on the circumstances; I'll give everything I have to Grillo so that he'll be good enough not to notice this little stratagem." Henceforth all of Fabrizio's happiness was attached to the possibility of performing this task, and he could think of nothing else. "If I can just manage to see her, I'm a happy man. . . . No," he said to himself, "she must also see that I see her." All night long, his head was filled with carpentry stratagems, and he may not have thought even once of the Court of Parma, of the Prince's anger, and so on. We confess that he also did not think of the sufferings that must be overwhelming the Duchess. He waited impatiently for the next day, but the carpenter did not reappear: apparently he was regarded in the prison as a Liberal; it was found necessary to send someone else, a mean-faced fellow who made no reply except to grumble ominously in response to all the agreeable things Fabrizio could think up to say. Some of the Duchess's many attempts to correspond with Fabrizio had been discovered by the Marchesa Raversi's numerous agents, and by her General Fabio Conti was daily informed, alarmed, and put on his mettle. Every eight hours, six soldiers of the guard relieved those in the great hall with the hundred columns; moreover, the Governor posted a special jailer at each of the three iron gates along the corridor, and poor Grillo, the only man who actually saw the prisoner, was condemned to leaving the Farnese Tower only every eight days, which distressed him a good deal. He revealed his ill humor to Fabrizio, who had the wit to reply by no more than these words: "Plenty of *nebiolo d'Asti,* my friend," and gave him some money.

"Well! Even this, which consoles us for every ill," exclaimed the outraged Grillo, his voice barely audible to the prisoner, "we're forbidden to take, and I should refuse it, but I'm going to take it; besides, it's a waste of money; there's nothing I can tell you about anything. You must be nice and guilty; the whole Citadel is in a frenzy on account of you; the Duchess's goings-on have managed to get three of us dismissed already."

"Will the shutter be ready before noon?" Such was the great question which made Fabrizio's heart pound all that long morning; he counted every quarter of an hour which chimed from the Citadel's clock-tower. Finally, when the last quarter before noon was striking, the blind had not yet arrived; Clélia reappeared to tend her birds. Cruel necessity had given wings to Fabrizio's boldness, and the danger of no longer seeing her seemed so overpowering that he dared, as he stared at her, to make the gesture of sawing the shutter with his finger; it is true that immediately after having perceived this gesture, so seditious in a prison, she faintly bowed and withdrew.

"What is this?" exclaimed Fabrizio. "Can she be silly enough to see an absurd familiarity in a gesture dictated by the most imperious necessity? I wanted to ask her to deign, whenever she comes to tend her birds, to glance occasionally at the prison window, even when she finds it covered by an enormous wooden shutter; I wanted to show her that I would do whatever is humanly possible to manage to see her. Good God! Can it be that she won't come tomorrow because of this one indiscreet gesture?"

This fear, which troubled Fabrizio's sleep, was completely justified; the next day Clélia had not appeared by three o'clock in the afternoon, when the huge blinds were put in place over Fabrizio's windows; the various planks had been raised, starting from the esplanade of the great tower, by means of ropes and pulleys attached outside to the iron bars of the windows. It is true that, hidden behind a shutter in her own apartment, Clélia had followed in anguish every action of the workmen; she had clearly seen Fabrizio's mortal anxiety, but had nevertheless had the courage to keep the promise she had made to herself.

Clélia was a little devotee of Liberalism; in her childhood she had taken quite seriously all the Liberal notions she had heard in the company of her father, whose only thoughts were of establishing his position in society; she had then gone on to hold in scorn and virtually in horror the courtier's supple character: hence her antipathy to marriage. Since Fabrizio's arrival, she was filled with remorse: "Now," she said to herself, "my unworthy heart sides with people who seek to betray my father! And he dares make me a gesture of sawing through a door! ... But," she immediately said to herself, her soul overwhelmed, "the whole town is talking of his imminent death! Tomorrow may well be the fatal day! With the monsters who govern us now, anything in the world is possible! What sweetness, what heroic serenity in those eyes which may be about to close forever! Lord! What agonies the Duchess must be suffering! They say she's in complete despair. If I were she, I'd go stab the Prince, like that heroine Charlotte Corday ..."

During this whole third day of his imprisonment, Fabrizio was crazed with anger, but solely for not having seen Clélia reappear.

"Anger for anger, I should have told her that I loved her," he exclaimed to himself, for he had arrived at this discovery. "No, it's not out of greatness of soul that I am ignoring my prison and belying Blanès's prophecy; such honor does not fall to me. In spite of myself I am dreaming of that sweet glance of pity Clélia cast upon me when the police were taking me out of the guard-room; that glance has erased my entire past life. Who could have told me that I should find such gentle eyes in such a place! And just when I had my own eyes sullied by the physiognomy of a Barbone and by that of Signor Governor-General. Heaven appears amidst these vile creatures. And what am I to do if I am not to love beauty and seek to see it again? No, it is not by greatness of soul that I am indifferent to all the little vexations with which prison overwhelms me." Fabrizio's imagination, rapidly considering all the possibilities, arrived at that of being restored to liberty. "No doubt the Duchess's friendship will work miracles for me. Well! I shall thank her for my freedom with no more than my lips; these places are not the sort to which one returns! Once out of prison, separates socially as we are, I shall probably never see Clélia again! And as a matter of fact, what harm has prison done me? If Clélia deigned not to overwhelm me with her anger, what else would I have to ask of Heaven?"

The evening of that day when he had not seen his lovely neighbor, a great idea occurred to him: with the iron cross of the rosary given to each prisoner upon entering prison, he began, and successfully, to bore a hole in the blind. "This may be rash," he said to himself before he began. "Have the carpenters not said in my presence that after tomorrow they will be replaced by painters? What will these workmen say if they find a hole in the shutter over the window? But if I do not commit this rash act, tomorrow I cannot see her. Can it be by my own fault that I shall pass a single day without seeing her! And especially when she left me in anger!" Fabrizio's rash act was rewarded; after fifteen hours of labor, he saw Clélia, and to complete his happiness, since she did not suspect she was being watched by him, she remained motionless for a long time at her window, staring fixedly at the enormous blind; he had plenty of time to read in her eyes the signs of the tenderest pity. At the end of her visit she even obviously neglected to tend her birds, remaining for whole minutes motionlessly staring at his window. Her heart was profoundly troubled; she was thinking of the Duchess whose extreme misfortunes had inspired such pity in her, and yet she was beginning to hate her. She understood nothing about the deep sadness which was overwhelming her spirit; she was annoyed with herself. Two or three times, during this visit, Fabrizio was so impatient as to try shaking the blind; it seemed to him that he was not happy so long as he could not indicate to Clélia that he had seen her. "Still," he said to himself, "if she knew that I saw her so easily, timid and reserved as she is, no doubt she would remove herself from my sight."

He was much happier the next day (out of what miseries does love not create its happiness!): while she was sadly staring at the huge blind, he managed to thrust a tiny piece of wire through the hole his iron cross had made, and with it made signs which she obviously understood, at least insofar as they meant: I am here and I see you.

Fabrizio was unlucky on the days that followed. He wanted to cut out of the enormous blind a piece of wood the size of his hand, which he could replace at will and which would allow him to see and be seen, in other words to speak, by signs at least, of what was occurring in his heart and soul; but it so happened that the noise of the very imperfect little saw he had made out of his watch-spring serrated by the iron cross aroused Grillo, who came to spend long hours in his room. He imagined he noticed, it is true, that Clélia's severity seemed to diminish in inverse proportion to the material difficulties which opposed any communication; Fabrizio could see quite well that she no longer pretended to lower her eyes or to look at her birds when he tried to give her some sign of his presence with the help of his wretched bit of iron wire; he had the pleasure of seeing that she never failed to appear in the aviary precisely when the last quarter-hour before noon chimed from the clock-tower, and he was nearly presumptuous enough to regard himself as the cause of this regular punctuality. Why? This idea seems scarcely rational, but love observes nuances invisible to the indifferent eye, and from them draws infinite consequences. For instance, since Clélia no longer saw the prisoner, almost immediately upon entering the aviary she looked up toward his window. This was during those funereal days when no one in Parma doubted that Fabrizio would soon be put to death: he alone was unaware of it, but this dreadful idea never left Clélia's mind, and how could she have blamed herself for her excessive interest in Fabrizio? He was going to die! And for the cause of freedom! For it was too absurd to execute a del Dongo for running through a mere player. It is true that this lovable young man was attached to another woman! Clélia was profoundly unhappy, and without precisely admitting to herself the sort of interest she was taking in his fate. "Of course," she said to herself, "if he is put to death, I shall withdraw to a convent and never again participate in court life—how it horrifies me! Fine-mannered murderers!"

The eighth day of Fabrizio's imprisonment, she had a good cause for shame: she was staring fixedly and quite absorbed in her sad thoughts at the shutter concealing the prisoner's window; that day he had not yet given any sign of his presence; suddenly a tiny piece of the shutter, slightly bigger than a man's hand, was removed: Fabrizio stared at her with a happy expression, and she met the greeting in his eyes. She could not sustain this unexpected ordeal, and quickly turned back to her birds and began tending them; but she was trembling so violently that she spilled the water she was giving them, and Fabrizio could see her emotion quite clearly; she could not endure this situation, and decided to run out of the room.

This moment was incomparably the finest in Fabrizio's life. With what transports he would have rejected freedom, had it been offered to him then!

The following day was the day of the Duchess's great despair. The entire city was convinced that it was all over with Fabrizio: Clélia lacked the mournful courage to show him a hardness which was not in her heart; she spent an hour and a half in the aviary, stared at all his signs, and frequently answered them, at least by the expression of the liveliest and sincerest interest; she left him at certain moments in order to hide her tears. Her woman's coquetry was intensely aware of the imperfection of the language employed: had they managed to speak, in how many different ways might she not have sought to divine the precise nature of Fabrizio's feelings for the Duchess! Clélia was now almost unable to deceive herself; she hated Signora Sanseverina.

One night, Fabrizio happened to think somewhat seriously about his aunt: he was amazed, and scarcely recognized her image, so completely had his memory of her altered; for him, at this moment, she was fifty years old.

"Good God!" he exclaimed with enthusiasm. "How right I was not to tell her I loved her!"

He had reached the point of virtually no longer being able to understand how he had come to find her so pretty. In this regard, little Marietta made an altered impression that was less distinct: the fact was that he had never imagined that his soul counted for anything in his love for Marietta, while frequently he had imagined that his whole soul belonged to the Duchess. The Duchess of A—— and Marietta now had the effect on him of two young doves whose entire charm was in their weakness and innocence, while the sublime image of Clélia Conti, in seizing his whole soul, reached the point of inspiring him with terror. He was all too aware that the eternal happiness of his life would oblige him to reckon with the Governor's daughter, and that it was within her power to make of him the most wretched of men. Each day he was in mortal fear of seeing end, abruptly, by a whim without appeal from his own will, this sort of singular and delicious life which he found himself living so close to her; yet she had already filled with happiness the first two months of his imprisonment. This was the period when, twice a week, General Fabio Conti would say to the Prince: "I can give Your Highness my word of honor that the prisoner del Dongo is not speaking to a living soul, and is spending his days overcome by the deepest despair or in sleep."

Clélia came two or three times a day to tend her birds, occasionally for only moments at a time: if Fabrizio had not loved her so much, he would certainly have perceived that he was loved; but he had mortal doubts in this regard. Clélia had had a piano moved into the aviary. While touching the keys, so that the sound of the instrument might acknowledge her presence and beguile the sentries who paraded under her windows, her eyes responded to Fabrizio's questions. On only one subject did she make no reply, and even, on certain great occasions, took to flight and occasionally vanished for a whole day; this was when Fabrizio's signs indicated sentiments the import of which it was too difficult not to understand: on this point she was inexorable.

Thus, although closely confined in a rather narrow cage, Fabrizio was leading a very busy life; it was entirely given over to seeking the solution to this terribly important problem: "Does she love me?" The result of thousands of constantly renewed observations, though also constantly cast into doubt, was this: "All her deliberate gestures say no, but everything that is involuntary in the movement of her eyes seems to admit that she feels a certain friendship for me."

Clélia was indeed hoping never to reach the point of an avowal, and it was to defray this danger that she had repelled, with excessive anger, a plea Fabrizio had made to her on several occasions. The wretchedness of the resources employed by the poor prisoner ought, it would seem, to have inspired greater pity in Clélia. He sought to communicate with her by means of letters he drew on his palm with a piece of charcoal of which he'd made the precious discovery in his stove; he would have formed the words letter by letter, in succession. This invention would have doubled the means of conversation in that it would have permitted saying specific things. His window was about twenty-five feet away from Clélia's; it would have been too risky to speak to each other over the heads of the sentries parading in front of the Governor's *palazzo*. Fabrizio doubted whether he was loved; had he had some experience of love, no such doubts would have remained; but no woman had ever occupied his heart; moreover he had no suspicion of a secret which would have reduced him to despair had he known it: there was serious question of the marriage of Clélia Conti to the Marchese Crescenzi, the richest man at Court.

Chapter Nineteen

General Fabio Conti's ambition, exalted to madness by the difficulties which had just arisen in Prime Minister Mosca's career and which appeared to herald his fall, had led him to create violent scenes with his daughter. He repeated to her incessantly, and angrily, that she would be the ruin of his fortunes if she did not finally decide upon a husband; at over twenty, it was time to make a match; this state of cruel isolation into which her unreasonable stubbornness had plunged the General must be brought to an end, and so forth.

It was initially to avoid these constant fits of rage that Clélia had sought refuge in the aviary, which could be reached only by a steep and narrow wooden staircase constituting a serious obstacle for the General's gout.

For several weeks, Clélia's soul was so agitated, she was so uncertain of what she ought to want, that without quite making any promises to her father, she had virtually allowed herself to become engaged. In one of these fits of rage, the General had exclaimed that he might well send her to cool her heels in the gloomiest convent in Parma, where he would leave her to sulk until she deigned to make up her mind.

"You know that our family, old as it is, cannot muster an income of six thousand lire a year, while the Marchese Crescenzi's annual fortune amounts to over a hundred thousand scudi. Everyone at court agrees that he has the best disposition; he has never given anyone reason for complaint; he's handsome, young, in favor with the Prince, and you would have to be mad to reject his advances. If this rejection were the only one, I might tolerate it; but here are five or six suitors, among the first men at Court, whom you refuse, like the little fool that you are. And what would become of you, pray tell, were I to be retired on half-pay? What a victory for my enemies if I were seen living in some second-floor apartment, often as I was considered for the Ministry! No, a thousand times no! My good nature has led me to play the part of a Cassandra long enough. Either you'll give me some good reason for turning down this poor Marchese Crescenzi, who's had the kindness to fall in love with you, to agree to marry you without a dowry, and to make you a settlement of thirty thousand lire a year, on which at least I could have a roof over my head—you'll give me a reason or by God you'll marry him in two months . . ."

One phrase in this whole speech caught Clélia's attention: the threat of being sent to a convent and consequently removed from the Citadel, and just when Fabrizio's life seemed to be hanging by no more than a thread, for not a month passed without the rumor of his imminent death running once again through Court and town alike. No matter how she reasoned, she could not bring herself to take such a risk: to be separated from Fabrizio, and just when she was trembling for his life! That in her eyes was the greatest misfortune of all, or at least the most immediate.

Not that, even were she not separated from Fabrizio, her heart foresaw any prospect of happiness; she believed him loved by the Duchess, and her soul was lacerated by a deadly jealousy. She kept brooding over the advantages enjoyed by this woman, so universally admired. The extreme reserve she imposed upon herself with regard to Fabrizio, the sign-language to which she had confined him, lest she fall into some indiscretion—everything seemed to combine to deprive her of the means of reaching some clear understanding of his relations with the Duchess. So every day she felt ever more cruelly the dreadful misfortune of having a rival in Fabrizio's heart, and every day she dared less and less to expose herself to the peril of giving him the chance to tell the whole truth about what was going on in his heart. But what a delight it would be to hear him confess his true feelings! What happiness for Clélia to be able to dispel the terrible suspicions poisoning her life.

Fabrizio was fickle; in Naples, he had the reputation of charming mistresses quite readily. Despite all the reserve imposed upon the role of a young lady, ever since she had become a Canoness and attended Court, Clélia, without ever asking questions but by listening attentively, had managed to learn the reputations of the young men who had, one after the next, sought her hand in marriage; well then, Fabrizio, compared to all the others, was the one who was least trustworthy in affairs of the heart. He was in prison, he was bored, he paid court to the one woman he could speak to—what could be simpler? What, indeed, *more common?* And this was what plunged Clélia into despair. Even if, by some full revelation, she might have learned that Fabrizio no longer loved the Duchess, what confidence could she have in his words? Even if she could have believed in the sincerity of his speeches, what confidence could she have had in the lasting nature of his feelings? And finally, to complete the prospect of despair in her heart, was not Fabrizio already far advanced in an ecclesiastical career? Was he not on the verge of committing himself to eternal vows? Did not the greatest dignities await him if he adopted such a life? "If the slightest gleam of sense still remained in my heart," the wretched Clélia was telling herself, "should I not beg my father to lock me up in some faraway convent? And the last stroke of misery, it is precisely the fear of being taken away from the Citadel and being shut up in a convent which governs everything I do! It is this terror which obliges me to dissimulate, which compels me to the hideous and shameful lie of pretending to accept the arrangements and the public attentions of Marchese Crescenzi."

Clélia's character was a profoundly rational one; her whole life long, she had never had to reproach herself for a single rash action, and her behavior in the present case was the height of irrationality:

imagine her sufferings! ... They were all the worse in that she permitted herself no illusions. She was attached to a man who was wildly loved by the handsomest woman at Court, a woman who, on so many counts, was Clélia's superior! And this very man, had he been free, was incapable of a serious attachment, while she, as she felt all too well, would never have but one attachment in all her life.

So it was with a heart agitated by the deepest remorse that Clélia, every day, came to the aviary: compelled to this place as if in spite of herself, her anxiety changed its object and became milder, her remorse vanished for a while; she waited, her heart pounding, for the moment when Fabrizio might open the sort of transom he had made in the huge shutter covering his window. Often the presence of the jailer Grillo in his room kept him from conversing with her by sign-language.

One night, at about eleven, Fabrizio heard the strangest noises in the Citadel: after dark, lying on the window-sill and poking his head through the transom, he could manage to distinguish the louder noises made on the great staircase known as the three hundred steps, leading from the first courtyard inside the round tower to the stone platform on which the governor's *palazzo* and the Farnese prison had been built.

About half-way up, at a height of a hundred and twenty-five steps, this staircase crossed from the south side of a huge courtyard to the north, where there was a very narrow iron catwalk, in the center of which a turnkey was posted. This man was relieved every six hours, and he was obliged to stand up and move to one side in order to let anyone pass on the catwalk which he was guarding and which was the only way to get into the Governor's *palazzo* and the Farnese Tower. It sufficed to give two turns to a spring, the key of which the Governor kept in his possession, to cast this iron catwalk into the courtyard more than a hundred feet below; this simple precaution taken, since there was no other staircase in the whole Citadel and since every midnight a sergeant brought to the Governor's residence, and put in a cabinet reached through his bedroom, the ropes of all the wells, he remained quite inaccessible in his *palazzo*, and it would have been equally impossible for anyone to reach the Farnese Tower. This is what Fabrizio had distinctly noticed the day he had entered the Citadel, and what

Grillo, who, like all the jailers, loved boasting about his prison, had explained to him several times: thus he had little hope of escaping. However he recalled one of Abbé Blanès's sayings:

> A lover thinks more often how to reach his mistress than a husband how to protect his wife; a prisoner thinks more often how to escape than a jailer how to lock his cell; thus, whatever the obstacles, lover and prisoner will triumph.

That night, Fabrizio quite distinctly heard a large number of men crossing the iron catwalk known as the slave's bridge, because once a Dalmatian slave had managed to escape by throwing the catwalk guard down into the courtyard.

"They're coming to take someone away, maybe they're going to take me out to be hanged; but there may be some disorder, and I must make the most of it." He had armed himself, and was already taking his money out of its various hiding-places, when suddenly he stopped. "What a funny creature man is!" he exclaimed, "There's no denying it: what would an invisible spectator say, watching these preparations? Would I be thinking of making my escape? What would happen to me the day after I managed to get back to Parma? Would I not do anything in the world to return to Clélia? If there's some disorder, let's take advantage of it to slip into the governor's *palazzo;* maybe I'll be able to speak to Clélia, maybe under cover of the confusion I'll manage to kiss her hand. General Conti is as suspicious as he is vain, and keeps five sentries guarding his *palazzo,* one at each corner of the building and a fifth at the main door, but luckily it's a very dark night." Stealthily, Fabrizio went over to see what his jailer Grillo and his dog were up to: the jailer was sound asleep in an oxhide slung from the ceiling by four ropes and encased in a coarse netting; the dog Fox opened his eyes, stood up, and crept toward Fabrizio to lick his hand.

Softly our prisoner went back up the six steps leading to his wooden chamber; the noise at the foot of the Farnese Tower, and right in front of the door, was becoming so loud that he was sure Grillo would wake up. Fabrizio, armed to the teeth and ready for action, was imagining he was destined, this very night, for great adventures, when all of a sudden he heard the opening bars of the loveliest symphony in the world: a serenade being played for the General, or for his daughter. Fabrizio fell into a fit of hysterical laughter: "And I was planning to use my dagger! As if a serenade were not infinitely more commonplace an event than a rebellion or an abduction requiring the presence of eighty men in a prison!" The music was excellent, and sounded delicious to Fabrizio, whose spirit had not had distraction of this sort for so many weeks; it caused him to shed many gentle tears; in his delight, he made the most irresistible speeches to lovely Clélia. But the next day, at noon, he found her so deeply melancholy, and so pale, and in her glances he read such flashes of rage, that he did not feel sufficiently justified in questioning her about the serenade; he was afraid of seeming discourteous.

Clélia had good reason to be melancholy; the serenade was being given her by the Marchese Crescenzi: so public an action was a kind of official announcement of their engagement. Until the very day of the serenade, and until nine that evening, Clélia had put up the best possible resistance, but she had had the weakness of yielding to her father's threat of sending her immediately to a convent.

"Then I should never see him again!" she had said to herself through her tears. It was in vain that her reason added: "I should never again see this person who would be my downfall in any case; I should never again see the Duchess's lover; I should never again see a man who has had ten known mistresses in Naples and who has betrayed them all; I should never see this young careerist who, if he does survive the sentence that hangs over his head, will take holy orders anyway! It would be a crime for me to see him again once he is outside the Citadel, and his natural frivolity will spare the temptation to do so; for what am I to him? An excuse for distracting himself for a few hours of each of his days in prison." Amidst all this abuse, Clélia managed to remember the smile with which Fabrizio had observed the police surrounding him when he left the turnkey's office to climb up to the Farnese Tower. Tears filled her eyes: "Dear friend, what wouldn't I do for you! You will ruin me, I know you will, it is my fate, I am ruining myself by listening to this dreadful serenade this evening; but tomorrow, at noon, I shall see your eyes once more!"

It was precisely on the day after that day when Clélia had made such great sacrifices for the young prisoner whom she loved so passionately; it was the day after that day when, realizing all his faults, she had sacrificed her life to him, that Fabrizio was cast into despair by her coldness. If even by employing no more than the imperfect language of signs, he had done the slightest violence to Clélia's soul, she probably would not have been able to restrain her tears, and Fabrizio would have obtained a confession of all that she felt for him; but he lacked boldness, he was too mortally afraid of offending Clélia; she might inflict too severe a punishment upon him. In other words, Fabrizio had no experience of the kind of emotion produced by a woman one loves; it was a sensation he had never felt, even in its faintest nuance. It took him eight days, after the night of the serenade, to return to the familiar footing of simple friendship with Clélia. The poor girl armed herself with severity, dying of fear lest she betray herself; and to Fabrizio it seemed that he was more remote from her each day that passed.

One day—some three months since Fabrizio had been in prison without having any communication with the outside world, and yet without feeling particularly unhappy—Grillo remained late into the morning in his room; Fabrizio did not know how to get rid of him; he was in despair; finally the second quarter after noon had already chimed when he was able to open the two little trap-doors about a foot high which he had cut into the fatal shutter.

Clélia was standing at the aviary window, her eyes fixed on Fabrizio's transom; her drawn features expressed the most violent despair. No sooner had she caught sight of him than she signaled that all was lost: she rushed to her piano and, pretending to sing a recitative from an opera popular at the moment, she told him, in phrases interrupted by despair and fear of being understood by the sentries parading under the window: "Good God, and are you still alive? Thanks be to Heaven! Barbone, that jailer whose insolence you punished the day you came here, had vanished, was no longer in the Citadel: the night before last he returned, and since yesterday I have reason to believe he is attempting to poison you. He comes prowling into the private kitchens of the *palazzo,* which supply your meals. I know nothing for certain, but my chambermaid believes that this hideous person never enters the kitchens except with the intention of taking someone's life. I was perishing with anxiety, and not seeing you appear, I believed you dead. Refrain from all nourishment until further notice; I shall do everything possible to send you a little chocolate. In any case, at nine tonight, if it is Heaven's will that you possess a piece of string, or that you can form the strips of your sheets into a ribbon, let it down from your window to the orange-trees, I shall attach a cord to it which you will pull up to yourself, and by means of this cord I shall be able to supply you with some bread and chocolate."

Fabrizio had preserved as a treasure the piece of charcoal he had found in the stove of his room; he hurriedly took advantage of Clélia's emotion and wrote on his hand a series of letters which, taken in order, spelled out these words:

I love you, and life is precious to me only because I see you; above all things, send me some paper and a pencil.

As Fabrizio had hoped, the extreme terror he had read in Clélia's features kept the girl from breaking off the interview after this bold expression *I love you;* she was content merely to show a good deal of annoyance. Fabrizio had the wit to add:

The high winds blowing today keep me from hearing clearly the advice you have sung to me, the sound of the piano drowns out your voice. What is that poison, for instance, that I believe you mentioned?

At this word, the girl's terror reappeared full strength; hastily she began drawing huge letters in ink on the pages she tore out of a book, and Fabrizio was transported with delight to see established at last, after three months of attempts, this means of correspondence he had so vainly sought. He took care not to abandon the little ruse which had worked so well for him; he hoped to write real letters, and kept pretending not to grasp the words of which Clélia was showing him the successive letters.

She was obliged to leave the aviary to join her father; above all she was in terror he might come looking for her; his suspicious genius had been quite dissatisfied with the close proximity of this aviary window and the shutter masking the prisoner's. Clélia herself had had the notion a few moments earlier, when Fabrizio's non-appearance had plunged her into such anxiety, that it would be possible to throw a pebble wrapped in a piece of paper toward the upper part of this shutter; if Chance would have it that the jailer in charge of Fabrizio at that moment did not happen to be in his room, then this would be a sure means of correspondence.

Our prisoner made haste to construct a ribbon out of strips of his sheets, and that evening, shortly after nine, he clearly heard some tapping on the tubs of the orange-trees under his window; he let down his ribbon, which brought him back a very long slender cord, by which he was first able to pull up a supply of chocolate and then, to his inexpressible satisfaction, a roll of paper and a pencil. It was in vain that he let down the cord again; he received nothing more; apparently the sentries had come near the orange-trees. But he was intoxicated with joy. He hastened to write an endless letter to Clélia; no sooner was it finished than he fastened it to his cord and sent it down. For over three hours he waited in vain for it to be collected, and several times drew it up again to make changes in his text. "If Clélia does not see my letter tonight," he said to himself, "while she is still moved by her ideas about poison, tomorrow morning she may well have nothing to do with the idea of receiving a letter from me."

The fact is that Clélia had not been able to avoid going down into the city with her father: Fabrizio had virtually guessed as much when he heard the General's carriage returning, two quarters after midnight; he recognized the sound of the horses' hooves. What was his joy when, a few minutes after having heard the General cross the esplanade and the sentries present arms, he felt a tug on the cord, which he kept wrapped around his arm! A heavy weight was attached to this cord; two little tugs gave him the signal to pull it up. He had some difficulty in getting the heavy object he was pulling up around the jutting cornice under his window. This refractory object proved to be a carafe filled with water and wrapped in a shawl. It was with ecstasy that this poor young man, who had lived so long in such complete solitude, covered this shawl with kisses. But we must abandon describing his emotion when at last, after so many days of vain hopes, he discovered a tiny piece of paper pinned to the shawl:

Drink only this water, live on chocolate; tomorrow I will do all I can to send you some bread, I will mark it all around with little ink crosses. It is horrible to say, but you must know: Barbone may be assigned to poison you. How could you help knowing that the subject you mention in your penciled letter is certain to displease me? Therefore I should not be writing you, were it not for the extreme danger which threatens you. I have just seen the Duchess; she and the Count are both very well, but she has grown much thinner; do not write to me again on this subject: are you trying to make me angry?

It was a great effort of virtue, on Clélia's part, to write the penultimate line of this letter. Everyone was claiming, in court circles, that Signora Sanseverina was becoming very friendly with Count Baldi, that handsome man, the former lover of the Marchesa Raversi. What was certain was that he had broken with the latter in the most scandalous fashion, though for six years she had been more than a mother to him and had established him in society.

Clélia had been obliged to begin this hastily written little note over again, because her first version betrayed something of these new amours which public malice attributed to the Duchess.

"How vile of me!" she had reproached herself, "to say something bad to Fabrizio about the woman he loves . . . !"

The next morning, long before daybreak, Grillo entered Fabrizio's room, set down a heavy package, and vanished without saying a word. This package contained a good-sized loaf of bread speckled on all sides with tiny ink crosses. Fabrizio covered them with kisses; he was in love. Next to the loaf was a roll of something wrapped in many folds of paper; it held six thousand francs in sequins; and last of all, Fabrizio found a handsome brand-new missal: a hand he was beginning to know had written these words in the margin:

Poison! Be careful about water, wine, any kind of food; live on chocolate, try to make the dog eat the dinner you won't touch; if you reveal that you suspect something, the enemy will try some other means. Nothing foolish, in God's name! No frivolity.

Fabrizio hurriedly effaced these beloved words which might compromise Clélia, and tore out a great many pages of the missal, with the help of which he made several alphabets; each letter was carefully drawn with crushed charcoal soaked in wine. These alphabets were dry when at three-quarters past eleven Clélia appeared two steps back from the aviary window. "The great thing now," Fabrizio said to himself, "is to get her to use them." But luckily it so happened that she had many things to say to the young prisoner concerning the attempted poisoning: a dog belonging to one of the serving-girls had died from having eaten a dish intended for him. Clélia, far from offering objections to using the alphabets, had prepared a splendid one with ink. The conversation undertaken by this means, quite inconvenient in its initial phrases, lasted no less than an hour and a half, in other words all the time Clélia could remain in the aviary. Two or three times when Fabrizio permitted himself forbidden subjects, she did not answer, and left for a moment to give her birds the care they needed. Fabrizio had persuaded her that after dark, when she sent him water, she should include one of the alphabets which she had drawn in ink and which was much easier to read. He lost no time in writing a very long letter in which he was careful not to express any tender thoughts, at least not in a fashion which might give offense. This stratagem succeeded; his letter was accepted.

The following day, in their conversation by alphabets, Clélia made him no reproaches; she informed him that there was less danger of poison now; Barbone had been attacked and almost killed by some men who were courting the serving-maids in the governor's kitchen; it was likely that he would not dare reappear there. Clélia confessed that for Fabrizio's sake she had dared steal an antidote from her father; she was sending it to him: the important thing was to refuse any food served to him which seemed to taste strange.

Clélia had put many questions to Don Cesare, without managing to discover the provenance of the six hundred sequins Fabrizio had received; in any case, the gift was an excellent sign; the severity of his supervision was diminishing.

This episode of the poison enormously advanced our prisoner's interests, yet he could never obtain the least avowal which might resemble love, though he had the felicity of living on the most intimate terms with Clélia. Every morning, and frequently in the afternoons, there was a long conversation with the alphabets; each evening, at nine, Clélia accepted a long letter, and occasionally answered it with a few words; she would send him the newspaper and some books; finally Grillo had been won over to the point of permitting Fabrizio some bread and wine, which were delivered daily by Clélia's chambermaid. The jailer had concluded from this that the Governor was not in agreement with the men who had ordered Barbone to poison the young Monsignore, and he was relieved to think so, as were all his comrades, for it had become proverbial in the prison that "you need only look into Monsignore del Dongo's eyes for him to give you money."

Fabrizio had grown quite pale; the complete lack of exercise was bad for his health; with this exception he had never been so happy. The tone of his conversations with Clélia was intimate, and occasionally very merry. The only moments of Clélia's life which were not haunted by dreadful forebodings and remorse were those which she spent in such dialogues. One day she was rash enough to tell him: "I admire your delicacy; knowing I am the Governor's daughter, you never mention your desire to regain your freedom."

"That is because I am careful not to have any such nonsensical desire," Fabrizio answered. "Once back in Parma, how would I see you again? And then life would be unendurable if I couldn't tell you everything I think. . . . No, not quite everything I think, you have seen to that; but after all, despite your cruelty, living without seeing you every day would be a much worse torment than this prison! I've never been so happy in my life! . . . Isn't it funny to discover that happiness was waiting for me in a prison?"

"There are many things to say in that regard," replied Clélia with an expression suddenly very serious and almost sinister.

"What do you mean?" cried Fabrizio, suddenly alarmed. "Am I

likely now to lose this tiny place which I've been able to win in your heart and which constitutes all the happiness I have in this world?"

"Yes," she told him, "I have every reason to believe that you have failed to be truthful with me, though you may be regarded in society as a man of honor; but I do not wish to discuss this subject today."

This singular opening cast a pall of embarrassment over their conversation, and frequently his eyes or hers filled with tears.

Chief Justice Rassi was still aspiring to a change of name: he was quite tired of the one he had made for himself and longed to become Baron Riva. Count Mosca, for his part, was endeavoring with all the skill he possessed to strengthen this venal judge's passion for the title, even as he sought to redouble the Prince's mad hope of becoming Constitutional Monarch of Lombardy. These were the only means he could devise to delay Fabrizio's death.

The Prince said to Rassi: "Fifteen days of despair and fifteen of hope—it is by such a regime, patiently followed, that we shall succeed in overcoming the character of this haughty woman; it is by such alternating harshness and gentleness that even the fiercest steeds are tamed. Apply the caustic firmly."

Indeed, every fortnight a new rumor circulated in Parma announcing Fabrizio's imminent execution. This report plunged the unhappy Duchess into the deepest despair. Loyal to her resolve not to drag the Count to his ruin, she was punished for her cruelty toward this poor man by the continual alternations of black despair in which her life was now spent. In vain Count Mosca, overcoming the cruel jealousy inspired by the handsome Count Baldi's attentions, wrote to the Duchess whenever he was unable to see her and kept her abreast of whatever information he owed to the future Baron Riva's zeal; the Duchess, in order to resist the terrible rumors that kept circulating about Fabrizio, would have needed to spend her every waking moment in the company of a man of heart and wit comparable to Mosca himself; Baldi's emptiness, leaving her to her thoughts, afforded a dreadful style of existence, and the Count failed to communicate to her his own reasons for hope.

By means of various ingenious excuses, this Minister had managed to persuade the Prince to deposit in a friendly castle near Saronno, in the very heart of Lombardy, the archives of all the highly complicated intrigues by means of which Ranuccio-Ernesto IV nourished the utterly absurd hope of becoming Constitutional Monarch of that fair region. More than twenty of these highly compromising documents were in the Prince's hand or signed by him, and in the event of Fabrizio's life being seriously threatened, the Count had planned to inform his Highness that he would communicate these documents to a great power who, by a word, could crush him.

Count Mosca regarded himself as sure of the future Baron Riva, and feared only poison; Barbone's attempt had greatly alarmed him, and to such a degree that he had decided to risk an action quite insane to all appearances. One morning he arrived at the Citadel gates and asked for General Fabio Conti, who came down as far as the bastion over the gates; here, strolling in a friendly fashion after a bittersweet and conventional little preface, the Count did not hesitate to remark: "If Fabrizio dies under suspicious circumstances, this death may well be laid to my account; I shall pass for a jealous man, which would be an abominable absurdity for me, one I should be determined not to accept. Therefore, and to clear myself of it, were Fabrizio to die of some sickness, I should kill you with my own hands, you may count on that."

General Fabio Conti made a splendid reply and spoke of his own valor, but he could not get the Count's expression out of his mind.

A few days later, and as if he had conspired with the Count, Chief Justice Rassi allowed himself a singular indiscretion for such a man. The public scorn attached to his name which was proverbial among the common people had sickened him ever since he had nourished some definite hopes of being able to escape such a label. He sent General Fabio Conti an official copy of the sentence condemning Fabrizio to an imprisonment of twelve years in the Citadel. According to the law, this is what should have been done the very day after Fabrizio entered the prison; but what was unheard-of in Parma, that realm of secret measures, was that the courts should permit such a step without the Sovereign's express orders to do so. Indeed, how to encourage hopes of redoubling the Duchess's alarm every fortnight, and of taming this proud nature, as the Prince put it, once an official copy of the sentence had left the Chancellery of Justice? The day before the day when General Fabio Conti received Chief Justice Rassi's official communication, he learned that the clerk Barbone had been badly beaten upon returning somewhat late to the Citadel; from this he concluded that there was no longer any question in certain quarters of doing away with Fabrizio; and by a touch of prudence which saved Rassi from the immediate consequences of his folly, he made no mention to the Prince, upon the first audience he obtained with him, of the official copy of the prisoner's sentence which had been transmitted to him. The Count had discovered, fortunately for the poor Duchess's peace of mind, that Barbone's clumsy attempt had been no more than an impulse of private revenge, and he had caused that clerk to be given the warning already mentioned.

Fabrizio was quite agreeably surprised when, after one hundred and thirty-five days in prison, in a rather narrow cell, the good chaplain Don Cesare arrived one Thursday to take him for a stroll on the esplanade of the Farnese Tower: Fabrizio had not been there ten minutes when, overcome by the freshness of the air, he was taken ill.

Don Cesare made the incident an excuse to grant Fabrizio half an hour's such exercise every day. This was a piece of folly; such frequent strolls soon restored to our hero a strength which he abused.

There were several more serenades; the punctilious Governor permitted them only because they involved the Marchese Crescenzi with his daughter Clélia, whose character now alarmed him; he vaguely realized that there was no point of contact between her and himself, and still feared some action on her part. She might take refuge in a convent, and he would be quite helpless to prevent it. Furthermore, the General feared that all this music, whose sounds could penetrate to the deepest dungeons reserved for the blackest Liberals, might contain signals. The musicians themselves roused his jealousy for their own sake; hence no sooner was the serenade over than they were confined in the great lower halls of the Governor's *palazzo,* which by day served as staff offices, and released only the next morning in broad daylight. It was the Governor himself who, standing on the slave's bridge, had them searched in his presence and restored their liberty, not without repeating several times that he would immediately hang any man who might have the audacity to bear messages of any kind to any prisoner. And it was known that in his fear of giving offense he was a man to keep his word, so that the Marchese Crescenzi was obliged to pay his musicians three times their usual fee, so distressed had they been to spend the night in prison.

All that the Duchess could obtain, and this with the greatest difficulty, from the cowardice of one of these men, was that he would take a letter which would be delivered to the Governor. The letter was addressed to Fabrizio, and in it the writer deplored the fatality which so arranged matters that after he had spent more than five months in prison, Fabrizio's friends in the world outside had been unable to establish any correspondence with him whatsoever.

Upon entering the Citadel, this bribed musician flung himself at General Conti's feet and confessed that a priest unknown to him had so insisted that he take a letter to Signor del Dongo that he had not dared refuse; but that knowing his duty, he now made haste to put it into His Excellency's hands.

His Excellency was highly flattered: he knew the resources at the Duchess's disposal, and was terrified of being hoaxed. In his delight, the General went so far as to present this letter to the Prince, who was delighted.

"So, the firmness of my administration has afforded me my revenge! This haughty woman has been suffering for five months! But one of these days we'll have a scaffold built, and her wild imagination will not fail to believe that it is intended for young del Dongo!"

CHAPTER TWENTY

One night, toward one o'clock in the morning, Fabrizio, leaning on his window-sill, had pushed his head through the opening cut in the shutter, and was contemplating the stars and the vast horizon to be enjoyed from the top of the Farnese Tower. His eyes, sweeping the countryside toward the lower Po and Ferrara, happened to notice an extremely small but rather bright light apparently emanating from the top of another tower. "That light cannot be visible from the plain," Fabrizio said to himself, "the tower's thickness keeps it from being seen from down below—it must be some signal for a distant point." Suddenly he noticed that this light appeared and vanished at very close intervals. "It must be some girl communicating with her lover in the next village." He counted nine successive flashes: "That's an *I*," he decided, "since *I* is the ninth letter of the alphabet. And then, after a pause, there were fourteen flashes. "That's an *N*"; then, after another pause, a single flash: "That's an *A*; the word is *Ina*."

What were his delight and his amazement when the successive flashes, always separated by brief pauses, then completed the following words: INA PENSA A TE. Evidently, "Gina is thinking of you!" He immediately answered with successive flashes of his lamp through the opening in his shutter: FABRIZIO T AMA ("Fabrizio loves you!") The communication continued until daybreak. This night was the hundred and seventy-third of his captivity, and he now learned that for four months these signals had been made every night. But anyone could see and decipher them; from this night on, abbreviations were devised: three flashes in rapid succession indicated the Duchess; four, the Prince; two, Count Mosca; two quick flashes followed by two slow ones meant *escape*. It was agreed that in the future they would use the old alphabet *alla monaca*, which in order not to be understood by outsiders changes the usual order of the letters and gives them an arbitrary numbering; *A*, for instance, is represented by ten; *B* by three; in other words, three successive flashes of the lamp means *B*, ten flashes means *A*, etc.; a moment's darkness constitutes the space between words. An appointment was made for the following night at one o'clock, and the following night the Duchess came to this tower, which was a quarter of a league outside the town. Her eyes filled with tears seeing the signals made by the very Fabrizio whom she had so often believed to be dead. She told him herself by flashing her lamp: *I love you   Courage   Keep up your hopes   Exercise within your room   You will need the strength of your arms*. "I have not seen him," the Duchess said to herself, "since that concert of Fausta's, when he appeared at my salon doors in a footman's livery. Who could have guessed then what Fate held in store for us all!"

The Duchess had signals sent which told Fabrizio that soon he would be released, *thanks to the Prince's kindness* (these signals could be read); then she went back to sending messages of affection; she could not tear herself away from him! Only the remonstrances of Ludovic, who because he had been of use to Fabrizio had become her own factotum, could convince her, when day was dawning, to break off the signals which might attract the attention of someone hostile. This announcement of an imminent release, repeated several times, cast Fabrizio into a deep melancholy: Clélia, noticing this the next day, was so indiscreet as to ask him the reason.

"I am about to give the Duchess serious grounds for annoyance."

"What could she ask of you that you would deny her?" exclaimed Clélia, carried away by the most burning curiosity.

"She wants me to leave this place," he answered, "and that is something I shall never consent to do."

Clélia could not answer, she stared at him and dissolved into tears. If he had been able to speak to her at close range, perhaps then he might have obtained the avowal of feelings concerning which his uncertainty frequently plunged him into the deepest discouragement; how intensely he felt that life, without Clélia's love, could be nothing for him but an endless round of bitter disappointments or unbearable tedium. It seemed to him that it was no longer worth living to rediscover those same delights which had seemed so interesting before he had known love, and although suicide had not yet become fashionable in Italy, he had thought of it as a last resort, if fate were to separate him from Clélia.

The following day he received a very long letter from her:

My friend, you must know the truth: very often, since you have been here, all Parma has supposed that your last day was upon you. It is true that you were condemned to no more than twelve years' imprisonment in the Fortress; but unfortunately it is beyond doubt that an all-powerful animosity is still determined to pursue you, and I have twenty times dreaded lest poison put an end to your days on this earth: therefore take advantage of any possible means of escape from this place. You see that on your behalf I am failing in my most sacred duties; judge the imminence of the danger by the things I venture to tell you, and which are so out of place on my lips. If it is absolutely essential, if there is no other means of safety, then flee. Every minute that you spend in this fortress can put your life in the greatest danger; you must realize that there is a faction at Court which the prospect of crime will never turn from its intentions. And don't you see all the schemes of this faction constantly foiled by Count Mosca's superior skill?

Now, however, a sure means of exiling the Count from Parma has been found, to the Duchess's despair; and is it not all too certain that this despair will be intensified by the death of a certain young prisoner? This word alone, which is unanswerable, ought to make you see your situation clearly. You say that you regard me with affection: consider first of all that insurmountable obstacles stand between this sentiment and any firm basis for it between us. We may have met in our youth, we may have held out a helping hand to each other during an unfortunate period; fate may have placed me in this place of punishment in order to reduce your sufferings;

but I should never forgive myself if certain illusions, which nothing warrants nor shall ever warrant, were to lead you to fail to grasp any possible occasion to release your life from such a dreadful danger. I have lost my peace of mind by the cruel indiscretions I have committed by exchanging with you certain signs of true friendship: if our childish games with alphabets were to lead you to such ill-founded illusions which, indeed, might have such fatal effects, it would be useless for me to justify myself by recalling Barbone's attack on you. I shall have cast you myself into a much more serious danger and a much more certain one, by imagining I was shielding you from a momentary peril; and my indiscretions are eternally unforgivable if they have generated in you sentiments which might lead you to resist the Duchess's advice.

Look what you compel me to say to you once more; make your escape, I command you . . .

This letter was very long; certain passages, such as the *I command you . . .*, which we have just transcribed, afforded moments of delicious hope to Fabrizio's love. It seemed to him that the basis of the feelings it expressed were quite tender, for all the remarkable discretion of their phrasing. At other moments, he paid the penalty for his complete ignorance in this sort of combat; he saw no more than friendship, or even simple humanity, in this letter from Clélia.

Moreover, everything she told him did not change his plans for an instant: supposing that the dangers she was describing were quite real, was it excessive to purchase, by a few momentary dangers, the happiness of seeing her every day? What kind of life would he be leading once he had again taken refuge in Bologna or in Florence? For, by escaping from the Fortress, he could not even hope for permission to live in Parma. And even if the Prince were to change his mind to the point of releasing him (which was highly unlikely, since he, Fabrizio, had become, for a powerful faction, a means of bringing down Count Mosca), what kind of life would he lead in Parma, separated from Clélia by all the hatred which divided the two factions? Once or twice a month, perhaps, chance would bring them to the same salons; but even then, what kind of conversation might he have with her? How would he regain that perfect intimacy which every day now he delighted in for hours at a time? What would salon conversation be, compared to the words they were exchanging with their alphabets? "And when I might purchase this life of delights and this one occasion for happiness by a few little dangers, what would be the harm in that? And would it not be one more happiness to find thereby a faint opportunity of giving her a proof of my love?"

Fabrizio regarded Clélia's letter as no more than the opportunity of asking her for a meeting: this was the sole and constant object of all his desires; he had spoken to her only once, and one other moment when he had entered the prison, and that had been over two hundred days ago.

An easy means of meeting with Clélia offered itself: the good Abbé Don Cesare granted Fabrizio half an hour's exercise on the terrace of the Farnese Tower every Thursday during daylight hours; but the other days of the week, this exercise, which might be observed by all the inhabitants of Parma and the surrounding area, and seriously compromise the Governor, occurred only after dark. In order to reach the terrace of the Farnese Tower, there was no staircase but that of the little steeple attached to the chapel so lugubriously embellished with black and white marble, which the reader may perhaps recall. Grillo used to lead Fabrizio to this chapel, would open the door to the steeple stairs: his duty would have been to follow him up it, but since the evenings were beginning to be chilly, the jailer allowed him to climb the stairs on his own, locking him into that steeple which led to the terrace, and returning to warm himself at the fire in his own room. Very well then, might not Clélia make her way some evening, escorted by her own chambermaid, to the black marble chapel?

The whole long letter by which Fabrizio answered Clélia's was calculated to produce this meeting. Moreover, he confided to her in all sincerity, and as if another person were involved, all the reasons which convinced him not to leave the fortress:

> I would expose myself daily to the prospect of a thousand deaths in order to have the felicity of speaking to you, with the help of our alphabets, which no longer impede us for a moment, yet you want me to commit the deception of exiling myself in Parma, or perhaps in Bologna or even in

Florence! You expect me to take a single step away from you! You must realize that such an effort is impossible for me; it is futile for me to make such promises, I could never keep them.

The result of this request for a meeting was an absence on Clélia's part which lasted no less than five days, during which time she came to the aviary only when she knew Fabrizio could not make use of the little opening cut into the shutter. Fabrizio was in despair; he concluded from this absence that despite certain glances which had made him conceive certain wild hopes, he had never inspired in Clélia any feelings but those of simple friendship. "In which case," he asked himself, "what does life matter to me? Let the Prince take it from me, he is welcome to it; one reason the more for not leaving the fortress!" And it was with a profound sentiment of disgust that, night after night, he answered the signals of the little lamp. The Duchess believed he had gone quite mad when she read, on the transcription of the signals which Ludovic brought her every morning, these strange words: *I do not wish to escape; I want to die here!*

During these five days which were so cruel for Fabrizio, Clélia was still more unhappy than he; she had had this inspiration, so poignant for a generous spirit: "It is my duty to take refuge in a convent, far from the fortress; when Fabrizio learns that I am no longer here, which I shall have him learn through Grillo and the other jailers, then he will consent to make an attempt at escaping." But going into a convent was abandoning forever all hopes of seeing Fabrizio again; and renouncing such hopes when he was giving such evident proofs that the sentiments which might once have linked him to the Duchess no longer existed! What more touching proof of love could a young man give? After seven long months in prison, which had seriously altered his health, he was refusing to regain his freedom. The frivolous being whom the courtiers had described to Clélia would have sacrificed twenty mistresses to leave the fortress even one day sooner; and what would he not have done to get out of a prison where poison might have ended his life from one day to the next!

Clélia's courage failed her; she committed the signal error of not seeking refuge in a convent, which at the same time would have given her the most natural reason in the world for breaking off with the Marchese Crescenzi. Once this mistake was made, how could she resist a young man so lovable, so sincere, so tender, who was exposing his very life to dreadful dangers in order to obtain the simple happiness of glimpsing her from one window to another? After five days of dreadful struggles, mingled with moments of contempt for herself, Clélia decided to answer the letter in which Fabrizio sought the happiness of speaking to her in the black marble chapel. In point of fact, she refused him, and in rather harsh terms, but from this moment on, all tranquillity was lost for her, at every moment her imagination depicted Fabrizio succumbing to the symptoms of poison; she came six or eight times a day to the aviary, feeling the passionate need to assure herself with her own eyes that Fabrizio was still alive.

"If he is still here in the Fortress," she said to herself, "if he is exposed to all the horrors which the Raversi faction may be devising for him with the intent of destroying Count Mosca, it is solely because I have been so cowardly as not to take refuge in a convent! What excuse could he have to remain here, once he was convinced that I had left the place forever?"

This girl, at once so timid and so proud, reached the point of risking a rejection on the part of the jailer Grillo; furthermore, she exposed herself to all the observations the man might have made on the strangeness of her behavior. She sank to that degree of humiliation where she sent for him, and told him in a tremulous voice which betrayed her whole secret, that in a few days Fabrizio would be receiving his order of release, that the Duchess Sanseverina was engaging with this intention in the most active enterprises, that often it was necessary to have the prisoner's immediate reply to certain propositions that were being made to him, and that she was requesting him, Grillo, to permit Fabrizio to cut an opening in the shutter which covered his window, in order that she might communicate with him by certain signs the instructions which she was receiving from the Duchess several times a day.

Grillo smiled and assured her of his respect and his obedience. Clélia was infinitely grateful to him for not adding another word; it was obvious that he was quite aware of everything that had been going on for the last few months.

No sooner had this jailer left her quarters than Clélia gave the signal which had been agreed upon to call Fabrizio on important occasions; she confessed to him all that she had just done.

"You want to die by poison," she added; "I hope to have the courage one of these days to leave my father and to bury myself in some faraway convent; that is what I shall be indebted to you for; then I hope that you will no longer resist the plans which may be made to assure your release from this place; so long as you are here, I suffer dreadful and irrational torments; in all my life I have never intentionally harmed a living soul, and it seems to me that I am the reason for your death here. Such a notion with regard to a perfect stranger would reduce me to despair; imagine my feelings when I conceive that a friend, whose irrationality gives me grave reasons for distress, but whom after all I have seen every day for such a long period, is at this moment subject to the pains of death! Sometimes I feel the need of hearing from your own lips that you are still alive . . .

"It is in order to free myself from this dreadful suffering that I have just sunk to asking for a favor from a servant who might well refuse me, and who may even betray me. Furthermore, I should perhaps be glad if he were to denounce me to my father; at that moment I should leave for some convent, no longer the involuntary accomplice of your cruel follies. But believe me, this cannot last long, you will obey the Duchess's orders. Are you satisfied, cruel friend? It is I who am urging you to betray my own father! Call Grillo and pay him off!"

Fabrizio was so deeply in love, the simplest expression of Clélia's will plunged him into such terror, that even this strange communication afforded him no certainty that he was loved. He summoned Grillo, whose past favors he had rewarded generously, and, as for the future, told him that for each day he permitted the use of the opening cut in the shutter, he would receive a sequin. Grillo was delighted with these conditions.

"Monsignore, I'm going to speak to you quite frankly: are you willing to eat a cold dinner every day? That is a simple enough means of avoiding poison. But I must ask you for the greatest discretion—a jailer must see all and acknowledge nothing, and so on. Instead of one dog, I shall employ several, and you yourself will let them taste each dish you plan to eat; as for the wine, I shall give you my own, and you will drink only out of the bottles I have already begun. But if Your Excellency wants to ruin me forever, you need merely confide these same arrangements to Signorina Clélia; women are women always and if she were to quarrel with you tomorrow, she would take her revenge by disclosing these stratagems to her father, whose dearest pleasure would be to have some reason to have one of his jailers hanged. After Barbone, he is perhaps the nastiest customer in the whole fortress, and this is what constitutes the true danger of your position; he knows how to handle poison, you can be sure of that, and would not forgive me for this notion of employing three or four little dogs."

There was to be another serenade. This time Grillo answered all of Fabrizio's questions; he had determined, however, to be discreet on all occasions, and not to betray Signorina Clélia, who, according to him, while on the verge of marrying the Marchese Crescenzi, the richest man in the State of Parma, was nonetheless making love, insofar as prison walls permitted it, with the generous Monsignore del Dongo. He had answered all the latter's questions concerning the serenade, when he was stupid enough to add: "They say he'll be marrying her soon."

It is easy enough to imagine the effect of this sentence upon Fabrizio. That night he answered the lamp signals only by reporting that he was ill. At ten the next morning, Clélia having appeared in the aviary, he asked her with a ceremonious tone quite new between them, why she had not frankly told him that she loved the Marchese Crescenzi and that she was about to marry him.

"Because there is not a word of truth in the whole story," Clélia replied with some impatience.

It is also true that the rest of her answer was less categorical: Fabrizio pointed this out to her and took advantage of the occasion to repeat his request for a meeting. Clélia, who saw her good faith being doubted, granted it almost immediately, though informing him that she would be dishonoring herself forever in Grillo's eyes. That evening, after dark, she appeared, accompanied by her chambermaid, in the black marble chapel; she stopped in the middle of the chapel, beside the sanctuary lamp; Grillo and the chambermaid retreated some thirty paces toward the door. Clélia, trembling in every limb, had prepared a fine speech; her intention was to avoid any compromising avowal, but the logic of passion is urgent; its burning interest in learning the truth forbids all vain pretense, while at the same time its extreme devotion to its objects allays any fear of giving offense. At first Fabrizio was dazzled by Clélia's beauty; in nearly eight months he had not been so close to anyone but his jailers. But the name of the Marchese Crescenzi revived all his anger, which increased when he distinctly observed that Clélia replied with no more than tactful evasions; the girl herself realized that she was intensifying his suspicions instead of dispelling them. This sensation was too cruel for her to bear.

"Will you be pleased," she said to him with a degree of anger and with tears in her eyes, "to have made me exceed the bounds of all that I owe myself? Until August third of last year, I had felt nothing but aversion for the men who were my suitors. I had a limitless and probably exaggerated contempt for the nature of all courtiers, and everything that was acceptable at this Court was repellent to me. On the other hand, I recognized remarkable virtues in a prisoner who on August third was brought into this fortress. I experienced, without at first realizing what it was, all the torments of jealousy. The attractions of a charming woman, and one quite familiar to me, were so many dagger-thrusts in my heart, for I believed, and still tend to believe, that this prisoner was attached to her. Soon the persecutions of the Marchese Crescenzi, who had asked for my hand, redoubled; he is extremely wealthy and we have no fortune at all; I was quite prepared to reject him when my father uttered the fatal word *convent;* I realized that if I were to leave the fortress I could no longer protect the life of the prisoner whose fate so interested me. The triumph of my stratagems had been that until this moment he suspected none of the dreadful dangers which threatened his life. I had promised myself never to betray either my father or my secret; but this woman so resolved upon such admirable action, of a superior intelligence and a terrible determination, who was protecting this prisoner, offered him, as I imagined it, means of escape; he rejected them and sought to convince me that he was refusing to leave the Fortress in order not to lose me. Then I made a great mistake; I struggled for five days, when I should have instantly left the Fortress and taken refuge in a convent: this step would have offered me a ready means of breaking with the Marchese Crescenzi. I lacked the courage to do so, and I am now a lost soul; I have declared an attachment to a frivolous man: I know how he lived in Naples; and what reasons would I have for supposing that he has altered his character? Confined in a harsh prison, he has paid court to the only woman he could see, she has been a distraction for his tedium. Since he could speak to her only with certain difficulties, this amusement has assumed the false appearance of a passion. This prisoner having made a name for himself in the world by his courage, he supposes he can prove that his love is something more than a passing fancy by exposing himself to such great dangers in order to continue seeing the person he imagines he loves. But once he is at liberty in the city, surrounded once again by all the seductions of society, he will return to being what he has always been, a man of the world given over to dissipations, to gallantry, and the poor companion of his imprisonment will end her days in a convent, forgotten by this frivolous man, and suffering the mortal regret of having made him this confession."

This historic speech, of which we are presenting only the principal features, was, as may well be supposed, twenty times interrupted by Fabrizio. He was desperately in love, as well as quite convinced that he had never loved before having seen Clélia, and that his life's destiny was to live for her alone.

The reader can doubtless imagine the fine things he was saying when the chambermaid warned her mistress that the clock had just struck half-past eleven, and that the General might return at any moment; their separation was cruel.

"I may be seeing you for the last time," said Clélia to the prisoner: "A measure in the interest of the Raversi faction may afford you a cruel way of proving that you are not unfaithful."

Clélia left Fabrizio choking with sobs and dying with shame at being unable to conceal them altogether from her chambermaid or, especially, from the jailer Grillo. A second conversation was possible only when the General would announce his intention of spending another evening at court; and since Fabrizio's imprisonment and the interest it had inspired in the courtiers' curiosity, he had found it a matter of discretion to suffer an almost continual fit of the gout, and his excursions into town, subject to the demands of a vigilant policy, were often decided only at the moment of getting into his carriage.

Since that evening in the marble chapel, Fabrizio's life had been a series of joyous raptures. Great obstacles, of course, still seemed to stand in the way of his happiness; but finally he knew the supreme unhoped-for joy of being loved by the divine creature who occupied all his thoughts.

The third day after this interview, the lamp signals ended quite early, virtually at the stroke of midnight; the moment they ended, Fabrizio's skull was nearly cracked by a huge ball of lead which, hurled through the upper part of his window-shutter, came crashing through its paper panes and fell into his room.

This huge ball was not nearly so heavy as its size suggested; Fabrizio easily managed to open it and found a letter from the Duchess. Through the intervention of the Archbishop, whom she had skillfully flattered, she had won over a soldier in the Fortress garrison. This man, expert in the use of a catapult, managed to evade the notice of the sentries posted at the corners and the door of the Governor's Palace, or else had come to some sort of agreement with them.

You must escape by means of ropes: I shudder even as I give you this strange advice, and for over two months have hesitated to say as much to you; but the official prospect continues to darken, and we have worse to look forward to. For this reason, start signaling again with your lamp to show us that you received this dangerous letter; signal P, B, and G *alla monaca,* in other words four, twelve, and two; I shall not breathe until I have seen this signal; I am in the tower, and will reply by N and O, seven and five. Once the reply has been received, make no further signals and concern yourself exclusively with the meaning of my letter.

Fabrizio hastened to obey, and sent the arranged signals, which were followed by the indicated replies; then he went on reading the letter.

We may expect the worst; I have heard as much from the three men in whom I place the most trust, after I made them swear on the Gospels to tell me the truth, however cruel it may be to me. The first of these men threatened the surgeon who denounced you in Ferrara that he would attack him with a knife; the second is the one who told you, when you came back from Belgirate, that it would have been wiser, actually, to have used your pistol on the footman who came singing through the woods leading that skinny horse; you don't know the third man, who is a highwayman of my acquaintance, a man of action if ever there was one, and as brave as yourself; that is why I have asked him, in particular, to tell me what you should do. All three have told me, each without knowing that I consulted the other two, that it would be better to risk breaking your neck than to spend another eleven years and four months in the continual fear of a very likely poisoning.

You must continue exercising in your room for a month, climbing up and down a knotted rope. Then, when the Fortress garrison has been given a holiday ration of wine, you will make the great attempt. You will have three silk-and-hemp ropes the thickness of a swan's quill, the first eighty feet long, by which to get down the thirty-five feet from your window to the orange-trees, the second of three hundred feet, which is a problem because of its weight, to get down the hundred and eighty feet of the wall of the great tower; and a third rope thirty feet long is to be used to get you down the ramparts. I spend my life studying the great wall on the eastern side of the tower, that is, toward Ferrara: a gap caused by an earthquake has been filled by a buttress which forms an inclined plane there. My highwayman tells me that it would be easiest to get down on this side, risking no more than a few bruises, if you slide down the inclined plane formed by this buttress. The vertical distance is no more than twenty-eight feet to the bottom; this side is the least well guarded.

However, all things considered, my highwayman, who has escaped from prison three times and whom you would like if you knew him, though he has no use for people of your sort—my highwayman, who I assure you is as nimble and clever as you yourself, thinks it would be better to get down on the west side, exactly opposite the little Palace once occupied by Fausta, as you well know. What determined this choice is that the wall, although very steep, is covered with bushes; there are branches as big as your little finger which might easily scratch your eyes out if you're not careful but which are also good things to hold on to. This very morning I was studying this west side with a spyglass; the place to choose is just under a new stone that was set in the upper parapet two or three years back. Directly under this stone, you will find first of all a bare space of some twenty feet; here you must proceed very slowly (you can imagine how my heart pounds as I give you these terrible instructions, but courage consists in knowing how to choose the lesser evil, dreadful though it appears); after the bare space, you will find eighty or ninety feet of big bushes where you can see birds flying around, then a space of thirty feet where there is nothing but grass and vines and wall-flowers. Then, closer to the ground, twenty feet of bushes, and finally twenty-five or thirty feet of newly plastered wall.

The reason for preferring this side is that here, straight down from the new stone in the upper parapet, there is a wooden shack built by a soldier in his garden, and which the captain of the Fortress engineers wants to have pulled down; it is seventeen feet high, and has a thatched roof which abuts onto the main wall of the Fortress. It is this roof which tempts me; in the dreadful case of an accident, it would break your fall. Once you get to this point, you are inside the circle of ramparts that are not very well guarded; if you are stopped here, fire your pistol and defend yourself for a few minutes. Your friend from Ferrara and another trusty fellow, the one I call my highwayman, will have ladders and will lose no time scaling this low rampart and flying to your rescue.

The rampart is only twenty-three feet high, and an easy slope. I will be at the foot of this last wall with a good number of armed men.

I have every hope of getting five or six letters into your hands by the same means as this one. I shall keep repeating the same things in other words, so that we are sure to reach an understanding. You can guess my feelings when I tell you that the man who said it would have been better to shoot the footman, who after all is the best of fellows and is dying of remorse, thinks that you will get off with no worse than a broken arm. The highwayman, who has more experience in such enterprises, thinks that if you climb down very carefully, and above all without hurrying, your freedom will cost you no more than a few bruises. The big problem is to get you the ropes; this has been my sole thought for the last fifteen days, during which this tremendous project has obsessed my every waking moment.

I have no answer to make to that madness, the only senseless thing you ever said in your life: "I don't want to escape!" The man who advised shooting the footman exclaimed that boredom had driven you mad. I shall not conceal from you that we fear an imminent peril which may hasten the day of your escape. To warn you of this danger, the lamp-signal will tell you several times in succession: The castle is on fire! and you will answer: Are my books burned?

This letter contained another five or six pages of details; it was written in microscopic characters on extremely thin paper.

"All this is very fine and very well thought out," Fabrizio said to himself; "I owe eternal gratitude to the Count and the Duchess; they may believe that I am afraid, but I shall not attempt to escape. Who has ever escaped from a place where he is rapturously happy to fling himself into a dreadful exile where he lacks everything, including the air to breathe? What would I do after a month in Florence? I would assume some disguise to come back and prowl around the gates of this Fortress and try to catch one of her glances!"

The next day, Fabrizio was indeed afraid; he was at his window, around eleven in the morning, considering the splendid landscape and waiting for the happy moment when he might see Clélia, when Grillo came into the room quite out of breath.

"Quick, quick! Monsignore, throw yourself on your bed, pretend to be sick, there are three judges coming up the stairs! They're going to question you: think carefully before you answer; they're coming to *snare* you!" As he said these words, Grillo hurriedly closed the opening in the shutter, pushed Fabrizio onto his bed, and threw two or three coats over him. "Tell them you're very sick and don't talk much—above all make them repeat their questions to give yourself time to think!"

The three judges entered. "Three escaped jailbirds," Fabrizio said to himself as he glanced at these vile countenances, "and not three judges at all"; they were wearing long black gowns. They bowed gravely, and without a word sat down in the three chairs that were in the room.

"Signor Fabrizio del Dongo," said the oldest one, "we are grieved by the melancholy mission which we must perform in your regard. We are here to inform you of the death of His Excellency, Signor the Marchese del Dongo, your father, Second Grand Major-domo Major of the Lombardo-Venetian Kingdom, Knight Grand Cross of the Orders of . . ." etc., etc., etc.

Fabrizio burst into tears; the judge continued. "Signora the Marchesa del Dongo, your mother, has written to inform you of this news by a hand-written letter, but since she has included in her missive certain unsuitable reflections, by a decree issued yesterday, the Court of Justice has decided that her letter would be imparted to you only in extracts, and it is this extract which Signor Bona, Clerk of the Court, will now read to you."

Once this reading was concluded, the judge came over to Fabrizio where he lay and showed him in his mother's letter the very passages of which copies had just been read to him. Fabrizio saw in the letter the words *unjust imprisonment . . . cruel punishment for a crime which is no such thing . . .* and realized what had motivated the judges' visit. However, in his scorn of magistrates without honor he said no more than these specific words: "I am ill, gentlemen, and perishing of weakness, and you will excuse me for not standing . . ."

Once the judges had left, Fabrizio wept a good deal more, and then said to himself: "Am I such a hypocrite? It seems to me I never loved him at all."

On that day and those following, Clélia was extremely sad; she called to him several times, but scarcely had the heart to say more than a few words. The morning of the fifth day after this interview, she told him that she would come that evening to the marble chapel.

"I can only say a few words to you," she told him as she came in. She was trembling so much that she had to lean on her chambermaid for support. After having sent the girl to the chapel entrance, she added in a voice that was scarcely audible: "You must give me your word of honor—your word of honor that you will obey the Duchess, and attempt to escape on the day she tells you to do so, in the way she will instruct you, or tomorrow morning I shall take refuge in a convent, and I swear to you here and now that I shall never speak another word to you in all my life."

Fabrizio remained silent.

"Promise," said Clélia, tears in her eyes and almost beside herself, "or else we are speaking here for the last time. The life you are forcing me to lead is dreadful: you are here on my account, and each day may be the last of your life." At this moment Clélia was so weak that she was compelled to support herself on a huge armchair that had long ago been placed in the middle of the chapel for the use of the imprisoned Prince; she was on the point of fainting.

"What must I promise?" Fabrizio asked, looking overcome.

"You know."

"All right, I promise to fling myself knowingly into dreadful misfortunes, and to condemn myself to live far from all that I love in the world."

"Promise real things."

"I promise to obey the Duchess and to make my escape when and how she tells me to. And what will become of me, once I have lost you?"

"Promise to escape, whatever may happen."

"Then you have made up your mind to marry the Marchese Crescenzi once I am no longer here?"

"Oh, Heavens! What kind of heart do you think I have? . . . But promise, or my soul won't have another moment's peace."

"All right, I promise to escape from this place when the Duchess Sanseverina tells me to, and whatever may happen between now and then."

Having obtained this promise, Clélia was now so faint that she was compelled to leave, once she had thanked Fabrizio. "Everything was prepared for my flight tomorrow morning," she told him, "had you persisted in remaining. I would have seen you now for the very last time in my life, I had made a vow to the Madonna. Now, as soon as I am able to leave my room, I shall go examine that terrible wall under the new stone in the parapet."

The next day, he found her so pale as to alarm him. She told him from the aviary window: "Let us not deceive ourselves, dear friend; as there is something sinful in our relationship, I cannot doubt that some sort of misfortune awaits us. You will be discovered when you attempt to escape, and lost forever, or worse; yet we must satisfy what human prudence asks of us—it asks us to make every effort. To get down the outside of the great tower, you will need a strong rope over two hundred feet long. For all my efforts since I learned of the Duchess's plans, the only ropes I've been able to obtain add up, altogether, to no more than fifty feet. The Governor has issued orders that all the ropes found in the Fortress be burned, and every evening they remove the well-ropes, which are so weak that they often break in bringing up nothing heavier than their buckets. But may God forgive me, I am betraying my father and working, unnatural daughter that I am, for his eternal grief. Pray to God for me, and if your life is saved, promise to dedicate every moment of it to His glory.

"One idea has occurred to me: in eight days I'll be leaving the Fortress to attend the wedding of one of the Marchese Crescenzi's sisters. I shall be back that same evening if I can, but I shall do everything possible to return only very late, and perhaps Barbone will not dare search me too closely. All the greatest ladies of the court will attend this wedding of the Marchese's sister, no doubt including the Duchess Sanseverina. In God's name, have one of these ladies give me a bundle of ropes tightly packed, not too heavy and not too big. Were I to expose myself to a thousand deaths, I shall use every means, even the most dangerous, to bring this bundle inside the Fortress, in defiance, alas! of all my duties. If my father learns of it I shall never see you again; but whatever my fate, I shall be happy within the limits of a sister's friendship if I can help to save you."

That very evening, by the nocturnal signals sent by lamp flashes, Fabrizio informed the Duchess of the unique opportunity of getting a sufficient length of rope into the Fortress. But he begged her to keep the secret from the Count himself, strange as it seemed. "He is mad," the Duchess thought, "prison has changed him, he is taking things tragically now." The next day, a ball of lead, catapulted into his room, brought the prisoner the news of the greatest possible danger; the person responsible for bringing ropes into the Fortress, he was told, would literally be saving his life. Fabrizio hastened to give this news to Clélia. This ball of lead also brought Fabrizio a very precise plan of the western wall down which he was to climb from the top of the great tower into the space enclosed within the bastions; from this place, it was easy enough to escape afterward, the ramparts being only twenty-three feet high and scantily guarded. On the back of the plan, written in a tiny, delicate hand, was a splendid sonnet; a generous soul exhorted Fabrizio to make his escape, and not to let his spirit be corrupted and his body wasted by the years of captivity which still remained for him to endure.

Here a necessary detail, one which partly accounts for the Duchess's courage in advising Fabrizio to attempt such a dangerous course, compels us to interrupt, momentarily, the story of this bold enterprise.

Like all factions not in power, the Raversi party was not closely united. Cavaliere Riscara detested Chief Justice Rassi, whom he accused of having forced him to lose an important case in which, as it had happened, Riscara himself had been in the wrong.

Through Riscara, the Prince received an anonymous message informing him that a copy of Fabrizio's sentence had been officially addressed to the Governor of the Fortress. The Marchesa Raversi, that adroit leader of her party, was exceedingly annoyed by this misstep, and immediately informed her friend the Chief Justice about it; she regarded it as natural enough that he should have wanted to secure something from Count Mosca so long as Mosca remained the Minister in power. Rassi presented himself quite intrepidly at the Palace, imagining that he would be let off with a few slaps on the wrist; the Prince could not do without a skilled jurisconsult, and Rassi had managed to banish, as Liberals, a judge and a barrister, the only men in the country who might have replaced him.

The Prince, beside himself with rage, covered Rassi with insults and advanced upon him with the intention of delivering a blow.

"Really, Sire, it's no more than a clerk's error," Rassi replied quite coolly; "the thing is laid down by law, it should have been done the day of Signor del Dongo's confinement in the Fortress. The over-zealous clerk imagined he had forgotten about it, and made me sign the covering letter as a matter of form."

"And you expect to make me believe lies like that?" shrieked the outraged Prince. "The fact is that you've sold yourself to that rascal Mosca, which is why he's given you your Cross. By God, you won't get off with a few kicks—I'll have you brought to justice and publicly disgraced."

"I defy you to bring me to justice!" Rassi replied quite confidently (knowing that this was a sure method of calming the Prince). "The law is on my side, and you don't have another Rassi to get around it for you. You won't disgrace me, because there are times when your nature is severe; then you crave blood, but at the same time you want to keep the esteem of reasonable Italians, which is a *sine qua non* of your ambition. So you will recall me for the first severe action your nature requires of you, and as usual I shall obtain for you a perfectly regular sentence passed by timid and quite honest judges which will nonetheless satisfy your passions. Find another man in your State as useful as myself!"

On these words, Rassi made his escape; he had been let off with a sharp reprimand and a few kicks. Once he left the Palace he set out for his estate of Riva. He was somewhat apprehensive of a dagger-thrust in the first impulse of the Prince's rage, but also had no doubt that before two weeks had passed a courier would recall him to the capital. He employed his time in the country in organizing a reliable means of correspondence with Count Mosca; he was madly in love with the title of Baron, and felt that the Prince had too much regard for that sublime thing, nobility, ever to confer it upon him; while the Count, all too proud of his birth, respected only nobility proved by titles which dated from before the year 1400.

The Chief Justice had not been mistaken in his anticipations; he had been not more than eight days on his estate when one of the Prince's friends, who happened to pass by, advised him to return to Parma without delay; the Prince received him with a smile, then assumed a very serious expression and made him swear on the Gospels that he would keep the secret concerning what he was about to confide to him; Rassi swore in all seriousness, and the Prince, his eyes inflamed with hatred, exclaimed that he would not be master in his own house so long as Fabrizio del Dongo was alive.

"I can neither," he added, "banish the Duchess nor endure her presence; her eyes defy me and my life is poisoned by her."

After allowing the Prince to explain himself at great length, Rassi, pretending to be extremely embarrassed, finally exclaimed: "Your Highness will be obeyed, of course, but the case is horribly difficult: there is no likelihood of condemning a del Dongo to death for the murder of a Giletti; it is already a remarkable achievement to have managed to put him away in the Fortress for a dozen years. Moreover, I suspect the Duchess has discovered three of the peasants who were working at the Sanguigna diggings and who happened to be outside the trenches at the moment when that ruffian Giletti attacked del Dongo."

"And where are these witnesses?" inquired the furious Prince.

"Hidden somewhere in Piedmont, I imagine. It would take a conspiracy against Your Highness's life . . ."

"That has its dangers," said the Prince; "it puts the idea of such a thing in people's heads."

"Nonetheless," said Rassi with mock innocence, "that is the only weapon in my official armory."

"There's always poison . . ."

"But who would administer it? Not that idiot Conti?"

"But from what I understand, it wouldn't be his first attempt . . ."

"He'd have to be roused to anger," Rassi interrupted, "and besides, when he did away with the captain, he wasn't yet thirty, and he was in love and infinitely less cowardly than he is nowadays. Of course, everything must yield to reasons of state, but taken unawares and at first glance, I can think of no one to execute the Sovereign's orders but a certain Barbone, the registry clerk at the prison whom Signor del Dongo happened to knock down the day he was sent there."

Once the Prince was put at his ease, the conversation went on endlessly; he concluded it by granting his Chief Justice a month in which to act; Rassi sought two. The next day he received a secret gift of a thousand sequins. For three days he reflected; on the fourth he reverted to his original notion, which to him seemed self-evident: "Only Count Mosca will have the heart to keep his word to me, *primo*, since by making me a Baron he is giving me nothing he respects; *secundo*, by warning him, I am probably saving myself from a crime for which I am more or less paid in advance; *tercio*, I shall be taking revenge for the first humiliating blows ever received by Cavaliere Rassi."

The following night, he informed the Count of his entire conversation with the Prince.

The Count was secretly paying his court to the Duchess; it was quite true that he still did not see her at her own house more than once or twice a month, but almost every week, and whenever he could manage to create occasions for speaking of Fabrizio, the Duchess, accompanied by Cecchina, would come, late in the evening, to spend a few moments in the Count's garden. She was even able to deceive her own coachman, who was devoted to her and imagined she was visiting in a house nearby.

The reader can imagine whether the Count, having received the Chief Justice's terrible confidence, immediately gave the signal that had been prearranged with the Duchess. Though it was very late at night, she had Cecchina request him to come to her immediately. The Count, delighted as a lover by this appearance of intimacy, nonetheless hesitated to tell the Duchess everything: he feared seeing her driven mad by grief.

After casting about for veiled expressions by which to mitigate the fatal announcement, he nonetheless ended by telling her everything; it was not in his power to keep a secret which she sought from him. In the last nine months, extreme misfortune had had a great influence upon this ardent spirit; it had strengthened her, and the Duchess no longer burst into sobs or lamentations.

The next night she had Fabrizio sent the signal of great danger:

The castle is on fire.

He answered quite properly:

Are my books burned?

That same night she fortunately managed to get a letter to him inside a ball of lead. This was eight days after the marriage of the Marchese Crescenzi's sister, where the Duchess committed an enormous indiscretion of which we shall give an account in its proper place.

CHAPTER TWENTY-ONE

Almost a year before the period of her misfortunes, the Duchess had made a singular acquaintance: one evening when she was, as they say in these regions, moonstruck, she had taken it into her head to visit her villa at Sacca, on a hillside beyond Colorno, overlooking the Po. She enjoyed improving this estate; she loved the great forest which crowned the hill and reached the villa; she busied herself laying out paths in picturesque directions.

"You'll get yourself carried off by brigands, my lovely Duchess," the Prince had said to her one day. "It's impossible that a forest you are known to walk in should remain deserted." The Prince glanced at the Count, whose jealousy he hoped to arouse.

"I have no fear, Your Serene Highness," the Duchess replied with an innocent look, "when I walk in my woods; I am reassured by this thought: I have never done harm to anyone—who could hate me?" The remark was considered a bold one, for it recalled the insults offered by the Liberals of the country, an insolent lot if ever there was one.

The day of the stroll in question, the Prince's words came back to the Duchess's mind as she noticed an extremely ill dressed man following her at a distance through the woods. At a sudden turn she took as she went on with her walk, this stranger came so close to her that she was alarmed. Her first impulse was to call her game-keeper, whom she had left about half a mile behind, in a flower-bed near the villa. The stranger had time to approach and flung himself at her feet. He was young, extremely handsome, but wretchedly dressed; his clothes were in rags, with rents in them a foot long, but his eyes burned with the fire of an ardent soul. "I am under sentence of death, I am Doctor Ferrante Palla, and my five children and I are dying of hunger."

The Duchess had noticed how dreadfully thin he was, but his eyes were so fine and filled with so tender an exaltation that they obliterated any notion of crime from her mind. "Pallagi," she thought, "might have given such eyes to the *Saint John in the Desert* he has just painted in the Cathedral." The idea of Saint John was suggested to her by Ferrante's incredible attenuation. The Duchess gave him the three sequins that were in her purse, apologizing for offering him so little, having just paid her gardener his wages. Ferrante thanked her effusively. "Alas!" he exclaimed. "I once lived in the city, and I would see elegant women; since I performed my duties as a citizen, I have lived in the forests, and I was following you not to ask for charity or to rob you, but like a savage fascinated by angelic beauty. It has been so long since I've seen a pair of lovely white hands!"

"Please get up," the Duchess said to him, for he had remained on his knees.

"Allow me to remain as I am," Ferrante said to her; "this posture proves to me that I am not at this present moment engaged in stealing, and that calms me; for you must know that I rob others in order to live ever since I have been forbidden to practice my profession. But at this moment I am a simple mortal who worships sublime beauty."

The Duchess realized that the man was slightly mad, but she was not at all frightened; she saw in this man's eyes that he possessed a good and ardent soul, and moreover she was anything but indifferent to remarkable countenances.

"You see, I am a doctor and I was in the habit of making love to the wife of Sarasine the apothecary, in Parma; he took us by surprise and drove her out of his house, along with three children he rightly suspected were mine and not his. We have had two more since then. The mother and our five children live in the most abject poverty in a shack I built with my own hands here in the forest, about a league away. For I must avoid the police, and the poor woman chooses to remain with me. I was sentenced to death, and quite justly; I was conspiring. I loathe the Prince, who is a tyrant. I did not take flight for lack of money. My woes are much greater than that, and I ought to have killed myself a thousand times over; I no longer love the unfortunate woman who has given me these five children and has ruined herself for my sake: I love someone else. But if I do away with myself, the mother and the five children will literally starve to death." The man spoke with the accents of sincerity.

"But how do you manage to live?" the Duchess asked, moved by his story.

"The children's mother spins; the oldest daughter has been brought up on a farm belonging to Liberals, where she tends the sheep; myself, I steal from people on the road from Genoa to Piacenza."

"How do you reconcile robbery with your Liberal principles?"

"I keep track of the people I rob, and if I ever have any money, I return what I have taken from them. I consider that a Tribune of the People like myself performs a labor which, by reason of its danger, is worth a good hundred francs a month; so I am careful never to take more than twelve hundred francs a year. No, that's wrong; I do steal a little more than that, for with this extra sum I pay to have my works printed."

"What works are those?"

"*Will —— Ever Have a Chamber and a Budget?*"

"What!" exclaimed the Duchess in amazement. "Then you, Signor, are one of the greatest poets of the age—you are the famous Ferrante Palla!"

"Famous, perhaps, but most unfortunate, that is for certain."

"And a man of your talents, Signor, must steal in order to live!"

"That may be the reason I have any talent. Hitherto all our authors who have become well known were people paid by the government or by the religion they sought to undermine. Myself, *primo,* I risk my life; *secundo,* Signora, imagine the feelings that wrack my soul when I am about to commit a robbery! Am I justified in doing this, I ask myself. Is a Tribune's office really worth a hundred francs a month? I have two shirts to my name, the suit you see on my back, a few worthless weapons, and I am sure to end my days on the gallows: yet I dare to believe I am an honest man. I would be a happy one without this fatal love which now permits me to find only misery at the side of my children's mother. Poverty weighs upon me by its ugliness: I am fond of fine clothes, of white hands . . ." He stared so intensely at the Duchess's that she was alarmed.

"Farewell, Signor," she said to him. "Can I do anything for you in Parma?"

"Think, on occasion, of this dilemma: his job is to rouse hearts and to waken them from that false and altogether material happiness afforded by Monarchies. Does the service he renders his fellow citizens deserve a hundred francs a month? . . . My misfortune is to be in love," he said very softly, "and for nearly two years my heart has been filled with you alone, though hitherto I have gazed upon you without frightening you." And he took to his heels with a prodigious speed which amazed and also reassured the Duchess.

"The police would have a hard time catching him," she mused; "he really is a madman."

"He's a madman," her servants informed her; "we've all known for a long time that the poor fellow has been in love with the Signora; when the Signora is here, we see him wandering in the high ground of the woods, and once the Signora leaves, he invariably comes to sit in the same places where you have been; he is sure to pick up the flowers that might have fallen from your bouquet, and he keeps them fastened in that dreadful hat of his."

"And you've never mentioned these follies to me," the Duchess said, almost reproachfully.

"We were afraid the Signora might tell the Minister Count Mosca. Poor Ferrante is such a good fellow—he's never done any harm to anyone, and just because he loves our Napoléon they've sentenced him to death."

The Duchess did not say a word to the Count about this encounter, and since this was the first secret she had kept from him in four years, she found herself obliged to stop short in the middle of a sentence ten times over. She returned to Sacca with gold, but Ferrante did not appear. She returned fifteen days later: Ferrante, having followed her for some time, hiding from tree to tree, at a distance of a hundred paces, burst upon her with the celerity of a sparrow-hawk, and once again flung himself at her feet.

"Where were you fifteen days ago?"

"In the mountains beyond Novi, robbing a mule-team coming back from Milan, where they had been selling olive oil."

"Take this purse." Ferrante opened the purse, took out a sequin, which he kissed and thrust into his bosom, then gave it back to her.

"You give back my purse and you commit highway robberies!"

"Certainly; it is my rule never to have more than a hundred francs in my possession; now at this moment the mother of my children has eighty francs and I have twenty-five; I am five francs over, and if I were hanged right now I would feel remorse. I have accepted this sequin because it comes from you and because I love you." The intonation of this simple speech was perfect.

"He really does love," the Duchess said to herself.

That day he seemed quite distracted. He said that there were people in Parma who owed him six hundred francs, and that with such a sum he would repair the shack where his poor children now were catching cold.

"But I'll lend you those six hundred," said the Duchess, deeply moved.

"But as a man in public life, the opposing party could slander me and say I've sold myself out."

Won over, the Duchess offered him a hiding-place in Parma if he would promise her that for the time being he would not exercise his magistrature in Parma and that above all he would carry out none of the death-sentences which he claimed to have passed *in petto.* "Supposing I were hanged as a consequence of my carelessness," Ferrante said quite seriously; "all these enemies of the people would live on for years, and whose fault would that be? What would my father say to that, when he greets me in Heaven?"

The Duchess spoke to him at length about his children, to whom the damp might cause some fatal illness, and he ended by accepting her offer of a hiding-place in Parma.

In the only half-day the Duke Sanseverina had spent in Parma since his marriage, he had shown the Duchess a remarkable hiding-place in the southern corner of his *palazzo*. The outer wall, which dates from the Middle Ages, is eight feet thick; it has been hollowed out to create a hiding-place some twenty feet high, but only two feet wide. It is right beside the splendid reservoir mentioned in all the travel literature, a famous construction of the twelfth century, built during the siege of Parma by the Holy Roman Emperor Sigismund, and later enclosed within the walls of the Palazzo Sanseverina.

This hiding-place is entered by sliding aside a huge block of stone on an iron pivot which runs through its center. The Duchess was so touched by Ferrante's madness and by the fate of his children, for whom he stubbornly rejected any present having some value, that she allowed him the use of this hiding-place for some time. She saw him next the following month, once again in the Sacca woods, and since on that day he was a little calmer, he recited to her one of his sonnets, which she found equal or superior to the finest produced in Italy in the last two hundred years. Ferrante obtained several interviews; but his exalted affections became importunate, and the Duchess realized that this passion followed the laws of all loves granted the possibility of conceiving a glimmer of hope. She sent him back to the forest and forbade him to speak to her again: he obeyed at once and with utter docility.

This was how matters stood when Fabrizio was arrested. Three days afterward, at nightfall, a Capuchin appeared at the door of the Palazzo Sanseverina; he had, he claimed, an important secret to communicate to the mistress of the place. The Duchess was so wretched by then that she had the man brought in: it was Ferrante.

"A new iniquity is occurring here, of which the Tribune of the People must take cognizance," said the lovesick man. "Moreover, acting as a private citizen," he added, "I have nothing to give the Duchess Sanseverina but my life, and I present it to her now."

Such sincere devotion on the part of a madman and a thief deeply touched the Duchess. She spoke a long while to this man who passed for the greatest poet of northern Italy, and wept a good deal. "Here is someone who understands my heart," she said to herself. The following day he reappeared, again at nightfall, disguised as a footman wearing her livery. "I have not left Parma; I have been told of a horror which my lips refuse to repeat, but here I am. Consider, Signora, what you are refusing. The being you see before you is not a court doll, but a man!" He was on his knees as he spoke these words with an expression of utter conviction. "Yesterday," he added, "I said to myself: she has wept in my presence; therefore she is a little less unhappy."

"But Signor, just think what dangers surround you—you will be arrested in this city!"

"The Tribune will say to you: Signora, what is life when duty calls? The wretched man, who has the misfortune of no longer feeling passion for virtue now that he is burning with love, will add: Signora Duchess, Fabrizio, a man of feeling, may be about to perish; do not repulse another such man who offers himself to you! Here is a body of iron and a soul which fears nothing in the world but your displeasure."

"If you speak to me once more of your feelings, I shall close my door to you forever."

It occurred to the Duchess that evening to inform Ferrante that she would provide a small pension for his children, though she was afraid that he would leave her straightaway and kill himself.

No sooner had he left than she said to herself, overcome by sinister presentiments: "I too may die, and would to God I might, and soon! if I could find a man worthy of the name to whom I might entrust my poor Fabrizio."

The Duchess had an idea: she took a piece of paper and acknowledged in a text which included whatever legal terminology she knew that she had received from Signor Ferrante Palla the Signora Sarasine and her five children. The Duchess added: "Further, I bequeath a life-annuity of some of twenty-five thousand francs, on the express condition of paying a life-annuity of fifteen hundred francs to three hundred francs to each of his five children on condition that Ferrante Palla provides his services as a physician to my nephew Fabrizio del Dongo, and will be to him as a brother. Such is my request." She signed the document, predated it by a year, and folded the sheet.

Two days later, Ferrante reappeared. This was at the moment when the entire city was agitated by the rumor of Fabrizio's imminent execution. Would this sad ceremony take place in the Fortress or under the trees of the public promenade? Several men of the people went strolling that very evening in front of the Fortress gates to see whether the scaffold was being erected there: this spectacle had moved Ferrante. He found the Duchess drowned in tears, and scarcely in a condition to speak; she greeted him with a wave of her hand, and pointed to a chair. Ferrante, disguised that day as a Capuchin once again, was splendid; instead of taking a seat he flung himself on his knees and prayed to God in a devout whisper. When the Duchess seemed a little calmer, without shifting his position he interrupted his prayers a moment to murmur these words: "Once again he offers his life."

"Just think what you are saying," exclaimed the Duchess with that haggard look in her eyes which, after sobs, indicates that anger is overcoming tenderer feelings.

"He offers his life to avert Fabrizio's doom, or to avenge it."

"There is a certain circumstance," the Duchess answered, "when I might accept the sacrifice of your life." She stared at him attentively. A flash of joy lit up his face; he quickly rose to his feet and held his arms to Heaven. The Duchess went to find the paper hidden in the secret drawer of a great walnut cabinet. "Read this," she said to Ferrante. It was the legacy to his children which we have mentioned. Tears and sobs kept Ferrante from reading to the end; he fell to his knees once more. "Give the paper back to me," the Duchess said, and before his eyes she burned it in the candle. "My name," she added, "must not appear should you be captured and executed, for this is a matter of life and death."

"It is my joy to die for the defeat of the tyrant, and a much greater joy to die for you. Let this be understood, and kindly make no further mention of this detail concerning money; I should regard it as an insulting doubt."

"If you are compromised, I may be as well," the Duchess replied, "and Fabrizio after me: it is for that reason, and not because I doubt your courage, that I insist that the man who has rent my heart be poisoned and not stabbed. For the same reason that is so vital to me, I command you to do everything within your power to save your own life."

"I shall carry out your will swiftly, faithfully, and discreetly. I foresee, Signora Duchess, that my own vengeance shall unite with yours: were it to be otherwise, I should still obey swiftly, faithfully, and discreetly. I may not succeed, yet I shall employ all the human strength I possess."

"You must poison Fabrizio's murderer."

"I had guessed as much, and for the past twenty-seven months that I have been leading this abominable vagabond life, I have often conceived such an action on my own account."

"If I am discovered and condemned, as an accomplice," the Duchess continued in a proud tone of voice, "I do not want it to be imputed to me that I have seduced you. I command you not to attempt to see me again before the time of our revenge: there must be no question of putting the man to death before I have given you the signal to do so. His death at this moment, for instance, would be catastrophic for me, rather than useful. Most likely his death must not occur for several months, but it will occur. I insist that he die by poison, and I should prefer letting him live to seeing him shot down. For interests which I choose not to explain to you, I insist that your own life be preserved."

Ferrante was delighted by this authoritative tone the Duchess was taking with him: his eyes glittered with joy. As we have said, he was dreadfully thin; but it was apparent that he had been extremely handsome in his early youth, and he imagined himself to be still what he had once been. "Am I mad?" he asked himself, "or can it be that the Duchess intends, on the day when I have given her this proof of my devotion, to make me the happiest of men? And indeed, why should this not be so? Am I not worth every bit as much as that doll of a Count Mosca, who when the moment came was unable to serve her in this matter, not even to enable Monsignore Fabrizio to escape?"

"I may require his death tomorrow," the Duchess continued, still with the same expression of authority. "You know that huge reservoir at the corner of the *palazzo,* close by the hiding-place you have occasionally used; there is a secret means of causing all that water to flow into the street; indeed, that will be the signal of my revenge. You shall see, if you are in Parma, or you will hear, if you are living in the woods, that the great reservoir of the Palazzo Sanseverina has collapsed. Act at once, but by means of poison, and, above all, expose your own life as little as possible. No one must ever know that I am involved in this business."

"Words are useless," Ferrante replied with ill-concealed enthusiasm, "I have already decided upon the means I shall use. The life of this man becomes more odious to me than it was, since I shall not dare see you again so long as he lives. I shall await the signal of the reservoir's collapse." He bowed abruptly and left the room. The Duchess watched him leave. When he was in the next room she called him back.

"Ferrante!" she exclaimed. "You magnificent man!" He returned, as though impatient at being recalled; his face at this moment was sublime. "And your children?"

"Signora, they will be wealthier than I; you may perhaps grant them some little pension."

"Here," the Duchess said as she handed him a big olive-wood case, "here are all the diamonds I have left; they are worth fifty thousand francs."

"Ah, Signora! You humiliate me!" said Ferrante, with a gesture of horror, and his expression changed completely.

"I shall never see you again before this deed is done: take this, I wish it," the Duchess added with an arrogant expression that overwhelmed Ferrante. He put the case in his pocket and left, shutting the door behind him. Once again the Duchess called him back; he came into the room with an anxious expression: the Duchess was standing in the center of her salon; she flung herself into his arms. A moment later, Ferrante had almost fainted with happiness; the Duchess released herself from his embrace, and with her eyes indicated the door.

"There is the only man who has understood me," she said to herself; "that is how Fabrizio would have acted, if he could have understood me."

There were two traits in the Duchess's character: what she wanted once she wanted forever; she never gave further thought to a decision once she had made it. In this regard she used to quote a remark of her first husband's, the charming General Pietranera: "What insolence to myself!" he used to say. "Why should I suppose I have more sense today than when I made up my mind?"

From this moment, a sort of gaiety reappeared in the Duchess's nature. Before the fatal decision, at each step that her mind had taken, at each new thing she saw, she had the feeling of her inferiority with regard to the Prince, of her weakness and her gullibility; the Prince, she believed, had pusillanimously deceived her, and Count Mosca, in accord with his courtier's genius, however innocently, had furthered the Prince's designs. Once her vengeance was determined, she felt her strength; each step her mind had taken gave her a certain happiness. I am inclined to think that the immoral delight Italians experience in taking revenge is a consequence of their power of imagination; people of other countries do not, strictly speaking, forgive; they forget.

The Duchess did not see Palla again until the last days of Fabrizio's imprisonment. As the reader may have guessed, it was he who came up with the plan of escape: there existed in the forest, some two leagues from Sacca, a half-ruined medieval tower over a hundred feet high; before mentioning escape a second time to the Duchess, Ferrante begged her to send Ludovic, with picked men, to arrange a series of ladders around this tower. In the Duchess's presence, he climbed up by means of these ladders, and came down with a simple knotted rope; he repeated the experiment three times, then he again explained his plan. Eight days later, Ludovic too was willing to climb down this old tower by a knotted rope: it was then that the Duchess communicated this plan to Fabrizio.

In the final days before this attempt, which might well lead to the prisoner's death in more ways than one, the Duchess could find no moment of rest unless Ferrante was at her side; this man's courage electrified her own; but it was evident that she must conceal this singular companionship from the Count. She feared not that he would object but that she would be distressed by his objections, which would have doubled her anxieties. What, to take as her most intimate adviser an acknowledged lunatic and a man under sentence of death as well!

"And," the Duchess added, speaking to herself, "a man who subsequently might do such strange things!" Ferrante happened to be in the Duchess's salon just when the Count came to inform her of the conversation the Prince had had with Rassi; and when the Count had left, it was all she could do to keep Ferrante from proceeding then and there to carry out a frightful plan! "I am strong now!" exclaimed this madman. "I no longer have any doubt as to the legitimacy of the deed!"

"But in the moment of rage which will inevitably follow, Fabrizio will be put to death!"

"But thereby he would be spared the danger of that terrible descent: it is possible, it is even easy," he added, "but the young fellow lacks experience."

The wedding of Marchese Crescenzi's sister was celebrated, and it was at the party given on this occasion that the Duchess encountered Clélia and was able to speak to her without awakening suspicions among the fashionable onlookers. The Duchess herself handed Clélia the bundle of ropes in the garden, where these ladies had gone to take a breath of air. These ropes, woven with the greatest care, half of hemp and half of silk, with knots at regular intervals, were very slender and quite flexible; Ludovic had tested their strength, and, throughout their length, they could bear a load of eight hundredweight without breaking. They had been coiled up to form several bundles in the shape of a quarto volume; Clélia took it from the Duchess and promised that everything that was humanly possible would be accomplished to bring these bundles inside the Farnese Tower.

"Yet I fear the timidity of your nature; and furthermore," the Duchess added politely, "what interest can you have in the fate of a man who is a stranger to you?"

"Signor del Dongo is in distress, *and I promise you that he shall be saved by me!*"

But the Duchess, relying very little upon the presence of mind of a young person of twenty, had taken other precautions she was determined not to share with the Governor's daughter. As it was only natural to suppose, this Governor happened to be at the party given for the wedding of the Marchese Crescenzi's sister. The Duchess said to herself that if she could administer a strong narcotic to him, it would initially be supposed that he was suffering an attack of apoplexy, and then instead of employing his own carriage to return him to the Fortress, she might, with a little skillful management, be able to suggest a better idea, that he be put into a litter which just happened to be in the house where the party was being given. Here there would also be a number of picked men dressed as servants for the party who in the general confusion would obligingly offer to carry the sick man to his lofty residence. These men, under Ludovic's direction, would be carrying a considerable quantity of ropes, cunningly concealed under their uniforms. It is evident that the Duchess was quite out of her senses since she had seriously envisaged Fabrizio's escape. The danger of this beloved being was too great for her soul, and in addition was lasting too long. By an excess of precautions she nearly caused this escape to fail, as we shall see. Everything proceeded according to her plan, with the one difference that the drug produced too powerful an effect; everyone believed, even those of the medical profession, that the General had had an apoplectic stroke.

Fortunately Clélia, in despair, had not the slightest suspicion of so criminal an attempt on the part of the Duchess. The confusion was such, at the moment that the litter containing the half-dead General entered the Fortress, that Ludovic and his men passed in without challenge; they were perfunctorily searched at the slave's bridge. Once they had carried the General to his bed, they were taken to the kitchen quarters, where the servants entertained them lavishly; but after this meal, which was not over until nearly dawn, it was explained that prison rules required that they be locked in for the remainder of the night in the lower rooms of the *palazzo;* they would be released the following day by the Governor's deputy.

These men had managed to hand Ludovic the ropes they had brought in with them, but Ludovic had great difficulty in catching Clélia's attention, even for a moment. Finally, when she was passing from one room to the next, he showed her that he was leaving the bundles of rope in a dark corner of the first-floor salons. Clélia was greatly struck by this strange circumstance and immediately conceived the most dreadful suspicions. "Who are you?" she asked Ludovic. And on receiving his extremely ambiguous reply, she added: "I ought to have you arrested—you or those other men of yours have poisoned my father!... Confess this instant the nature of the poison you have used, so that the Fortress doctor can administer the proper antidotes—confess this instant, or else you and your accomplices will never get out of this Fortress!"

"There is no cause for the Signorina to be alarmed," Ludovic replied with perfect ease and politeness; "there has been nothing like poison; someone has been careless enough to give the General a dose of laudanum, and it appears that the servant accused of this crime put a few too many drops in the glass; you have our eternal apologies, but the Signorina may be assured that, Heaven be thanked, there is no danger whatever: the Governor must be treated for having, by mistake, imbibed an excessive dose of laudanum; but I have the honor to repeat to the Signorina that the servant accused of the crime made no use of real poisons, as did Barbone when he sought to poison Monsignore Fabrizio. No one has attempted to avenge the danger incurred by Monsignore Fabrizio; the clumsy servant was merely entrusted with a bottle containing some laudanum, I can swear as much to the Signorina! Of course it must be understood that if I were to be officially questioned, I should deny everything.

"Moreover, if the Signorina should speak to anyone about laudanum and poison, even to the excellent Don Cesare, Fabrizio will be done to death by the Signorina's own hand. For she renders impossible forever any and every attempt at escape; and the Signorina knows better than I that it is not with simple laudanum that the Monsignore was to be poisoned; she also knows that someone has granted only a month for the commission of this crime, and that it has already been over a week since the fatal order was received. Therefore, if the Signorina has me arrested, or merely speaks a word of the matter to Don Cesare or anyone else, she will be delaying our enterprises by much more than a month, and I have every reason to say that she will be killing Monsignore Fabrizio with her own hand."

Clélia was terrified by Ludovic's strange tranquillity. "So here I am having a perfectly ordinary conversation with my father's poisoner," she said to herself, "who is employing polite euphemisms in order to address me! And it is love which has brought me to all these crimes...!"

Her remorse scarcely allowed her the strength to speak; she said to Ludovic: "I am going to lock you into this salon, and then I shall run to inform the doctor that it is merely laudanum; but good God! how shall I tell him that I have found this out? Afterward, I shall return to release you. But," said Clélia, running back from the door, "did Fabrizio know anything about the laudanum?"

"Heavens no, Signorina, he would never have agreed to such an expedient. And besides, what would have been the use of such an unnecessary confidence? We are acting with the strictest discretion in order to save Monsignore's life, who will be poisoned within the next three weeks; the order to do so has been given by someone whose wishes generally meet with no obstacle; and to tell the Signorina the whole truth, it is said that it was the terrible Chief Justice Rassi who received these instructions."

Clélia fled, horror-stricken: she so relied on Don Cesare's utter probity that, while taking certain precautions, she dared inform him that the General had been given laudanum and not something else. Without answering, without questioning, Don Cesare hurried to the doctor.

Clélia returned to the salon in which she had locked Ludovic, intending to question him further about the laudanum. She no longer found him there: he had managed to escape! On a table she saw a purse full of sequins, and a little box containing various kinds of poison. The sight of such things made her tremble. "Who is to say," she thought, "that it is only laudanum that my father has been given, and that the Duchess has not sought to take revenge for Barbone's attempt? Good God! Here I am in contact with my own father's poisoners! And I have let them escape! And perhaps this very man, if put to the question, would have confessed to something more than laudanum!" Clélia fell to her knees, dissolved in tears, and prayed fervently to the Madonna.

Meanwhile the Fortress doctor, surprised by what Don Cesare had told him, according to whom he had no more than laudanum to deal with, gave the suitable antidotes, which soon dispelled the most alarming symptoms. The General gradually came to himself as day was breaking. His first deed indicating consciousness was to hurl insults at the colonel who was his second in command and who had taken it upon himself to issue the simplest orders while the General was unconscious.

The Governor then went into a towering rage against a kitchen-maid who, as she served him a bowl of bouillon, happened to pronounce the word *apoplexy.*

"Am I of an age," he shouted, "to have apoplectic fits? It is only my sworn enemies who can delight in spreading such rumors. Moreover, have I been bled, that slander itself should dare speak of apoplexy?"

Fabrizio, absorbed in the preparations for his escape, could not comprehend the strange noises that filled the Fortress at the moment the half-dead Governor was carried in. At first it occurred to him that his sentence had been changed, and that he was to be put to death. Then, seeing that no one appeared in his room, he decided that Clélia had been betrayed, that upon her return to the Fortress the ropes she was probably bringing had been taken from her, and that henceforth all his plans for escape were out of the question. At daybreak he saw an unknown man come into his room, who without a word set down a basket of fruit; under the fruit was hidden the following letter:

Filled with the keenest remorse for what has been done, not, Heaven be thanked, with my consent, but on the occasion of an idea that had occurred to me, I have vowed to the Blessed Virgin that if, by her holy intercession, my father is saved, I shall never refuse to obey any of his orders; I shall marry the Marchese as soon as he tells me to, and I shall never see you again. Nonetheless, I believe it is my duty to complete what has been begun. Next Sunday, upon return from the Mass to which you will be taken by my request (remember to prepare your soul, you may meet death in the difficult undertaking that is to come), upon return from Mass, as I was saying, delay your return to your room as much as you can; you will find what you require for the enterprise you have in mind. If you perish, my heart will be broken! Could I be accused of having contributed to your death? Did not the Duchess herself repeat to me on several occasions that the Raversi party is gaining the upper hand? They seek to bind the Prince by a cruel deed which will separate him forever from Count Mosca. The Duchess, through her tears, swore to me that this one resource remains: you will perish if you do not make the attempt. I cannot look at you again,

I have made my vow; but if, on Sunday evening, you see me dressed all in black at the usual window, that will be the signal that the following night everything will be in readiness, insofar as my means allow. After eleven, perhaps only at midnight or at one in the morning, a little lamp will appear at my window, this will be the decisive moment; commend yourself to your Patron Saint, make haste to put on the priest's clothes you will be provided, and be off.

Farewell, Fabrizio, I shall be at my prayers, and shedding the bitterest tears, you may be certain of that, while you incur such great dangers. Should you die, I shall not survive you; good God! What am I saying? But if you make your escape, I shall never see you again. On Sunday, after Mass, you will find in your prison the money, the poisons, the ropes sent by that terrible woman who loves you so passionately and who has told me three times over that this is what must be done. May God and the Blessed Madonna preserve you!

Fabio Conti was an ever-uneasy jailer, always troubled, always dreaming that one or another of his prisoners was escaping: he was hated by everyone in the Fortress, but, misfortune inspiring the same resolve in all men, the wretched prisoners, even those chained in the dungeons three feet high, three feet wide, and eight feet long, in which they could neither sit nor stand—all the prisoners, even these, as I say, conceived the notion of ordering a *Te Deum* sung at their own expense when they learned that their Governor was out of danger. Two or three of these wretches composed sonnets in honor of Fabio. Oh, the influence of misery upon these men! Let him who blames them be led by his fate to spend a year in a dungeon three feet high with eight ounces of bread a day and *fasting* on Fridays!

Clélia, who left her father's bedroom only to pray in the chapel, said that the Governor had decided that the rejoicings would be limited to Sunday. That Sunday morning, Fabrizio attended Mass and the *Te Deum;* that evening there were fireworks and in the lower rooms of the *palazzo* the soldiers received a ration of wine four times the quantity the Governor had stipulated; an unknown hand had even sent several casks of brandy, which the soldiers broached. The generosity of these drunken soldiers refused to permit the five soldiers on sentry-duty around the *palazzo* to suffer from their posting; as soon as they arrived at their sentry-boxes, a trusty servant gave them some wine, and it is not known by what hand those who were posted as sentries at midnight and for the rest of the night received a glass of brandy as well, while the bottle was in each case forgotten beside the sentry-box (as was proved in the subsequent investigation).

The confusion lasted longer than Clélia had expected, and it was only toward one in the morning that Fabrizio, who for the last eight days had sawed through two bars of his window, the one which did not face the aviary, began to take down the shutter; he was working almost directly above the sentries guarding the governor's *palazzo*, but they heard nothing. He had made only a few new knots in the enormous rope necessary to get down from that terrible height of a hundred and eighty feet. He coiled this rope like a bandolier around his body: it hampered his movements a good deal, for its bulk was enormous; the knots kept it from forming a compact mass, and it protruded over eighteen inches from his body. "This is the main obstacle," Fabrizio said to himself.

Once he had arranged the first rope as best he could, Fabrizio took the other one, with which he planned to get down the thirty-five feet which separated his window from the terrace where the Governor's *palazzo* stood. But since, however intoxicated the sentries might be, he could hardly climb down over their heads, he emerged, as we have said, out of the second window of his room, the one which overlooked the roof of a sort of vast guard-room. By a sick-man's caprice, as soon as General Fabio Conti could speak, he had posted two hundred soldiers in this former guard-room that had been abandoned for over a century. He said that after having been poisoned, he would probably be murdered in his bed, and these two hundred soldiers must be on guard against any such attack. One may imagine the effect this unforeseen measure produced upon Clélia's heart: this pious girl was fully conscious of the extent to which she was betraying her father, and a father who had been nearly poisoned in the interests of the prisoner she loved. She almost regarded the unexpected posting of these two hundred men as an act of Providence which was keeping her from proceeding any further in Fabrizio's liberation.

But everyone in Parma was talking about the prisoner's imminent death. This melancholy subject had even been discussed at the party given on the occasion of Signora Giulia Crescenzi's wedding. Since for such a trifle as a clumsy sword-thrust given to an actor, a man of Fabrizio's birth was not released after nine months' imprisonment, it was evident that politics had something to do with his case. And in that event, it was futile to think further about the matter, people were saying; if it was not suitable for the authorities to execute him publicly, he would soon die of some disease. A locksmith who had been summoned to General Fabio Conti's *palazzo* spoke of Fabrizio as of a prisoner long since despatched, and whose death was being concealed for political reasons. This man's words caused Clélia to make up her mind.

Chapter Twenty-two

During the day Fabrizio was beset by several serious and disagreeable reflections, but as he heard the hours strike which brought him nearer to the moment of action, he began to feel ready and cheerful. The Duchess had written him that he would be surprised by the fresh air and that once outside his prison he might find it impossible to walk; in that case, it would be better to risk being recaptured than to hurl oneself one hundred and eighty feet down a wall. "If this misfortune occurs," Fabrizio said to himself, "I will lie down against the parapet, sleep an hour, then start all over; since I've given Clélia my promise, I'd rather fall from the top of the ramparts, high as they are, than forever be obliged to brood over the taste of the bread I am eating. What horrible pains one must experience before the end, when one dies of poison! Fabio Conti will not stand on ceremony; he will have me given the arsenic used to kill the rats in his Fortress."

Toward midnight, one of those dense white fogs the Po occasionally flings over its banks spread first through the city and then reached the terrace and the bastions in the center of which rose the huge tower of the Fortress. Fabrizio estimated that from the terrace parapet, the young acacia-trees surrounding the gardens planted by the soldiers at the base of the hundred-and-eighty-foot wall would no longer be visible. "Which is a good thing," he realized.

Shortly after half-past twelve had struck, the signal of the little lamp appeared at the aviary window. Fabrizio was ready to act; he crossed himself, then tied to his bed the shorter rope intended to lower him the thirty-five feet separating him from the terrace on which the Governor's *palazzo* stood. He landed without difficulty on the roof of the guard-room, occupied since the night before by the reinforcement of two hundred soldiers we have already mentioned. Unfortunately, these soldiers, by a quarter to one, had not yet fallen asleep; while he was tip-toeing across the curved-tile roof, Fabrizio could hear them saying that the Devil was up there on the roof, and that they ought to try killing him with a round of musket-fire. Several voices claimed that this enterprise would be a great impiety, others that if a shot were fired without killing something the Governor would throw them all in jail for having alarmed the garrison to no purpose. The whole argument sent Fabrizio scurrying across the roof as fast as he could go, making even more noise. The fact is that at the very moment when, dangling from his rope, he passed in front of the windows—luckily at a distance of four or five feet because of the roof's projection—they were bristling with bayonets. Some people have claimed that Fabrizio, mad as ever, had conceived the notion of playing the Devil's part and that he tossed these soldiers a handful of sequins. What is certain is that he had scattered sequins on the floor of his room, and also on the terrace on his way from the Farnese Tower to the parapet, in order to distract the soldiers who might have come in pursuit of him.

Having landed on the terrace, where he was surrounded by sentries who normally called out every fifteen minutes the one sentence *All's well around my post,* Fabrizio made for the western parapet and began looking for the new stone.

What seems incredible and might make one doubt the facts, if the result had not had an entire city for witness, is that the sentries posted along the parapet did not see and arrest Fabrizio; as it happened, the fog just mentioned was beginning to rise, and Fabrizio has said that when he was on the terrace, the fog already seemed to have reached half-way up the Farnese Tower. But this fog was not thick, and he could see the sentries quite clearly, some of whom were walking back and forth. He added that, impelled as though by a supernatural force, he boldly took up a position between two sentries quite close to him. He calmly unwound the long rope which was coiled round his body and which twice became tangled; it took him a long time to straighten it out and spread it on the parapet. He heard the soldiers talking all around him and determined to stab the first man who approached. "I wasn't at all worried," he added; "it seemed to me I was performing a ceremony."

He attached his rope, once it was disentangled, to an opening cut in the parapet for the release of rain-water, climbed up onto this same parapet, offered God a fervent prayer, and then, like a hero of the age of chivalry, thought for a moment of Clélia. "How different I am," he said to himself, "from the frivolous libertine who entered this prison nine months ago!" At last he began to descend that dizzying height. He was acting quite mechanically, he said, and as if he were climbing down in broad daylight, in full view of friends, to win a wager. About half-way down, he suddenly felt his arms losing their strength; he even thinks he let go of the rope for a second, but immediately recovered it; perhaps, he says, he grabbed onto the bushes which he was dropping through and which were scratching him. Now and then he felt a searing pain between his shoulders, which nearly took his breath away. There was an extremely uncomfortable swaying motion; he was constantly swung against the bushes and was even brushed by several large birds which he had wakened and which flew right at him. The first times, he imagined he was being seized by men pursuing him down the Fortress wall in the same fashion he was descending, and he prepared to defend himself. Finally he landed at the base of the huge tower with no worse problem than bleeding hands. He says that the slope of the lower half of the tower walls was very helpful—he brushed against the wall as he came down, and the plants growing between the stones greatly retarded his descent. Landing in the soldiers' gardens at the bottom, he fell into an acacia-tree which from above seemed four or five feet high and which was actually fifteen or twenty. A drunken man lying asleep there took him for a thief. Falling out of that tree, Fabrizio nearly dislocated his right arm. He began running toward the parapet but, according to him, his legs seemed to have turned to cotton-wool; he had no strength left. Despite the danger, he sat down and drank a little of the brandy which remained. He dozed off for a few minutes and lost consciousness of where he was; waking, he could not understand how he could be seeing trees in his room. At last the terrible truth returned to his memory; immediately he walked over to the rampart and climbed up onto it by a broad flight of steps. The sentry posted quite close by was snoring in his box. Fabrizio found a cannon lying in the grass; to this he tied his third rope, though it was a little too short, and dropped into a muddy ditch where there might have been a foot of water. While he was climbing out and trying to discover where he was, he felt himself seized by two men: for a moment he was terrified, but he soon heard a voice close to his ear whispering: "Ah, Monsignore! Monsignore!"

He vaguely realized that these were the Duchess's men, and immediately fainted dead away. Some time later he sensed that he was being carried by men walking very fast and in complete silence; then they stopped, which caused him great anxiety. But he had no strength to speak or even to open his eyes; he felt he was being embraced; suddenly he recognized the scent of the Duchess's garments. This fragrance revived him; he opened his eyes and managed to utter the words "Ah, dear friend!!" Then he fainted dead away once again.

The faithful Bruno and a squad of police loyal to the Count were waiting two hundred paces away; the Count himself was hidden in a tiny house very close to the place where the Duchess was waiting. He would not have hesitated, had it been necessary, to wield his sword alongside several retired officers, his intimate friends; he considered himself somehow obliged to save Fabrizio, whose life seemed to him in great jeopardy and who would have had his pardon signed by the Prince had he, Mosca, not been so foolish as to attempt to spare his Sovereign from writing an indiscreet document.

Since midnight the Duchess, surrounded by men armed to the teeth, had been pacing up and down in deep silence close to the Fortress ramparts; she could not stand still and believed she would have to fight in order to rescue Fabrizio from his pursuers. Her ardent imagination had taken a hundred precautions too complicated to describe here, each of an incredible rashness. It has been estimated that over eighty agents were on duty that night, all in readiness to fight for an extraordinary purpose. Fortunately, Ferrante and Ludovic were leading this party, and the Minister of Police was not hostile; yet the Count himself observed that the Duchess had not been betrayed by anyone, and that as a Minister he himself knew nothing of these arrangements.

The Duchess lost her head completely upon seeing Fabrizio again; she hugged him convulsively, then despaired upon seeing him covered with blood: it had come from his hands, but she imagined him to be seriously wounded. With the help of one of her men, she had removed his coat to bandage him when Ludovic, who fortunately happened to be there, insisted on putting Fabrizio and the Duchess into one of the little carriages which had been concealed in a garden near the city gates, and they crept away in order to cross the Po near Sacca. Ferrante, with twenty armed men, made up the rear guard and had faithfully promised to stop any pursuers. The Count, alone and on foot, left the neighborhood of the Fortress only two hours later, when he saw that no one was stirring. "Here I am, committing high treason!" he said to himself, wild with joy.

Ludovic had the inspired idea of putting in another carriage a young surgeon attached to the Duchess's household who happened to have a build similar to Fabrizio's. "Make your escape," he told this man, "in the direction of Bologna; be clumsy about it, try to get yourself arrested; then contradict yourself in your answers, and at the end confess that you are Fabrizio del Dongo; do everything you can to gain time. Be clever at being clumsy, you'll get off with a month in prison, and the Signora will give you fifty sequins."

"Who thinks of money in the Signora's service?"

He set off and was arrested several hours later, affording great joy to General Fabio Conti and to Chief Justice Rassi, who, along with Fabrizio's danger, saw his baronage taking flight.

The escape was discovered at the Fortress only around six that morning, and it was not until ten that anyone dared inform the Prince of the matter. The Duchess had been so well served that despite Fabrizio's deep sleep, which she took for a dead faint and made the carriage stop three times, she crossed the Po in a boat as the hour of four was striking. There were relays of horses on the left bank which covered another two leagues with great speed, until they were stopped for over an hour for the inspection of passports. The Duchess had every kind of passport for herself and for Fabrizio, but she was quite irrational that day and took it into her head to give ten napoleons to the Austrian police-clerk, and to take his hand as she burst into tears. This clerk, greatly alarmed, began the inspection all over again. They then traveled by post; the Duchess paid so extravagantly that she aroused suspicion everywhere in a country where any stranger is suspect. Ludovic again came to her aid, saying that Signora the Duchess was overcome with grief on account of the protracted fever of young Count Mosca, son of the Prime Minister of Parma, whom she was taking to consult doctors in Pavia.

It was only when they were some ten leagues beyond the Po that the prisoner fully recovered consciousness; he had a dislocated shoulder and a good many scratches and bruises. The Duchess was still behaving so oddly that the innkeeper of the village where they stopped for a meal imagined he was dealing with a Princess of the Imperial House, and proceeded to offer her the honors he believed were her due, when Ludovic told the man that the Princess would surely send him to prison if he undertook to have the church bells rung.

Finally, around six that evening, they reached Piedmontese territory. Here for the first time Fabrizio was in complete safety; he was taken to a tiny village off the main road; his hands were bandaged, and he slept a few hours more.

It was in this village that the Duchess permitted herself an action not only dreadful in the eyes of morality but also fatal to her peace of mind for the rest of her life. A few weeks before Fabrizio's escape, and on a day when all Parma was at the Fortress gates trying to glimpse the scaffold being erected in his honor in the courtyard, the Duchess had revealed to Ludovic, now the factotum of her household, the secret by means of which one could remove, from a quite inconspicuous little iron frame, a stone forming part of the pavement of the famous reservoir of the Palazzo Sanseverina, a thirteenth-century structure of which we have already spoken. While Fabrizio was asleep in this village *trattoria*, the Duchess sent for Ludovic, who supposed she had gone mad, so strange were the glances she kept darting at him. "You must be expecting," she told him, "that I'm going to give you many thousands of francs. Well, not at all! I know you, you're a poet and you'd run right through such an amount of money. I'm going to give you the little estate of La Ricciarda, a league outside Casalmaggiore."

Ludovic flung himself at her feet, wild with joy, and protested with heartfelt accents that it was not in hope of gain that he had helped save Monsignore Fabrizio; that he had always loved him dearly since he had had the honor of driving him, once, in his office as the Signora's third coachman. When this man, who was genuinely warm-hearted, believed he had occupied such a great lady's attention long enough, he took his leave; but she, with tears in her eyes, cried: "Wait!"

She was pacing back and forth, silent now, in that village inn, occasionally glancing at Ludovic with incredible eyes. At last this man, realizing that there was to be no end to this strange exercise, decided to address his mistress. "The Signora has given me so extravagant a gift, one so much beyond anything a poor man like myself could imagine, worth so much more than the poor service I have had the honor to perform, that I believe in all conscience I cannot keep her estate of La Ricciarda for myself. I have the honor to return it to the Signora, and to request that she grant me a pension of four hundred francs."

"How many times in your life," she asked him with the grimmest hauteur, "how many times have you ever heard that I have abandoned a plan once I have decided upon it?" After this sentence, the Duchess paced a few more minutes; then, suddenly coming to a halt, she exclaimed: "It is by accident, and because he managed to attract that young girl, that Fabrizio's life has been saved! If he hadn't been so lovable, he would be dead. Can you deny it?" she asked, walking up to Ludovic, her eyes glittering with the blackest fury.

Ludovic recoiled a few steps and was now certain she was mad, which gave him the liveliest anxiety for the proprietorship of his estate of La Ricciarda.

"Well?" continued the Duchess in the gentlest and gayest tone of voice, utterly transformed. "I want my good people of Sacca to have a holiday, one they won't forget for a long time. You will return to Sacca now, if you don't mind. Do you imagine you'll be running any risk?

"None to speak of, Signora: no one in Sacca will ever admit that I was in Monsignore Fabrizio's service. Besides, if I may say as much to the Signora, I am burning to see my property of La Ricciarda: it seems so strange to think of myself as a landowner!"

"Your high spirits please me. The present tenant of La Ricciarda, I believe, owes me three or four years' rent; I'll make him a present of half of what he owes me, and the other half of his arrears I'll give to you, but on one condition: that you'll go to Sacca, that you'll say that the day after tomorrow is the feast of one of my patron saints, and that the evening after you arrive you'll have my *palazzo* illuminated in the most splendid fashion. Spare neither money nor effort—just consider that it will all be for the greatest happiness of my life! I have been preparing this illumination for a long while; over the last three months I have collected in the *palazzo* cellars everything that might serve for this noble festival; I've put in the gardener's hands all the fireworks necessary for a magnificent display—you must have it take place on the terrace overlooking the Po. I have eighty-nine barrels of wine in those cellars; I want eighty-nine fountains of wine flowing in my grounds; if there is a single bottle that has not been drunk the next day, I shall say you do not truly love Fabrizio. When the wine-fountains, the illuminations, and the fireworks are all under way, you will take care to make yourself scarce, for it is possible—indeed, it is my hope—that all these splendid things will be regarded, in Parma, as an act of insolence."

"Indeed it is not merely possible, it is certain—as it is certain that Chief Justice Rassi, who has signed Monsignore's death sentence, will explode with rage. And in fact . . . ," Ludovic added timidly, "if the Signora would choose to give more pleasure to her poor servant than by granting him half the arrears of La Ricciarda, she might allow me to play a trick on the Chief Justice . . ."

"You are a fine fellow!" exclaimed the Duchess rapturously. "But I absolutely forbid you to do anything to Rassi; I have plans to have him publicly hanged, later on. As for yourself, try to keep from being arrested at Sacca; everything will be ruined if I lose you."

"Lose me, Signora! Once I've said I'm celebrating the feast of one of the Signora's patron saints, even if the police were to send thirty officers to spoil our plans, you can be sure that before they reached the red cross in the middle of the village, not one would still be on his horse. They're no fools back there in Sacca—past-masters at smuggling, every one, and all of them worship the Signora..."

"Well then," the Duchess continued with a singularly detached expression, "if I give wine to my good people of Sacca, I want to give water to the inhabitants of Parma; the same evening my house is illuminated, take the best horse in my stable and gallop to my *palazzo* in Parma and ... open the reservoir!"

"Ah, what a splendid idea of the Signora's!" cried Ludovic, laughing like a madman. "Wine for the good people of Sacca and water for the bourgeois of Parma, who were so certain, the wretches, that Monsigore Fabrizio would be poisoned like poor L——" Ludovic was beside himself with delight; the Duchess complacently watched his fits of laughter; he kept repeating: "Wine for the good people of Sacca, and water for the bourgeois of Parma! No doubt the Signora knows better than I that when they were rash enough to drain the reservoir twenty years ago, there was at least a foot of water in several streets of the city."

"And water for the bourgeois of Parma," the Duchess echoed, laughing. "The promenade in front of the Fortress would have been filled with people if they had beheaded Fabrizio. . . . Everyone calls him *the great culprit.* . . . But be sure you do this carefully; no one alive must realize that the flood was caused by you, and ordered by me. Fabrizio and the Count himself must know nothing of this little joke of ours. . . . But I was forgetting the poor of Sacca: go and write a letter to my agent, and I'll sign it; tell him that for the festival of my patron saint, he is to distribute a hundred sequins to the poor of Sacca, and that he must do whatever you ask with regard to the illumination, the fireworks, and the wine; and above all, there must not be one full bottle left in my cellars the next day."

"The Signora's agent will have no difficulties except on one point: in the five years since the Signora has had the villa, she has not left ten poor people in Sacca."

"*. . . And water for the bourgeois of Parma,*" crooned the Duchess. "How will you manage this joke of ours?"

"My plans are all made: I leave Sacca around nine, at half-past ten my horse is at the inn of the Three Simpletons on the road to Casalmaggiore and to *my* estate of La Ricciarda; at eleven I'm in my room at the *palazzo,* and at a quarter past eleven: water for the bourgeois of Parma, and more than they'll need to drink to the health of the great culprit. Ten minutes later I leave town by the Bologna road. I make a deep bow as I pass the Fortress, which Monsignore's courage and the Signora's wit have just dishonored; I take a path through the fields, one I know well, and make my entry into La Ricciarda." Ludovic glanced at the Duchess and was alarmed: she was staring fixedly at the bare wall six paces in front of her, and it must be confessed that her gaze was horrible. "Ah, my poor estate!" Ludovic reflected. "No doubt about it, the lady is mad!"

The Duchess looked at him and guessed his thoughts. "Ah, Signor Ludovic, great poet as you are, you'd like a deed in writing: run and find me a sheet of paper."

Ludovic had no need to be told twice, and the Duchess wrote out a long deed of gift, predated by a year, in which she acknowledged receipt from Ludovic San Micheli of the sum of eighty thousand francs, and as security for said sum gave him in pledge the estate of La Ricciarda. If after the interval of twelve months the Duchess had not returned the said eighty thousand francs to Ludovic, the estate of La Ricciarda would remain his property.

"It is a fine thing," the Duchess mused, "to give a faithful retainer nearly a third of what I have left for myself. . . . Now then," she said to Ludovic, "after the entertainment of the reservoir, I'm giving you only ten days to relax at Casalmaggiore. For the deed to be valid, you must say that it's a transaction which dates back more than a year. I want you to join me at Belgirate, and as soon as you can; Fabrizio may be going to England, and you'll be with him." Early the next day, the Duchess and Fabrizio were at Belgirate.

They took up residence in that enchanting village; but a deadly grief awaited the Duchess on the shores of that lovely lake. Fabrizio was altogether transformed; from the first moments when he awakened, still somewhat lethargic from his sleep, the Duchess noticed that something extraordinary was taking place within him. The deep feeling he so carefully concealed was quite strange, for it was nothing less than this: he was in despair at being out of prison. He took pains to conceal this source of his melancholy, for it would have led to questions he had no desire to answer.

"Can you explain it to me?" the startled Duchess asked him. "That horrible sensation when hunger forced you to eat in order to remain alive, swallowing one of those hateful dishes furnished by the prison kitchens—the sensation that *perhaps at this very moment I am poisoning myself*—didn't that fill you with horror?"

"I thought of death," Fabrizio answered, "the way I suppose soldiers think of it: it was a possibility I was certain I could avoid by using my wits."

What anxiety, then, what suffering for the Duchess! This adored, singular, lively, original being was henceforth, before her very eyes, a prey to some impenetrable reverie; he even preferred solitude to the pleasures of frank discussion with the best friend he had in the world. Yet he was polite, attentive, grateful to the Duchess; as before, he would have sacrificed his life for her a hundred times over; but his soul was elsewhere. Often they would stroll four or five leagues along that sublime lake without speaking a word to each other. Their conversation, the exchange of the cold thoughts henceforth possible between them, might have seemed pleasant to others; but they still remembered, the Duchess particularly, what such conversation had been before that fateful fight with Giletti, which had separated them from each other. Fabrizio owed the Duchess an account of his nine months in that dreadful prison, yet he had only a few brief and fragmentary remarks to make concerning his entire sojourn there.

"Well, it had to happen sooner or later," the Duchess would tell herself grimly. "Distress has aged me, or else he is truly in love, and I have no more than second place in his heart." Humiliated, overwhelmed by this greatest of all possible sufferings, the Duchess would sometimes reflect: "Had it been the will of Heaven that Ferrante had gone quite mad or lost his courage, it seems to me I should be less miserable than I am." From that moment, this semi-remorse poisoned the Duchess's esteem for her own character. "There it is," she said to herself bitterly, "I am repenting a resolution I have already made: then I am no longer a del Dongo! It must be Heaven's will," she continued; "Fabrizio is in love, and what right have I to want him not to be? Has a single word of real passion ever been exchanged between us?"

Reasonable as it was, this notion deprived her of sleep, and in fact what revealed that age and a flagging heart had come upon her along with the prospect of an illustrious revenge was that she was a hundred times more unhappy at Belgirate than at Parma. As for the person who might be the cause of Fabrizio's strange reverie, it was scarcely possible to entertain reasonable doubts: Clélia Conti, that pious child, had betrayed her father by consenting to make the garrison drunk, and Fabrizio never mentioned Clélia! "But," the Duchess added, striking her breast in despair, "if the garrison had not been made drunk, all my ingenuities, all my schemes would have been useless; so it is she who has saved him!"

It was with the greatest difficulty that the Duchess obtained from Fabrizio details concerning the events of that night, "which," as she said to herself, "would in the old days have constituted the subject of an endless discussion! In those happy times he would have talked all day long and with what ever-renewed verse and gaiety about the merest trifle I might have brought up."

As it was necessary to anticipate every possibility, the Duchess had installed Fabrizio at the port of Locarno, a Swiss town at the end of Lake Maggiore. Every day she would call for him in a boat, and they would make long excursions around the lake. Well! Once when she had determined to visit his apartment, she found the walls covered with views of Parma he had sent for from Milan or from Parma itself, a city he ought to have held in abomination. His little sitting-room, transformed into a studio, was crowded with all the apparatus of a watercolor painter, and she found him completing a third view of the Farnese Tower and the Governor's *palazzo*.

"The one thing you must do now," she said to him with a frown, "is to paint from memory the portrait of that friendly Governor who wanted nothing better than to poison you. But now that I think of it," the Duchess continued, "you ought to write him a letter of apology for having taken the liberty of escaping and making a mockery of his Fortress."

The poor woman had no idea how truly she spoke; no sooner had he reached a place of safety than Fabrizio's first concern had been to write an altogether polite and in some sense absurd letter to General Fabio Conti, in which he asked pardon for having escaped, offering as an excuse his discovery that a certain prison underling had been ordered to give him poison. Little though he cared what he wrote, it was Fabrizio's hope that his letter would fall under Clélia's eyes, and his face was wet with tears as he wrote it. He ended with a rather amusing sentence, venturing to say that, finding himself a free man, he often had occasion to regret his little room in the Farnese Tower. This was the main burden of his letter, which he hoped Clélia would understand. While the writing fit was still upon him, and in hopes of being read by someone, Fabrizio addressed his thanks to Don Cesare, that kind chaplain who had lent him books on theology. A few days later Fabrizio commissioned the little bookseller of Locarno to travel to Milan where, as the friend of the famous bibliophile Reina, he purchased the most magnificent editions he could find of the works Don Cesare had lent Fabrizio. The kind chaplain received these volumes and a fine letter informing him that in moments of impatience, pardonable perhaps in a wretched prisoner, the margins of his books had been covered with absurd notes. He was requested, consequently, to replace them on his library shelves by these volumes, which the deepest gratitude took the liberty of offering.

It was quite modest of Fabrizio to give the simple name of *notes* to the endless scribbling with which he had filled the margins of a folio copy of the works of Saint Jerome. In hopes that he might return this book to the kind chaplain and exchange it for another one, he had written in the margins day by day a very specific journal of all that had happened to him in prison; the great events were nothing but the ecstasies of *divine love* (this word *divine* was the substitute for another he dared not write). Sometimes this divine love led the prisoner to deep despair, sometimes a voice in the spaces above him offered some hope and produced transports of happiness. All this, fortunately, was written in *prison ink*, consisting of wine, chocolate, and soot, and Don Cesare had merely glanced at it as he replaced the volume of Saint Jerome on his shelves. Had he perused those margins, he would have seen that one day the prisoner, believing himself poisoned, congratulated himself on dying less than forty paces away from what he loved most in all the world. But eyes other than those of the kind chaplain had read this page since Fabrizio's escape. That fine notion—*to die near what one loves best!*—expressed in a hundred different ways, was followed by a sonnet in which it appeared that the soul, separated after cruel sufferings from the fragile body it had inhabited for twenty-three years, impelled by that instinct for happiness natural to all that once knew life, would not mount to Heaven to mingle with the angelic choirs as soon as it was free, and supposing that God's terrible judgment granted pardon for its sins; but rather, happier after death than it had been in life, it would go only a few paces from the prison, where it had languished so long, to be united with all it had loved in this world. "And thus," the last line of the sonnet asserted, "I shall have found my paradise on earth."

Though Fabrizio was mentioned in the Fortress of Parma only as an infamous traitor who had violated the most sacred duties of man, the good priest Don Cesare was nonetheless delighted by the sight of the fine volumes sent to him by some stranger; for Fabrizio had taken care to write only several days after sending the books, lest his name cause the whole bundle to be indignantly returned. Don Cesare made no mention of these kind attentions to his brother the Governor, who fell into fits of rage at the mere name of Fabrizio del Dongo; but since the latter's escape, Don Cesare had resumed all his former intimacy with his affectionate niece; and since he had once taught her a little Latin, he now showed her the fine volumes he had received. This had been the fugitive's hope. Suddenly Clélia blushed deeply, for she had just recognized Fabrizio's handwriting. Long narrow strips of yellow paper had been placed as bookmarks in various parts of the volume. And just as one might say that in the midst of the sordid pecuniary interests and the insipid chill of the vulgar thoughts which fill our lives, the actions inspired by a real passion rarely fail to produce their effect; as if a propitious divinity were taking care to lead them on, so Clélia, guided by this instinct and by the thought of but one thing in the world, asked her uncle to compare the old copy of Saint Jerome with the one he had just received. How to express her delight amid the grim melancholy into which Fabrizio's absence had plunged her, when she found on the margins of the old Saint Jerome that sonnet we have just mentioned as well as the day-by-day memoirs of the love he had felt for her!

From that first day, she knew the sonnet by heart; she sang it, leaning on her window-sill, in front of the now blank window where she had so often seen a little opening appear in the shutter. That shutter had been taken down to be placed on the judge's desk in the courtroom, to serve as evidence in an absurd trial which Rassi was instituting against Fabrizio, now accused of the crime of having escaped or, as the Chief Justice himself said with a smile, *of having removed himself from the clemency of a magnanimous prince!*

Each of Clélia's actions had been for her the object of intense remorse, and now that she was unhappy, such remorse was all the more intense. She sought to ease her self-reproach by recalling her vow *never to see Fabrizio again,* made to the Madonna at the time of the General's semi-poisoning and subsequently renewed every day.

Her father had been made ill by Fabrizio's escape, and furthermore had come very near to losing his position when the Prince, in his rage, had cashiered all the jailers of the Farnese Tower and sent them as prisoners to the city jail. The General had been saved from this fate in part by the intercession of Count Mosca, who preferred to see him shut up on top of his Fortress rather than as an active rival maneuvering in Court circles.

It was during the fifteen days of uncertainty concerning the disgrace of General Fabio Conti, who was really ill, that Clélia found the courage to perform the sacrifice she had announced to Fabrizio. She had had the wit to fall ill on the day of the general rejoicings, which was also the day of the prisoner's escape, as the reader perhaps remembers; she was ill the next day as well, and, in a word, was so skillful in her behavior that with the exception of the jailer Grillo, whose special duty it was to guard Fabrizio, no one had any suspicion as to her complicity, and Grillo held his tongue.

But though Clélia had no further anxieties in this regard, she was still cruelly wracked by her just remorse: "What argument in the world," she would ask herself, "can diminish the crime of a daughter who betrays her father?"

One evening, after a day spent almost entirely in the chapel and in tears, she begged her uncle Don Cesare to accompany her to the bedside of the General, whose fits of rage terrified her all the more in that any and every topic produced new imprecations against Fabrizio, that abominable traitor.

Once in her father's presence, she summoned the courage to tell him that if she had always refused to grant her hand to the Marchese Crescenzi, it was because she felt no inclination toward him, and that she was certain to find no happiness in such a union. At these words, the General flew into a rage, and Clélia had some difficulty continuing with what she had to say. She added that if her father, tempted by the Marchese's great fortune, believed himself bound to give her strict orders to marry this man, she was prepared to obey. The General was quite amazed by this conclusion, which he was far from expecting; yet he managed to rejoice over it. "So," he remarked to his brother, "I shall not be reduced to second-floor lodgings, should that scoundrel Fabrizio make me lose my place by his wicked actions."

Count Mosca did not fail to show himself utterly scandalized by the escape of that scoundrel Fabrizio, and repeated at every opportunity the phrase coined by Rassi concerning the base conduct of this entirely vulgar young man, as it turned out, who had removed himself from the Prince's clemency. This witty phrase, consecrated by the best society, found no echo among the populace. Left to their own good sense, even while believing Fabrizio entirely culpable, the people of Parma admired the resolve it must have taken to have flung oneself over so high a wall. Not one creature of the Court admired such courage. As for the police, so greatly humiliated by this escape, they had officially discovered that a troop of twenty soldiers in the pay of the Duchess—a cruelly ungrateful woman whose name was no longer uttered save with a sigh—had provided Fabrizio with four ladders tied together, each one forty-five feet long: having lowered a rope tied to the ladders, Fabrizio had had no more than the extremely vulgar merit of pulling the ladders up to his cell. A few Liberals known for their imprudence, among them the physician C——, an agent paid directly by the Prince, added (though compromising themselves by doing so) that these wretched police officers had had the barbarity to execute eight of the unfortunate soldiers who had facilitated that ingrate Fabrizio's escape. He was then blamed even by the true Liberals for having caused, by his rashness, the death of eight poor soldiers. It is thus that petty despotisms reduce to nothing the value of public opinion.

CHAPTER TWENTY-THREE

Amidst this general uproar, only Archbishop Landriani appeared loyal to his young friend's cause; he ventured to repeat, even at the Princess's court, the legal maxim according to which, in every trial, one must keep an ear free of all prejudice in order to hear the arguments of an absent party.

The day after Fabrizio's escape, several persons had received a clumsy sonnet celebrating this flight as one of the finest actions of the age, and comparing Fabrizio to an angel alighting on earth with outspread wings. The following evening, all Parma was repeating a sublime poem. This was Fabrizio's monologue as he slid down the rope, passing judgments on the various incidents of his life. This sonnet gave him an eminence in public opinion on account of two magnificent verses, in which every connoisseur recognized the style of Ferrante Palla.

But here I must seek an epic style: where else might I find colors to limn the torrents of indignation which suddenly flooded all respectable hearts when they learned of the dreadful insolence of that illumination of the villa at Sacca? There was but a single outcry against the Duchess; even the true Liberals declared that this action cruelly compromised the wretched suspects being held in the various prisons of the realm, and needlessly exasperated the Sovereign's heart. Count Mosca declared that the Duchess's old friends had but one recourse, which was to forget her. The chorus of execration was therefore unanimous: a stranger passing through the city would have been struck by the vehemence of public opinion. But in this country where people know how to appreciate the pleasures of revenge, the illumination at Sacca and the splendid celebration given on the grounds to some six thousand peasants enjoyed an enormous success. Everyone in Parma was talking about how the Duchess had distributed a thousand sequins to her people; this accounted for the somewhat harsh welcome given to the thirty or so officers the police had been so foolish as to send to this little village, thirty-six hours after the sublime evening and the general intoxication which had followed it. The officers, welcomed by a shower of stones, had taken to their heels, and two of them, fallen from their horses, had been thrown into the Po.

As for the bursting of the great reservoir of the Palazzo Sanseverina, it had gone virtually unnoticed: it was during the night that several streets had been more or less flooded; the next day one would have said that it had rained. Ludovic had been careful to break the panes in one of the *palazzo* windows, to suggest that robbers had broken in.

A little ladder had even been discovered. Only Count Mosca recognized his friend's genius.

Fabrizio was quite determined to return to Parma as soon as he could; he entrusted Ludovic with a long letter to the Archbishop, and this loyal servant returned to post at the first Piedmontese village, Sannazzaro to the west of Pavia, a Latin epistle which the worthy prelate addressed to his young protégé. We shall add one detail which, like several others no doubt, will seem tedious in countries where there is no longer a need for precautions. The name of Fabrizio del Dongo was never written; all the letters sent to him were addressed to Ludovic San Micheli, at Locarno in Switzerland, or in Belgirate in Piedmont. The envelope was made of coarse paper, the seal clumsily applied, the address barely legible, and occasionally embellished with directions worthy of a cook; all the letters were dated from Naples, six days before the actual date.

From the Piedmontese village of Sannazaro, near Pavia, Ludovic lost no time in returning to Parma: he was entrusted with a mission which Fabrizio regarded as of the greatest importance, nothing less than getting into Clélia Conti's hands a silk handkerchief on which was printed a sonnet by Petrarch. It is true that one word of this sonnet had been altered: Clélia found it on her table two days after having received the thanks of the Marchese Crescenzi, who proclaimed himself the happiest of men, and it is unnecessary to say what impression this mark of an ever-growing remembrance produced upon her heart.

Ludovic was to try to obtain every possible detail concerning what was happening in the Fortress. It was he who gave Fabrizio the sad news that the Marchese Crescenzi's marriage now seemed to be definitely settled; almost no day passed without some sort of party given for Clélia inside the Fortress. A decisive proof of the marriage was that the inordinately rich and consequently avaricious Marchese, as is the custom among the wealthy class of northern Italy, was making vast preparations, though he was marrying a girl *without dowry*. It is true that General Fabio Conti's vanity, outraged by this observation, the first to occur to all his compatriots, had just purchased an estate worth over 300,000 francs, and this estate he had paid for, though he was virtually penniless, in ready money, apparently out of the Marchese's funds. Then the General had declared that he was giving this estate as a wedding-present to his daughter. But the charges for the documents and other matters, amounting to over 12,000 francs, seemed an absurd expense to the Marchese Crescenzi, an eminently logical person. For his part he was having woven in Lyons a set of magnificent tapestries in carefully matched colors calculated to delight the eye, designed by the famous Bolognese painter Pallagi. These tapestries, each of which contained some aspect of the armorial bearings of the Crescenzis, who as the world well knows are descended from the celebrated Crescentius, the Roman Consul in the year 985, were to furnish the seventeen salons forming the ground floor of the Marchese's palace. The tapestries, clocks, and lusters sent to Parma cost over 350,000 francs; the cost of the new mirrors, added to those the house already possessed, amounted to two hundred thousand francs. With the exception of two salons, the work of the famous Parmigianino, the greatest painter of the region after the divine Correggio, every room on the first and second floor was now occupied by celebrated painters from Florence, Rome, and Milan, who were decorating them with frescoes throughout. Fokelberg, the great Swedish sculptor, Tenerani from Rome, and Marchesi from Milan had been working for a year on ten bas-reliefs representing as many feats of Crescentius, that truly great man. Most of the ceilings, thus frescoed, also made some allusion to his life. Particularly admired was the ceiling on which Hayez, from Milan, had represented Crescentius received in the Elysian Fields by Francesco Sforza, Lorenzo the Magnificent, King Robert, the Tribune Cola di Rienzi, Machiavelli, Dante, and the other great figures of the Middle Ages. Admiration for these distinguished spirits was taken as a witty epigram at the expense of those presently in power.

All these magnificent details monopolized the attention of the nobility and the bourgeois of Parma, and pierced our hero's heart when he read about them, described with naïve admiration, in a long letter of over twenty pages which Ludovic had dictated to a customs-officer in Casalmaggiore.

"And I, poor wretch that I am!" Fabrizio kept saying to himself. "With a yearly income of no more than four thousand lire! What an impertinence for me to dare aspire to Clélia Conti, for whom all these miracles are being wrought!"

Only one item in Ludovic's long letter, though this one written in his own wretched hand, informed his master that he had encountered that evening, and in the condition of a fugitive, poor Grillo his former jailer, who had been imprisoned, and then released. This man had asked for the charity of a sequin, and Ludovic had given him four in the Duchess's name. A dozen of the former jailers, recently liberated, were preparing a little reception with knives (*un trattamento di coltellate*) to the new jailers their successors, should they ever manage to encounter them outside the Fortress. Grillo had said that serenades were given almost daily at the Fortress, that Signorina Clélia was very pale, frequently ill, *and other things of this kind.* This absurd phrase caused Ludovic to receive, by return post, orders to return to Locarno. He did so, and the details he gave in person were even more melancholy for Fabrizio.

One may judge of the latter's consideration for the poor Duchess; he would have suffered a thousand deaths rather than utter Clélia Conti's name in her hearing. The Duchess held Parma in abhorrence; while for Fabrizio, all that betokened this city was at once sublime and touching.

Less than ever had the Duchess forgotten her revenge; she had been so happy before the incident of Giletti's death! And now what was her fate—she was living in expectation of a dreadful event of which she was determined not to utter a word to Fabrizio, she who once, during her transactions with Ferrante, had supposed she would delight Fabrizio by telling him that one day he would be avenged.

One can now form some notion of the amenity of Fabrizio's conversations with the Duchess: a gloomy silence reigned between them almost all the time. To increase the pleasures of their intercourse, the Duchess had yielded to the temptation of playing a little trick on this all too beloved nephew. The Count was writing her almost daily; apparently he was sending couriers as in the time of their *amours,* for his letters invariably bore the stamp of some Swiss canton or other. The poor man was tormenting his wits to avoid speaking too openly of his feelings, and attempting to make his letters entertaining; they were scarcely glanced at by a distracted pair of eyes. What avails, alas! the faithfulness of an esteemed lover, when one's heart is riven by the coldness of the man one prefers to him?

In two months' time the Duchess answered him only once, and that was to ask him to determine the Princess's susceptibilities and to see whether, despite the insolence of the fireworks display, a letter from the Duchess would be well received. The letter he was to deliver, if he judged it suitable, asked the Princess for the position of Lord-in-Waiting, which had fallen vacant recently, for the Marchese Crescenzi, and requested that it be awarded him in consideration of his marriage. The Duchess's letter was a masterpiece of the tenderest and the most eloquent respect; this courtly style did not admit the slightest word of which any consequence, however remote, might not be agreeable to the Princess. Hence the reply breathed a tender friendship to which separation was a torment.

My son and I, *the Princess told her,* have not spent a single tolerable evening since your abrupt departure. Does my dear Duchess no longer remember that it is she who effected my participation in choosing the officers of my household? Does she then believe herself obliged to give me reasons for the Marchese's position, as if any desire of hers were not the best of reasons for me? The Marchese will have the position, if I have any say in the matter; and there will always be a place in my heart, a prominent one, for my beloved Duchess. My son employs just the same expressions, however strong they may sound from the lips of a great boy of twenty-one, and asks you for samples of the minerals of the Val d'Orta, near Belgirate. You may address your letters, frequent as I hope they will be, to the Count, who is still vexed with you and whom I particularly cherish on account of such sentiments. The Archbishop too has remained faithful to you. We all hope to see you again one of these days: remember that it is your duty. The Marchesa Ghisleri, my Mistress of the Robes, is preparing to leave this world for a better one: the poor woman has given me a great deal of trouble; she is giving me more by departing so inopportunely; her illness reminds me of the name I would have put with such pleasure where hers is now, if only I could have obtained that sacrifice of independence from the one woman who, by leaving us, has taken with her all the joy of my little court, and so on.

Hence it was with the awareness of having sought to hasten, as much as it lay within her power, the wedding which was filling Fabrizio with despair that the Duchess saw him every day. Sometimes, therefore, they would spend four or five hours sailing around the lake, without exchanging a single word. Fabrizio's good will was complete, but he was thinking of other things, and his naïve and simple soul afforded him nothing to say. The Duchess saw this, and it was agony to her.

We have forgotten to mention, in its proper place, that the Duchess had taken a house in Belgirate, a charming village which keeps the promise of its name (*i.e.,* a fine turn around the lake). From the French windows of her salon, the Duchess could step out into her boat, quite an ordinary one which she had rented and for which four oarsmen would have sufficed; she hired a dozen, and managed to include a man from each of the villages around Belgirate. The third or fourth time she found herself in the middle of the lake with all these carefully selected men, she ordered them to stop rowing. "I regard you all as my friends," she told them, "and I want to entrust you with a secret. My nephew Fabrizio has escaped from prison; and perhaps, treacherously, an attempt will be made to recapture him, right here on your lake, that country of freedom. Keep your ears cocked, and inform me of anything you happen to learn. I authorize you to enter my rooms by day or night."

The oarsmen responded enthusiastically; the Duchess knew how to make herself loved. But she did not believe there was any question of recapturing Fabrizio: it was for herself that she was taking all these precautions, and before the fatal order to open the reservoir of the Palazzo Sanseverina, she would not have dreamed of such a thing.

Her prudence had also committed her to rent an apartment for Fabrizio at the port of Locarno; every day he came to see her, or she herself crossed over into Switzerland. One may judge of the vitality of their perpetual tête-à-têtes by this detail: the Marchesa and her daughters came to see them twice, and the presence of these "strangers" gave them pleasure; for despite the ties of blood, we may call a person who knows nothing of our dearest interests and whom we see but once a year a stranger.

The Duchess happened to be at Fabrizio's apartment in Locarno one evening, with the Marchesa and her two daughters; the district Archpriest and the parish priest as well had come to pay their respects to these ladies: the Archpriest, who had interests in a commercial establishment and kept abreast of current happenings, suddenly ventured to say: "The Prince of Parma is dead!"

The Duchess turned very pale; she had scarcely the courage to say: "Have any details been made known?"

"No," the Archpriest replied; "the report merely cites the death, which is certain."

The Duchess looked at Fabrizio. "I have done this for him," she said to herself; "I would have done a thousand worse things, and here he is, in front of me, indifferent and dreaming of another!" It·was beyond her powers to endure this dreadful thought; she fell into a dead faint. Everyone hastened to her assistance; but as she came to, she noticed that Fabrizio was less concerned than the Archpriest and the curate; he was daydreaming as usual.

"He's thinking of returning to Parma," the Duchess said to herself, "and perhaps of breaking off Clélia's wedding to the Marchese; but I'll be able to keep him from doing that." Then, remembering the presence of the two priests, she made haste to add: "He was a great Prince, and has been greatly maligned! This is a great loss for us all!"

The two priests took their leave, and the Duchess, in order to be alone, announced that she was taking to her bed. "No doubt," she said to herself, "prudence would have me wait a month or two before returning to Parma; but I feel that I shall never have such patience; I am suffering too much here. This continual daydreaming of Fabrizio's and this silence are an intolerable spectacle for my heart. Who could have predicted that I would find it tedious to sail around this delightful lake, the two of us together, and just when I have done more to avenge him than I can ever tell him! After such a spectacle, death is nothing. I am paying now for those childish transports of happiness I was taking in my *palazzo* at Parma when I received Fabrizio there on his way back from Naples! Had I spoken one word, everything would have been settled, and perhaps, involved with me, he would not have given a thought to that little Clélia; but that word was deeply repugnant to me. Now it overwhelms me. What could be simpler? She is twenty and I—transformed by anxiety, ill as I am, I am twice her age! . . . One must die, end it all! A woman of forty is no longer something for the men who have loved her in her youth! Now I shall find no more than the pleasures of vanity; and do they make life worth living? All the more reason for going to Parma, and for amusing myself. If matters took a certain turn, I should lose my life. Well! What's so bad about that? I'd die a splendid death, and before it was over, but only then, I'd say to Fabrizio: 'Ingrate! It was for you!' . . . Yes, only in Parma can I find something to do with what life remains to me; I'll play the *grande dame* there. What a blessing if I could be aware now of all those distinctions which used to be the bane of the Raversi's life! In those days, in order to see my own happiness, I needed to look into the eyes of envy. . . . My vanity has one satisfaction; with the exception of the Count perhaps, no one can have guessed the event that has put an end to my heart's life. . . . I'll go on loving Fabrizio, I'll be devoted to his interests; but he must not break off Clélia's wedding and marry her himself. . . . No, that must never be!"

The Duchess had reached this point in her mournful monologue when she heard a loud noise in the house. "Good!" she said to herself. "Now they're coming to arrest me; Ferrante will have let himself get caught, he must have confessed. And so much the better! Now I'll have an occupation: fighting for my life. But first of all not to let myself be captured." Half-dressed, the Duchess fled into her garden: she was already planning to climb over a little wall and escape into the countryside; but she noticed that someone was entering her bedroom. She recognized Bruno, the Count's confidential servant: he was alone, along with her chambermaid. She approached the French door. The man was telling the chambermaid about the wounds he had received. The Duchess entered her room; Bruno virtually flung himself at her feet, imploring her not to tell the Count the absurd hour he had chosen to make his appearance. "Right after the Prince's death," he added, "the Signor Count gave orders to all the posting-stations not to furnish horses to the subjects of the State of Parma. So I reached the Po on our own horses, but when I was getting out of the boat, my carriage was overturned, broken, smashed to bits, and I had such serious bruises that I couldn't ride a horse, as was my duty."

"Even so," said the Duchess, "it is three in the morning: I'll say you arrived at noon; you won't contradict me."

"I am grateful for the Signora's kindness."

Politics in a literary work are a pistol-shot in the middle of a concert, a crude affair though one impossible to ignore. We are about to speak of very ugly matters, which for more than one reason we should rather suppress, but which we are forced to discuss by events which fall within our province, since the hearts of our characters constitute their theater.

"But for God's sake, how did the Prince happen to die?" the Duchess asked Bruno.

"He was out shooting migratory birds in the marshes along the Po, two leagues from Sacca. He fell into a hole concealed by a tuft of grass; he was perspiring heavily, and caught a chill; he was taken to a lonely farmhouse, where he died in a few hours. Some people claim that Signors Catena and Borone died as well, and that the whole business happened because of the copper pots in the peasant's farmhouse where they were—pots filled with mold. They had eaten food out of them. And of course the excitable people, the Jacobins, say what they like and talk of poison. . . . I know that my friend Toto, a groom at Court, would have died if it hadn't been for the generous care of a country bumpkin who seemed to have considerable medical knowledge and supplied him with some very strange remedies. But people have already stopped talking about the Prince's death: the truth is, he was a cruel man. When I left, a mob was gathering to slaughter Chief Justice Rassi: they wanted to go and set fire to the gates of the Fortress, in order to try to save the prisoners. But it was claimed that Fabio Conti would fire his cannons. Other people declared that the Fortress cannoneers had poured water over their gunpowder, being unwilling to massacre their fellow citizens. But what's more interesting is that while Sandolaro was tying up my poor arm, a man came from Parma saying that people had found Barbone in the streets—you know, that famous clerk of the Fortress—and had beaten him and then hanged him from the tree on the promenade closest to the Fortress. The people were on the way to break that fine statue of the Prince which stands in the Court gardens, but the Signor Count took a battalion of the Guard, posted it in front of the statue, and announced that no one entering the gardens would leave alive, and people were afraid. But the strangest thing of all, which that man from Parma, who is a former police-officer, told me several times, is that the Signor Count actually kicked General P——, in command of the Prince's Guard, and had him taken out of the gardens by two fusiliers, after tearing off his epaulettes."

"I know my Count!" exclaimed the Duchess in a transport of joy she would not have believed possible a moment earlier. "He would never

permit an offense to our Princess; and as for General P——, in his devotion to his legitimate masters, he would never consent to serve the
usurper, while the Count, being less delicate, fought in all the Spanish
campaigns, which he was frequently reproached for at Court."

The Duchess had opened the Count's letter, but interrupted her
reading to ask Bruno a hundred questions. The letter was highly entertaining; the Count used the most lugubrious terms, yet the liveliest
pleasure broke through at each word; he avoided details concerning
the manner of the Prince's death, and ended his letter with these
words:

> No doubt you will return, my angel! But I advise you to wait a day or two
> for the message which the Princess will be sending you, as I hope, either
> today or tomorrow; your return must be as splendid as your departure was
> bold. As for that great criminal who is with you, I certainly count on hav-
> ing him judged by a dozen magistrates summoned from all parts of this
> State. But in order to have this monster punished as he deserves, I must
> first be able to tear the first sentence to shreds, if it exists.

The Count had reopened his letter to add:

> Now for a very different business: I have just had cartridges distributed to
> two battalions of the Guard; I shall do battle and deserve as best I can that
> sobriquet "the Cruel" with which the Liberals have honored me for so
> long. That old mummy General P—— has dared to speak in the barracks
> of parleying with the people, who are more or less in rebellion. I write you
> from the middle of the street; now I'm going to the Palace, which shall be
> entered only over my dead body. Farewell! If I die, it will be as your votary,
> even as I have lived! Don't forget to take the three hundred thousand francs
> left in your name at the banker D——'s, in Lyons.
>
> Here is that poor devil Rassi, pale as death and without his wig; you
> can't imagine what he looks like! The people are determined to hang him,
> which would be doing him a great wrong, he deserves to be drawn and
> quartered. He sought refuge in my *palazzo*, and has run after me into the
> street; I'm not sure what to do with him. . . . I don't want to lead him to
> the Prince's Palace, which would cause the rebellion to break out there.
> F—— will see how much I love him; my first word to Rassi was: I must

have the sentence of Signor del Dongo, and all the copies of it you can obtain, and I want you to inform all those iniquitous judges who are the cause of this rebellion that I'll have them all hanged, like yourself, my dear friend, if they breathe a word of this sentence, which has never existed. In Fabrizio's name, I'm sending a company of grenadiers to the Archbishop. Fare-well, my angel! My *palazzo* will be burned to the ground and I shall lose my charming portraits of you. I'm off to the Palace to strip that wretched General P—— of his rank, who is up to his usual tricks; he is basely flatter-ing the populace, as he used to flatter the late Prince. All these generals are scared out of their wits; I believe I shall have myself made Commander in Chief.

The Duchess was unkind enough not to have Fabrizio wakened; she felt a burst of admiration for the Count which closely resembled love. "All things considered," she said to herself, "I must marry him." She wrote him immediately, and sent one of her men with the letter. That night, the Duchess had no time to be unhappy.

The next day, around noon, she saw a boat manned by ten oarsmen rapidly cleaving the waters of the lake; she and Fabrizio soon recognized a man wearing the livery of the Prince of Parma: indeed this was one of his couriers, who, before disembarking, shouted to the Duchess: "The rebellion has been put down!"

This courier handed her several letters from the Count, an admirable communication from the Princess, and a decree of Prince Ranuccio-Ernesto V, on parchment, which created her Duchess of San Giovanni and Mistress of the Robes of the Dowager Princess. This young Prince, so learned in mineralogy and whom she had supposed an imbecile, had possessed sufficient wit to write her a brief note; but there was love at the end of it. The note began as follows:

The Count tells me, Signora Duchess, that he is pleased with me; the fact is that I have withstood a few rifle shots beside him, and that my horse was grazed: considering the fuss made over such trifles, I am particularly eager to participate in a real battle, but not one against my own subjects. I owe everything to the Count; all my generals, who have no experience of warfare, behaved like so many hares; I believe that two or three have fled as far as Bologna. Since a great and deplorable event has put me in power, I have signed no decree which has been so agreeable to me as the one which appoints you my mother's Mistress of the Robes. My mother and I well recall that one day you admired the fine view to be had from the *palazzetto* of San Giovanni, which once belonged to Petrarch, or so it is said; my mother has desired to present you with this little estate; and I, uncertain what to give you, and not daring to offer all that belongs to you—I have made you Duchess in my country; I do not know if you are so learned as to know that Sanseverina is a Roman title. I have just awarded the Grand Cordon of my Order to our worthy Archbishop, who has shown a resolve rare in men of seventy. You will not disapprove my having recalled all the ladies who were banished. I am told that I must no longer sign my name without having written the words *your affectionate:* I am vexed that I must lavish assurances which are not quite true except when I write you.

Your affectionate
Ranuccio-Ernesto

Who would not have said, judging from this language, that the Duchess was to enjoy the highest favor? Yet she found something quite odd in other letters from the Count, which she received two hours later.

Without offering any further explanation, he advised her to postpone her return to Parma for several days, and to write to the Princess that she was quite unwell. Nonetheless, the Duchess and Fabrizio left for Parma immediately after dinner. The Duchess's purpose, which she still did not acknowledge, was to hasten the Marchese Crescenzi's marriage; Fabrizio, for his part, made the journey in transports of wild joy, which seemed quite absurd to his aunt. He had hopes of seeing Clélia again soon; and was counting on carrying her off, even against her will, if that were to be the only means of breaking off this marriage.

The journey of the Duchess and her nephew was very gay. At the posting station before Parma, Fabrizio stopped a moment in order to change into his ecclesiastical habit; ordinarily he was dressed in mourning. When he came into the Duchess's room, she said to him: "I find something inexplicable and rather sinister in the Count's letters. If you want my advice, you'll spend a few hours here. I'll send you a courier once I've spoken to that great Minister."

It was with great reluctance that Fabrizio followed this reasonable advice. Transports of joy worthy of a boy of fifteen marked the reception the Count gave to the Duchess, whom he addressed as his wife. It was some time before he was willing to talk politics, and when at last he did, they discovered the sad reason for this:

"You were quite right to keep Fabrizio from arriving officially; we are in the grip of reaction here. Can you guess the colleague the Prince has bequeathed me as Minister of Justice? It's Rassi, my dear, Rassi, whom I've treated as the ruffian that he is, on the day of our grand adventure. By the way, I must inform you that everything that has taken place here has been suppressed. If you read our gazette, you will see that a clerk of the Fortress, one Barbone, has died from a fall from a carriage. As for the sixty-some rascals I had shot, when they attacked the Prince's statue in the gardens, they are enjoying the best of health, but happen to be traveling abroad. Count Zurla, Minister of the Interior, has himself gone to the residence of each of these unfortunate heroes, and has bestowed fifteen sequins to their families or to their friends, with orders to say that the deceased is traveling, and threatens a term in prison if any mention is made that the man was shot. A man in my own Ministry of Foreign Affairs has been sent on a mission to the journalists of Milan and Turin so that no mention will be made of the *unfortunate event*, which is the consecrated phrase; this fellow will push on to Paris and London, in order to place a denial in every newspaper, semi-officially, of anything that might be said of our troubles. Another agent has headed for Bologna and Florence. I merely shrugged my shoulders.

"But the amusing thing, at my age, is that I have experienced a moment of enthusiasm in speaking to the soldiers of the Guard and in ripping the epaulettes from that booby General P——. At that moment I would have given my life, without a qualm, for the Prince; I now confess that it would have been a very stupid way of ending it. Today, the Prince, fine young man that he is, would give a hundred scudi for me to die of some disease; he does not yet dare ask me to resign, but we speak to each other as seldom as possible, and I am sending a quantity of little reports in writing, as I did with the late Prince, after Fabrizio's imprisonment. Apropos, I have not yet torn up the sentence signed against him, for the good reason that our scoundrel Rassi has not yet given it back to me. So you did the right thing to keep Fabrizio from arriving here officially. The sentence is still in effect; though I don't believe that Rassi would dare to have your nephew arrested now, it is still possible that he will do so in a fortnight. If Fabrizio insists on returning to the city, let him come and stay with me."

"But what is the reason for all this?" exclaimed the Duchess in amazement.

"The Prince has been convinced that I am giving myself the airs of a dictator and a savior of the fatherland, and that I want to lead him about like a child; furthermore, in alluding to him, I am reported to have pronounced the fatal word: this *child*. Which may be quite true, I was overexcited that day: for instance, I saw him as a great man because he wasn't too frightened at the first gunshots he had ever heard in his life. He's not entirely without brains, he certainly has a better style than his father: in short, I can't say it too often, his heart is sound; but this sound young heart hardens when someone tells him of a nasty trick and he imagines that one must have a very dark soul himself to realize such things: consider the education he has been given . . . !"

"Your Excellency should have realized that one day he would be master here, and put an intelligent man at his side."

"First of all, we have the example of the Abbé de Condillac, who when summoned by the Marchese di Felino, my predecessor, made his pupil nothing better than a King of Simpletons. He walked in the processions and, in 1796, he failed to come to terms with General Bonaparte, who had tripled the area of his States. In the second place, I have never believed I would remain Minister for ten years in succession. Now that I am entirely without illusions, and this for the last month, I want to amass a million, before leaving to its own devices this bedlam I have rescued. Without me, Parma would have been a republic for the last two months, with the poet Ferrante Palla as its dictator."

At this the Duchess blushed. The Count knew nothing of what had happened.

"We're going to revert to the typical eighteenth-century Monarchy:

the confessor and the mistress. At heart, the Prince cares for nothing but mineralogy and perhaps for you, Madame. Since he has been in power, his valet, whose brother I happened to have promoted to captain nine months ago—this valet, I repeat, has managed to put it into the Prince's head that he should be happier than other men because his profile appears on the coinage. This fine idea has been followed by a certain amount of boredom.

"Now he requires an aide-de-camp to conjure away his boredom. Well, even if he were to offer me that famous million we require to live decently in Naples or Paris, I would not be his remedy for boredom and spend four or five hours every day with His Highness. Moreover, since I have more brains than he, at the end of a month he would take me for a monster.

"The late Prince was a wicked and envious man, but he had fought in battle and commanded an army corps, which gave him a certain bearing; he was regarded as having the substance of a Prince, and I could be his Minister, for better or worse. With this decent fellow of a son, truthful and truly kind-hearted, I am compelled to be an intriguer. Here I am the rival of the most insignificant little woman in the Palace, and indeed a very inferior rival, for I should despise a hundred necessary details. For instance, three days ago, one of those women who puts clean towels in the rooms every morning took it into her head to make the Prince lose the key to one of his English desks. Whereupon His Highness refused to concern himself with all the business dealt with by the papers that happened to be in that desk; now, for twenty francs you can have the boards removed from the bottom of the desk, or else use skeleton keys; but Ranuccio-Ernesto V told me that would be to inculcate bad habits in our Court locksmith.

"Hitherto it has been quite impossible for him to retain the same opinion for three days running. Had he been born Signor Marchese So-and-so, with a certain fortune, this young Prince would have been one of the most estimable men of his court, a sort of Louis XVI; but now, with all his pious naïveté, how can he resist the various cunning traps that surround him? And the salon of your enemy the Raversi is more powerful than ever; the discovery has been made there that I— I who gave orders to fire on the populace and who was resolved to kill three thousand men if necessary rather than to let the statue of the Prince who had been my master be desecrated—I am a raging Liberal, that I wanted him to sign a Constitution, and a thousand such absurdities. With such notions of a Republic, the madmen would keep us from enjoying the best of all possible Monarchies.... In short, Signora, you are the only member of the present Liberal party of which my enemies account me the leader, on whose account the Prince has not expressed himself in offensive terms; the Archbishop, still an entirely honest man, having spoken in reasonable terms of what I have done *on that unhappy day,* is in deep disgrace.

"The day after the day which was not yet called *unhappy,* when it was still true that the rebellion existed, the Prince remarked to the Archbishop that, in order to spare you assuming an inferior title in marrying me, he would make me a Duke. Today I believe that it is Rassi, ennobled by me when he was selling me the secrets of the late Prince, who is to be made a Count. In the face of such a promotion, I should cut a poor figure."

"And the poor Prince a worse one."

"No doubt: but ultimately he is the *master* here, a circumstance which in less than fifteen days causes *absurdity* to vanish. And so, dear Duchess, let us proceed as in the game of backgammon: *let us withdraw.*"

"But we shall be anything but rich."

"As it happens, neither of us has any great need of luxury. If you give me, in Naples, a seat in a box at the San Carlo and a horse, I am more than satisfied; it will never be wealth which will afford the two of us our due, but rather the pleasure which the intelligent souls of wherever we may be will take in coming to you for a cup of tea."

"But still," the Duchess continued, "what would have happened, that *unhappy day,* if you had kept aloof as I hope you will do in the future?"

"The troops would have fraternized with the people, there would have been three days of bloodshed and incendiarism (for it will take a hundred years in this country for a Republic to be anything but an absurdity), then two weeks of pillage, until two or three regiments supplied from abroad came to put a stop to it. Ferrante Palla was in the midst of the populace, full of courage and high words, as usual; he probably had a dozen friends who were in collusion with him, out of which Rassi will make a splendid conspiracy. What's certain is that, while wearing an incredibly dilapidated coat, he was distributing gold by the handfuls."

Amazed by all this news, the Duchess lost no time in going to thank the Princess.

The moment she appeared, the Lady of the Bedchamber handed her the little golden key to be worn at her belt, which is the mark of supreme authority in the Princess's part of the Palace. Clara-Paolina hastened to dismiss the company and, once alone with her friend, persisted for several moments in expressing herself somewhat obscurely. The Duchess was uncertain what was being said, and answered with the greatest reserve. Finally the Princess burst into tears and, flinging herself into the Duchess's arms, exclaimed: "My days of misery are beginning all over again: my son will treat me worse than his father ever did!"

"I shall see to it that such a thing never happens," retorted the Duchess, "but first of all," she continued, "I beg Your Most Serene Highness to accept here and now the homage of all my gratitude and of my profound respect."

"What can you mean?" exclaimed the Princess, filled with anxiety and fearing a resignation was in order.

"What I mean is that whenever Your Serene Highness allows me to turn to the right the nodding chin of that mandarin on her mantelpiece, she will also permit me to call things by their proper names."

"Is that all, my dear Duchess?" cried Clara-Paolina, rushing to put the mandarin in the proper position. "Speak freely then, Signora Mistress of the Robes," she said in a charming tone of voice.

"Your Serene Highness," continued the Duchess, "has understood the situation perfectly; the two of us are in the greatest danger; the sentence against Fabrizio is not revoked; consequently, the day someone wishes to get rid of me and to offer an offense to you, he will be thrown in prison again. Our position is as bad as ever. As for myself personally, I am marrying the Count, and we shall settle either in Naples or in Paris. The last trait of ingratitude of which the Count is presently the victim has entirely disgusted him with public affairs, and were it not for the interest of Your Most Serene Highness, I should advise him to remain in this bedlam only so long as the Prince bestowed upon him an enormous sum of money. I shall ask Your Highness's permission to explain to her that the Count, who had one hundred and thirty thousand francs to his name when he took up the Ministry of Foreign Affairs, now possesses an income of scarcely twenty thousand lire. In vain have I urged him to give some thought to his fortune. During my absence, he has picked a quarrel with the Prince's tax-collectors, who were scoundrels; the Count has replaced them by other scoundrels who have given him eight hundred thousand francs."

"What!" exclaimed the Duchess in amazement. "Good Heavens, how vexed I am to hear such a thing!"

"Madame," the Duchess replied coolly, "am I to turn the mandarin back to the left?"

"Good Heavens, no!" cried the Princess. "But I am vexed that a man of the Count's character should have thought of such methods of enriching himself."

"Without that theft, he would be despised by all honorable men."

"Good Heavens! Is it possible?"

"Your Serene Highness," the Duchess continued, "except for my friend the Marchese Crescenzi, who has an income of three or four hundred thousand lire, everyone here steals; and who would not steal in a country where the recognition of the greatest services lasts no more than a month? It means that nothing is real and that nothing survives disgrace except money. May I permit myself, Your Highness, the liberty of some terrible truths?"

"I myself permit you," said the Princess with a deep sigh, "painful to me as they are."

"Well then, Your Highness, the Prince your son, an entirely honorable man, is capable of making you much happier than his father did; the late Prince had a character more or less like the common run of humanity. Our present Sovereign is not certain of desiring the same thing three days in a row; consequently, in order to be sure of him, one must live with him continually, allowing him to speak to no one. Since this truth is not difficult to perceive, the new *ultra* party, led by those two splendid figures Rassi and the Marchesa Raversi, will seek to supply the Prince with a mistress. This mistress will have permission to make her fortune and to distribute certain minor positions, but she will have to answer to the party for the constancy of her master's will.

"For my part, if I am to be properly established at Your Highness's Court, I require that Rassi be disgraced and banished; furthermore I wish Fabrizio to be judged by the most honest judges that can be found: if these gentlemen acknowledge, as I hope, that he is innocent, it will be only natural to grant His Grace the Archbishop that Fabrizio will be his Coadjutor with eventual succession. If I fail in this, the Count and I shall retire; hence in parting I leave Your Most Serene Highness with this piece of advice: she must never pardon Rassi, nor must she ever leave her son's realm. At close hand, this good son will never do her serious harm."

"I have followed your arguments with the close attention they demand," the Princess answered with a smile; "am I to assume the duty, as well, of furnishing my son with a mistress?"

"No indeed, Madame, but make certain first of all that your salon is the only one where he enjoys himself."

The conversation drew to a close in this fashion, the scales having fallen from the eyes of the innocent and witty Princess.

One of the Duchess's couriers went to tell Fabrizio that he could enter the city, though in concealment. He was barely noticed: he spent his entire time disguised as a peasant living in the wooden shed of a chestnut-seller, opposite the gates of the Fortress, under the trees of the promenade.

CHAPTER TWENTY-FOUR

The Duchess organized some delightful parties at the Palace, which had never seen so much gaiety; never had she been more charming than she was that winter, yet she was living amidst the greatest dangers; but also, during this critical period, she never stopped to think twice with any noticeable regret about the strange transformation in Fabrizio.

The young Prince would appear quite early at the lively at-homes given by his mother, who kept telling him: "Now go and *govern;* I imagine there are dozens of reports on your desk awaiting a yes or a no, and I don't want all Europe blaming me for making you a Wastrel King so I can rule in your place."

Such counsels had the disadvantage of invariably being offered at the most inopportune moments, that is, when His Highness, having overcome his timidity, was taking part in some charade, the performance of which greatly entertained him. Twice a week there were outings in the country to which, on the pretext of enabling the new Sovereign to win his people's affection, the Princess invited the prettiest women of the middle classes. The Duchess, who was the heart and soul of this merry court circle, hoped that these lovely bourgeois ladies, all of whom regarded the good fortunes of the parvenu Rassi with mortal envy, would inform the Prince of some of this Minister's countless rascalities. For, among other childish notions, the Prince prided himself on a *moral* ministry.

Rassi was too astute not to feel how dangerous to him were these brilliant parties of the Princess's Court, concocted as they were by his enemy. He had not been able to bring himself to hand over to Count Mosca the quite legal sentence passed on Fabrizio; hence it was inevitable that either Rassi or the Duchess must vanish from the Court.

The day of that uprising among the people, the very existence of which it was now in good taste to deny, money had been distributed to the populace at large. Rassi started from this point: even more shabbily dressed than usual, he would enter the city's poorest houses and spend hours in serious conversation with their wretched inhabitants. He was well rewarded for his pains: after a fortnight of such a life he was convinced that Ferrante Palla had been the secret leader of the insurrection, and moreover that this creature, poor all his life as a great poet would be, had sent nine or ten diamonds to be sold at Genoa.

Among others were mentioned five valuable stones which were actually worth over forty thousand francs and which, *ten days before the Prince's death,* had been given up for thirty-five thousand francs because, so the seller said, *the money was needed.*

How to describe the Minister of Justice's raptures at making this discovery? He realized that he was being made a daily laughingstock at the Princess Dowager's court, and more than once the Prince, discussing business with him, had laughed in his face with all the naïveté of youth. It must be confessed that Rassi's manners were singularly common: for instance, as soon as a discussion interested him, he would cross his legs and clasp one of his shoes; if his interest increased, he would spread his red cotton handkerchief over his knee, and so on. The Prince had laughed heartily at the joke made by one of the prettiest middle-class women at court who, quite aware of the shapeliness of her own leg, had proceeded to imitate the Minister of Justice's elegant gesture.

Rassi requested an extraordinary audience, and said to the Prince: "Would Your Highness be willing to give a hundred thousand francs to discover for sure how his august father met his death? With such a sum, justice would be in a position to apprehend the guilty, if such there be."

The Prince's reply left no room for doubt.

Soon afterward, Cecchina informed the Duchess that she had been offered a huge sum to allow her mistress's diamonds to be examined by a jeweler; she had indignantly refused. The Duchess scolded her for refusing, and, a week later, Cecchina had the diamonds to show. On the day chosen for this exhibition of the jewels, Count Mosca posted two trustworthy men in every jewelry-shop in Parma, and by midnight he was able to inform the Duchess that the inquisitive jeweler was none other than Rassi's own brother. The Duchess, who was extremely gay that evening (a *commedia dell'arte* was being performed at the Palace, in which each character invents the dialogue as the piece proceeds, the plot being posted in the wings)—the Duchess, who was to play a role, had as her lover in the play Count Baldi, a former lover of the Marchesa Raversi, who was also present. The Prince, the shyest man in his realm but a fine-looking young fellow with the tenderest heart, was studying Count Baldi's part, which he wanted to act at the next performance.

"There's not much time," the Duchess said to the Count; "I go on in the first scene of the second act; let's go into the guard-room."

There, among twenty bodyguards, all wide awake and quite attentive to the words exchanged by the Prime Minister and the Mistress of the Robes, the Duchess said to her friend with a laugh:

"You always scold me when I tell you unnecessary secrets. It was on my account that Ernesto V was called to the throne; I had to avenge Fabrizio, whom I loved then much more than I do today, though always quite innocently. I know of course that you find it hard to believe in such innocence, but what does that matter, since you love me in spite of my crimes. Well! Here's a real crime: I've given all my diamonds to an extremely interesting sort of lunatic named Ferrante Palla, I even kissed him if he would cause the death of the man who sought to have Fabrizio poisoned. Where is the harm in that?"

"Ah, so that's where Ferrante got the money for his uprising!" exclaimed the Count, somewhat amazed. "And you're telling me all this here in the guard-room."

"I have no time, and here is Rassi on the heels of the crime. Of course the word *uprising* never crossed my lips, I abhor Jacobins. Consider the matter, and tell me your thoughts after the play."

"I'll tell you right now that you must make the Prince fall in love with you.... But quite honorably, of course!"

The Duchess was given her cue, and she hurried away.

Some days later, the Duchess received in the post a long, absurd letter, signed by one of her former ladies-in-waiting; this woman requested employment at Court, but the Duchess had recognized at first glance that the letter was in neither her handwriting nor her style. As she unfolded the sheet to read the second side, the Duchess found at her feet a tiny miracle-working image of the Madonna, folded up in a printed page of an old book. After glancing at the image, the Duchess read a few lines of the printed page. Her eyes shone when she found these words there:

> The tribune has taken one hundred francs a month, no more; with the rest it was sought to reawaken the sacred fire in souls which were chilled by egoism. The fox is on my heels, that is why I have not sought to see the adored being one last time. I told myself, she has no love for the Republic, she who is my superior in mind as much as in grace and beauty. Moreover, how to create a Republic without republican citizens? Could I be deceiving myself? In six months, I shall traverse all the towns of America, bearing a microscope and on foot; I shall see if I must still love the one rival you have in my heart. If you receive this letter, Signora Baroness, and no profane eye has read it before you do, have them break one of the young ash-trees planted twenty paces from the place where I first dared address you. Then I shall bury, under the great box-tree in the garden which you noticed one time in my happier days, a casket containing some of those things which cause slander to men of my way of thinking. Of course, I should never have written had the fox not been on my heels, and risked endangering this heavenly being; look under the box-tree in a fortnight.

"Since he has a printing-press at his command," the Duchess said to herself, "we'll soon be getting a sonnet-sequence; Lord knows what name he'll give me!"

The Duchess's coquetry led her to make a trial of her strength; for a week she was indisposed, and the Court had no more amusing parties. The Princess, quite scandalized by everything which her fear of her son had compelled her to do since the first moments of her widowhood, went to spend this week in a convent attached to the church where the late Prince was buried. This interruption of the parties left the Prince with an enormous burden of leisure to dispose of, and charged a notable failure to the account of the Minister of Justice. Ernesto V realized all the tedium which would threaten him if the Duchess were to leave the Court, or merely ceased to shed gaiety within it. The parties began again, and the Prince showed himself increasingly interested in the *commedia dell'arte*. He planned to take a part, but dared not confess this ambition. One day, blushing deeply, he said to the Duchess: "Why shouldn't I act too?"

"We are all at Your Highness's orders here. If Your Highness deigns to command me, I shall have the plot of a comedy arranged, so that all Your Highness's brilliant scenes will be opposite me, and since during the first days everyone is somewhat shaky, if Your Highness will pay me close attention, I shall provide him with all the appropriate lines."

Everything was arranged, and with infinite skill. The shy Prince was ashamed of being shy; the pains the Duchess took not to offend this innate timidity made a profound impression on the young Sovereign.

The day of his debut, the performance began half an hour earlier than usual, and there were present in the salon, at the moment they took the stage, only eight or ten elderly ladies. Such an audience had little or no effect upon the Prince, and moreover, brought up in Munich on true monarchical principles, they always applauded. Invoking her authority as Mistress of the Robes, the Duchess locked the door through which the commonplace courtiers had access to the play. The Prince, who had a certain *literary* turn of mind and a handsome countenance, acquitted himself nicely in his first scenes; he repeated quite intelligently the phrases which he read in the Duchess's eyes, or which she whispered to him. In a moment when the scant audience was applauding with all their might, the Duchess made a sign, the door of honor was opened, and the theater was filled in a moment by all the prettiest women of the court, who, judging the Prince both handsome and expressive, began applauding; the Prince blushed with pleasure. He was playing the part of the Duchess's lover. Far from having to suggest words to him, soon she was compelled to shorten the scenes; he spoke of love with an enthusiasm which frequently embarrassed the actress; his speeches lasted five minutes. The Duchess was no longer the dazzling beauty she had been the year before; Fabrizio's imprisonment and, even more, the sojourn on Lake Maggiore with a Fabrizio turned morose and silent had given another ten years to the lovely Gina. Her features had become marked, and showed more intelligence and less youth. They now revealed a girlish animation only rarely; but on the stage, with makeup and all the assistance which art affords an actress, she was still the loveliest woman at court. The impassioned speeches the Prince poured out to her alerted the courtiers, and that evening people remarked to each other over and over: "There's *la Balbi* of this new reign."

The Count took silent umbrage. The play over, the Duchess said to the Prince before the whole court: "Your Highness acts too well; people will be saying that you are in love with a woman of thirty-eight, which will spoil my arrangement with the Count. So I shall act no more with Your Highness, unless the Prince swears he will speak to me only as he would to a woman of a certain age—to Marchesa Raversi, for instance."

The same play was performed three times; the Prince was wild with pleasure; but one evening, he seemed extremely anxious. "Either I am greatly mistaken," said the Mistress of the Robes to her Princess, "or our Rassi is trying to play some trick on us; I should advise Your Highness to choose a play for tomorrow; the Prince will act badly, and in his despair, he will say something to you . . ."

Indeed, the Prince acted very badly; he was scarcely audible, and couldn't manage to end his sentences. At the end of the first act, he was almost in tears; the Duchess was standing beside him, but cold and motionless. The Prince, happening to be alone with her for a moment in the green room, went to close the door.

"Under no circumstances," he said, "can I get through the second and third acts; I have no desire whatever to be applauded out of mere politeness; the way they were clapping for me tonight cut me to the quick. Give me some advice—what must be done?"

"I shall go out on stage, curtsy to Her Highness, then to the audience, like a real impresario, and announce that the actor performing the role of Lelio being suddenly indisposed, the performance will conclude by some pieces of music. Count Rusca and the Ghisolfi girl will be delighted to show off their squeaky little voices to such a brilliant audience."

The Prince took the Duchess's hand and kissed it rapturously. "If only you were a man," he exclaimed, "you would give me good advice: Rassi has just laid on my desk a hundred and eighty-two depositions against my father's alleged murderers. As well as these depositions, there is a formal accusation of over two hundred pages; I must read all this, and moreover I have promised not to mention a word about it to the Count. That leads straight to executions; already he wants me to have extradited from France, near Antibes, that great poet Ferrante Palla, whom I admire so greatly. He's living there under the name of Poncet."

"The day you have a Liberal hanged, Rassi will be bound to the Ministry by chains of iron, which he desires above all things; but Your Highness will no longer be able to announce a promenade two hours in advance. I shall mention to neither the Princess nor the Count the cry of pain which has just escaped you; but since I am under oath to keep no secrets from the Princess, I should be glad if Your Highness were to say to his mother the very things which have just been uttered to me."

Such a notion somewhat mollified the distress of the *failed actor* which had overcome the Sovereign.

"Very well, inform my mother; I shall be waiting in her study." The Prince left the wings, crossed a salon adjoining the theater, and abruptly dismissed the Chamberlain and his aide-de-camp, who were following him; quite as hurriedly, the Princess left the performance; in the Princess's study, the Mistress of the Robes curtsied deeply to both mother and son and left them alone. One may imagine the agitation of the Court: these are the things which make Court life so entertaining.

After an hour, the Prince himself appeared at the study door and summoned the Duchess; the Princess was in tears; her son's countenance had quite altered.

"What weak creatures these are," the Mistress of the Robes marveled to herself, "always in a temper and looking for some excuse to be angry with someone." At first mother and son vied for the opportunity to describe matters to the Duchess, who took great pains to keep her responses quite neutral. For two endless hours, the three actors in this tedious scene played out the roles we have just suggested. It was the Prince himself who went to fetch the two enormous portfolios Rassi had left on his desk; as he emerged from his mother's study, he found the whole Court waiting for him.

"Go away, leave me in peace!" he exclaimed, in a tone that was quite unprecedented. The Prince didn't want to be seen carrying the two portfolios—a Prince carries nothing. The courtiers vanished in the twinkling of an eye. As he walked on, the Prince encountered only the footmen who were snuffing the candles; he dismissed them angrily, as well as poor Fontana, the aide-de-camp on duty, who had been tactless enough to remain, out of zeal.

"Everyone is doing his best to vex me this evening!" he exclaimed crossly to the Duchess as he returned to the study. The Prince considered her highly intelligent and was annoyed by her evident insistence upon not offering an opinion. For her part, the Duchess was determined to say nothing until her advice was *expressly* requested. A good half-hour passed before the Prince, who had the sense of his own dignity, brought himself to say: "But Signora, you say nothing!"

"I am here to serve the Princess, and to forget instantly whatever is said in my presence."

"Well then, Signora," the Prince said, blushing deeply, "I order you to give me your advice."

"Crimes are punished so that they will not be repeated. Was the late Prince poisoned? This seems highly unlikely. Was he poisoned by the Jacobins? That is what Rassi would like to prove, for then he becomes a permanently necessary instrument to Your Highness. In that case, Your Highness, who is setting out on his reign, may indulge himself in many evenings like this one. The majority of your subjects say, and quite veraciously, that Your Highness has a kind nature; so long as Your Highness will not have some Liberal hanged, he will enjoy such a reputation, and certainly no one will dream of planning poison for you."

"Your conclusion is obvious!" the Princess exclaimed. "You don't want my husband's assassins punished!"

"It is all too clear, Signora, that I am bound to them by the tenderest affection."

From the Prince's expression the Duchess realized that he believed her to be in complete agreement with his mother on some line of conduct. There was a swift series of sharp exchanges between the two women, after which the Duchess protested that she would not speak another word, and she kept her promise; but the Prince, after a long argument with his mother, once again commanded the Duchess to give her opinion.

"That is what I swear to both Your Highnesses I shall not do!"

"This is mere childishness!" the Prince exclaimed.

"I beg you to speak, my dear Duchess," said the Princess with great dignity.

"That is what I implore you to excuse me from doing, Signora; but Your Highness," the Duchess added, turning to the Prince, "reads French perfectly; in order to calm our agitated minds, why not read us *all* one of La Fontaine's fables?"

The Princess found this "all" rather insolent, but she looked both amazed and amused as the Mistress of the Robes, who had gone quite coolly to the bookshelves, returned with a volume of La Fontaine's *Fables;* she turned the pages for a few moments, then remarked to the Prince as she handed the volume to him: "I beg Your Highness to read the *whole* of this fable."

THE GARDENER AND HIS LORD

A man in love with gardening
—a sort of bourgeois peasant—
cultivated in his village
a tidy garden and the field nearby.
Thorny bushes hedged it in,

and among the vegetables grew
flowers enough for Margot's fête,
thyme and all the other herbs. . . .
And when this paradise of his
  happened to be invaded
  by a greedy nibbling hare,
the gardener complained to his lord:
"This wretched beast devours his fill
  day and night, and laughs at traps—
sticks and stones are of no use:
he is, I wager, possessed." "Possessed?"
the lord replied, "the Devil himself
would be halted by my hounds:
I promise you'll be rid of hares!"
"When, Sir?" "Tomorrow for sure!"
Next day, as promised, came the lord
with all his men: "Now as for lunch—
how tender are your pullets?" Then
the hunters followed, what a din
  their horns and trumpets made!
  The gardener was deafened, and
  you should have seen the garden!
Farewell beds and farewell rows—
no more turnips, no more leeks,
nothing left to make the soup!
  Quoth the gardener: "This
  they call the sport of kings!"
But no one paid him any mind,
  and men and dogs in an hour
  wrought far worse damages
  to the wretched garden
than all the region's hares could do
by nibbling for a century. . . .

Young Princes, settle your disputes
among yourselves, and don't commit
the folly of resorting to kings:
thus will your gardens thrive!

This reading was followed by a long silence. The Prince walked up and down the study, after having gone to put the book back on the shelves himself.

"And now, Duchess," the Princess said, "will you deign to speak to us?"

"Certainly not, Your Highness. So long as the Prince has not appointed me his Minister, I should in speaking run the risk of losing my place as Mistress of the Robes."

Another silence, for a quarter of an hour. At last the Princess thought of the part once played by Marie de Médicis, the mother of Louis XIII: for some days past, the Mistress of the Robes had had the Court Reader read aloud Monsieur Bazin's excellent *History of Louis XIII*. Though quite annoyed, the Princess realized that the Duchess might well leave the country, and then Rassi, of whom she was dreadfully afraid, might well imitate Richelieu and cause her own son to send her into exile. At that moment, the Princess would have given anything in the world to humiliate her Mistress of the Robes, but she could not do so: she stood up and came, with a rather exaggerated smile, to take the Duchess's hand and say: "My dear Duchess, prove your affection for me by speaking now."

"Very well, but only these words: toss into this very fireplace all the papers collected by that viper Rassi, and never reveal to him that they have been burned." In a whisper, and quite familiarly, she added in the Princess's ear: "Rassi may be a Richelieu!"

"What the Devil! Those papers are costing me over eighty thousand francs!" exclaimed the irritated Prince.

"My dear Prince," the Duchess replied energetically, "you see what it costs you to employ such rascals of low birth. Please God you may lose a million and never lend credence to the low scoundrels who kept your father from sleeping during the last six years of his reign."

The words *low birth* greatly pleased the Princess, who felt that the Count and his mistress had too exclusive an esteem for intelligence, always a little too closely related to Jacobinism.

During the brief moment of profound silence, filled by the Princess's reflections, the Palace clock chimed three o'clock. The Princess stood up, curtsied deeply to her son, and said: "My health does not permit me to extend this discussion any longer. No minister of *low birth*—ever! You will never free me of the notion that your Rassi has stolen half the money he has made you spend on spying!" The Princess took two candles out of their sconces and put them in the fireplace, so that they did not go out; then, coming close to her son, she added: "La Fontaine's fable wins out, in my mind, over the just desire to avenge a husband. Does Your Highness permit me to burn these *writings?*"

The Prince remained motionless.

"He really has a stupid face," the Duchess said to herself; "the Count is right: the late Prince would not have made us stay up till three in the morning before making up his mind."

The Princess, still standing, added: "That little lawyer would be quite proud, were he to know that his miserable papers, stuffed with lies and arranged for his own advancement, have occupied the two greatest personages in the Kingdom all night long!"

The Prince hurled himself like a madman on one of the portfolios and emptied its entire contents into the fireplace. The mass of papers was about to extinguish the two candles; the room filled with smoke. The Princess saw in her son's eyes that he was tempted to take up a carafe and save these papers, which had cost him eighty thousand francs.

"Then open the window!" she shrieked at the Duchess angrily. The Duchess hastened to obey; immediately all the papers caught fire at once; there was a great roar in the fireplace, and soon it was apparent that the chimney was on fire.

The Prince had a petty nature with regard to all money matters; he saw his Palace going up in flames, and all the treasures it contained destroyed; he ran to the window and summoned the guard in a voice quite different from his usual one. At the sound of the Prince's voice, the soldiers rushed into the building in great confusion, and he returned to the fireplace, which was drawing air from the open window with a really terrifying noise. He lost patience, swore, walked back and forth in the study a few times like a man beside himself, and finally ran out of the room.

The Princess and her Mistress of the Robes remained standing, facing each other, preserving a profound silence.

"Is there going to be another fit of rage?" the Duchess asked herself. "My word, I've won my case." And she was preparing to be quite impertinent in her replies when a sudden thought struck her; she saw the second portfolio intact. "No, my case is only half won!" And she said quite coolly to the Princess: "Does Her Highness order me to burn the rest of these papers?"

"And where will you burn them?" the Princess asked crossly.

"In the salon fireplace; if they are tossed in one by one, there will be no danger."

The Duchess put the portfolio crammed with papers under her arm, took up a candle, and walked into the adjoining salon. She had time to notice that this portfolio was the one filled with depositions, put five or six bundles of paper in her shawl, and carefully burned the rest, then vanished without taking leave of the Princess. "There's a fine piece of impertinence," she said to herself laughing; "but with all that woman's affectations of inconsolable widowhood, she nearly caused me to lose my head on the scaffold."

Hearing the sound of the Duchess's carriage, the Princess was filled with rage against her Mistress of the Robes.

Despite the lateness of the hour, the Duchess had the Count summoned; he was observing the fire at the Palace, but soon appeared with the news that it was all over. "The little Prince actually showed a good deal of courage, and I offered him my warmest compliments."

"Give a quick look at these depositions, and then burn them at once."

The Count read and turned pale. "My word, they were getting quite close to the truth; this business is cleverly put together, they're right on Ferrante Palla's heels; and if he talks, we're in a tight spot."

"But he won't talk!" the Duchess exclaimed. "He is a man of honor, that Ferrante. Burn them, burn them!"

"Not yet. Allow me to copy out the names of twelve or fifteen dangerous witnesses, whom I shall take the liberty of removing, if our Rassi ever tries to begin again."

"May I remind Your Excellency that the Prince has given his word to say nothing to his Minister of Justice concerning our nocturnal escapade."

"Out of cowardice and fear of a scene, he will most likely keep it."

"Now, my friend, this has been a night which brings our wedding a good deal closer; I would not have chosen to bring you a criminal file as a dowry, and especially for a sin which my interests in another man have made me commit."

The Count was a man in love; he took the Duchess's hand and uttered a great cry; there were tears in his eyes.

"Before leaving, give me some advice as to how I must behave with the Princess; I am dying of fatigue, I acted on the stage for an hour, and for five in that woman's study."

"You have taken sufficient revenge for the Princess's nasty remarks, which were no more than weakness, by the impertinence of your departure just now. Tomorrow you will resume with her the tone you employed this morning; Rassi is not yet in prison or in exile, we have not yet torn up Fabrizio's sentence. You were asking the Princess to reach a decision, which always makes Princes and even Prime Ministers cross; after all, you are her Mistress of the Robes, which is to say, her servant. By a reaction which is infallible in weak people, in three days Rassi will be in higher favor than ever; he'll try to have someone hanged: so long as he hasn't compromised the Prince, he's sure of nothing. . . . There was a man hurt in the fire tonight, a tailor who showed, upon my word, extraordinary bravery. Tomorrow I shall oblige the Prince to take my arm and accompany me on a visit to that tailor; I'll be armed to the teeth and I'll keep my eyes open; moreover this young Prince is not yet hated. But I want to get him used to walking in the streets—it's a trick I'm playing on Rassi, who will certainly succeed me and who will no longer be able to indulge in such rashness. On our way back from the tailor, I shall have the Prince pass in front of his father's statue; he will notice the places where stones have broken the Roman toga that imbecile sculptor has wrapped around him; and finally the Prince will be quite a fool indeed if he doesn't make this reflection on his own: 'That's what one gains by hanging Jacobins.' To which I shall reply: 'You must hang ten thousand or none: Saint Bartholomew's Massacre destroyed the Protestants in France.' . . . Tomorrow, dear friend, before my promenade with the Prince, have yourself announced at his Palace and tell him: 'Last night I served you as a Minister and gave you certain advice, and on your orders I have incurred the Princess's displeasure; you must pay me for that.' He will be expecting a request for money, and will frown; you will leave him plunged in this misery as long as you can, then you will say: 'I beg Your Highness to order Fabrizio to be judged *in contraddittorio*'—which means he himself will be present—'by the twelve most respected judges in your Realm.' And without wasting any time, you will ask him to sign a little text written in your own lovely hand, and which I shall dictate to you; I shall include in it, of course, the clause to the effect that the former sentence is quashed. There can be only one objection to this; but, if you proceed swiftly enough, it will not occur to the Prince. He may say to you: 'Fabrizio must be made a prisoner in the Fortress.' To which you will reply: 'He will give himself up to the municipal prison.' (You know that I am master there, and your nephew will come to see you every evening.) If the Prince answers you: 'No, his escape has tainted the honor of my Fortress, and for form's sake, I must have him return to the room where he was,' you will answer in your turn: 'No, for there he will be at the mercy of my enemy Rassi.' And by one of those womanly phrases which you know how to insinuate so well, you will lead him to understand that in order to make Rassi yield, you might indeed tell him about tonight's *auto-da-fé*; if the Prince insists, you will inform him that you are going to spend a fortnight on your Sacca estate.... You will have Fabrizio summoned and will consult him about this procedure which may put him back in prison. Let us anticipate all possibilities: if, while your nephew is under lock and key, Rassi has me poisoned in a fit of impatience, Fabrizio may run certain dangers. But that is highly unlikely; you know that I have hired a French cook, the merriest of men and inclined to punning; now, punning is incompatible with murder. I've already told our friend Fabrizio that I've collected all the witnesses of his fine and courageous action; it was clearly Giletti who wanted to kill *him*. I haven't mentioned these witnesses to you because I wanted to surprise you, but that plan fell through; the Prince refused to sign. I told our Fabrizio that of course I would obtain a high ecclesiastical office for him; but I shall have great difficulties if his enemies can provide the papal court with an accusation of murder.... You realize, Signora, that if he is not tried and judged quite formally, the name Giletti will cause him trouble for the rest of his life. It would be a great piece of cowardice not to be tried and judged, when one is certain of one's innocence. Moreover, even if he were guilty, I would get him off. When I spoke to him, the hot-headed young man did not even let me finish; he took up the official almanac, and together we chose the twelve most learned and honorable judges; the list is drawn up, and we have erased six names, which we replaced by six learned attorneys, my personal enemies, and since we could discover only two such enemies, we have filled the list by four rascals devoted to Rassi."

This proposal of the Count's greatly alarmed the Duchess, and with good cause; at last she saw reason, and at the Minister's dictation, wrote the document naming the judges.

The Count did not leave her until six in the morning; she attempted to sleep, but in vain. At nine o'clock, she breakfasted with Fabrizio, whom she found burning with a desire to be tried; at ten o'clock she waited on the Princess, who was not to be seen; at eleven she saw the Prince, who was holding his levee, and who signed the document without the slightest objection. The Duchess sent the document to the Count, and retired to bed.

It would perhaps be amusing to describe Rassi's rage, when the Count compelled him to countersign, in the Prince's presence, the document the latter had signed earlier that day; but the pressure of events forbids . . .

The Count discussed the merit of each judge, and offered to change the names. But the reader is perhaps a trifle weary of these procedural details, no less than of these Court intrigues. From all such matters, the moral can be drawn that the man who approaches a Court compromises his happiness, if he is happy, and in any case risks making his future depend on the intrigues of some chambermaid.

On the other hand, in America, in the Republic, one must waste a whole day in paying serious court to the shopkeepers in the streets, and must become as stupid as they are; and over there, no opera.

The Duchess, at her evening levee, had a moment of intense anxiety: Fabrizio was not to be found; finally, around midnight, at the Court performance, she received a letter from him. Instead of committing himself to the municipal prison, where the Count was master, he had gone back to his old room in the Fortress, only too happy to be living a few feet away from Clélia.

This was an event of enormous importance: in such a place he was more exposed to poisoning than ever. This folly reduced the Duchess to despair; she forgave the cause of it, the passionate love for Clélia, because in a few days' time the girl would be marrying the rich Marchese Crescenzi. This mad action restored to Fabrizio all his old influence over the Duchess's heart.

"It is that cursed paper which I obliged the Prince to sign which will cause Fabrizio's death! How insane these men are with their notions of honor! As if there was any reason to consider honor under absolute governments in realms where a Rassi is Minister of Justice! We ought to have accepted there and then the pardon the Prince would have signed just as readily as he signed the order convening that extraordinary tribunal. After all, what does it matter if a man of Fabrizio's birth is more or less accused of having taken up a sword and killed an actor like that Giletti with his own hand!"

No sooner had she received Fabrizio's letter than the Duchess ran to the Count, whom she found pale as death.

"Good God! My dear Duchess, I have an unlucky touch with that boy, and you'll be angry with me all over again. I can prove to you that I summoned last night the jailer of the municipal prison; every day, your nephew could have come to take tea with you. The dreadful thing is that it is impossible for you and for me to tell the Prince that we fear poison, and poison administered by Rassi; such suspicion would seem to him the height of immorality. Yet if you insist upon it, I am ready to go to the Palace; but I am sure of the answer. I can tell you more; I offer you a means which I would not employ for myself: since I have held power in this realm, I have not put a single man to death, and you know that I am so sensitive in this regard that sometimes, at dusk, I still think of those two spies I had shot a little too lightheartedly in Spain. Well! Do you want me to get rid of Rassi for you? The danger he represents to Fabrizio is limitless; he has there a sure means of getting rid of *me*..."

The Duchess was greatly tempted by this proposal, but she did not accept it. "I cannot endure," she said to the Count, "under that beautiful Neapolitan sky of ours, that you should suffer from such dark thoughts when night comes on."

"But my dear friend, it seems to me that we have no choice except among dark thoughts. What will become of you, what would become of me indeed, if Fabrizio is carried off by some sickness?"

The discussion continued anew on this point, and the Duchess brought it to a close with this remark: "Rassi owes his life to the fact that I love you more than Fabrizio; no, I would not poison all the evenings of the old age we are going to spend together."

The Duchess hurried to the Fortress; General Fabio Conti was delighted to present her with the formal text of the military regulations: no one can enter a State prison without an order signed by the Prince.

"But Marchese Crescenzi and his musicians come to the Fortress every day . . ."

"That is because I have obtained an order for them from the Prince."

The poor Duchess was not aware of all her misfortunes. General Fabio Conti had considered himself personally dishonored by Fabrizio's escape: when he saw him arrive back at the Fortress, he ought not to have admitted him, for he had no orders to do so. "But," he said to himself, "it is Heaven which sends him to me to reconstruct my honor and save me from the ridicule which would spoil my military career. Here is an opportunity which must not be missed: no doubt he will be acquitted, and I have only a few days for my revenge."

Chapter Twenty-five

Our hero's arrival filled Clélia with despair: the poor girl, pious and sincere as she was, could not conceal from herself that she would never find happiness apart from Fabrizio; yet she had vowed to the Madonna, at the time of her father's near poisoning, that she would offer him the sacrifice of marrying the Marchese Crescenzi. She had vowed never to see Fabrizio again, and already she was prey to the cruelest remorse for the admission she had been led to make in the letter she had written to Fabrizio on the eve of his escape. How to describe what occurred in that melancholy heart, so sadly occupied with watching her birds fluttering to and fro and habitually and tenderly glancing up toward the window from which Fabrizio used to gaze at her, when she saw him there once again, greeting her with tender respect?

She imagined it to be a vision Heaven granted for her punishment; then the cruel reality dawned upon her reason. "They have recaptured him," she said to herself, "and he is lost!"

She recalled the remarks made in the Fortress following that escape; the humblest of the jailers regarded himself as mortally offended. Clélia looked at Fabrizio, and in spite of herself that gaze depicted the whole of the passion which filled her with despair.

"Do you suppose," she seemed to be saying to Fabrizio, "that I shall find happiness in that sumptuous Palace they are making ready for me? My father never tires of telling me that you are as poor as we are; but good God! how eagerly I should share that poverty! Yet alas! we must never see one another again."

Clélia lacked the strength to make use of their alphabets: as she gazed at Fabrizio she suddenly felt ill and sank into a chair next to the window. Her chin was resting on the sill and, since she had sought to glimpse him until the last moment of consciousness, her face was turned toward Fabrizio, who could see her clearly. When she opened her eyes again, after a few seconds, her first glance was for Fabrizio: she saw tears in his eyes, but these were the effect of extreme joy; he was discovering that absence had not made her forget him. The two poor young people remained some while as though enchanted by the sight of each other. Fabrizio even dared to sing, as though he were accompanying himself on the guitar, a few improvised verses, which said: "*It is to see you once more that I have returned to prison; I am to be tried and sentenced.*"

These words appeared to waken all of Clélia's virtue: she swiftly stood up, hid her eyes, and by sudden gestures sought to convey to him that she was never to look upon him again; she had vowed as much to the Madonna, and it was in a moment of forgetfulness that she had just looked at him. When Fabrizio dared express his love once more, Clélia fled, offended, swearing to herself that she would never look at him again, for such were the precise terms of her vow to the Madonna: *My eyes shall never look upon him again.* She had written them on a slip of paper which her uncle Don Cesare had allowed her to burn upon the altar at the moment of the offertory, while he was saying Mass.

Yet despite all these vows, Fabrizio's presence in the Farnese Tower had reawakened all of Clélia's old habits and actions. Usually she spent all her days by herself, in her room. No sooner had she recovered from the unexpected agitation which the sight of Fabrizio had provoked in her than she began to move about the *palazzo* and renew acquaintance, so to speak, with all her humble friends. One garrulous old woman who worked in the kitchen said to her with an air of mystery: "This time, Signor Fabrizio will not leave the Fortress."

"He will not repeat the mistake of climbing over the walls," Clélia said, "but he will leave by the door, if he is acquitted."

"I am telling Your Excellency, and I have good reason for saying so, that he will not leave the Fortress except feet first."

Clélia turned as pale as death, which was noticed by the old woman, who cut short her eloquence there and then. She said to herself that she had been wrong to speak in such a fashion before the Governor's daughter, whose duty it would be to say to the world that Fabrizio had died of some disease. On her way back to her room, Clélia encountered the prison doctor, an honest man if a timid one, who said to her with a frightened expression that Fabrizio was quite ill. Clélia could scarcely keep on her feet; she searched everywhere for her uncle, the kind Abbé Don Cesare, and found him at last in the chapel, where he was praying quite fervently; his expression seemed quite troubled. The dinner-bell rang. At table, not one word was exchanged between the two brothers until the end of the meal, when the General spoke quite sharply to his brother. Don Cesare glanced at the servants, who left the room.

"General," Don Cesare said to the Governor, "I must inform you that I shall be leaving the Fortress; this is my resignation."

"*Bravo! Bravissimo!* To make me the object of suspicion! . . . And your reason, if you please?"

"My conscience."

"Why, you are no more than a cassock—what do you know about honor?"

"Fabrizio is a dead man," Clélia said to herself; "he has been poisoned at his dinner tonight, or tomorrow at the latest." She ran to her aviary, determined to sing, accompanying herself on the piano. "I shall go to confession," she said to herself, "and I shall be forgiven for having broken my vow in order to save a man's life." Imagine her consternation when, at her aviary, she saw that the shutters had been replaced by boards fastened to the iron bars! Overwhelmed, she attempted to warn the prisoner by a few words screamed rather than sung. There was no reply of any kind; a deathly silence already reigned in the Farnese Tower. "Everything is over," she said to herself. She ran downstairs, beside herself, then back up in order to supply herself with what money she had, and some little diamond earrings; she also snatched up, in passing, the bread that remained from dinner which had been set on a sideboard. "If he is still alive, it is my duty to save him." She walked on with a proud expression toward the little door of the Tower; it was open, and eight soldiers had just been posted in the pillared hall of the ground floor. She stared quite boldly at these soldiers; Clélia intended to speak to the sergeant in command: the man was not there.

Clélia dashed up the narrow iron staircase that spiraled around a column; the soldiers watched her in amazement, but apparently because of her lace shawl and bonnet, dared say nothing. On the first landing, there was no one, but when she reached the second floor, at the entrance to the corridor which, the reader may recall, was sealed by three iron-barred doors and led to Fabrizio's room, she found a turnkey unknown to her who told her in a terrified tone of voice, "He has not yet eaten."

"I am quite aware of that," Clélia said haughtily. The man dared not stop her.

Twenty paces farther on, Clélia found sitting on the first of the six wooden steps leading up to Fabrizio's room another turnkey, elderly and very red in the face, who said to her firmly, "Signorina, do you have an order from the Governor?"

"Don't you know who I am?" At this moment Clélia was inspired by a supernatural strength, and was quite beside herself. "I am going to save my husband," she said to herself.

While the old turnkey exclaimed: "But my duty doesn't permit . . ." Clélia ran up the six steps; she flung herself against the door: an enormous key stood in the keyhole; it required all her strength to make it turn. At this moment, the half-drunk old turnkey grabbed the hem of her dress; she rushed into the room, closed the door behind her, tearing her dress, and as the turnkey was pushing against it to enter after her, she shot the bolt that was under her hand. She glanced around the room and saw Fabrizio sitting in front of a tiny table, where his dinner was laid. She dashed to the table, knocked it over, and, seizing Fabrizio's arm, asked him: "My love, have you eaten anything?"

This form of address enchanted Fabrizio. In her agitation, Clélia was forgetting, for the first time in her life, all feminine discretion, and revealing her true feelings.

Fabrizio had been on the point of beginning this fatal meal; he took her in his arms and covered her with kisses. "This dinner was poisoned," he thought; "if I tell her I have not touched it, her religious feelings will overcome her again and Clélia will run away. If on the other hand she believes I am dying, I shall convince her not to leave me. She wants to find a way to get out of her dreadful engagement—fate has granted it to us: the jailers will come up here and break down the door, and there will be such a scandal that the Marchese Crescenzi will surely be offended, and the marriage broken off." During the moment of silence filled by these reflections, Fabrizio felt that already Clélia was attempting to free herself from his embrace. "I feel no pains as yet," he told her, "but soon they will cast me at your feet; help me to die."

"O my only friend!" she answered him, "I shall die with you," and she clasped him in her arms with a convulsive movement.

She was so lovely just then, her gown slipping off her shoulders and in such a state of extreme passion, that Fabrizio could not resist an almost involuntary movement. Which met with no resistance . . .

In the enthusiasm of passion and of generosity which followed extreme rapture, he murmured to her quite foolishly: "No unworthy falsehood must cast a shadow over the first moments of our happiness: had it not been for your courage, I should be no more than a corpse, or be in the throes of the cruelest agony; but I was just about to begin dining, when you came in, and I have not yet touched this food." Fabrizio dwelt on these these dreadful images in order to dispel the indignation he was already reading in Clélia's eyes. She gazed at him for a few seconds, overcome by two violent and opposing emotions, then flung herself into his arms. There was a loud noise in the corridor; the three iron-barred doors were opened and shut with great violence; men were shouting as they ran.

"Oh, if I had weapons!" Fabrizio exclaimed. "They took mine from me when I turned myself in. Now they must be coming to end my life! Farewell, my Clélia, I bless my death, since it has been the occasion of my happiness."

Clélia kissed him and slipped into his hand a tiny ivory-handled dagger, whose blade was scarcely longer than that of a pen-knife. "Don't let them kill you," she said, "defend yourself to the very end; if my uncle the Abbé hears all this noise, he has the courage and the virtue to come to your rescue; I shall appeal to them . . ."

And with these words, she rushed to the door. "If you are not killed," she said with exaltation, keeping the bolt closed with her hand and turning to face him, "let yourself starve to death rather than touching any food whatever. Keep this bread with you always."

The noise was coming closer. Fabrizio put his arm around her, stood beside her at the door, and, yanking it open, rushed down the six wooden steps. In his hand he held the tiny ivory-handled dagger, and he was on the point of stabbing the waistcoat of General Fontana, the Prince's aide-de-camp, who quickly stepped back, exclaiming in terror: "But I'm coming to rescue you, Signor del Dongo!"

Fabrizio ran back up the six steps and cried into the room, "It's Fontana, he's come to rescue me." Then, returning to the General on the wooden steps, he discussed the situation with him quite coolly. First, and at great length, he begged him to forgive his initial impulse of anger. "I was about to be poisoned by this dinner, which is here before me; I had the wit not to touch it, but I confess that such an undertaking has given me a shock. When I heard you coming up the stairs, I imagined that someone was coming to finish me off with a dagger. . . . Signor General, I request you to give orders that no one is to enter this room: we shall remove this poison, and our good Prince shall be informed of everything."

Pale and abashed, the General transmitted the orders Fabrizio had suggested to the picked jailers who had followed him: these men, crestfallen at the discovery of the poison, hurriedly ran back down the stairs; they seemed to be hurrying ahead in order not to delay the Prince's aide-de-camp on the narrow staircase, but they actually wanted to make their escape and disappear. To General Fontana's great amazement, Fabrizio stopped for a good quarter of an hour on the little iron staircase that spiraled down to the ground floor; he wanted to give Clélia time to hide on the first floor.

It was the Duchess who, after several wild attempts, had managed to send General Fontana to the Fortress; it was quite by accident that she had succeeded. As she left Count Mosca, who was certainly as alarmed as she was, she had run to the Palace. The Princess, who regarded with marked repugnance any display of energy, which she found vulgar, thought she had gone mad and scarcely seemed disposed to engage in any unusual measures on her behalf. The Duchess, beside herself, was weeping bitter tears, unable to do anything but repeat over and over: "But Signora, in a quarter of an hour, Fabrizio will be poisoned!" Observing the Princess's perfect composure, the Duchess went mad with grief. It did not occur to her to make that moral reflection which would not have escaped a woman brought up in one of those Northern religions which encourage self-scrutiny: "I was the first to use poison, and now it is I who shall be destroyed by poison." In Italy, such reflections, in moments of passion, are taken as the sign of a vulgar sensibility, much as a pun would be regarded in Paris in similar circumstances.

The Duchess, in desperation, risked going into the salon where the Marchese Crescenzi, who was in attendance that day, happened to be. On the Duchess's return to Parma, he had effusively thanked her for the title of *Cavaliere d'Onore*, to which, without her intervention, he would never have had any claim. There had been no lack of protestations of limitless devotion on his part. The Duchess addressed him with these words: "Rassi is prepared to poison Fabrizio, who is in the Fortress! I want you to put some chocolate in your pocket, and a bottle of water which I shall give you. Go up to the Fortress and save my life by telling General Fabio Conti that you'll break off your engagement to his daughter if he does not allow you to give Fabrizio this water and this chocolate with your own hands."

The Marchese turned pale and his face, far from being animated by these words, revealed the crassest embarrassment; he could not believe in so dreadful a crime in a city so law-abiding as Parma, ruled by so great a Prince, etc.; moreover he uttered these platitudes with singular deliberation. In a word, the Duchess was confronting an honest man but a very weak one unable to bring himself to act. After twenty such phrases interrupted by the Duchess's shrieks of impatience, he hit upon an excellent notion: the oath he had taken as *Cavaliere d'Onore* forbade him to take part in any actions against the government … Who could conceive the Duchess's anxiety and her despair, conscious as she was that time was flying?

"But at least go see the Governor, tell him I shall pursue Fabrizio's murderers to hell itself!"

Despair seconded the Duchess's natural eloquence, but all her intensity merely alarmed the Marchese further and increased his irresolution; after an hour, he was less disposed to take action than at the first moment.

The wretched woman, now in the extremities of desperation and realizing that the Governor would refuse nothing to so wealthy a son-in-law, went so far as to kneel at his feet, whereupon the Marchese Crescenzi's cowardice seemed to increase further; he himself, viewing this strange spectacle, feared to be unwittingly compromised; but a singular thing happened: the Marchese, a good man at heart, was touched by the tears and by the position at his feet of so lovely and especially so powerful a woman. "I myself, noble and rich as I am," he said to himself, "may one day also be at some Republican's feet!" The Marchese began to shed tears, and finally it was agreed that the Duchess, in her capacity as Mistress of the Robes, would present the Marchese to the Princess, who would grant permission for him to give Fabrizio a little basket, the contents of which, he would declare, he was entirely ignorant.

The previous evening, before the Duchess knew of Fabrizio's folly of presenting himself at the Fortress, there had been a *commedia dell'arte* performance at court, and the Prince, who always insisted on playing the lover's part with the Duchess, had spoken of his feelings with such passion that he would have been quite ridiculous if, in Italy, a passionate man or a Prince could be any such thing!

The Prince, quite shy yet invariably taking any matter concerning love with the greatest seriousness, happened at that moment to encounter the Duchess in one of the corridors of the Palace; she was accompanying the Marchese Crescenzi, who appeared to be quite upset, to the Princess's apartments. So dazzled was he by the beauty, height-ened by despair, of the Mistress of the Robes that for the first time in his life the Prince showed some character: with a more than imperious gesture, he dismissed the Marchese and proceeded to make the Duchess a formal declaration of love. No doubt the Prince had arranged his words long in advance, for some of them were fairly sensible.

"Since the conventions of my rank forbid me to grant myself the supreme happiness of marrying you, I swear to you on the Blessed Sacrament never to marry any other woman without your written permission. I am quite aware," he added, "that I am causing you to forfeit the hand of a Prime Minister, a clever and agreeable man; but after all, he is fifty-six years old, and I am not yet twenty-two. I should be offering you an insult and deserving your refusal were I to refer to certain advantages which have nothing to do with love; but all who take some interest in money matters at my court speak admiringly of the proof of his love which the Count bestows upon you by making you the custodian of all he possesses. I would be only too happy to imitate him in this regard. You will make better use of my fortune than I myself, and you shall have the entire disposition of the annual amount which my Ministers hand over to the Intendant-General of my Crown; so that it shall be you, my dear Duchess, who will determine the sums I shall expend each month."

The Duchess found all these details very long; Fabrizio's perils were piercing her to the heart. "But don't you understand, my dear Prince," she exclaimed, "that at this very moment Fabrizio is being poisoned in your own Fortress? Save him! I believe all you say!"

Everything about this little speech was ill-advised. At the mere mention of poison, all the enthusiasm and good faith which this poor high-principled Prince had put into his words vanished in a twinkling; the Duchess realized her blunder only when there was no longer time to remedy her words, and her desperation increased, a phenomenon she would have imagined impossible. "If I had not mentioned poison," she said to herself, "he would have granted Fabrizio his freedom for my sake. O beloved Fabrizio!" she added. "It is fated, then, that I must be the one to stab you to the heart by my stupidity!"

It took the Duchess a long time and a great many coquetries to bring the Prince back to his speeches of impassioned love; but he re-

mained deeply offended. It was his mind alone that was speaking; his
heart had been frozen by the notion of poison first of all, and then by
that other notion, quite as unflattering as the first was terrible: "Poison
is being used in my realm, and without my being informed of it! Rassi
intends to disgrace me in the eyes of all Europe! And God knows what
I shall be reading next month in the Paris newspapers!"

Suddenly this shy young man's soul fell silent within him; an idea
had occurred to him. "My dear Duchess! You know how attached to
you I am. Your horrid notions about poison are quite unfounded, I like
to think; but at least they lead me to certain conclusions, they almost
make me forget, for a moment, my passion for you, which is the only
one I have felt in all my life. I feel that I am not attractive; I am no more
than a boy who is deeply in love; but at least put me to the test." The
Prince grew quite animated in using such language.

"Save Fabrizio, and I shall believe it all! No doubt I have been carried away by maternal feelings; but send for Fabrizio at this very moment, have him taken from the Fortress so that I may see him. If he is
still alive, send him from this Palace to the municipal prison, where he
will remain for months on end, should Your Highness require it, until
the date of his trial."

With despair, the Duchess saw that the Prince, instead of immediately granting so simple a request, had turned quite morose; he
blushed deeply, stared at the Duchess; then he lowered his eyes and his
cheeks grew pale. The inopportune mention of poison had suggested
an idea worthy of his father or of Philip II, though he dared not put it
into words.

"Listen to me, my dear Duchess," he said at last as though against
his will and in a tone that was anything but gracious, "I am quite aware
that you regard me as no more than a boy, and a graceless one to boot:
I am now going to say something horrible to you, but something suggested to me at this very moment by my true and deep passion for you.
If I believed for an instant in this matter of poison, I should already
have taken action, as my duty commands; but I can see nothing in your
request but a caprice of passion, of which, if I may say so, I do not entirely comprehend the significance. You want me to take action without consulting my Ministers, though I have been reigning for no more

than three months! You ask me to make a great exception to my usual mode of conduct, which I have always regarded as quite reasonable. It is you, Signora, who are Absolute Sovereign at this moment, it is you who give me hopes for the matter which is everything to me; but in an hour, when this fantasy of poison—when this nightmare—will have vanished, my presence will become importunate to you, and you will withdraw your favor from me. So I must have a promise: swear to me, Duchess, that if Fabrizio is restored to you safe and sound, I shall obtain from you, within the next three months, all the felicity my love can desire; you shall guarantee the happiness of my whole life by putting an hour of your own at my disposal, and you shall be wholly mine."

At that moment, the Palace clock struck two. "Ah! It may be too late," thought the Duchess. "I swear it," she exclaimed, with a wild look in her eyes.

At once the Prince became a different man; he ran to the far end of the gallery, which led to the room of his aides-de-camp. "General Fontana, go to the Fortress immediately; as fast as you can, get up to the room where Signor del Dongo is being held, and bring him here to me, I must speak to him within twenty minutes—in fifteen if possible."

"Ah, General!" exclaimed the Duchess, who had followed the Prince. "A single minute may determine my whole life. No doubt it is a false report which makes me fear that Fabrizio is being poisoned: shout to him as soon as you are within hearing that he is to eat nothing. If he has begun his meal, make him vomit—tell him I wish it, use force if necessary; tell him that I am following close behind you, and I shall be in your debt for life."

"Your Grace, my horse is saddled, I am regarded as something of a horseman, and I am off at a gallop. I shall be at the Fortress eight minutes ahead of you."

"And I, dear Duchess," the Prince exclaimed, "ask you for four of those eight minutes." The aide-de-camp had vanished, a man whose sole merit was knowing how to ride. No sooner had the door closed behind him than the young Prince, who appeared to have acquired some character, seized the Duchess's hand. "Consent, Madame," he said in a passionate tone of voice, "to accompany me to the chapel." At a loss for the first time in her life, the Duchess followed him without uttering a word. She and the Prince hurried along the whole length of the Grand Gallery, the chapel being at the far end. Once inside the chapel, the Prince fell to his knees, almost as much in front of the Duchess as before the altar. "Repeat your oath," he said passionately. "If you had been fair, if this unfortunate accident of princely rank had not been my undoing, you would have granted out of pity for my love what you now owe me because you have sworn it."

"If I see Fabrizio again, and not poisoned, if he is still alive in eight days, if His Highness appoints him Coadjutor and next in succession to Archbishop Landriani, I shall give up my honor, my dignity as a woman—I shall sacrifice everything and give myself to His Highness."

"But *dear friend*," said the Prince with a mixture of timid anxiety and tenderness which was quite appealing, "I fear some unforeseeable stratagem which might destroy my happiness—that would be the death of me. If the Archbishop opposes me with one of those ecclesiastical arguments which postpone such matters for years on end, what will become of me? You see that I am acting in entire good faith; are you playing the little Jesuit with me?"

"No, in good faith, if Fabrizio is rescued, if with all your powers you make him Coadjutor and eventually Archbishop, I shall dishonor myself and belong to you. . . . Your Highness undertakes to write *approved* in the margin of a request that Monsignor the Archbishop will present to you within eight days."

"I shall sign a blank sheet for you—rule me and my country as well!" exclaimed the Prince, blushing with happiness and truly beside himself.

He insisted upon a second oath. He was so moved that he forgot the shyness so habitual to him, and in that Palace chapel where they were alone together he whispered things to the Duchess which, spoken three days earlier, would have quite changed her opinion of him. But the desperation Fabrizio's danger had inspired in the Duchess now gave way to horror of the promise which had been wrested from her.

The Duchess was overwhelmed by what she had just done. If she did not entirely realize the dreadful bitterness of the promise she had given, it was because her attention was fixed on one question: had General Fontana reached the Fortress in time?

In order to free herself from the impassioned speeches of this boy and to change the subject somewhat, she launched into extravagant praises of a famous canvas by Parmigianino hanging over the chapel's high altar. "Kindly allow me to send it to you," said the Prince.

"I accept," the Duchess replied; "but now, permit me to leave you in order that I may meet Fabrizio." In distraction, she told her coachman to set off at a gallop. On the bridge over the Fortress moat, she met General Fontana and Fabrizio, emerging on foot.

"Have you eaten?"

"No, miraculously enough."

The Duchess flung her arms around Fabrizio's neck and fell into a faint which lasted an hour and at first inspired fears for her life and later for her reason.

Governor Fabio Conti had turned pale with rage at the sight of General Fontana: he had been so slow in obeying the Prince's orders that the aide-de-camp, who imagined that the Duchess would soon be in the position of reigning mistress, had finally lost his patience. The Governor was intending to extend Fabrizio's malady two or three days, "And now," he said to himself, "this courtier General will find the insolent fellow writhing in the agony which is my revenge for his escape."

Fabio Conti, deep in thought, stopped in the guard-room on the ground floor of the Farnese Tower, from which he made haste to dismiss the soldiers; he wanted no witnesses for the scene which was about to occur. Five minutes later he was petrified with astonishment at hearing Fabrizio's voice and seeing him, alive and alert, describing the prison to General Fontana. He vanished.

Fabrizio revealed himself the perfect gentleman in his interview with the Prince. First of all, he had no desire to seem to be a child frightened by everything and nothing. With kind condescension the Prince asked him how he was feeling.

"Like a man, Your Most Serene Highness, dying of hunger, and having, fortunately, neither breakfasted nor dined."

After having had the honor of thanking the Prince, he sought permission to see the Archbishop before presenting himself at the municipal prison. The Prince had turned prodigiously pale when it became apparent to his childish mind that poison was not entirely a chimera of the Duchess's imagination. Absorbed in this cruel thought, he at first made no answer to Fabrizio's request to see the Archbishop; he then felt obliged to make up for his distraction by an excess of graciousness. "Go out alone, Signor, walk unguarded through my capital's streets. At ten or eleven, you may present yourself at the prison, where I hope you will not remain for long."

The morning after this great day, the most remarkable of his entire life, the Prince fancied himself a little Napoléon; he had read that this great man had been shown kindness by several of the beauties of his court. Once established as a Napoléon by such treatment, he recalled that he had also been a Napoléon under fire. His heart was still exalted by the decisiveness of his behavior with the Duchess. Consciousness of having done something difficult made him an altogether different man for a fortnight; he became susceptible to general ideas; he achieved some character.

He began that day by burning the patent creating Rassi a Count, which had been on his desk for over a month. He dismissed General Fabio Conti, and requested the truth about the poisoning from his successor, Colonel Lange. The latter, a fine Polish soldier, terrorized the jailers and told the Prince that there had been an attempt made to poison Signor del Dongo's breakfast, but too many persons would have had to be made party to the secret. Measures were taken for the dinner, and had it not been for General Fontana's arrival, Signor del Dongo was a dead man. The Prince was dismayed; but since he was deeply in love, it was a consolation to be able to tell himself: "I have actually saved Signor del Dongo's life, and the Duchess will not dare break the promise she has given me." Another idea occurred to him: "My calling is a good deal more difficult than I had thought; everyone agrees that the Duchess is infinitely witty, and here policy is at one with my heart. It would be divine for me were she willing to be my Prime Minister."

That evening, the Prince was so vexed by the horrors he had discovered, that he was unwilling to take a part in the play. "I should be overjoyed," he told the Duchess, "if you consented to reign over my State as you do over my heart. To begin with, I shall tell you how I have spent my day." And he then described very accurately the burning of Rassi's patent, the appointment of Lange, his report on the poisoning, and so on. "I realize that I have very little experience as a Sovereign. The Count humiliates me by his witticisms; he even makes jokes in the Council of State, and in my court he makes remarks whose veracity you shall now contest: he says that I am a child he leads where he likes. Being a Prince, Madame, does not mean one is any less a man, and such things are a tribulation. In order to give the lie to the stories Signor Mosca may tell, I have had to appoint that dangerous scoundrel Rassi to the Ministry, and now there is this General Conti who considers Rassi still so powerful that he dares not confess that it was Rassi or Marchesa Raversi who made him order your nephew's death; I have a good mind simply to send General Fabio Conti before the court; the judges will determine whether he is guilty of attempting murder by poisoning."

"But Your Highness, have you such judges?"

"What do you mean?" asked the Prince in astonishment.

"You have learned jurists who walk the streets with solemn faces; moreover they will always pass the judgment which will please the ruling party of your court."

While the scandalized young Prince uttered phrases which revealed his candor much more than his sagacity, the Duchess said to herself: "Does it really suit me to let Conti be disgraced in this fashion? Surely not, for then his daughter's marriage to that bore Marchese Crescenzi becomes impossible."

On this subject, there occurred an endless dialogue between the Duchess and the Prince. The Prince was overwhelmed with admiration. In consideration of Clélia Conti's engagement to the Marchese Crescenzi, but on this sole condition, which he angrily declared to the ex-Governor, he offered him a pardon for his attempt to poison Signor del Dongo; but on the Duchess's advice, he exiled Conti until the time of his daughter's wedding. The Duchess believed she was no longer in love with Fabrizio, but she still passionately desired Clélia Conti's marriage to the Marchese; there was, in this, a vague hope that gradually she would see Fabrizio's obsession fade away.

The Prince, in a transport of happiness, wanted to disgrace Rassi publicly that very evening. The Duchess laughed and said to him: "Do you know Napoléon's saying? *A man in a high position, on whom all eyes are fixed, ought never to allow himself violent impulses.* But it is too late for such things tonight in any case. Let us put off all business until tomorrow."

She wanted to give herself time to consult the Count, to whom she described quite precisely the evening's dialogue, though suppressing the Prince's frequent allusions to a promise which was poisoning her life. The Duchess flattered herself that she would make herself so necessary to the Prince that she might obtain an indefinite postponement by saying: "If you have the barbarity of seeking to submit me to this humiliation, for which I shall never forgive you, I shall leave your realm the very next day."

Consulted by the Duchess as to Rassi's fate, the Count showed himself highly philosophical: General Conti and he would go on a long journey through Piedmont.

A singular difficulty arose for Fabrizio's trial: the judges wished to acquit him by acclamation, and at the first session. The Count had to employ threats to make the trial last at least eight days and the judges take the trouble to hear all the witnesses. "These people are always the same," he said to himself.

The day after his acquittal, Fabrizio del Dongo at last took possession of the office of Grand Vicar to the worthy Archbishop Landriani. That same day, the Prince signed the dispatches necessary to have Fabrizio named Coadjutor with eventual succession, and less than two months afterward, he was installed in that position.

Everyone complimented the Duchess on her nephew's solemn demeanor; the fact is that he was in despair. The day after his release, followed by the dismissal and exile of General Fabio Conti and of the Duchess's rise to the highest favor, Clélia had taken refuge with her aunt, Countess Contarini, an extremely elderly and extremely rich woman solely concerned with the condition of her health. Had she wished to do so, Clélia might have seen Fabrizio, but anyone who had known of her previous commitments and who saw how she now behaved, might have supposed that her love for Fabrizio had ceased with her lover's dangers. Not only did Fabrizio pass as often as he decently could in front of the Palazzo Contarini, but he had even managed, with infinite difficulty, to rent a little apartment opposite its first-floor windows. On one occasion, Clélia, having thoughtlessly gone to the window to watch a procession pass, immediately withdrew, as though terror-stricken; she had noticed Fabrizio, dressed in black but as a poor workman, watching her from one of the windows of the wretched lodgings which had oiled paper for windowpanes, like his room in the Farnese Tower. Fabrizio would have liked to persuade himself that Clélia was evading him as a consequence of her father's disgrace, which people attributed to the Duchess; but he knew all too well another cause for this remoteness of hers, and nothing could distract him from his melancholy.

He had been moved neither by his acquittal nor by his installation in high office, the first which he had filled in his entire life, nor by his splendid position in society, nor finally by the assiduous court paid to him by all the ecclesiastics and all the devout laity of the diocese. The charming apartment reserved for him in the Palazzo Sanseverina was no longer found to be adequate. To her delight, the Duchess was obliged to offer him the entire second story of her Palace and two fine salons on the first, which were constantly filled with persons awaiting the moment to pay court to the young Coadjutor. The clause of *eventual succession* had produced a surprising effect in the region; people now counted as virtues all those firm qualities in Fabrizio's character which once had so scandalized the poor, foolish courtiers.

It was a great lesson in philosophy for Fabrizio to find himself quite indifferent to all these honors, and much more unhappy in that splendid apartment, with ten footmen wearing his livery, than he had been in his wooden chamber in the Farnese Tower, surrounded by ugly jailers and constantly in fear for his life. His mother and his sister, Duchess V———, who came to Parma to see him in his glory, were struck by his deep sadness. The Marchesa del Dongo, now the least romantic of women, was so profoundly upset that she imagined that he had been given some sort of slow poison in the Farnese Tower. Despite her extreme discretion, she felt she must speak to him about this extraordinary melancholy of his, and Fabrizio answered her only with tears. A host of advantages, the consequence of his brilliant position, produced no effect on him save to put him out of temper. His brother, that vain soul gangrened by the vilest selfishness, wrote him a more or less official letter of congratulation, to which was attached a draft for fifty thousand francs, so that he might, said the new Marchese, purchase horses and a carriage worthy of his name. Fabrizio sent this money to his younger sister, who had married disadvantageously.

Count Mosca had had a splendid translation made, in Italian, of the genealogy of the Valserra del Dongo family, originally published in Latin by that Archbishop of Parma, Fabrizio del Dongo. He had it printed magnificently with the Latin text *en face;* the engravings had been replaced by splendid lithographs made in Paris. The Duchess had wanted a fine portrait of Fabrizio to be bound opposite that of the original Archbishop. This translation was published as the work of our Fabrizio during his first imprisonment. But every source of pleasure was poisoned for our hero, even the vanity so natural to all mankind; he did not venture to read a single page of this work attributed to his labors. His position in the world made it an obligation for him to present a splendidly bound copy of it to the Prince, who, feeling that he owed some compensation for the cruel death to which he had come so close, granted him the right of entry to his Grand Levees, a favor which confers the title of *Excellency.*

CHAPTER TWENTY-SIX

The only moments when Fabrizio had some chance of emerging from his deep melancholy were those he spent hidden behind a pane of glass he had substituted for a square of oiled paper in the window of his apartment opposite the Palazzo Contarini, where as we know Clélia had taken refuge; the few times he had seen her since he had emerged from the Fortress, he had been deeply distressed by a striking change, one which seemed to him to bode no good. Since her lapse, Clélia's countenance had assumed a quality of nobility and seriousness that was quite remarkable; she looked like a woman of thirty. In this extraordinary transformation Fabrizio perceived the reflection of some fierce resolve. "At every moment of the day," he said to himself, "she is swearing to be faithful to that vow she made to the Madonna, and never to lay eyes on me again."

Fabrizio guessed only a part of Clélia's misfortunes; aware that her father, now deeply in disgrace, could return to Parma and reappear at Court (without which life for him would be impossible) only on the day she married the Marchese Crescenzi, she wrote her father that she desired this marriage. The General had at this time retired to Turin, quite prostrated with grief. In truth, the effect of this heroic resolve had been to add ten years to her age.

She soon discovered that Fabrizio had a window opposite the Palazzo Contarini; but she had had the misfortune to glimpse him only once; as soon as she saw a turn of the head or a man's figure at all resembling his, she immediately shut her eyes. Her deep piety and her confidence in the Madonna's aid were henceforth her only resource. She had the pain of feeling no esteem for her father; her future husband's character struck her as entirely commonplace and appropriate to the sentiments of worldly society; finally, she adored a man she must never see again, though he had certain rights over her. This accumulation of disasters struck her as the worst of fates, and we must confess she was right: after her marriage, she would have to go and live two hundred leagues from Parma.

Fabrizio was aware of Clélia's profound modesty; he knew how much any extraordinary undertaking—one that, if discovered, might constitute a subject of gossip—was certain to distress her. Yet impelled to extremity by the depths of his melancholy and by those glances of Clélia's which kept turning away from him, he ventured to bribe two of the servants of Signora Contarini, Clélia's aunt. One day, at nightfall, Fabrizio, dressed as a country gentleman, presented himself at the door of the Palace, where he was awaited by one of the servants he had bribed; he had himself announced as arriving from Turin with letters for Clélia from her father. The servant went to deliver the message, and showed him upstairs into an enormous antechamber on the first floor of the Palace. It was in this room that Fabrizio passed perhaps the most anxious quarter of an hour in his entire life. If Clélia rejected him, he would know no further peace nor hope. "In order to cut short the importunate cares my new dignities have heaped upon me, I shall spare the Church a bad priest and, under an assumed name, go bury myself in some Carthusian monastery!" Finally the servant came to inform him that Signora Clélia Conti was willing to see him. Our hero's courage quite failed him; he was on the point of collapsing with fear as he made his way up the staircase to the second floor.

Clélia was sitting at a little table on which stood a single candle. No sooner had she recognized Fabrizio under his disguise than she took flight and hid at the far end of the salon.

"This shows how much you care about my salvation," she exclaimed, hiding her face in her hands. "Yet you know, when my father was on the verge of death from poison, I vowed to the Madonna never to see you again. I have broken that vow only on that one day, the most wretched in all my life, when I felt bound by conscience to save you from death. It is already a great deal more than you deserve if, by some distorted and probably criminal interpretation of my vow, I consent to listen to you."

This last remark so amazed Fabrizio that it took him several seconds to be delighted by it. He had expected to be met with the deepest anger, and to see Clélia run away from him; finally he regained his presence of mind and snuffed the one candle. Though he believed he had understood Clélia's orders, he trembled in every limb as he walked toward the end of the salon where she had taken refuge behind a couch; he had no idea whether he would offend her by kissing her hand; she herself was quivering with love, and flung herself into his arms. "Dear Fabrizio," she said to him, "how long it has taken you to get here! I can only speak to you for a moment, for it is certainly a great sin; and when I promised never to see you again, no doubt I also meant to promise never to speak to you. But how could you be so barbarous as to pursue my poor father's notion of taking revenge? For after all, it was he himself who was nearly poisoned to make possible your escape. Shouldn't you do something for me, now that I've jeopardized my own good name in order to save you? Besides, now you are quite committed to Holy Orders; you wouldn't be able to marry me, even if I were to find some way of getting rid of this hateful Marchese. And then how could you dare, on the very evening of the procession, try to see me in broad daylight, thereby violating in the most outrageous way the sacred oath I've sworn to the Madonna?"

Fabrizio crushed her in his arms, beside himself with amazement and delight.

A conversation which began with such a quantity of things to be said was not to end for a long while. Fabrizio told Clélia the precise truth as to her father's banishment; the Duchess had had nothing to do with it, for the simple reason that she had not for a moment supposed that the notion of poison had occurred to General Conti; she had always assumed it was an inspiration of the Raversi faction, which sought to get rid of Count Mosca. This historical truth, developed at great length, made Clélia happy indeed; she had been wretched at having to hate anyone related to Fabrizio. Now she no longer regarded the Duchess with a jealous eye.

The happiness established by this one evening lasted only a few days.

The worthy Don Cesare arrived from Turin; plucking up courage from the perfect honesty of his own heart, he ventured to have himself presented to the Duchess. After requesting her on her word of honor not to abuse the trust he was about to place in her, he admitted that his brother, misled by a false point of honor and believing himself flouted and ruined in public opinion by Fabrizio's escape, had felt bound to seek revenge.

Don Cesare had not spoken for two minutes before his case was won: his perfect virtue had touched the Duchess, who was quite unaccustomed to such a spectacle. He delighted her as a novelty.

"Hasten the marriage of the General's daughter to the Marchese Crescenzi, and I promise you I shall do everything I can for the General to be received as if he were returning from a journey. I shall invite him to dinner; are you satisfied? No doubt there will be a certain chill at first, and the General must on no account be in a hurry to claim his office as Governor of the Fortress. But you know that I have a friendly feeling for the Marchese, and I shall nurse no rancor for his father-in-law."

Armed with these words, Don Cesare came to tell his niece that she held in her own hands her despairing father's life: for several months, he had not appeared at any Court.

Clélia determined to visit her father, hiding under an assumed name in a village near Turin; for he had imagined that the Court of Parma would require his extradition from that of Turin, in order to bring him to trial. She found him ill and half-mad. That very evening she wrote a letter to Fabrizio, breaking off with him forever. Upon receiving this letter, Fabrizio, who was developing a character quite similar to his beloved's, went into retreat at the Charterhouse of Velleja, in the mountains ten leagues outside Parma. Clélia wrote him a letter ten pages long; she had once sworn never to marry the Marchese without Fabrizio's consent; now she asked it of him, and from the depths of his retreat at Velleja, Fabrizio granted it to her by a letter filled with the purest friendship.

Upon receiving this letter in which the sentiment of friendship, it must be confessed, irritated her considerably, Clélia herself decided upon the day of her marriage, the festivities surrounding which occasion enhanced still further the brilliance of the Parmesan court that winter.

Ranuccio-Ernesto V was a miser at heart; but he was desperately in love, and he hoped to attach the Duchess to his Court; he begged his mother to accept a considerable sum with which to give a number of parties. The Mistress of the Robes succeeded in making admirable use of this great increase in funds; the parties at Parma, that winter, recalled the great days of the Court of Milan and of that charming Prince Eugène, Viceroy of Italy, whose kindness has left so lasting a memory.

The Coadjutor's duties had recalled Fabrizio to Parma; but he declared that for reasons of piety, he would continue his retreat in the little apartment which his protector, Monsignore Landriani, had obliged him to take at the Archbishop's Palace; and he shut himself up there, accompanied by a single servant. Hence he attended none of the brilliant festivities at Court, which won him an enormous reputation for sanctity in Parma and in his future diocese. One unexpected consequence of this retreat, to which Fabrizio had been inspired entirely by his deep and hopeless melancholy, was that the worthy Archbishop Landriani, who had always loved him and who, as it happened, had had the notion of making him Coadjutor, now conceived a slight jealousy of him. The Archbishop rightly supposed that he must attend all the Court festivities, as is the custom in Italy. On these occasions, he wore his ceremonial costume, which was more or less the same as the one he wore in the choir of his own Cathedral. The hundreds of servants gathered in the series of antechambers of the palace did not fail to rise

and seek the blessing which the Monsignore was delighted to stop and bestow upon them. It was during one of these moments of solemn silence that Monsignore Landriani heard a voice saying: "Our Archbishop goes to the ball, and Monsignore del Dongo never leaves his room!"

At this moment the enormous favor Fabrizio had enjoyed at the Archbishop's Palace came to an end; but he now could fly with his own wings. That very behavior which had been inspired solely by the despair into which Clélia's marriage had plunged him passed for the effect of a sublime and elementary piety, and the faithful read as a work of edification that translation of his family's genealogy which displayed no more than the most insane vanity. The booksellers produced a lithographed edition of Fabrizio's protrait, which was sold out in a few days, particularly among the people; the engraver, out of ignorance, had reproduced around Fabrizio's countenance several of those ornaments which should appear only in the portraits of Bishops and to which a Coadjutor has no claim. The Archbishop saw one of these portraits, and his rage knew no bounds; he summoned Fabrizio, and addressed him with the harshest observations, in terms which passion at times rendered extremely coarse. Fabrizio had no difficulty, as may easily be conceived, in conducting himself as Fénelon would have done on such an occasion; he listened to the Archbishop in all humility and with all possible respect; and when this prelate had ceased speaking, he recounted the whole history of the translation of that genealogy made on Count Mosca's orders, at the time of Fabrizio's first imprisonment. It had been published with worldly intentions, which he had ever regarded as unsuitable for a man of his condition. As for the portrait, he had been entirely ignorant of the second edition, as of the first, indeed; and the bookseller having sent to the Archbishop's Palace, during his retreat, twenty-four copies of this second edition, Fabrizio had sent his own servant to purchase a twenty-fifth; and having learned by this means that his portrait was selling for thirty soldi, he had sent a hundred francs as payment for the twenty-five copies.

All these explanations, though set forth in the most reasonable tone by a man who had many other sorrows in his heart, increased the

Archbishop's rage to the point of madness; he went so far as to accuse Fabrizio of hypocrisy.

"That is what all these common people are like," Fabrizio said to himself, "even when they have some intelligence!" He now had a more serious cause for worry to contend with, derived from his aunt's letters, which absolutely insisted that he return to his apartment in the Palazzo Sanseverina, or at least that he come visit her on occasion. Fabrizio was certain to hear of the splendid parties given by the Marchese Crescenzi on the occasion of his marriage, and this was what he was not sure he could manage to endure without creating a scene.

When the wedding took place, there were eight whole days during which Fabrizio had vowed himself to complete silence, after ordering his servant and the Archbishop's men never to utter a word to him. When Monsignore Landriani learned of this new affectation, he summoned Fabrizio much more frequently than was his custom, and sought to engage him in extremely long conversations; he even obliged him to hold conferences with certain provincial canons who were claiming that the Archbishopric had infringed their privileges. Fabrizio responded to all these incidents with the perfect indifference of a man whose mind is on other things. "I would be better off," he said to himself, "if I were a Carthusian; I would suffer less among the rocks of Velleja."

He went to see his aunt, and could not restrain his tears as he embraced her. She found him so transformed—his eyes, even larger on account of his extreme thinness, seemed to be starting out of his head, and he himself seemed so pinched and wretched in his frayed little soutane of a simple priest that at first the Duchess too could not restrain her tears; but a moment afterward, when she realized that this entire transformation in the appearance of this handsome young man was caused by Clélia's marriage, she experienced sentiments almost equal in vehemence to the Archbishop's, though more skillfully concealed. She was cruel enough to speak at length of certain picturesque details which had characterized the delightful parties given by the Marchese Crescenzi. Fabrizio made no answer, but his eyes closed momentarily in a convulsive movement, and he grew even paler than he had been, which at first would have seemed impossible. In such moments of intense sorrow, his pallor assumed a greenish tinge.

Count Mosca arrived, and what met his eyes, a thing which seemed to him quite incredible, finally and altogether cured him of the jealousy which Fabrizio had never ceased to inspire in him. This able man employed the most delicate and ingenious turns of phrase to attempt to revive some interest in Fabrizio for the things of this world. The Count had always regarded him with a good deal of esteem and a certain friendliness; this friendliness, no longer counterbalanced by jealousy, became at this moment something quite akin to devotion. "There's no denying it, he's paid dearly for his good fortune," he said to himself, numbering his disasters. With the excuse of showing him the painting by Parmigianino which the Prince had sent to the Duchess, the Count took Fabrizio aside. "Now, my friend, let us speak man to man: can I be of some help to you? You have no questions to fear from me, but perhaps a certain sum of money can be of use to you, or a certain amount of power? You have only to say the word and I am at your service; if you prefer to write, write to me."

Fabrizio embraced him warmly and discussed the painting.

"Your behavior is a masterpiece of diplomacy," the Count remarked to him, returning to the easy style of polite conversation; "you are arranging a fine future for yourself—the Prince respects you, the people venerate you, your frayed little black soutane gives Monsignore Landriani some sleepless nights. I have some experience in such matters, and I can assure you I have no advice to offer which might improve what I see. Your first step in the world at the age of twenty-five has brought you to the pinnacle of perfection. You are spoken of a great deal at Court, and do you know to what you owe this distinction which is altogether unique at your age? To that frayed little black soutane. The Duchess and I possess, as you know, that old house which once belonged to Petrarch, on the woody hillside above the Po; if you are ever weary of the wretched little stratagems of the envious, it has occurred to me that you might be Petrarch's successor there—his renown will only increase your own."

The Count was racking his brains to produce a smile on that anchorite's face, but was unable to do so. What made the transformation more striking was that until recently, if Fabrizio's countenance possessed one defect, it was to present now and then, quite inappropriately, an expression of pleasure and gaiety.

The Count did not let Fabrizio leave without telling him that notwithstanding his retreat, there might be some affectation in not appearing at Court the following Saturday, which was the Princess's birthday. These words stabbed Fabrizio to the heart. "Good God!" he thought. "What am I doing here in this Palace!" He could not think without shuddering of one encounter he might have at Court. This notion absorbed all others; he realized that his sole recourse would be to arrive at the Palace just when the doors of the salons would be opened.

And so the name of Monsignore del Dongo was one of the first to be announced on the evening of the gala reception, and the Princess received him with the greatest possible distinction. Fabrizio's eyes were fixed on the clock, and as soon as it indicated the twentieth minute of his presence in that salon and he stood up to take his leave, the Prince entered his mother's apartments. After paying his respects for some moments, Fabrizio by a clever stratagem once again approached the door, when there occurred, to his misfortune, one of those Court incidents which the Mistress of the Robes was so good at bringing about: the Chamberlain-in-Waiting ran after him to say that he had been chosen to make up the Prince's whist table. In Parma, this was a signal honor, one far above what the rank of Coadjutor ordinarily received in society. To make up the Prince's whist table was a sign of favor, even for the Archbishop. At the Chamberlain's words, Fabrizio felt his heart give way, and though a mortal enemy of any public scene, he was about to observe that he was suffering from a sudden spell of dizziness; but he realized that he would be subject to questions and to sympathies even more intolerable than the card-game. On that day, he had a horror of speaking.

Fortunately the Father Superior of the Minorite Brothers happened to be among the great personages who had come to do honor to the Princess. This cunning monk, a worthy emulator of the Fontanas and the Duvoisins, had taken up his position in a remote corner of the salon; Fabrizio went over to stand in front of him so as not to notice the doorway into the room, and began talking of theological matters. But he could not help hearing Signor the Marchese and Signora the Marchesa Crescenzi being announced. Fabrizio, to his surprise, felt a violent impulse of anger. "If I were Borso Valserra," he said to himself (this was one of the generals of the first Sforza), "I would go over and stab that fat Marchese here and now, with the very ivory-handled dagger that Clélia gave me on a certain happy day, and that would teach him to show himself with his Marchesa in a place where I happen to be!"

His countenance changed to such a degree that the Father Superior of the Minorite Brothers inquired: "Is Your Excellency feeling unwell?"

"I have a dreadful headache . . . these bright lights are hurting my eyes . . . and I'm still here only because I've been asked to make up the Prince's whist table."

At this remark, the Father Superior of the Minorite Brothers, who was of bourgeois extraction, was so disconcerted that, no longer knowing what to do, he began to bow to Fabrizio, who, for his part, much more troubled than the Father Superior of the Minorite Brothers, began speaking with a strange volubility; he realized that a great silence was forming around him, and he did not want to look. Suddenly a bow tapped a music-stand; a *ritornello* was played, and the famous Signora P—— sang that once-popular aria by Cimarosa:

Quelle pupille tenere!

Fabrizio withstood the first measures, but soon his anger vanished, and he felt an overpowering need to shed tears. "Good God!" he said to himself. "What an absurd scene! And in my soutane as well!" He believed it was the better part of valor to speak about himself: "These terrible headaches, when I try to resist them, as I am doing this evening," he said to the Father Superior of the Minorite Brothers, "end with floods of tears which might provide food for scandal in a man of our condition; in consequence, I beg Your Most Illustrious Reverence to permit me to weep as I look your way without paying me any special attention."

"Our Father Provincial at Catanzara is afflicted with the same infirmity," observed the Father Superior of the Minorite Brothers. And he began whispering an endless story.

The absurdity of which, including details of the evening meals of this Father Provincial, brought a smile to Fabrizio's lips, a phenomenon which had not occurred in a long while; but soon he ceased attending to the Father Superior of the Minorite Brothers. Signora P—— was singing, with heavenly talent, an aria by Pergolesi (the Princess was fond of old-fashioned music). There was a slight noise close to Fabrizio, and for the first time that evening he looked around. The armchair which had just produced this tiny creak on the parquet floor was occupied by the Marchesa Crescenzi, whose tear-filled eyes now met Fabrizio's, which were in no better condition. The Marchesa looked down; Fabrizio continued to look at her for a few seconds: he was studying that lovely head covered with diamonds; but his gaze expressed rage and disdain. Then, telling himself: ". . . *and my eyes shall never look upon you.*" he turned back to his Father Superior and said: "Now my infirmity is troubling me worse than ever."

Indeed, Fabrizio wept bitter tears for over half an hour. Fortunately, a Mozart symphony, dreadfully mangled, as is the custom in Italy, came to his rescue and helped him dry his tears.

He stood fast, and did not glance at the Marchesa Crescenzi; but Signora P—— sang once again, and Fabrizio's soul, relieved by tears, achieved a state of perfect repose. Life then appeared to him in a new light: "How can I claim," he asked himself, "to be utterly forgetting her in these very first moments? Could such a thing be possible?" This notion occurred to him: "Can I be any more unhappy than I have been these last two months? And if nothing can increase my sufferings, why resist the pleasure of seeing her? She has forgotten the vows she has made; she is frivolous—are not all women like that? But who could deny her heavenly beauty? The look in her eyes fills me with ecstasy, while I must force myself to pay any attention to women who are considered the loveliest in Parma! Then why not let myself be enchanted; at least it will be a momentary relief."

Fabrizio had some knowledge of men, but no experience of the passions, otherwise he would have realized that this momentary pleasure, to which he was about to yield, would render futile all the efforts he had been making to forget Clélia for the past two months.

The poor girl had come to this party only because her husband had obliged her to; after half an hour, she declared she was not feeling well and wanted to leave, but the Marchese told her that to send for his carriage to take her departure, when so many were still arriving, would be quite unprecedented and might even be interpreted as an indirect criticism of the Princess's party. "As *Cavaliere d'Onore*," he added, "I must remain at the Princess's orders here in her salon until everyone has left: there may be, and indeed there doubtless will be, all kinds of orders to be given to the servants, they are so careless! And would you have a mere Equerry usurp that honor?"

Clélia resigned herself; she had not yet seen Fabrizio and still hoped he had not come to this party. But at the moment the music was about to begin, the Princess having permitted the ladies to be seated, Clélia, who paid no attention to such matters of precedence, let all the best chairs near the Princess be taken and was obliged to look for a place at the back of the room, in the very corner where Fabrizio had taken refuge. As she reached her chair, the singular costume in such a place of the Father Superior of the Minorite Brothers caught her eye, and at first she did not notice the slender man wearing a simple black soutane who was talking to him; yet a certain secret movement attracted her glance to this person. "Everyone here has uniforms or gold-embroidered coats: who can this young man in black be?" She was giving him a closer look when a lady, coming to take a seat beside her, caused her chair to move. Fabrizio looked around: she did not recognize him, so changed was his countenance. At first she said to herself: "There's someone who looks like him, it could be his older brother; but I thought he was only a few years older, and this is a man of forty." Suddenly she recognized him from a twitch of his lips. "How the poor fellow must have suffered!" she said to herself, and she looked down in distress—not in order to keep her vow. Her heart was overcome by pity. "He didn't look anything like that after nine months in prison!" She did not look at him again; but without exactly turning her eyes in his direction, she noticed all his movements.

After the concert, she saw him go over to the Prince's card table, placed a few steps from the throne; she breathed again when Fabrizio was now some distance away from her.

But the Marchese Crescenzi had been deeply offended to see his wife relegated to a place so far from the throne; all evening he had been busily persuading a lady who was sitting three chairs away from the Princess and whose husband owed him money that she would do well to change places with his wife. When the poor lady resisted, as was only natural, he went to look for the indebted husband, who enabled his better half to hear the sad voice of reason, and at last the Marchese had the pleasure of effecting the exchange, and went to find his wife. "You're always too self-effacing," he told her; "why walk that way with your eyes down? People will take you for one of those middle-class women who is surprised to find herself here and whom everyone else is surprised to see here as well! That madwoman of a Mistress of the Robes is always doing such things! Yet people talk of keeping Jacobinism down! You must realize that your own husband occupies the first position among gentlemen at the Princess's Court; and even if the Republicans managed to suppress the Court, and the nobility as well, your husband would still be the richest man in the country! That is a notion you never keep sufficiently in mind."

The chair in which the Marchese had the pleasure of installing his wife was only six paces away from the Prince's card-table; she could see only Fabrizio's profile, but she found him grown so thin, and above all seeming to be so far above anything likely to happen in this world, he who once let no incident pass without commenting upon it, that Clélia ended by coming to this dreadful conclusion: Fabrizio had altogether changed; he had forgotten her; if he was now so thin, that was the effect of the severe fasting to which his piety subjected him. She was confirmed in this sad conclusion by the conversation of everyone around her: the Coadjutor's name was on everyone's lips; everyone speculated as to the signal favor of which he was the object, young as he was, to make up the Prince's whist party! People admired the polite indifference and the look of pride with which he tossed down his cards, even when he was trumping His Highness. "That's really incredible!" exclaimed some old courtiers. "His aunt's favor has completely turned his head ... but thanks be to Heaven, it will not last; our Sovereign hates people to assume those little airs of superiority."

The Duchess approached the Prince; the courtiers who were standing at a respectful distance from the card-table, unable to hear more than a few random words of the Prince's conversation, noticed that Fabrizio was blushing a good deal. "His aunt must be teaching him a lesson," they were thinking, "about those grand airs of his." Fabrizio had just heard Clélia's voice; she was answering the Princess, who, in making the rounds of the ballroom, had addressed the wife of her *Cavaliere d'Onore*. The moment came when Fabrizio had to change places at the whist table; he now found himself directly opposite Clélia, and abandoned himself repeatedly to the pleasure of looking at her. The poor Marchesa, feeling his eyes upon her, was quite embarrassed. Several times she forgot about her vow altogether: in her desire to discover what was happening in Fabrizio's heart, she fixed her eyes upon him.

Now that the Prince's game of whist was finished, the ladies stood up to proceed into the room where supper was being served. There was a moment of confusion. Fabrizio found himself close to Clélia; he was still quite determined, but he happened to recognize a very faint fragrance which she used on her gowns; this sensation overcame all his resolutions. He approached her and repeated in a whisper, as though to himself, two lines of that sonnet by Petrarch which he had sent her from Lake Maggiore, printed on a silk handkerchief:

Happiest was I when all believed me sad,
How changed today is all my lot in life!

"So he has not forgotten me," Clélia exulted, in a transport of joy. "That beautiful soul has never wavered!" And she ventured to murmur to herself two more lines of Petrarch:

No, never shall you see a change in me,
Fair eyes that have taught me what love is.

The Princess withdrew immediately after supper; the Prince had followed her to her apartments, and did not return to the reception rooms. As soon as this became known, everyone sought to leave at the same time; there was utter confusion in the antechambers; Clélia found herself standing quite close to Fabrizio; the deep melancholy ingrained in his features moved her to pity. "Let us forget the past," she said to him, "and keep this souvenir of *friendship.*" And with these words, she put out her fan so that he could take it from her.

Everything changed in Fabrizio's eyes; in an instant he was another man; the very next day he declared that his retreat was concluded, and he returned to occupy his splendid apartment in the Palazzo Sanseverina. The Archbishop said and believed that the favor the Prince had shown him in inviting him to his whist-table had completely turned this new saint's head; the Duchess realized that he had come to some agreement with Clélia. This thought, coming to redouble the misery afforded by the memory of a fatal promise, quite determined her to absent herself from Court. Her caprice was marveled at: What! Leave the Court just when the favor she was enjoying seemed to have no bounds! The Count, entirely happy since he believed that there was no such thing as love between Fabrizio and the Duchess, said to his friend: "Our new Prince is virtue incarnate, but I used to call him *that child—*will he ever forgive me? I see only one way of returning to his good graces, which is to disappear. I shall show myself to be a model of good manners and the deepest respect, after which I shall be ill and request a leave of absence. You will allow me this, since Fabrizio's fortunes are now assured. But will you make this great sacrifice for me," he added with a laugh, "of exchanging the sublime title of Duchess for a much inferior one? For my own amusement, I am leaving affairs here in incredible confusion; I had four or five workmen in my various Ministries—I have pensioned them off during the last two months, for reading the French newspapers, and they have been replaced by incredible dummies. . . . Following our departure, the Prince will find himself in such difficulties that despite his horror of Rassi's character,

I have no doubts he will be compelled to recall him, and I myself am merely awaiting orders from the tyrant who disposes of my fate to write a letter of tender friendship to my friend Rassi, informing him that I have every reason to hope that justice will soon be done to his true merits."

CHAPTER TWENTY-SEVEN

This serious conversation took place the day after Fabrizio's return to the Palazzo Sanseverina; the Duchess was still appalled by the joy so luminous in all of Fabrizio's actions. "Incredible!" she said to herself. "That pious little ninny deceived me! She couldn't hold out against her lover for even three months."

The certainty of a happy outcome had inspired that cowardly creature, the young Prince, with the courage to love; he had heard something of the preparations for departure being made at the Palazzo Sanseverina; and his French valet, who put little trust in the virtue of great ladies, encouraged him with regard to the Duchess. Ernesto V permitted himself to take a step which was severely reproved by the Princess and indeed by every sensible member of the Court; by commoners it was regarded as the seal of the remarkable favor the Duchess enjoyed. The Prince came to see her in her own *palazzo*.

"You are leaving," he said to her in a serious tone which the Duchess found odious; "you are leaving: you are betraying me and breaking your word! And yet if I had delayed ten minutes in granting you Fabrizio's pardon, he would have been a dead man. And you leave me a wretched one! I must confess that without your promises I should never have had the courage to love you as I do! Have you no sense of honor?"

"Just think a moment, Your Highness. In your entire life has there ever been a period equal in happiness to the four months which have just passed? Your glory as a Sovereign and, I daresay, your happiness as a man of feeling have never risen to such a pitch. Here is the compact I propose: if you deign to consent to it, I shall not be your mistress for a fleeting moment and by virtue of a promise extorted from me by fear, but I shall devote every moment of my life to procuring your happiness, I shall always be what I have been the last four months, and perhaps love will come to crown friendship. I would not swear to the contrary."

"Well then," said the Prince, delighted, "play another part, be still more than you have been, rule both me and my Kingdom—be my Prime Minister; I offer you the kind of marriage permitted by the regrettable conventions of my rank; we have an example of such a thing close at hand: the King of Naples has just married the Duchess of Partana. I offer you all I can—a marriage of the same sort. I shall add a distressing political consideration to show you that I am no longer a child, and that I have given the matter some thought. I lay no stress on the condition which I impose on myself of being the last Sovereign of my house, and suffering the disappointment of seeing in my lifetime the Great Powers control my succession; I bless these very real disadvantages, since they offer me a further means of proving to you both my esteem and my passion."

The Duchess did not hesitate for a second; she found the Prince tedious and the Count quite lovable; to him there was only one man in the world she could prefer. Moreover, she ruled the Count, whereas the Prince, yielding to the demands of his rank, would have ruled her, more or less. Then too, he might well turn unfaithful and take mistresses; the difference in their ages might seem, in a few years, to entitle him to take such a step.

From the very first moment, the prospect of boredom had settled the whole matter; nonetheless the Duchess, who sought to be as charming as possible, asked for time to reflect. It would take too long to record here the quasi-tender turns of phrase and the infinitely gracious terms in which she managed to swathe her refusal. The Prince lost his temper; he saw all his happiness escaping him. What would become of him once the Duchess had left his Court? Besides, how humiliating to be rejected! "After all, what will my French valet say when I tell him of my defeat?"

The Duchess managed to calm the Prince, and little by little to bring the negotiations to her actual terms. "If Your Highness deigns not to demand the fulfillment of a fatal promise, one that is horrible in my eyes, obliging me, as it does, to incur my own contempt, I shall spend my life at his Court, and this Court will always be what it has been this winter; my every moment will be dedicated to contributing to your happiness as a man, and to your glory as a Sovereign. If Your Highness requires me to keep my promise, you will have spoiled the rest of my life, and immediately afterward will see me leave your realm, never to return. The day I shall have lost my honor will also be the last day I shall ever see you."

But the Prince was stubborn, like all cowards; moreover, his pride as a man and as a Sovereign was vexed by the rejection of his hand; he thought of all the difficulties he would have had to gain acceptance for such a marriage, which he was nonetheless determined to vanquish.

For three hours the same arguments were repeated on either side, frequently mingled with very strong language. The Prince exclaimed: "Do you wish to persuade me, Signora, that you have no sense of honor? Had I hesitated so long the day General Fabio Conti gave poison to Fabrizio, you would even now be erecting a tomb to him in one of the churches of Parma."

"No, not in Parma, this country of poisoners."

"Very well then, go, Signora Duchess," the Prince retorted angrily, "and take my contempt with you."

As he was leaving, the Duchess said to him in a whisper: "All right, come here at ten tonight, in the strictest incognito, and you shall have your fool's bargain. You will then have seen me for the last time, though I would have devoted my life to making you as happy as any absolute monarch can be in this Jacobin age. Just think what your Court will be like when I am no longer here to extricate it by force from the boredom and spite which are its natural conditions."

"For your part, you reject the crown of Parma, and more than the crown, for you would not have been any ordinary Princess, married for dynastic reasons without love; my heart is entirely yours, and you would have seen yourself ever the absolute mistress of my actions as of my government."

"Yes, but the Princess your mother would have been in a position to regard me as a vile scheming woman."

"In that case I would have banished the Princess with a pension."

There followed another three-quarters of a hour of sharp exchanges. The Prince, who had a sensitive soul, could not bring himself either to use his rights or to allow the Duchess to leave. He had been told that after a first success was obtained, no matter how, all women come round.

Dismissed by the indignant Duchess, he ventured to reappear, trembling and altogether wretched, at three minutes to ten. At ten-thirty, the Duchess stepped into her carriage and left for Bologna. She wrote to the Count once she was beyond Parma's borders:

> The sacrifice has been made. Do not ask me to be cheerful for the next month. I shall not see Fabrizio again; I await you at Bologna, and whenever you wish, I shall be Countess Mosca. I ask only one thing of you: never force me to reappear in the country I am leaving, and always remember that instead of an income of one hundred and fifty thousand lire, you will have thirty or forty thousand at most. All the fools were watching you open-mouthed, and for the future you will be respected only insofar as you condescend to sink to their petty level. Tu l'as voulu, Georges Dandin!

Eight days later, the wedding was celebrated in Perugia, in a church where the Count's ancestors have their tombs. The Prince was in despair. The Duchess had received three or four couriers from him, and had not failed to return his letters, in fresh envelopes, with their seals unbroken. Ernesto V had granted the Count a magnificent pension, and awarded the Grand Cordon of his order to Fabrizio.

"That is what pleased me most in his farewells. We parted," said the Count to the new Countess Mosca della Rovere, "the best of friends; he awarded me a Spanish Grand Cordon, and gave me some diamonds worth every bit as much as the Cordon. He told me he would make me a Duke, but wanted to keep that in reserve in case he might tempt you back to his realm. So I have the responsibility of informing you—a fine mission for a husband—that if you deign to return to Parma, even if only for a month, I shall be made a Duke, under any name you choose, and you will have a fine estate."

Which the Duchess refused with every appearance of horror.

After the scene which had occurred at the Court ball, and which seemed quite decisive, Clélia seemed no longer to remember the love she had appeared to share so briefly; the most violent remorse had seized this virtuous and pious soul. This Fabrizio understood quite well, and despite all the hopes he attempted to sustain, the blackest misery filled his soul. This time, however, such misery did not lead him into retreat, as at the period of Clélia's marriage.

The Count had requested *his nephew* to keep him well informed as to what was happening at Court, and Fabrizio, who was beginning to realize all he owed him, had promised to carry out this mission in all good faith.

Like everyone in town and at court, Fabrizio had no doubt that his friend intended to return to the Ministry, and with even more power than he had previously wielded. The Count's anticipations very soon proved to be accurate: less than six weeks after his departure, Rassi was Prime Minister; Fabio Conti, the Minister of War; and the prisons, which the Count had nearly emptied, were teeming once again. The Prince, summoning such men to power, believed he was taking his revenge on the Duchess; he was madly in love and especially detested Count Mosca as his rival.

Fabrizio had a great deal to do; Monsignore Landriani, at the age of seventy-two, had fallen into a dreadful lethargy, and almost never left his Palace, so that it was up to his Coadjutor to perform virtually all his functions.

The Marchesa Crescenzi, overwhelmed with remorse, and alarmed by her spiritual director, had found an excellent way of avoiding Fabrizio's attentions. Taking as an excuse the last months of her first confinement, she had turned her own Palace into a sort of prison; but this Palace had an enormous garden. Fabrizio managed to make his way there, and placed on Clélia's favorite path bouquets of flowers arranged such a way as to convey a message, just as she had once done for him on his last evenings of imprisonment in the Farnese Tower.

The Marchesa was extremely annoyed by this effort; her emotions were swayed now by remorse, now by passion. For several months she did not permit herself to venture into her own Palace garden; she even had scruples about looking down into it.

Fabrizio was beginning to believe he was separated from her forever, and despair seized his soul as well. The world in which he was spending his life seemed to him mortally offensive, and had he not been intimately convinced that the Count could find no peace of mind outside the Ministry, he would have withdrawn to his little apartment in the Archbishop's Palace. He would have found it sweet to live alone with his thoughts, and no longer to hear human voices, save in the official exercise of his functions. "But," he said to himself, "in the interests of Count and Countess Mosca, no one can take my place."

The Prince continued treating him with a distinction which placed him in the first rank at Court, and such favor he owed in large part to himself. The extreme reserve which, in Fabrizio, derived from an indifference mounting almost to disgust for all the affectations or the petty passions which fill men's lives, had pricked the young Prince's vanity; he frequently said that Fabrizio was quite as witty as his aunt. The Prince's candid nature half realized the truth: which is that no one approached him with the same feelings at heart as Fabrizio. What even the most vulgar courtiers could not help noticing was that the consideration accorded Fabrizio was not at all what was due to a mere Coadjutor but even surpassed the attentions which the Sovereign granted the Archbishop. Fabrizio wrote to the Count that if ever the Prince had wit enough to recognize the chaos to which his Ministers Rassi, Fabio Conti, Zurla, and others of that ilk had reduced his affairs, he, Fabrizio, would be the natural channel by which he might alter the situation without excessively compromising his self-esteem.

Were it not for the fatal words "that child," *he wrote to Countess Mosca*, applied by a man of genius to an august personage, the august personage would already have exclaimed: Return at once and rid me of all these scoundrels. As of today, if the wife of the man of genius deigned to take a step, however insignificant it might be, the Count would be rapturously recalled; but he might enter through a far nobler door if he would wait till the fruit was ripe. Moreover, everyone is bored to tears in the Princess's salons, the only amusement being Rassi's folly, who since his ennoblement to the distinction of a Count has become maniacal about the degrees of nobility. Strict orders have just been given that anyone who cannot prove eight quarterings of nobility may no longer venture to appear at the Princess's evenings (these are the precise words of the text). Those already entitled to enter the Grand Gallery during the morning levees and to stand where the Sovereign passes on his way to Mass will continue to enjoy this privilege; but new arrivals must provide some proof of eight quarterings. Whereupon it was remarked that Rassi is evidently a man who gives no quarter . . .

It may be imagined that such letters were not to be entrusted to the post. Countess Mosca replied from Naples:

We have a concert every Thursday, and a *conversazione* every Sunday; our salons are so full you cannot move. The Count is delighted by his excavations, he spends twenty thousand francs a month on them, and has just sent for workmen from the Abruzzi mountains, who will cost him only twenty-three soldi a day. You should certainly come to see us. It must be more than twenty times now, ungrateful sir, that I have extended this invitation.

Fabrizio had no intention of obeying: the simple letter he wrote daily to the Count or to the Countess seemed an almost unendurable burden to him. The reader will forgive him when it is realized that a whole year passed in this fashion, without Fabrizio's being able to address a single word to the Marchesa. All his attempts to establish some sort of correspondence had been repulsed with horror. The habitual silence which, in his boredom, Fabrizio maintained everywhere except in the exercise of his clerical functions and at court, joined to the unblemished purity of his conduct, had gained him such extraordinary veneration that he finally determined to obey his aunt's advice:

The Prince has so much esteem for you, *she wrote him,* that you must soon expect a fall from grace; he will lavish signs of indifference upon you, and the cruel scorn of the courtiers will follow. These petty despots, honest though they may be, are as fickle as fashion itself, and for the same reason: boredom. You can find the strength to face up to the Sovereign's whims only in preaching. You know you improvise so nicely in verse—try speaking for half an hour about religion; you may utter heresies at first, but hire a learned and discreet theologian to help you write your sermons, and point out your faults to you, which you will set right the following day.

The kind of misery which a frustrated love creates in the soul makes a cruel burden of whatever requires action or attention. But Fabrizio told himself that his credit with the people, should he acquire any, might eventually be of use to his aunt and to the Count, for whom his respect increased every day, as affairs at Court afforded him some familiarity with human wickedness. He determined to preach some sermons, and his success, ensured by his extreme slenderness and his frayed cassock, was unparalleled. People found in his speech a fragrance of profound melancholy which, combined with his attractive countenance and the report of the high favor he enjoyed at Court, won every woman's heart. It was decided that he must have been one of the bravest captains in Napoléon's army. Soon this absurd fact was beyond all possible doubt. People reserved seats in the churches where he was to preach; the poor would take possession of them as a speculation from five o'clock in the morning.

So great was his success that Fabrizio finally conceived the idea, which altered everything in his soul, that the Marchesa Crescenzi, if only out of simple curiosity, might some day come to hear one of his sermons. Suddenly the delighted public discovered that his talent had increased twofold; he indulged himself, when he was moved, in images whose boldness would have made the most experienced orators hesitate; sometimes, forgetting himself, he yielded to moments of impassioned inspiration, and his entire audience dissolved in tears. But it was in vain that his *aggrottato* eye sought among so many faces upturned toward the pulpit the one whose presence would have constituted so great an event for him.

"But if ever I know such happiness," he told himself, "I shall either fall ill or lose my powers of speech entirely." To prevent the latter eventuality, he had composed a sort of tender and impassioned prayer, which he always kept beside him in the pulpit, on a stool; it was his intention to begin reading this text should the Marchesa's presence ever put him at a loss for words.

One day he happened to learn, through those of the Marchese's servants he had bribed, that orders had been given that the box of the *Casa Crescenzi* was to be prepared for the next night's performance at the principal theater of the town. It had been a year since the Marchesa had appeared at any public occasion, and it was a tenor who was creating a furor and filling the house every evening who was causing this departure from her habits. Fabrizio's first impulse was of extreme delight. "At last I'll be able to see her for a whole evening! They say she's very pale." And he tried to imagine what that charming countenance might look like, its colors half erased by the soul's conflicts.

His friend Ludovic, quite upset by what he called his master's madness, managed with great difficulty to find a box in the fourth ring, almost opposite the Marchesa's. An idea occurred to Fabrizio: "I hope to put it into her head to come to my sermon, and I shall choose a very small church, in order to be able to get a good look at her." Fabrizio usually preached at three in the afternoon. On the morning of the day the Marchesa was to go to the opera, he let it be known that since his duties would keep him at the Archbishop's Palace all day, he would preach as a special exception at half-past eight in the evening, in the little church of Santa Maria della Visitazione, located just opposite one of the wings of the Palazzo Crescenzi. Ludovic, on his behalf, offered a huge quantity of candles to the nuns of the Visitation, with a request to illuminate their church as bright as day. He had a whole company of Grenadier Guards, and one sentry was placed, bayonet at the ready, in front of each chapel, in order to prevent thieving.

The sermon was announced for half-past eight only, and by two o'clock the church being entirely filled, one can imagine the uproar produced in the quiet street over which towered the noble architecture of the Palazzo Crescenzi. Fabrizio had given notice that in honor of Our Lady of Pity he would preach on the pity a generous soul ought to have for someone in misfortune, even when he is guilty.

Disguised with infinite care, Fabrizio reached his box at the theater precisely when the door were opened and when there were still no lights. The performance began around eight, and a few moments after the hour he had that delight which no one can conceive if he has not experienced it, of seeing the door of the Crescenzi box opening; the Marchesa came in, whom he had not seen so well since the day she had given him her fan. Fabrizio feared he would faint with delight, feeling impulses so extraordinary that he said to himself, "Perhaps I'm about to die! What a delightful way of ending this melancholy existence! Perhaps I shall collapse in this box; the flock gathering at the Church of the Visitation will never see me arrive, and tomorrow they will learn that their future Archbishop fainted away in a box at the opera, disguised, moreover, as a servant and wearing livery! Good-bye reputation! And who cares anyway?"

Yet around quarter to nine, Fabrizio made an effort, and pulled himself together; he left his box in the fourth ring and with great difficulty managed to make his way on foot to the place where he was to get rid of his livery and put on a more suitable outfit. It was only around nine o'clock that he reached the Church of the Visitation, in a state of such pallor and weakness that the rumor spread through the church that the Signor Coadjutor would be unable to preach that evening. One can imagine the attentions lavished upon him by the nuns, at the grille of their inner parlor, to which he had retired, These ladies chattered a great deal; Fabrizio asked to be alone a few moments, then hurried to his pulpit. One of his assistants had informed him, around three o'clock, that the Church of the Visitation was entirely filled, but with people belonging to the lower classes, apparently attracted by the spectacle of the brightly lighted church. Entering the pulpit, Fabrizio was agreeably surprised to find all the seats occupied by young people of fashion and personages of the greatest distinction.

A few words of apology opened his sermon, received with stifled cries of admiration. Then came the impassioned description of the wretch on whom pity must be taken in order worthily to honor the *Madonna della Pietà,* who herself had suffered so on earth. The orator was greatly moved; there were moments when he could scarcely utter the words so as to be heard throughout this little church. In the eyes of all the women and of many of the men, he himself seemed to be the wretch on whom pity must be taken, so extreme was his pallor. A few minutes after the phrases of apology by which he had begun his discourse, it was noticed that he was not in his usual condition: his melancholy, that evening, appeared to be much deeper and more tender than usual. On one occasion, tears were seen in his eyes: at that moment there arose among his hearers a universal sigh so loud that the sermon itself was interrupted.

This first irregularity was followed by ten more; cries of admiration broke out, floods of tears were shed; at every moment such phrases as *"Ah, Santa Madonna!"* and *"Ah, Gran Dio!"* could be heard. Emotion was so general and so overpowering in this select audience that no one was ashamed of uttering such cries, and the people who were carried away did not seem ridiculous to their neighbors.

At the interval customarily allowed in the middle of the sermon, Fabrizio was told that absolutely no one was left in the theater; only one lady was still to be seen in her box, the Marchesa Crescenzi. During this interval, suddenly there was a great clamor in the church: the faithful were proposing to put up a statue to the Signor Coadjutor. His success in the second part of the sermon was so wild, and so worldly, the impulses of Christian contrition were so completely replaced by cries of quite profane admiration, that he felt he must offer, as he left the pulpit, some sort of reprimand to his auditors. Whereupon all of them left at once with a singularly shamefaced movement; and out in the street, everyone began applauding furiously and shouting: *"Evviva del Dongo!"*

Fabrizio hurriedly glanced at his watch and ran to a tiny barred window which illuminated the narrow passageway from the organ to the interior of the convent. As a concession to the incredible and unprecedented crowd which filled the street, the porter of the Palazzo Crescenzi had set a dozen torches in those iron fists one sees emerging from the outer walls of medieval Palaces. After a few minutes, and long before the cries had ceased, the event Fabrizio was awaiting so anxiously occurred: the Marchesa's carriage, returning from the theater, appeared in the street; the coachman was obliged to stop, and it was only at the slowest pace, and by means of many shouts, that the carriage could reach the door.

The Marchesa had been touched by the sublime music, as is the way of sorrowing hearts, but even more the perfect solitude of the performance when she had learned the reason for it. In the middle of the second act, while the splendid tenor was on stage, even the people in the pit had suddenly abandoned their places to try their luck and attempt to enter the Church of the Visitation. The Marchesa, seeing that she was blocked by the crowd before her own door, burst into tears. "I did not make the wrong choice!" she said to herself.

But precisely on account of this moment of tenderness, she firmly resisted the urgings of the Marchese and all the friends of her house, who could not imagine that she would not go to hear so amazing a preacher. "After all, he outdraws the best tenor in Italy!"

"If I see him, I am lost!" the Marchesa said to herself.

It was in vain that Fabrizio, whose talent seemed more brilliant every day, preached several more times in that little church so close to the Palazzo Crescenzi; he never caught sight of Clélia, who ultimately took offense at this insistence on coming to disturb her quiet street, after having already driven her out of her own garden.

Glancing at the faces of the women who listened to him, Fabrizio had noticed some while back an extremely pretty dark little face, with eyes that seemed to dart flames. These splendid eyes were usually bathed in tears by the eighth or ninth sentence of the sermon. When Fabrizio was obliged to say things he himself found overlong and tiresome, he gladly rested his gaze on this countenance whose youth delighted him. He learned that this young person was called Anetta Marini, and that she was the sole daughter and heiress of the richest cloth merchant in Parma, who had died a few months earlier.

Soon the name of this Anetta Marini, the cloth merchant's daughter, was on everyone's lips; she had fallen madly in love with Fabrizio. When the famous sermons began, her marriage had just been arranged with Giacomo Rassi, the elder son of the Minister of Justice, whom she found by no means unattractive; but no sooner had she heard Monsignore Fabrizio a couple of times than she declared that she no longer wished to marry; and when asked the reason for such a singular change of heart, she replied that it was not suitable for an honorable girl to marry one man when she had fallen madly in love with another. At first her family sought to learn, without success, who this other man might be.

But the burning tears Anetta shed during the sermons led them to the truth of the matter; her mother and her uncles having asked her if she loved Monsignore Fabrizio, she boldly replied that since the truth had been discovered, she would not demean herself by a lie; she added that, having no hope of marrying the man she adored, she wished at least no longer to offend her eyes by the sight of the Contino Rassi. This flouting of the son of a man pursued by the envy of the entire bourgeoisie of Parma became, in two days, the talk of the town. Anetta Marini's reply was thought charming, and was repeated by everyone. It was mentioned in the Palazzo Crescenzi, as everywhere else.

Clélia was careful not to open her mouth on such a subject in her own salon; but she put certain questions to her chambermaid, and the following Sunday, after hearing Mass in her Palace chapel, she took her chambermaid with her in her carriage and went in search of a second Mass in Signorina Marini's parish. There she found all the town gallants assembled, attracted by the same object; these gentlemen were standing close to the door. Soon, from the great stir made among them, the Marchesa realized that Signorina Marini must be entering the church; Clélia found herself quite advantageously placed to see her, and in spite of her piety, paid little or no attention to the Mass. She found this bourgeois beauty to have a certain look of self-confidence which, she considered, might have been more suitable in a woman married for a number of years. Aside from that, she was pretty enough, in her petite way, and her eyes, as people say in Lombardy, seemed to make conversation with the things they looked at. The Marchesa escaped before the Mass was over.

The following day, the friends of the Crescenzi household, who came regularly to spend the evening, had a new extravagance of Anetta Marini's to gossip about. Since her mother, fearing she would do something foolish, granted her only the tiniest allowance, Anetta had gone to offer a fine diamond ring, which her father had given her, to the famous Hayez, then in Parma decorating the salons of the Palazzo

Crescenzi, and had asked him to paint a portrait of Signor del Dongo; but she wanted this portrait to show him dressed simply in black, and not in clerical garb. Now, the evening before, little Anetta's mother had been quite surprised, and even more scandalized, to find in her daughter's bedroom a magnificent portrait of Fabrizio del Dongo, set in the finest frame that had been gilded in Parma in the last twenty years.

CHAPTER TWENTY-EIGHT

Swept away by the course of events, we have had no time to sketch the comical race of courtiers who swarmed at the Court of Parma and made asinine comments on the incidents we have related.

What, in this country, makes a minor nobleman, provided with an income of three or four thousand lire, worthy to figure in black stockings at the Prince's levees is first of all never to have read Voltaire and Rousseau: this stipulation is anything but difficult to fulfill. Next, he must be capable of speaking sympathetically about the Sovereign's cold, or of the latest crate of mineral specimens just received from Saxony. If, after this, he does not miss a single day's Mass all year long, if he could count among the number of his intimate friends two or three fat monks, the Prince would deign to address him once a year, a fortnight before or a fortnight after New Year's Day, which would grant him great distinction in his parish, and the tax-collector would not dare harass him excessively if he happened to be in arrears with the yearly sum of a hundred francs with which his small estates were taxed.

Signor Gonzo was a poor devil of this sort, noble indeed, who, beyond the fact that he possessed some small fortune, had obtained through the influence of the Marchese Crescenzi a splendid post, bringing in eleven hundred and fifty thousand francs a year. This man could well have dined at home, but he had one passion: he was only at his ease and happy when he found himself in the salon of some great personage who would snap at him from time to time: "Hold your tongue, Gonzo, you're nothing but a fool." This judgment was prompted by bad temper, for Gonzo almost invariably had more brains than the great personage. He would speak on every topic and quite gracefully: moreover, he was ready to change opinions according to a frown from the master of the house. In truth, though quite astute with regard to his own interests, he hadn't an idea in his head, and when the Prince happened not to have a cold, he was occasionally at a loss for words upon entering a salon.

What had won Gonzo a reputation in Parma was a magnificent *tricorne*, embellished with a rather moth-eaten black plume, which he wore even with evening-dress; but you had to have seen the way he carried that plume, either on his head or in his hand; here was his talent, and his whole importance. He inquired with authentic anxiety after the the health of the Marchesa's little dog, and had the Palazzo Crescenzi caught fire, he would have risked his life to save one of those fine gold-brocaded armchairs which for so many years had snagged his black-silk breeches, whenever it so happened that he ventured to sit down on one for a moment.

Seven or eight individuals of this species came at seven every evening to the Marchesa Crescenzi's salon. No sooner were they seated than a lackey magnificently appareled in daffodil-yellow livery all covered with silver braid, as well as the red waistcoat which completed such magnificence, came to collect the hats and canes of these poor devils. He was immediately followed by a footman bearing an infinitesimal cup of coffee on a silver-filigree stem, and every half-hour a majordomo, wearing a sword and a splendid coat in the French style, passed around ices.

Half an hour after the threadbare minor courtiers, there would arrive five or six officers talking in loud voices and in a very military manner, usually discussing the number and the type of buttons which ought to be on a soldier's uniform if the commanding general was to win victories. It would not have been discreet to allude in this salon to a French newspaper; for even when the news was found to be quite agreeable—for example, fifty Liberals shot in Spain—the bearer of such news nonetheless remained convicted of having read a French newspaper. The crowning stroke of all these people's skill was to obtain every ten years an increase of one hundred and fifty francs in their pensions. It was in this fashion that the Prince shared with his nobles the pleasure of ruling over the peasantry and the bourgeoisie of Parma.

The chief personage, without question, of the Crecenzi salon was Cavaliere Foscarini, an entirely honest man who had therefore been in prison, off and on, under every regime. He was a member of that celebrated Chamber of Deputies which, in Milan, had rejected the Registration Edict presented by Napoléon, an action of extremely rare occurrence in history. Cavaliere Foscarini, after having for twenty years been the friend of the Marchese's mother, had remained the influential man of the household. He always had some amusing tale to tell, but nothing escaped his shrewd notice; and the young Marchesa, who felt herself guilty at heart, trembled before him. As Gonzo had a veritable passion for the great nobleman, who would say rude things to him and reduce him to tears once or twice a year, his compulsion was to seek to do him little services; and had he not been paralyzed by the habits of extreme poverty, he might have succeeded occasionally, for he was not lacking in a certain degree of finesse and a much greater amount of effrontery.

Gonzo, as we know him, quite disdained the Marchesa Crescenzi, for she had never in her life spoken a rude word to him; but, after all, she was the wife of that famous Marchese Crescenzi, the Princess's *Cavaliere d'Onore,* who once or twice a month would say to Gonzo: "Hold your tongue, Gonzo, you're nothing but a fool."

Gonzo noticed that everything people said about little Anetta Marini momentarily drew the Marchesa out of her state of revery and indifference in which she remained habitually plunged until the stroke of eleven, when she would make tea and offer a cup to each man present, addressing him by name. Whereupon, at the moment of retiring, she seemed to find a brief spell of gaiety, which was the time people chose to recite to her certain satirical sonnets.

Excellent things of this kind are composed in Italy: it is the only kind of literature which still shows a little life; in truth it is not subject to the censor, and the courtiers of the *Casa Crescenzi* would invariably preface their sonnet by these words: "Will the Signora Marchesa permit the recitation of a very poor sonnet?" And when the sonnet had met with laughter and been repeated two or three times, one of the officers never failed to exclaim: "Our Minister of Police certainly ought to see to it that the perpetrators of such infamies are hanged!"

Bourgeois circles, on the contrary, greeted these sonnets with open admiration, and the lawyers' clerks would sell copies of them.

From the sort of curiosity shown by the Marchesa, Gonzo realized that the little Marini girl's beauty had been excessively praised—after all, she had a huge fortune besides—and that the Marchesa was jealous. Since with his incessant smile and his utter effrontery toward everything that was not noble, Gonzo made his way everywhere, the very next day he entered the Marchesa's salon carrying his plumed hat in a certain triumphant manner which was observed in him only once or twice each year, when the Prince had said to him: "*Addio,* Gonzo."

After respectfully greeting the Marchesa, Gonzo did not withdraw as was his habit to take his place on the armchair which had just been pushed forward for him. He stood in the center of the group and exclaimed abruptly: "I have seen the portrait of Monsignor del Dongo!"

Clélia was so surprised that she was obliged to lean on the arm of her chair; she attempted to withstand the storm, but was soon compelled to abandon the salon. "You must admit, my poor Gonzo, that you are exceptionally clumsy sometimes," haughtily exclaimed one of the officers who was finishing his fourth ice. "How could you not know that the Coadjutor, who was one of the bravest colonels in Napoléon's army, once played a criminal trick on the Marchesa's father by walking out of the Fortress where General Conti was in command, as if he had walked out of the Steccata?" (The Steccata is the principal church in Parma.)

"Indeed there are many things I do not know, my dear Captain, and I am a poor imbecile who makes blunders all day long."

This retort, quite in the Italian style, produced laughter at the brilliant officer's expense. The Marchesa soon returned; she had plucked up her courage and was not without some vague hope of being able herself to admire this portrait of Fabrizio, which people said was so fine. She praised the talents of its creator, Hayez. Without realizing it, she offered charming smiles to Gonzo, who was glancing slyly at the officer. Since all the other courtiers of the household were indulging in the same pleasure, the officer made his escape, vowing a deadly hatred to Gonzo, who had triumphed over him and who, when taking his leave later that evening, was invited to dinner the following day.

"And here's another piece of news!" exclaimed Gonzo after dinner the next day, when the servants had left the room. "It seems that our Coadjutor has fallen in love with the little Marini girl!"

One can imagine the distress which filled Clélia's heart upon hearing such an extraordinary sentence. Even the Marchese was moved. "But Gonzo, my friend, you're completely off the track, as usual! And you really should speak a little more discreetly about someone who has had the honor of playing whist with His Highness some eleven times!"

"Well, Signor Marchese," Gonzo replied with the coarseness of people of this sort, "I can assure you that he would just as soon play a game or two with the little Marini girl. But it is quite enough that such details displease you—they no longer exist for me; more than anything else in the world I would not distress my dear Marchese."

Regularly, after dinner, the Marchese would retire to take a nap. Today he had no such intention; but Gonzo would rather have cut out his tongue than have added a single word concerning the little Marini girl; and each time he began to speak, he managed it so that the Marchese might hope he was returning to the Marini girl's *amours.* Gonzo possessed to a superior degree that Italian form of wit which consists in exquisitely postponing all mention of the longed-for word. The poor Marchese, dying of curiosity, was obliged to make the advances; he said to Gonzo that, when he had the pleasure of dining with him, he invariably ate twice as much. Gonzo failed to understand, and began describing a splendid gallery of paintings being collected by the Marchesa Balbi, the mistress of the late Prince; three or four times he mentioned Hayez, with the deliberate accents of the profoundest admiration. The Marchese said to himself: "All right, now he's coming to the portrait commissioned by the Marini girl!" But this was precisely what Gonzo was careful not to do. The clock struck five, which greatly vexed the Marchese, who was in the habit of ordering his carriage at five-thirty, after his nap, to drive to the *Corso*. "This is where your stupid chatter takes you," he said harshly to Gonzo; "you're making me get to the *Corso* after the Princess, whom I serve as *Cavaliere d'Onore* and who may have orders to give me. All right, be quick about it! Tell me in so many words, if you can, about this so-called love-affair of Monsignore the Coadjutor!"

But Gonzo wanted to keep this story for the ears of the Marchesa, who had invited him to supper; hence he rushed in a very few words through the episode asked of him, and the Marchese, half asleep, hurried off to take his nap. Gonzo assumed a very different manner with the poor Marchesa. She had remained so young and naïve amidst her high estate, that she supposed it was her obligation to make up for the rudeness with which the Marchese had just spoken to Gonzo. Charmed by this success, the latter recovered all his eloquence, and made it a pleasure, no less than a duty, to enter with her into an infinity of details.

Little Anetta Marini would give as much as a sequin for each seat that was reserved for her at the sermons; she always came with two of her aunts and her father's old bookkeeper. These seats, which she had reserved the night before, were usually chosen almost facing the pulpit, but slightly to one side of the high altar, for she had noticed that the Coadjutor frequently turned toward the altar. Now, what the public had also noticed, was that *not infrequently* the young Coadjutor's eloquent eyes readily paused as they encountered the piquant beauty of the young heiress, apparently quite attentively, for once he had met her eyes, his sermon became more learned, the quotations abounded, and there were no longer those gestures that come from the heart; and the ladies, for whom the sermon's interest ceased almost at once, began staring at the Marini girl and speaking unkindly about her.

Clélia insisted on hearing all these singular details three times over. At the third repetition, she became quite dreamy; she was calculating that it had been precisely fourteen months since she had seen Fabrizio. "Would there be anything so terribly wrong," she asked herself, "in spending an hour in church, not in order to see Fabrizio but to hear a famous preacher? Besides, I'll take a seat far away from the pulpit, and I'll look only once at Fabrizio when I come in, and then one other time at the end of the sermon. . . . No," Clélia said to herself, "it's not Fabrizio I'm going to see, I'm going to hear the remarkable preacher!" Amidst all these rationalizations, the Marchesa suffered some remorse; her behavior had been so irreproachable for fourteen months! "Well," she said to herself in order to gain some peace of mind, "if the first woman who comes tonight has been to hear Monsignore del Dongo preach, I'll go too; if she hasn't gone, then I'll stay away."

Once this decision was made, the Marchesa made Gonzo a happy man by saying to him: "Try to find out what day the Coadjutor is preaching, and in what church. Tonight, before you leave, I may have a little errand for you to run for me."

No sooner had Gonzo left for the *Corso* than Clélia went to take a breath of air in the garden of her *palazzo*. She failed to consider the objection that for ten months she had not set foot out there. She was lively now, animated; there was color in her cheeks. That evening, as each boring visitor entered the salon, her heart pounded with emotion. Finally Gonzo was announced, who saw at the first glance that he was going to be an indispensable man for the next week. "The Marchesa is jealous of the Marini girl, and my word, it would be as good as a play," he said to himself, "with the Marchesa acting the heroine, and little Anetta as the soubrette, and Monsignore del Dongo the lover! My word, the seats would be worth two francs and cheap at the price!" He was overjoyed, and for the whole evening he interrupted everyone and told the most preposterous stories (for example, about the famous actress and the Marquis de Pequigny, which he had heard the evening before from a French traveler). The Marchesa, for her part, could not sit still; she walked about the salon, passed into an adjoining gallery where the Marchese had hung no painting that cost less than twenty thousand francs. These pictures spoke so clear a language that evening that they exhausted the Marchesa's heart with high feelings. Finally she heard the double doors open; she ran back to the salon; it was the Marchesa Raversi! However, even as she was offering her the customary compliments, Clélia felt herself losing the power of speech. The

Marchesa obliged her to ask her question twice: "What do you think of our fashionable preacher?"

"I used to think he was nothing but a petty intriguer, a worthy nephew of the illustrious Countess Mosca; but the last time he preached, you know, it was at the Church of the Visitation, just across the road there, he was so sublime that all my antagonism vanished and I found him to be the most eloquent man I have ever heard."

"So you attended one of his sermons?" Clélia asked, trembling with happiness.

"Why, my dear," laughed the Marchesa, "weren't you listening to what I said? I wouldn't miss such an occasion for anything in the world. They say his lungs are affected, and that soon he won't be preaching anymore!"

No sooner had the Marchesa left than Clélia summoned Gonzo to the gallery. "I have almost decided," she told him, "to hear this preacher they talk so much about. When will he be preaching?"

"Next Monday, which is to say, in three days; and it's as though he had guessed Your Excellency's intentions, for he's coming to preach at the Church of the Visitation."

Not everything was settled, but Clélia could no longer control her voice; she walked up and down the gallery five or six times, without adding another word. Gonzo said to himself: "That must be vengeance working inside her. How could anyone be so insolent as to escape from prison, especially when you have the honor to be jailed by a hero like General Fabio Conti!" And he added aloud, with splendid irony, "Moreover you must make haste; his lungs are affected. I heard Doctor Rambo say that he doesn't have a year to live. God is punishing him for having broken his bond by treacherously escaping from the Fortress."

The Marchesa sat down on a divan in the gallery and signaled to Gonzo to do the same. After a few moments she handed him a tiny purse in which she had put several sequins. "I want you to reserve four seats for me."

"May poor Gonzo be permitted to slip in among Your Excellency's suite?"

"Of course; reserve five places. . . . I don't care at all," she added, "about being close to the pulpit; but I'd like to get a look at Signorina Marini, they say she's so pretty."

The Marchesa could scarcely live through the three days separating her from the famous Monday, the day of the sermon. Gonzo, for whom it was a signal honor to be seen in public in the company of so great a lady, had put on his French coat with his sword; nor was this all: taking advantage of the proximity of the Palazzo Crescenzi, he had had carried into the church a splendid gilded armchair for the Marchesa, which was regarded as the last insolence by the bourgeois parishioners. The reader may well imagine the poor Marchesa's feelings when she caught sight of this chair, which had been placed just opposite the pulpit. Clélia was so embarrassed, lowering her eyes and shrinking back into a corner of this enormous armchair, that she had not even the courage to glance at the little Marini girl, whom Gonzo pointed out to her with an effrontery she could not get over. Any person not of noble birth was absolutely nothing in this courtier's eyes.

Fabrizio appeared in the pulpit; he was so thin, so pale, so *consumed,* that Clélia's eyes immediately filled with tears. Fabrizio spoke a few words, then stopped, as if his voice had suddenly failed him; in vain he attempted to begin one sentence after another; he turned away and took up a written sheet.

"Brethren," he said, "a wretched soul and one worthy of your entire compassion implores you through my lips to pray for the end of his torments, which will cease only with his life."

Fabrizio read the remainder of his sheet very slowly; but so expressive was his voice that before the middle of the prayer everyone was in tears, even Gonzo. "At least no one will notice me," the Marchesa said to herself as she burst into tears.

While he was reading the writing on the sheet of paper, Fabrizio happened upon two or three ideas concerning the state of the unhappy man for whom he had come to seek the prayers of the faithful. Soon his thoughts came to him in abundance. Seeming to address the public, he was speaking only to the Marchesa. He ended his sermon a little sooner than was usual because, despite all his efforts, his tears overcame him to such a degree that he could no longer speak intelligibly. The best judges found this sermon singular but equal at least, with regard to pathos, to the famous one preached with the lighted candles. As for Clélia, no sooner had she heard the first ten lines of the prayer read aloud by Fabrizio than she considered it as a hideous crime to have been able to spend fourteen months without seeing him. Returning home, she went to bed in order to be able to think of Fabrizio in perfect freedom; and the next day, quite early, Fabrizio received a note in the following words:

> We rely upon your honor; find four *bravi* whose discretion you can count on and tomorrow, on the stroke of midnight at the Steccata, be waiting outside a little door at number 19 in the Strada San Paolo. Remember that you may be attacked, do not come alone.

On recognizing this heavenly handwriting, Fabrizio fell to his knees and burst into tears. "At last!" he exclaimed. "After fourteen months and eight days! Farewell my sermons!"

It would take too long to describe the various kinds of folly which beset, that day, the hearts of Fabrizio and Clélia. The little door indicated in the note was none other than that of the orangery of the Palazzo Crescenzi, and ten times during the day Fabrizio found a way to go look at it. He armed himself, and alone, just before midnight, walking fast, he was passing close to this door when to his inexpressible delight he heard a familiar voice say to him in almost a whisper: "Come in here, friend of my heart."

Cautiously Fabrizio entered and found himself in the orangery itself, but opposite a heavily barred window raised some three or four feet above the ground. The darkness was intense. Fabrizio had heard some sort of noise up in this window, and when he explored the grille with his hand, he felt a hand thrust through the bars to take his own and raise it to lips which gave it a kiss.

"It is I," said a beloved voice, "who have come here to tell you I love you, and to ask if you are willing to obey me."

The reader may imagine Fabrizio's answer, his joy, and his amazement; after the first raptures, Clélia said to him: "I have made a vow to the Madonna, as you know, never to see you; that is why I am receiving you in this darkness. I want you to know that if you ever forced me to look at you in daylight, everything would be over between us. But first of all, I do not want you to preach before Anetta Marini, and do not imagine that I could have had so foolish an idea as to have an armchair brought into the house of God."

"My angel, I shall never preach again before anyone! I only preached in the hope of one day seeing you."

—

Here we shall ask permission to pass, without saying a single word about them, over an interval of three years.

At the period our story resumes, it had already been a long while since Count Mosca had returned to Parma as Prime Minister, and more powerful than ever.

After these three years of divine happiness, Fabrizio's soul underwent a caprice of affection which managed to change everything. The Marchesa had a charming little boy two years old, *Sandrino,* who was his mother's joy; he was always at her side or in the Marchese Crescenzi's lap; Fabrizio, on the contrary, almost never saw him; he could not bear the idea of the child's loving another father. He conceived the notion of taking the boy away before his memories had grown quite distinct.

In the long hours of each day when the Marchesa could not be with her lover, Sandrino's presence consoled her; for we must confess a thing which will seem strange north of the Alps: despite her transgressions, she had remained faithful to her vow; she had promised the Madonna, it may be recalled, *never to see* Fabrizio; such had been her very words: consequently she received him only by night, and there was never any light in the apartment.

But every evening, he was received by his beloved; and what is admirable, in the midst of a Court devoured by curiosity and boredom, Fabrizio's precautions had been so skillfully calculated, that this *amicizia,* as it is called in Lombardy, was never even suspected. Such love was too intense for there not to have been quarrels; Clélia was too subject to jealousy, but almost invariably the quarrels proceeded from another cause. Fabrizio had taken advantage of some public ceremony in

order to be in the same place as the Marchesa and to look at her; she then made some excuse to leave at once, and for a long while she banished her lover.

Many people at the court of Parma were astonished that no intrigue should be known in connection with a woman so remarkable for her loveliness and for the loftiness of her soul; she roused passions which inspired any number of follies, and Fabrizio was frequently jealous.

The good Archbishop Landriani had died long since; Fabrizio's exemplary conduct and eloquence had caused him to be forgotten; his own older brother had died, and all the family property had reverted to him. It was at this time that he distributed annually, to the vicars and parish priests of his diocese, the hundred and some thousand francs which the Archbishopric of Parma brought him in.

It would have been difficult to conceive of a life more honored, more honorable, and more useful than the one Fabrizio had created for himself, when everything was upset by this unfortunate caprice of affection.

"Because of this vow which I respect and which nonetheless constitutes the bane of my existence, since you refuse to see me by daylight," he said to Clélia one night, "I am obliged to live constantly alone, having no other entertainment but work; and even work fails me. Amidst this melancholy and austere way of spending the long hours of every day, one idea has come to me, which is indeed my torment and which I have vainly fought against for six months: my son will never love me; he never even hears my name. Raised amidst the agreeable luxuries of the Palazzo Crescenzi, he scarcely knows who I am. The rare occasions when I do see him, I think of his mother, of whose heavenly beauty he reminds me and whom I cannot look upon, and he must find my face a serious one, which for children means sad . . ."

"Now," said the Marchesa, "what is all this alarming speech of yours leading to?"

"To having my son back; I want him to live with me; I want to see him every day, I want him to learn to love me; I want to love him myself, at my leisure. Since a doom unique in all the world deprives me of that happiness enjoyed by so many loving hearts, and since I do not spend my life with everything I love, at least I want to have at my side the being who recalls you to my heart, who replaces you, in some sense. Men and affairs weigh upon me in my obligatory solitude; you know that *ambition* has ever been an empty word for me, from the moment I had the happiness to be locked up by Barbone, and all that is not felt in the soul seems absurd to me in the melancholy which, in your absence, overwhelms me."

The reader can imagine the intense suffering with which her lover's grief filled poor Clélia's soul; her sadness was all the more intense in that she felt that Fabrizio was partly justified. She went so far as to wonder whether she ought to try breaking her vow; but she also felt that so worldly an arrangement would not put her conscience at peace, and perhaps an angry Heaven would punish her for this new crime.

On the other hand, if she agreed to yield to Fabrizio's entirely natural desire, if she tried not to hurt that affectionate soul she knew so well, and whose peace of mind her singular vow so strangely compromised, what likelihood was there of abducting the only son of one of the greatest noblemen in Italy without the deception being discovered? The Marchese Crescenzi would spend enormous sums, would himself lead the investigations, and sooner or later the abduction would be found out. There was only one means of warding off this danger, which was to send the boy far away—to Edinburgh, for instance, or to Paris; but to this a mother's affection could never consent. The other means suggested by Fabrizio, and indeed the more reasonable solution, had something sinister about it, and almost more alarming in this desperate mother's eyes; they would have to feign the child's illness, said Fabrizio; he would grow steadily worse, and finally die in the Marchese Crescenzi's absence.

A repugnance which, in Clélia, amounted to terror, caused a rupture which could not last.

Clélia claimed that they must not tempt God; that this beloved son was the fruit of a crime, and that if they further roused the fire of Heaven, God would not fail to take the boy for his own. Fabrizio spoke once again of his strange destiny:

"The station in life to which chance has called me," he said to

Clélia, "and my love compel me to an eternal solitude; I cannot, like most of my fellow men, enjoy the sweetness of an intimate society, since you will receive me only in a darkness, which reduces to no more than moments, actually, that part of my life I can spend with you . . ."

Many tears were shed. Clélia fell ill, but she loved Fabrizio too greatly to refuse forever the terrible sacrifice he asked of her. To all appearances, Sandrino fell ill; the Marchese quickly summoned the most renowned physicians, and at this moment Clélia encountered a terrible difficulty she had not foreseen; she had to prevent this beloved child from taking any of the remedies prescribed by the doctors; it was no small matter.

The child, kept in bed more than was good for his health, became really ill. How to explain to the physician the cause of this sickness? Torn by two conflicting interests both so dear to her, Clélia was on the verge of losing her mind. Must she consent to an apparent recovery, and thereby sacrifice the whole consequence of a long and painful deception? Fabrizio, for his part, could neither forgive himself for the violence with which he ruled his beloved's heart nor renounce his plan. He had found a way to be admitted every night to the sick child's room, which had produced a further complication. The Marchesa came to nurse her son, and on some occasions Fabrizio was compelled to see her by the light of the candles, which seemed to Clélia's poor sick heart a terrible sin which presaged Sandrino's death. It was in vain that the most renowned casuists, consulted as to obedience to a vow in a case where the fulfillment of that vow would obviously be harmful, had replied that the vow could not be regarded as broken in a criminal fashion, so long as the person bound by a promise to God dissolved that promise not for the idle pleasure of the senses but in order not to cause an obvious evil. Yet the Marchesa was in despair nonetheless, and Fabrizio saw the moment approaching when his strange idea would effect the deaths of both Clélia and his son.

He had recourse to his intimate friend Count Mosca, who, old diplomat that he was, was touched by this love story, most of which was quite unknown to him.

"I can arrange the Marchese's absence for you for five or six days at least: when do you want this to happen?"

Some time afterward, Fabrizio came to tell the Count that every-thing was in readiness for him to take advantage of such an absence.

Two days later, as the Marchese was returning from one of his es-tates near Mantua, certain "brigands," apparently hired to carry out a personal vendetta, abducted him though without in any way mistreat-ing him, and placed him in a boat which took three days to make its way down the Po, covering the same route Fabrizio had taken so long ago after the famous Giletti business. On the fourth day, the brigands deposited the Marchese on a desert island in the Po, after being care-ful to rob him completely and to leave him no money or belongings of any value whatever. It took the Marchese two whole days to return to his *palazzo* in Parma; he found it draped with black, and his entire household in mourning.

This abduction, so skillfully arranged, had a deadly consequence: Sandrino, established in secret in a large and splendid house where the Marchesa came to see him almost every day, died after several months. Clélia believed she had been stricken by a just punishment, for having been unfaithful to her vow to the Madonna: so often had she seen Fa-brizio by candlelight, and even twice in broad daylight, and with such tender raptures during Sandrino's illness! She survived this beloved son no more than a few months herself, though she had the sweetness of dying in her lover's arms.

Fabrizio was too much in love, and too much a believer, to resort to suicide; he hoped to meet Clélia again in a better world, but he was too intelligent not to feel that he had a great deal for which to atone.

A few days after Clélia's death, he signed several settlements by which he assured a pension of a thousand francs to each of his ser-vants, and kept a similar pension for himself; he gave estates worth an income of nearly a hundred thousand lire to Countess Mosca; a simi-lar sum to the Marchesa del Dongo, his mother; and whatever might remain of the paternal fortune to one of his sisters who had married impecuniously. The following day, after having sent to the proper au-thorities his resignation of the Archbishopric and of all the positions which the favor of Ernesto V and the friendship of his Prime Minis-ter had successively heaped upon him, he retired to the Charterhouse of Parma, situated in the woods bordering the Po, some two leagues from Sacca.

Countess Mosca had strongly approved, at the time, her husband's resumption of his Ministry, but she herself had never been willing to set foot within the State of Ernesto V. She held Court at Vignano, a quarter of a league from Casalmaggiore, on the left bank of the Po, and consequently within Austrian territory. In that magnificent Palace of Vignano, which the Count had built for her, she was at home on Thursdays to all the high society of Parma, and every day to her many friends. Fabrizio would not have let a day pass without coming to Vignano. The Countess, in a word, united all the appearances of happiness, but she lived only a very short time after Fabrizio, whom she adored and who spent but one year in his Charterhouse.

The prisons of Parma were empty, the Count enormously rich, Ernesto V adored by his subjects, who compared his government to that of the Grand Dukes of Tuscany.

TO THE HAPPY FEW

NOTES

Parma: Stendhal probably
selected Parma as the site of
his novel's chief action because he had found here the
initial *donnée* of his narrative
in an ancient chronicle concerning the origins of the
greatness of the Farnese
family which had ruled over
Parma since the sixteenth
century. Further, Stendhal
had visited the city in 1811
and again in 1814; he knew
it well enough to speak of it
readily, little enough to feel
hampered by any strict
accuracy in describing its
topographical details. Then,
too, Parma was the city of
Correggio, perhaps Stend-
hal's favorite painter; in his
letter of thanks to Balzac he
observes: "The entire character of the Duchess San-
severina is copied from
Correggio (that is, produces
on my soul the same effect
as Correggio)."

4 **Gros:** Antoine-Jean, Baron
Gros, 1771–1835. A pupil of
David, introduced in 1793
by Josephine into Napoleon's
entourage; he was made a
baron by Charles X.

5 **Lieutenant Robert:**
Though he appears only in
the novel's first pages, this
character is of great impor-

tance, since Stendhal has on three or four occasions indicated that he was Fabrizio's real father. All of Stendhal's young heroes have a similarly questionable paternity, perhaps a logical consequence of Stendhal's resentment of his own father.

9 **Italian Legion:** In 1797 Napoleon created an Italian Legion, consisting of some seven hundred infantry and three hundred cavalry.

Directory: The Directory succeeded the Convention in October 1795 and governed until Napoleon seized power in November 1799.

Marengo: In the Battle of Marengo (in Piedmont, Northern Italy) on June 14, 1800, Napoleon won a decisive victory over the Austrians.

10 *bocche di Cattaro:* An inlet on the Adriatic coast south of Dubrovnik.

Many serious authors: Stendhal's ironic reference to Sterne's procedure in *Tristram Shandy.*

18 **Beresina:** During the retreat from Moscow (1813), Napoleon's armies were attacked while crossing the River Beresina; some ninety thousand men were lost during this retreat. Stendhal himself, bearing dispatches from Josephine, was one of the survivors.

26 **Gulf of Juan:** Having escaped from Elba, Napoleon and some seven hundred French troops had landed on the southern French coast on March 1, and would reach Paris within three weeks.

27 **famous poet Monti:** Vincenzo Monti (1754–1828). A classicizing poet who in the lines Fabrizio paraphrases laments the death of Mascheroni, who had welcomed the Napoleonic liberation of Italy.

32 **Piedmont:** Piedmont was part of the French Empire, and its male inhabitants subject to conscription.

36 **napoleon:** A gold coin worth twenty francs.

61 **Fénelon:** François de La Mothe-Fénelon (1651–1715), theologian, wrote a celebrated pedagogical romance *Télémaque* in 1699 for the grandson of Louis XIV, of whom he had been appointed tutor; in 1695, he was made Archbishop of Cambrai.

74 **Silvio Pellico** (1789–1854): His account of his years of imprisonment by the Austrians, *My Prisons*, was published in 1832.

82 **Signor Andryane:** Author of another account of imprisonment under the Austrians, *Memoirs of a Political Prisoner in the Spielberg*. The Spielberg was an Austrian fortress-prison in Brünn (Brno).

83 **Bayard:** Chevalier de Bayard (c. 1473–1524), *"le chevalier sans peur et sans reproche"* (the fearless and blameless knight).

87 **Pietragrua:** Stendhal lists names of women he had known in Milan, specifically Angela Pietragrua with whom he had been in love.

89 *Constitutionnel:* A French newspaper representing Liberal opinion and banned throughout Austrian territory.

106 *scagliola:* inlaid marble.

Joseph II (1741–1790): King of Germany and Holy Roman Emperor.

107 **Lafayette:** Stendhal had met Lafayette on several occasions and was impressed by his "noble affability."

112 **Canoness:** An honorary title conferred on lay persons by certain religious communities.

131 *Monitore* (*Moniteur*): A Liberal French daily founded in 1789.

Marchesa San Felice: During the occupation of Naples by the French, the Marchesa de San Felice (1768–1800) was instrumental in disclosing an anti-Republican plot. When the Royalists regained control of Naples in 1799, the Marchesa was arrested and condemned to death, and executed in 1800.

132 **Polyeucte:** Character in a tragedy by Corneille produced in 1643, in which Polyeucte, the governor of Armenia under the Emperor Decius, is baptized and suffers martyrdom. The story became the substance of many operas, notably by Donizetti.

144 *La Locandiera:* In this play of 1753, regarded as Goldoni's masterpiece, the mistress of an inn is betrothed to a young man called Fabrizio.

172 **Themistocles:** In Napoleon's letter of July 14, 1815, to the Prince Regent, he seeks protection under British law and compares himself to Themistocles, the Athenian general exiled from Athens and seeking asylum with his former enemy the king of Persia.

190 **Charterhouse of Velleja:** Stendhal's invention.

201 **Madonna of Cimabue:** No Madonna by the thirteenth century Italian painter exists in the church at San Petronio.

baiocchi: A copper coin of low value, comparable to a penny.

210 *Cascata del Reno:* The falls on the river Reno, west of Bologna.

211 **Bouffes Parisiens:** A theatre company, initially Italian, specializing in comedy.

212 **Tancred** (Tancredi): A hero of Tasso's *Gerusalemme liberata.*

214 **Burati** (1778–1832): A satirist and poet writing in Venetian dialect, whom Stendhal knew personally.

252 **Parmigianino** (1503–1540): A Mannerist painter noted for his portraits and religious paintings.

Intelligenti pauca!: [Latin] A word to the wise is sufficient!

270 **Judith:** In the Apocrypha, a Hebrew maiden who saves her town of Bethulia by seducing the besieging general, Holofernes, and beheading him while he sleeps.

279 **Rasori:** Giovanni Rasori (1766–1837), a physician of

liberal sympathies whom Stendhal had known in Milan.

285 **Almaviva:** Count Almaviva and his servant the barber Figaro, characters in Stendhal's favorite operas, Mozart's *Marriage of Figaro* and Rossini's *Barber of Seville,* both based on plays by Beaumarchais (1732–1799).

Armida: An enchantress in Tasso's *Gerusalemme liberata.*

296 *aquetta di Perugia:* A poison consisting of arsenic, lead, and antimony.

298 **Vanvitelli** (1700–1773): A famous Neapolitan architect.

299 **Alessandro Farnese** (1545–1592): appointed Governer of the Netherlands by Philip II of Spain, and sent to assist the French Catholics in their struggle with Henri IV.

303 **Alfieri:** Vittorio Alfieri (1749–1803), a leading Italian poet and dramatist of the Romantic period.

310 **Charlotte Corday:** Charlotte Corday d'Armont

(1768–1793) came to Paris and stabbed Marat, a Revolutionary leader, to death in his bath on July 13, 1793, and was guillotined four days later.

356 **Pallagi:** Pallagio Pallagi (1775–1860), a Bolognese painter.

360 **The Holy Roman Emperor Sigismund:** Sigismund came to Parma in the fifteenth century, not the twelfth. Stendhal is probably confusing him with the Emperor Frederick Barbarossa (1122–1190).

386 **Reina:** Francesco Reina (1770–1826) of Milan.

394 **Fokelberg, Tenerani, Marchesi, Hayez:** Artists living in Italy at the time of the novel.

421 **Marie de Médicis:** Mother of Louis XIII; she lost her influence to Cardinal Richelieu, the King's principal minister after 1624.

424 **Saint Bartholemew's Massacre:** The massacre of Huguenots in the major cities of France on Saint Bartholo-

mew's Eve (August 23, 1572), said to have been instigated by Catherine de Médicis, mother of Charles IX.

457 **the Fontanas and the Duvoisins:** Churchmen renowned for their learning during the Napoleonic era.

Signora P——: Probably Giuditta Pasta (1798–1865), a great opera singer of her day who had sung this aria ("Those gentle eyes") in Paris in 1823.

461 **Petrarch:** Actually four lines by the poet Metastasio (1698–1782), also quoted in Rousseau's *Nouvelle Héloïse* (1761).

468 **Tu l'as voulu, Georges Dandin!:** An allusion to Molière's comedy *Georges Dandin:* "You asked for it, Georges Dandin!" (and it serves you right).

479 **Gonzo:** In Italian, a *gonzo* is a fool or clown.

481 **Registration Edict:** A measure introduced to facilitate the raising of war taxes.

494 **the Charterhouse of**
–95 **Parma:** This charterhouse actually existed, not in the forest of Sacca but northeast of Parma. The monks having been expelled from their monastery in the middle of the eighteenth century, the edifice was empty when the French armies were billeted there, along with a supply depot. It was subsequently utilized as a cigar factory, and today serves as a reformatory.

495 **To the Happy Few:** Readers of Stendhal will recognize this phrase at the conclusion of at least three of his major works, including *The Red and the Black.* Its source is in part Shakespearean (*Henry V,* IV, iii: "We few, we happy few"), but more probably a recollection of a phrase in Goldsmith's *Vicar of Wakefield,* the first chapters of which Stendhal had learned by heart to familiarize himself with the English language.

Afterword

by Richard Howard

English-speaking readers invariably characterize Stendhal's works, and especially *The Charterhouse of Parma*, by the words *gusto, brio, élan, verve, panache*. These are, of course, all foreign terms, never translated, though so necessary that they have been readily naturalized. It will be the translator's aim, indeed the translator's responsibility, so to characterize any future translation of Stendhal, who wrote his last completed novel in fifty-two days, a miracle of gusto, brio, élan, verve, panache.

Like miracles generally, the novel is mysterious, beginning with its title: the Carthusian Monastery of Parma, the Charterhouse, appears only on the last page of the book, three paragraphs from the end. To this sequestration Fabrizio del Dongo retires, lives there a year, dies there (he is twenty-seven years old—the age of the oldest French generals in Napoleon's army entering Milan in Chapter One). Stendhal had initially wanted to call his novel *The Black Charterhouse*, a clue: in the prison from which Fabrizio so spectacularly escapes, there is indeed a *black chapel*. Fabrizio's *nine months' imprisonment* in the Farnese Tower—more than one critic has observed—is analogous to the Carthusian monks' discipline in their monastery: by this means he is reborn, he achieves freedom, happiness, and love.

Throughout the novel, incidents and details recur, repeat themselves, recall some earlier instance. Certain verbal echoes may keep the reader conscious of the pattern: Fabrizio's first imprisonment and his night with the jailer's wife will "become" Fabrizio in the Farnese Tower, loving Clélia; the del Dongo castle at Grianta towering above Lake Como "becomes" the Citadel of Parma; the astronomy lessons on the platform of one of the castle's gothic towers "become" Abbé Blanès's observatory on top of the town bell tower, then the platform of the citadel on which the Farnese Tower is erected. Towers, platforms, windows; height, imprisonment, flight; divination, hiding, vision: these images and themes weave the novel together. The same words are used in widely separated situations: the translator must make sure they recur in his version. . . .

Nothing fixed. "The man," Nietzsche said, "was a human question-mark." And he suggested the tone, the reason for it and the consequence of it: "Objection, evasion, joyous distrust, and love of irony are signs of health; everything absolute belongs to pathology."

Consider Gina's two husbands: Count Pietranera, who prefers living in poverty to political compromise, and Count Mosca, for whom politics is a game and any conviction a liability. All political life is marked by incoherence. As Professor Talbot puts it, conservatives become liberals when out of power, and liberals become conservatives when in power.

Consider, again, Fabrizio's roles; in the first third of the novel he claims to be a barometer merchant, a captain of the Fourth Regiment of hussars, a young bourgeois in love with that captain's wife, Teulier, Boulot, Cavi, Ascanio Pietranera, and an unnamed peasant. Further, he will assume a disguise to visit Marietta's apartment, will use Giletti's name and passport to go through customs, assume another disguise as a rich country bourgeois; then claim to be Ludovic's brother, then Joseph Bossi, a theology student. With Fausta, he passes himself off as the valet of an English lord; in the duel with Count M—— he calls himself Bombace. And under all this, his conviction that he is a del Dongo. Nor is he even that—he is the son of a French lieutenant named Robert billeted in the del Dongo palace in Milan during the French occupation; therefore Gina is not his aunt, though on one occasion early in the novel she passes Fabrizio off as her *son!* . . . Evading the love of a woman he believes to be his aunt, Fabrizio ends in a prison originally built to house a crown prince guilty of incest. Nothing fixed: Fabrizio is not a soldier, though he may have fought at Waterloo; not for a moment do we believe he is a cleric, though he is made archbishop of Parma; he is pure becoming, and the language he uses must show him to us in that form, that formlessness. . . . Translate this book to exorcise the fetishism of the Work conceived as an hermetic object, finished, absolute . . . (Beyle, the anti-Flaubert). Nothing in this novel, "complete" though it may be, is quite closed over itself, autonomous in its genesis, and its signification. Hence Balzac's suggestion to erase Parma altogether and call the book something like "Adventures of a typical Italian youth. . . ." Remember that the novel opens as the story of the Duchess Sanseverina. And ends with the "throttled" disappearance (Beyle's phrase, in protest against the publisher's insistence that the book fit in two volumes) of everyone but Mosca, "immensely rich." Such vacillation is never satisfied. More than *Vanity Fair,* this is a Novel Without a Hero, without a Heroine, a novel without . . .

Realism, but no reality. The first text by him I ever translated, for Ben Sonnenberg's *Grand Street,* was that extraordinary list of twenty-three articles headed *Les Privilèges.* That ought to have done it: God would exist and Beyle would believe in Him if he never had to suffer a serious illness, only three days' indisposition a year. . . . If his penis would be allowed to grow erect at will, be two inches longer, and give him pleasure twice a week . . . If he could change into any animal he chose . . . If he would no longer be plagued by fleas, mosquitoes, and mice . . . etc., etc.

Then I translated one of the dozens of unfinished books "by" one of dozens of pseudonyms (as many as Kierkegaard, as many as Pessoa!), texts abandoned after no more than a torso had been molded, the armature of inspiration forsworn once the rapture waned (*The Pink and the Green*).

The invitation in both these texts, preposterous and unfinished alike, to enter (and for the translator, it is virtually a welcome) into the banausics of the affair . . . A kind of painful tension under the disguise of the driest, or the wettest, style. What Valéry calls the restlessness of a superior mind; in any case an ineloquent one. You could "place" Stendhal by saying he is utterly alien to eloquence (Hugo, who had no use for him, said he lacked "style"; Stendhal delighted in the compliment, as in this scribbled note: "A young woman murdered right next to me—she is lying in the middle of the street and beside her head a puddle of blood about a foot across. This is what M. Victor Hugo calls being bathed in one's own blood"). An author who must be continually *reread*, for he never repeats, and as Alain observes, never *develops*.

It's not style he lacks, but rhythm: Stendhal never sweeps you away—he doesn't want to sweep you away: that would be against his principles. He engages your complicity, and for that you must be all attention. Follow him down the page, in the sentence, across the synapses of the amazing clauses, and the sense, the wit, the *literature* occurs in the gaps between the statements, very abruptly juxtaposed:

> A man of parts, he had formerly shown courage in battle; now he was inveterately in a state of alarm, suspecting he lacked that presence of mind commonly deemed necessary to the role of ambassador—M. de Talleyrand has spoilt the profession—and imagining he might give evidence of wit by talking incessantly.

Grasshopper prose, and there is no pleasure to be taken in it if it is not attended to by *presence of mind*. As the reference to Talleyrand suggests, we are being taken into the author's confidence, entrusted with the supposition of intellect—what other author flatters us to this degree?

A translator observes that the scansion of the Stendhal phrase is almost always dependent on that tendency of the French language to accent its abstract nouns on the final syllable: *la logique, le bonheur, l'esprit* (the Beylist trinity). This gives a certain determination to the run of the words, a certain *frappe*, as if the words were minted by a very sure mind. In a language so disposed, may the translator find means to afford evidences of an analogous *mentality*, a power which separates, which suspends, which excludes.

Reading aloud the chapters of *The Chartreuse* to Ben Sonnenberg as

I translated them, week by week (fifty-two days to write, twenty-eight weeks to translate), I reveled with him in Beyle's strange elevation of bastardy, the rejection of the Father, the return, with Italy always, to the Mothers. Silly often, goofy even, but always *on*. Adored by Proust, envied by Gide ("He is the cuttlebone on which I sharpen my beak—what I envy in him is that he doesn't have to put on his track shoes before he starts running"), Stendhal withstands translation yet again, a stage in his continued life.

A NOTE ON THE TYPE

The principal text of this Modern Library edition
was set in a digitized version of Janson,
a typeface that dates from about 1690 and was cut by Nicholas Kis,
a Hungarian working in Amsterdam. The original matrices have
survived and are held by the Stempel foundry in Germany.
Hermann Zapf redesigned some of the weights and sizes for Stempel,
basing his revisions on the original design.